# THE ANOMALY

# THE ANOMALY

Wendy Joyce

RED HOUR INK

Capitol Electronic Reporting
obo Red Hour Ink
10100 Fair Oaks Blvd., #G
Fair Oaks, CA  95628

ISBN-13:    978-1-937338-02-2

This is a work of fiction. Names, characters, places, and events are products of the author's imagination or are used fictitiously and are not to be construed as real.

Grateful acknowledgment is made for permission to reprint excerpts from the following:

(LET ME BE YOUR) TEDDY BEAR
Words and Music by Kal Mann and Bernie Lowe, Copyright © 1957; Renewed 1985
Gladys Music (ASCAP). Worldwide Rights for Gladys Music Administered by Cherry Lane
Music Publishing Company, Inc. International Copyright Secured. All Rights Reserved.
Reprinted by permission of Hal Leonard Corporation.

TOTAL ECLIPSE OF THE HEART
Written by Jim Steinman. Used by permission of Edward B. Marks Music Company
on behalf of Lost Boys Music.

WHAT A WONDERFUL WORLD
Words and Music by George David Weiss and Bob Thiele, Copyright © 1967 by
Range Road Music, Inc., Bug Music-Quartet Music and Abilene Music, Inc. Copyright
renewed and assigned to Quartet Music, Inc., Range Road, and Abilene Music LLC.
International Copyright Secured. All Rights Reserved. Reprinted by permission of:
Hal Leonard Corporation
Larry Spier Music LLC obo Abilene Music LLC
Range Road Music, Inc.

Cover design by Adrian Michael Designs.
Photography courtesy of Imgorthand, NejroN, and Klosa.

For Pop,

whose departure streaked
my Soul inky-blue.

*Thank you...*

...Marky D.—always the skeptic, but never the cynic—for dogging me with your infuriating logic. You were right, though, all the way down the line.

...Kristin R., for confirming what I had only hoped to be true.

...Kelly R., for persuading me to reset the front matter.

...Kevin Miller, a wonderful editor, for going beyond editing.

...Deborah Carter, for tearing my tethers to PTP.

...Joyce Bahnsen, a celebrated artist, for your direction in design.

...Terry & Kevin R., and Holly & Joe C., for your critiques and insight.

...Donna Poppenhagen, a seasoned writer, for your wisdom, which brought the chapters together.

...Arthur Tait, a remarkable attorney, for your 24/7 advice and for tolerating my serial TUIs.

...Kathy Moon, *especially Kathy Moon*, for redirecting my path. (...and for getting us out of The Sand Trap—*powk, powk, powk*—the moment the bark sprayed.) A better friend, no Soul ever had.

# THE ANOMALY

# ORDERS:

## April 3, 1898—Chilkoot Pass, Alaska

Beneath his feet, a mound of stones and ice entombed his Charge's empty shell, and above his head, snow flurries shimmered in the flickering lights of concerned Guides. Those of a sensitive nature had asked, "Romal, would you like me to stay?" Others, more given to pointedness, had said, "Romal, your Charge left hours ago; why do you hover above the shell?"

Whether tactful or direct, all Guides shared genuine concern. Quite endearing, Romal thought, but also foolish and unnecessary. With a gracious smile, Romal ushered their leave. Apparently, though, they needed more ushering. Romal wagged his finger at them. "Do you intend to linger overhead until the Players glimpse your lights? And what absurdity will they conclude your lights to be? I suggest you see to your Charges' Awakenings before your imprudent delays create a ridiculous legend within the Players' history books."

Instantly, sixty-two Guides vanished. Romal sighed, his eyes now turning toward Haven. "Well, One, so begins this corner of your tapestry."

A team of rescue workers trudged past, their shoulders sagging, their steps stumbling. They were valiant men, but thoroughly fatigued. Still, how much effort did it take to turn their chins and notice the plot of snow they were leaving unsearched? Romal flinched at his selfish thought. The Players' hands were blistered, their toes frostbitten. Their pain deserved regard; a Player's shell did not. A Player's shell had less value than a Player's clothing. Shells always returned to dust; clothing, at least, could be worn again. Eventually, the workers would uncover the rest of the buried shells. Romal looked across the plateau to count just how many shells remained.

*One?* Romal cleared his throat of a grumble. Zia's shell was the *only* body to have escaped their notice. Often lost as a Soul, always lost as a Player, Zia had now left a shell to be lost as well. Romal found no humor in this irony.

He peered into the lives of the rescue workers—natives, stampeders, and one retired detective, the eldest of the group. The man had a powerful stride—or so his companions perceived. In truth, arthritis knotted the man's knees; his steps came down hard or they wouldn't come down at all. Years of bone hitting bone had sunken the man's cheeks into a permanent wince. Though the cold winds bit into the man's joints, a complaint never left the man's lips. Romal issued a vibration to the man's heart. "Turn around."

A group of tired heels were dragging up the icy slope when the detective's chin jerked up, his steps halting, his spine straightening. Briefly, he held still, listening. He then swiveled, his hand shielding his eyes from wind and snow.

A stampeder nudged him. "Franklin, you coming?"

Franklin nodded but didn't move. He saw the evidence of a thorough search—shallow holes and deep craters, dirt mounds and rock piles, boulders and tree limbs still wrapped in their hoisting ropes. *Thorough*, he told himself, but a queer feeling—an instinct, he figured—disagreed.

He waved the stampeder on and headed back.

Standing in the center of the searched area, Franklin noticed an embankment shadowing a mound of snow left undisturbed. "Darn." He started toward it. A few feet from the spot, a blast of heat rushed into him. His steps faltered, but he caught himself quickly, his knees now bending freely and painlessly. He straightened with renewed vigor, but had no time to ponder this odd return of his health; he had work to do. He began to dig.

Over and over, dirt and ice flung from his shovel. Eventually, a body emerged—a body encased in red snow.

Franklin wiped the frost from his brow, his squint shifting from the blood on his shovel to the blood on the half-buried man. He knelt on the frozen mud for a closer look. "I'll be darned." He pulled off a glove.

Tailed to a frigid gust came a stampeder's call, "You got a live one?"

His left hand railing the dirt and stones, his right hand probing the hole in the dead man's chest, Franklin hadn't a free arm to signal, no.

Stampeders, hopeful, hurried to Franklin, their shovels, canteens, and gurneys clanging.

Franklin got to his feet, his blood-soaked hand tightening into a fist.

When the rescue workers saw the body, they rested their shovels. A questioning look passed among them before it settled on Franklin.

"You suppose a tree branch got him?" a stampeder asked. "I bet that's what got him. A tree branch came down and—"

"Diller, hush up," Franklin said. "Ain't no tree branch killed this man. He was good and dead before the avalanche."

"Before the avalanche? What do you suppose stuck him in the chest?"

Franklin held up what his fist had enclosed. "A bullet."

# Book I

*A*t your prior request, we honored your Charge, Gell-Mann, and look where that led. We now refer to a pinnacle particle by a ridiculous name. Quark! That's hardly a word; it's a belch. Perhaps we should honor all Player-physicists and rename the skios the God-particle. Or, as your Charge would have it, the goddamn particle.

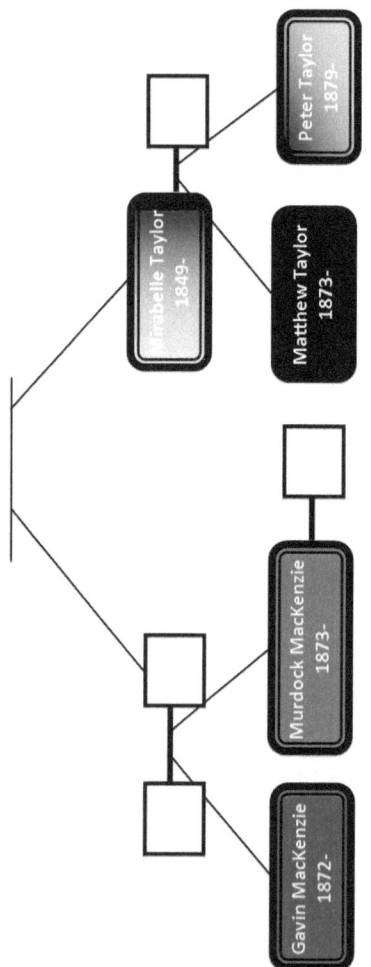

# 1

## April 6, 2002 —Haven

Canine columns of ribbed teeth lined the jaw to the monster's salivating mouth where we hid within a cavity. Any minute, we would be chewed, swallowed, digested and—

"Stop your pacing." Romal yanked me into the seat beside him. "And harness your reckless imagination before it bests you. This is a pleasant room within the Parity Halls, not a rotted cranny within a monster's tooth."

I slouched low, boneless and sinking.

Romal jostled me upright. "Zia, how you present yourself is a choice. Will you present yourself as a slab of skioses melting over a chair? Or will you present yourself as a gracious Yin Soul brimming with purpose?"

"Is this a test?"

Romal frowned. "Attempted humor?" He leaned in, separating our noses with a scolding finger. "The ArchGuide has a record of your every thought, whether spoken or sparked, and of your every deed, whether taken or forsaken. He will compare your skewed decisions of a hundred years ago to the Soul you choose to present today." He rested back, eyes closed. "Little chance of a favorable comparison if you present yourself as a clown."

I tried to sit still, but my heel began thumping. "Hey, Romal, can I ask a question?" He didn't answer, so I tapped him, "hey, hey, hey," until one of his eyes reopened. "Can I ask one lousy question?"

"One? Unlikely, but I'll applaud the effort."

"How come—If other—When I—" Dozens of questions bombarded my head, each question screaming, *pick me, pick me*. But no amount of conjunctions could join those questions into one. An aimless stare fell to my lap.

Romal nudged me. "Out with it. I'd rather hear your torturous chatter than untangle your tortuous thoughts."

"How come I'm the only Soul who doesn't know stuff?"

Romal shifted uneasily.

I bounded to my feet. "You were supposed to say, 'oh, no, Zia, that's all in your head.' But it's not, is it? Everybody *does* know stuff. How? How did they learn it? Did I miss a meeting? A manual?"

"No, no," Romal said, though his eyes dodged mine, and he fidgeted like a doctor tasked to deliver terminal news.

"I knew it." I sank to my chair. "I have a celestial disease. I just knew it."

"You know nothing."

"You're right." My head limbered sideways to rest on Romal. "Ignorance is part of the disease."

"Sit up." Romal scraped me off his shoulder. "Other than an incurable imagination, you have no illness."

"Oh. But you said—"

"Whatever you think I said, I said nothing of the sort."

"Oh. Then how come—"

"For ten minutes, a mere ten minutes, please sit still and be quiet."

Having been Romal's Charge for centuries, I knew his two moods, cranky and *very* cranky. To return him to *just cranky*, I twisted an imaginary key on my lips. After waiting ten minutes, I said, "How come—"

"Zia, I asked for ten minutes, not 30 seconds."

"I gave you ten minutes, ten *Earth* minutes." My rationale brought back Romal's pinched face of *very* cranky. "Fine," I told him. Leaning back, I kept quiet for 11 minutes, the extra minute serving as an apology. "Romal, now will you tell me?"

"I have nothing to tell. Souls have no manual, and you have no malady."

"Then how do billions of Souls, throughout all eleven Orders, automatically know stuff? They didn't learn it as Players; their knowledge of dos and don'ts predates the first Determinant on Earth. I need the answer, Romal. I bet it will explain my small size and mismatched lights."

"Mismatched? Ridiculous. Your colors are interesting."

I clutched a hank of the purple lights spinning down from my head. "This is supposed to mimic hair, wavy and shiny, not electrocuted." I stretched the kinks flat across my green shoulder. "See that? Purple and green clash. They don't belong on the same Energy."

"Nonsense. They're the colors of a petunia."

"They're the colors of a chopped up toad."

"Really, Zia, now isn't the time—"

"I knew it." My palms flew up. "It's never the time. Just forget it." My feet shuffled to the dimensional window. Earth had reached its farthest point in orbit and appeared smaller than a tennis ball. For a while, I reflected on my eleven lives—although Guides count twelve, but avoid that subject, too—until, one by one, each memory lowered my chin. "Crap."

Immediately, Romal stood at my side, his arm stretching across my back to give a comforting squeeze. His other arm swept across the window to shift the view. The forefront dimension, now Divisional, spotlighted the Awakening and Descending Fields. While Romal gazed out the window, a rolling *ahhh* leaked from his lips. "Extraordinary, don't you think?"

*Extraordinary?* I craned toward the window, but saw what I always saw—fleeting lights from Awakening Parties crossing in and out of Transitional fields, cords popping up and disappearing, brigades of Souls arriving and descending, their lights flashing, blinking and merging. "Looks like an LA freeway times ten. Well, maybe five."

"Long ago, before time measured, that region cradled all of your kind, all ten billion bundles of Energy, each with a Ribbon of Life, but none with a spark to—"

"To self-awaken. I know the story. Everything and everybody existed within the Nucleus Power. Half the Nucleus wanted to spark our awareness; the other half wanted us catatonic. Then *BOOM,* or as the Players tell it, *BANG!* But boom or bang, the Power split into Pure Positive and Pure Negative—One and beelzeButt."

"BeelzeNiine."

"Jeez, I *know.* Even *I* know about the Great War. It resulted in a bunch of Hands-Off rules for Guides and a list of Do-Not-Interfere laws for us."

"All to safeguard your Free Will. To appreciate that, you must learn the difference between innascible, which you are, and invincible, which you are not. Regardless, after the Great War, the Council of Genesis awakened the Souls, secured them into Orders, and paired them with Guides."

"Wait. What Council? Alpha told me that One selected the Orders."

"Alpha told you no such thing. He said One selected *your* Order. You then assumed One selected every Soul's Order; am I correct?"

He was, but I shrugged instead of nodding, tired of always being wrong.

Romal continued, "I served on the Council of Genesis, a daunting task to say the least. We labored through the expanse of Energies while centuries blurred into lonely millenniums. Quite often, our work felt eternal, as though we might never come to the last Soul."

"And did you?"

Romal winced. "Of course we did! December 1631, the recorded date on Earth and a bittersweet moment for the Council. In earlier times, Souls shared their fascinating stories about their adventures in play. And the Council listened, enraptured, thrilling vicariously with their successes and paining deeply with their defeats. But by 1631, much had changed, sadly changed for the Council. Souls, no longer neophytes, were rather busy progressing to the side of their choice—be it One or be it Niine. Life after life, Energy to Player, Player to Energy, Souls had little time for chitchat. Between their lives, a Soul might manage a cordial wave to the Council." His fingers wiggled pathetically at the window. "Rarely more."

"Okay, I get it. Thank you? Sorry? Uhm, call home more often?"

Romal snorted.

"Fine," I said, "I don't get it."

"The hell you say." Romal brushed aside my purple lights that supposedly mimicked hair. His eyes met mine. "In 1631, we finally approached the last Energy, a small whirl of Yin, and we sparked her Awakening. Her atoms unfurled and reassembled without issue. Then we waited."

"Waited for what?"

"Matter, but not another particle belonged to the Soul. Though half the size of any other, she was complete—a sea green Yin topped in maroon lights, or as you see it, purple."

"Whoa, you mean—" I thumbed my chest.

"Yes, yes, you were the last grain of Energy to awaken. Unfortunately, the millenniums had drained the Council's patience, and we bickered over securing your Order. One member, noting your strong voice, proposed the Warriors. Another member suggested the Counters, an Order predisposed to oddities. Then a wise and distinguished member offered the Order of Teachers, but his idea was met with dissent. Rude dissent I might add."

"I could have been a Teacher?"

Romal shuddered. "No, no, no. Certainly not. Desperation spawns bad ideas. Unthinkable." He went back to his chair and sat. "Fortunately, One solved the matter by sending a message through our dear friend Alpha. 'Eleventh Order,' Alpha told us, 'Zia, Order of Agitators.' Naturally, no Council member had suggested the Order, but now—"

"Why?" My question startled Romal. "Sorry for interrupting, but why?"

"What do you mean, why? Why not another obstinate, caustic recluse? Is that your question?"

I nodded.

Romal pinched the bridge of his nose, his lips nibbling out mumbles, "Yes, yes, I set myself up for that one. Yes, indeed." After a while, his hand came down. "Zia, picture ten billion Energies. If that gives you trouble, think of ten billion grains of sand. Upon waking, an Energy emanated love, wonderment, and tranquility. All ten billion woke in peace...all except you."

"Except me?" I glided to Romal. "What does that mean? I'm peaceful. Damn peaceful."

"Yes, yes, I'm certain you think so. But you woke with aggression, flares of burgundy we had never seen and shrieks of antimatter we had never heard. We harnessed the vibrations as quickly as possible, but unfortunately, we missed a few. Mount Vesuvius erupted in an unscheduled explosion."

My mouth opened but no words came out.

With two fingers, Romal nudged it closed. "The Council began to list each Agitator's placement to find and consider those Guides having the fewest. Nothing personal, you understand, just a fair distribution of a difficult Order. But while we tallied, Alpha's brilliant orange eyes dimmed with concern. Well, I couldn't have that. Although I'm merely an Interim Guide, I declared myself your Guide. Alpha, in a burst of gratitude, twitched in a moment less dour." Romal smiled. "And there you have it."

"I have it? What do I have?" I sat with a thud. "I'm a freak?"

"No such beast, not with the attachment you give it. Life itself refuses boundaries, always has, always will, and it throws us an anomaly to remind us of such. Think of the hummingbird, capable of backward flight."

"I'm backwards?"

"Hmm, but not my point. Consider the misunderstood platypus, classed as a mammal, yet it lays eggs."

"Isn't it poisonous?"

"Oh, that's right. So it is."

"For chrissake, Romal, is this your idea of a pep talk? Toasting drunks lift more spirits."

Romal's eyes thinned. "Fair warning, Zia, when you address the ArchGuide, you had better drop the sarcasm and watch the language. Refrain from any act or comment that you would later defend as humor. No antics."

"Antics? That was the Zia of ages ago."

"No, that was the Zia of moments ago on the Parity Hall steps. Did you think Novella would find your waders amusing?"

"I was kidding around."

"Shouting, 'Bring on the floods,' wretchedly distasteful."

"It was a joke."

"It was an insult. Novella takes great pride in having served as Noah."

"He built one lousy ark. Big deal. It's not as though the entire world actually flooded. Besides, what has he done since? Nothing. So I tease him. I always tease him. And Novella always fashions a stick and—"

"A staff."

"A stick, a staff, the Holy freakin' Grail. Whatever it is, he wags it at me. Except, come to think of it, he didn't this time. Did you notice that? This time, he acted weird. He smiled. He never smiled at me before. And he reached out like he was going to pat my head. Did you see that?"

"I saw you duck, tuck, and roll."

The more I thought about Novella, the more I recalled receiving smiles from other Souls, too. Smiles I had never received before. "Hey, how come everyone is acting weird toward me?"

"Oh look," Romal said, "the door is opening."

When I turned and looked, the door was still shut. "No, it's not—"

Then it opened.

Romal stood. "Come along. It's impolite to keep an ArchGuide waiting."

When I got up, Romal circled me twice to inspect. Then his hands folded over mine. "Zia, we've had our differences, scores of bruises and apologies. At times, you thought ill of me; at times, I thought I had failed you. Though Souls design themselves from an eternity of choices—skills to select or toss, elements to polish or purge—Guides serve one purpose." He released my hands, stepped back, and bowed. "I hope I have served you well."

An inky-blue lump caught in my throat; Romal had never failed me. Never. He's cranky, sure, but he's also patient, loving, and crazy smart. I bet he was Noah Webster's Guide because he uses words that the Players' dictionaries have long ago deleted or have yet to include, *innascible* and *skios* to name two.

For centuries, I had given him hell, but I had never known, until that moment, that I had given him heartache, too. I should have known. Had I been a better Soul, more deserving of Romal, I *would* have known.

I bounded forward, knocking him backward, my arms roping his neck. "You're the best, Romal. You never failed me. You served me great. Nobody nowhere yammers better than you. Nobody. Between my lives, I'll give you better than a wave. I promise. In fact, I'll make sure every Soul gives you better than a lousy wave."

"No, no, quite unnecessary." Between his returned squeezes, he tried to pry free. "Come now, Zia, no need for this. A smidgeon of decorum, please."

I let go.

He smoothed aside my purple kinks, poked back my shoulders, and bumped up my chin. "Remember, Zia, confine the story to the relevant facts. Don't elaborate. And for the love of One, do not curse and do not lie."

"Lie? *Me?* I don't where you get your informa—"

"DO NOT LIE!" He swiveled me toward the door. "Let's go."

When we entered, I thought we had the wrong room. Where was the marble? The chandeliers? The sculptures? It wasn't even a room. Rooms have walls and ceilings. This place did not.

From way up high, a stream of light flowed down and lit a small wooden table where a thin, slate-gray ArchGuide sat opposite two empty chairs. That's it. No color, no sound, no nothing. Just a blank canvas inviting my imagination...and the dimness darkened into oily shadows, and the oily shadows twisted into ominous threats. My eyes widened; my legs locked.

Romal leaned into my ear. "Control it, Zia. It's a choice. Choose to control your imagination."

"I will. I will." But as we glided to our seats, I bunched into Romal, nearly tripping him.

When Romal bowed, I did, too, and when he sat, I did the same.

The ArchGuide watched us, but he didn't say a word. I stared into the round black pits of his eyes.

When Romal elbowed me, I started talking. "Hello, Sir. I'm Zia, Order of Agitators. With the hope that you'll grant my request, I'm here to tell you what happened that spring. And I will, but first—" I crossed my fingers, preparing to rush my words, hoping that a quick offense was a tiny offense. "Can I say one thing? Just one thing? I need to say one thing first. Please?"

Romal cupped his forehead and let out a disparaging, "*Nooo.*"

"Sir, I just want you to realize that the season of consequence rippled for a hundred years. Not five. Not fifty. But a hundred years. Okay? Straight up, I take full responsibility. Yes, Sir. But I get it now, okay? Back then, I didn't get squat. Just compare my thoughts of 1898 to those of my last life. When you do, you'll know that what I'm telling you is true. Okay? *Okay?*"

The ArchGuide glanced at Romal.

"Wait," I said, "I'm not telling you how to do your job. Hell no. I mean, no, Sir. But the comparison is important. Damn import—I mean, darn important. But you probably know that, right? *Right?* Uhm, maybe you could nod? Maybe blink? Okay, maybe not. I'm a little nervous. Romal told me to look at you when I'm talking, but that's hard. Oh, jeez, I don't mean you're hard to look at, like you're ugly or something. Because you're not. Not ugly, I mean. Not that I'm checking out your looks. I don't care how you look. I mean, I care, but—"

Romal rapped the table. "Zia, the event in Alaska, please."

"Yeah, okay. That's when I saved my brother's life. I mean—"

Instantly, the ArchGuide's hand came up—the signal for silence—and he turned to Romal for what I knew was a thought-to-thought chat.

I picked my fingers.

A moment later, Romal stood, bowed to the ArchGuide, and tugged up on my elbow. "Come along, Zia. Time to go."

"Go? Go where? What about my request?"

"Denied," Romal said. "Come along."

"Huh?" It happened so fast, my head filled with a buzzing din, as if a thousand bees had made a hive of it. Though numb and confused, I collected myself and followed Romal.

At the doorway, Romal paused. "It's respectful to thank the ArchGuide."

"Thank him?"

"For his time."

"His time?" I looked back at the pompously pious ArchGuide who hadn't given me the chance to retract or explain my bad choice of words.

Romal waited...and the ArchGuide seemed to be waiting, too. "Romal, did he tell you to remind me?"

"Zia, it's respectful whenever—"

"He did!" Red sparks flared and fell from my forehead. Ignoring Romal's calls to stop, I marched back to the ArchGuide. "You got some nerve. You want Romal to teach me respect? He ought to teach YOU! Maybe I messed up, but I'm nervous. I'm wired nervous, made worse by having to stare into your big, black bugeyes. That's right, bugeyes. Now, that's my excuse; what's yours? Fifty times, I asked, 'Right? Right?' Would it have killed you to answer?

One peek into my Soul and you would have known I wasn't being a smart-ass. But, hey, if you want to deny me, fine. You got the power. But first—" I thumped into the chair, my arms crossing. "Respectfully, Sir, I came to state my story, and that's just what I'm going to do. If you raise your hand, I'll shut up, but I won't leave. I'll sit here through eternity until your hand lowers. And if you pelt me with your white light, that's fine, too. From wherever I land, I'll drag my sorry Soul back to this chair. Get it? I've been walloped by better than you and for a whole lot less. Let me know when you're ready to listen."

Ebony eyes doubled in size, but I didn't look away. If he was scanning my thoughts, all he was hearing was, *oh crap, I'm in deep, deep shit.*

I felt Romal's presence to the side. Without a blink from the ArchGuide, I groped for Romal's arm, found it, and gripped it.

Loosening my fingers, Romal sat again. As he turned my chin toward his, my eyes strained at the corner to keep watch on the ArchGuide. "Zia, look at me," Romal said. "Come now, turn your attention to me."

My focus volleyed a few times before it stayed on Romal.

"That's better," Romal said. "Calm now?"

I nodded.

"Splendid," he said. "You have another chance."

Up shot my triumphant fist.

Just as quickly, Romal smacked it down...and clamped it. Before I could spit out an apology, Romal's thumb grazed my forehead, and my eyes struggled to stay open. "Let them close," Romal said, so I did. "Zia, listen carefully, very carefully. Somewhere within your Soul lies a fragment of wisdom. It's undoubtedly small, a speck perhaps, but it does exist, and it's staid, grave, earnest, and true. I want you to find that fragment and clutch it. Should you think it's dissolving or slipping free of your grasp, or should you begin to doubt that you've grasped it at all, I want you to trust that you have it and to keep a tight hold. That sliver of wisdom will carry you through, from the first word of your story to your last utterance of truth. Do you understand?"

I nodded.

After a while, I heard a queer voice. It came out of me—I knew it was me—but it sounded nothing like me. It sounded frighteningly truthful.

In the summer of 1897, we heard the rumors. *Everyone* heard the rumors. They rose from the seaports in California and Oregon, and they spread like a virus, passing from lip to lip over clotheslines, through barbershops, and outside churches, infecting millions across the states.

Before we could figure the truth of it, the rumors broke into worldwide headlines—*Gold in the Klondike.*

Murdock smacked the newspaper against my chest. "Get packed, brother. We got a destiny in the arctic."

By *destiny,* I thought he meant we would strike gold in the Yukon and return to Utah as wealthy men. *Destiny* implies fortunes gained and dreams realized; otherwise, you're supposed to call it fate. Had Murdock said, "...*fate* in the arctic," I would have set a course for the equator. *Fate* is never good.

We weren't the only ones infected by a gold-fate destiny. Overnight, lines of buggies, horses, and wagons clogged the westbound trails and roads. Hoards of others amassed at train depots, burgeoning and toppling the railroad schedules. Fifty thousand men and women moved across the landscape like an unstoppable herd of buffalo migrating west—that's how the press described it, calling the herd *stampeders.*

When Murdock said we were joining the stampede, I told him, "We ain't got train fare to Seattle. And if we managed that, how we gonna get from Seattle to Alaska? Swim?"

He punched me, not because of the sarcasm—Murdock never understood sarcasm—but because he couldn't swim a lick, and he figured I was poking fun of him. Had he been able to swim, he would have taken my sarcasm for serious and insisted we save money by swimming.

As it was, he couldn't swim, and we didn't have money. But across town, our Taylor cousins, Matthew and Peter, had plenty of money, enough to pay for all of us...once Murdock convinced them to come along.

We were in our twenties—Peter, just barely—and we shared the same grandfather, but that's all the MacKenzies and the Taylors shared. Well, that and our feelings for Mirabelle, their mother, our aunt. She was a widow, tiny but sturdy, hardworking and God-fearing, and she was the kindest woman I had ever known. Matthew gave her love and respect, but Peter, the apple of her eye, gave her crap. She forgave him, but I didn't. Had Mirabelle been my mother, I would have been a better man...and I wouldn't have given her crap.

Murdock averted eye contact with our aunt; she made him nervous. Her lips pursed at every word leaving Murdock's mouth. "A man can never have too much money," Murdock said. "And seein' that you're family, it's only right we let you share in the gold. Hell, ain't no other reason for asking you along."

Matthew refused—his mother needed a son's hand to help with the chores—but Peter leapt the stairs, two at a time, to start packing. He didn't even notice the tears welling in his mother's eyes. After she dabbed them dry, she hardened them on Murdock. "Go on and help Peter," she told him. "You started the fuss, now make yourself useful." She tried to push him, but Murdock had the girth of two men and the weight of three. Mirabelle's hand fell against him like a feather falls against a brick. "Are ya deaf?" she said, her voice loud with insistence. "Go help your cousin pack up his gear."

Murdock lumbered toward the stairs. Matthew and I started to follow, but Mirabelle's arm swung out to corral us in place.

After Murdock disappeared into the loft, Mirabelle fixed her gray eyes on me. "I don't much listen to gossip," she said, "but I've heard troubling talk about your brother. Folks say he's a thief and a liar. Some call him a shill for the devil." She tugged my chin sideways and eyed the fleshless groove at the corner of my mouth and the long puckered scar that snaked to my cheekbone. I swallowed hard, praying she wouldn't ask.

And she didn't ask...because she already knew. "He's got a devil's temper to boot." She pulled my chin back to hers. "Gavin Dearg MacKenzie, I want the truth. Is Murdock sewn from one decent thread of my sainted sister, or is he cut from the sinful cloth of your father and his father before him?"

If only I could turn back time...I answered with a shrug.

A strange sadness washed over my aunt. "For shame," she whispered. "A spoken lie is a forgivable sin, but an unspoken truth is a harbinger of evil. Can ya figure the reason, Gavin? Can ya?"

I can now...about a hundred years too late.

For Mirabelle's peace of mind, "See that no harm comes to your brother," Matthew packed, too, promising to watch over Peter.

In a tavern near the Seattle Port, Murdock bumped into several incoming travelers. A commotion erupted when those travelers later discovered their money-clips missing. Murdock's sleight of hand had escaped everyone's notice—everyone except Peter.

Jittering to tell, Peter saddled beside me at the bar and ordered a whiskey. When it came, Peter threw it to the back of his throat and then coughed and choked like the non-drinking kid he was. "Know what I saw?" he sputtered.

"Don't care," I told him.

Peter went on anyway. "Your brother is mighty slick. I never seen a faster hand. It just slipped in and out of those pockets without nobody feeling nothing. Hey, you suppose Murdock would teach me?"

Murdock loathed Peter, but since I was bored and wanting entertainment, I told him, "Sure. Go on and ask," and then I turned in my seat to watch.

Peter strode to Murdock's table. Seconds later, Murdock rose like a bull, his weight bending the tavern's floor boards. "Get away from me." His sweeping arm hit squarely across Peter's chest.

Gangly Peter bounced off a nearby table and landed on the floor.

Red-faced and disheveled, he returned to the stool beside me. He stared at the counter, not talking, not drinking, and not jittering with excitement anymore. After a while, he muttered, "Don't know why he got so mad. I ain't gonna tell nobody nothing. Kin don't turn against kin. Ain't that right? Shoot, you know it better than anyone. You learned it the hard way." When I looked at Peter, he ran a finger down his cheek. "Ain't that how you got that scar?"

My face heated, now wishing Murdock had thrown Peter through the barroom window.

"Your daddy was teaching you a lesson, right?"

My *daddy* had nothing to do with it, but I kept my mouth shut.

"To make you more like Murdock," Peter said. "That's what I figure, 'cause Murdock is plenty smart and powerful strong."

Yep, smart and strong like a rhino, both getting their way by plowing through men. That's what I should have said. Instead, I said nothing at all.

"He don't take guff from nobody."

Nobody gave him guff; Murdock was meaner than a snared wolverine.

"I bet if I work hard and do what he tells me, he'll—"

CRAACK. My shotglass hit hard on the bar top. "He'll what? *Respect* you? Peter, that ain't gonna happen. Get that through your thick skull. He don't like you. He ain't never gonna like you. He thinks you're a sissy-boy."

"But I ain't."

"Don't matter. You could bed a hundred whores, but it wouldn't change Murdock's mind none...if he has a mind." I threw back the last of my drink, sleeved my mouth, and then flagged the bartender. "Another whiskey. And bring another for my cousin here, the goddam dullard."

Peter jumped up. "I ain't no dullard, and I ain't no sissy-boy." He kicked the barstool aside to lean into me. "And I don't need no whores to prove it. I got another way. You'll see." He marched out of the tavern.

On March 9th, we boarded the steamship Farallon bound for Alaska.

A few miles from port, Peter started that *I-got-a-secret* kind of jittering again. The minute Matthew and Murdock left for the deck, Peter locked the cabin door. Then he showed me what he bought in Seattle—a side-strap holstering a Colt 45. "Ain't it a beauty?"

It was! It was silver and gleaming and polished to a mirror shine. He said he bought it to stop looters from taking our gold. "I'll give them a helluva surprise." He kept drawing the gun, swinging it, aiming it, and holstering it. "When I protect our gold, I betcha Murdock will think better of me."

"Did you tell Matthew?" I asked only to rattle Peter, who was no less a fool than I was an opportunist. Obviously, Matthew knew nothing of the gun. A died-in-the-wool stalwart, Matthew hadn't come for the gold. He had come because he had promised his mother he would babysit Peter. Had Matthew known about the gun, he would have been boxing Peter's ears back to Utah.

"Gavin, you ain't gonna tell him, are you?"

"That depends," I said, reeling him in. "Can I shoot it?"

Then, and every evening thereafter, Peter and I met at a secluded spot on deck, and we fired at whales, dolphins, and everything else bobbing in the sea.

Our fun ended seven days later when we stepped off the planks in Alaska and learned of a new law. Armed Canadian Mounties, tired of burying starved and frozen bodies, refused entry into the Yukon unless a man could prove a year's worth of provisions. At best, our sacks weighed fifty pounds, a pittance to the four tons we needed. Falling in among the masses—the masses of the ill-prepared—we hiked the Chilkoot trail.

Twelve miles later, we pitched our tents at Sheep Camp, a roughed-in town with two saloons, three log buildings, and one swarm of prospectors. Within days, Matthew, Peter, and I had jobs hauling cargo between Dyea and Sheep Camp. We trudged back and forth, back and forth, sixty miles of back and forth for each ton of supplies we advanced one mile on the trail.

Our frozen bones ached, our Utah boots peeled, and our empty bellies growled in constant complaint. Cheechakos, that's what the natives and sourdoughs called us. Cheechakos, meaning newcomer or tenderfoot— literally tenderfoot if you didn't know about mukluks.

While my cousins and I worked as packers, Murdock claimed to work Long Hill. "For a better wage," he said jiggling a bag of coins twice the weight of ours.

Those who worked Long Hill deserved double pay. Long Hill ascended north from Sheep Camp and ended at the Scales, the tent-town weighing supplies. Although Long Hill only stretched a few miles, the pass spiraled at a near vertical angle—up, over, and around giant blocks of granite—to reach a height of 1600 feet. Stampeders didn't walk Long Hill; they climbed it. Sometimes crawled. Carcasses of stumbled mules littered the gulches.

In truth, Murdock didn't work Long Hill. To gain his money, he hid in a shallow vein above the main trail and ambushed returning prospectors.

I told no one.

By early spring, we had stockpiled the required supplies to cross over the border. One load after the next, we moved our packs to the Scales. Once weighed, we joined the single file line at the bottom of the Golden Stairs. That's what they called the 1500 steps grooved into the mountain's ice—The Golden Stairs. For accuracy, they should have called it, The Staircase To Hell.

After a slow, arduous climb up the icy steps, we cached our packs at the summit, and then we prepared to descend to get the next load. *Prepared* meant steeling your nerves because the descent was worse than the climb. Stampeders slid down chutes that were shovel carved into the snow and ice. Except nobody slid. Everybody plummeted. *Floop, floop, floop.*

Pitching, rolling, and bouncing, we ricocheted off the sides and plunged into the man ahead. Our legs flapping, our arms twisting, we tumbled, skidded, and flailed. *Floop, floop, floop.* We shot from the chutes like snow covered cannonballs, bloodied and bruised.

Matthew estimated forty-two round trips to move our tonnage from the Scales to the summit. Murdock figured it different. "When we've cached enough up there for the two of us, we're crossing into Canada."

A block of ice rocked in my head where a brain should have been; otherwise, I wouldn't have asked, "What about Matthew and Peter?"

Murdock's fist took out my last canine tooth.

On our 15th round-trip, Matthew remained at Sheep Camp to pack another load for the Scales. Murdock, Peter, and I climbed the Golden Stairs. Once more at the summit, we cached our supplies, and then Peter positioned at a chute, but only Peter. He noticed and scooted back, questioning Murdock.

Murdock didn't like questions, and he liked them even less coming from Peter.

Their voices rose.

I stepped aside. Frostbitten and chilled to the Soul, I listened without hearing, watched without seeing, and felt only the northern wind as it cut through my jacket and rattled my bones.

Their shouts grew into blows. Peter fell and his arm struck a boulder. Clutching his elbow, Peter wailed, howled, and writhed, making a big fuss over an elbow, just a lousy elbow.

"Gavin," Murdock shouted, "let's go."

The shout brought Peter staggering to his feet. His glove disappeared into his jacket and then reappeared brandishing the gun. "You ain't going nowhere except down the chute."

After a stunned pause, Murdock looked my way, no doubt scrutinizing my reaction.

My face showed surprise, candid surprise. Through the months of hauling, climbing, and freezing, I had forgotten about the Colt.

Turning again to Peter, Murdock said, "Only a woman hides a gun." He spat. "Women and sissy-boys."

Peter began trembling, which caused Murdock to grin. "A gun won't make a man out of a sissy-boy." He started toward Peter. "You better grow a spine real quick 'cause I'm going to shove that gun up your sissy-boy ass."

Peter's trembling became a violent shaking. A dark circle emerged on the front of his pants.

Murdock roared with sardonic laughter. "Sissy-boy wet himself."

His cheeks flushed, his eyes swimming in unspilled tears, his mouth ratcheting with stutters, "I'm—I'm not—You—You better—I have—" Peter cocked the gun.

I watched, disconnected and numb.

My surreal detachment began when I shrugged to Aunt Mirabelle, but then it ended when I saw Peter's finger quiver near the trigger.

In a split-second of insight, I realized how my silence had paved the path to where we now stood.

In the next split-second, I tried to reverse it; I lunged for the gun.

In a Player's instinct to keep control, Peter's hand squeezed.

The gun fired, pitching me into darkness.

Insight had already fled; my last thought as Gavin centered on myself. *Finally, warm toes.*

# 2

*His unassuming nature, Boy Scout honesty, and quick willingness to lend a hand or loan a buck earned him a town full of buddies.*

## 1901 - Divisional

After my Awakening, an irritable Romal left me in Divisional instead of taking me to Haven. He muttered, "Then wait here," and took off. *Then*, as if in reply to something, although I hadn't said a word.

Centuries earlier, after I woke from my seventh life, Romal had said, "all right, *then* stay." After my eighth, he had said, "So be it, *then* remain." Both times, like now, he had left me in Divisional.

This time, I shouted, "Hey, Romal, you're hearing voices. I never said I wanted to stay. Romal? *Romal?* Aw, forget it."

I envisioned a pillow and stretched out. Whatever was causing Romal's crankiness, it had nothing to do with my ninth life. Not a chance. I had lived a decent life, despite my lousy gender. A thousand times I had told Romal to give me Yin lives only, but Romal never listens. He picks out cords connecting to Yang, and then he complains when I mess up.

This time, though, Romal had nothing to complain about. As Gavin, I had made a few mistakes, but they were teensy mistakes, the kind Romal usually fixed with a lecture while I pretended to listen. For sure, I hadn't hurt another Player. Not directly. I sure hadn't shot anyone. Just the opposite. I stepped in front of the gun, and that stupid Peter Taylor ended my life.

Despite a few details I might have overlooked while rethinking my life as Gavin, I knew two facts for certain: One, my life ended in a noble act; I had saved Murdock's life by sacrificing my own. And two, Romal would never agree with number one; somehow, he would give my noble act a bitter slant.

Centuries ago, after completing my first life, Romal hollered about a ripple effect, blaming me for the death of my crew, as if I had forced the men at gunpoint to board the ship. When I brought up Free Will, Romal rubbed his temples as if his head hurt, not from his own hollering, but from my arguing.

Just thinking about his short fuse made me glad that he had left me...left me in my favorite spot in Divisional. It's a good distance from the Awakening Field's hustle and bustle, yet it's close enough to the Earth's dimension for a front row view of their solar system. From here, I can watch the comets whirl, the stars explode, and the planets spin like gigantic tops—all the planets, from Mercury to Neptune and the three planets beyond that the Players have yet to discover and name.

Most Souls don't share my appreciation. They wake, celebrate, and leave for Haven. To them, this section feels desolate and lonely, which is a bit melodramatic, but that's how everyone describes it, everyone except me and Counters. But Counters don't count; they're too precise to describe anything right. I once asked a Counter a simple question, "If Saturn melted, would the ring dissolve?"

The Counter rambled on and on about ice particles, chilled velocities, and frozen gas. Everything cold. I waited to hear a *yes* or a *no*, but instead, I heard *furthermore*, *if*, and *unless*. My eyes glazed over in a fog of boredom. When the Counter asked if I understood, I nodded. The second I nodded, my sparks twinkled brightly in their changed color—the color of lies.

The Counter laughed. I don't know what he found funny about my polite lie, and I still don't know if Saturn's ring would dissolve.

*Whooshummm.* Earth rumbled past, so I sprawled out for sweet daydreams. No use thinking about weird Counters and irritable Guides—or my life as Gavin. All lives are too brief to make any difference anyway.

"Hello, Zia. Are you waiting for Romal?"

I jumped up, excited by the presence of my best friend, Awen, Order of Messengers, a seven-foot, dark blue Soul with thick, black lights atop his head. "Romal wouldn't take me to Haven," I said. "That's a bad sign, isn't it?"

Awen didn't seem to hear me. He peered at something beyond me, something across space. I wondered why he hadn't come to my Awakening, but I didn't want to put him on the spot by asking. I just wanted to do whatever Awen wanted to do. My green shoulder nudged into Awen's blue chest, and together, we surveyed the galaxy. Earth, covered in swirling particles of whites and grays, pressed against a navy backdrop glittered with stars—a heavenly view for Awen and me. Nothing else mattered.

"Are you waiting for Romal?" he asked again, strangely and quietly. Way too quietly.

I backed up to study my friend. "Awen, you just asked me that. Awen?"

His distant gaze neither fell to me nor tracked the Earth. His robust blues were fading, nearly transparent. "Awen, what's wrong?" I tugged on his arm. "Tell me what's wrong." Conflicting hues of confusion recolored my sparks.

Awen noticed and his face grew sadder.

*Damn, how I hate the tattletale sparks.* "Awen, don't worry about me. I'm fine. But you—Well, you don't look too good. What happened?" Then it hit me, and it was so obvious, I smacked a palm against my forehead. "Awen, you have a terrible message to give to some poor Soul, don't you? That's why you look awful, right? Hey, I know you're a caring Messenger, but you care too much. They caused the bad news, not you. Quit taking their problems so much to heart. Just deliver it quickly, like ripping off a bandage."

Awen stared into space, no doubt reworking some god-awful message into a softer blow. He's a sympathetic Soul, the best in his Order, but he's also a Dyad, which stinks. His other half is Ereo, which also stinks. Romal said that Dyads have specially designed relationships when they're in play. Always. It's some dumb rule, strictly for Dyads, supposedly to protect them, which makes no sense. Awen can protect himself. He doesn't need Ereo flitting in the background or hovering overhead. It's annoying. I had to train myself to ignore her. Good training, too, or I might have noticed her absence before that moment. "Hey, Awen," I tapped him, "where's your sidekick?"

Instantly, inky-blue sparks streaked his cheeks.

"Aw, jeez, sorry, sorry." I zoomed across the region, east then west, in a zigzagging search for Ereo.

I found no trace of her.

I swept to Awen's side, reached up, and blotted the blue from his face.

His eyes scrunched tight as if he were bearing an unbearable pain.

"Talk to me," I said. "Is this about Ereo? Did she abandon you? You can tell me. I'll understand. Whatever she did, it's not your fault."

"Zia," he whispered with so much buttery softness, I dizzied.

"Yes, Awen?"

"I know your Soul."

"Yes, go on."

"I know you intend no harm."

"Yes, go—Wait. Wait. Harm? *Harm?*"

"We are friends and that will never change."

*Uh-oh.* Dread surged, kicking away balance. I stumbled backwards. "Your message is for me? *ME?*"

# 3

*Zia will wink and say she has got it, and then she will go out and create a magnificent disaster that redefines peril.*

Romal retreated to his *Corner of the Universe,* or so he titled it after hearing the expression among Players and finding it quaint, despite its literal inaccuracies. For some time, visiting Souls and Guides looked for a corner in Romal's circular room, and they pointed out the dimensional distance to the universe. At that, Romal had rolled his eyes and had shaken his head, much like he was shaking his head now, only this time, to clear it from the unpleasant scenes of Zia's tenth life.

At the doorway, a Soul from the Order of Messengers stood waiting, her brow glistening with tricolored sparks of faith and distress. Her distress, Romal shared; her faith, he admired. He gave her a commiserating nod as he glided to the Dimensional Window.

As Earth approached, the window widened for an expanded view. Spiraling out from three continents were five thick life-cords, each cord encasing a Niine Determinant's Ribbon of Life.

Briefly, the ethereal tentacles untangled, giving view to another cord. Romal recounted. Yes, yes, six cords now, the sixth Determinant having just descended. His arrival on Earth completed the second set of six Niine Determinants—the first set having lived the prior millennium, the third set awaiting the upcoming millennium.

Romal tapped his chin, thoughtfully. Could Zia have ignited a ripple effect at a time more troubling? Sadly, no. All of Haven's Peril Guides were needed to counter the Determinants' influence on Players. Could Zia have ignited a ripple carting a greater consequence? What greater loss could there be than to lose the Dyads' cord, and with it, Haven's right to preserve humanity?

Regaining the cord required the skill of a Peril Guide; to that, Romal agreed. That the Peril Guide should be Alpha, Romal disagreed. "Your first Entity?" Romal argued. "But Alpha leads the Peril Guides in our present battle. Yes, yes, of course you're aware of that."

Initially, Romal perceived an inequity of concern—more being given to the future Players and less being given to the current Players—but his perception changed when he was given insight into another issue, one more profound, one rooted in the Great War.

As Earth crossed the dimensional window, the cords stretched and lashed, one grazing the pane.

Romal pressed into the window. "Such audacity."

"Shall I bring Alpha?" the Messenger asked.

"Yes, yes," Romal said without a glance from the cords. "Wait. Just wait." Every moment he delayed was another moment Alpha would have to thrash those Determinants. Or hinder them at least; Alpha wouldn't have time for a proper thrashing. The cords whipped across the window as if they were sensing Romal's stare and attempting to strike him.

Romal peered harder, unmoving, unblinking, until the cords shrank back, coiling into themselves. The planet rolled away.

When Earth had become a blot in the distance, Romal turned from the window, "Yes, I suppose now is—" and bumped into Alpha, tall and thin, his face deeply etched, his disposition sullen if not morose. But Alpha cast a light all his own. His eyes were fashioned of fire—two eternally burning orange flames. When Romal looked into those flames, he warmed with joy, love, and pride, though he spared no effort to conceal it. To that end, he restrained the urge to embrace Alpha. Emotional displays caused Alpha unease, especially when displayed in the presence of others—the *other,* at the moment, being a Messenger who deserved a chastising frown, which Romal readily gave.

The Messenger responded with an innocent smile. "I heard 'yes,' so I left. Did you say something more?"

"Indeed." Romal dismissed her. He then turned to Alpha, whose skills with complex strategies would not be afforded to the current, global travesty. Instead, only one travesty awaited Alpha—a small, green Agitator with maroon hair. "My delay in sending for you," Romal said, "was to allow another minute or two for you to thrash those Niine Determinants."

"Andromnis now leads the battle against the Determinants of today," Alpha said. "I am tasked to the Determinants of tomorrow, both to battle Niine's and to protect One's."

"*If* there's a One Determinant to protect. Half a Dyad stumbled toward Niine. With her choice went our right to the Dyads' future cord. The right now hangs in the balance, and in the balance, it will stay, until the Dyads and the three Souls complicit in her stumble gather at the Neutral Point for the Dyads to make their choice whole. Regrettably, the outcome depends on a very undependable Agitator."

"Zia?"

With an indignant huff, Romal shook an accusatory finger overhead. "Yin Messengers, you're chatterboxes, every last one of you."

Alpha pressed down gently on Romal's arm. "The Messenger did not inform me. I have felt Zia's vibrations since her initial Awakening."

"Really? Since 1631, you have *felt* her vibrations? Then you, my friend, suffered dearly...because that Agitator's vibrations played for Niine."

Alpha blinked with surprise.

Romal gave a curt nod. "You heard correctly; she played for Niine." His hands knotting at his backside, Romal began a slow, thoughtful pace. "Zia caused a ripple effect that returned four of our Players home—Zia included. Their deaths empowered Murdock MacKenzie, the Soul named Triite, Player for Niine, Order of Persuaders, and a formidable Persuader at that. He gained the admiration of his cousin, Peter Taylor, our Dyad, and that admiration grew unabated. Had Zia opened her mouth to plant one seed of truth, or had she cared an iota to—"

"She is an Agitator; an Agitator's nature is apathetic not caring."

Romal's pacing halted. His shoulders drew back. "Am I to understand that *you* are informing *me* of an Agitator's nature? Well, Alpha, you may be the Teacher of Peril Guides and quite the Peril Guide yourself, but I believe I am the expert on the Eleventh Order, am I not?" Romal raised a finger and a cactus appeared. "Eleventh Order Basics: Both Agitator and cacti thrive under desolate conditions, flourish with minimal attention, and bloom after lengthy solitude. If you desire a fragrant garden, you should plant lavender and roses. If a cheerful flowering is more to your liking, you should nurture the hollyhocks and mums. But if you cultivate cacti or guide an Agitator, you should keep your distance or expect to be pricked. That is their nature." Romal twitched and the cactus disappeared. "And that is page one of one thousand in the Comparative Chronicles, a resource most Guides respect to this day."

"As it deserves," Alpha said. "Your compilation is a mastery of—"

"Yes, yes, a mound of praises, which you'll top with an apology, which I'll claim none due, which you won't accept until I accept an apology not due. Glad we chatted. Now let's get to the crux of the problem, namely Zia.

Alpha, her Soul does not bloom. Regardless of the condition or the amount of attention, her Soul refuses to bloom. When disagreeable, most Agitators proffer a sharp but well-mannered complaint. Zia, however, shrieks. Not an ordinary shriek, mind you, but a shriek vexed with antimatter."

"Respectfully, Romal, address the event that shifted our right to the cord."

"Why?" Romal cast a look of reproach. "If that were all you needed to know, then that would be all I would tell you. And if that were all that I told you, then our Players will choose at the Neutral Point as they chose in Alaska. If you're to succeed in changing their decisions, you had better focus less on the culminating event and more on the underlying issue—Zia."

A contrite looking Alpha said, "Continue."

"Geminus's Charge, Ereo, served as Peter Taylor, the Dyad who made very poor choices. Poor indeed. Against the good sense of Geminus's whispers and under the foolish notion of impressing Murdock, Peter bought a gun. Zia knew of the gun, but against my whispers, chose to keep quiet. Peter hid the gun, later pulled the gun, and in Peter's hand, that gun fired, returning Zia home and sweeping the cord into neutral."

"When will the Neutral Point take place?"

Romal summoned The Book of Measure and a podium to set it on. Pages whirled. When they finally settled, Romal's finger scrolled to the bottom. "Neutral Point, one hundred years, 1998. Awen returns to Earth in 1973 and Ereo in '74." Romal looked up. "The Book still reflects a destined relationship, but it no longer records them as husband and wife."

"What year will the cord rise?"

Romal drew in a long breath; what he was about to suggest would undoubtedly stun Alpha, perhaps even shock him. "Alpha, consider steering our Players away from the Neutral Point."

Alpha's eyes brightened; his head cocked.

"Calm yourself," Romal said, "and get that look off your face. I haven't changed sides. I'm not asking you to do it; I'm asking you to consider it. If our Players don't arrive at the Neutral Point, the Dyads cannot make their choice whole. Half a Dyad is half a choice, and the cord remains neutral."

"One's Determinant cannot descend a neutral cord."

"Neither can Niine's!" Romal's outburst did not punctuate his point; it merely perplexed Alpha. And why would it not? Alpha didn't really know Zia. Even if Alpha could sense her vibrations, he couldn't possibly know the extent or the depth of the risk she posed. "Alpha, consider the consequence of our losing at the Neutral Point. Niine gains the cord and completes the third set of six Determinants *two centuries* ahead of schedule. We're unprepared for a 21st Century battle. We're prepared to win that war in the 23rd. If beelzeNiine gains the cord, and I suspect he'll spare no power to do so, our Players won't suffer another Holocaust; they'll suffer annihilation."

Alpha shook his head. "If One's Determinant cannot descend in the 21st Century, by the 22nd, no Player will care about a 23rd. What year will the cord rise?"

Romal glanced again at The Book. "2002. Because Zia's vibrations played for beelzeNiine, their side receives a ten-fold advantage for the Neutral Point. Three parities comprise the advantage." He read aloud:

*"Parity One: So as the Agitator withheld her voice,
so shall her voice fall on deaf ears, ten-fold."*

Romal paused to consider. "This parity might work to our benefit. Deaf ears ten-fold and Zia lies ten-fold, perhaps it's a wash."

"Then Zia's truths must multiply twenty-fold."

"Hmm, from zero-fold to twenty-fold. Good luck with that."

"To level disparities—"

"No, no. Around Zia, water within a glass won't level. Your whispers won't change that. The second she's plucked from the womb, she runs amok. On this side, Souls avoid her. All Souls, including those of her own Order. Her only friend is Awen, the Dyad to Ereo. Without a shred beyond truth, Zia's inner Soul is—well, it's disturbing. I've scrutinized her Soul and can state with absolute certainty that her vibrations are incorrect. Yes, yes, no such thing; nevertheless, her vibrations are unequivocally incorrect. Alpha, suppose for a moment, the violence in her initial Awakening was not an anomaly, not in and of itself, but rather, a symptom of one, of an intrinsic anomaly. It might explain her unfruitful lives. Observe the ten."

With a touch to Alpha's forehead, Romal transferred the images of Zia's lives. He rested a hand on Alpha's shoulder to watch the scenes roll under Alpha's control.

In Zia's first life, late 1600s, Alpha slowed the images near the time of her death. Zia had designed and built a cargo ship, but she set sail, knowing it wasn't seaworthy. It sank on its maiden voyage; terrified men floundered in the sea. Romal muted the sound; he had heard their screams countless times.

"Forty-two drowned," Romal said, "including Zia. "It would have been eighty-eight, but resourceful Guides created obstacles to boarding."

"During Zia's Life Review, how did she account for her decision?"

"Hear for yourself." Romal held up a finger, and Zia's words blared overhead.

*Hey, I'm not responsible. Players do whatever they want, whenever*
*they want. Free Will, that's what you call it. Free Will!*

"Further," Romal said, "she blames Guides for her behavior. She accuses us of having placed her in the wrong Order. Numerous times, I've tried to explain—"

"You *explain?*" Alpha blinked rapidly. *"Explain* what she intrinsically *knows?"*

Romal released a long, tired sigh. Not only did he *explain* matters to Zia, matters she would inherently know, but he would now have to explain this oddity to Alpha; moreover, he would have to explain it repeatedly because Alpha was a Guide of logic, and the oddity defied logic.

"When Zia feigns ignorance, she hasn't a spark of deception. How is that possible? Her entirety is skioses; she *is* knowledge. Nonetheless, when she pretends to lack knowledge, she hasn't a spark of deception to indicate otherwise. She's like a Player who insists, 'Only water runs in my veins.' Preposterous, of course. So, you draw your knife, you give them a good nick, and you are prepared to say, 'see, there's your blood,' only the joke is on you—out spurts water."

"Zia does not spark deception?"

"Of course she does, more sparks than a match lit in a powder keg. But when she denies even knowing the truth, she hasn't a flicker."

Alpha moved the scenes along: Early 1700s, lives two and three, both males, both slaves, and both ended in execution before her twentieth year.

"According to Zia," Romal said, "Agitators have no business as slaves, and I should have expected those lives wasted."

Lives four and five appeared and disappeared as short-stays—lives less than eleven years. Romal groaned. "Short-stays cause her a tirade. Believing she has had an inequitable number, she ordered the Counters to run a tally. Naturally, the Counters laughed, mistaking her absurdity for humor."

Alpha reversed the scenes, rechecking the start of each life.

"What is it?" Romal asked. "What concerns you about her births?"

"When descending into a male fetus, she hesitates."

"Hesitates if we're lucky. Before her sixth life, she disappeared. Dozens from the Order of Seekers went out in search. At the dimension's edge, they found her chasing Figments. We kept the poor mother in labor for three days, three *Earth* days. Zia still balked at the cord because she hasn't a shred of appreciation for the Yang perspective. 'Gender-matched lives only,' she tells me. So I told her, 'Do we look like a haberdashery? Do you think we tailor genders to fit one's request?' And she shouts, 'Well, why not? Why? Why? Why? And what the hell'—her words mind you—'is a haberdashery?'"

Alpha examined the sixth life, late 1700s. Imbued with artistic talent and placed in Paris, Zia had two loving parents, a well-rounded childhood, and a mentor for her gift. But at age seventeen, Zia began sipping absinthe. Within a few years, her talent and her life dissolved.

Alpha backtracked to a scene in a cafe where Zia sat at a table, her glass held high. Across from her, a buxom woman, her hair tousled, tipped her glass to clink Zia's. From the woman's head rose a life-cord containing the mottled Ribbon of a Niine Player. Before Alpha could lift the veil to identify the Soul, Romal said, "It's Triite."

"Two lives connecting to Zia?"

"No. Three. Move on."

Alpha forwarded to Zia's seventh life—Apache, born 1843.

By 1860, Zia had aligned herself with a Player named BlackDog. Zia's thoughts corrupted. Her apathy escalated to viciousness.

Removed 1864.

Alpha focused on BlackDog.

"Triite again," Romal said. "Born 18 months after Zia."

"Why Zia? What purpose does it serve to pursue Zia?"

"I've pondered the same, innumerable times, but I've yet to fathom a reason. Zia is a harmless Agitator, reckless at best. Triite is an accomplished Persuader, able to coerce hundreds, even thousands, during one lifetime. Why would Niine send a powerful Persuader against Zia?" Romal shook his head, distressed by the thought. "And yet, they did. They most certainly did."

Alpha moved past another short-stay and onto Zia's next life—Gavin MacKenzie.

"An excellent placement," Romal said, "or so I thought and so it began. Because Zia deafens her Soul to my whispers, I positioned her close to Awen, her friend. At first, it worked well; Zia intuitively felt her friend's vibrations. As such, Gavin respected his Aunt Mirabelle very much, though not quite enough to impart the truth at the critical moment. Regardless, Zia's placement appeared safe; all peripheral positions belonged to our side. Well, all except two—Gavin's father, whom Niine had already beset with illness, and Gavin's future brother, whose life-cord would snake to Hades within the year. And what demon did they choose? Triite! Unquestionably, Niine targeted my Charge. But I countered. Yes, yes, I countered. In 1873, as the life-cord rose from Mirabelle's womb, I stopped Ereo's descent and sent Phoenix in her stead."

"Romal, you changed the Dyads' designed relationship?"

"The Book stated, mother and son, not mother and eldest son. Mirabelle was destined for two sons, so Ereo became the younger son, Peter. I believed the switch imperative to protect my Charge. Phoenix is a worthy Healer with a sterling record of defeating Triite. Zia, on the other hand, can barely descend a life-cord. Instead of gliding smoothly through a cord and slipping gently into a womb, Zia corkscrews down, smacks the womb, jars the mother, and flips the fetus. Nearly every birth is breech. She's no match for a Persuader, let alone this one. Further, Zia carries a sizeable fragment of hatred toward Triite."

"Zia should not learn a Niine Player's identity."

Romal swept in a deep breath to fortify his patience. It was going to be a long Century, a *very* long Century. "Yes, Alpha. Zia *shouldn't* quite a lot of things. She *shouldn't* spy on a Player's Awakening because the Soul might be a Niine Player, and it was. She *shouldn't* sneak to Earth to ride a tornado because it might jumble her particles, and it did. And she *shouldn't* take pride in updating her invectives because it might offend the listener, and it has. Her latest—crap, shit and chrissake."

"I do not understand."

"'Crap' and 'shit' are slang for a Player's excrement. 'Chrissake,' is a slur referencing a One Determinant, though I could be mistaken. I'm not an etymologist of the profane."

"I understand the language; I do not understand her purpose."

"Her purpose? That's a question best posed to Zia."

Alpha took another count of Zia's lives. "Romal, you stated ten lives but imparted nine."

"Review the moments before her last short-stay. You'll see the fiasco."

Alpha reversed the scenes to the minutes before Zia's short-stay.

A Seeker and Zia stood side by side, each holding a cord rising from a twin—a male and a female. Peering into her cord, Zia gasped, "I have a tail!"

True to the Seeker's nature, he sparked curiosity.

Zia held out her cord. "See for yourself." She offered to hold the Seeker's cord while he had a look. The moment he handed her the cord, down Zia went. Immediately, Guides seized her and brought her back.

Zia never touched the womb.

Alpha froze the image and looked at Romal. The inevitable question hung in the space between them, *How did that count as a life?* Alpha didn't ask it aloud, and Romal appreciated that; he needed time to steady himself before answering. "Pull up the image at the point where we stopped her descent. Zoom in on her eyes."

Upon rechecking the image, Alpha noticed a dark blue particle leave Zia's eye—wide and fixed on the female twin. The particle dotted the womb.

"Her great desire for a gender-match cost her a life," Romal said. "I pleaded with One, 'Do not count that tear as a life. This Soul needs every moment we can afford her to prepare for her Twelfth.'" Romal coughed into a fist to rid the quake from his voice. "One always answers, but not always the answer prayed for. The tear touched the womb; the life stands."

Alpha looked expectantly at Romal, but Romal turned away. He had nothing more to say on the subject, other than to repeat, "The life stands; One decreed it."

As Romal glided to the dimensional window, he felt the heat from Alpha's eyes tracking him and imploring him to explain further. Romal shook his head. "Let it go, Alpha."

For a long while, neither spoke. "Romal," Alpha said, his voice barely breaking a whisper, "do you doubt Zia to choose One in her Twelfth Life?"

Romal tightened. His issues with faith were private matters, not matters for discussion. But before he could state as much, Alpha presumed the answer and began citing rules, laws, and protections that the Covenants afforded—matters well known to Romal. What wasn't well known—or was rarely seen—was this side of Alpha, an Alpha attempting to impart cheer. Or perhaps comfort. Though an awkward attempt—Romal had written half the laws—Romal found it touching all the same.

In due propriety, Romal fashioned a chair, sat, and allowed Alpha to continue uninterrupted...until Alpha said, "A Guide of Niine cannot interact with a Twelfth Life Player. The Covenants forbidding it have not changed."

"But the world did." Romal motioned at Earth spinning away in the dimensional window. "The world changed. A Guide has no need to interact with any Player beyond his own Charge. It's simply inefficient. Back when Earth had a scant population and the majority of Souls were reaching their Twelfth Life, the Hands-Off Law served them well. When a Guide from Niine commanded, 'Plunder that village,' he had better get comfortable for he had a long wait. His Players had to heat up the irons, pound the metals, fashion the swords, gather the horses, and draw up the maps. That took decades. Often, the soldiers arrived as old men with forgotten goals.

"All that is moot now. Players are plentiful, widespread, and skilled. Incredibly fast, too. Within a single day, a Player can cast a net of influence across an entire continent. For Guides of both sides, One and Niine, the most expeditious means of affecting the maximum number of Players is for a Guide to affect his own Charge.

"The Twelfth Life Covenants are pointless now, no better than an archaic law that forbids the use of a slingshot against—"

"A giant?"

Romal frowned; he didn't appreciate the parallel. Not one bit. "Zia is hardly a David. And from my viewpoint, she is sorely disadvantaged through no fault of her own. She didn't change the world, didn't write the Covenants, and didn't choose to be the only Soul who has yet to live a Twelfth Life. By 333 years, she's the only Soul yet to consecrate. If a Niine Player coerces her decision— If he persuades her path for— for—" His voice was breaking. He should have clipped the issue at the start. *Right at the start!* Had he done so, he would be articulating his point, not stammering his worries that he never intended to share.

He paused to regain himself. "Yes, yes, I'm certain all is fair. Somehow. If Zia consecrates to Niine, well then, we'll just pray for her turnabout in a following life—life 13 or 14. Perhaps life ten thousand. After all, consecrated Niine Players change sides all the time."

Alpha's brows bunched in a questioning look.

Romal sighed. "Alpha, I was being facetious. My struggle with faith is my concern; moreover, it was quite predictable. Guides band to their Charges. Not Peril Guides, of course. You have no Charges. You have melees to quell and disasters to avert...and then you move on. For all other Guides, including Interim Guides such as myself, we must guard against bias for we connect to our Charges, even those Charges who make a mockery of our guidance."

With a sweep of his arm, Romal stretched a mural of igloos across the room. The memory gave him a smile. "South Pole. I scoured the Earth for the perfect location for Zia's Twelfth Life. Well, it's not to be. So much for perfect placements."

"Romal, isolation would not have protected her."

Romal's smile bent. "The hell you say. I sought to protect others. As I previously told you, when Zia shrieks, atoms burst. Eardrum atoms as well." He pointed to the natives. "Their entire tribe is genetically deaf." He disposed of the mural and returned to The Book of Measure.

*"Parity two: So as the Dyad bonded to the Persuader,*
*so shall that bond increase, ten-fold."*

Romal tapped the page. "A parity most upsetting to Geminus. His whispers failed to penetrate Peter's attachment to Murdock, and this parity strengthens that attachment ten-fold."

"What breaks the attachment?"

"Truth. Unfortunately, the truth must come from Zia and must occur within the Neutral Point. At no other time and from no other Player will the truth break the tethers to the initial event." Romal read:

*"Parity Three: So as limits of knowledge preceded the*
*initial event, so shall limits of knowledge precede the*
*Neutral Point. Peripheral Players may not acquire knowledge*
*prior to the Dyad. The Dyad may not acquire knowledge*
*prior to nor beyond the knowledge proffered by the*
*Agitator within the Neutral Point."*

He closed The Book. "There you have it, three parities for the Neutral Point. If unchained from the initial event, the Dyads will return the Cord to One. Of that, I'm confident. But if they're still tethered to the ignorance they held in Alaska, they'll replay their previous decisions, only this time, with a devastating result for mankind; Niine gains the cord."

Alpha looked out the dimensional window, his eyes casting a reddish haze over Earth's sunrises and sunsets. Romal waited patiently, knowing Alpha's thoughts were churning, sorting, and absorbing all that he had heard. Romal only hoped Zia was waiting patiently as well. Awen had gone to join her and his presence would anchor Zia in Divisional...unless a Figment had happened by first. Was Zia now gallivanting across the universe to wherever that Figment tumbled?

Wanting to speed things along, Romal peeked into Alpha's thoughts. They centered on Phoenix, the Soul inside Matthew.

"Caught in the ripple effect," Romal said. "Matthew gained knowledge of Murdock's character at the most inopportune time—April 3rd, 1898. Despite our best efforts, we could not keep Matthew off the Chilkoot Pass." Romal smiled apologetically. "Excuse the intrusion, but prudence dictates a bit of haste."

"Haste?"

"Zia." Romal gestured toward Divisional. "I couldn't bring her home. It's another oddity to her Soul. She pretends a desire for Haven, but her inner Soul staunchly refuses. More than once, I've had to leave her in Divisional. Sometimes she stays, more often, she wanders off. She loves to chase Figments. I'm hopeful that Awen is with her, although the poor Dyad can barely speak. Half his atoms are missing, and the remaining half, a fretful scattering, circle and dart, round and round, in a pitiful search for their missing pair. Geminus, quite heartbroken for his Charges, pressed his desire for Awen to remain in Haven. But Awen wouldn't hear of it. He's more concerned for Zia's welfare than he is for his own. Geminus relented, partly to please Awen and partly to keep Zia from chasing Figments. I'm grateful for that. Please repay the favor; the moment you see Awen, send him home."

Alpha bowed. Romal tipped his head to acknowledge the bow. Then— Alpha's unease be damned—Romal pulled the somber Guide into a quick embrace. "A bit of advice," Romal said, "Zia spits on all courtesies, common or otherwise. Strangely, however, she respects the signal for silence. Don't question it, be thankful for it, and keep your hand free. You'll need to raise it quite often."

Alpha vanished.

When the orange glow from Alpha's eyes had faded from the dimension, Romal looked toward Haven. "Yes, yes, your infinite wisdom deems this path necessary for his self-forgiveness. Splendid. For I, too, await the day he permits himself joy; however, in my ever-so-humble opinion, the path seems rather harsh and the stakes quite high."

# 4

"Am I going to Hades?"

"No," Awen said before his vacuous stare returned.

"*Whew!* You had me scared for a—Wait. Are you?"

His head rocked side to side, a zombie-like motion for no.

I tugged him, "Awen?" but he didn't blink.

I gripped his shoulders, ready to give him a good shake, but then I reconsidered; jostling him might cause a permanent trance the way slapping a cross-eyed Player causes permanent cockeyes. I couldn't risk it. I slid to his feet and formed Tiddledy-Winks.

A while later, I heard him mumble. When my head tilted back, I caught a splash of inky-blue. I got to my feet. "Awen, I can take it. Just tell me. It can't be that bad. I've eliminated the two worst possibilities."

Before he could answer, a Guide appeared. Awen moved aside because he respects all Guides, even Guides with lousy timing.

"Is that your Guide?" I asked Awen.

His head rocked, no.

"Good," I said, "I'll get rid of him." I started toward the Guide. "Hey, private meeting here. Souls only, get it? Just take your—"

With a dip of his head, the Guide dismissed Awen.

I whipped around, but Awen had already disappeared.

I stormed up to the intruder. "Why did you do that? Huh? Couldn't you tell something was wrong? Why did you dismiss him? For chrissake, Awen is my friend. You ruined everything. WHY?"

The Guide, stiff as a tree—a big, ugly Redwood tree—prodded me back with his branch-like finger.

"You're in trouble," I told him. "Got that? You stopped a Messenger in the middle of his duty. That's right, a Messenger. You didn't know that, did you, Tree-Guide? Yep, you're in big trouble. When Awen's Guide hears about this, he'll prune you."

The Guide's hand rose.

Wow, what nerve! My mouth shut with a deliberate snap. Then I waited and waited—because when a Guide raises their hand, they're supposed to talk. But this Guide didn't know that either; he didn't say a word. Sparks of impatience shimmered on my outstretched arms that were jerking, *Well? Well?*

The Guide squinted, as if he didn't get it, as if he had never seen a Soul before. My foot tapped, my fingers clicked, I alternated from cupping my ear to pointing at my sparks.

The Guide looked at me more queerly.

I gave up. Eventually, my red sparks fizzled away. Only then did the Guide lower his hand.

He introduced himself as Alpha, my new Guide.

*New?* Jeez, after more than 200 years, Romal had pawned me off...and to a rookie, a *new* Guide.

Romal hadn't even said goodbye, good luck, or good riddance. Nothing. I palmed each eye—upset about Awen not Romal. Romal had tossed me aside like one tosses aside a rotting turnip. But I wasn't hurt. Not a bit.

"Untrue," said the newbie Guide. "You are hurt, but mistakenly so. Romal has grave concerns for your welfare."

"STAY OUT OF MY HEAD! Got that? I'm upset about Awen. Only Awen." I sized up the Alpha-Guide—freakishly tall, seriously glum, reddish-brown face resembling carved bark that would splinter if he smiled. His eyes, weirdest of all, sizzled like smoldering coals—coals of orange. Orange! Orange is no color for eyes. Orange is only good for oranges.

"Listen up," I said. "Let's get a few things straight. You're supposed to guide me when I'm down there." I pointed to Earth. "That's your job. You're not supposed to interfere when I'm on this side. That's not your job. Get it?"

He squinted again, his head tilting.

Being new, he probably hadn't come across a green Soul with purple hair before. I glided up to his nose. "I don't like anyone staring at me. Get it?"

A scorching light flashed from his eyes and singed my cheeks. I swept back, "You're not nice," then glided meters away.

I sat with my arms crossed and my back turned on the grim Guide who had called for my silence but hadn't talked, and who had burned my cheeks but hadn't apologized. To hell with him. And to hell with Romal for dumping me without even a lousy goodbye.

Hours later, I glanced over my shoulder.

Alpha was still there, still staring, still thinking his orange eyes scared me. "Won't work," I mumbled knowing that all Guides eavesdrop on mumbles. To prove my indifference, I whistled, *whrr-whrr-whrrrr*, until I grew tired of puckering. Again, I glanced back.

Alpha was still there.

I envisioned Tiddledy-Winks. Halfway into my winning game, *whish*, my Winks disappeared. I remade the Winks. A second later, they vanished, too. I shouted over my shoulder, "GO AWAY!"

He stayed. And he stayed quiet. Romal would have yelled—not that I missed Romal or his yelling, because I didn't. I just think yelling beats silence. Anything beats silence, especially when you don't have a Wink to flip.

I scooted sideways to look up at him. I'm not sure why I said it or why it came out like I was hacking up sand. "I—M—sau—sau—sau—sorry."

His heated orange eyes cooled. He bent down and poked my forehead; that's how Guides start Life Reviews, except the trainee Guide did it wrong. "You're supposed to use your thumb," I told him, my lids lowering. "Romal always used his thumb. And you slide it across my forehead. Slide not jab."

My Life Review started with scenes from childhood, which dragged on and on, pushing my boredom to the brink of a coma. When manhood started, I said, "Just so you know, Romal promised to give me gender-matched lives from now on. No more Yang, got it?" I peeked from one eye. My sparks glimmered in the colors of lies—*Damn*.

When we reached the Alaskan scenes, I started to shiver. My hand paddled for Alpha to hurry things along, get to my death and get out of this life. But instead of fast-forwarding, the pictures slowed. Eventually, they centered on Peter Taylor, stupid Peter Taylor, who was yelping and fussing over an elbow, just a goddam elbow.

My heroic moment was coming next, so I bumped Alpha and told him to watch closely. "I'm about to save my brother's life."

In a blur of moments, Peter pulled the gun and aimed it at Murdock. Heroically, I jumped in front of the gun and wrestled for control.

Peter shot me.

A tiny starburst signals the end of a Life Review, but the new Guide didn't know that because he stopped the images before the starburst came.

I rubbed my eyes open. "You're supposed to wait for the little starburst. Life Reviews start with a sliding thumb and end with a starburst. Didn't they teach you anything in Guide School?"

"We have not completed the review."

"Sure we have. Gavin died. I'm proof. Life over. Jeez."

"Zia, when Mirabelle inquired into Murdock's nature, why did you choose silence?"

"What difference does it make? I took the goddam bullet."

Alpha's face crunched up so tight, I thought it would crack. "In my presence, you will refrain from slurs and profanities."

I half-shrugged, half-nodded.

"Zia, why did you keep secret Peter's gun?"

"I didn't. I told, uhm, Matthew." Lies flickered—*stupid sparks*—but I slapped them off. "I can't help it if Matthew didn't hear me. Maybe his eardrums were frozen, or the wind was howling, *Whrrr*, like that."

"Why did you keep secret Murdock's character?"

"Why? You're asking *why?*" Despite all the objects I could fashion—pillows, yo-yos, Tiddledy-Winks—I could never get a cue card of excuses to appear. "Well, because—because I don't gossip. Yeah. I don't gossip."

"Murdock assaulted, robbed, and ended the lives of returning prospectors. True?"

*Ut-oh.* A queasy feeling started ringing bells and sounding alarms—Warning! Warning! A trainload of trouble is coming down the tracks. Prepare to dodge it or derail it. "Uhm, who?"

"Murdock MacKenzie."

I bit my lip and turned toward Saturn. An icicle storm was pelting its ring. I wanted to be there. Or be anywhere—anywhere else than where I sat.

Alpha didn't repeat the question. He just leaned down and poked my forehead—*again, poked!* I got stuck with a slow learner.

The scene began with an audible clip of my last thought as Gavin; *finally, warm toes.* Then Peter fell to his knees and bawled. Jeez, he cried so hard, I almost felt sorry for him—almost, but not quite, because Peter had also bawled over an elbow.

Murdock walked over to my lifeless body, nudged a boot into my side, and then—"*Whoa!* Back it up! Stop the scene. Did you see what Murdock did? Back it up. After I saved his life, that ungrateful bastard spat on me!"

Alpha let the pictures roll. In the next scene, Peter was tying supply planks together for a makeshift gurney. Others offered to help, but Peter refused. When they pointed to the quickening storm, Peter said, "Leave me alone." They walked away, shaking their heads.

When Peter finished the gurney, he used the last of the ropes to secure me on top. "What's he thinking?" I tapped Alpha. "He can't climb down from the summit without a tethering line. How does he expect to—*Oooh.*"

Down the Alaskan chute, Peter tobogganed, his arms clutching my corpse, his legs locked to the gurney, and his face bouncing against the hole in my chest. I began rooting for Peter, *hold on, hold on*, while he thumped and bumped over the grooves and pocks and the ice-packed mounds, until finally, *pa-whoshh*, out from the chute's mouth he came. The sled rambled a ways before it stopped. Slowly, a shaken Peter sat up looking much like a cannibal, my blood dripping from his chin.

The picture then switched to Sheep Camp where several men had carried news of the shooting to Matthew. Immediately, Matthew set out. When he reached the first bend, an Indian woman blocked his path and started jabbering in Tlingit.

"Alpha, fast-forward," I said. "Matthew doesn't know a lick of Tlingit."

"Nor did he hear Tlingit." Alpha replayed the scene, only this time, the Indian spoke English.

"Turn around," she said. "The snow is wet, the mountain angry. Twice, the mountain warns gently." She swiped the front of herself as if brushing off crumbs. "Soon hard." She smacked her chest. "Cheechakos will die."

"Hold on a minute," I said. "I thought she spoke Tlingit."

"Matthew heard English."

"How? Did Guides do that?"

"True."

"What for? A mad mountain?"

"Avalanches."

"Avalanches? We had a couple of hill slides in the morning, but no one was hurt. Right?"

Alpha wouldn't answer, which brought back my queasy feeling of impending trouble. "Forget it," I said. "Let's just hurry this along, okay?"

In the next scene, Matthew pushed past the Indian.

The Indian called after him, "Cheechakos will die."

Minutes before noon, a mile before the Scales, Matthew hugged a sorrowful Peter.

My nerves relaxed and my chewed fingers left my mouth to settle on my lap. Any moment, the starburst would come. *Finally* come.

But that didn't happen.

What happened was a loud, sharp crack, followed by a low, menacing rumble. Half the mountainside tore free and curled like a white tsunami.

Stampeders shouted and shoved in a scrambling panic to get off the hill. But the slab of ice and Earth—its height eclipsing the sun and its breadth stretching ten acres—enveloped them all, burying some to depths of fifty feet. Their cries and screams ended abruptly. Dead silence, except for the suffocating gasps of dying men.

Fixed on the spot where Matthew and Peter had been standing, I whispered, "Come on, dig out, dig out. *Please,* dig out."

Nothing stirred.

Sheep Camp emptied as stampeders became rescue workers. Still, more than sixty Players returned to Energy, Matthew and Peter included.

Before I could even hope for the starburst, the picture switched to my Aunt Mirabelle, a devout Catholic, who was in church honoring Palm Sunday the day of the avalanche.

Nine days after receiving news of her sons' deaths, Aunt Mirabelle scrubbed her house, end to end, and then crossed herself as she rested back in her favorite rocking chair. At first, I thought she was napping, but then I noticed her chest had stopped rising and falling.

From the Player's shell, a Soul reached up—a fist of navy blue.

"Awen?"

The fist seized its life-cord...

"Awen, no!"

...and snapped it.

The starburst came.

*Did someone burn her with holy water?*

Alpha found the Agitator more perplexing than Romal had described. Like all Souls, Zia was a structure of skioses—fused particles of awareness. From that structure, she would instantly realize every consequence attaching to each choice she had made as Gavin. She would know this more acutely than a Player would know their own physicality—the appearance of their face, the sound of their voice, the recognition of their body. Life Reviews were merely an accounting, not a discovery.

But strangely, Zia had no concept of herself, as if she were staring in a mirror and denying the reflection as her own. When Alpha queried her on Gavin's choices, Zia lied and mumbled. Her evasions ended abruptly when Awen emerged from Mirabelle.

Distraught, Zia hugged her knees against her chest and rocked. Ribbons of dark blue sparks cascaded from her face and pooled around her bottom.

Alpha placed a comforting hand on Zia's back. "Zia, do you understand how your vibrations played for Niine?"

Zia whirled away from Alpha's touch. "I didn't do squat for Niine," she said. "Peter did! That dim-witted ninny shot me. And he got himself and Matthew killed. Because of him, Awen broke his cord."

Never in Alpha's eternal existence was he more amazed; not one of Zia's sparks evidenced a lie. Molecular awareness without awareness. Alpha imagined a Player under a physician's knife. Upon the first cut, the physician expects to find blood...*only the joke is on you—out spurts water.*

For the physician to save the patient, he must set aside what is possible and impossible and address what is...and transfuse water instead of blood.

Similarly, Zia required *given* knowledge. For now, Alpha would have to accommodate—*transfuse water*—and explain all matters.

"Zia, so as you trust our Warriors to defend not slaughter, our Constructors to create not sabotage, and our Seekers to search not stagnate, so as they trust our Agitators to expose, not conceal. A silent Agitator is a Niine Agitator. Your vibrations served Niine, ten-fold."

Zia frowned as if angry, but her lights showed otherwise; they sparkled in the variegated shades of bewilderment.

To learn the depth of her unawareness, Alpha posed an elementary question. "Zia, what is the spark of knowledge that awakened the Souls?"

"Don't you know? Are you sure you're a Guide?"

"Answer the question."

Zia grumbled irritably, but after a minute, she perked. "An electron?"

Again, her answer drew to Alpha's mind the picture of a Player's vein spurting water. He had hardly shaken free from astonishment when Zia said, "I've answered your question, now answer mine. Who played Murdock?"

"Murdock is not your issue."

"The hell he's not. I saved his skin. And while my blood was melting the snow, he spat on me. He spat on his dead brother. I want his name. I demand his name *and* his Order."

"Your duty is to Ereo."

"*Ereo?*" Her tongue clucked as though the name had sullied her mouth. "*Ereo* left Awen. Forget Ereo."

A pink spark fell from Zia's forehead. She caught it, buried it within a fist, and began whistling as she turned toward Saturn, her arm stretching downward, her wrist snapping.

*Concealing the spark?* Her nonsense grated on Alpha. He glided to the front of her. "When you cleaned your Soul after Awakening, you missed a negative fragment, one that propagates jealousy."

"My Soul is my business."

"Zia, it is far less troublesome to remove a fragment than to conceal its effect. You should remove it immediately, lest you forget and carry it into your next life."

"Forget about fragments. Forget about Ereo. Just tell me who...played... MURDOCK?" Red sparks splintered from between her clenched teeth and struck Alpha's nose.

Wholly appalled, Alpha blasted a torrent of atoms from his gaping mouth. Earth's wind chimes trembled. Zia toppled backwards.

Alerted by the shock waves, a Peacekeeper appeared. "Sir?" She addressed Alpha, but kept a cautious watch on Zia.

Dazed, Zia fumbled and flopped.

Alpha checked Earth's calendar; months had passed. Months wasted toward the Neutral Point, time moving swiftly on Earth to the hours passing in Divisional. But in Zia's present state, her choices at the Neutral Point would replay her choices in Alaska...and the Dyads' cord would shift to Niine.

Hearing the echo of Romal's advice—*you had better focus less on the culminating event and more on the underlying issue*—Alpha cleared his mind of the Dyads, the Neutral Point, and the cord. Paramount now was finding the reason for Zia's blocked awareness.

"Sir?"

"Do not bind," Alpha told the Peacekeeper. "Just subdue."

The Peacekeeper frowned. "Only subdue?"

Because of her Order's innate ability to detect Niine threaded Souls, the Peacekeeper's frown troubled Alpha. "She is not a Niine Soul," he told her.

The Peacekeeper did not reply, nor did she have to. Her skepticism vibrated clearly...*if you say so*...and she went to Zia.

Still wobbling, Zia squinted up. "Back off. This is a private—"

From the Peacekeeper's hand, spirals of white light descended like radiant cords, first muzzling Zia's mouth, then encircling her downward.

Her eyes closing, Zia's head lulled above a glowing cocoon.

"When Earth reenters this region," Alpha said, "return and awaken her."

The Peacekeeper stretched to gauge Earth's distance. "Sir, permit me to stand guard or secure the binds."

"That is unnecessary." He thanked the Peacekeeper before she vanished.

Standing over Zia, Alpha tried to view her Ribbon, but her dark red lights, thick and tangled, mimicked hair whipping in a storm. Alpha willed the tresses to part and settle.

Swaying from Zia's crown was a wispy band of vibrant colors—Zia's Ribbon of Life. It greeted Alpha, flowing and curling around his fingers.

To Alpha's relief, Zia hadn't damaged her Ribbon. Though a Player's choices prior to their Twelfth Life had no effect on their Ribbon, an Energy's choices did—and Zia spent much time as an Energy.

Despite that time, she had kept her Ribbon smooth and luminous.

Encouraged, Alpha entered the first layer of Zia's Soul.

# 6

*...a mortuary of crawlers with pincers and of flyers with stingers that most people paid good money to exterminate.*

*D*own...*down*...*down*...

Alpha descended toward the Soul's nucleus...

...*down*...*down*...*down*.

...through layers of vibrations that bore no resemblance to vibrations at all. Instead of lowering through misty rainbows, velvety and sheer, Alpha was descending through a smokestack, stifling and sooty.

When Alpha touched the last level, the protective barrier, he looked for the radiance that shines up from the Soul's center, but he saw only murky shadows of filtered light.

Concentrating, Alpha sensed his way to the opening—a square.

When he lowered through the square, his eyes widened. Instead of a well-lit meadow—pristine, bright, tranquil—Zia's Soul resembled an abandoned battlefield where the weapons had been fashioned from glass. Only they were not glass—Alpha shook his head, dismayed—they were fragments. Hundreds and hundreds of fragments. Lifetime after lifetime, Zia had kept her biases, conflicts, and fears she formed while in play. When carted into Energy, they crystallized into prisms.

Across the surface of her core, green boulders rolled like cannonballs and knocked against purple blades. A twisting fence of yellow swords and crimson spikes encircled brown slivers and white needles, some embedded so deeply, only their tips protruded. A wilderness of negative fragments was blanketing Zia's inner light.

Alpha picked up a fragment, peered into the prism, and saw a stairway carved in ice. The Golden Stairs, he realized, an aversion gleaned during her last life. That, he understood; why she had kept it, he did not. Why had she chosen to cripple her Soul and burden a following life?

He picked up another prism.

It contained a sound so he held it to his ear.

Apparently, a vulgarity.

He released it.

For weeks in Divisional's time—months on Earth—Alpha examined prisms, explored vibrations, and scoured the Soul in search of answers.

What he found only raised more questions.

As Romal had said, Zia's vibrations were incorrect. Alpha felt this, too. Undeniably, the vibrations were incorrect. But how? Why? And in what way? Her Soul offered no answers.

Fighting despair, Alpha's arms spread upward, his head tilted back, but he kept his prayer silent and his vibrations restrained. *What Soul is this who darkens their inner light? What is the purpose for their self-injury? What is—is—*

His nose rumpled.

"—THAT SMELL?" From his mouth, two vibrations spilled, *that* and *smell.* They drifted up like pastel veils caught in a breeze.

At Alpha's feet, a dislodged fragment contained something gray and lumpy. Alpha nudged it.

Up came another burst of the putrid stench.

Alpha reeled, immediately switching off his olfactory senses. He wished to leave—leave immediately—but first, he had to gather and remove the two vibrations he had released.

Reaching up, he collected the first vibration, *that*, or what should have appeared as *that.* Half the vibration was missing. Severed.

Alpha gently scooped the second vibration, *smell.* It, too, had changed. Not sliced in half, but certainly distorted.

He weighed the benefits of what expelling and examining more vibrations might reveal against the risk of what overlooking and leaving a vibration would mean—Free Will compromised, a breach to the Covenants.

Preparing to take the risk, Alpha added as much light to the core as possible, and then he readied himself to seize the vibrations before they could scatter or hide. In a firm voice, Alpha issued three more vibrations. "The Great War."

*The* barely materialized before it thinned and...*dissolved?*

Quickly, Alpha caught *Great* and *War* mid-drift, pinned them beneath a fragment, and then scanned every particle of Zia's Soul for the first vibration...because a Guide's vibrations do not, *cannot,* dissolve.

But it had dissolved; Alpha's search confirmed it.

Alpha examined the two remaining vibrations, *Great* and *War.*

He found nothing peculiar about *War*. It had the correct density and weight, and it vibrated the correct meaning.

*Great*, however, had changed, both in shape and in color. Alpha pressed it to his chest; *Great* now vibrated *trivial*. A small dent marred the vibration's center as if it had...*imploded?*

Alpha peered into the concave; all particles were there, but they now spun in reverse.

Not imploded, he realized, but *inverted!*

He considered the resulting effect of having an inverted vibration. *Reverse knowledge?* Though Zia *had* knowledge, it ran counter to intrinsic knowledge, counter to her welfare, counter to advice and truth. Alpha's thoughts slowed; *counter knowledge* emulated a particular group of Players, a group he rarely intervened with—the adolescents.

No sooner had Alpha grasped this theory when the prisms quivered; Zia was waking. Alpha swept from her Soul.

He thanked and dismissed the Peacekeeper.

Alpha crouched beside a groggy Zia and spoke in his gentlest voice. "Zia, do you know why an Energy's form simulates a Player's body?"

Zia rolled her eyes. "Do I have to teach you everything? *We* don't look like Players; Players look like *us.*"

Backward logic. Momentarily, Alpha lost his words. Though he had anticipated an incorrect answer, he had assumed it would at least begin with *because.*

Rethinking, Alpha asked a question that could only be answered if Zia forced her logic to move forward. "What purpose is served by an Energy's nose, ears, mouth, and legs?"

"Pretty obvious," she said, her tone condescending. "Isn't it?"

With amazed curiosity, Alpha shook his head.

"Jeez, why do you think?" she said. "So we can smell, hear, talk, and run."

"But Energies do not—Your speech is not—No breath is needed for—" But to each clipped statement, Zia sparked genuine puzzlement. Though patently illogical, the idea that an Energy's form served a physical purpose was exactly what Zia believed.

Alpha reconsidered his approach. If he provided the answers, would she then rework her logic? "Zia, among Souls for One, the singular purpose of an Energy's form is to provide a familiar means to express love—smiling mouths, approving eyes, embracing arms. Your form, however, expresses strife and anger." He touched a dark blue spark glistening on her cheek. "And an abundance of frustration."

Zia bristled. "STOP STARING AT ME!"

Alpha straightened.

Zia jumped up, her fists swinging wildly at empty space, her screeches demanding Murdock's name and Order.

Alpha's continued refusal enraged Zia more. She stomped and cursed and spat. She envisioned rocks only to kick them.

But as her tantrum went on, no Peacekeeper appeared; Alpha made certain of that. To each of Zia's caustic vibrations, Alpha attached a vibration of his own; *It is this Soul's nature to wake wickedly. Do not interfere.*

For now, Alpha would not advise or guide Zia. Rather, he would employ the Players' tactics for directing a petulant youth. Given that Zia was an Energy, not an adolescent, Alpha considered the method repugnant.

"I WANT MURDOCK'S NAME!" She shouted. "Until I get it, I'm not leaving."

Repugnant but necessary. "True," Alpha told her. "You will remain here. Right here. You will stay in this spot until I return."

"Oh, I ain't leaving until—wait. What?"

To quell a foreseeable argument, Alpha lifted his hand. "Your time in Divisional will serve purpose. You will examine each of your lives, and you will document in writing the source of every negative fragment in that shambles you call a Soul. Further, you will define the fragment, describe its consequence, and explain your purpose for holding it."

"Huh?"

"Begin with your last life and work backwards. Do not fill the pages with empty chatter, falsehoods, or invectives. Do you understand?"

Her mouth agape, she gave a slight nod.

Slowly, very slowly, Alpha lowered his hand.

Zia appeared dumbstruck, a reaction that supported Alpha's theory. To prove or refute his entire theory, he would have to re-analyze each of Zia's lives. He rechecked Earth's time and then vanished.

# 7

*Zia, try to stay in this world, okay?*
*Will you do that for your Poppa?*


*S* *wooosh.* Earth ruffled my backside, rousing me from a stupor—a stupor caused by the new Guide's attitude flip. Instead of *suggesting* what I should do, the Alpha-Guide *told* me what to do. *Told!* I was sure that broke a Guide-rule, but who could I ask, *hey, can he do that?* Even if I knew someone to ask, I'd have to bring up Alpha's jibber-jabber about fragments. Any mention of fragments causes queer looks—*you have fragments?* It's asked with disgust like, *You have cooties?* Then I'd rotate, "Do you see any fragments?" But not once has anyone ever pointed out something disgusting clinging to me.

Nearby a flurry of atoms shifted and shaped, so I quickly fashioned a scorecard for my favorite game, *Name That Myth.* But before I could identify the Figment, it scattered—*Damn!* Figment one, Zia zero. It's a great game, but better played *before* you learn where Figments come from. *Players' beliefs create the Figments,* Romal had said. *When Players give up the belief, the Figment crumbles.* I asked him, "Then how come the beautiful beliefs—unicorns, fairies, angels— never last as long as the hideous beliefs—trolls, ghouls, devils?"

Romal didn't answer. He just shook his head, looking a little sad.

Centuries earlier, a grotesque creature came tumbling by. It must have been a legend retold through generations because it kept its shape across the dimension. I followed it. Given more time, I would have identified it, too, but a group of Seekers interrupted me. They claimed I had a life waiting in France...*Now!* They insisted on escorting me back to Divisional, even though I knew the way. For all their fuss, you would think someone would have been happy to see me. Instead, the Seekers were pissy, and Romal was fuming. That's all I get from Guides and Souls—mixed messages.

Alpha was the same—giving mixed message—talking about fragments when nothing was clinging to me. I envisioned my good, old pillow, punched it, and snuggled down for Divisional-bliss, which beats Player-hell any day. In fact, I couldn't think of one reason to ever accept another life. If that meant giving up Haven, then I'd give up Haven. Nobody wanted to take me there anyway. But I didn't care. Nope. I didn't care if I ever went home.

*Home*—That stupid thought brought on sparks of inky-blue.

When I swiped my eyes, I should have glimpsed the Earth. Instead, I saw a huge, white moon. I sat up, rubbing my eyes. No, it was not a moon. It was a ten-foot ball of paper—the printing press roll for The Daily Universe.

It quaked, *Document in writing the source of every*—

"HELL NO!" I kicked the ghostly paper-roll as it echoed Alpha's demands. "I'm not doing it," I told the universe. "Get it? Do you hear me?"

Nobody answered. I kicked the image again. Its size insulted me. How could Alpha think I had this much to list? Most of my lives had been stupid, dull, and quick. My mistakes would fit on a postcard.

Ignoring the roll, I played Tiddledy-Winks. When I had flipped my Winks into the cup for the thirteen time, I caved to the paper-roll, tired of being overshadowed by a big, fat ball. I glanced around for somebody watching, somebody finding this funny, somebody spying. It could happen. Spying is how I discovered BlackDog's identity.

I hid on Earth to spy on BlackDog's Awakening. He had caused me a mess of trouble, and I intended to tell him so. But Niine Guides came. I had never seen a Niine Guide before, and I hope I never see one again. They're angular, drawn, and mean looking, not the ugly kind of mean, but the intimidating thin-lipped kind of mean.

And I froze, the holy-shit kind of froze.

From BlackDog's body rose the Soul of Triite.

My shock came out in an audible gasp. The Awakening Party turned.

*JA-ZOOOMMM;* I rocketed past the sound waves and into Divisional where I reheard my gasp.

Spotting no spies now, I tore off a sheet to start the dumb assignment. "Life one, shipbuilder."

Writing appeared, *Alaska*.

"NO! I'm not working backwards. We do it my way or we don't do it at all. Get it? Shipbuilder, shipbuilder, SHIPBUILDER!"

Finally, the paper displayed, *Shipbuilder*.

"Strengths: I hired a hundred men to build that damn ship."

My words appeared except for the *damn*. Good! Self-editing paper would save a little time. Relaxing back, I began dictating. "Weaknesses: My selfless desire to make people happy caused problems. Bankers and backers wanted the ship sailed on a certain date. I wanted to please them, so we sailed on their deadline. The ship sank…because they rushed me. A few men drowned."

I craned forward to check the paper. My last four words were missing. Figuring I dropped my voice, I hollered, "A few men drowned."

Still nothing. Romal had crabbed about this life, but I couldn't remember why. I asked the paper, "Did more than a few men drown?"

Writing appeared; *Forty-two men drowned.*

I blinked and blinked, trying to process the number. I had thought most of the men had swam to shore. "Forty-two? Are you sure?"

The line repeated—*twice*—as if to blame me. I had taken enough blame from Guides; I sure wasn't going to take it from a paper wad. I shredded the sheet. Little white flecks trickled into space and disappeared.

Before I could decide whether to continue or to forget it, another sheet slipped from the roll and floated to my lap. "This stinks."

The paper showed, *This is necessary.*

"Hey, I drowned, too. Did you know that? Did anyone care that I sucked in saltwater? NO! Salty-shit went up my nose and down my lungs. Then a goddam shark feasted on my limbs and picked its teeth with my bones. Who cared about that? NOBODY! I'm going back as a shark hunter to kill—"

I stopped, rethought, and then ripped up that sheet, too. "Scratch that," I yelled to any eavesdropping Guides. "No more seaside placements, get it? I hate the ocean and all the salt-swilling shit that lives in it."

I stretched out, my back to the roll. A moment later, the roll fronted me again. I flipped sides. The roll dogged my turns. I punched it. "I'm not going to follow your rules. I'm not—"

"And why should you?"

The intruder's voice startled me upright. It seemed to have come from the far side of the solar system, from the edge of Divisional, and it seemed to croak more than talk, a raspy croak that rang a familiar bell.

I held still, listening. Just when I thought I had imagined the voice, it came again. "Choose freedom. We cherish Agitators. Praise them. Choose—"

"TRIITE!" I busted through the roll, but I couldn't spot him. While I scanned the region, the roll started to reassemble in front of me.

I tore through that one, too.

Again, it started to reshape.

I shot through it, "YOU COWARDLY MAGGOT!" and sped after Triite.

*From the moment he saw her, he hated her.*
*Strangely and completely.*

Triite skirted behind Jupiter before he called again. "I hear the passionate fury of a Niine Soul. You sing it...*well.*" Triite cringed; his lie was too obvious. Even a dolt like Zia wouldn't believe she did something well. She couldn't even gauge distance and was now scouring Saturn's ring.

Triite skipped across 38 of Juniper's moons before Zia finally noticed.

She bolted straight for him...and at an impressive speed.

Triite shot across light-years and then slipped into the Orion Arm. When cloaked by an ice belt, he called again. "One doesn't want you, Zia. Hasn't Haven made that blatantly clear? They have forsaken you, discarded you, but beelzeNiine grieves your abandonment and would welcome you."

While waiting for her to catch up, Triite preened his claws, sharp and shiny, filed by teeth and buffed by tongue. He raised them high, admiring their razor tips and imagining the surrounding ice blades melting in envy.

His grooming complete, Triite expanded his chest for the baritone voice of believable concern. "Your side lied to you, Zia. You do understand that, don't you? Your lives deserved praise and recognition, but you've received only rebuke and scorn. When you questioned their reasons, how did they respond? They banned you from Haven." He scratched himself and yawned. "Their injurious treatment victimizes you, which pains beelzeNiine deeply."

He listened but heard no response.

Minutes ticked by. The only sound breaking the stillness was the growl rising in Triite's throat. Why wasn't Zia answering? Was her silence meant to provoke him? She was a lowly Yin from the lowliest of Orders—Agitators, cosmic pumice stones, scratching and grating the skin off of others.

Yet, for some reason, for some inexplicable reason, his Guide, Kaane, thought Zia important. Kaane had mistaken Zia for another Agitator, Triite believed, because Zia was a bungling idiot, and Kaane was too savvy to squander a Persuader's skills on an idiot.

While reviewing his life in Paris, Triite became convinced that Kaane had erred. "Why did you waste my skills on that Agitator? She's not a challenge; she's a buffoon."

Immediately, Triite's hands thinned into claws, his legs bowed backwards, his spine curved into a hump, and his head melted into a lopsided knob.

As a Player, Triite would have wealth, beauty, and charm—Kaane promised. But as an Energy, Triite would return to a bulbous shape for having questioned his Guide.

Triite's next two lives—BlackDog and Murdock—only strengthened his conviction about Zia, but he held his tongue, his disfigurement reminding him to do so.

Somehow Zia had warped Kaane's judgment—Kaane, first Entity of beelzeNiine, leader in the Great War, and the only Guide victorious in a battle against Alpha, first Entity of One.

Inspired by his accomplished Guide, Triite's voice lifted again. "BeelzeNiine sends his personal regard."

"COWARD!"

Triite jumped; Zia was close. Too close.

When the ice belt tipped, Triite fled.

Zia pursued.

Leaping and sprinting from moons to nebulas, and whispering and shouting from flattery to threats, Triite lured Zia farther and farther from the Milky Way. No challenge about it...until they reached Divisional's edge.

Zia stopped, peered back, and began gnawing her thumb and sparking ambivalence.

Triite issued a string of coercions.

Zia refused to budge.

Triite snarled quietly, "Follow me, Zia. Follow me, follow me." They had so many more light-years to travel.

But Zia's sparks of indecision dominated her sparks of rage.

Triite beat on his temple; time was wasting. What scorn would stoke her anger and smite her doubts?

Kaane expected success from Triite, and he had every right to expect it.

Triite was a master manipulator, shrewd and cunning, and a prodigy of his Order. Matching him against an Agitator was like matching a lion against a porcupine. At worst, the lion suffers a few inconvenient quills. The porcupine, however, suffers death.

Triite intended to make Kaane proud—the fearless, ever-watchful Kaane—and also to amuse him. For several minutes, Triite worked on crafting a unique, intellectual insult, one that would entertain Kaane. If Triite excelled in his delivery, a very impressed Kaane might reconsider Triite's bulbous form.

When confident of his prose, Triite raised a voice deplete of guile. "Zia, become part of us. Rise above your kindred contagions."

Triite smiled, listening for Kaane's approval and for Zia's retort.

Hearing neither, Triite's claws clinked together in nervous wringing. "Zia, did you hear me? Rise above your kindred contagions."

"My what?" she yelled.

Triite flinched. He had neglected a Persuader's most basic tenet—know your audience. In styling the insult to impress Kaane, he had overlooked his intended audience—the idiot, Zia. "Your kindred contagions. Kindred contagions. KINDRED CONTAGIONS!"

She didn't answer.

His hatred burning, Triite's teeth began snapping and breaking. He spat out the pieces, cursing her name. "FIND ME, YOU MORON!" he exploded. "Is that clear enough? It's four words. *Four Words!* Do you need me to spell it? F-I-N—"

An ice pick struck the side of Triite's head. Kaane's voice followed, "I gave you the bait. USE IT!"

Triite nodded and nodded, and swallowed several times to regain a congenial tone. "Zia, excuse my outburst. You deserve my gratitude. Thank you for taking the bullet. You enabled my riches and ensured my wealth undivided; neither a brother nor a cousin to share in my gold."

"MURDOCK!"

Triite heard the shout and heard nothing more. He glanced from hiding— just in time.

Zia was blazing from Divisional and heading straight toward him.

Triite soared across hundreds of light-years.

Zia stayed winged at his heels.

At one point, Triite gained too much distance so he slowed beside a comet, "Enough gold to buy a town," then ducked into the comet's crater.

Zia whipped furiously through the stellar dust. When she came close, Triite bolted.

Within seconds, Zia blazed the same trail.

Dimension after dimension, through spiraling galaxies and blinding novas, Zia hounded Triite. She never paused or looked back...or gave thought to the changing landscape.

For thousands of miles, parasitic particles darted and bobbed and lined into vines, but Zia swept them aside and rushed after Triite.

Triite snickered and laughed, luring Zia deeper and deeper into the region. Soon, the vines thickened into an immobilizing web, and Zia couldn't see beyond a few feet. A slow awareness caused her to stop.

A vine eased around her ankle. As Zia reached down to remove it, the particles drew apart and scurried up her calves.

Triite screeched, hysterically thrilled. He imagined himself shattering her atoms, and he dreamed of her agony, her torment, her pleas. But his dreams would never be realized—such a shame. Players in science had it wrong; Energy cannot annihilate Energy. Such a shame. Such a shame.

A hollow tube whipped up and thumped the back of Triite's head. He turned with a snarl.

It was a life-cord.

Triite had to leave for Earth and he had to leave now.

Infuriated by the timing, he let out a jackal's howl. *"Aruuu."*

Zia glanced up, but barely that. Her lights flickered an array of colors—anger, confusion, worry—though colors devoid of fear. Triite hoped Kaane was noticing that, too, for it proved Triite correct—Zia was an idiot. If she had an ounce of intelligence, her every spark would evidence terror.

She grabbed a fistful of vines, turned her hand sideways, then loosened her grip. Nothing poured.

When she snapped her wrist, the particles scattered up her arm and attached to her neck.

Triite roared, "FOOL!"

The life-cord smacked him again.

Triite grabbed it, shook it, and thought of biting it in half, but then thought better. Kaane was watching. Kaane was always watching.

Grudgingly, Triite descended to Earth, his Ribbon of Life filling, expanding, and straightening the cord.

The cord disappeared.

# 9

*Like the moron in a cheap slasher flick—*
*Look, blood on the stairs; let's check out the attic—*
*I walked up to disaster.*

*Uh-oh.* Chasing Triite might have been a bad idea. Wherever I turned, I faced zillions and zillions of colored beads. They looked like drops of mercury, wet and slick, felt like balls of rubber, soft and squishy, and smelled like buckets of dead earthworms, a stench unrivaled.

I clutched a fistful to see whether they would dribble like BBs or would flow like water. Instead of pouring from my hand, the beads spurted between my knuckles and scampered up my arms. When I flicked my wrists, the buggers flew to my neck and peppered my cheeks. Although they rolled and tumbled with slippery ease, they also stuck like sap wads. Smaller than peas, bigger than sand, the beads, by the millions, flitted and swooned like brightly colored gnats. Millions more lined into vines, beads piling onto beads of the same color. Yellow ropes hung over my head, blue tendrils swayed at my sides, red chains matted beneath my feet. What a weird dimension—a jungle of zillions and zillions of sticky, smelly beads.

Close by, Triite called me a fool and then howled. After that, the place fell eerily quiet.

Pulsating like arteries, the vines covered the area as far as I could see, which wasn't very far. No sun. No planets. Not even a twinkling star to light my way home.

While thinking hard of what to do, my hand rose to chew on a thumb. Instead of a cuticle—*Auuk, auuk*—I bit a bead.

BILE! It tasted like bile or vomit or whatever that acidic juice is that a stomach gurgles up for a throat to swallow down. I spat and coughed, but I couldn't swipe my tongue. Bile-soaked beads gloved my hands.

Their stench was also poisonous; what else could be making me sick? Even before I bit the bead, a queer nausea had come over me. I felt like puking, but that couldn't be right. I was Energy; I *couldn't* be Player-type sick.

Soon, the rolling nausea became a stabbing pain. *Pain?* But pain can't—
*Ohhh*, my knees buckled—I guess pain could.

Hunched and gripping my stomach, I started a wobbling glide in the
opposite direction of Triite's howl.

Miles later, the vines thickened and the beads plumped. I had a nagging
feeling that I should turn around, but I kept going.

The beads rushed to vibrations; that much, I had figured out. Any sudden
movement caused tentacles of stink-beads to rope my legs. Gently and
slowly, with feet dragging weights of beaded slippers, with sap-drenched hair
curtaining my face, and with a stomach heaving like a hung-over Player, I
eased between the vines and plodded on.

While I slogged through the thicket of stink-beads, creepy Figments
appeared, startled me, and scattered. Had they formed in Divisional, I would
have lost the game, *Name That Myth;* the Figments, gruesome and perverted,
surpassed my knowledge of folklore and legend.

Ignoring the Figments, I splayed the vines and kept going and going, until
I couldn't go forward any longer. The vines, so thick, so many, were now a
barricade that I couldn't push through. *Crap.* For the hundredth time, I
swished them off my face. I had to turn around. No use fighting it; I had to
head back.

For eons, I trudged through the sticky beads and the sappy vines. Eons,
that's how it felt, though it was probably months. Maybe years. Without an
orbiting planet to gauge time, I had no way to know for sure.

Eventually, I arrived at the spot where I had heard Triite's yelp. At least
that's how the place looked. Nothing marked the spot, but the beads seemed
smaller, the vines fewer. I pushed ahead.

*Crap!* Within seconds, *seconds this time,* the vines latched onto me. Their
deposits of gluey beads scurried up my nose, rolled into my ears, and
squeezed under my lids.

Blinded and stumbling, I fell back to my starting point.

Before I could dig the suckers out of my face, I had to scrape them off
my hip to make a bead-free place for my fingers to wipe against. What a god-
awful dimension. When clean enough, I floated straight up.

From a hundred yards high, I tumbled straight down, webbed in stink-
beads. I popped them out of my eyes, snorted them out of my nose, and
spliced them out of my bottom.

I glided straight down.

A moment later, I climbed back up, coated in sap beads.

Frantic, I tried every angle—vertical, horizontal, diagonal—but each angle ended in a blanket of beads.

*Immobilized?* My legs wobbled, my forehead sparked hysterics.

The beads swarmed on the flickers. I heard thirsty sounds and, *Oh jeez,* sucking sounds, too.

Vampire beads!

Dizziness swirled and I stumbled—*Nooo*—but refused to fall. If I collapsed, the parasites would smother me. If my mouth opened to scream, they would bunch into my throat and choke off my cries...like they had done to Triite. He was sneering and laughing and having a great time...until he howled. Then the beads converged into his big, fat mouth and clogged up his lumpy, crooked windpipe.

*Hmm...*Good!

Somewhere nearby, Triite was hacking up stink-beads.

Good! Good! Good!

But if I didn't escape, I'd suffer Triite's fate. My chin tipped down, my eyes closed tight, and my hands folded together, squashing shit-balls between my palms. "One, this is Zia. I know you're sore at me because I never talk to you, but I'm talking to you now, okay? I need your help to get out of here. And if you help me, I promise to talk to you more often. I swear it. Just help me, please. And, uhm, could you hurry? Because the sooner I'm out of here, the more time I'll have to talk to you. Thanks for listening. Zia, Order of Agitators."

My eyes struggled to reopen against sap-beads weighting my lids. I started to cry, but the beads drank the inky-blue then wiggled into my tear-ducts to hunt for more.

I bit back the tears. No more feeding the parasites. Time to Yin-up!

I stood straight and tall and unfaltering, and I would stand that way for eternity if I had to, but I would not surrender to stink-beads.

Yep, eternity.

More slurping sounded as more inky-blue spilled because, *jeez,* eternity would feel like forever.

# 10

*Darwin minced my words. 'No, no, no, you're a matter of shape and weight, not a ladder from ape and fate.'*

"Y**ou did *WHAT?*"** Romal said, though he held up his hand to stop Alpha from repeating it. Romal had heard enough. He glided to the dimensional window to have a few words with One. *Did you hear what your first Entity did? He deliberately cast vibrations into an Energy. What could have possessed him? What indeed. Well, I hope you're—*

"Romal, I left no vibration."

"Irrelevant." Romal turned abruptly. "I want to know why, Alpha. Why a Guide, a Peril Guide no less, would risk creating a peril by scattering vibrations in the one place prohibited? A single, overlooked vibration taints the Soul's Free Will, and in turn, violates the Covenants. What in Haven possessed you?"

"A pungent odor."

"A pungent odor is a poor excuse for—"

"Initially."

*"Initially?"* A resigning groan left Romal. As he suspected, it was going to be a long century, a very long century indeed. Romal darkened the dimensional window and then fashioned a comfortable chair for himself. "All right, let's have it."

Alpha began espousing a theory—a remarkable, bizarre theory that made little sense to Romal. Was Alpha speaking of Energies or of Players? Alpha was mixing the two states...and mixing up Romal.

"Stop," Romal said. "Let's be clear." Romal formed two images—a Yin Energy and a female Player. He pointed to the Energy. "Impulses and currents bonded by skioses, a Soul is aware, ageless, and complete." Romal's finger swept to the Player. "Bone and blood surrounded by tissue, a Player is unaware, limited, and incomplete." His arm lowered. "Now, does your theory address a Soul's intrinsic state or their transient condition?"

Alpha corded the images and then touched the Energy.

The Energy began shrinking. As it did so, the connected woman changed to a girl. "I excised a third of the Energy's vibrations," Alpha said. "I left one-third and inverted one-third."

"I see," Romal said, his tone flat. "So you've whittled one image to craft a—a what? A teenager? In any event, what point begs my understanding?"

"These remaining vibrations, the intact third and the inverted third, reflect Zia's Soul."

"Alpha, nobody chopped up Zia's vibrations. Nobody can, nobody did."

"True, for it is her own skioses dissolving and inverting the vibrations. The result likens her to an adolescent Player."

"A teenager?" Romal rubbed his temples. "A teenage *Energy?*"

"Like all Souls, Zia designs herself by selecting elements of her being to enhance or detract. Unfortunately, her dissolved vibrations limit her awareness while her inverted vibrations steer her choice of design—an artful liar, sarcastic and profane. Her selected design is unknown among Souls, but it is well known among Players. It parallels many of their adolescents."

Romal began pacing. When Alpha pressed for understanding, Romal shook his head and held a finger to his lips. He needed time to absorb this theory. Did it support or contradict what he knew about Zia? Did it give reason to her oddities? He supposed that it did. But what had corrupted her skioses to behave with such trickery?

Alpha blocked Romal's pacing. "Romal, you suspected a more profound anomaly. You were correct."

"Well, if your theory is correct, though I'm still unconvinced, but if it proves true, how do you propose we fix Zia?"

"Zia is not aberrant; she is distinct, her Soul complete. We cannot alter an Energy. We can only guide them within their parameters."

"Really?" Romal's arms crossed. "So what parameters exist for a backward Soul lacking awareness? If Zia doesn't contain the truth, she can't provide the truth, let alone provide it ten-fold. Within the Neutral Point, her half-truths will gift the cord to Niine, or do you expect better than a disaster to come of her life?"

"It was not her lives that honored One. It was her deaths."

Romal gave a scoffing grunt. "Well, go on. Explain yourself."

"As a result of the inverted vibrations, Zia's deaths, all but the last, furthered other Players toward One."

His hand on Romal's shoulder, Alpha drew up the images of Zia's lives, starting with her first. "Do not focus on Zia," Alpha said. "Instead, pinpoint the ship and expand the view."

Once centered on the ship, Romal slowly and carefully widened the view. Onto the screen came a stout, cheerful fellow, dressed in finery, greeting beggars and bankers alike, but sporting a Ribbon of Life curdled in malice— a Niine Player's Ribbon.

"A stranger to Zia," Alpha said, "and the anonymous financier for building the ship. A few years after Zia's removal, the citizens, having no others to blame, held that Player accountable for the crew's death. His reputation and influence collapsed."

"Yes, I see that," Romal said, fully intrigued and advancing the years. "Extraordinary."

"Move to Zia's second life, then forward one score and widen threefold."

When Romal did so, he saw an expanding Niine cluster.

"The cluster inherited the property," Alpha said, "including the slaves. Zia's execution seeded dissent. That dissent became a revolt that damaged the family's power. You returned Zia quickly. Her second execution provoked another rebellion, which destroyed the cluster entirely."

"Yes, yes. Amazing. Quite amazing." Thoroughly engaged now, Romal jumped from event to event, from life to life, pivoting the views, widening the scopes, switching the angles. Scenes raced forward and backward and zoomed in and out, stretching across families and continents.

Romal began chuckling. "You must appreciate the irony. While bungling our plans, Zia inadvertently crippled Niine's. In France, her death—or the perception of it—inspired an addiction center, which multiplied. That ruined much of Niine's groundwork and spring-boarded thousands of Players through three generations toward One."

Romal's chuckling quieted upon noticing his especially grim friend. "Come now, Alpha. You don't think—You can't possibly believe—"

"Niine interpreted Zia's acts as deliberate."

"Nonsense!" Romal stated, irritated by the idea. He vanquished the scenes. "Utter nonsense. Not even a Determinant, nor a Guide for that matter, can know the mind and will within thousands of Players spanning multiple generations. Further, Zia's deaths did not benefit One; the Players' faulty assumptions did. I doubt the slaves would have titled her a hero had they known she was the owners' informant and was executed for prattling off twisted truths. And in France, Zia neither died of an overdose nor painted the picture that hangs in her honor."

"True. And from your perspective, a Player's truths and virtues in life honor One."

"Of course. Certainly so."

"Yet, when Zia shifted Souls to One, she did so from Niine's coveted field—death. And she used Niine's preferred weapon—deception. Or as you stated it, the Players' faulty assumptions. From Niine's vantage point, Zia is using their weapons and desecrating their grounds to further One. They believe she acts with intent."

"No, no, no. She acts with foolishness. Foolishness!"

"Niine targets Zia out of revenge."

"Ridiculous."

"Romal, they countered with their most skilled Persuader."

Romal couldn't stop shaking his head, though Alpha's words rang true. He glided to the dimensional window and removed the darkness. Foolish Zia. How could any entity mistake her for a threat? How could Kaane? *Kaane?* Romal tapped his lip; he could no longer delay in telling Alpha.

"Alpha, about Triite's Guide—" But as he turned from the window, he saw Alpha slumping and holding his head. "Alpha, what is it?"

When Alpha's hands came down, Romal saw a sprinkling of bumps dotting Alpha's forehead. Romal helped Alpha straighten. "Alpha, what is it?"

"Triite is in play," Alpha said. "Request the Order of Seekers to map all upcoming positions peripheral to Triite's placement."

"Yes, yes, certainly, but—"

Alpha vanished.

# 11

*She gabs and gabs, but no one gets out of her car because no one is in her car.*

"**I** want·to go home."

My bead stuffed ears perked.

"Don't you?"

Oh *jeez*, I wasn't alone! Someone—or something—was near. Maybe it was the thing creating the freakish Figments, maybe the King Bead.

With much effort, I lifted my arms, reached to my face, and scooped fistfuls of beads from over my eyes. I saw only squirming vines. Parting the tentacles, I glided a little ways before the beads amassed over my peepholes again.

Once more, I carved two holes into the beads and then managed another few feet.

The beads swarmed, weighting my legs in cement trousers.

"I want to go home," the voice came again.

I froze, expecting the beads to fly from me and head for the new vibration. Yep, any second, if I just held still, my load of beads would lighten.

"Don't you?"

I didn't move a twitch.

Neither did the beads.

Not a single bead left for the new vibration, which made no sense.

Why didn't they leave? Why? Then, as if I were a ramming a cattle prod into a dark sky, *'ya think that's a storm cloud?'* the answer came in a jolt.

*Crap!* The beads weren't drawn to random vibrations; the beads attacked. Jeez, how dumb could I be? And their attack was personal.

*Damn!*

Even worse, Triite was probably alive and well and not puking up shit-balls. *Damn! Damn! Damn!*

My hands clenched into fists.

Stink-beads squirted from between my fingers.

The image of Triite gagging and choking was replaced by an image of Triite sneering and laughing.

*Laughing...laughing...laughing.*

*"AURG!"* My fists swung. "I've been poisoned worse than this," I punched and kicked, "and by better than you."

The vines whirled and roped. I spun and tore. Sparks ignited faster than the vampire beads could eat them.

A clump of vines coiled into a makeshift fist. Before I could duck, it plunged into my face, knocking me backwards and shoving a bead clot into my mouth.

I flipped onto my knees then up to my feet. With both hands bracing my stomach, I crunched down.

Acidic shit-balls burst.

A liquid odor dripped out my nose and oozed between my teeth, but I kept grinding and mashing, crunching and chewing.

I spat out the chunks, then spat again for spite.

A clump of vines joined together and swooped back, preparing to charge.

I crouched, preparing to meet the charge headlong.

We shot forward, slammed together, and it was arms against tentacles, flinging and swinging, beads against bites, whipping and kicking, Energy against stink-beads.

In a sudden trick, the vines lurched up and rounded out, forming an arch. Or tunnel. Or maybe a throat! I spun with readied fists for whatever intended to fling me down that gullet.

I swiveled, again and again, alert and ready, but the vines stayed pinned. In my next jump and turn, I fronted the tunnel. *Huh?* The arcing vines had created a path to the voice. And there it was. Or there *she* was—a Soul still wearing her Player's costume of a little girl.

*Oh for chrissake, a Wanderer.*

After scraping beads from my hand, I nibbled on the side of my thumb while staring at the girl.

She sucked on her middle fingers while staring at me.

I had met wandering Souls before, but not many and never a kid. Botched Awakenings, that was my term for when a spooked Soul flies from Divisional and their Awakening Party pursues.

But this wasn't Divisional, and no Awakening Party was going to venture into the Badlands of Beads.

I waited for the usual questions: *Where am I? Is this heaven? Am I dead?*

But she just sucked her fingers, seemingly content.

My feet shuffled, unsure what to do. The last Wanderer I tried to help was a hunter. Blood poured from a hole in his thigh. I figured he shot himself and bled to death, and I felt bad because that's a dumb way to die. When I started toward him, he clasped his hands and dropped to his knees. "Mercy, Lord, save me from the devil."

He meant me. Damn rude. If his Awakening Party hadn't shown up, I would have given Mr. Marksman the devil he expected.

But this little girl presented an image of health, not a speck of blood on her to suggest she had seen her body broken, mangled, or bruised. Her pink, puffy cheeks and her mops of curly hair argued against a lingering disease.

However she had died, she hadn't seen it coming.

She looked about eleven or twelve—ten at least, thirteen at most—with big olive eyes that fixed on me, *jeez*, as if she expected me to do something.

Her free hand clasped her hip. Yep, she definitely expected me to do something. I looked at the curved ceiling of bubbling vines. With fingers crossed, I stepped into the tunnel.

Her palms flew up.

"What's the matter?" I said. "I'm coming for you."

"No," she told me before her slobbery fingers returned to her mouth— fingers she hadn't checked for beads. *Jeez*, stink-beads were crawling in my head or I would have realized immediately that the kid was bead-free. Dozens circled like hornets, but not one touched her. Somehow, her Player's illusion repelled beads.

I dredged up my costume as Gavin. The illusion assembled for two seconds—without repelling one bead—and then vanished. I tried another costume from an earlier life, but it vanished, too.

"I want to go home," she said. "Don't you?"

"Hey, a little patience, okay?" I concentrated like crazy to bring up every shell I had ever worn, but as quickly as they appeared, they disappeared.

*Crap!* My angry snort ejected a string of green beads.

"I want to go home. Don't you?"

"Hold your horses, Missy." In Divisional, if she so much as flickered a wish to be elsewhere, she would have been gone. Lucky for me, she wasn't going anywhere. Thoughts of flight didn't work in bead space... *Oh crap*...didn't work for me, the uncostumed Soul, but might work for her, the costumed. Because the Soul believed itself a little girl, the Soul would frighten like a little girl, too, and she was already upset, nearly crying, and maybe a thought away from disappearing.

My stomach cramped; I did not want to be alone again.

With eyes straining to the top of their sockets, I considered the nest of suspended beads. I swallowed hard—like the tunnel would swallow me if that kid left. *Jeez-oh-jeez.* I snapped my fingers to hold her attention. "Hey, little girl. Tell me something, okay? Okay?"

"What?"

"Uhm, well, how did you die*eeeeee*—" I thumped my forehead, *bad question, bad question.* "—dye, yeah, dye your pretty smock?" I followed my great save with a casual smile.

She grimaced like she were looking at a loon. "My smock is white."

"Oh, well, sure it is, but dyed white?"

She sighed with a quick eye roll. "I want to go home. Don't you?" Her heel thumped as if she were perturbed, as if, for years and years, she had been asking me to take her home, and as if, for years and years, I had been denying her. What a kooky, little Wanderer.

To keep eye contact, I stood in stork pose and slid one foot down the other leg to scrape away beads before I glided forward.

"No," she said.

"No? Again, no?" I scratched my head. "Don't you want my help?"

"I want to go home. Don't you?"

"Stop saying that!" Irritation flickered, but I controlled the sparks by reminding myself that kids don't mean to be annoying—this one, very annoying. She was just scared. I squatted, which was the least threatening pose I could think of. "I'll crawl to you, okay?"

"No."

"For chrissake why?"

"Because."

"Because why? Huh? Why?"

"Because you're green."

"What?" My jaw dropped. Beads took advantage.

I coughed them out before my lips pressed together to muzzle frustration. *Great, just goddam great. Lost in space, surrounded by stink-beads, and stuck with a brat, older than Mars, who dislikes my shade of green.* "GODDAMMIT!"

My sparks flared into flames.

The kid shrieked, and I mean SHAA-RIEKED, a genuine, high-pitched, earsplitting, never-ending screech that only a kid can make. *IYEEEEEEE.*

It sliced through atoms. Vines quivered and ripped. Beads jittered and burst. The entire jungle trembled, including me. I clasped my head and shouted, "I'M SORRY, I'M SORRY, I'M SORRY."

The second she let up, my hands fluttered in a crisscross. "No more fire. I swear. Calm down. Just calm down. I'll make the fire go away. Watch."

I ransacked my memory for something cheerful. I spotted a rainbow, tackled it, grabbed some picnickers, too, and plastered that scene across the forefront of my thoughts. "There! That's nice. Damn nice."

But my rainbow darkened. A thunderstorm exploded. Lightning shattered the picnickers' skulls, tornadoes scattered their limbs, and a hurricane flung their brains out to sea. Stupid rainbows, but I didn't say that. "Hold on, little girl, hold on. I'm trying."

I shifted to flowers, sweet, innocent flowers. But sweet flowers became sweetbriers, and sweetbriers brandished their razor thorns. The mini-daggers gouged my eyes, minced my flesh, and blinded me in blood. "BIRDS," I shouted, then much quieter, "Birds, come on birds."

A white feathered flock chirped and swooned and that was nice. Nice, nice, nice—until they crapped on my head. *Jeez,* I wasn't cut out for pleasantries. "Hey, little girl, you know what? You know what?"

"What?"

"You're right." My squat crumbled. "I am green. Puke-green. I'm a puke-green girl with purple hair who can't hold a pleasant thought to save her skin. But I'm nice." My arms opened and my fingers wiggled. "Trust me. Please?"

She glided up to me and smiled. "Jade green and garnet red." Then the color-blind kid nestled her drool-soaked palm into my hand.

Instantly, chunks of beads shriveled and dropped with tiny squeaks, whispered cries, and ghostly squeals, as if I were stomping on a village of microscopic people. I squeezed the kid's hand in case the weird noise was giving her the heebie-jeebies, too.

Although I wasn't bead-free, my stomach settled and my head cleared. I stood and started tugging the kid to the left. "Okay, let's go."

She anchored.

I tugged again, "Come on," but she wouldn't budge.

"Listen, little girl, here's how it works. You have to want to move, get it? So want to move, okay?"

"I want to go home."

"I KNOW! I mean, yes, I know."

"Don't you?" She pointed to the right.

"Oh, please, that is the worst—"

The blockade of vines parted.

I looked from the vines to the little girl and then to the parted vines again. Keeping our hands gripped, I angled her to my backside before I stretched into the hollow. "How did you do that? Huh? How the hell did you—"

"I want to go home." She tapped my back. "Don't you?"

I straightened. "Lead the way."

Her fingers laced to mine, we took off. Upon our approach, vines arched and spread, but after we passed, vines whipped at my rear, *my* rear only. After a dozen times of getting whacked, I twisted half-circle, "Son of a bitch," hoping to grab the vine and shred it.

The kid yanked on our clasped hands, spinning me straight.

She was crazy strong.

Eventually, the vines dwindled and the beads shrank. Light-years later, all traces of the jungle disappeared except for a handful of beads still clinging to the nape of my neck. Although we hadn't reached the Milky Way, I thought we should stop and celebrate.

The kid thought different. Her grip tightening, she pulled me along.

"Aw, come on," I said jostling our hands. "What's your hurry? Let's have some fun. Let's celebrate."

She ignored me.

I asked her name.

She ignored that, too. During our entire journey, she hadn't said a word.

Her silence bugged me. "Hey, if you don't want to talk to me, that's fine. Just say so. I've been snubbed worse and by better than you."

Her speed increasing, she whirled us through dimension after dimension.

Soon, our arms were stretched to their limit, mine stretching forward, hers stretching backward as if she were dragging dead weight...or the weight of an Energy who wanted to stop and celebrate.

Galaxies later, she unfastened our hands and sprinted away.

"Hey," I hollered, "slow down. Wait for me."

She shot across space, flashing through light-years.

I struggled like crazy to keep up. "WAIT!"

# 12

*Cura te ipsum, my friend. Please. Cure thyself.*

Earth had circled more than 20 times before Alpha returned. Romal had studied the requested maps and was prepared to summarize their contents. Alpha, however, seemed distracted, his focus lifting from the maps and drifting to the window. "Shall I darken it?" Romal asked.

Alpha apologized, though his attention stayed fixed on the window. "Is every Wanderer accounted for?"

Romal pulled him around. "What an absurd question. We've never lost sight of a Wanderer, neither on Earth nor in Divisional."

"Perhaps an Awakening Party trails at a distance beyond a Soul's purview."

"Ridiculous. What prompts such absurdities?"

"I sense—"

"A Wanderer?"

"I sense Zia perceives a Wanderer."

Romal relaxed. "Her perception is based on interpretation, and Zia interprets quite a lot of things incorrectly. It could be a Figment or a stellar dust ball or a meteor carved with a face. One only knows what it could be, but it is certainly not a Wanderer."

When Alpha's full attention returned to the maps, Romal pointed to Triite's new position. "Placed in California, Triite is now Monique, the granddaughter of Murdock MacKenzie."

"Triite is his own granddaughter?"

Romal nodded. "Murdock built quite a powerful cluster armed with wealth and influence. His cluster merged with another formidable cluster and changed to a matriarch. It's now a fortress, really, nearly impenetrable. Of the integral positions affecting the cluster, only two belong to our side, a cord in 1936, which will eventually become Monique's stepdaughter, and a cord in 1945, Monique's future son."

As Alpha leaned closer to the maps, Romal reminded him, "The Energies needn't return into play until the '70s."

"Untrue," Alpha said. "Only the Dyads will wait for the Neutral Point. Phoenix and Zia, like Triite, will return now."

"For sound reason, I assume," Romal said, uneasy with the idea of sending a vibration-challenged Zia anywhere until absolutely necessary. "Care to share your plans?"

Above the maps, Alpha held up an image of the Taylors—Matthew, Peter and Mirabelle—and of the MacKenzies—Murdock and Gavin. He drew three rippling lines; the first line from Gavin to Matthew, the second from Gavin to Peter, and the third from Matthew to Murdock. And he drew one straight line, which connected Peter to Mirabelle.

He pointed to the line spanning from Gavin to Peter. "This ripple weighted the parities ten-fold. That we cannot change." His finger tick-tock'd between Mirabelle and Peter. "When a Dyad's path conflicts with their other half, we have a Neutral Point. That, too, we cannot change."

Alpha erased the image of Peter and Mirabelle and the lines between Gavin and Peter. What Romal now looked at were squiggly lines threading from Gavin to Matthew and from Matthew to Murdock.

"This ripple is mutable," Alpha said, "and can be reversed before the Neutral Point. Gavin's death led to Matthew's removal. Matthew's removal empowered Murdock. Murdock's empowerment created this cluster." He pointed to the map reflecting Triite's current position as Monique. "If the ripple continues, by the time of the Neutral Point, Triite will have immeasurable effectiveness and Phoenix will have no effectiveness at all."

Romal tapped the 1945 position—Monique's future son. "For Phoenix?"

"Untrue." Alpha highlighted the 1936 position, Monique's eventual step-daughter. "Phoenix served as the elder of the Taylor brothers; Phoenix must serve as the elder again."

Realizing the position left for Zia, Romal's hands washed over his face. "Alpha, you cannot send Zia into Triite's womb. Undoubtedly, he carries a fragment against Zia, and his fragment likely dwarfs hers. If so, Triite will sense her Soul, and his hatred will override prudence and maternal instinct, and he will kill her."

"That is hoped for."

"You *hope* Triite removes her?"

"True." Alpha redrew the chart, replacing squiggles with arrows and adding the expected result of a reversed ripple.

*Zia* → → → *Zia (Gavin) Removed*
↓
*Phoenix (Matthew) Removed* → → → *Triite (Murdock) Power Enabled*

*Zia Removed* ← ← ← ← *Triite*
↓
*Triite (Monique) Power Disabled* ← ← ← *Phoenix Lives*

"The death that empowered the cluster—Matthew's death—becomes the life that will destroy it—the stepdaughter's life."

"Conjecture." Romal pushed aside the chart. "Don't state it as a fact."

"To keep Zia from Monique's womb, Hades lured Zia—"

Romal swiveled toward Divisional, but just as quickly, Alpha clutched Romal's arm. "She is unharmed," Alpha said. "But Hades' attempt to harness Zia supports my...conjecture. As you stated, Triite *will* sense Zia's Soul, and he will have a great urge to remove her. If he does, the ripple reverses—Phoenix lives, gains power, and disables the cluster. BeelzeNiine believes this as well."

Romal massaged his forehead. Much more than Zia was functioning in reverse—Niine striving against removal, Alpha hoping for it, weapons and tactics switching sides. Topsy-turvy and backwards. He looked out the dimensional window. Thankfully, the Earth remained on course, orbiting as it had always orbited, steady and constant...and fast. "1936 approaches," Romal said. "If Phoenix is to descend, you had better inform the Healers immediately."

"Who guides Phoenix?"

"Willow."

"Who guides Triite?"

"Triite? Oh, yes, yes." Romal turned away, tugging thoughtfully on his chin. Should he offer the name casually as if he were unaware of the relevance to Alpha? No, quite insulting. Perhaps he should deliver it with a lecture. Perhaps not, equally insulting. *Any suggestions, One?*

"Romal?"

Before turning to Alpha, Romal did his best to raise stern eyes, but an aged sorrow kept causing them to sag and blink. "Alpha, know thyself," Romal said quietly. "Examine the root of your every decision. For if you raise the blade of vendetta, you will fall on your own sword...again."

Alpha's eyes torched, the fire tinting the room blood-red. "Kaane."

# 13

*Oh my God, I'm the monster!*

Whether I dashed straight toward her or I strolled in her general direction, I couldn't catch the kid. Somehow, she kept a measured distance between us. I got the message; she didn't want to be friends. She hadn't wanted to talk, hadn't wanted to sing, and probably didn't even know how to whistle. Despite her faults, I would have taught her Tiddledy-Winks and *Name that Myth*, but to hell with her. Instead of thanking me for rescuing her from stink-beads, the kid was ditching me.

I sat and formed Tiddledy-Winks.

The kid, standing in the distance, held out her hand. *Finally*, she wanted my company again. "Come here," I told her. "I'll teach you Tiddledy-Winks."

"I want to go home," she said, "don't you?"

Preferring her company over the Winks, I got up and started toward her. But for every inch I moved forward, she glided backward, still facing me, still offering her hand. Baiting me.

"Little Missy," I shouted, "you ought to learn some manners." Then, like a second place runner with the finish line in sight, I hoisted speed from the bottom of my Soul, and I tore after her. "STOP!" I hollered zooming across universes. "STOP! STOP!" I split through star belts, meteor showers, and cosmic clouds. Galaxies flipped like pages. Suns, moons, and planets blurred.

*Planets?* I halted. *Oh jeez, oh jeez.* I was back in my wonderful area of Divisional where Earth lumbered and Mercury spun and Venus rolled and good old Saturn, my favorite planet, shimmered in ice.

To the side, the paper roll hovered, still waiting to edit my words. It could wait longer; a celebration could not. With hands on hips, I skipped and sang,

*"Camptown ladies sing this song, doo-dah, doo-dah*
*Camptown racetrack five miles long, oh-dah-doo-dah-day..."*

My singing blared through Divisional and jiggled the ghostly roll.

Surprisingly, the little girl rushed back to me.

I grabbed her hands to teach her to dance. She jerked free.

Fine! I sang anyway, bellowing every *dah* into her glum little face.

*"I come down there with my hat caved in, doo-DAH, doo-DAH*
*I go back home with a pocket full of tin, oh-dah-doo-dah day..."*

"Hey, watch my fancy feet." Then I jigged the best jig ever. "Want to know who taught me to dance? Frozen Toes. Yep. Frozen Toes in Alaska. Get it?" I ripped into laughter.

The kid stood expressionless.

Figuring she was a little slow upstairs, I explained, "Frozen Toes says, move 'em or lose 'em, because Frozen Toes is Alaska, not a person. Get it?"

She smiled, but it was a mischievous smile. "I know a song," she said.

"You're kidding. If you know a song, then why aren't you singing it?"

Then, skipping in a circle around me, she sang,

*"Zia, Zia with a blade of strife,*
*pecked and nicked at her Ribbon of Life,*
*when she saw what she had done,*
*she turned the blame on everyone.*
*Zia, Zia with a blade of strife..."*

"STOP THAT! That's a terrible song. Horrible. Who taught you that?"

"You did," she said, sweeping up to my ear, "get it?" Then she thumbed my forehead. Instantly, I saw myself ablaze in crimson sparks as I hunted Triite across galaxies and into oblivion. Flames of hatred shot up from my head, then dripped down, staining and grooving my Ribbon. Misery followed as I sloshed through bile-beads, then raw despair as I pleaded for One's help. The scenes displayed in horrific detail. "STOP IT!"

The images vanished.

My neck craned back. *Ohhh.* My fingers wiggled through the misty vapors, but the burs weren't shadows; my once lively aurora was now scathed and tattered. "Did I do that?"

But the little girl was gone.

I dragged myself to the paper roll. Alpha would want to know how I marred my Ribbon. But if I told him the truth, the roll would swell in size to adjust for my latest mistakes. I tore off a sheet and said, "Focus, focus."

*Focus, focus* appeared.

But how could I focus on my Player mess-ups when the mother of all blunders flagged over my head. "I don't think we understand a damn thing more on this side than what we understand on the Player side."

My statement appeared, except the *we's* were *I's* and the *damn* was missing.

# 14

*Zia, you might be in trouble, serious trouble.*
*Perhaps mortal jeopardy.*

Before I could dictate more, Alpha arrived. I had a load of questions—questions about bead space and vines and about a wandering kid who can thumb a forehead—but my mouth stayed shut because my questions would raise his questions, and I had plenty to explain already; Alpha would expect to see my written pages. Gathering my humblest voice, I said, "An asteroid carried off my work."

Instead of calling me a liar, he said, "Zia, you are returning to Earth."

"NOW? Didn't I just get here? I mean, whew, finally. I've been here for ages...right?" I once asked Romal why Divisional's time differed from Earth's time, but his answer started with, *dimensions splice time*, so I spliced his lecture with, *good enough*, to dodge what sounded like the start of something boring. So now, I had no idea how much time had elapsed, and I couldn't ask. To be safe, I cleared out all thoughts of bead space, Wanderers, and time. If Alpha snooped in my head, he would find absolutely nothing.

He looked at me funny. "Nothing?"

Unsure whether he was reading my thoughts or monitoring my empty head, I switched the subject. "Hey, how come I have to go now?"

"To assist the Dyads."

"Awen? I'll do anything for Awen."

"Awen and Ereo."

I blew a little raspberry and began counting stars.

"The Dyads require your assistance," Alpha said.

"Twenty-two, twenty-three, twenty—no, that's a planet. Where was I?"

"Zia, the Dyads require your assistance."

"What does Awen want me to do?"

"Help Ereo."

I only half believed him, but wholeheartedly wanted to please Awen. "Is that why you're sending me? My life will help Ereo?"

"Your life?" Alpha squinted upward, as if he were trying to solve an unsolvable puzzle.

"Yes or no?" I said. "Will my life help Ereo?"

He still didn't answer, seemingly stumped by my simple question.

"Jeez, Alpha, am I or am I not going to Earth to help Ereo?"

"True," he answered with quick enthusiasm.

That bugged me. "You're supposed to answer right away," I told him. "It's in the Guide-book. And speaking of Guide-books, Romal made it a rule that I get gender-matched lives only. So, this upcoming life, I'm a female, right?"

"Male."

"NO!" I hurled a big rock. "That's not fair. I'm Yin! YIN! I don't want the male brain. It's gummed up with ego and poisoned by testosterone."

Alpha grunted. "Your dramatics serve no purpose."

"Alpha, pa-*leeease*, give me a gender match. Pick another baby, and then do your hocus-pocus, manipulating things from this side so that I mix with whomever I should mix with on that side. I'll help Ereo, I swear it, but I'll do it as a female, okay?"

Alpha shook his head.

"Crap." I formed long blades of grass, the kind yanked from the ground with dirt clogs attached. I chucked these weed-bombs at passing meteors and winking stars. "Ereo aside, who are the other Souls near my position?"

"Their identities are not your issue."

I chucked more dirt-bombs. "Then let me peek at my next family."

He hesitated, which meant I had a chance. "Come on, Alpha, please? I just want a few minutes to observe them. What can that hurt? Their Souls will be hidden by their Players' costumes, so how could I learn their identities? Maybe some Souls can identify another Soul by their Ribbon's colors, but I can't. Hell, I can barely recognize my ow*hhhh*." My hands clapped over my stupid, stupid mouth.

Alpha's eyes brightened.

Feeling my purple lights parting, my bottom lip disappeared under a top row of teeth, and my head tipped back. An orange glow was illuminating my scuffed up band. "We'll discuss this later," I said. "I have a life to live."

"Zia."

"My Ribbon is a bit scratched up, but I can explain. Seriously. It's a long, crazy story about a fiery comet careening to Earth, but I stopped it. Yep, without a thought to my own safety, I shot into the comet and altered its course. I guess my Ribbon got a little banged up, huh? Well, it's a small sacrifice for mankind. At least I survived."

My story stank—too damn long—and bathed me in lie-colored sparks.

Alpha raised an eyebrow. "Zia, why do you attempt deception when—"

"Why do you get to know?" I said, irritated by Guides always forcing my lies. "Why do you get to know everything, but I get to know shit? Huh? Even if I don't open my mouth, my sparks tell everybody everything. Failing that, you stick your nose into my thoughts. But I can't invade your privacy to learn what you're thinking or how you're feeling. Hell, I don't even get to know who the Players are in my lives, not before, during, or after. And rarely do I care. But this time, this one time, I want a peek at where I'm going." My foot stomped, my arms crossed. "Or I'm not going anywhere."

Alpha reached out and gripped my shoulder. Instantly, we stood outside the back entrance to a three-story Victorian, neatly restored. It was the home of my dreams, the home of all Players' dreams, a mansion centered on acres of manicured grasses and gardens, a palace with columns and archways painted in mauves and trimmed in pinks.

I clutched my chest, "For *meee?* Wow-oh-wow. This is perfect. A perfect home. *My* home. Finally, a decent placement." I elbowed Alpha. "Aw, you wanted to surprise me, right? Hey, I'm surprised. And you won't be sorry; I'll make you proud. I'll make everyone proud. Thank you. From the bottom of my Soul, thank you. I'm going to have the best life I've ever—"

A breeze rolled in carting a familiar sting. My tongue flicking out, I confirmed the worst—*salt!* Crap-infested sea salt. The fog swallowing the property's far end was *coastal* fog. I started gliding.

"Zia?"

No one realizes the sinister sea, no one feels its viciousness. No one gets the ocean...no one but me.

A stone path snaked across the grass, through the hedges, around the roses, and between the herb gardens and the fruit trees. The path ended on a sandy bluff. Chewing my lip, I floated over the edge...*PA-Woosh*...and was sucker-punched by a wave.

Coughing and sputtering, I glided higher, beyond the ocean's reach. It crashed back against the rocks and recoiled.

"You want me?" I spread my arms. "Here I am. Come and get me."

A wave thundered up, stretching high and swinging strong. When it smacked the ridge top, its saline breath pickled the air.

"You can't get me," I said. "You'll have to wait for me to come to you...and I will never, ever come to you."

The ocean flung another white-capped fist, but when it reached my feet, its foamy knuckles had thinned to spit.

I spat, too. "Never, ever will I come to you."

We stared at each other—the ocean and me—in a silent exchange of our foulest obscenities.

Much later, a hand brushed my cheek. Alpha's hand. His face held a look of pity.

"Jeez, it's nothing," I told him while I blotted my eyes. "I just hate the ocean." I spat at the dark waters below. "And all the salt-infested microbes within it."

Together, Alpha and I glided back to the mansion, but I paused at the door. "Hey, you know what I was thinking?" I used my matter-of-fact voice while peering at a thread of ants marching through my toes. "That cliff is pretty steep. Maybe you should whisper in somebody's head to put up a wall or a fence." I pretended to study the ants. "I mean, not that I care, because I don't. I'm just worried about my family's safety." I looked up.

Alpha still had a sorrowful face.

"Aw, forget it." I shoved past him and into the house.

Inside, everything was as elegant as the outside promised. "Persian," I said pressing a cheek against the hand-woven rug that dressed the marble floor. "Tell Romal I knew that. He thinks I never learned a thing from any life."

Ruby-red drapes covered arched windows and cast a pinkish light over a staircase spiraling to the second and third story. Hating staircases, frozen or otherwise, I stayed downstairs where the only thing twanging my nerves was a row of aquariums spanning the living room wall.

Somebody had a severe interest in sea-crap.

I explored the woodwork, sculptures and paintings.

"Hey!" I pointed to a picture of horses. "Alpha, come see this. That's the work of my old friend Theo, Theodore Gericault. I called him Theo to make him mad; He called me Monsieur Mad to make me mad. Is he famous?"

"His artistry endured."

"Yeah?" I stared at the canvas, reflecting. "Oh. Well, uhm, good for Theo." I raised a poor excuse for a smile. "Hey, I got a right to be miffed. The idea for one of his most celebrated paintings came from me, but Theo, gave me zero of the glory. See, whenever I sipped a bit too much absinthe, I would ramble on and on about my repeating nightmare. In it, a ship sank and a whole lot of people drowned. Theo took notes. Months later, the frigate, La Méduse, sank. Theo, crazy superstitious, thought I had foretold of the disaster as a spiritual message for him to paint the scene. So he did. The painting was pretty good, too, but it was my nightmare, my story, my—"

"Jealousy."

"Jealousy? Jealous of Theo? Naw."

"Zia, you harbored ill-will for The Raft of Medusa, did you not?"

For a few seconds, I snorted and scowled, but my act was humiliatingly transparent. I flopped across the rug, the Persian rug, not that any Guide cares that I know such things. I plucked at the wool fibers while wishing I had never lived one life.

"Zia," Alpha said, his tone rife with sympathy, which made me feel worse.

"Don't. Just don't." I needed a few minutes to get a grip on self-loathing for having destroyed my Paris life. "The thing is, The Raft of Medusa stirred a fit among political bigwigs. Get it?" I looked up at Alpha. Yep, he got it. My focus returned to the rug. "All I ever stirred was a drink. My own fault. I know that. I just wish—wish like hell—I could relive that life. Or regain that talent. I was a painter, you know, and a damn good one. But that's all gone. Poof. Never again. But I'm glad for Theo. I am. His work should be admired. Honestly, Theo deserves the fame." Having said that, I started to feel it, too. And feeling good for Theo came with a good feeling for me. Go figure.

Alpha bent down and touched my shoulder. "You inspired a series of Theodore's later paintings."

"I did? No foolin'?"

"He painted them shortly after your removal."

I jumped up. "Poke the pictures into my head. Show me. I want to see them." I held still, but Alpha's jab never came. "Alpha, what's the matter? Are the paintings lousy? I don't care. I want to see them anyway. Come on, show them to me."

"Zia, the Players are depicted as—as troubled."

"Troubled? *Troubled?*" My pride sank like Theo's ship. "Oh, I get it. You mean nuts."

Alpha sighed.

"I guess Theo wasn't teasing when he called me Mad. He meant insane-mad. Damn. I should have known." And before Alpha could make a dopey-sad face again, I said, "Forget it. I'll take it up with Theo, if I find his Soul."

"Yin, Eleventh Order."

"Theo is an Agitator?"

"True."

I smiled, big and wide. "That figures."

A door creaked open and curls of auburn hair poked through. Big, brown eyes flitted left and right before the little girl, in a velveteen coat, scampered across the room to huddle behind the Queen Anne sofa. She reminded me of the kid in bead space, but I couldn't share that with Alpha. When her coat parted, a puppy's wet nose popped out and whined. "Hush, Plato," she said. "Don't cry. You'll get me in trouble."

The puppy whined louder. The girl pulled a chunk of meat from her pocket. The puppy sniffed once, gobbled it, and nuzzled her coat for more.

"Is she my sister?" I asked.

"True."

"And she's Ereo, right?"

Silence.

"Okay, don't tell me. And don't tug on your ear if I'm right." I watched for Alpha's ear tugging, but I guess he never heard of codes. "Fine," I said. "We'll do it your way; I'll pretend I don't know."

The girl bounced to her knees, peeked over the sofa, and then ducked down with her puppy. She did that every few minutes—fed scraps to the dog, giggled at the thankful licks, and peeked nervously over the couch.

I followed her line of sight—two big swinging doors that probably led to the kitchen. The doors had captivated Alpha, too. He stood with statue-like stillness, his unwavering stare highlighting those doors.

Was I to be the only one left out of a great mystery?

Alpha reached toward me. "We must go."

I dodged his transporting hand and swept toward the doors.

"ZIA!"

"Hang on. I just want to see—"

*WHAM*, the doors punched open.

*BAMM*, they smacked the walls.

Alpha bolted towards me.

"JENEVIEVE!" shouted behind me.

I spun.

A tall, angry woman marched right through me.

My breath left. My legs jellied. I started to fall.

I felt a pinch and it was over.

Sort of.

Back in Divisional, I collapsed, face down, gasping and swallowing from a burst of fear. I had glimpsed the pregnant woman for less than two seconds —didn't even know the color of her eyes—but when her Soul passed through mine, I learned more than I wanted to know.

My chin tipped up. "Nice knowing you."

"Zia."

"OH HELL NO!" I rolled onto my back. "Find yourself another patsy. You're not sticking me in that thing. I know what it is. That thing is a Niine Determinant. This must be the early Twentieth Century, right? That's when another set of those Determinant-things will be running around on Earth. That's what Romal once told me. He also said that those Determinant-things change the tapestry of the world. Global stuff."

"True; however—"

"However nothing. No way, no how. I draw the line on tapestry-changing parents. Get it? Even if she were a One Determinant, I'd still refuse. *Waaay* too much pressure. Whatever this tapestry is, you just thread me onto the fringe. Better yet, weave me out of it."

"Zia."

"NO! Save the argument. Why not just boot my butt straight to Hades. That's where you're sending me, straight to Hades."

"She is not a Niine Determinant."

I looked at him hard. "Are you sure? You're not supposed to lie, you know. They taught you that in Guide School, right? No take-backs."

"Zia, the Determinants were leading armies in Europe, not furnishing mansions in California."

"But I felt her Soul. She has no conscience."

"She is a Niine Player, nothing more. Niine suppresses her conscience to unshackle a callous intent. That is a common weapon of Niine."

Immediately, I thought of Triite—but it couldn't be. I had just left that ogre days ago. Or was it years? Questions flurried with another bundle of *should haves:* I should have fessed up to leaving Divisional in pursuit of Triite; I should have asked about the vampire beads and the wandering kid; I should have explained how I bruised my Ribbon. Too late now. "Alpha, straight up, my previous mothers played for One, and I still messed up my lives. Talk to Romal. He'll tell you."

"Zia, all Players live among Players for both sides, One and Niine."

"Sure, bakers, doctors, and neighbors, but not mothers, not mine anyway."

An empty cord wiggled up at my side. I slapped it. "Alpha, what if I fail? I'll go to Hades."

Alpha made a strange face again, his eyes squinting, his head tilting, as if he were trying to interpret gibberish. "Zia, you cannot go to Hades unless you choose to do so; however, you cannot make that choice until your consecrating life."

"My what?"

"Zia, this is only your Eleventh life."

*Eleventh?* "Alpha, you're scaring me worse than that mother. This is my tenth life. TENTH! Why don't you know that? What kind of Guide are you? Can't you even count? How can I trust anything you say?"

In the middle of my blustering panic, Alpha poked my forehead. The image of a monster-mother was replaced by the picture of a faded Awen.

"Yeah, I get it." I grabbed the cord. "But I'm doing this for Awen, okay? Not Ereo. Got that? And while I'm down there, don't leave me for a second. In fact, forget about whispering. Just holler!"

I snaked the cord, watching big squiggles ripple into smaller ones. "Stupid gender, stupid ocean, stupid mother. This life already stinks." I lashed the cord vertically, creating mountains that cascaded into hills. Then I whipped the cord, round and round, a circling lasso. When I tried a figure eight, the cord tangled.

"Descend now," Alpha said in a tone I didn't care for, "or the child will be stillborn."

"Stop rushing me." After a one-eyed peek down the tube, I held it to my lips and blew Taps. *To-ta-tooo, to-ta-tooo.*

"Zia."

I saluted. *To-ta-to, to-ta-to, to-ta-tooo.*

"Zia."

*To-ta-tooo, tooo-taaa-tooo.*

"ZIA!"

"I'M GOING." *To-ta-to.*

Filling the cord with my skinned-up Ribbon, I descended into the belly of the beast.

# Book II

*After one or two skinned knees, a precocious child learns that a Superman cape won't enable them to fly. Granted, Zia endures countless bloodied knees and several fractured limbs before she quits retesting the cape.*

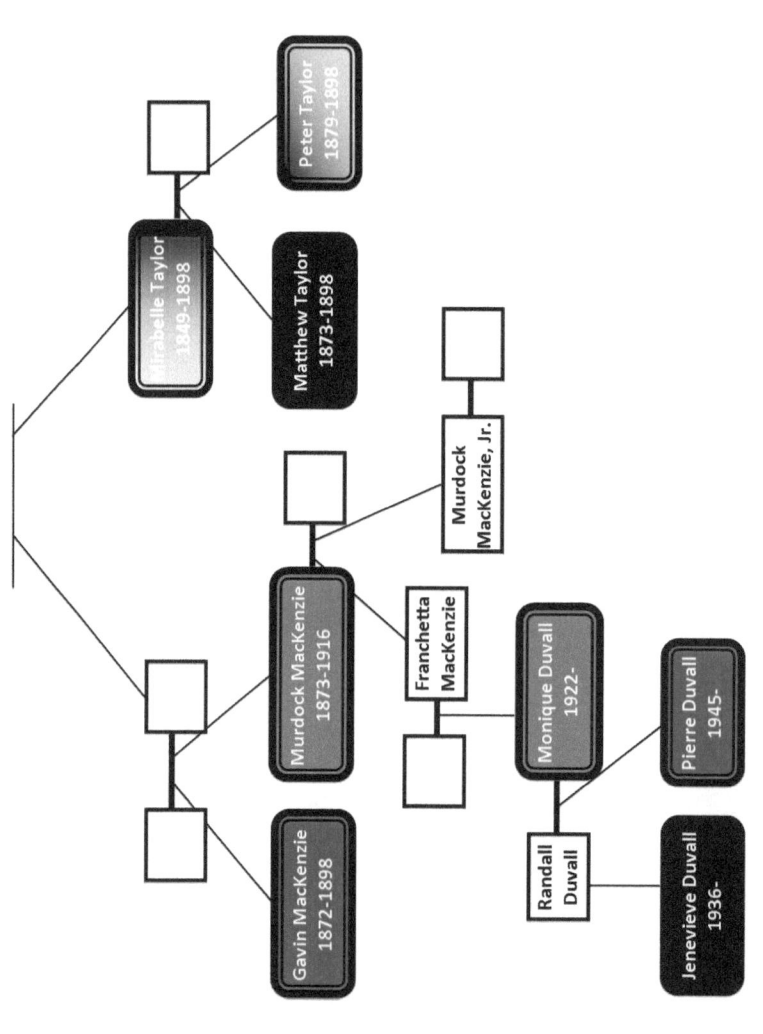

# 15

*As a Player, Triite would have wealth,*
*beauty, and charm—Kaane promised.*

## 1950 - California

Inside the Duvall mansion, seated at a desk, Mr. Perriman studied the last page of the will to appease Monique Duvall. Her phone calls and letters had accused the Executor's firm of disreputable intent. Behind him, Monique paced alongside a row of saltwater tanks.

"'Treasures from the sea,'" she said bending to peer at a toadfish, "'a gift for my precious pearl.' Lies. Despicable lies."

"I'm sorry?" Mr. Perriman said.

"That, too, is a lie." Monique tapped the glass. "Men are never sorry. Randall built these aquariums to symbolize captivity. My captivity. Marine life imprisoned by glass, and my life imprisoned by Randall's seed. His so-called gift was a veiled apology for deforming my belly."

"With Pierre? He's a fine boy, certainly worth—"

"Worth what? A million dollars? That's a paltry share of this estate."

"No, I wasn't referring to Pierre's financial worth. I was referring to—"

"Matters that don't concern you with opinions that don't interest me. Your job is to correct mistakes in this will."

"Mrs. Duvall, there are no mistakes. Understandably, the terms are upsetting, but the will is painstakingly clear. Though you didn't attend the will's reading, I mailed you a certified copy, which came back, delivery refused. As I tried to explain on the phone before the call ended abruptly, your late husband set up an increasing inheritance based on your years of marriage, starting on your seventh anniversary. Although the percentage increased on every anniversary thereafter, the point is moot. Your husband's death legally ended the marriage. According to the will, if the marriage terminates two days or two minutes before your seventh anniversary, it's all the same. You're not entitled to a dime of—"

"WRONG!" Monique marched to the Executor and leaned into his nose. She steeled her threatening eyes onto his blinking ones. "Randall's seed festered into eleven pounds that issued in a coat of sticky white filth. He destroyed my womb. And you sit here, trying to tell me that I suffered for nothing? No, Mr. Perriman, you are wrong. Read the will again. And keep reading until you find my entitlement or until your eyes bleed from the strain. Am I understood?" Her red fingernails clicked the mahogany desk. "Well? Find your tongue. Am I understood?"

Mr. Perriman nodded, quickly and continuously.

The lean, six-foot Monique straightened again. "Very well."

Mr. Perriman withdrew a handkerchief, dabbed his brow, then flipped the papers to the start.

Monique went to one of nine basins, each set beside a door and steaming with water. For the third time that hour, her hands underwent a brutal scrubbing. Pink flesh peeled into a blistering red before she gently towel-dried each raw and scalded finger. She strode back to the aquariums. "Randall, if you weren't dead, I'd filet your heart and feed it to the eels."

She tossed the towel and crossed her arms. Her thoughts still on Randall, her sharpened nails cut into her ivory forearms. Blood dotted her fingers. She licked the tips as her heels pounded back to the basin.

Mr. Perriman listened for her distance. When the water splashed, he closed the folder and fumbled into his coat. "The estate is held in trust until Jenevieve's twenty-first birthday. You are allowed—"

"ALLOWED?" Monique whirled. Before Mr. Perriman could adjust his fedora, Monique was across the room. Her arms bladed in muscles, Monique blocked the front door, *click-click-click,* her razor nails pricking a threatening beat on the doorframe. "Allowed?"

"I—I meant no insult." Mr. Perriman glanced over his shoulder hoping to spot a cook or a housekeeper, but he saw no one. Again, sweat beads popped on his brow. He was a slight man with limited strength, a man given to numbers, not a man firmed for battle, especially a battle against a strong, unstable woman. "Mrs. Duvall, if you choose to live here, you may. The trust maintains the estate, including the groundskeepers, caretakers, cooks and staff. All recurring debts are provided for until Jenevieve's age of majority. Then Jenevieve will control the estate, but I'm sure she'll see that all your needs are met. She's a delightful girl, so well-mannered and poised."

"She's a dandy," Monique said dully. "What becomes of the estate should something happen to either child?"

"I'm sorry?"

"No, you're not sorry. You're dim. I'm referring to something unfortunate, Mr. Perriman. Must I be crude?"

"If something unfortunate happens to Pierre before his age of majority, well, his million dollar inheritance becomes yours. With Jenevieve, all assets are to be liquidated and granted to The Institute of Marine Research."

The tendons in Monique's neck thrummed. She glared at the sweaty little man who had just declared her a pauper. She ought to rip out his useless orbs for failing to see her entitlement. Yes, that's just what she would do if he didn't open his eyes to see what she had endured. She started toward him.

Mr. Perriman backed up.

Monique unzipped her skirt and nudged it down to expose her lower abdomen. "Do you see this, Mr. Perriman?" But he turned his reddening face, testing Monique's patience. "LOOK! Look at these marks."

The Executor cleared his throat, adjusted his glasses, and forced himself to look. Three thin lines, two inches long, grooved Monique's belly.

"Mrs. Duvall, they're barely noticeable. My wife has stretch marks, too."

Monique re-zipped her skirt. "I don't give a damn about your wife. Your wife is a hag. A common drudge. And it's your fault, Mr. Perriman, because that's what men do. All men. They marry beautiful young girls whose tender bodies can be claimed, soiled, and imprisoned by the man's planted seed. 'Cook for me, clean for me, bear my children,' until her beauty is spent, her lot is servitude, and her desires match those of a mongrel dog yearning for a master's approval and attention. And then, Mr. Perriman, what do men do? After he commits these atrocities on her, what do men do?" The irony started Monique laughing. "*He* blames *her*, blames *her* for becoming a pathetic worn-out rag, and his eye wanders to the next pretty victim. That's what men do, Mr. Perriman. They sanction their iniquities by calling it love."

Blood had drained from the Executor's face leaving him a wet and sallow man whose mouth opened and closed like a shored fish gasping for water. Monique might have savored the briny scent of fear wafting through the air had Mr. Perriman been a challenge and not a pathetic turtle-man hunched into his shoulders. Monique stepped aside. "Dismissed."

As Mr. Perriman hurried to leave, Monique heard him mumble. Her arm lashed across the exit. "What did you say?"

"Nothing. I—I merely offered condolences."

"You mentioned timing."

"An untimely tragedy of fate. Now, please, the office expects me."

*Fate?* Monique's arm slowly lowered.

The Executor swung the door open and rushed from the house. Monique, heavy in thought, eased the door closed. *Untimely tragedy of fate?* It was certainly untimely. Randall's death had occurred the morning before their seventh anniversary, thereby denying Monique of her multimillion-dollar inheritance. Was *fate* responsible? Her beloved mother, Franchetta, had taught that fate colludes in acts of three.

Monique went to her desk, gathered a pencil and paper, and drew a triangle. In the center, she printed the result—*death*. At the triangle's peak, she wrote an act of fate—*bee*. A bee had chosen that particular morning to perch itself on Randall's glass of orange juice. At the triangle's left point, she wrote the second act of fate—*idiot*. Randall, still groggy from sleep, had stupidly mouthed the bee.

For a long while, she pondered the triangle's right point, but nothing seemed to fit. She was about to give up when she spotted her mistake. Such an obvious mistake, too. It was right in the triangle's center. Zero inheritance was the result, not death. Randall's death she intended, though intended for the following day. Had Randall sipped Monique's tea—a brew that had been aging for weeks—he would have agonized for hours instead of dying within minutes from anaphylactic shock.

She erased *death* from the center. In its place, she drew a dollar sign with a slash. Now the third act of fate became clear. Across the triangle's right point, she wrote *flawed*. All physical maladies were flaws, all marks of contamination; Jenevieve's asthma, Pierre's lazy eye, and Randall's allergy to bee venom. If not for the third fate, the bee would have delivered a swollen lip, not a premature death. Fate had indeed colluded to seize her fortune.

Monique crumpled the paper and rested her head on folded arms. "Ma mére, even fate has turned against me. I need you."

Loneliness came with memories of Franchetta. Loneliness and love. While other mothers had raised their daughters to become obedient drudges, Franchetta had taught Monique a legacy of wisdom—the Formulas of Four. Monique specialized in toxic herbs, and by twelve, she knew what to grow, when to harvest, and how long to steep. When her skills advanced, Monique learned to brew deadly teas, sweet and untraceable.

At sixteen, she served her first lethal brew to her father.

Death swooped in quickly, his fingers still clasping the cup. Franchetta, a proud mother, declared Monique gifted. Franchetta's first tea had merely caused her own father a headache. Franchetta had to rework the formula several times before her father, Murdock MacKenzie, succumbed to death.

When Monique heard the story, she tried to comfort her mother. "Ma mére, it's not your fault. Grandfather MacKenzie was Scottish. Father was French. It's harder to kill a bear than to kill a fox."

When Monique turned eighteen, she knew how to choose, seduce, and properly dispose of a husband. Her mother had purged many husbands, as did her grandmother and her great-grandmother. This great lineage of women filled Monique with pride. Pride and bitterness. Monique had no daughter to bestow her legacy of wisdom. Her nails drummed the desk. *Click -click-click, click-click-click.*

Although Jenevieve came from another bloodline, she was pliant, intelligent, and female. In seven years, Jenevieve would control the Duvall wealth. Then greedy men would fill her head with filthy lies. Naive Jenevieve would fall victim to drudgery—*click-click-click*—unless Monique saved her.

Monique nodded; yes, she would save Jenevieve. She would open Jenevieve's eyes, force her compliance, and teach her the ancestral wisdom. Spared from a man's enslavement, a grateful Jenevieve would return what rightfully belonged to Monique—the Duvall estate.

Pierre, on the other hand—*click-click-click, click-click-click*—a clumsy little oaf, whose right eye was brown and weepy, and whose left eye was green and rolling, had poisoned Monique's womb. Monique shuddered. Fate had issued Pierre and fate had invited his return—a million dollars for his return. Without that money, Monique was less than a guest in her own home, her purchases approved and disapproved at Mr. Perriman's discretion, and later, at Jenevieve's whim—a sickening thought.

Monique went to a basin to cleanse her hands. The water felt maliciously cold. "CARLOS."

He came quickly, nodding incessantly. "Yes, ma'am. Yes, ma'am."

"Did you boil the cleansing water for twenty minutes before you refilled the basins?"

"Yes, ma'am."

"You're lying. I think you removed the kettle before the water boiled."

"No, ma'am. The water boiled for twenty minutes to the second."

Monique searched his face for a hint of deception. "From now on, refill the basins every 15 minutes with water boiled for 30. Am I understood?"

"Yes, ma'am."

"Carlos, do you remember an invitation to a benefit dinner? Some charity for cripples."

"Yes, ma'am, a banquet and silent auction to raise funds for a children's hospital."

"Next Saturday night, correct?"

"Yes, ma'am, but you told me—"

"I don't care what I told you before. I'm telling you now that I plan to attend. Either dig through the trash until you find the invitation or have the hospital issue a new one. Reserve my table, party of one."

"Yes, ma'am."

"And have the chauffeur draw up a map."

"Ma'am?"

"I know how to drive. The chauffeur better know how to draw up a map. If I lose my way, he will lose his job. Additionally, tell the staff, including the children's au pair, to vacate the premises for that weekend. I wish to grieve my husband in private. Anyone stepping foot on these grounds between Friday evening and Monday morning will be dismissed. You'll go, too. Am I understood?"

"Yes, ma'am."

Monique turned her back, but kept a keen eye on Carlos's reflection in the window. "Dismissed."

Carlos bowed. "Thank you, ma'am."

Monique smiled, recalling her mother's good advice; *keep a watch for deception at your back.* "Oh, ma mére, everything is clear now. I have the answer. Tell me you're proud."

Monique listened for the companion voice in her head she was certain came from her mother. This time, however, she didn't hear Franchetta's soft and approving whispers. Instead, she heard what sounded like anxious chanting. *No, child, no, no, no.*

# 16

W hile keeping watch over Phoenix, Willow witnessed Kaane's many attempts to stop Monique from removing Pierre.

When Monique's slippery hands dropped the uncapped bottle, the pills rolled and rolled until they found their way to the drain.

A few nights later, an unseasonable frost killed Monique's nightshade.

When Alpha appeared, Willow gestured to the withered plants beneath Jenevieve's window. "Monique's determination frustrates Kaane," she told Alpha. "He destroyed the entire garden, both deadly root and harmless bloom."

The warmth from Alpha's gaze fell upon Willow's profile.

"Phoenix is a worthy Healer," Alpha said.

Willow nodded, appreciating Alpha's intent, but finding no comfort in his comment. "At the moment," Willow said, "Phoenix is Jenevieve, a defenseless child within the lair of a Niine Persuader." She paused to let Alpha absorb the gravity of her statement. "Each time one of my Charges descends a cord, I grip my faith and I say a prayer, and I don't stop praying until my Charge returns home."

"I understand," Alpha said.

"No, you don't." Willow gave a quick smile. "But you will."

A week later, two Guides from Niine joined Kaane in a sudden move toward the mansion.

"It's a triad," Willow said. "A Niine triad." Her worried eyes swept from the triad to the sleeping Jenevieve. "Alpha, hurry. Godspeed."

But Alpha had already left to intervene.

# 17

*He chose the knife because
acquiring apologies would take time.*

Acres of gardens separated the main house from the servants' quarters. On Friday night, staff cleared the grounds, all staff except Kathryn, the au pair. She lingered at the kitchen's back door.

"Oh, but the children," she said to Monique, "they'll be expecting me in the morning. If it's the noise that worries ya, we'll be quieter than church mice. Ya won't be disturbed."

Monique checked her watch. "In three minutes, you won't have a job." She inspected her nails.

She loathed the way Kathryn looked at her. For that matter, she loathed the way Kathryn looked at all. Kathryn waddled more than walked, squinted indoors, and spoke with a doltish accent that grated on Monique's nerves. "Dismiss her," Monique had told Randall. "Just to embarrass me, Kathryn calls herself a nanny, but she's neither a Brit nor a goat. Get rid of her." But Randall refused, claiming Kathryn was family and would always have a place in their home.

Monique glanced at her watch again. "Two minutes."

"But surely you'll be needing me tomorrow night. Are ya not attending a fancy dinner?"

"Are you prying into my affairs?"

"Oh, no, ma'am. I wasn't meaning to pry. But if you'll pardon me for asking, you're not planning on leaving the children alone, are ya?"

Monique heated. "You are not pardoned. Jenevieve is fourteen, old enough to care for herself and watch over Pierre. She's too old for a—for an au pair, a title you don't deserve. You have two weeks to find employment elsewhere."

"No, ma'am, you can't be serious." Kathryn's squinty eyes suddenly widened. "The children need me. Jenevieve is tearful and clinging to me skirts wherever I go. And Pierre, oh, he's a lovely boy, but he's such a sad boy. He misses his father dearly, and he don't wear his patch without reminding. Ma'am, I love these children. Love them like they were me own."

"But they're not your own, are they, Kathryn? You chose the lot of a servant, a common nursemaid, whose services are no longer required. Since you don't appreciate two weeks' notice, you now have one. And if you say another word, I'll have you removed from the property this minute."

Kathryn's jaw clenched. Reluctantly, she walked out and started toward the servants' quarters.

"Kathryn," Monique called, "I've reconsidered." When joy had risen in Kathryn's face, Monique said, "You have three days' notice." Monique slammed the door and then peered through the side window to witness a devastated Kathryn slumping. "So much for nannies." Monique dug into her pocket, withdrew a skeleton key, and headed to the study.

Steam twined above a freshly filled basin sitting on a pedestal at the library's entrance. Monique scoured her hands until her ivory skin had turned red-raw clean. Stepping into the study, she sniffed the air, but detected no dust; only illiterate pigs allowed dust to settle on their books.

Thousands of leather bounds lined the shelves, floor to ceiling, and spanned three walls, each wall with its own rolling ladder. The arts, classics, and illustrated fiction—Randall's section—Monique intended to purge. Like Kathryn, they were unnecessary. Randall's historicals, however, would stay. Monique revered history; only fools did otherwise.

The east and west shelves held Monique's collection passed down from nine generations and grouped into the Formulas of Four: Earth—botany, entomology, mineralogy, ornithology, herpetology; Wind—chemistry, physics, astronomy, meteorology; Water—aquaculture, oceanography, ichthyology; and Fire—psychology, theology, metaphysics.

Monique rolled the oak ladder out of the way. From the bottom shelf, she pulled the Brewer's Anthology-3. Yellow and brittle with age, the folio ripped. Monique cursed fate's relentless battle to stop her.

Earlier, a clumsy misstep had sent all but two of her sleeping pills tumbling down the sink. With those pills went Monique's contrived excuse that her contentious child had mistaken the pills for candy. Then she went to the garden for a deadly but palatable herb, but her garden had withered under a killing frost.

Monique carried the folio to the heirloom desk where she keyed the lower drawer. She pulled out an amber vial topped with a cork. It contained the brew meant for Randall. Monique would have to alter the formula for Pierre. Toxins left traces in the eyes. Although difficult to detect in an adult's hardened corneas, Pierre's eyes, young and two-colored, attracted attention, and likely more attention during an autopsy.

She opened the book. Sprinkled throughout the text were handwritten corrections from her lineage of mothers.

*Eye of newt*, three little words often written into stories with witches stirring cauldrons. Like many legends and fables, a factual premise gave rise to the three words...as Monique's grandmother knew when she crossed out the word, *eye*, and printed the word, *egg*. Years later, Franchetta added a note, *California*. Monique smiled; fairy tale witches would have had a deadly brew had their cauldrons contained *Egg of California newt*.

Monique turned the page. Under the light of a table lamp, she scanned pages and pages of notes and drawings, then she gathered more books to interpret language, search meanings, and analyze symbols.

Hours into the night, the lights flickered and then died.

Monique lit a candle. With bloodshot eyes, she kept reading.

At three a.m., she found the correct passage to alter the brew. She drew the candle closer to the book. Melted wax spilled from the holder and spread across the unread page. Monique jumped up and desperately tried to wipe off the wax, but the brittle paper ripped and crumbled.

"Ma mére," Monique cried out, "why have you left me? WHY?" With both hands, she flung the book.

It smacked the shelves, jarring free Aquatic Deep.

When Monique went to return the two books to the shelves, she noticed the picture on the parted page of Aquatic Deep. "Odessa." A tired but grateful smile came to her face. All along she had had the means for ridding Pierre. Clear and simple, the means lived within her saltwater tanks.

Her head tipped back. "Thank you, ma mére, thank you."

She retired for the night.

Kaane appeared beside Alpha in the empty room.

"Interfering?" Kaane asked, but only to goad a response. He knew Alpha hadn't stirred Monique to throw the book, nor had Alpha caused Aquatic

Deep to tumble. Alpha had parted the pages, true, but that was fair play...and well played. What a shame Alpha had chosen the wrong side.

Kaane suspended the candle's flame before it could burn the last of its wax. "We were once brethren," Kaane whispered turning to the flames of Alpha's eyes. "One created our battle, not beelzeNiine. Had One agreed to divide the Energies as beelzeNiine had proposed, we would still be brethren."

"Energies choose their state of being."

An aggravated hiss issued from Kaane, "Free Will." How could Alpha be so blind, so stubborn, so fooled? Suckling on Kaane's face were clusters of atoms, each cluster resembling a bead, small and round, but each composing a Soul. Kaane scraped a handful from his cheek and held it out. "This is what you gave Free Will—spats of particles."

The Souls bleated and squawked in Kaane's palm.

"BeelzeNiine sought only half," Kaane said. "Half! A fair and equitable division. But One sought more than half. Tell me, which Power is greedy?" With two fingers, Kaane pinched the Soul until it squealed. "Pain, the fault of One. Had we  gathered the Energies into our state of being, they would have never known a moment of agony. Instead, One creates this miserable planet, 'Here's your vehicle; drive yourself to a state of being.' Tell me, which Power lacks compassion?" He returned the Souls to his face. "When this vehicle is destroyed, Energies will have no method to achieve any state of being. Their existence will equate to celestial dust. And they'll be aware of that, Alpha, because they're aware of themselves. One woke them, not beelzeNiine. Tell me, which Power is cruel?"

Alpha turned to leave.

"Your moment of intemperance," Kaane said quickly.

Alpha stilled.

Kaane circled to the front of him. "Battling for eons in The Great War had taken a toll on all Guides. After eons and eons, who among us was battling with full rationale? Not one. Not one Guide from either side. So who could blame you for your one rash act of drawing a weapon from the Negative Power? Not I, Alpha, even though you wielded that weapon against me. But One, supposedly so wounded, so hurt, nearly extinguished existence. We stand here today only because beelzeNiine conceded to this mistake you call Free Will. Tell me, Alpha, which Power is rigidly self-serving?"

"BeelzeNiine." Alpha vanished.

# 18

*Unless he travels in the astral plane,*
*Fikus was more than five hundred miles away.*


Within seconds of touching the velvet bedspread, Monique melted into sleep. In her dreams, she saw her mother, her grandmother, and her great-grandmother. The three mothers, hunched and gray, shook their heads and wagged their fingers, desperate and scolding.

To Monique, they were bothersome. They blocked her view of what stood in the distance—a tall, umber figure, its eyes casting a coppery light. On the figure's shoulder was a dove. When Monique lifted to her toes for a better look, the mothers began waving their arms and flagging for attention. Monique returned to her heels. "Move aside," Monique said. "Let me see what it is."

The mothers whirled and scowled.

Franchetta stepped forward clutching an eye-patch.

"Oh that?" Monique said. "That's a problem solved."

Franchetta lifted the patch high, then lowered it to her forehead, raised it again, then back to her forehead. The gesture continued while the other mothers wrung their hands.

"You're confusing me," Monique said. "Forehead is life."

The cronies tittered and nodded anxiously.

"Pierre?" Monique stared at the patch. "You want Pierre to—to—"

The dove took flight, stealing Monique's attention. "Oh, look! Look!"

The mothers spun around. And in the timeless motion captured in dreams, the mothers pitched and whirled against the bird's fluttering wings. Feathers showered down, thousands and millions of feathers. They swelled into clouds, blinding Monique and clogging her throat.

She tried to scream, tell the mothers to stop, hold still. Couldn't they see she was choking? *Whack!* Monique shot upright, gasping and fingering her mouth for feathers. Cold sweat had darkened the velvet covers from violet to plum. Saliva ringed her down-filled pillow. She flung the pillow and twisted to the bed's edge. Her temples throbbed from the nightmare. Her mouth parched, she lifted the bedside water glass, and then set it down empty. Her mothers had visited her dream; that much, she recalled. When she pressed her memory for more, the nightmarish feathers resurfaced. A shiver ran down her spine. She had nearly died in the fluffy down. *Died!*

Curious about the noise that had awakened her, she eased from the bed and over to the window. If Carlos had forgotten to secure the shutters, he'd lose a week's pay.

She swept aside the drapes. Her heart tripped. Stuck on the outside pane above the closed shutters was a white feather. Monique rapped the glass until the feather dropped. She lifted the window, unlatched the shutters, and looked down.

A dove twitched and flapped, bickering with death. When it caught Monique's eye, it surrendered. Monique drew back, oddly nervous. "Horrid thing." She quickly closed the window.

From the den, the Grandfather Clock chimed noon. After bathing, Monique spent four hours fixing her hair and applying her makeup until the mirror reflected perfection. Wearing an evening gown, she went downstairs.

Giggles rose from the kitchen. Frivolous giggles from children who were breaking Monique's rule; children should be seen and not heard. Monique pelted the doors to announce her entrance. Jenevieve was stirring a pot of bubbling oatmeal while Pierre sat kicking the table legs.

"Stop your nonsense," Monique told them.

The children froze, their smiles disappeared, and their heads lowered. Monique turned to Pierre. "I've warned you to sit still at the table. After your oatmeal, you're to go right to your room. And take off that idiotic eye-patch. It announces to the world your shame."

Pierre looked at his sister, who gave a quick nod. Pierre slipped a finger under the band, plucked off the patch, and pushed it across the table.

"Jenevieve, see that Pierre is in bed by eight, yourself by nine."

"Where's Katy?" Jenevieve asked.

"Kathryn has better things to do than coddle the two of you." Monique pushed into her ivory gloves, smoothing the satin to her elbows. "I expect every basin scrubbed and refilled with boiling water. Am I understood?"

"Yes, ma mére," Jenevieve said, "boiled for twenty minutes."

"Thirty." Monique smiled at her protégé. "I left your asthma medication on the counter. Remember to take it before bed."

After a silent minute, Monique said, "Jenevieve, where are your manners? When someone shows you consideration, such as setting out your medicine to keep you from wheezing throughout the night, what do you say?"

"Thank you, ma mére."

"That's better." Monique studied them until they respectfully trembled. She marched from the kitchen. When the swinging doors settled, she listened for the sound of laughter or deception at her back. Satisfied by their continued silence, Monique went to the entryway mirror to check her appearance. Flawless. The black sequined gown defined her narrow hips and revealed a tasteful plunge of cleavage. She tousled her golden hair, admiring its contrast to her gown's ebony sparkles. Perfect. She swayed side to side.

"Tonight, ma mére, I'll rid the fates." She twirled. "Gone, gone, gone." A pestering insect buzzed her ear, *nooo, nooo, nooo*. Monique swatted it.

The drive to the benefit should have taken thirty minutes, but the Packard lurched for two miles before the motor quit, stranding Monique.

Soon, however, an old truck, towing a small boat, rambled up the road. A tall, weathered fisherman got out of the truck and offered assistance.

Monique told him to hurry. While the fisherman inspected the engine, Monique re-powdered her nose. Suddenly, the motor hummed. But it seemed to Monique that the man had done nothing more than shine a bright flashlight beneath the hood. When the hood closed, Monique noticed the fisherman's hands were empty. She cracked the window. "If you left your flashlight sitting on the motor—"

"Untrue."

"Very well. I suppose you expect to be paid."

"Untrue."

"Whether true or not, the proper reply is yes or no." Monique hit the gas. Miles later, she lowered the window. Instantly, the gust sucked out the map. Monique was unconcerned; she had memorized the directions. She arrived at the event, parked on a side street, and then hurried up the steps.

While awaiting announcement, Monique peeked into the ballroom. Sitting at linen covered tables topped with rose bouquets and set with china for eight were celebrities, politicians, and tycoons. On one side, under the shimmering lights of crystal chandeliers, a twenty-piece orchestra led couples in a waltz. On the opposite side were the treasures to be auctioned.

Some of the guests had attended Randall's funeral. Once again, Monique would have to tolerate their boorish sympathies.

"Mrs. Monique Duvall," the Announcer proclaimed, turning all heads.

A tuxedoed escort came to Monique's side, bowed, and offered the crook of his arm. Her chin high, Monique accepted with a delicate hand.

While crossing the room, Monique noticed a crude display of jealousy; guests were turning their backs as she approached. To the few who properly ogled Monique, Monique graced them with a cupped wave and an approving nod. Midway through the room, as Monique strolled past a table of eight, she heard, "Gold digger."

Monique swiveled back. She firmed a stance behind the large bosomed shrew who had uttered the insult. A few chairs over, a man discreetly elbowed his wife, who then looked up. She passed along the hushing nudge to the still gossiping Marilyn Camford. Marilyn glanced over her shoulder and then quieted with a sip of champagne.

Ignoring her escort's tug, Monique glared at each seated man until, one by one, they budged to their feet and waited for permission to sit. When no permission came, Mr. Camford excused himself and left. The remaining men, still standing, gave expectant looks to Marilyn.

With a put-upon sigh, Marilyn set down her flute of champagne, lifted a smile, and then twisted in her chair. "Oh, Mrs. Duvall, so wonderful to see you, dear." She offered her hand.

Monique recoiled openly, as if the offered hand were diseased.

Marilyn flushed, her rejected hand rising to adjust an earring. "I'd invite you to join us, but as you can see, our table is full."

"Marilyn, we didn't have a chance to talk at Randall's funeral."

"Yes, very unfortunate. I'm terribly sorry for your loss. All of us are." Impassive sympathies mumbled around the table. "Do let us know if you need anything." She brushed the air and shifted back to her friends.

Monique's nostrils flared; the pompous swine had the nerve to dismiss Monique Duvall. Monique dug into her clutch, retrieved a business card, and slapped it down beside Marilyn's plate. The other ladies leaned over to glimpse the card before Marilyn picked it up. "What is this?"

"Randall's physician. Before Randall died, he made me promise to give you the doctor's card."

Marilyn turned sideways. "Whatever for?"

"Randall had syphilis. Have yourself checked."

Around the table, jaws fell like a circle of dominoes. Marilyn jumped up, toppling her chair. "How DARE you! You're a damn liar."

"Oh, come now, Marilyn. Let's not pretend shock when your health is at stake. Every husband has an occasional dalliance. And every intelligent wife understands that fact; isn't that correct, ladies?" The women chilled with frigid glares to their squirming husbands. "And speaking of affairs, where is that delicious Mr. Camford?"

Marilyn reached back and grabbed a water glass. "WHORE!" But as she brought the glass around, Monique blocked the arm mid-swing. Forearm to forearm collided launching the water glass high into the air.

Heads tipped back.

Two tables away, the glass crashed on a plate. A woman sprang with a shriek. Baffled guests bumped into other guests, their eyes searching the ceiling for what had fallen. The clamor of rising voices caused other guests to hush, their ears perked, their drinks suspended halfway to their lips. The dancing slowed, the music stuttered, and the nervous conductor looked to the Announcer for direction. The Announcer gestured, *keep playing...keep playing!* Then he motioned to Monique's escort, *Get going!*

Monique felt a firm hand press on the small of her back. Having dispensed with Marilyn Camford, Monique allowed the escort to usher her along. When they reached Monique's table, the escort pulled a chair, but before Monique sat, he walked away.

"Good evening," Monique said to the only guest at her table. The woman stood, dabbed a linen to her lips, and then followed the path of the escort. "Lovely waltz," Monique said to those at a neighboring table. "I believe it's Chopin, isn't it?"

They frowned and turned their backs to Monique. Obviously, they wanted to hide their musical ignorance. Monique fluffed a napkin to her lap and waited for others to join her.

Nobody came.

Monique sighed; isolation is the plight of the perfect...and they saw her as perfect. How could they not? Monique blushed.

Throughout the evening, she placed several bids in the auction box, some double the item's value. At one a.m., bids would be opened and winners announced.

Monique checked her watch. Ten. She left the ballroom and strolled down the hallway toward the ladies' room. At the doorway, Monique lingered, pretending to check her clutch. When the hallway was clear, Monique hurried out the side exit.

# 19

The buzzing of a tenacious mosquito challenged Monique's drive home. Twice she swerved, once skimming a guardrail. By the time she parked in the breezeway, she was bitten and angry, "insufferable insect." She slammed the car door, immediately cringing and scolding herself for making such a racket. Obscurity was difficult enough from the moonlight flickering off her sequined dress.

Keys in hand, she hurried up the pathway and entered through the back door. The aquariums tinted the living room a neon green and droned in a percolating rumble. Monique started toward the kitchen, but then stopped and hurried back into the shadows.

Jenevieve had forgotten to draw the front drapes. Parts of the room were exposed to late night strollers with prying eyes. Monique couldn't risk closing the drapes now. Someone might have already noticed them open and would state as much if questioned later.

Indignantly, Monique removed her heels. In a half-stoop, she scurried to the kitchen.

Under the glow of nightlights, she gathered a wide-mouthed jar and a small fishnet. After a peek from the kitchen, she rushed past the windows and over to the tanks. "Odessa," she sang softly, "where are you?" She filled the jar with saltwater before setting it aside. Using the net, she combed the tank, poking and prodding behind rocks and underneath coral. "Come out, come out, wherever you are."

In the adjacent tank, a parrotfish darted at the glinting sequins, *tink-tink-tink*. It hit the glass, retreated, then attacked again.

"You're irritating me, Kaiser." Monique swept the net toward Kaiser's tank. Sand from the bottom lifted and swirled, uncovering a timid octopus. "Oh, there you are, you pretty little girl. It's time to go home."

The octopus inched toward the rocks.

"Don't be difficult. I'm not going to hurt you." Monique scooped up Odessa and plopped her into the jar. She set the jar on top of the tank. "I'll be back for you later."

Once more, Monique ducked past the windows.

She went upstairs to Jenevieve's bedroom. When she cracked the door, moonlight seeped into the hall. Monique clenched; Jenevieve had forgotten to lower her bedroom shade.

Monique skirted past the window and over to Jenevieve, who wasn't tossing or turning or making rhythmic sounds of life. Monique felt Jenevieve's wrist for a pulse.

Nothing. Monique sucked in a quick breath, her desperate fingers working across Jenevieve's neck. Finally, she found a heartbeat. Though weak and sluggish, the heart was beating. Monique dropped the wrist to pat her own chest, relieved.

On Jenevieve's nightstand was a porcelain figurine of a dove perched on the shoulder of a crying angel. 24k gold outlined the angel's wings and dotted the angel's tears. The dove was solid gold.

Monique recalled when Randall presented the figurine to Jenevieve. "Your mother cherished this guardian angel," he had told her. "Whenever you were troubled, she placed it at your bedside. When you woke, you always seemed much better."

Monique turned the statue over and over. Jenevieve should have drawn the drapes and lowered her shades. With a firm grip, Monique smacked the figurine against the dresser's edge. Half the angel tumbled to the rug. "It's for your own good." She looked at the sleeping Jenevieve. "I'm sparing you from your kindred contagions."

Twelve chimes echoed up from the Grandfather Clock. Monique returned half an angel to the nightstand. "Someday, you'll thank me."

She smiled down at the fortunate girl who now had Monique for a mother. "Sleep tight. You have much to learn." Monique slipped from the room and quietly closed the bedroom door. When she turned to the hallway, she bumped into her disheveled son.

"Owww."

"Hush," Monique said. "What are you doing out of bed?"

Pierre fisted his eyes. "I heard something. I want Jen." He tried to squeeze between Monique and the wall, but she sidestepped. Pierre whined louder, "Nooo, I want Jen. I want—"

"Pierre, listen to me." She pushed him back. "Tonight, you and I are going to send Odessa home. We'll take her to the ocean and set her free. Won't that be fun?"

"Whaaat?"

"I said—"

"Can Jen come?"

"No, Jen doesn't feel well."

"But I want Jen. Why can't Jen come?"

"I told you, she doesn't feel well. Can't you leave your poor sister alone? And can't you speak without whining?"

Pierre choked in little sobs.

Disgusting tears and snot ran down Pierre's face—a face Monique would have to touch in order to nudge the boy's chin up. "Pierre, listen to me. Let's show your sister what a big boy you are. Let's free Odessa, and when we come back, we'll take a plate of cookies to Jen. How does that sound?"

"Cookies? Cookies?"

"Plates and plates full of cookies."

"Can we have—"

"Whatever you like. But we need to go now. Odessa is waiting."

Pierre's strong eye looked from his mother to Jen's bedroom, then back to his mother. "Is it dark outside?"

"Yes, but big boys aren't afraid of the dark. Are you a big boy?"

Pierre nodded.

"Very well. Let's hurry now, so we can all have cookies."

Pierre followed Monique to the staircase landing.

Crouching, Monique hastened over to the tanks, took the jar, and then motioned for Pierre to come along.

Mimicking his mother's game, Pierre ran half-stooped.

When the back door closed, Monique wiggled into her heels and pointed to the muddy shoes lining the porch. "Choose something."

Pierre shook his head. "They're dirty." A fleshy finger wiggled into a nostril.

Monique slapped his hand. "If you don't pick something other than your nose, you'll walk barefoot to the beach."

Pierre chose his red boots.

Monique winced—blazing red boots on a moonlit night—but she had no time to argue. Red boots or not, full moon or not, time was running out.

Pierre booted his feet and grasped his mother's finger. Monique offered no more than a finger knowing that Pierre's hands had been in filthier places than his nose.

He held tight as she led him along the stone path toward the ocean.

When they reached the ridge, Monique poured out Odessa and then threw the jar over the cliff. Odessa curled on the ground. "Pick her up, Pierre. Pick her up so I don't soil my gloves. Pierre, are you listening? Pierre?"

The thundering waves had hypnotized Pierre. He stood expressionless, strangely entranced. Monique followed Pierre's line of sight, but saw nothing out of the ordinary. She saw only an ocean clipped by a moonlit horizon. She shook him. "Pierre? What is the matter with you? Pierre?"

His eyes began blinking again. "Huh?"

"Look at Odessa. Poor Odessa. Pick her up. She doesn't like the dirt."

Pierre picked up the octopus. Immediately, the octopus's blue rings brightened. "Oooh!" Pierre's brown eye lifted from the octopus to Monique.

"She likes you," Monique said. "Now let's go set her free."

His hands cupping the slippery animal, Pierre followed his mother down the trail leading to the beach. He stopped a distance from the sea and held the octopus out.

"Pierre, the ocean can't come to you. You must take Odessa to the sea."

Pierre slowly shook his head, the hypnotic glaze returning to his face.

Monique pushed her disobedient child. "You're wearing boots. Give Odessa a fighting chance. Take her to the water."

When the sea rolled back, Pierre walked out. But when the sea swirled in and touched Pierre's boots, he threw Odessa, spun around, and tried to run.

But he stumbled. "I don't *feeel* good."

Pierre's head cocked to examine his palm.

It was bleeding.

He held it up to show his mother. "Odessa bit me."

Then Pierre's brown eye rolled like his green one.

He fell backwards.

The tide rushed in to soften Pierre's fall.

Monique looked up at the stars. "This is your fault, Randall, your miserable fault. I wanted a daughter, but you selfishly planted a son. Well, there's your son; I'll take your daughter. Now we're even."

She hiked up the trail and went to the cliff's edge. Red boots bobbed with the tide's ebb and flow. "Even."

She brushed the sand from her dress.

When she turned to leave, she saw a white, billowing nightgown moving toward her. Adrenaline surged, her heart galloped.

Thinking quickly, she screamed with calculated volume, loud enough for the intruder's ears, but too quiet to attract further attention. "My baby, my poor Pierre. Help, somebody help me."

The figure now ran.

When Kathryn reached the ridge, she nearly collapsed. Panting and wheezing, she hunched with one arm bracing a leg, the other arm waving desperately for support. "Wha—Wha—What is it? Is—Is Pierre—Where is—Pierre? I saw—saw boots. Red boots. Pierre is—" Kathryn's muscles seized. She couldn't draw enough breath to speak, and she couldn't straighten her spine to see Monique's face—a face of indifference.

Kathryn only saw Monique's lowered finger pointing to the cliff.

Kathryn ambled to the edge and looked over. Both hands flew to her cheeks. "Oh, sweet Jesus! Sweet Jesus!" She crossed herself.

The moment Kathryn turned, Monique rammed her in the chest.

Kathryn's arms flew forward, then flapped wildly as she fell backward.

When her trailing scream ended, Monique peered over the ledge.

Like the dove that had smacked Monique's window, Kathryn jerked and twitched, arguing the inevitable, bickering with death.

Seconds later, her mangled body stilled, her eyes wide, her mouth open.

"Dismissed," Monique said. She checked the time—12:29—then sprinted back to the Packard. When seated inside, she opened her compact mirror, reapplied her lipstick, and fingered her hair.

"Well, ma mére, are you proud?" She snapped the compact closed. "I know you are, but I would love to hear it."

She listened for her mother's approving whispers.

She heard an injured animal's high-pitched wail.

# 20

*What kind of change?*
*Do we change into a rabbit or a fish?*

Eldon, having resumed Randall's form, cradled the sleeping Pierre.

Alpha stood in a nearby dimension, watching and waiting. He had expected a quick Awakening—short-stays rarely bond to the physical plane—but Earth had already circled twice during Zia's Transitional Sleep.

On the heels of Earth's third pass, Dharlin arrived and immediately dressed into Kathryn. Alpha told her, "Zia's Soul wishes to stay asleep."

"Let me trade places with Eldon," Dharlin said. "Pierre attached to me more than he attached to his father."

While Alpha considered, Pierre's eyelids fluttered open.

"Hello there, son," Randall said.

Pierre frowned and tried to bite his father's arm.

Alpha whispered to Dharlin, "It is this Soul's nature to wake wickedly."

Dharlin smiled. "So *I* shouldn't worry."

"True. Undue concern serves no purpose."

Pierre wiggled off his father's lap.

Randall remained seated. "Come give your father a hug."

"Uh-uh." Pierre shifted from foot to foot. "Where's Katy?"

"Katy will be along soon. Now come give—"

"Nooo."

"Don't you want—"

"Nooo. Jen said you went to heaven." Pierre scooted away.

To coax Pierre closer, Randall cupped his ear. "What's that? These old ears don't hear too well. What did you say?"

Pierre bent forward. "Jen said you went—"

"What's that? Still can't hear you."

Pierre stammered. He wished his father could hear him. And the moment he wished it, his lips were grazing Randall's ear. "JEN SAID YOU WENT TO HEAVEN."

Pierre tapped his father until his eyes reopened. "Did you hear me?"

"That I did, son. That I did."

Alpha turned to Dharlin, but before he could speak, Dharlin said, "I know, I know, her nature is loud."

"True."

With Randall's promise of a root'n-toot'n bronco ride, Pierre climbed onto his father's knee. His arms outstretched, his legs locked around his father's legs, Pierre said, "I'm ready. Go. Go."

Randall's knee thumped. Pierre swirled off balance. Randall caught him and settled him upright. Pierre bounced up and down. "Go, go."

So Randall's knee rocked, bumped, and swerved, and Pierre's giggles became squeals of laughter. "Do it again. Do it again."

When Randall slowed the game, hoping to stimulate Pierre's reflection, Pierre's heels jabbed as though he were spurring a horse. "Gitty-up, gitty-up."

Hours later, Randall shot an imploring look to Dharlin. She answered with a baffled shrug. Then Dharlin noticed Alpha's faint smile and his finger swaying in harmony to Pierre's swoops and spills.

"Alpha," Dharlin said, "respectfully, it was a short-stay."

Alpha's smile straightened. "Pierre has known little happiness."

"Pierre is now an Energy, timeless and tireless. He will bounce on a knee for eternity, unless we awaken the Soul."

"Do you accuse me of bias?"

Dharlin sparkled *yes*, but she said, "I'm from the Order of Teachers. I wish to learn how this delay benefits the Soul."

After a moment of thought, Alpha resigned with sigh. "Intervene."

Kathryn stepped into Pierre's dimensional view. Immediately, Pierre cried out, "KATY!" From his instant wish, he was clutching her thighs and burrowing snuffles and sobs into her belly. "Katy, where were you? I couldn't find you. Where did you go? WHERE?"

Kathryn rubbed and patted Pierre's little back. "Ooh, your Katy is here. Right here." She curled to his head and planted little kisses. "Oh, stop your fussin' now. I'm right here."

"I couldn't find you." His neck craned back, revealing a face of pitiful hurt. "Where were you?"

"Where was I? I might ask ya the same. Ya run off, so I come to find ya."

"You did?"

"Do ya doubt me?"

Pierre shook his head. "But—But—" He skirted behind Kathryn, then pointed at Randall. "He didn't go to heaven."

"Course he did. And we're having a lovely visit, aren't we?"

"Huh?"

"Haven't ya noticed? We're surrounded in charming beauty." She pried him from her legs. "Go on, Pierre, out with ya. See for yourself."

Timidly, Pierre glided a little ways, then looked back at Kathryn. She winked. "Glorious, ain't it?"

Pierre turned again to the silken clouds that veiled the planets and shrouded the stars. It seemed familiar. Familiar, too, were the ice crystals that wedded a glimmering ring around Saturn. He knew about ice crystals—how? He knew they were fun—in what way? Pierre glanced over his shoulder. His father now stood beside Katy, both surrounded in iridescent lights.

"I'm right here," Kathryn said, but Pierre wasn't afraid. Even the idea of fear now seemed...*stupid?* He knew this place, though not from pictures or dreams. He sensed a familiarity, a sense that grew stronger as he looked across the billions of stars lighting the heavens.

"I belong here," Pierre said, though the voice didn't sound like his own. That's odd, Pierre thought and then giggled; what did he know about odd, for chrissake? He giggled again.

His knees and shins tingled. Sparks of pink flesh peeled away revealing green underneath. When Pierre bent to brush the flecks from his feet, he noticed that his arms were also shedding.

He straightened, feeling strangely taller. A maroon strand toppled from his head and tickled his cheek. Pierre examined it. Then his eyes closed and visions flooded—shipbuilding, slaves, families, France, Alaska. All the images from prior lives flurried. They ended with Pierre's last thought—*Odessa bit me.*

With a sharp inhale, Zia's eyes opened, fully awake. She spread her arms and soared straight up, miles high, twirling ecstatically, spinning joyously, as if to embrace the stars. The stars brightened as if to welcome her home.

But Zia descended slowly, her shoulders rounding, her head shaking, and her stare firmly fixed on Kathryn.

She would never see Katy's illusion again. Not ever.

Reading Zia's vibrations, Kathryn whispered, "It's okay. Let it go."

Zia's lips quivered, struggling to give voice to her vibrations, *Katy, I love you*, but she pained so deeply, all she managed was, "Ka—Katy, I—" with a spillage of inky-blue.

# 21

*Hey, God, this is Zia Schatz.
Listen up; your system stinks.*

**B**efore Eldon and Dharlin shed their costumes, I choked. Even though I was fully awake, I cried like crazy when Katy's illusion disappeared.

The Soul, Dharlin, Order of Teachers, tried to comfort me by comparing the transition of Awakenings to the aging process of Players.

When babies grow into adults, the baby is gone. Or changed. Either way, the parents will never see the infant's form again. It's now an adult. The parents have the adult to love. Energies have Energies to love...forever.

I could have argued the obvious—a gradual change versus an abrupt change—but I didn't because it was Katy.

As a Player, she had been round and thick with white hair and freckled skin. As an Energy, she was a chocolaty Soul with mulberry tresses. But no matter how changed, whether Player or Soul, one life to the next, to me, Katy would always be Katy. *My Katy.* I guess that was her point.

Excluding Alpha, who stood in the distance, my Awakening Party numbered two—which was two more than usual.

Eldon, Order of Seekers, had been my father, Randall. He told seafaring tales of enormous waves that rolled up and down, up and down.

I turned a deeper shade of green.

Dharlin hushed Eldon and then asked me, "Would you like us to go?"

I half-shrugged. "But Katy—I mean, Dharlin, how did you die?"

She glanced in Alpha's direction before answering. "Zia, that's not your... problem."

I shot a glare to Alpha. "You mean issue, right?"

Dharlin turned my chin back to hers. "Ease up on Alpha, okay?"

"Hey, you don't know what he put me through. Alpha needs to go back to Guide School and practice on gophers before taking on Souls."

"Meaning what?"

I cupped my mouth for a discreet whisper, "He's new."

"He's what?"

I coughed into a fist. "*Hawk*-new. New guide."

Eldon chuckled.

Before I could find out what was so funny, Dharlin wrapped me in a lasting hug, which I made last even longer. When we released, I said, "Katy, uhm, you know." I examined my nails, wishing Dharlin still looked like Katy to make it less awkward.

"I love you, too," Dharlin said, and I nodded.

Eldon spread his arms. I guess he wanted a hug, too. Not having spent much time with my father, I offered a handshake. "Thank you, Eldon."

He smiled, we shook, and then Dharlin and Eldon glided away.

When Alpha approached, my sparks reddened. "YOU TRICKED ME! That life helped nobody. Not only did you sucker me into another Yang life, but you tricked me into a short-stay—and removed me by drowning! Goddamn drowning. I gulped cell-infested shit-water loaded with saline bloated microbes that dug into my ears, puckered my eyeballs, and munched on my brains. I sucked in devil's piss."

"No matter the length, each life serves purpose."

"That's a bunch of crap. Goddamn spirit-babble. You set me up."

"Your anger, however, serves no purpose."

"It serves mine, which beats the hell out of serving as a pawn in some stupid cosmic game where suffering seems to be the purpose. Ask One if I suffered enough for His purpose."

"Careful, Zia."

"Agony, misery and suffering—that's the real Trinity. Kindness, love and compassion—that's the rhetoric Guides use to muzzle the whining of suffering Souls."

Alpha's hand started to rise, but I knocked it down. "Tell One and Niine to recheck their purposes; I think they're working off the same set of plans."

"ENOUGH!"

"No, I'll tell you when—"

*WHAPOOSH!* An explosion of white light flung me backward. I landed in a heap, dazed and warbled and surrounded by...*fireflies?*

Through the haze of twinkling lights, I saw Alpha's hand rise and his eyes torch. I quickly and repeatedly nodded my compliance to shut-up.

"Not a word of advice has given you pause," Alpha said. "When it is time for you to speak, you lie. When it is time for you to listen, you chatter. When it is time for your selflessness, you complain. Which of these admirable traits invites your debate?" His hand lowered.

"You're giving me a bad slant. Maybe—"

"QUIET!" He shouted, seriously shouted. "My question was rhetorical. It does not require your answer; it requires your consideration." His glare, like swirling suns, nearly singed my atoms. "For the last time, Zia, I will placate your faithlessness, but I will not do so again. You did not drown."

My mouth opened in protest—I *know* I swallowed sea-crap—but Alpha leaned into my face. His brow raised, his lips pursed, he dared me to peep. My mouth closed.

Alpha straightened. His fingers laced at his back, Alpha glided in tight circles around me. "Your fragment containing a fear of the ocean creates multiple illusions—a sea with wicked intent and a false memory of drowning. But illusions are no more tangible than the Figments you chase. That fragment is only one among hundreds in that deplorable squalor you call a Soul. As I previously advised, either remove the fragments—an arduous task, but one of your own making—or expect to trip repeatedly over your negative debris. But trip quietly, Zia, because it is your choice to trip at all."

He lectured like a schoolmaster beaned by a spitball, and I squirmed like the kid who had launched it.

"Male or female, privileged or poor, fit or frail, each placement serves a purpose, not a whim. To have or not have faith in that purpose is a choice, your choice to make. But choosing to lack faith does not sanction recriminations against One. Utter blasphemy. A Player's reproach is understandable, their perspective limited, and therefore, forgivable. But on this side, Zia, *on this side*, you have no such excuse for impieties."

Inky-blue welled, but I swiped my eyes and then balled my hands into my lap. "I'd have faith, tons of it, if you would just prove that my short-stay helped Awen."

"Proof negates faith."

"I don't care what it negates. Did I help Awen?"

"Zia, you hold a negative fragment that taints your attachment to Awen. If that same fragment contained a bird, your injurious attachment would severe the bird's wings to keep it from flying."

"Awen is not a bird."

"But a bird shares atoms with its wings, and Awen shares atoms with Ereo. Not all birds can fly, and not all Dyads pair in every life. For those birds capable of flight, their wings provide the means. For those Dyads destined to pair in a life, their cord provides the means for a Determinant's descent."

"A Determinant?" I looked up, amazed. "Does Awen know?"

Alpha sighed. "True." He crouched beside me, which is never a good sign.

My gaze fell again to my lap. Alpha tried to lift my chin, but I pushed his hand away. "Just say it."

"Zia, Players grieve removals."

"Aw, jeez, *more* lectures? *Now?*"

"When their grief aggravates into a relentless anguish, the removed Soul has the choice of whether or not to console the Player."

I raised cockeyes of impatience. "Grief, anguish, got it."

"They console through vibrational whispers—"

Just then, I noticed the planet behind Alpha. "Hey!"

"—until the anguish subsides or the Player is removed."

"Pluto?"

"If it is the latter, the consoling Soul oversees the Awakening. Zia?"

"Hang on a second." I tugged Alpha around. "You see that planet? Between my last two lives, Players discovered it. They named it Pluto. Jen told me. She made a solar system out of Tinker Toys." With a one-eyed squint, I pointed a tad to the right. "But they missed Pluto's sidekick. See it? And if they can't spot that one, they'll never discover those other two. Nope." My arm relaxed. "Too far away, I guess."

I looked again at Alpha...a very sour-faced Alpha. "What's wrong?" I asked. "I was listening. You were talking about...Anguish? Awakenings?"

He frowned.

"Removals? Whispers?"

His eyes narrowed; his mouth squeezed.

"Well, I can't quote you verbatim, but I got the gist. Somewhere, some-how, somebody caused someone grief. Uhm, was it me?"

"Undeniably, true." He clenched my shoulder—a whole lot harder than what was necessary—and, *floop*, took us to Earth.

In front of us, an alleyway stretched between two brick buildings. One side had illuminated letters, *St. Luke's Children's Hospital.* The other building had chipped and peeling paint, *Oncology Center.*

"Follow me," Alpha said before he drifted down the alley, which was dark and wet and smelled like pee and rancid meat.

Midway through the alley, we came to a metal door on the hospital side. A few feet past it, overstuffed garbage pails and bulging plastic bags leaned against the wall. In the middle of the trash, scratched-up legs wiggled from the mouth of an overturned can. One sock had a scrap of pink lace on it, so I figured the legs belonged to a girl. She was rummaging through the garbage, banging and scraping the metal can. When the clanging paused, I heard lips smacking.

"Okay, Alpha, I get it. You made your point. You want me to appreciate my lives, right? Be thankful I'm not her. Okay. I'm thankful. Now can we get out of here?"

He didn't answer. I guess he had more for me to learn. Maybe a lesson in patience. So I waited and waited, wondering how long this patience-thing was going to take.

After a while, the girl crawled out from the can. She smelled like a forgotten bluegill in a fisherman's pocket. Greasy hair clumped over her face and shriveled peelings and bluing bread clung to her arms and legs. She didn't seem to care, though, because she had found something to eat—a yellow, spongy loaf of crap.

After tossing the wrapper, she swept aside her hair.

"Jen?" I looked at Alpha, then back to the girl. "My sister Jen?"

# 22

*I'm lousy at offering cheer. Or comfort. Or sympathy.*

"What happened to her?" I picked and poked, but the oily crud remained on her cheeks. "She's ten years older."

"Five."

"Five?" Sparks of worry splintered into anger. "Who did this to her? I want a name. And for chrissake, why is she eating—*that?*"

"Past events cannot change. Present choices seed the future."

"Spare me the gibberish. Open your bag of tricks and start your hocus-pocus. HELP HER!"

Alpha pointed to Jen's life-cord encasing her Ribbon of Life. Her bright, silky band of colors had stripes and stains of inky-blue. "She's devastated," I said. "This is your fault. When you removed Katy, what did you expect?"

"She grieves Pierre."

"Me? What is she grieving me for? You're wrong. I was just a goofy kid, a pesky brother."

"For a short breadth of time."

I looked again at Jen. "Ereo? Ereo, stop missing me. I treated you like crap. Well, not as Pierre, but I didn't have time. I'm sorry I ignored you, Ereo. I didn't do it on purpose. Not always. Okay, I did, but I'm sorry."

Though I wanted to see her as Ereo—Awen's irritating shadow—I saw her only as Jen—my older sister, who loved and protected me, and who taught me the name of Pluto.

I tried to hug her, but my arms swished through her body and met themselves. "I wish you could hear me and know I'm okay...and know that I'm sorry, damn sorry for the nasty way I treated you. Forgive me, Ereo." I kissed her cheek. "You were the best sister I ever had. I love you, Jen."

Looking up, I saw Alpha smiling. "What are you looking at? Huh?"

His finger circled, gesturing me around. One of Jen's inky-blue threads had lightened. "OH MY GOD! Did I do that? Did I?"

"True. A pure and unselfish intent formed a vibration that—"

"Yeah, yeah." My cheek flat to the cord, I searched Jen's Ribbon for more dark threads that I had lightened. "Hey, behind the gold strands, I think I see another—Oh, no, wait. Hmm. I guess I only lightened one. But still—" I sat back, a little proud. "I made a difference."

"Do you choose to console?"

"Console? Jen needs help, real help, Player-type help or Guide-type help."

"She is tethered to anguish. It is your choice whether or not to console."

"*My* choice? I smell another set up."

"If you accept the duty of a consoling Soul, you will impart positive whispers into the moments before she dreams and into the minutes before she wakes. You will continue to do so until she unbinds from anguish."

I peered hard at Jen's Ribbon and its thick streaks of inky-blue. She wouldn't be unbinding from anguish any time soon. "*Positive* whispers?"

"Solace and love."

"I'm not good at that. My deluge of sappiness only lightened one thread among thousands. Can't you find someone who's better at the solace-stuff? How about a Healer? I've heard Healers are annoyingly cheerful."

"She grieves for you. Your vibrations can assist her. Another Soul's cannot."

*Damn.* Like I always suspected, nothing good comes from somebody liking you. "Yeah, I'll do it. Jen would do it for me. I'll Yin-up and do it for her." My sparks flickered doubt.

"Zia?"

"No, you're reading it wrong. I want to help Jen. I do." And my lights proved that to be true. "But hanging around Earth is—" I rubbed my hanging head. "—bound to be lonely."

"Are you not lonely in Divisional?"

"No, I'm alone in Divisional. Here, I won't be alone, but I won't be part of anything either. It's like starving at a banquet because you don't have a mouth. Get it?" I looked up to see if he got it. "Alpha?"

Alpha was gone.

I sprang to my feet. "Alpha, where did you go? You can't just leave me. I've never done this before. I need guidance. That's your job. Check the Guide-book. Alpha? *ALPHAAA?*"

Jen's moan interrupted my scream.

*Crap.*

I envisioned a basket of oranges.

# 23

*...now you must tolerate the intolerable*
*—a patch of winking daisies.*

Romal scratched his head. "Why on Earth is she attacking fruit?"

Alpha's brow furrowed. "It serves no purpose."

"Purpose aside, Zia typically kicks rocks. Why delicious oranges?" He looked at Alpha, whose eyes spun like mandarin pinwheels. Romal cleared his throat. "Never mind."

When Zia reached the last orange, she backed up, and then charged the orange. In her furious kick, her leg swept too high, spilling her backward.

Alpha's arms shot out, but then instantly swept to his sides. He glanced at Romal, whose mouth hung open. Alpha turned his reddening face.

"Incredible," Romal said. "You were about to catch her."

"That is not...relevant."

"I think it is. I think you reacted—dare I say it—without purpose, as if you thought to spare her from injury, as if injury were possible. Admit it, Alpha, you acted without purpose."

Tensing, Alpha glided a few meters away.

Romal chuckled as he shadowed Alpha. "Such stubbornness. Alpha, you've intervened with Warriors rampaging toward the innocent, Seekers prying into Niine's piranha ponds, Messengers imparting secrets to—"

"State your point."

Grinning broadly, Romal poked Alpha's chest. "That small, reckless Agitator burrowed herself into your somber heart."

"I am guiding her."

"Yes, yes, you certainly are. And you're parenting her as well."

Alpha grunted. "Untrue."

"Really? Prior to serving Pierre, had you ever served a Player child? Peril Guides intervene when a Player unwittingly becomes a menace, but isn't that always within their adulthood?"

Silence.

"Alpha, it's not a blight on your record to admit such inexperience. No one doubts your abilities. When a Constructor's plans would have blown Earth into little moons around Neptune, your name was the first on everyone's lips, and you handled the situation admirably."

"Do you not have a Charge requiring your assistance?"

"Certainly. So stop interrupting and delaying my leave. When you prayed for guidance to prepare Zia for the Neutral Point, you couldn't have anticipated the answer you received. You, a teacher of Peril Guides and the first Entity of One, asked to stand aside for the skills of another. And that 'other' isn't even a Guide. He's a Soul. Understandably, you're upset."

"I am not—"

"You are." Romal swiveled Alpha about face. "Your restraint can't hide it from me."

Alpha gave a reticent nod, his focus shifting to the Hospital. "He is a worthy Finisher."

"Yes, yes. Trust Malachi. No Finisher is more gentle yet firm, nor more skilled yet humble."

"Nor more robust."

Romal laughed. "That too. Profoundly large."

# 24

*I had a filthy chakra—*
*that's what the girl said when she offered to clean it for free.*

A winter wind swept through the alley. Cigarette butts and wadded tissues cycloned.

Jen wrapped herself with newspapers and curled against the wall.

I glided to the metal door, but when I tried to knock, my hand fell through. Slowing the motion didn't work either. "Jen, get up. Pound on this door. They'll feed you and give you a place to—"

The newspapers jittered from Jen's shivering.

"Okay, stay here. I'll get help." Beyond the door, a supply room's shelves bowed under sacks of grain and cans of food. Trying to grab a box of crackers was like trying to knock on the door—a waste of time. I glided out the opposite door and into a noisy blizzard of sounds and smells.

Greasy steam dampened the foreheads of nurses topped in pointy caps and of girls dressed in pink stripes. Some gathered at tables to eat and to chitchat and to wink at the blue-coated doctors touting harrumph-harrumph faces. Others meandered at a counter and pointed to lumpy stuff.

Behind the counter, a lady and a girl, their hair tucked under black nets, dropped spoonfuls of goop onto plates. Doctors grunted their thanks then clattered their trays along a metal rail.

Although few visitors sprinkled the room, one group, at a table by themselves, wore the black and white getup of the weird farmers who paint hexes on barns. In my last life, I had avoided their kind. Avoiding their kind now, I moved across the room, through the double-doors, and into a hallway.

I wandered the hospital's maze of corridors while sidestepping the hustling staff. I had never been in a hospital, not in any life, but I had pictured them as dim and quiet. Here, lights flickered, doctors and nurses sprinted, carts and gurneys jangled, and phones rang and rang and rang.

I lifted above the crowd. From the ceiling grate beside me, a voice suddenly blasted, *DR. SOBEL, Emergency Room, STAT,* rocketing me three floors up. I settled in a room with a funny smell—a blend of baby powder and penicillin. Above the doorway, crooked felt letters tagged the place, *Game Town*. And Game Town swarmed with little people—kids with red-rimmed eyes, snot stuffed noses, and drool slicked chins. Some wiggled on tiny chairs at miniature tables, a few sprawled on the floor to play cards, three slept on gurneys, two whined, and one puked.

In the center of the room, kids bunched on a couch to stare at what looked like a life review screen. I glided closer. "WOW! A television box! A real television box. You kids are so lucky." Their weepy eyes blinked-blinked. "Lucky except for the sick thing."

On the screen, a lady poured liquid stuff onto a spoon and then plunked the spoon into her mouth. It must have tasted like crap; her face skewed. *Get your Vitamita Vegemin today. It's so tasty, too. Tastes just like candy.* She teetered and swooned. "Hey, make it louder," I said. "Turn it up."

A kid flagged an attendant, but instead of asking for volume, she asked for a blanket. She was cold...*like Jen!* I bolted straight down, hit the basement, flew up a floor, and then rushed down hallways, through the cafeteria, and into the alley. Jen was still asleep, still bundled in trash, still shivering.

"Sorry, Jen, sorry, sorry. I swear, I'll get help." I went back to the cafeteria, pulled in a big breath, and then shouted, "HELP!"

"Claire," a doctor called from across the room. When the lady behind the counter looked up, the doctor raised a metal creamer. "It's curdled."

One by one, noses sniffed beneath lids and fingers rose sporting curds. Claire apologized, but insisted she had refilled the creamers that morning.

"Forget the cream," I told them. "My sister needs *HEEEEEELP!*"

Everyone reeled from their coffee cups, cereal bowls, and biscuits with gravy. What horrible luck to need attention at the exact moment that cream and milk were flipping into cheese. Worsening matters, the weird farmer went mad, insane-mad. "A devil is present," he shouted. "A devil sours the milk."

He hurried his family out the double doors. Obviously, the farmer had a few straws missing from his haystack; if a devil were near, I would be the only one to know.

Just then, a planet of a woman with two orbiting assistants barreled into the room, her mammoth breasts heaving beneath her embroidered name— *Head Nurse Gruer.*

She had a round, moon-like face, a thin, lipless mouth, and a small, wadded nose. The thick lenses of her glasses enlarged her pin-sized eyes into big, black marbles. "NURSES," she hollered, "I need nurses on the floor. Let's move it, people, MOVE IT!"

The staff scrambled, muttering curses. Minutes after Gruer stomped out, only Claire and the other net-head remained. They spurted soap into water-filled buckets before they grabbed their mops and rags. I would have yelled again, but Claire switched on the radio and began singing, *Crazy, crazy for you.*

Claire could have been thirty or she could have been sixty; her unlined face conflicted with her gray speckled hair. "Rosa," she said to the younger net-head, "stack the garbage bags in the storage room. Harold comes in at midnight and takes out the garbage."

"Miss Claire," Rosa said, "I can take the bags out myself."

"You do that," I told Rosa. "Take them out to the alley and find Jen."

"Honey, you have your job," Claire dunked a sponge into sudsy water, "let Harold do his. Just stack the trash by the door."

As Rosa entered the storage room, I hollered, "Take out the garbage!"

Rosa dropped the bags to bat her hair, *swat-swat-swat*, as if her hair had trapped a bee. Maybe if I slammed against the door and made it creak or rattle, the noise would stir Rosa's curiosity, and she would look into the alley and spot Jen. When Rosa left to get more bags, I bent into a runner's lunge.

When Rosa returned, I charged full force at the door—and sailed right through it. I tumbled across the alley and landed in the neighboring building, the *Oncology Center.*

"Clamp, scalpel, clamp," came from the masked doctors above me.

I unwrapped from their legs and started to stand—*Uh-oh.* I froze half-stooped, surrounded by aghast looks from an Awakening Party.

Slinking backwards, "sorry, sorry," I returned to the alley.

Long ago, Romal had warned, *never disturb an Awakening.* Though I tuned out the Soul-sapping sermon that followed his warning, I don't think he defined what was meant by *disturb.* Would one quick question create a disturbance? All I needed was one quick answer, or even a tip, on how to get food and shelter for Jen. For several minutes, I practiced my opening line—the apology. When I had it down, I turned to Jen, "How does this sound—" but her trembling had worsened into spastic shakes. *Damn.* To hell with apologies and excuses, I marched back into the operating room. "Hey, I need some he*lll*...Hello?"

Gone. Everyone was gone. Not a Player, Soul, or Guide to be found. On the table was a sheet draping over a small, empty Player-shell. I dragged myself back to the alley where Jen shivered and shook because I was too worthless to help. My frustration blew. "*Aurggg.*"

A rat bolted from the garbage. It scurried along the wall and then wiggled through a crack in the doorjamb. Within seconds, shouts and bangs erupted from the cafeteria. The rat squirted back through the crack and scampered into the safety of an empty bean can.

I hovered above the can. "What did you do? Did you stir up trouble?"

Whiskers poked out, swishing.

"That's no excuse, got it? You have no business taking your flea-ridden fur into a hospital. You're nothing but a big—"

"Miss Claire!" Rosa stood in the alley, her hands balled at her chest.

"I could kiss you," I told the rat. His snout tipped upward. "Whoa, take it down. I meant, I could kiss you if you weren't disgusting, but you are. And there's a bean on your head."

Claire rushed into the alley, but stopped abruptly beside the stricken Rosa. "Honey, it's just a mouse."

Rosa gave a terse headshake and pointed at the jostling trash.

Claire moved cautiously toward Jen. Leaning down, Claire grabbed a fistful of the news. With a nervous jump, she whipped it off Jen's legs. "Oh, mercy, mercy."

Claire waved for Rosa's help. Together, they unburied the rest of Jen.

"She ate something bad," I told them. "Yellow, spongy crap. But she'll be okay, right?"

Claire felt Jen's cheeks. "She's burning up."

"She's sick?" I asked. "Jeez, get a doctor. Hurry up, get a doctor."

Rosa was about to get help, but Claire grabbed her arm. "Nurse Gruer will send this child to County General. That's the policy, but it ain't right. The good Lord led this child to our hospital for a reason, so here this child will stay. Wait here while I close the cafeteria."

Claire hurried back inside.

Rosa cleared some trash and sat beside Jen.

Jen's bleary eyes parted, "leave me alone," then shut again.

"You don't mean that," Rosa said. "We're going to help you." Humming, she tweezed litter from Jen's face.

"Thanks, Rosa," I said.

"No problem," she said, causing me a startled stumble as I took off after Claire.

# 25

*Intent vibrates into the result.*

W hile we were outside, four nurses had taken seats at a table. Claire eyed them.

"What are you waiting for?" I said. "Boot them out."

Instead, Claire smoothed her dress, fashioned a smile, and strolled to the nurses. When she spoke, three pointy caps tipped back, but the fourth cap tilted. That nurse smirked. Stitched on her dress was the name, *Nurse Reichert,* with a heart dotting the *i*.

I didn't like her. And it had nothing to do with her heart-dotted *i*. Nothing. It had to do with her smirk and stalling questions—*Why did they have to leave? Why was the cafeteria closing over a mouse? Why couldn't Claire mop around her table of friends.*

"Slap her," I told Claire. "Give her what-for."

Instead of what-for, Claire's smile sweetened. "I do apologize for the inconvenience." She gestured toward the door.

Three of the nurses got up, and they prodded Reichert to follow.

Reichert grumbled but gave in. While they were filing out, Claire tugged one nurse aside. "Ask Nurse Logan if she wouldn't mind coming down here." Claire locked the door behind the nurses and then headed back to the alley.

"Wait, Claire. Stop! Look!" But Claire didn't hear me...nor did she see Reichert's snoopy face pressing against the window set high in the door.

"GO AWAY!" I shouted at Reichert, but every few seconds, she lifted to her toes for another peek. Waving my arms did not block her view. Shouting, "LEAVE," in her face only caused her to brush at her ear like one brushes aside a pestering mosquito. Minutes later, Reichert's peek became a lasting stare. She was watching Claire and Rosa coming in from the storage room. They were bracing a wobbling Jen.

Feeling miserably ineffective, I sunk to the floor at Reichert's feet.

On the baseboard, an overgrown wolf spider clutched its meal.

"I don't want your lousy fly," I told it.

The spider reared, two legs pinching the air aggressively.

"You can't hurt me," I told it. "I'm Energy. You can only bite—" I looked at Reichert's long, naked legs. "Hey, spider, want to know what's tastier than a fly? Soft, fleshy tissue." I pointed up Reichert's dress. "It's up there, up at the curve."

The spider dropped the fly and hopped onto Reichert's shoe. Four of its eyes looked up the dress, the other four eyes fixed on me. I slapped my inner thigh to show the spider where to bite. "Remember, wait for the curve before you bite. And bite real hard."

At first, the spider climbed slowly. Then Reichert bounced to the balls of her feet, and the spider scurried. It disappeared beneath her hem.

Seconds later, "*EeeOwww*," Reichert smacked down on her heels and sent a frantic hand pawing up her dress.

Walking toward us was a lean, no-nonsense-looking nurse. She wore the name-tag *Regina Logan*. "Nurse Reichert, is something wrong?"

Reichert glowered at Logan as if Logan had delivered the bite.

Clutching her thigh, Reichert hobbled toward the restroom.

Logan pulled out a key, unlocked the door, and went into the cafeteria.

I flew after Reichert.

With her dress hiked and cinched by an elbow, Reichert angled a mirror on a reddening swell.

I sat on the bathroom sink, my arms crossed. "Serves you right for smirking and spying...and for dotting your *i* with a stupid heart. Now mind your own business or you'll get far worse than a wolf spider bite. You'll get a widow. Get it?"

All the way back to the cafeteria, I threw victory punches into the air.

At the far end of the vending machines, voices rose from behind a door marked *BreakRoom*.

Inside, Jen rested on a cot. A damp towel cooled her forehead and a thermometer parted her lips.

At her side, Rosa stirred a bowl of chicken soup. She looked expectantly at Claire, but Claire was busy timing Jen's pulse while Logan moved a stethoscope across Jen's chest.

"She's hungry," Rosa said. "She'll feel better after she has had some of my soup."

Claire and Logan exchanged a look of concern that I didn't understand. So when Claire withdrew the thermometer, I bobbed to read it. But Claire was too quick; she glimpsed the mercury line then flicked her wrist, returning the thermometer's reading to normal.

Using four fingers, Logan pushed on multiple spots across Jen's belly. Each time she pushed, she asked, "Does it hurt when I press here?"

And each time, Jen shook her head.

"Broth only," Logan told Rosa. "No crackers." Then to Claire, she said, "Let's talk in private."

Logan and Claire walked out.

Humming cheerfully, Rosa began straining the soup and tipping the broth into Jen's willing mouth. "Thank you," Jen whispered between each teaspoon. "Thank you, thank you."

Although the door was shut, snippets of a squabble filtered in—*Fire me—send to County General—Gruer will—Gruer won't—Gruer will.*

Rosa hummed louder to drown out the quarreling, but I got the gist; the beady-eyed Gruer was mean.

"Don't worry," I said to Rosa. "I'll handle Gruer. You take care of Jen."

"Nothing to worry about," Rosa told Jen. "We'll take care of you." She blotted a napkin to Jen's chin.

Later, Claire came in holding a hospital gown. "Rosa, help me get her undressed." They propped up Jen and peeled off her clothes.

At first, Jen didn't mind, but then, *"Waaait,"* she began struggling and stretching toward her pants. Her hand clenched and unclenched. "My picture. Please. My picture."

Rosa dug into the pockets. Beneath lint and peanuts, she found a creased photograph and handed it to Jen.

Jen fell back to her pillow. "My brother. My baby brother."

Before her lids dropped, she turned the photo face up. All of us leaned in to have a look. I winced, just like Claire and Rosa winced. It was the kind of wince you make at the backs of parents who think their homely kid is cute. My mouth was crooked, my shoulders were sloped, and my eye was patched. My apple of looks had rolled pretty far from the stunning good looks of my parents.

"Honey," Claire tapped Jen lightly, "I need a few answers before you fall asleep. Are you allergic to any medications?"

Jen shook her head.

"That's good," Claire said. "Now tell me your name. Please, baby, you can trust us."

"Jen—Jennifer. Jennifer Smith."

"No, Jen, you're feverish," I said. "Think hard. You're Jenevieve Duvall."

"How old are you?" Claire asked.

"Twenty-two."

*Twenty-two?* I did a quick calculation. "No, Jen, you're 19."

Logan returned with a black leather bag. From it, she whipped out a syringe.

"Whoa," I said. "Hold on a minute. Isn't this a bit drastic? How about pills? Don't you have pills?"

Holding the needle straight up, Logan tapped the tube until an air bubble loosened and rose. She pressed the plunger gently until liquid spurted from the needle's tip.

She signaled Claire.

"Honey," Claire said, "you have a mighty high fever that needs to come down. We're going to roll you onto your side so Nurse Logan can give you a shot. Is that all right?"

"NO," I said, but Jen countered with a nod. They tipped her. I swallowed. "What about pills? PILLS!" The silver sliver lowered. My eyes squeezed tight. Jen squealed—well, somebody squealed. "Are you done yet? Are you done yet? Are you done yet?"

When my eyes reopened, Logan was handing Claire a bottle of pills.

"Give her two of these tonight," Logan said, "then one every six hours. When my shift ends, I'll be back to check on her."

"Regg, I appreciate this." Claire slipped the bottle into her pocket. "I just couldn't see losing her to County General."

"Can you see losing your job?" Logan asked. "Because if Gruer finds out, she'll fire us, and I'll lose my license."

# 26
*There are two paths, but one is not good.*

Claire brought down another cot. For the first few nights, she slept beside Jen. While medicine and soup were mending Jen's body, I was trying to mend Jen's Soul, "Quit grieving, okay?" but without much success. Her threads remained inky-blue, but her cheeks blossomed into a rosy pink.

Within the week, Jen was pleading to repay Claire's kindness. "At least let me wash the dishes."

But standing caused Jen headaches. Although Jen tried to hide her sudden cringing and pained squinting, Claire noticed and insisted Jen return to the cot. "Baby, you need more rest," Claire said. "My home is just down the road. It ain't much, but it's comfortable. There's a spare room with a warm bed and a pantry with plenty to eat."

Jen thanked her, but said no.

Days later, Claire offered again, now sounding as though Jen would be doing Claire the favor by accepting. Jen thanked her but still refused.

A week after that, Claire asked a third time. Jen burst into tears with an adamant, "NO!" and fled to the breakroom.

Claire and I scratched our heads, equally baffled.

Crazy stubbornness didn't fit Jen's nature—sweet, protective, gentle. Although my opinion formed within a baby-brother's heart, when I looked at Jen, it still felt true. Claire must have shared my opinion because she didn't pressure Jen. Instead, Claire brought in boxes of toiletries, bags of clothes, and crates of books.

Jen gushed, "Oh, this is too much."

"It ain't nothing," Claire said, and she motioned for Rosa.

Rosa stepped forward with a ceramic frame. "It's for your picture."

Taking the frame slowly, Jen's blinking eyes moistened. Then her spindly arms wrapped around portly Rosa. Claire beamed as she watched Jen and Rosa's friendship cement.

"You can help in the kitchen," Claire said, "but stay out of the cafeteria. Curious eyes might cause a fuss. Can you do that?"

"She can, she can," Rosa said, and Jen wholeheartedly agreed.

"Just for the time being," Claire said. "I have a few things to work out." But the girls weren't listening. They were too busy turning the breakroom into Jen's makeshift home.

While Jen spent her days in the kitchen, I spent mine watching the television box in Game Town. At night, I read over Jen's shoulder until she turned out the lights. Then Jen cried. Always. Not hard or loud, but choking sobs and sniffled murmurs, "Pierre, I'm so sorry," she cried night after night.

"Quit it, Jen," I whispered. "If you keep adding to your inky-blue, I'll never get out of here. Feel good, okay? Quit missing me, all right? Jen? Jen?"

*Cauk-shoo.*

I should have been assigned as a sleep aid.

I envisioned a pillow, settled on the floor, and stared at the ceiling. No meteors to count. No Figments to chase. No television box. No company. Just hours and hours of inescapable boredom.

"This is hell!" I shouted. "Absolute hell. No Soul ever had it worse."

Then an image popped into my head—a Wanderer, then two Wanderers, then three. Some were Wanderers in Divisional where Awakening Parties pursued, but others were Wanderers on Earth—ghosts—off-limits to intercept. But whether in Divisional or on Earth, the Wanderers were lonely, confused, and scared. I felt them, felt their misery, and I realized they had it worse than me.

"From this moment on," I vowed aloud, "I promise to be kind to every Wanderer no matter who they are, where they are, and what they call me...even if they mistake me for the devil. I swear it."

Unwilling to wallow in loneliness any longer, I took off. I had no idea what I was searching for; I only knew that I wouldn't find it on the breakroom floor. I glided through hallways and corridors, peeking into darkened rooms and rechecking an empty Game Town.

Late in the night, I spotted a beacon of moonlight shining in through sliding glass doors. The doors opened to a cobblestone courtyard set with tables, benches, and chairs. Surrounding the courtyard was a high brick wall, and at the top of the wall, cats were playing and mating. Beneath them, slugs and snails roamed the shrubbery while ants and cockroaches foraged beneath tables for crumbs. The night life of these nocturnal creatures was the only nightlife to be found.

Disappointed, I was about to move on when, in the center of the courtyard, the snout of the alley-rat poked up from the water drain. I rushed outside. "Are you crazy? Do you want to be cat-chow? Get out of here! GO!"

*Swish.* The rat plunked below the grate. I dropped to my knees and stuck my head into the drain. "What the hell were you thinking? Do you have a death wish? Can't your big nose smell the cats? What's the matter with you?"

Its snout stretched toward me.

"Stop that! For chrissake, I'm not going to kiss you. I'm an Energy. You're a rodent. Rodents are disgusting. You'll have to accept that. Now get your tail back to the alley. Get it?"

*Swish, swish,* went his whiskers. He got it.

I pulled from the drain, sat back, and became aware of the gleaming eyes watching me—cockroaches, spiders, beetles, lizards, snails, slugs, a snake, and a row of cats, their tails slapping the bricks. I wasn't sure what the tail-slapping meant, but I was pretty sure I wouldn't like it. "Stop staring at me."

They kept on staring.

"Look, I owed the rat. End of story. Get it?"

A calico jumped down from the wall. *Meow.*

Then all the cats meowed—*meow, meow, meow*—in what sounded like applause. When the beetles, *click-click-click*'d, I knew it for certain. Flattered, I held up a gracious hand and nodded. "Aw, no big deal. Just forget it."

Except I couldn't forget it; I returned to my courtyard friends nightly.

I pushed my thoughts into slugs and snails, but they crawled too slow to be much fun. Cockroaches were too skittish, ants were too small, spiders had too many eyes, and rain beetles were too much work. When I tried to align the beetles into the letters of my name, they lumbered and tottered and took all night just to form the Z.

When I greeted the reptiles, the lizards turned their backs and the garden snake coiled. "Hey, I just want to be friends. Get it?" Concentrating, I sent them assurances that I meant no harm—*friends, friends, friends.*

*Krrzzz,* a static jolt bounced me off a table. Instead of them feeling me, I felt them...and they were not very nice—*Leave us alone.* I didn't need a second shock. Not then, not ever. I steered clear of reptiles, even turtles.

Dozens of stray cats came to the courtyard each night to hunt, feed, and mate. Curious creatures, they kept trying to brush against me.

"You can't," I told them, "until I'm in play. That's when I'm human. Right now, I'm an Energy. Get it?"

Their throaty *errrrs* of feline laughter grew louder. To cats, all matter fits into one of four groups—cat, threat, food, entertainment. They classed me as entertainment.

"That's stupid," I said.

Fur bristled and claws uncurled.

"Uhm, stupid to disagree." I didn't mind the role of courtyard jester because cats are great listeners. Hardened skeptics, sure, but great listeners.

Then one morning, as I was tweaking a tale about one of my lives—"So, I told him, 'Leo, you call that a painting? Put some teeth in Mona's smile'"—Gruer showed up with a newspaper and coffee. One glimpse of the cats, and she hissed and stomped and swung the paper until the last cat fled.

Although I couldn't stop her, I could get even. At midnight, I gathered the felines. "Spray the grounds, benches, and tables. Spray everywhere and everything until you've sprayed your last drop."

The next morning, in a courtyard slick with stench, Gruer took one step outside and slipped. Her arms flung out, one whacking the glass door, the other dousing her dress in coffee.

Nurses came quickly. Holding their breaths, they hoisted Gruer onto her feet. Gruer was clutching her elbow and panting out moans, "Ohh, ohh, ohh." Pain seemed to radiate in her face, but how could it?

"It's just an elbow," I told her. "Just a dumb elbow."

In Game Town, I sprawled on the floor to watch the television box. Cartoons were on, but I didn't find them funny. My thoughts kept drifting to Gruer. She was mean. Mean people are supposed to have Niine Ribbons. But after glancing Gruer's Ribbon—smooth and bright—I turned away, wishing I had never looked at her Ribbon at all.

Mornings later, I missed the window for whispers because I had stayed too long in the courtyard and because Jen had risen earlier than usual. She and Rosa were busy decorating the cafeteria in holiday cheer. Crayoned Santas and watercolored snowmen plastered the walls, and popcorn swags and candy garlands looped the metal railings.

Staff rattled the entrance doors. "Five more minutes," Claire called as she set out metal bins full of eggs, potatoes, and bacon. "Open in five minutes." Claire hurried to the storage room. When she returned, she had a Christmas package. "This can't wait," Claire said handing the gift to Jen.

"Hurry up and open it," Rosa said as the cafeteria doors rattled again.

Jen opened the package and pulled out one of three dresses, each embroidered with *Jennifer Smith*. Jen started welling up with gratitude, but Rosa hooked her arm and pulled her toward the breakroom. "Cry later," Rosa said. "You're serving today."

"I am?" Jen turned excitedly to Claire.

"Properly dressed," Claire said. "Now get yourself changed. We have turkeys to order and cranberries to boil."

While Claire worked the cash register, Jen and Rosa giggled and chatted and scooped food onto plates.

Then Reichert came in. While she pushed her tray along the railing, her eyes steeled on Jen. "How long have you been working here?"

"Uhhh." That's all Jen said. "Uhhh."

"Started today," Rosa said as she hip-bumped Jen.

Bony Jen spun sideways, caught herself, and moved to the opposite end of the counter. Reichert's stare followed her.

"Pig," Rosa said.

Reichert's attention jerked to Rosa. "Excuse me?"

Rosa held up tongs dripping with bacon. "Pig?"

They mirrored a tight-lipped smile, then Reichert scooted her tray.

At the register, Reichert gave Claire a ten dollar bill, then tipped her head toward Jen. "New gal, huh? Don't we have a hiring freeze?"

Claire quickly handed over the change. "Oh, I hired Miss Smith a month ago, a week before the freeze."

"Is that so." Reichert's mouth twisted in a nasty smirk. "Does she live nearby?"

Claire slammed the register's drawer closed. "I don't see how that's any of your business."

Reichert walked off, still carting a smirk.

"I'm warning you," I told Reichert as she picked at her eggs. "Don't you cause trouble, or I'll cause trouble for you." Noticing the time, I hurried to Game Town for the last few hours of morning cartoons.

But the television box was off. Assistants and aides were rearranging the room, pushing toy bins aside and unfolding chairs—rows and rows of chairs. "We'll put the gurneys over here," an aide said. "Let's move the couch."

"What's going on?" But no one heard me, so no one answered. I glided from one conversation to the next until I had pieced the puzzle together. A special movie was playing that night, so rearranging the room had pre-empted morning cartoons. I hung around anyway, kibitzing card games and checkers.

Late afternoon, I went back to the cafeteria, wondering if Claire, Jen, and Rosa were coming to Game Town to watch the big-deal movie. All three were shelving inventory in the storage room. A scattering of visitors and staff sat drinking coffee and tea at the tables.

Reichert was walking up from the far end of the vending machines. She had nothing in her hands, neither a candy bar nor the coins to buy it with.

She wore a smug smile.

The breakroom door was ajar.

Rushing after Reichert, I tried like crazy to knock something over, tumble a chair, spill a glass of water. Anything to trip her. If she fell, maybe she would whack her head and forget what she saw. But as hard as I tried, I couldn't budge anything solid. "I WARNED YOU!"

Reichert left uninjured.

That evening, I bunched in among the kids on the floor to watch the big-deal movie. Souls, dressed as Players, clanked chains, howled, and threatened a tight-fisted old man. Terrorized, the old man fell to his trembling knees. I sprang up, "They're not Wanderers. They're wide awake and scaring you on purpose. Don't take their crap!"

In the midst of my rant, the intercom blared, drowning out the old man's mutterings. Hoping he was giving the Souls what-for, I leaned into the television box. The old man thought the Souls were an undigested bit of beef, a blot of mustard, a crumb of cheese...and a fragment of an underdone potato. *A fragment?* I sat back on my heels, thinking about all the times I had been lectured about fragments. Not once had anyone ever mentioned a potato...or cheese or mustard or beef. Somehow, food connected to bad fragments. Got it! I tucked away my new knowledge.

The intercom sounded again, *Claire Brown and Jennifer Smith, report to the Head Nurse's Office.*

# 27

*A crack-smoking bear!*

*J*ennifer and Claire? Head nurse's office? That was Gruer's office.

I raced to the kitchen, but Jen and Claire were gone.

Rosa was scrubbing a table. She dunked a rag into soapy water and scrubbed the same spot over and over.

"Rosa, trust me," I said. "I'll figure something out."

Rosa nodded. "Everything will work out."

"Dammit, Rosa, can you hear me? CAN YOU?" Mimicking the movie, I envisioned chains, rattled them, and howled.

*Splosh.* Rosa re-dunked the rag and rescrubbed the table. She couldn't hear me. Who can hear a moth fluttering in a windstorm? I started off to search for Claire and Jen. "Rosa, I'll take care of things. Don't worry."

*Splosh.* "I'm not worried."

The main hallway veined into smaller halls leading to a lab, an Emergency Room, and a gift-shop. The second and third floors housed kids. The fourth floor housed kids and Game Town. I bolted outside to count the floors, *one, two, three, four, five.* I shot into the fifth floor and into a room where a very unhappy man was holding his head, tapping his pencil, and scrolling a long, narrow paper.

"Stop complaining," I said. "You should see the paper roll waiting for me in Divisional."

But this man's paper didn't have lessons or confessions. It had numbers that the man copied into a book. An accountant! And accountants sit in offices near other offices—offices like Gruer's. While flurrying through the hallways and darting into offices and labs, I discovered a secret place...that wasn't secret enough, not for what the doctor and the nurse were doing. "For chrissake," I told them, "there are kids and nuns around here."

They didn't care. They were too busy petting and murmuring and bending into positions I hadn't known possible. I inched closer, tilting sideways.

*Womp.* I was suddenly back in the hallway.

I glided forward again. *Womp.* I bounced back like a rubber ball hitting a stone wall. I reached out and touched a cosmic barrier. *Ohhh.* I got it; whether the couple knew it or not, they were fashioning a life-cord. And somewhere in the Awakening Field, a Soul was preparing to descend.

While I knew cord-making was private, I always wondered how that privacy was enforced. I figured Guides policed the Earth for gawking Souls, then tapped them on the shoulder, *All right, pal, let's move it along, nothing to see.* Apparently, I figured wrong.

Corridors later, I spotted Claire's tall frame towering beside Jen's hunched shoulders. They were entering an office that a nurse was exiting—Nurse Reichert. "WITCH!" I hollered. "You two-bit, rotten witch."

She strolled right through my flinging fists. Dogging her through the halls, I kicked and spat and hurled rocks and cow shit. "This isn't over. Not by a long shot. I got friends. Friends that will do far worse than a spider bite. You got that, Reichert? You just wait. This isn't over."

I kept flinging and swinging, but by the time she entered the elevator, I was puffing and panting, "Whoa." My stomach seized, the universe spun, and I hit the wall. Only in bead-space had I felt this kind of pain. "Reichert, you lousy—*YEOW.*" A sharp jab struck me dead center.

For several minutes, I stood slumped and still, my eyes on the floor. Occasionally, my blurry vision lifted from the floor to check for dizziness. On one such time, I thought I saw that weird girl from bead space. She was standing down the hallway among a whole bunch of Players' legs. My head tipped down again to steady myself. When it lifted, the kid was gone. Or maybe she had never been there. I wasn't seeing too well.

When the pain eased, I started back to Gruer's office. I glided slowly at first, but then my speed quickened with thoughts of the villainous Gruer and with plots of my revenge—revenge must nastier than cat spray.

I swept down the last few halls and whipped around the remaining corner. "Gruer, you're not sending Jen away. I'll blind you with bird shit. I'll slide you on ice." In a furious blaze, I shot headlong through the office doors. "I'll knock you flat on your—"

"You'll do nothing of the sort!" a voice boomed.

My arms flew out, my heels skidded, but I slammed into knees. *Knees?* Knees as big as my head, which slowly limbered back, *oh jeez, oh jeez.*

Sitting on the edge of Gruer's desk was a mountainous Yang Energy, a giant smoking a pipe. Turquoise strands—more fur than hair—danced from his neck to his toes, but not a single strand sprouted from his head. This Goliath-Soul had arms and legs thicker than my waist. His yellow eyes were bigger than my gaping mouth.

He paddled the air, gesturing me to step back—*move away from the Players*.

I did so, quickly.

His legs crossed like knotted cables, he rose like a carpetless genie. When he reached the ceiling, he relit his pipe and seemed fully satisfied smoking it, *puff, puff, puff*, showing no interest in me.

I stammered, *Uh, uh, uh,* then eventually, "Uhm, Mister, uh, I have to do something. See, that woman is about to—"

"I don't care what you think she's about to do." His head cocked, one luminous eye enlarged and spotlighted me. "You won't send a spider to bite her leg, nor will you spill any water to provoke her fall." *Puff, puff, puff.*

"Mister, you don't understand. I'm here to help—"

"Help?" Smoke furled from his nostrils. "By inciting cats to mark the good woman's bench?"

"Cats? Cats?" I scratched my head. "No, I don't remember any—"

"Lapse in good judgment? I had assumed you were a benevolent Yin Soul, tasked in the welfare of another. Had I believed otherwise, I would have taken issue immediately."

"That's what I'm trying to tell you. I'm here to help her." I pointed at Jen. "Her real name is Ereo. She's a Dyad. It's a long story, but I don't have time to explain." My finger shifted to Gruer. "That awful—"

A sudden spark shot from the smoking-giant—a purple spark, the color of caution. It landed on my pointing finger. Though accidents happen, he didn't even say, excuse me. Instead, the giant turned a profile. *Puff, puff, puff.*

I brushed off the spark. "Mister, that awful—"

Another spark fired. I flinched. My lip tingled and I dabbed it. A purple light twinkled on my fingertip. My teeth clenched. The giant had sparked deliberately, and he had aimed it, too.

My anger flared, but Sanity rushed in to douse the flames. *Are you crazy? You're a dribble of pea soup against a bear.* I mumbled, "but the bear started it," and Sanity retorted, DON'T POKE THE BEAR.

My heel thumped the floor. "Mister, as I started to say, that awfully nice woman wants to remove Jen. I don't mean *removed* removed. I mean—"

"I know what you mean. I've lived a life or two."

"But Jen has no place to go. Claire and Rosa love her, and she loves them. I can't let that—that awfully nice woman, uhm, dismiss her. Jen depends on me. Her partner, Awen, is depending on me, too. Get it?"

He looked me up and down, then he leaned right and left. I hate being sized up, but now wasn't the time to tell him so. Or to tell him anything at all.

When he finished eyeing me, he *hmm*'d, like one *hmm*s over lumpy gravy when the dinner guests are knocking at the front door. *Hmm*—make do or do without. "Hmm."

Gruer's voice rose. "How is this girl paid? There's no record of her in accounting. How are you hiding her wage? Under phony receipts? And at a time when a parking ticket would break our budget. Explain yourself."

Claire apologized, but Gruer didn't want to hear it. Claire tried for understanding, but Gruer grumbled. Wanting to hear the words in her grumble, I inched closer.

The giant's eyes flashed a warning.

I scooted back. "Please," I said, "I only want to—"

"Help?" *Puff, puff, puff.* "I witnessed your help."

My heel thudded again. "All right, fine, I did the cat-thing, okay? I admit it. I'm sorry. I didn't know Gruer was your friend. I didn't know she had any friends. But don't let Jen suffer for what I did. She needs Claire and Rosa. Help me do something before—"

His pipe vanished and his arm rose. Although he wasn't a Guide, I hushed. He wiggled a finger over his shoulder.

A wall picture jumped its hook. *KRRCKLLG.*

The room silenced.

Except for the giant, all heads turned. In the middle of the splintered glass was a photograph of a toddler clutching a teddy bear.

Gruer lumbered over to the mess. She brushed aside the shards. Clutching the photo, she waddled back to her chair. She dropped the picture into a drawer, then sat, hands folded. Her pained eyes locked with Claire's sympathetic ones. Although they weren't Guides, somehow, Gruer and Claire were talking without words.

Jen glanced from face to face as if she shared my confusion.

The smoking-man released his pipe. With forearms resting on his knees, his lids lowered half-mast, and he began chanting under his breath. At first, I thought he was peering at Jen's cord and noticing her grief. But I was wrong. The slits from his eyes highlighted Gruer's Ribbon and its blades of midnight blue. I shrank to the corner, feeling worse than rotten; I felt like a pile of slippery crap that had tripped a blind woman.

Claire tapped Jen. "Go on back to the cafeteria."

When the door closed behind Jen, Claire stretched an open palm across the table. "Margaret, please. We have history. We go back more than 30 years. That's longer than any two people on these grounds. Back then, we had a vision of what this hospital could mean for children. All children. And in my book, 22 is still a child. Jennifer needed what we could provide. I wasn't going to turn her away. We vowed that this hospital would never again turn away a child. After what happened to your little boy—"

"Don't you dare bring up my son. You think a day goes by that I—that I—" Her lips trembled. She slumped back, turned her face, and motioned for Claire to leave.

"I'm sorry, Margaret. I wasn't meaning to hurt you."

"You deceived me."

"I had to. You would have sent her to County General."

"She was sick? SICK?" Gruer's hands slapped the desk, and she lifted like a rising hurricane. "So, not a vagrant needing a job, but a sick girl needing treatment. How dare you."

"Margaret."

"How dare you place this hospital at risk."

"Margaret, listen to me."

"No, you listen, Claire. You crossed the line. You jeopardized this hospital's license, placed us at risk with the County and the Board. This time, you've gone too far."

"Please, settle down."

"I'll settle down when I'm good and ready. Tell me who treated her."

"I can't tell you."

"Can't or won't?"

"I can't...can't get through to you." Claire stood with a tired sigh. "Margaret Gruer, when you come down to the cafeteria, I treat you with the cold respect that makes you comfortable. I don't like it, but that's how you want it, so that's how it is. You have shut out every member of this hospital with your bullying. Not a Soul on these grounds even knows we were once friends, darn good friends, too. And in all these years, I never once told anyone what's chewing on your insides, why you are like you are. I've just been praying and waiting, believing and trusting, and having faith that someday you will work through your grief, open your heart, and allow love into your life again."

Gruer lowered into her chair.

"Margaret Gruer," Claire said, "if you send that girl packing—"

"Don't you threaten me."

"If you send that girl packing, then the Margaret I know is gone, killed by the bitterness of her own loss." Claire walked to the door and paused. "And I'll stop waiting for my friend."

*Jeez*, my eyes misted up with inky-blue. I got up to follow Claire.

Once again, the smoking-man was enjoying his pipe as if nothing else mattered, not even Gruer's misery.

"Excuse me," I said, but the giant didn't answer. "EXCUSE ME."

He turned slightly.

I pointed quickly at Gruer. "She needs you. Maybe you could whisper something nice to help her feel better."

"You are concerned?" *Puff, puff, puff.*

"Well, you know, look at her. She's sad. Soul-type sad."

"And this concerns you?" He still wouldn't face me.

Gruer tissued her eyes. She opened the desk drawer, withdrew the photograph, and tenderly touched the boy's cheek. Then she set it aside and got out a pen and paper. She muttered, "You brought this on yourself," and began writing.

"Yeah, it concerns me plenty," I said. "And I'm not talking about what she's writing. She's miserable, don't you get it?"

The giant's legs unknotted. He leapt to the floor. Had he been a Player, the building would have shook.

I swept back. "Okay, you get it. You get it. You made the picture drop, right? I'm impressed, damn impressed. I can blow out a candle, but it takes me eight hours. But you, wow, what talent. You just wiggled a finger and, boom, a picture fell. Right? Right?"

Flattery had no effect on the smoking-man.

"Look," I said. "I'm trying to thank you. Okay?"

"You're doing a poor job of it." He blew a smoke ring that traveled to the tip of my nose before it dissolved. "Start with a proper greeting."

"A greeting?"

"Of course. From any time period or language you fancy."

I shrugged. "Hi?"

"Modern. Pity." *Puff, puff, puff.* "Now introduce yourself."

"Okay. My name is Zia. I was Jen's brother, Pierre. Died at six." I stretched out a timid hand.

The giant smiled. The pipe and smoke vanished. He took my hand, but instead of shaking it, he kissed it.

When I withdrew my hand, I swiped it across my hip.

The giant laughed. I don't know what he found so funny and my irritation flickered.

"Dear Lady, I am Malachi, Order of Finishers." He bowed. "I have roamed these hallways for more than three decades. A mother's mourning, you understand, rather strong. Quite resolute." He motioned to the pile of broken glass.

"You were the boy in the picture?"

"Splendid deduction. Smart as a whip. Indeed, I died at three."

"And Gruer was your mother?"

"Brilliant reasoning. Yes, she was my mother. Does that surprise you?"

It did. When I looked at Gruer, it was hard to imagine her creating a life-cord.

Malachi rumbled as if he were reading my thoughts. "She didn't always appear as she does now. In her younger day, she was quite handsome."

*Handsome?* But I kept my mouth shut.

Gruer got up, her fist clenching the paper.

Malachi leaned over and whispered in her ear.

Gruer let out a pitiful moan. She dropped the paper into the waste-basket and walked out.

"No need to worry," Malachi said. "Your friend will stay."

"Just like that? How did you do that? How? Can you teach me?"

"Tenaciously eager. Charming. But no, Dear Lady, I cannot teach you." Malachi formed his pipe, lit it, and with a mouthful of smoke said, "Because I did very little. One is firmly planted in her heart. I simply brushed off a speck of dust." *Puff, puff, puff.* "So, Dear Zia, I assume you'll be staying for awhile."

I nodded.

"Very well, but I have a few rules. Let's start with the cats."

"No, no, I won't ask them to spray. I promise. I'll go talk with the cats tonight, or right now if you want."

Although he *hmm'd* again, I could tell he believed me. He blew his smoke rings to the side of my face instead of into it.

"My next rule," he said, "if you wish to injure your Ribbon by retaliating against Players, that's your affair. Mottle your Ribbon as much as you like, but not here, Dear Lady, not under this roof. Not around children who struggle each day for the love and compassion of positive vibrations."

"No, yeah. But I haven't—"

"Lady Reichert."

"Oh, she counts?"

His eyes narrowed.

"Okay, okay," I said. "I promise. Now can we be friends?"

"Of course. Tell me your Order."

"My Order? Uhm." I sparked nervousness.

"Dear Zia, you do remember your Order, don't you?"

"Yeah, and I'm proud of it, too." I stomped on the stupid sparks of lies. "Those sparks are wrong. I'm plenty proud. I'm from the Eleventh Order, Order of Agitators."

"Hmm, I never would have guessed." He broke into a belly laugh.

"What's so funny? Huh? You think Finishers are better? Ha-ha-ha, I'm laughing at Finishers, how do you like that?"

"Slow down, Dear Lady, contain yourself." Malachi held up a surrendering hand. "I'm not your enemy nor was I laughing at your Order. It was your reluctance to reveal your Order I found amusing. Amusing and charmingly modest. Most Souls chatter ad nauseam about such things."

"Oh. Well, some people don't like Agitators. Some think we're bad-tempered. Some call us troublemakers and rude."

"The nerve."

"Yeah." My arms crossed. "I'm never rude."

"I can see that. And I'm not *some* people now, am I?" Malachi winked. "Wasn't Lady d'Arc from your Order? Galileo, too? Marvelous Souls."

"They're different. They're the Greats. Every Order has their Greats." My feet shuffled. "I'm not one of them."

"You never know. You have many lives ahead of you, I'm sure."

"Honestly, Malachi, they put me in the wrong Order. I should have been a Warrior. I'd behead an army of demons." I envisioned a sword, slashed through the air, and cut his smoke ring in two.

"No, Dear Zia." Malachi's tone sobered. "Warriors must be highly disciplined and sharply focused, for within them rises a powerful sword to battle the blights of mankind. They are the most selfless of Orders, Dear Lady. They cannot afford the luxury of personal interest, much less a temper. Their sword must be keenly directed and their stamina unfaltering for their lives are challenged more often than all the Orders combined."

"Are you sure? Don't they just hack up the bad guys?"

Malachi fixed a serious eye on my sword.

"Oh." I let it dissolve.

Malachi drew on his pipe and blew smoke overhead. "Warriors shoulder a grave responsibility that neither you nor I would want to bear. Not at all. Be thankful for your placement with Agitators. They are every bit as valuable and magnificent as any other Order."

"But their reputation is—"

"Misunderstood, Dear Lady, simply misunderstood. But that's among Players not Energies."

I smiled, probably blushed, too. The smoking bear had called my Order valuable. Magnificent and valuable. I didn't want to leave my new friend, but it was time for Jen's whispers.

I thanked Malachi and gave him a light punch. "Will you be here tomorrow?"

"Yes, and for tomorrows to come. Bring me your questions, and I'll give you the answers to the best of my ability."

"Wow. How did you know I had a ton of questions?"

"Tomorrow, Dear Lady."

"Yeah, okay." I drifted toward the door. "Malachi, just one question for now. How come you form an old pipe and stinky smoke?"

His eyes twinkled. "Dear Lady, for the very reason you envision a pillow each night."

"Comfort?"

Malachi grinned—even his smoke ring stretched into a grin—and then he disappeared.

Halfway down the hall, it struck me. "Hey, wait a minute. How did you know about my pillow? Have you been spying on me?"

Out of thin air came a chuckle.

## 28

*I waited with patience for his grief to ease.*

**M**orning after morning, Zia popped into Gruer's office to present a list of questions to Malachi, although rarely the questions Malachi had expected. *How come you're so big? How come cartoons end at noon? If Saturn melted, would the ring dissolve?*

Her visits continued daily until the morning before Christmas. On that day, Zia didn't show.

Concerned, Malachi glided the hallways to find her. He was about to check Game Town when a distraught Zia came rushing out. "Leave me alone," she said. "I don't want to talk about it."

Late afternoon, the doctors and nurses trickled out of the hospital to join their families for Christmas Eve. By six p.m., only a handful of staff remained, even fewer by eight.

In her office, Gruer pored over charts and budgets, working later than usual. She reached beneath heavy rimmed glasses to rub at her eyestrain.

Overhead, Malachi puffed on his pipe. "Time to rest, Good Woman, time to go home."

Gruer pushed from her desk, pulled on her black wool coat, and opened her office door to leave. A present, leaning against the door, fell at her feet. The gift was wrapped in silver foil with red ribbons, topped with a green bow, and labeled with a blue cherub.

Gruer stretched into the empty hallway to look right and left. "Silly nonsense."

"Good Woman, no one is watching you, no one is witnessing your faked indignation. Now pick up the package and let's have a look."

Gruer bent, adjusting her glasses, and read, *To Margaret, my friend.*

She huffed with another check of the halls. Grabbing the present, she back-stepped into her office and shut the door. She sat again. While her fingers drummed the desk, she studied the gift.

"I doubt it will bite." Malachi reshaped smoke rings into hearts. "Chance it, Good Woman. Open the gift."

Gruer's tapping stopped. She untied the ribbon, and then her thick fingers slid under the tape to prod the paper free. Ten minutes passed before one end opened. Usually, Malachi wouldn't care if the unwrapping took hours. Or days. He was a patient Soul, abundantly patient, as is the gift of his Order. Tonight, however, Gruer needed rest. Exhaustion formed pink pillows beneath her eyes and carved marionette lines down from her mouth. She was fatigued to the bone, the type that doesn't loosen from a night of sleep, the type that worried Malachi.

"Good Woman," he whispered, "a bit of haste. We must get you home."

Gruer removed the wrapping and then spent five minutes hand-ironing the wrinkled foil before she folded it and tucked it neatly into her purse. She lifted the lid on the box and peeled back the tissue. Nestled on more tissue was a pewter frame adorned with scrolling. At the top, the inscription read, *No Child Denied*. A tiny gasp left her.

"If memory serves," Malachi said, "that was the theme of the nursing convention you and Lady Claire attended. Or was it the mantra that set the foundation for the hospital's reform after my removal? Either way, it rings a bell with us, doesn't it? There's more at the bottom. Read on."

Gruer blew her nose, then read the lower engraving, *Christian Daniel Gruer 1920-1923*.

"I am honored," Malachi whispered.

Gruer retrieved her son's photograph and positioned it into the frame. She hung it over the dusty outline left on the wall from the prior frame. She stood back, her eyes watering.

Malachi lowered to her side and put his arm around her shoulder. He appreciated the gift, but more particularly, he admired Claire's timing. Had Gruer received the frame before issuing the letter that allowed Jen to stay, Gruer would have rebuked the gift, viewing it as a bribe. But now, Claire's gift and its timing had oiled the brittle strings in Gruer's heart.

As always, Malachi walked Gruer home. They strolled through the pine scented night until winter winds hastened Gruer's steps. They passed a group of carolers whose throats strained in a crescendo. They smiled at the neon blinking Santa and his short-circuiting reindeers. And they read the riddle of the month on the New Ministries message board: *What is missing in Ch—ch?*

Blocks from the hospital, they arrived at the only darkened house on the street. Neither tinsel nor candle evidenced the holiday. Except for the unseen companion ever vigil at her side, Gruer was alone.

As was his custom, Malachi waited in the living room until Gruer finished bathing and retired for the night. Then, as always, he vanquished his pipe before entering her bedroom. After a kiss to her forehead, he whispered his love until her dreams set in.

Typically, Malachi sat on the rooftop and watched the stars until dawn. Tonight, however, he was troubled. Though he had left Zia alone as she had demanded, he had expected to see her later that day.

He hadn't.

Malachi returned to the hospital.

Other than the hum from the vending machines, the cafeteria was quiet. Malachi checked Game Town. Empty. He glided the halls, looking into the children's rooms and checking behind their curtains. No Zia.

"Dr. Rockmire, must speak to you. Must speak to you." The Ghost-Doctor waved a clipboard as he hurried up the hallway. He appeared in the form he had last viewed himself—white hair and wrinkled face, which matched the color and the creases of his lab coat. "Dr. Rockmire, a patient. Your patient. Terrible. Speak to you."

"Not now, good Doctor," Malachi said. "I'm searching for a friend."

The Ghost-Doctor slumped.

Instantly, Malachi regretted his haste. He touched the Ghost-Doctor's shoulder. "I'm terribly sorry. Quite thoughtless of me. Tell me your troubles, but quickly if possible."

But *quickly* wasn't possible, Malachi knew. For decades, Malachi had listened to the Ghost-Doctor's ramblings. It was never quick, and it was never coherent. Like all Wanderers, confusion plagued the Ghost-Doctor.

The Soul refused to wake up...because he shouldn't, or mustn't, not when so many children needed him. Scores and scores of children needed him to stop a murderous thief—Influenza.

It seeped into the children's lungs, stole their breaths, and ended their lives. So many, many lives.

The children trusted the Doctor, their inflamed eyes pleaded for his help. How could he rest when influenza was suffocating the children.

No, he would not rest. He must NEVER rest.

He must save the children....*save the children...save the children...*

But he couldn't.

Not all.

They died...a long, long time ago.

No child in the hospital suffered influenza.

Malachi was not, nor had ever been, Dr. Rockmire.

More than four decades had passed since 1918. For the Ghost-Doctor, however, not a single day had surrendered to a night. "Three patients, stat, wing two, ER."

"Yes, and you'll treat them with admirable consideration."

"Room five, coughing, fever. Hurry, room seven. Treatment."

Malachi drifted away as the Ghost-Doctor shouted orders to the echoes of his past. "Room two. Send nurse. Nurse, stat. Gangrene. Treatment."

*Gangrene?* Malachi turned swiftly. "Good Doctor, do you have a patient with gangrene?"

The Ghost-Doctor checked his clipboard. "Terrible, yes, green. Courtyard, yes. Gangrene." The Ghost-Doctor jotted a note, pocketed his pen, and glided off. "More nurses, more nurses."

Malachi formed his pipe.

# 29

*But motion slowed and time thickened in a wave of déjà vu.*

"Glorious night," Malachi said joining Zia on top the terrace wall. "Don't you agree?"

Zia shrugged. In the distance, carolers sang.

> *...I have no gift to bring, pa-rum-pum-pum-pum,*
> *that's fit to give our King, pa-rum-pum-pum-pum...*

Malachi fashioned his smoke rings into toy drums, but they floated off without Zia's notice. "Where's your friend?" Malachi asked.

Zia's mouth slanted in a scowl. "Jen turned down Rosa's party, a real party with dancing and buttered rum, to join Claire's dumb choir and sing in a dumb church. Who knows why. But she'll be back. Jen won't spend the night anywhere but here. Who knows why about that either. Go figure."

"They celebrate the birth of a One Determinant. Some celebrate with gaiety, some with prayer. A joyous time for most, but not for you?"

"They got the date wrong."

"And their mistake troubles you?" He reached to her cheek to dab a tear.

Zia pushed his hand away. "I don't need your pity," she said. "Players do; that's the point. Your mother and Jen wouldn't hurt so much if we could just tell them or show them that we're okay. But we can't."

"What else troubles you?"

"Nothing. That's it."

"Dear Lady, what more troubles you?"

> *...pa-rum-pum-pum-pum,*
> *rum-pum-pum-pum, rum-pum-pum-pum...*

Zia shook her head, her lips squeezed together, but after a stretch of time, Zia said, "The new kid in Game Town has a Ribbon rougher than sandpaper. Do you know what that means?"

"He has choices."

"Bull. After the doctors heal him, that Niine Player will grow up and slaughter our Players. Where are their choices? And we can't warn anyone.

That's just wrong. It's like watching a bunch of guppies swimming next to a shark. The guppies don't realize it's a shark until the shark chomps them in half. But we can see the shark. Why can't we warn our Players, 'hey, that kid is a monster'? But we can't, can we? So, if there's a reason to this never-ending crap, now would be a great time to tell me."

"Why do you suppose your friend accepted Lady Claire's invitation rather than attending Miss Rosa's party?" Malachi puffed a large circle, then pinched the bottom and dented the top. "Any idea?"

"Self-punishment? I don't know. Are you changing the subject?"

"Dear Lady, the answer to my question *is* the subject."

"Jeez, you sound like a Guide. Oh purpose purpose," Zia rumbled in a baritone voice. "Oh, negative fragments. Why, you call that a Soul? Harrumph-harrumph. I call it a shambles. Clean it up!"

"And have you done so?"

"What?"

"You cast aspersions on the universe, yet you disregard your own Soul."

"My Soul is fine."

"Dear Lady, Guides advise for our benefit, not for theirs. When a Guide informs you that you've overlooked a few fragments, you would be wise to recheck your Soul. You can't see the brilliance of a sunrise through a window covered in filth."

Zia curled her finger to bring Malachi closer. He withdrew his pipe and bent sideways. Zia whispered in his ear, "Maybe, just maybe, I don't know where to find these food-fragments."

"Food?" Malachi uprighted, saw she was serious, and quickly drew on his pipe, *puff, puff, puff,* to quell his laughter because Zia would have misunderstood. When the last bit of chuckle had cleared from his throat, he said, "Dear Lady, it's a wonderful night for tossing out fragments. Can't think of one better. Why don't we go into your Soul and tackle those fragments?"

"*We?* I thought only Guides could get inside Energies."

"Only Guides may enter without your permission." Malachi vanquished his pipe. His hands folded over Zia's. "Close your eyes and concentrate."

"Concentrate on what?"

"*Shhh.*"

When Zia appeared in her consciousness, Malachi called, "Follow my voice," and Zia descended through dark, swirling vibrations. When she spotted Malachi, she flashed to his side. Their hands locked.

*Down...down...down.* They descended through veils of gray, dusty white, and sooty brown. *Down...down...down.* Eventually, horizontal bands of forest green thickened beneath their feet. "Is this it?" Zia asked.

"No, this is the protective layer surrounding your core." Malachi slowly rotated. "Hmm. I don't see—"

"You don't see what? What are we looking for?"

"The light shining up from your center." Malachi's feet swished at the mist. "Hmm. Rather dense. Probably shrouding the opening. No matter. Our search begins. Keep your eyes on the surface for a square or a circle."

They moved through mounds of fog. After hours of roaming, Zia jostled their hands. "Hey, what if we get lost in here?" When Malachi failed a quick reply, Zia alarmed. "WE'RE LOST?"

"No, no, Dear Lady." Malachi scratched his head. "You're just well hidden. Come along." A while later, Malachi mumbled to himself, "Where in the world are you?" But Zia heard his mumble and again panicked. Malachi assured her, "All is well. You're just a delightful secret, a buried treasure." Thereafter, he was careful to keep his concerns unspoken.

Later, Zia stopped and kicked at a cloud of green. "Wait, I found something." Kneeling, she splayed the mist. "Look, Malachi, a square."

"So it is," Malachi said with much more relief than he let show.

Zia stuck her head down the opening. When she withdrew, her eyes were round and unblinking. "You know what? I think I've been in there before."

"Of course you have, Dear Zia. Fragments don't walk in by themselves." Malachi stretched along the square's edge and formed his pipe. *Puff, puff, puff.* "Well, what are you waiting for? Go find the offending fragments and remove them at once."

Again, Zia poked through the square. When she pulled back, she was biting her lip.

"Something troubles you?" Malachi asked.

"Sort of. What do fragments look like? Broken glass?"

"Prisms, yes, of course."

"What color?"

"All colors."

"*All* colors? All those shards and prisms are *fragments?*"

"Dear Lady, you're becoming distressed."

"No, I *am* distressed. Crazy stressed. There are hundreds down there. Maybe thousands. For chrissake, they're breeding."

Malachi snorted. "Is your fondness for hyperbole among them? If so, please remove it."

But Zia jittered and wrung her hands. Malachi sighed and pushed to his knees. "Very well. Move aside. Let's have a look."

Zia scooted.

"Let's count the few fragments that you claim is a thou*OUUUU*—" From his gaping mouth, the pipe fell and dissolved. "Good Heavens! You've been a busy little lady. Yes, indeed. Quite the collector, you are, a collector of all that is or ever was."

His nose crinkled, then burned. Immediately, he shut off vibrations to scent. "Dear Lady, what odor on Earth have you vilified?"

Zia took a whiff. "Oh. Oh that. Alaska's bird-sized mosquitoes won't bite if you smash up garlic and smear the juice over your skin. That's what the peddler said when he sold me a pot-full. I bathed in half and ate the rest. My clothes stunk and my sweat reeked. Indians held their noses, 'oh, Cheechako, pee-yew,' and stampeders insisted I pitch my tent downwind."

"Dear Lady, that smell is not garlic."

"Jeez, I KNOW! Mosquitoes nearly ate me alive. And each bite welted, and half the welts became infected and spewed pus. I was a stinky, pus-spewing Cheechako. I sure as hell know it wasn't garlic." She shook her head. "I bathed in a pot of rotten cauliflower. Boiled cauliflower looks like garlic."

Malachi nodded. "I suppose it does." Again, he peered into the square.

"Is it bad?" Zia tapped his shoulder. "I mean, compared to other Souls."

Malachi sat back, formed another pipe, and sucked voraciously while Zia waited for an answer. Malachi wanted to tell her—was prepared to tell her—that he had seen worse, only he hadn't. He hadn't seen a quarter of that many fragments within one Soul. He rubbed the back of his neck. "Dear Zia, 'bad' is such a relative term. Let's call it a worthy endeavor." He forced a smile. "Yes, a worthy endeavor. A challenge. And a challenge to be met without delay. Please, remove those culprits, one shard at a time."

"And put them where?"

"Up through this opening. Once outside your core, the fragments will dissolve. Now, go on."

Zia dropped through the square and started to descend. "Aren't you going to help?"

"No, Dear Zia, no one can remove another Soul's fragments. Not even a Guide. I can take you here and explain how it's done. The rest is up to you."

Zia lowered to the field of fragments. When her feet touched the core, she slowly rotated, looking all around.

"Don't ponder the entirety," Malachi said. "Start with one. Pull it from your center and begin a pile. When you have as much as you can carry, bring them up."

Zia sat. She picked up a fragment—*a stupid fragment*, Malachi heard. In place of the fragment came a pinhole of light. She sparked curiosity. Holding the shard over the light, she peered inside.

"What does it reveal?" Malachi asked.

Before answering, Zia studied all sides of the prism. "Snow. My poor frozen feet in Alaska." She shoved it aside. "I hate snow."

"Of course you do. But once you remove the fragment, you will see the beauty of a white-topped mountain and feel the tickle of a snowflake's kiss."

"Yeah, right."

Zia picked up another...then another...then another. To every fragment Zia picked, plucked, and added to her pile, a thread of light sprouted in the fragment's place. When the stack had grown to an armload, Zia carried them up to the opening.

She pushed the fragments out of the square. The fragments dissolved.

"Splendid, Dear Zia. Now go on. There's more work to be done."

Zia somersaulted backwards. For hours, she gripped, pulled, and pitched, but while she did so, she grumbled, spit, and cursed.

Wanting to improve her attitude, Malachi said, "Dear Lady, think of it as weeding a garden, a labor generously rewarded by spring blossoms."

When Zia tossed out the next stack, she said, "I'd pave the garden and never pull a stinking weed again." She did a back-dive.

*Puff, puff, puff.* Malachi, still determined to bring cheer to her task, complimented Zia's diving.

Zia fumbled, almost dropping the fragments as she neared the square. "What kind of diving? Huh? Not saltwater, right?"

When she said, *saltwater*, a crimson spark shot from her brow. Cued by the spark, Malachi said, "Freshwater pools, Dear Lady. Admirable diving into lakes and ponds and freshwater pools that haven't a pinch of salt."

Zia smiled, "Thanks," and she did a swan-dive back to her core.

A stubborn purple sliver caused her to struggle. She clutched it, dug in her heels, and after much effort, slid it free. She looked into the prism and frowned. She shook it, rapped it against her palm, then looked again.

Her frown deepened. She threw it onto a separate stack.

"Those fragments puzzle you?" Malachi asked.

"They're wooden nickels. Slugs. Not worm-slugs, I mean—"

"I know what you mean. I've lived a few lives. And I assure you, those prisms contain something."

Zia reexamined the purple prism. "And I'm telling you, they're empty."

"Hold it to your nose."

She did, then shrugged.

"Hold it to your ear."

Zia pressed it to her ear. Her head tipped back with a giggle.

"Don't keep me in suspense," Malachi said. "What do you hear?"

*"Shhh,"* Zia said now listening to each prism from her special pile.

"Young Lady, what in heavens do you hear? A tiger's roar? A cannon's blast? The crack of a whip? Please, tell me what you hear."

"Stuff. Just words. Words from lots of lives."

"Words?" *Puff, puff, puff.* "What words? Vulgarities?"

Zia's grin stretched. *"Maaaybeee."*

Malachi released an exasperated breath. "Dear Lady, please rid yourself of those indecorous epithets immediately."

Zia sorted the pile, then carried only a third to the opening. After she threw them out, her arms folded on the square's edge, her legs swimming in space. "Jeez, they're only words, just harmless strings of letters. That's all."

Malachi raised an eyebrow. "Inherently harmless, but poisoned by your vicious use."

"Still, they're just silly words."

"If you spoke them as such, you wouldn't find them among your negative fragments. But you tainted them, Dear Zia." Malachi formed a hammer. "In the hands of a builder, a hammer secures a nail; in the hands of a killer, it bludgeons a head. The user determines positive or negative, and the receiver feels it, whether a blow to the head or a wound to the heart."

Zia tilted her head back to show her cockeyes and lolling tongue.

"Charming," Malachi said, his tone flat. "Bring up the rest of the words."

"Nope, I'm keeping those. When I get mad, I don't want to be tongue-tied. Or worse, yammering, golly-gee-gosh." She took Malachi's hand, kneaded it like a pillow, then snuggled it beneath her cheek. "When you talk, I think of castles and knights. That's your way, your language. When my Guide talks, I think of monks, few words, no frills, no repeats. That's his way. My first Guide, Romal, talked rapid-fire, *rat-a-tat-tat-tat*, as if he invented language. I bet he did, too. He's that smart. So, I have my way of talking. It's lousy, but it's mine." She spun from the edge, twirled, and flipped into a dive.

With Malachi's prodding, Zia worked through the night, and then through Christmas Day and through the two days that followed. When she talked of leaving for her duty to Jen, Malachi said, "Whispers are far more effective from a cleansed Soul."

So Zia toiled on, plucking, gathering, and pitching fragments. Over time, the multitude of pinholes had turned her core into a field of light—almost. Three sunken prisms cast shadows across her surface like submerged boulders darkening a shallow lake. Only the fragments' triangular tips jutted above the surface—dorsal fins of red, blue, and green. Gripping the red one, Zia pulled and tugged. "Malachi, it's too big, buried too deep."

"Not so. Ease your arms down and around it. Rock it a bit until it loosens, then give a firm yank. That should do the trick."

As Zia's arms slid around the fragment, her face pressed into the prism. When she saw the contents, she pulled away. "This one stays."

"Dear Lady—"

"NO!" She spat on the shard. "It stays."

She moved to the blue tip. It proved too wide for her grasp. "Malachi, can you see how big this thing is?"

Unquestionably, it was the largest, but Malachi didn't want to discourage her. "Yes, Dear Lady, it's a worthy endeavor."

"Yeah? Just how worthy is this endeavor?"

Malachi hedged. "Measuring worthiness—"

"Save it." Zia swept high to see for herself. "Aw, crap." She descended slowly. "Worthiness nothing." She kicked the blue tip and huffed. And in that huff was a sniff. Uncertainty crossed her face. She knelt, clutched the blue tip, and sniffed again. "*Ohhh*," holding her stomach, she rolled away.

"Dear Lady, what ails you?" Hearing only incoherent mumblings, he leaned far into the square. What he heard made no sense—*Salt-sucking-microbes, crap-infested sea-shit*.

Zia crawled to the green shard. With a hard yank, she fell backwards, clutching half the fragment. She looked at the other half still embedded in her core. "I broke it."

"No, Dear Zia, bring it here and I'll explain."

Zia peered into the prism. "This is wrong. Love can't be negative."

"Dear Lady, what you hold is not love. It's possessiveness marbled with jealousy. Please release it, and you'll understand. Trust me."

"But this is Awen. *My* Awen." She nuzzled it. "Not Ereo's. Stupid Ereo. Stupid Jen."

The embedded piece expanded. "Oh heavens," Malachi said watching the dark green shadow spread beneath Zia's feet. "Dear Zia, lift your face off the triangle. Please, lift it at once. The fragment feeds your unkind thoughts. In turn, you create more. Please, lift your face from the fragment."

"No! Awen is my friend. *MINE!*"

"Dear Lady, am I your friend? Am I?" Although she mumbled, yes, Malachi said, "I cannot hear you. Please nod or shake your head."

Her face lifted from the fragment to give a sloshy nod.

"Then keep your eyes on me and your face off the prism. Bring it here."

Zia rose a few feet. "But this is Awen. *My* Awen."

"Awen would want this."

"He would? Are you sure?"

Malachi stretched as far as he could into the square. "I give you my word as a gentleman; Awen would want this. Trust me." He kept her attention long enough for the effect of the prism—a daze—to subside from her eyes.

She gave a firm nod, "You're a good friend, Malachi," then she pressed the fragment to her chest. Before Malachi could utter one word of alarm, she zoomed straight up, knocking a startled Malachi backward.

When he looked up, Zia was looking down through her still encircled arms where the fragment had dissolved. Malachi grinned and applauded. "Bravo. Bravo. A dazzling rocket of—what's the modern term? Gusto!"

Zia smiled, too, as she lowered to Malachi's side. Her forehead glistened with pride when she saw all the lights shining up from her core. "Wow."

"Wow indeed," Malachi said also appreciating the beautiful lights. "You conquered much, a glorious purging."

"I did, didn't I?" And her smile widened. "Let's get out of here."

"Leave?" Even from the square's edge, Malachi could see the face within the red prism and he knew the harm it would cause. Somehow, he had to convince Zia to remove it. "It was a glorious purging, indeed, but—"

"Stop," Zia said. "I did good. Damn good. Don't spoil your praise by adding a 'but.' In my entire existence, I've never received praise that didn't end in a 'but.' Can I receive it now? Please? Just this once, no buts. Okay?"

Reluctantly, very reluctantly, Malachi took her hand and they ascended.

## 30

*Zia carries a sizeable fragment
of hatred toward Triite.*

I avoided Malachi because he constantly nagged about the remaining fragments, even after I explained, "The red and blue are personal, and the green is no big deal. If it affected me, I wouldn't love Ereo, right? But I love her plenty. I love her whether she's Ereo the Soul or Ereo the Player Jen. No bad feelings."

"However—"

"No *however*s. It's a wooden nickel, not worth discussing."

*Puff, puff, puff.* He hovered at the ceiling in Gruer's office. "Dear Lady, then consider the red. It's a marvelous day to conquer the red fragment."

"Jeez, Malachi, I came to show you a trick I learned in Game Town. I didn't come here to be badgered about stupid fragments again, okay?"

Right then, Claire and Jen walked into the office, and Gruer told them to sit. "Ms. Smith, when I signed your employment papers, I did so on one condition. After the holidays, you were to find a suitable residence."

"Yes, ma'am."

"An employee cannot live in a breakroom."

"Sure they can," I said. "Jen proves it."

Gruer motioned to Claire. "Ms. Brown, you have the floor."

Bouncing a little with an excited smile, Claire turned to Jen and said, "Honey, four blocks away, there's a nice studio apartment coming available for a six-month lease. Nurse Gruer and I paid the deposit and a few months' rent. It's an early birthday present. Isn't that wonderful?"

Instead of a returned smile, Jen made a face as if she had eaten something bad. "I can't." She slumped in her chair. "I just can't."

"Don't be silly," Claire said. "Of course you can. It's a gift, not a loan. We bought you some furnishings, too—a table, some chairs, a little dresser and a nightstand. We even got a bed for you. It ain't much, but it beats a cot."

"No," Jen said. "You don't understand. I appreciate everything you've done for me, but I can't accept your gift."

"But Jennifer—"

"Claire." Gruer gave a terse head shake. She was leaning back, the tips of her pointer fingers tapping together an inch from her lips. She was studying Jen. "I believe Jennifer *can't* because she can't sign a lease. She's a minor."

"Honey, is that true?"

"I'm sorry, Claire. I hated to lie to you."

"How old are you?" Gruer asked.

"I'm almost twenty."

"Oh, baby," Claire said, "your family must be worried sick."

"You're my family. You and Rosa. I don't have anyone else, not anymore." Two of Jen's sky-blue threads became navy again; a month of my whispers went right down the drain.

"Let's have the truth," Gruer said. "Start with your name."

Jen squirmed. Gruer's tone hardened. "Your name, young lady."

"Jenevieve. Jenevieve Duvall."

The splotchy reds in Gruer's face turned ashen. "Duvall? Any relation to—" When Jen nodded, Gruer whipped out tissues to dab at the sudden sweat popping on her brow. "I remember reading about your father's death. Anaphylactic shock?"

"Yes. A bee sting."

Gruer turned to Claire. "It was five or six years ago. You were back east taking care of your mother."

"It reached our papers, too," Claire said. "I remember the headlines, *Tragedy strikes the Duvalls again.*"

Gruer shook her head. "The 'again' headline occurred later, about a week after Mr. Duvall's death. If memory serves, while Mrs. Duvall was attending a fundraiser benefitting hospitals—this hospital included—the recently fired governess returned in the middle of the night and stole the Duvall boy. Reporters called it a murder-suicide."

"They were wrong," Jen said.

"Completely wrong," I added.

Jen sat straight again. "Katy had been my au pair since the day I was born. She was my best friend and the only mother Pierre had ever known. Katy would have never hurt Pierre or me or anyone."

"That's right," I said. "Never in a billion years."

"My stepmother lied to the police," Jen said. "Everything she told them about Katy was a lie. After school, I went to the police station and told them the truth, but they didn't believe me. I'm just a teenager; she's Monique Duvall. I don't know why Katy jumped from the cliff, but I do know she didn't cause Pierre's death. I know it for a fact...because I'm to blame."

*What?* I tugged on Malachi, "What did she just say?"

He cupped his ear, signaling me to listen, and he held a finger to his mouth, telling me to shut up.

"I was babysitting Pierre," Jen said. "After I went to bed, he came into my bedroom and broke the little angel statue that I kept by my bedside."

"Your angel broke?" I turned to Malachi. "I didn't break her angel."

"He must have been scared," Jen said, "but I didn't wake up. I don't know why the sound didn't wake me. It should have, but it didn't. I don't know why it didn't. Why didn't I wake up? Why?" She looked anxiously from Claire to Gruer as if one of them might have the answer.

They didn't, but I did. "You were sick, Jen. Don't you remember?"

She pulled in a deep breath. "Pierre knew the angel meant a lot to me. I wish I had let him play with it. If I had, he wouldn't have been so upset when he broke it. He wandered outside and went down to the ocean."

"No, Jen," I told her. "You got it all wrong. Ma mére took me to the ocean. Ma mére."

Claire brushed aside Jen's bangs. "Honey, you can't blame yourself. You were just a little girl. It was an accident."

"It wasn't an accident," Jen said. "It was neglect. That was the first time my brother was left in my care. But I was so tired that night, I forgot so many things. I didn't draw the drapes or close my curtains, and I didn't lock the doors. Pierre couldn't reach the locks. The only way he could have left the house is if I had forgotten to lock the doors. His death is my fault. My fault."

Jen started sobbing.

Claire pulled Jen into a hug. "No, honey, no, you're not to blame. You were just a little girl. Just a little girl."

"This is all wrong," I told Malachi. "No wonder she's carved up in blue. Guilt. But it's all wrong. My mother took me to the ocean so we could release Odessa, her stupid octopus. I wanted Jen to come, but she was sick. We were going to take cookies to Jen after we set Odessa free, but the damn thing bit me. Then I slipped and—" I recalled Alpha's words, *You did not drown.* "I must have hit my head on a rock."

Gruer slid the box of tissues toward Jen. "Why did you run away?"

Jen pulled from Claire's arms, took a few tissues, and wiped her face. "You probably won't believe me, but my stepmother is—is insane. Insane and dangerous. Although she tolerated me, she hated Pierre. From the day he was born, she wouldn't touch him. Katy mothered him. I tried to protect him. And when he died, my stepmother forbade me to speak his name. After the funeral, she said I had work to do. She wanted me to memorize pages from her grandmothers' books. They were about plants and poisons. I told her no. The next day, she gave me a cup of tea, which blistered the roof of my mouth and closed my throat. I could barely breathe. When I reached for the phone, she ripped it from the wall."

Gruer's brows lifted briefly with a glance to Claire.

"I'm not making this up." Jen's voice became desperate and insistent, and her eyes volleyed between Claire and Gruer. "It's the truth. I swear it."

"Honey, we believe you," Claire said, but Gruer looked unconvinced.

"Ms. Gruer," Jen said, "a year after Pierre died, I ran away. That was the first time. I was 15. I hid at a friend's house. My stepmother's detectives dragged me back home. Within a month, my friend's house burned down from an electrical fire, a freak electrical fire. They lost their house and all their belongings. The insurance company wrote them a check but then canceled it. My friend's parents hired a lawyer. Two weeks later, the lawyer wouldn't return their calls. After that, my friend wouldn't return mine. My stepmother was behind it. She was punishing the whole family for having helped me."

She turned to Claire. "That's why I couldn't stay with you. I couldn't risk my stepmother finding out. I know what she would do to you. Something terrible. You would lose everything. I couldn't let that happen."

"Baby, nothing bad is going to happen to me, and we're not going to let anything bad happen to you."

"You don't know her," Jen said. "You don't know what she's capable of. When I turned sixteen, she took me out of school and locked me in my room. I wasn't allowed contact with the outside world. When I learned to recite certain pages, she brought me a tray of food, but often the food tasted strange. I didn't eat for days, but I didn't have an appetite anyway. I spent my childhood protecting Pierre. When he died, I felt I deserved my stepmother's abuse, and I would take her abuse for the rest of my life if it would bring back Pierre. But it won't. I can't change what happened. I broke through my bedroom window and ran away to protect myself."

"You don't have to run anymore," Claire said before she turned to Gruer. "Isn't that right?" Then everybody turned to Gruer.

"This is a hospital," Gruer said, "not a shelter for runaways." Before anyone could argue, Gruer held up a silencing palm. "Why here?" she asked Jen. "Why would you hide in this hospital...or any hospital, for that matter? With all your money—"

"I don't have any money. My father willed everything to my stepmother. All that I owned, or thought that I owned, became hers. She made sure that I knew it and appreciated her generosity. Every morning began with The Daily Gratitudes, a list she checked off while I recited my thanks: Thank you, ma mére, for my clothes; thank you, ma mére, for my food; thank you, ma mére, for sparing me from my kindred contagions."

"Your what?" All of us chorused.

"It makes no sense," Jen said, "but it was third on her list."

*Kindred contagions?* Where had I heard that stupid phrase before? I ransacked my memory. Had I heard it from ma mére? No, the voice didn't match. Ma mére's voice was smooth and commanding. In my recall, *kindred contagions* came from a grinding, crackly voice like...

*"TRIITE!"*

A siren began blaring and the room started to spin.

Voices melded into mumbles and slipped into the backdrop.

Someone was asking questions, someone was answering...and someone was shaking me, "Dear Lady, get hold of yourself," and speaking from far, far away. "Please, Dear Zia, stop...please don't...don't go."

# 31

*I had a strange sensation of déjà vu,*
*only this time, the feeling threaded to a payback.*

M alachi rose to the hospital's rooftop.
In the distance, Zia, ablaze in scarlet sparks, was gliding west.
Malachi fashioned his pipe. *Puff, puff, puff.*
"Sir Alpha," he called, "your Charge has left the premises."
He blew a smoke ring and painted it red.
"Still clouded by the fragment. I'm terribly sorry."

*Desperation spawns bad ideas.*

Alpha watched Zia move along the coast. She paused at the Victorian homes to compare each to the home in her memory before she moved on.

"She chooses Niine," Kaane said appearing beside Alpha. "A surprising but gratifying twist of events." Kaane erupted in laughter. Dozens of suckling Souls tumbled to Kaane's feet. Mewing and squeaking, the Souls rolled around blindly in search of another. When they bumped together, they clung, forming long, beaded strings. The strings bounded back to their host.

"How do you like Free Will now?" Kaane tipped his head toward Zia. "Despite my efforts, Monique removed her son. Despite your efforts, Zia seeks revenge, murderous revenge, as if she actually believes she can remove a Player. Her ability for self-deception is beyond fantastic; it's phenomenal, the apex of deception. She is a formidable Niine Soul."

"Untrue," Alpha said without a blink from Zia.

"Denial? I know you're in agony, Alpha, but denial is beneath you. Without your Agitator, you have no chance of success at the Neutral Point. You've lost the war before the first battle. I might allow our newly recruited Agitator to retain her form if you will answer one question. What did you hope to gain by removing Randall? Your strategy eludes me. Eventually, we would lead our Players to the hospital and force Jenevieve to return home. You would have anticipated that. You would have also known that your sweet Jenevieve would surrender the weapon of wealth to her persuasive mother. Your Healer is a poor adversary for our Persuader, as their lives in Alaska well proved. So, Alpha, what did you hope to achieve by Randall's removal? All you gained was a delay, which seems a weak strategy, unbefitting of you."

"Zia will not choose Niine."

Fronting Alpha, Kaane said, "She *is* choosing Niine."

"Zia will choose restraint."

"*Restraint?*" Kaane looked again at Zia. "Detonated dynamite sparks less."

His postured steeled, his eyes unrevealing, Alpha said, "I offer a wager."

"A wager?" Kaane's mouth fell open. "The Great Alpha offers a bet?"

"If Zia chooses restraint, you will remove your Player, Monique Duvall, before she takes her twelfth breath."

Behind Kaane's forced laughter and mask of indifference, Alpha saw intrigue, the reaction he had sought. "Let me understand the wager," Kaane said. "You want me to remove the matriarch of Niine's most powerful cluster, disabling a global agenda that spans generations, crosses oceans and continents, and envelopes the media, the politicians, and the lawmakers. What could you possibly offer to match this worth?"

"The first Entity of One—Myself."

Alpha expected Kaane's shock, not his fury. Kaane seized a handful of Souls and shook them at Alpha. "For this? THIS? You give yourself for THIS?" The Souls howled and squealed as Kaane crushed them within his fist. "Shats of particles." Kaane threw the clump at Alpha's feet. They drew apart, injured and crying. Soon, they would regain themselves, would always regain themselves, and would suffer another day. "You were never my brethren," Kaane said, his eyes raking over Alpha, his tone low with disdain. "Never. Let beelzeNiine do with you what he will."

"Then you accept?"

Kaane peered at Zia. Alpha knew he was assessing her sparks—crimson and burgundy, much anger, much hatred. It seemed a sure-win for Kaane, which only furthered Kaane's suspicions. "Restraint? That Soul hasn't a spark of restraint. Bets and trickery from a master strategist, I smell desperation."

Alpha turned as if preparing to leave. "Accepted," Kaane said, "with one caveat. We wager on her restraint, her *self*-restraint. No Guide coercion. Not a single whisper." Kaane thrust out his hand, palm side down. "Well?"

On the outside, Alpha maintained his composure, but on the inside, he faltered. He had intended to encourage Zia's restraint—she had so little of her own. He would have prayed for wisdom, but Zia's sparks were already dotting the walkway to the Duvall estate.

"I'm waiting," Kaane said, exuding more confidence with every second of Alpha's delay. "Have you faith in your Agitator's restraint or not?"

Alpha's eyes closed briefly—*One, forgive me*—then he placed his palm, side up, six inches beneath Kaane's. "Accepted."

Between their hands, molecules whirled and swirled and formed a spinning ball. When the ball filled the breadth of space between their palms, it split—Half soared to Haven, half spiraled to Hades.

O dessa, that slimy, blue-ringed blob, had delivered a lethal bite. I hadn't drowned, hadn't hit my head, and Alpha hadn't removed me. My mother, my monster-mother, Triite, had murdered me. For the betterment of Players, I would lance that ogre Triite right out of his shell.

When I found my old home, I flew inside. Nothing had changed except the aquariums were gone. Not a trace of marine life remained.

Faint singing rose from the kitchen. I started toward it, thinking of all the weapons a kitchen afforded. If Monique stood beneath the ropes tying the cast iron pots, I would concentrate on those ropes until the strands untwined, the iron pots fell, and Monique's head splattered. If that didn't work, I'd topple a candle and blow on the flame until the curtains caught fire and set the house ablaze.

Monique wasn't in the kitchen, as I should have known. She didn't cook or sing. An old radio was playing a waltz. Carlos, the only person I recognized, was dancing with a maid while cleaning girls clapped and waited a turn. I hated them all—all served the festering devil. "TRIITE," I shouted, "I'm coming for you. Wherever you are, I'll get you. DO YOU FEEL ME?"

"Oh my God!" a maid gasped. Briefly, she stared right at me, but then her pupils darted right and left as if I had disappeared. "Did you see it?" She asked again and again. "It was right there. *Right there!* A ghost. A little ghost!"

Everyone's eyes were scanning the room until the maid said, "She was green with red hair." Then most of the staff laughed, a few teasing her about aliens. "I know what I saw," she insisted. "A little green girl with red hair."

"PURPLE HAIR," I hollered, "and I'm not a kid."

I checked the library. No Monique. I glided up the staircase and to the master bedroom. No Monique. But as I turned to leave, I heard humming.

In the master bathroom, the devil was relaxing in a tub of bubbles. A pink mask covered her eyes, but nothing covered her Soul...not from me. Within the cloaking shell of Monique Duvall was the insidious maggot called Triite.

On the wooden ledge framing the tub, a radio played the same cheerful tune that played downstairs. Monique tapped and hummed with the music. She was relishing life, her last few minutes of life. I could hardly wait to see Triite's shock when he slithered from the Player's costume and saw that it was me, Zia, who had stripped him of his power and wealth and returned him to his hideous deformities.

I considered the means for his removal. Water on the floor? No. Players rarely die from a fall. Besides, slipping was too painless. I kept looking around, but I couldn't concentrate—the radio kept playing happy songs.

Stupid, damn radio. I wanted to rip out the cord, tear it from its socket.

*No.* Leave the cord intact and tumble the radio into the bathwater. *YES!*

Death by electrocution. Perfect!

If Malachi could wiggle a finger and cause a picture to fall, then I sure as hell could center my thoughts to knock a radio off a wooden ledge.

I closed my eyes and stoked the fires of hatred and rage, every negative spark within me. When my form glowed in a mass of purples and garnets, I directed my energy to the radio. *Move, move, MOVE!* My arms lashed out.

A thick stream of lava sparks struck the radio. It moved half an inch.

Again and again, I dug into my center, dredged up viciousness and malevolence, and then blasted it toward the radio.

*Thump.* Each time, the radio crept closer to the edge.

*BANG!* A blusterous wind kicked the bedroom shutters.

The noise jarred my attention and stopped Monique's humming. She lifted the corner of her eye-mask. "CARLOS! CLOSE THE SHUTTERS." She resettled with a grumble, "idiots."

The radio was one nudge away from frying the devil. I riled my fury for the final, killing blast.

"I want to go home."

I spun, half-circle.

"Don't you?"

Watching me with big, sad eyes was the little girl from bead space.

When my surprise let up, I said, "What the hell are you doing here?"

"I want to go home, don't you?"

"Where the hell is your Awakening Party?"

She shrugged.

I rushed to the window, looked up at the stars, and hollered, "HEY, what kind of slipshod Awakenings are you guys running up there?"

The little girl tapped me. "I want to go home, don't you?"

*Jeez*, this again. "Listen kid, you should have gone home a long time ago. A long, long time ago. You have to hurry back to Divisional. If you stay on Earth, they'll tag you as a Wanderer, the off-limits kind. You have to go. Go now. There's probably a huge Awakening Party searching everywhere for you. Don't you get it?"

Her head tilted sideways.

Nope, the dim-witted kid didn't get it at all. She just stared at me through her big, green eyes and repeated, "I want to go home, don't you?"

I punched the windowsill. "I can't go home. Don't you get that? I can't go home right now."

Her sad little face drooped with more sadness. She seemed on the verge of tears.

"Aw, crap." I knelt, met her eye-level, and clasped her shoulders. "Listen to me, kid. You have to wish to be where you belong. Not a big wish, like blowing out birthday candles, but just a teensy-tiny wish that comes from your Soul. Then you'll be where you belong. And where you belong is up there." I turned her toward the window and pointed. "See? Up there in the sky. Wait. Past the sky. Go for the stars. No, wait. You might overshoot. Think Saturn. Yeah, Saturn. They'll find you on Saturn. But you have to want to be there. Okay? So want it. Just...just want...*oooh*."

A tidal wave of sickness engulfed me. My hands slid from the kid and hit the floor.

*Jeez, oh, jeez.*

I held my belly and swallowed repeatedly.

*Jeez, oh, jeez.*

Jarring pain came with whirling dizziness that spiked, over and over, like an invisible army was beating the crap out of me—punches, blows, and kicks to my back, belly, and head.

On and on the pummeling continued, on and on.

After what felt like forever, the battering eased.

I lifted my head. The kid was gone, hopefully back to Divisional.

"Please, One, please don't lose her. I know she's annoying, but she's not bad. She's just not bright. So please, One, please don't lose her."

Bruised and aching, I pushed to my feet. In a bent-over stoop, I staggered to Monique. "Bitch. *EEYEOW!*" I nearly dropped to my knees again.

Hunched and hobbled, I started back to the hospital.

# 34

*Damn you, Zia, you and your infectious insanity.*

Kaane swirled to every side of Zia, then above and beneath her. "Where are the vibrations? I'll find them. I will!"

But no outside vibrations had entered the house.

Kaane could see that; Alpha could see that, too.

The child-thing was neither an Energy nor a Guide—"WHO WAS SHE TALKING TO?"—nor apparently visible to Kaane.

While Zia was dragging herself from the house, Kaane cracked the sky with lightning.

The windows rattled.

Monique stood up in the bathtub. With her ninth breath she screamed, "CARLOS, CLOSE THOSE DAMN SHUTTERS. CARLOS!"

She took her tenth breath as she stepped from the tub.

Kaane motioned.

Monique's eleventh breath was a gasp; she slipped and knocked the radio into the tub.

The houselights flickered, and then darkness enveloped the house.

Kaane and an Awakening Party carried off Triite.

○━┱

Geminus and Willow appeared beside Alpha. All three exchanged puzzled looks, but no one spoke.

Much later, Willow broke the silence. "Theories anyone? Anyone?"

"Zia perceives the child as a Wanderer," Alpha said.

Willow shook her head. "That was no Wanderer."

"Nor Figment," Alpha said.

"What's left?" Willow asked. "It certainly wasn't a Guide."

They turned to Geminus, who was still staring at the spot where the child-thing had stood.

"Geminus?" Alpha touched him. "Geminus?"

With a quick shiver, Geminus's attention returned to the Guides. "It was an echo."

"Impossible," Alpha said. "Zia is not a Dyad."

"Nor was it a Dyad's echo," Geminus said. "But it was an echo all the same."

⚷

"An *echo?*" With a disagreeable grunt, Romal changed the window's view from centering on the Guides to spotlighting Haven. "Really, One, did I complain about defiant skioses or reversed tactics? Well, perhaps I did, but only in passing. But now you throw in an echo? From a *non-Dyad?*" His arms crossed. "Hmm. If I didn't know better, I would think you were having sport of me."

With the same ease as crossing a hallway that divides two rooms, Romal stepped from his Corner of the Universe and entered the year 1631. At Zia's initial Awakening, Romal excised a tiny skios from her Soul. It attached to Zia's perception of color, more specifically, the color of the lights topping her head. In Zia's distorted view, she would see those lights as purple. She would never see her light's true color—dark red. Unfortunate, yes, yes, but unavoidable. It was the least consequential skios Romal could find.

"Echoes," Romal muttered as he re-entered his Corner of the Universe.

A Messenger waited.

Romal gave her the skios. "Deliver this to Andromnis. Have the Constructors map the skios's pattern, and then have the Seekers find every Soul, whether Energy or Player, who carries such pattern." He raised an irritable frown toward Haven. "Tell Andromnis that I suspect a third species."

# 35

*His few words about love and concern for others*
*annihilated my million excuses spewed through the night.*

I crawled into the hospital. "Jeez, who turned up the heat? Are we trying to melt the arctic?" I went to Game Town, but I lasted two minutes in the mugginess and stench. "Would somebody open a window?"

Nobody did, so I left for the courtyard. Above the sliding glass doors to the terrace, Malachi was puffing on a hookah pipe. Below him, a group of nurses huddled over a newspaper. "That poor family," a nurse said.

"What a shame," said another, and all nodded and *tsk-tsk'd*.

My head throbbed with their tsking.

Against the demonic glare of the overhead lights, I squinted up at Malachi and asked, "What's the big news?"

He pointed to the paper.

"Can't you just tell me? I'm seeing double."

He pointed again and sucked on his hookah pipe.

I read over the nurse's shoulder: *Monique Duvall Electrocuted.* I wanted to read more, but the nurse flipped the page. A much younger Jen appeared below the caption, *Missing Heiress Sought.*

"That's the girl in the cafeteria," a nurse said.

"No," said another.

"Yes, it is," the others agreed. I wedged in and skimmed the sub-heading: *Duvalls, a Family Plagued in Tragedy or a Family Cursed?*

"Cursed," I told them, "take it from me."

Gruer's footsteps thundered up the hall. Heads perked. The newspaper jostled closed and the staff hustled to look busy.

Malachi eyed me strangely.

"You got a problem?" I said. "If you have something to say, say it."

*Puff, puff, puff.* Only smoke came out his mouth.

"Malachi, I know what you're thinking, and you're wrong. I didn't kill her. But believe what you want; I'm too sick to argue."

Prickly heat started burning my neck and scorching my toes, enough heat to shame the sun. I had to get out, get away from the pulsating lights, the blaring intercoms, and the judgmental Malachi with his stupid pipe.

In the courtyard, I stretched flat across the top of the brick wall. On the tree branch above me, a male mockingbird meowed, crowed and brayed in an unending repertoire of irritating noises to attract a mate. My tolerance ended when I heard, *Azzie-azzie*, the mocking sound of a chainsaw. In my head, I kept screaming, *Shut up! Shut up!* But what left my parched mouth was a feeble, "Shoo. Shoo."

The bird shat on me.

I switched sides. Every part of me ached—ached ten times worse than my hangovers from sipping absinthe all night in France.

Malachi appeared beside the mateless mockingbird. "Miserable?"

I envisioned a cool cloth for my forehead, but it didn't help. "Not now, Malachi, I feel sick, sicker than a Player."

"Hmm. The residue of wickedness."

"Wickedness? *Wickedness?* Is that what this is?"

Malachi nodded. "Rather painful, I've heard."

"Only heard, huh? Why? You've never had a so-called wicked thought?"

"Dear Lady, when I'm a Player, I don't dine on lye and razors, and for much the same reason, when I'm an Energy, I don't ingest negativity and wickedness. It's quite unpleasant, as everyone knows."

"Everyone knows, huh? *Everyone?* Well, I DIDN'T KNOW!"

Malachi chuckled. "You certainly do now."

I lifted a droopy eye. "What do you want? Are you a sadist? Did you come to watch my misery? Take pleasure in my suf—my suf—" My throat seized, my stomach crunched. Icicles shot up my spine and a fire blazed in my head. My vision blurred creating three smoking Malachis when just the one bugged me plenty. I flopped to the pavement and pressed a hot forehead against the cold slate. Relief. An all-too familiar relief—cooling my face on a Paris sidewalk where thousands of shoes had left their dirty mark.

"Malachi, I didn't kill her." I hugged the brittle-cold stone. "You can see by my sparks, I'm not lying. I did not kill her."

"Of course not. Energies cannot remove Players."

"Wrong." I rolled onto my back. "This Energy could have and almost did. Monique had an electric radio by her bathtub, and I moved it. I saw it move. Another inch and—"

"And time would have hiccupped, the radio would have returned to the ledge, but you, Dear Zia, would not have returned to the hospital."

"But I—"

"Think it through, Dear Lady. Imagine a world where Energies could smite Players, where invisible hands could reach down to punish insults and avenge slights. The Player population would sink to zero. Thankfully, Energies cannot remove Players."

"But Guides do."

"Guides are not Energies. They are the fingers of One and Niine."

"Yeah? I know which finger Romal gave me. I guess Alpha is the pinky."

Malachi jiggled with restrained chuckles.

"Spit it out," I told him. "Laugh if you have to, then spit it out."

"Alpha is an extraordinary Guide. Exemplary."

"You got the wrong Alpha. My Alpha has a barkish face, orange eyes, talks like an antique, looks like the Grim Reaper. And he's new."

"He's your *new* Guide, not *a* new Guide. Most Souls are well acquainted with Alpha."

"They know him?" Ignoring the weights in my head, I lifted to my elbows. "How? How do other Souls know him?"

"Dear Lady, back when Energies lacked experience as Players, almost all required intervention during their first few lives. Intervening is tasked to Peril Guides—Peril Guides such as Alpha. Although most Souls became proficient Players well before the Bronze Age, Peril Guides continue to step in whenever an Energy becomes, well—" *puff, puff, puff,* "—a menace."

"A menace? *Me?* That doesn't make sense. I'm experienced. I've had lives all over the globe and under all kinds of conditions."

"Hmm, sounds as though you're still flunking the third grade." Malachi belly laughed, which jangled my nerves long after he vanished.

I crawled beneath a patio table to avoid more bird crap.

Within the hour, break-time began for the day shift. Books and newspapers slapped the tables, cigarette lighters clicked open and closed, and chairs screeched and scraped across the patio slate. A hand reached down and mashed gum under the table. The wad stuck for two seconds before it fell through my nose. Having no strength to even flick off a flea, I escaped the noisy crowd the only way I could; I lowered into my Soul.

While descending, my aches and pains disappeared and a blissful quiet surrounded. No Malachi poking fun, no Players slurping coffee, and no mockingbird trilling for a date. I drifted through swirls of greens and blues, focusing on the light shining up from my square and hoisting my stamina for what I intended to do. With a backward spin, I dove to my core.

Considering how it looked before, my Soul was pretty clean. I kicked aside a scattering of fragments because I hadn't come for them. And I hadn't come for the blue or the green fragment either. I had come for the red, and wow, how the red had grown. Portions now overlapped the blue, casting shadows of eggplant purple.

Kneeling, I looked into the red shard and saw the bulbous face of Triite, a creature I had first encountered after waking from my Paris life. I had ventured outside Divisional to chase what I thought was a Figment...until it cackled, "Still craving absinthe?"

I rushed back to Divisional, but I never told Romal.

Staring into the prism, I had an inkling of why Guides conceal Players' identities. If I hadn't spied on an Awakening, the prism wouldn't contain Triite as BlackDog. While returning from a hunting trip and crossing through a battlefield, BlackDog and I came upon two injured Confederate soldiers. BlackDog clutched one soldier by the hair, yanked the man's head back, and with an, *IEEEE*, slit the man's throat.

BlackDog whooped and danced until he noticed the other soldier, the one still alive at my feet. I admired BlackDog. I thought he was the strongest brave in our tribe. I was scrawny and skittish, and BlackDog's look of contempt caused me to cringe—cringe to my knees and withdraw my knife. With an, *Auieec-ec-ec,* more cough than battle cry, I tried to cut the man's throat. My trembling hand delivered a nicked up shave. I threw the knife and ran. BlackDog despised me. Wanting to regain his approval, I tortured animals and bullied kids.

Romal removed me.

Also in the prism was Triite as Murdock, another identity I wouldn't have learned had I listened to my Guide, stayed put, and not chased after Triite.

Although Murdock was my junior by a year, he was twice my size and weight. When I was fourteen, I told our mother that Murdock had skinned our cat. Days later, Murdock held me down, shoved a razor into my mouth, and tried to cut out my tongue. I fought like crazy, but I was no match for Murdock. The moment the blade pressed against flesh, Murdock whipped the razor, severing my cheek into two flaps.

Although I still had my tongue, I never told on Murdock again.

Finally, Trüte as Monique, *Look at Odessa. Poor Odessa. Pick her up.*

Connecting Trüte to Monique had caused the fragment to swell. The prism was now four times the size of the square's opening. Hour after hour, I broke apart the fragment and carried out the pieces.

When the last of the shards dissolved, euphoric excitement came over me...an excitement to tell Malachi. I climbed to consciousness.

My eyes opened to an enormous eye, two inches from my own, peering at me from behind a magnifying glass. "Gangrene, treatment. Stat. Terrible."

I sprang upright.

The ghost brandished a thermometer, "Won't hurt, won't hurt," and darted to my backside.

I spun around and smacked his hand. "Damn straight it won't hurt."

Malachi appeared. The ghost rushed to him, calling him Dr. Reckmile or Rockmore, something other than Malachi. They talked for a minute before the queer spirit took off muttering, "Nurse on four. Stat. Room three."

Malachi raised an eyebrow. "Be patient with the Good Ghost-Doctor."

"Ghost-Doctor? Do you know where your Ghost-Doctor wanted to stick his thermometer?"

Malachi bubbled with caged laughter.

"IT'S NOT FUNNY! Why doesn't he wake up and smell the year?"

"Dear Lady, in the bleak of night and for all to hear, you shouted a worthy promise to show compassion toward Wanderers."

"I did?"

"You did. Even to those Wanderers who mistake you for the devil. I should think a mistake of your health would be far less insulting."

"Oh. Oh yeah. So you heard that promise, huh? But I—"

"Promises gain merit, not when they're spoken, but when they're tested and held."

"Yeah, but he's creepy."

"If you cannot be compassionate, be tolerant. If you cannot be tolerant, avoid the Good Doctor entirely. He rarely leaves the hallways, and he never enters Game Town."

"Game Town? How come?"

"You'll find the Good Doctor's photograph and history among the pictorial display in the hospital's lobby." *Puff, puff, puff.* "Take interest."

Malachi vanished.

## 36

*But this summer, herds of spiritualists
contaminated our town.*

"Squawking reporters descended like a murder of crows." That was Gruer's way of apologizing to Perriman for mistaking him for a newsman and calling security.

But Perriman wasn't mad. The moment he glimpsed Jen, his hand fluttered in pats to his chest. "Oh, thank God, thank God." For years, his own investigators had searched for Jen, "unbeknownst to Mrs. Duvall," he said. "Mrs. Duvall insisted Jenevieve was visiting relatives."

Perriman's detectives could neither confirm nor refute Monique's story. So when a hospital worker leaked Jen's whereabouts to the press, Perriman cut his vacation short and caught the next flight to San Francisco.

Inside Gruer's office, Perriman explained that Randall bequeathed a generous monthly stipend to Jen until her 21st birthday. "Then the entire estate transfers to Ms. Duvall," Perriman told everyone.

His news didn't surprise Gruer, but it sure surprised Jen, though not in a good way. She wanted the life of Jennifer Smith, cafeteria worker, and that's all she wanted.

"Honey," Claire said, "you'll always be Jennifer Smith to me. Money won't change that. But money will help you get an apartment."

"She can buy the building," Gruer said.

"She can purchase the block," Perriman added.

Claire hushed them. "Jennifer, nobody is going to take away your job, and nobody can take you out of my heart. I promise."

With that assurance, Jen secured an apartment a few blocks from the hospital and lived on a pittance of her monthly allowance. She directed Perriman to give her unused balance to the St. Luke's Hospital Fund.

This bugged Perriman. "It was your father's wish that you should want for nothing."

"Then his wish came true," Jen said. "I'm happy and safe and working with people I love. That's all I want, a simple life."

But Jen didn't live the life she wanted.

Newsmen dogged her as she walked to and from the hospital. Jen pushed past, refusing to give interviews.

Desperate, reporters swarmed the cafeteria and waved money at nurses for gossip.

Claire called security.

After that, everyone had to show a tag that connected them to a patient or to the staff.

Still, a few reporters slipped past security so Claire stayed alert. When she or Rosa suspected a snoop, they rang a bell. Then Jen would duck into the breakroom while Claire determined the man's business.

Weeks later, Jen suffered a spell of headaches. Her staggering and aspirin-eating caught Claire's notice.

A frazzled Claire was then keeping one dubious eye on every stranger and one worried eye on Jen.

Despite everyone's efforts, a photographer weaseled into the kitchen and snapped a picture of Jen scrubbing the kitchen floor on her hands and knees.

He tore out of the cafeteria and ran across the parking lot. I stayed right above him. While he was fumbling for his car keys, I thought of asking a rabid squirrel to jump from a tree and lop off his nose.

I thought of it, I wanted it, and I came close to doing it.

But I didn't.

The pain of swallowing wickedness had nothing to do with my decision; that pain eventually goes away.

But if I broke my promise to Malachi, his disappointment would cause me a different kind of pain...the kind that lingers for a long, long time.

I kept my promise; I did not interfere.

# 37

*I never called a cop. Never.*
*I called a friend.*

Gruer shuffled the newspaper closed, her veins ridging her neck. "Good woman," Malachi whispered, "calm yourself." Though Gruer's life-cord was firmly attached, she was not immune to a debilitating stroke. "Slow down. Calm yourself." But Gruer thundered down the hall, her fist clenching the paper, her Soul ignoring Malachi's whispers, "Deep breaths. Easy now."

Gruer punched the cafeteria doors, marched to a table, and slapped down the morning news. Wings of paper spilled. "Claire, did you read this trash?"

Nurses scrambled to lid their coffees and make their escape.

Jen and Rosa froze. Claire untied her apron and handed her spatula to Rosa. "Honey, take over. I'll be in the breakroom with Nurse Gruer."

Gruer's face, now swollen and red, heightened Malachi's concerns. Back when Christian Gruer died, the Good Woman's color had drained, anguish stealing every spot of pink from her cheeks. Then the Good Woman ate...and ate...and ate...burying her broken heart beneath pounds of flesh.

Adrenaline now fought against that flesh.

The Good Woman was blistering red. Malachi's eyes blued.

In the breakroom, Claire coaxed Gruer into a chair. "You need a doctor."

"Nonsense. I can take care of myself."

Claire dampened two towels. She wrapped the first around Gruer's neck and used the second to cool Gruer's cheeks and forehead. "Margaret, you can't take care of nothing if you give yourself a heart-attack."

Gruer batted the hand. "Stop fussing. I'm not a child."

"Margaret, either you cool your forehead until your tomato face is a pretty peach or I will strap you down and get a doctor in here."

Gruer snatched the towel and began blotting her own face. "Did you see the front page? How in the world did they get that picture?"

"It was bound to happen."

"Half twisted truths. They don't care who they hurt."

"Margaret, it's just a filthy rag."

"Well, this filthy rag implied a competency hearing. *Duvall heiress, scullery worker; brainwashed or insane?* Worthless trash."

"We've had our share of bad publicity, and we've always handled it without a coronary. Is there something more upsetting you?"

Gruer looked away.

"Marvelous insight, Lady Claire," Malachi answered. "Please press on."

Claire pulled a chair around. "Come on, Margaret. What is it?"

"Mr. Perriman delivered a notable sum to my office. He said to expect the same on the first of every month. God knows we can use the money, but Claire, it doesn't feel right, nor does it look right in the eyes of the public. We have a millionaire minor on her hands and knees scouring kitchen floors while granting us sizeable amounts of her inheritance. This has to stop. In all good conscience, I cannot allow that child to be used as fodder for malicious gossip. And that's exactly what this world has come to—selfishness expected, selflessness attacked."

"I understand, but—"

"Don't argue with me, Claire. I've made up my mind. Jenevieve cannot mop floors. I know she wants to, but I cannot permit it. The publicity is too damaging, both for her and for this hospital's reputation."

"Margaret, let me speak. I agree with you; Jen shouldn't be mopping floors. And I think the pressure is giving her headaches."

"Headaches?"

"She tells me no, but she squints and flinches quite a bit. And I've seen her swallowing aspirin too many times. Maybe it's the long hours or the pressure of dodging reporters or the smell of the cleaning fluids. Most likely, it's everything combined. When I tell her to rest, she works harder. Lord, that bitty thing is as stubborn as you. But I have an idea."

Gruer snorted with cynicism, though she didn't say a word.

"Go on, Lady Claire," Malachi said. "The Good Woman is listening."

"On breaks and at quitting time," Claire said, "Jen goes upstairs and reads to the kids in Game Town. Regina Logan says that the little ones really take to her. The minute Jen enters the room, the kids light up, especially the foreign kids. Jen speaks French, German, and Spanish. So, why don't we move her upstairs, give her that empty office down the hall from yours, and call her a benefactor instead of a volunteer. Regina can train her to help with the nurses. As long as Jen feels needed, she won't feel rejected."

"Brilliant idea," Malachi said. "Bravo, Lady Claire, bravo."

But Gruer pondered the idea with twisted lips.

"It takes her off the kitchen floor," Claire said, "and it keeps her a working part of the hospital. Regina and the other nurses could sure use the help, and the kids could always use a little more attention. Everybody wins."

"Good Woman," Malachi whispered, "move beyond your ego. Though the solution springs from another, embrace it. It's an excellent idea."

"I'll think about it," Gruer said, "and *I* will make the decision."

*Schklink.* The sound of breaking glass came from the kitchen. "Enough of this nonsense," Gruer said. "I have work to do, and you have a butter-fingers to scold."

Claire returned to the kitchen. Gruer went to the sink, splashed cool water on her face, and then toweled her neck and forehead. When she set the towel down, she noticed one of Jen's books left on the counter. *The Little Prince.* She smiled.

Malachi smiled, too. "Oh yes, Christian Gruer's favorite story. Night after night, you, my Good Mother, read me that book. Though the pages became tattered, your eyes never faltered and my delight never waned. Such a marvelous message rose from those pages, a message of love."

Gruer's hand fleeted across the cover. "Chris," left her lips in an airy whisper.

Malachi hugged her. "Take strength, Good Woman, strength from all the love surrounding you."

Gruer wiped her eyes, pulled back her shoulders, and marched from the breakroom, her heels hitting hard across the cafeteria floor. At the swinging doors, she stopped, turned around, and shouted, "Miss Brown."

A hush fell over the room. All heads lifted.

"That Nursing School did the world an injustice. They should have waived your tuition. You would have made a fine nurse, Miss Brown. One of the best." She punctuated her statement with a sharp nod. "One of the best!"

Bewildered faces jogged back and forth between Gruer and Claire.

A nonchalant Claire cracked two eggs onto the grill. "Margaret Gruer, you're just an old sentimental fool."

Claire and Gruer exchanged a look. Though it lasted a split-second, Malachi caught its entire meaning. The spark in their eyes told of an enduring friendship, and it apologized, forgave, and embraced, all within a heartbeat.

# 38

*Despite Father-Time's best effort, there's a leftover tile.*
*It just doesn't fit. Not anywhere. Not anymore.*

Morning and evening, walking to and from work, Jen was confronted by a battalion of reporters. They yelled out questions, begged for her interview, and hurled accusations to goad her response. But Jen held tight, never uttering a word. She didn't want attention or fame; she wanted the simple life of Jennifer Smith. Everyone and everything attached to Jenevieve Duvall, Jen shut out...with one exception.

Jen hurried to answer the late-night knock. "Come in, come in." And in walked a dark-haired girl—*girl* this time, not even a woman—dressed in the modern-day garb of soothsayers; hoop earrings, grungy bandana, beaded necklace. The girl hugged Jen; their kind always hugged Jen. And Jen said, "I heard you're gifted," because Jen has always heard that they're gifted.

"She's full of crap," I told Jen, because they're always full of crap. "She just wants your money." But Jen gave her a check because all Jen wanted was an answer that either confirmed or absolved her guilt over Pierre's death. Despite my years of whispering, I had lightened only half of Jen's inky-blue.

The girl picked up the frame displaying the crumpled photo of Pierre. "Is this your brother?"

Instead of, *hey, you're the gifted girl, you tell me*, Jen said, "Yes."

"That's strange," the girl said, "because I'm sensing the spirit of a little girl, not a little boy." The soothsayer looked in my direction. I flitted to the ceiling. The girl's gaze followed. She mumbled, "An angry spirit."

*LIAR,* I shouted, startling the girl.

Jen wrung her hands. "Does she know Pierre?"

I moved to the far wall. The girl's pupils dogged me. "I'm not sure."

As soothsayers go, this one bugged me the most. Others fed Jen crap, and Jen slept soundly when well fed on crap. But this soothsayer confused everything. "No, it's not a little boy. I'm sorry. No, it's not your nanny, Katy. I'm sorry. It's a small spirit with bad vibes."

*STOP SAYING THAT!* My shout spilled the girl backwards.

When she got to her feet, she dug into her pocket and pulled out two thick bundles of tied leaves. She shoved them at Jen. "Burn them," she said. "The smoke gets rid of angry spirits." She hurried to the door. Jen pleaded with her to stay, but the girl said, "No way. Bad vibes." She threw down Jen's check, "Burn the smudge sticks tonight," and left.

Jen lit one of the bundles, started coughing, and then dumped the bundle into the sink. That night, she cried, but harder and longer than she had cried in months. I couldn't whisper anything nice because every atom in my being was cursing the soothsayers. *As One is my witness, I'm going to get those bullshitters. I swear it. When next a Player, I will break their crystal balls.*

The following morning at the hospital, Claire took Jen upstairs to an empty room. She said it was Jen's new office, which sounded to me like a promotion. But Jen didn't act that way. She stopped in the doorway. I flew right past and over to the window. "Jen, look, a courtyard view."

"Are you sure about this?" Jen asked. "Do they really need me up here?"

"Tell her yes," I coaxed Claire while jumping on the couch, *twang-twang-twang*, and imagining the sound of its springs. "Yes, yes, yes. Tell her an office with a courtyard view beats a kitchen with fat-filled steam any day."

Claire pulled two chairs together. "Let's talk." She scooped Jen's hands into her own. "Tommy O'Brien is walking on that prosthetic leg now."

I stopped bouncing, wondering where Claire was going with this.

"After his amputation," Claire said, "that child was mad at the world. He wouldn't talk, wouldn't walk, wouldn't eat. He just closed up inside of himself. But after you spent time with the boy, he's eating, gaining weight, and chattering so much, the nurses can't shush him up."

"I didn't do anything," Jen said. "All I—"

Claire pressed a finger to Jen's lips. "Baby, he's not the only child you've shined your light upon. Medicine might heal the body, but it doesn't restore the Soul. From the time I was a bitty girl, all I ever dreamed about was becoming a nurse. I pictured myself wearing that pressed linen dress and assisting the doctors and comforting the sick. I felt it so strongly, I thought it was my calling. But the Good Lord thought otherwise. And through the years, I've come to thank Him a thousand times." She squeezed Jen's hands. "Make that a thousand and one. Understand? I think the Good Lord has special plans for you, plans outside the kitchen. Just give it a try, honey. That's all I'm asking. Give it a try. All right?"

"But what will I do here?"

"Nurse Logan will train you to help on the floor. In your spare time, you could plan a reading program for the kids."

"I can do that?" Jen was finally getting excited. "A reading program?"

"Forget that," I told her. "You can sit back and relax all day."

While Jen was staring at the empty bookshelves, a huge smile spread across her face. "Claire, I'll come visit you at least once a day, every day."

"You better. But don't expect me to serve up your meals. You come behind the counter and get your own."

Jen's arms wrapped around Claire's neck. "I love you, Claire."

"I love you, too, baby," Claire said. "My goodness, such a fuss. You're on another floor, not on another planet. Get yourself settled in, then report to Nurse Logan. But don't forget to come down for supper. Okay?"

Jen nodded and looked again at the bookshelves. "It's kind of exciting."

Claire brushed Jen's cheek. "I want to hear that again after you've emptied your first bedpan." Claire kissed Jen's forehead and then walked out.

Jen spun around in her chair. She investigated the desk drawers and ran her hand across the bookshelf planks while I jigged a happy-dance. "Jen, this is great. GREAT!"

I flew after Claire to thank her.

Claire was around the corner, slumped against a wall. "What's wrong?" I asked because she was sniffling into cupped hands while tears leaked between her fingers. My tongue rummaged inside my cheek. *Crap.* I sank to the floor and examined the tiles. They needed waxing. Maybe replacing. Lots of gouges. I looked up—still crying—then back to the floor. Someone should fill in the grooves. Either clean the tiles or replace them. Stupid floor. I scraped at something sticky. Probably gum. Some slob put gum on the floor. I picked at it, glanced down the hallway, then picked at the gum again.

Finally, somebody noticed Claire and approached, "Are you okay?"

"Are you blind?" I said. "She's crying. FIX IT!"

"I'm fine," Claire said. "I just pinched my finger in a drawer."

*Pinched your finger?* I bobbed to see Claire's pinched finger, but she buried her hands into pockets and walked off.

Over time, Jen learned to cool foreheads, chart temperatures, and of course empty bedpans. When she finished her daily assignments, she sang nursery rhymes to the toddlers, taught phonics to the preschoolers, and read adventure stories to the older kids.

Whether toddler or teen, kids were equally mesmerized by Jen; they *ooh*'d and *aww'd* through Cheerio'd mouths.

Within the year, a new console television replaced the old Emerson box. Jen purchased Lincoln Logs and Tinker Toys then taught frail fingers how to create windmills and cabins. She bought Raggedy Anns for the girls and Mr. Potato Heads for the boys. The first time a kid stuck a pipe into the lopsided potato, I took a jab at Malachi. "Hey, this spud-face looks like you."

Malachi grinned. "You're too gracious. He's quite the Dapper Dan."

*Dapper Dan?* Malachi took all the fun out of insults.

On Jen's twenty-first birthday, she rolled a chunk of the Duvall estate into the Hospital Fund. Stalled plans for a north wing became a sudden flurry of funded construction. Later, diagnostic equipment, computerized lab machines, and state-of-the-art scanners transformed the once limping St. Luke's Hospital into a leading medical center—that's what Gruer called it— that attracted pediatric specialists. Five years after that came a building for research and teaching.

Rosa met and married an electrician who had been working on the new wing. Soon after, she became pregnant and stayed home to raise twin boys.

Jen bought an apartment complex and let student nurses stay rent-free. Over time, her timid gait became a confident stride. She stopped emptying bedpans and devoted fourteen hours a day to a program she developed called LITS, *Literature Inspires The Spirit.* But no matter how busy her schedule— charts, paperwork, meetings—Jen kept her promise to Claire and visited her daily in the kitchen. Both Claire and Gruer refused to retire.

Long ago, I had run out of questions for Malachi. So instead of bugging him for answers, I tried teaching him fun things to do—jigging, show-tunes, long-distance spitting. But in return, he tried to teach me boring stuff—chess, archery, Shakespeare. Plain and simple, Jen and Malachi were lousy at fun. Jen was always teaching; Malachi always preaching.

"Dear Lady, they are neither penguins nor crows," he lectured. "They are the good sisters of The Holy Cross."

"They're not that good or they would let us watch *The Three Stooges.*"

"Impressionable children imitate the injurious acts of—"

"Aw, jeez, it was one poked eye." I kicked a rock. "What's the big deal? The kid had two."

I languished on the floor in Game Town because nothing changed for me. Nothing. Nothing except the stupid programs on the television box.

# 39

*I was his only friend.*
*Well, me and a little fairy Will dreamed up.*

While Alpha was keeping watch on Zia, Romal appeared, "Ahem," and turned Alpha's attention. "You're misinterpreting Zia's vibrations."

"Untrue. They are vibrations of gravity."

"Yes, yes, they most certainly are...vibrations of grave loneliness."

Alpha's posture stiffened. "Untrue."

"Grave loneliness to the point of bitter stagnation."

"She has the companionship of the Finisher."

"Teachers and mentors are not companions in the eyes of an adolescent."

Alpha huffed. "She is not an adolescent."

"No, no, she certainly is not," Romal said. "But you drew the comparison. You would do well to honor it."

All day, kids camped in Game Town waiting for the evening movie. After dinner, nurses rolled in gurneys and wheelchairs strung with drips. Attendants unfolded dozens of chairs, and Jen lined the floor with cushions.

I sat on one arm of the sofa, an attendant sat on the other, and between us, four little boys fidgeted. When the movie began, the lights dimmed and the kids calmed. The film started in black and white, changing to color later. A brown haired girl, who looked like Young-Jen, landed in a place called Oz.

The movie captivated all the kids.

All except one.

The new boy, nine or ten years old, wore a scowl. When asked if he wanted a blanket or a glass of water, the kid snarled, "What's it to you?"

While watching the movie, I caught the kid glancing in my direction. Nobody was behind me or digging in the toy bins, so I shrugged it off.

When the wicked witch appeared on the screen, I checked for the kid's reaction. He was staring at me, not through me or past me, but right at me. "She's mean and green," he said, "like *you!*"

I fell off the couch.

When I popped back up, I glided over to the wall...and took the kid's attention with me. I pointed to my chest.

The kid's eyes narrowed...and he nodded!

"MALACHI, MALACHI, *MALACHIII.*"

Malachi appeared cupping his ears. "Good heavens, Dear Lady, what fiend has cursed the universe by endowing your shrill?"

I pulled Malachi around. "Watch the boy on the end. Watch him. Watch." I waved at the kid.

The boy stuck out his tongue.

I thumped on Malachi's chest. "He can see us. He can see us."

"Nonsense. He's simply bored with the movie."

"Yeah? You think so?" I glided to the ceiling. The boy's neck craned back. I moved across the room to the far wall. The boy wiggled onto his knees and twisted around to peer over the backside of the couch. When the attendant tried to straighten him, the kid jerked defiantly.

"Extraordinary," Malachi said. *Puff, puff, puff.* As he came to my side, he left a thick, chugging smoke trail across the room.

"Ditch the pipe," I told him. "If the kid thinks your smoke is real, he might start coughing."

"Unlikely, Dear Zia." Malachi squared a smoke ring by pinching it four times to fashion corners. He spooled up the bottom as if he were rolling up a shade. "The lad's veil is lifted for you."

"Veil? What veil? Malachi, if he can see me, then he can see you."

"Splendid reasoning, but you're confusing a Player's eye with a Mind's eye. The boy does not see me, and for that, Dear Lady, I am grateful. My form might frighten the child."

"Naw. Your form wouldn't frighten a flea. You're just a mountainous, turquoise, pipe-smoking teddy bear. Kids see that all the time."

Malachi chuckled. "While I fancy your description, I doubt the lad would share your view. He might mistake me for a moss-covered Big Foot, that mythical fellow who wanders the northern forests. Or he might believe I'm a Neanderthal, still stained with the algae of evolution."

While Malachi talked on, I made goofy faces at the kid, but I couldn't get him to laugh. I couldn't even get him to smile. "What's your name?" I asked. He didn't seem to hear me, so I hollered, "TELL ME YOUR NAME."

"He cannot hear you, Dear Zia, that is for certain."

"Why? If he can see me, why can't he hear me?"

"What does one have to do with the other? Veils cloak reality. You're real, but your words are not. An Energy's speech is an illusion to communicate in a familiar way. But a Player cannot hear us because we don't actually speak. Only a Guide's words are tangible."

I made another face at the kid.

Malachi started to drift away. "Good night, Dear Lady, I must attend to the Good Woman. Enjoy your new friend."

"Wait. If I scream or shout, will he—"

"Neither your insistence nor your volume will solidify your words. At best, the boy will hear a buzzing sound, the hymn of a mosquito or a bee."

"Wait."

"Really, Dear Zia, I've dallied long enough. I have obligations to keep."

"But the kid said—uhm, uhm." My fingers twisted and twined.

Malachi's huge hand cupped over my nervous fingers to hold them still. "What did the young fellow say?"

I swallowed. "That I'm—I'm green, ugly green, like the wicked witch in the movie. Tell me honestly, Malachi, am I puke-green?"

Malachi flickered with genuine surprise. His surprise was good enough for me, but not for Malachi. His burly arms swallowed me. "You are not puke-green. Such an atrocious term by any account. You are emerald green, a precious gem. Emerald green, do you hear me?"

I did, but he was squashing me against his chest. "Mooglegoogleurf."

"Why, your color is the honored color of the city that those characters seek."

I squirmed free. "They do?"

"They do, Dear Zia. Their destiny depends on it."

"No foolin'?" I listened intently to the television box. After a few minutes, I heard, *Emerald City.* They were heading to *Emerald City.*

I smiled at my big, bear friend.

He gave a reassuring nod. "EMERALD GREEN," he boomed, "that's what you are. Emerald green. Be *prrroud!*" He rolled his Rs like the lion in the movie, "*Prrroud,*" and disappeared.

## 40

*Billy jiggled, his eyes crossing, his tongue sputtering, and, dammit, I smiled; the kid had the loony-face down pat.*

The nuns called him William—*William, don't flick your peas at the nurses.* While tutoring his reading, Jen called him Will—*Will, if you don't like the book, I'll set it aside, but let's not rip out the pages.* And Game Town's attendant called him Little Man—*Lookin' good, Little Man, lookin' good.*

The attendant lied; Will never looked good.

His clay-gray skin sagged, and he wiggled and bobbed as though he were built without bones. And all that wiggling and bobbing caused him to puke—puke so often, an acrid odor seeped from his pores.

But I didn't care if he stank worse than limburger cheese because Will could see me. And I didn't care about his medical charts because I could see Will's life-cord, and that life-cord was thinning, and not just at the base where the cord connects to the head. Will's entire outer shell was dissolving.

I didn't know what was making Will sick, but I did know one thing for sure; he wouldn't be leaving the hospital as a Player.

At the start of our friendship, Will seized the top rank in the pecking order of kids. "I'm older," he said, and he thumbed his chest. "Okay?"

He was stealing the power position, the one who chooses the games to play and the channels to watch—the almighty power of the oldest. Even twins know the rules; the first from the womb will eventually declare, *I'm a minute older.* The second twin will try to argue, *minutes don't count.* But of course minutes count. Seconds count. Age dominates. And I was the oldest and deserved the top rank.

My heel thumped, my arms folded.

Will leaned into my face and hollered, "OKAY?"

*Jeez.* I caved, nodding.

To learn my name—or close to it—Will dumped a can of plastic letters. He told me to point, but I couldn't spot a Z on top of the heap. I motioned for Will to spread them out, but he didn't understand.

He insisted I hurry up, *hurry up!*

Feeling pressured, I pointed to an S, then to an I, then to an A.

Will lined up the letters. "RIGHT?" His hands clenched, his knuckles whitened, but he seemed more desperate than mad. I gave a thumbs up and Will relaxed, but only for a minute. His frustration reared again when he poked the letters, prodding them to speak.

Will couldn't read.

I pointed to the little girl on the couch.

After much head shaking and eye rolling, Will finally gave in and asked the little girl, "Lylah, what does that spell?"

Lylah craned toward the letters, but she spoke too soft for human ears.

"TALK LOUDER," Will shouted.

Lylah slid from the sofa and whispered, "Sia," whistling the S and using the long I.

Will turned to me and hollered, "RIGHT?"

I nodded and nodded. *Jeez,* Will was a tense kid.

"Who are you talking to?" Lylah asked.

"A green troll," Will said.

I let it go because I wasn't puke-green and I wasn't troll-green. I was emerald-green; Malachi had told me so.

Lylah was five or six and smelled of baby powder. Her tuffs of yellow fuzz covered an otherwise bald head. Her heart-shaped lips, red-rimmed eyes, and cotton-white skin reminded me of rose petals tossed in the snow. Unlike her life-cord, thick and strong, Lylah's voice was thin and urgent and never louder than a whisper. If a nurse asked Lylah what she had for dinner, Lylah's hands would flourish at her chest, and she would glance the room for eavesdroppers. "Rice and cheese," she would whisper as if imparting a dire secret or answering the great mystery of life. She followed her revelations with a quirky tip of her head, as if to say, *you know what that means?*

Nobody had a clue, but everybody nodded...and smiled. Lylah drew affection the way a little, white bunny draws affection; you just want to hold it, love it, and calm its urgent jittering.

Most of the kids steered clear of Will, but Lylah shadowed him. Later that week, Lylah tried to join Will and me as we struggled to play Go-Fish—struggled like always. Will would fan my cards, flash them an inch from my nose, and then slap them face down. He would ask for a number, honestly expecting me to have memorized those cards. If I pointed to the wrong card, or worse, I shrugged, Will called me stupid and dumb. Then he'd raise the cards for another two seconds, slap them down, and ask again, "Any sevens?"

God-forbid the wrath of Will should I shrug a second time. Will would throw the deck of cards into my face. That's how our games usually ended. But this time, our game ended when Lylah asked to play and Will shoved her. "Get away." He shoved her hard, too.

I went to the couch and sulked beside Lylah. Together, we watched Casper cartoons.

Several times, Will called me dumb. He got out the box of checkers—our favorite game because it's easily played by pointing. Then Will rolled back and forth, playing both sides of the board. He grumbled that he didn't want to play with a troll anyway. A dumb troll.

Lylah's thumb went into her mouth, and she snuggled down on the couch, her head landing on my lap.

Will perked, glowering, but I pretended not to notice. I patted Lylah's fuzzy head. "You're lying on a troll," Will told her. "She's going to bite you."

"Naw-uh," Lylah said. "You're just mean." Her thumb plunked back into her mouth.

Fuming, Will returned to his checkers. He looked at the black pieces, then at the red, then back and forth, as though he were trying to remember which side had the next move. "Dumb troll." He flipped the board over, ending his own game. After a minute, he lifted onto his knees. "Are you going to play with me or not?"

"I do want to play, but you—"

"NOT YOU!" Will hollered at Lylah before he jabbed a finger toward me. "YOU! Are you going to play with me or not?"

My mouth tightened, and I gestured to the head on my lap.

"NO!" Will said. "I don't want to play with her."

I turned again to the cartoons.

After much grumbling, Will said, "All *riiight*," as if he were making the mother of all sacrifices. "All *riiight*, Lylah, you can play with us."

Delighted, Lylah slid from the couch. Will pushed aside the checkers and brought out the cards. We played Go-Fish, only now, Lylah held my cards for me. "Do you got any Jacks?" Will said.

"Do you want me to check?" Lylah asked.

"No," Will told her. "Just hold the cards." He glared at me. "Any Jacks?"

I tapped the backside of a Jack.

Will plucked the card from Lylah's hand.

"Oooh!" Lylah's thick bunny-lashes fluttered. "Your troll is *reeeal.*" Her free hand patted her chest as if to remind her lungs to breathe.

I had never seen a kid more awed, and I guess Will hadn't either. He sat two inches taller, and his face wore a full blush. From then on, Will invited Lylah to join all of our games. Within weeks, the three of us were inseparable, although Will had rules to our friendship.

If I gave too much notice to Lylah, Will would order me off the couch. If Lylah asked too many questions about me, Will would tell her that I was a bloodthirsty troll that bites. But this Mean-Will was a Scared-Will—scared of losing his audience because Will loved to entertain. To that, Lylah gave Will something I couldn't—sound. Lylah's appreciation came in giggles, laughter, and applause. My appreciation was mimed.

When we watched the television box, Will wanted Lylah and me at opposite ends of the couch so he could sit in the middle, center stage. Then my bee-buzzing noise joined their two voices to sing the opening jingles of our favorite shows.

Weeks later, at the start of the *Beverly Hillbillies,* Will did more than just sing; he did something the nurses forbade him to do. He got up and tried to dance. *Tried,* but his limbs floundered and flopped. Then he puked.

He slipped in the vomit and sliced his neck on the table's metal railing.

The attendant, a few steps outside the doorway, heard Lylah's faint cry. He rushed in and took Will away.

Will didn't come back to Game Town for five days—five, quiet, worrisome days for Lylah and me. When Will finally returned, he posed like Superman—head turned, fists on hips—to show off the X's lining his throat.

After *oooh*ing, Lylah excitedly told Will about a new show called *Lost in Space* that featured a boy-astronaut named Will. "Will Robinson," Lylah said in her typical breathless whisper. She added her quirky head tip, *you know what that means?* Will and I nodded to make her happy.

*Lost in Space* became our favorite show, not only because Will shared the same name, but also because Will dreamed of becoming an astronaut.

At the end of each episode, Will and I horsed around, pretending to be characters in the show. I played the role of Penny, the snoopy girl who was always sticking her nose in places it didn't belong, and Will played the role of the robot, the mechanical guard with venting-hose arms that swung up and down when the robot warned, "Danger, Will Robinson, danger, danger."

Though Lylah was our sole audience, she laughed and clapped with more zeal than ten kids. As our bonds grew stronger, Will stopped calling me a troll, even when he was mad. Instead, he called me a fairy. The staff called me, *Will's pretend-friend*, with a *wink-wink*, as if the wink was part of the name.

I didn't mind, but Lylah sure did. "It's not pretend," she said in her loudest whisper. "It's *reeeal.*" Then she put a finger to her lips. Whether she was telling them to hush up or keep it a secret, Will and I didn't know. All the same, Will beamed, proud that Lylah believed and defended him.

He rewarded her loyalty by changing our positions on the couch. Lylah sat in the middle. At times, she even rested her head on my lap...and Will allowed it, sometimes even showing concern for me. "You're squishing the fairy."

Each day, Jen tutored Will in reading. When his lesson started, Jen would turn off the television box, and Lylah and I would move to the toy bins so we wouldn't distract Will. If Will focused on his schooling, he would finish in time for *Gilligan's Island.*

After forty minutes of Dick and Jane, the books closed. Lylah and I hurried to join Will on the couch. Instead of Jen turning on the box, she asked Will, "Tell me about your invisible friend."

Will shot a blaming frown at me for causing Gilligan's delay.

"It's a *fairrry,*" Lylah said.

"Lylah, can you see the fairy?" Jen asked.

Lylah shook her head. "Only Will."

"Will, can you describe the fairy?"

An irritable Will said, "Then can we watch Gilligan?"

"Sure," Jen told him.

As Will looked me over, Jen's eyes flitted about in my direction.

"I think it's a kid like us," Will said.

"Yeah," Lylah said, "only a *fairrry.*"

"A boy fairy or a girl fairy?" Jen asked.

*Ohhh,* I slumped, now realizing what was prompting Jen's questions. *Someday, I'm going to get those soothsayers;* I chiseled that promise into my core.

"A girl fairy," Will said. "Green all over, except for her hair. Her hair is dark red and really messy."

"It's purple," I muttered, though not really caring.

Jen tried to smile through her disappointment. "Don't forget to do your homework. I'll see you on Thursday."

Lylah reached out with wiggling fingers.

Jen swept her up, kissed her nose, and then set her down next to Will.

After turning on the box and changing the channel to Gilligan, Jen left.

I curled at the end of the couch. Nothing on the box registered. *As One is my witness, I'm going to break their crystal balls.*

A while later, a tiny finger touched my cheek. Briefly, a dab of inky-blue shimmered on Lylah's fingertip. "I see you," she whispered, her voice extra soft with awe. "You're not a fairy. You're an—an angel."

*Angel? Whoa!* No one had ever mistaken me for an angel. A devil, sure, a troll, lately, but an angel? Never. Never until now.

Lylah whispered for Will's attention, which was firmly fixed on Gilligan. Pulling in a big breath to muster volume, Lylah said, "Will, I can see the green angel. Will, look, look, she's crying."

I was gesturing and shrugging that it was no big deal, but Lylah wouldn't quit. "Will, Will, Will."

Then Will snapped, "WHAT?"

Lylah lifted to her knees and raised her little, pink nose to Will's stiff chin. "Angels...cry...blue." She gave her quirky nod—*you know what that means?*—jabbed a thumb into her mouth, and flopped backwards on the couch.

As Will looked at me, his breaths came huffing from his nostrils. He rapped his knuckles against his head, as if he were trying to figure out how to fix a great problem. Suddenly, he wagged a scolding finger at me. "Don't cry anymore. Okay? OKAY?"

That was all Will said, but that was all he needed to say. Good friends say a lot with very few words. I mouthed, *Okay.*

With a satisfied smile, Will turned back to the TV.

At the end of the show, the attendant, who always sat in the corner, left to check on the dinners. We were halfway through the next show when Will bowled over and blasted chunks. Steamy, acrid vomit landed on the floor and splashed on Lylah's legs. But Will puked so often, I said, "Jeez, give a girl some warning," before I saw Will's face. Green. The kind of green that should never be seen on a Player. Mucus bubbled at his mouth. *Damn.*

I hit the call button, but no bell rang. *Damn, Damn, Damn!* I started yelling—*Bzzzz*—but my bee-buzzing gained no attention.

Will's eyes closed, his body keeled sideways, and his head landed on Lylah's lap. I flew to the closest station and screamed at the shift nurse. *Bzzzz.* She batted her eyes at a doctor. I bit my lip and concentrated, *Go to Game Town....Go to Game Town...Go to Game Town..*

Finally, the nurse's wooing ended, and she strolled off to check on the kids. Will had spewed a bunch more times. Puke dripped from Lylah's ankles, though she didn't care. She was curled over Will, her lips grazing his earlobe as she sang him a show tune.

*"...you sit right back to hear a tale, a tale of a frightful ship..."*

Poor Will hadn't an ounce of strength or he would have yelled at her for singing it wrong.

When the nurse saw the piles of puke, she started shouting and hitting buttons that beeped and glowed. Immediately, the room filled with staff and upheaval. An attendant swooped up Lylah and set her on a rolling bed away from the chaos. I went to Lylah. With my hand resting on hers, we sang to stay strong.

*"...a tree at our door...a tree at our door..."*

My eyes closed to send off a vibration. "One, I know I promised to talk to you more, and I will...someday. But right now, I need a favor. Could you please help Will? If he's going to stick around, can you ease up on his pain? It probably hurts an awful lot to barf so much. But if Will is going home, can you keep an eye on his Awakening? I would hate to see him wandering like the Ghost-Doctor. Thanks for listening. Zia, Order of Agitators."

When my eyes reopened, Will and most of the staff were gone.

"Is Will going to heaven?" Lylah asked.

How could I answer? If I nodded and Will recovered, Lylah would think I had lied. If I shook my head and Will never returned, Lylah might think he had gone to hell. The nuns, a common sight in the hospital, told kids there were four places for the dead—heaven, hell, purgatory, and limbo. Other than heaven, their descriptions were pretty horrific and unfit for tiny ears, especially sick, tiny ears.

Lylah touched my cheek and then cooed at the twinkling spark of inky-blue. "Are you going to say goodbye to Will?"

I nodded.

"Tell him goodbye for me, too."

I nodded again.

Lylah slipped a thumb into her mouth and rolled onto her side. I kissed her temple. Her tiny lids fluttered. "Don't forget," she said, drool seeping alongside her thumb, "say goodbye for me, too."

I took off to find Will. If they were planning to remove him, I wanted to watch his Awakening Party lift him safely into Transitional Sleep.

# 41

*He slapped his chest and raised two fingers—me, too.*

When the Good Woman had slipped into dreams, Malachi retreated to the rooftop. The warm summer night carried the scent of stinkweed—an unworthy name for such an intoxicating fragrance. He inhaled through his nostrils and held it appreciatively. He was about to relax and fashion his pipe when Alpha appeared. "Good evening, Sir Alpha," Malachi said. "Your company is always a pleasure, though an unexpected pleasure at this time. I had assumed you would be attending William's Awakening."

"William's Guide has already received my gratitude for lifting the veil."

"And Sweet Lylah has a ruffled veil as well, I see. Quite generous of you."

"You disapprove?"

"Good heavens, I haven't the arrogance to approve or disapprove of your decisions. My respect is unyielding. Permit me to ask, do you fare well?"

"The hour draws near for Jenevieve Duvall's removal."

"Lady Duvall? Oh. Oh, I shall miss her. Then Dear Zia will also be leaving; I shall miss her especially. Yes, indeed." Malachi recalled their first encounter when Zia had barreled into the Good Woman's office and had crashed into Malachi's knees. He thought of the earlier years when his humor had irritated the poor girl. But gradually, over much time, her defenses came down and her smiles came up. Nearly 15 years of lectures, tears, arguments, and hugs. Indeed, he would miss her very much. Malachi dabbed his eyes. "Do forgive me. Lost in reflection, I'm afraid." He bowed with the deep bend of a gentleman. "Sir Alpha, I hope I have served you well."

"I am grateful, Malachi. My Charge could not have gained more from another Soul. You are a credit to your Order."

"Thank you, Sir, but I'm just a common Finisher, not extraordinary in the least. But like all those of my Order, I can sense unspoken questions. They scuffle the air like a tailless kite."

Alpha considered this and then smiled. "Undeniably, you are a worthy Finisher." He turned toward the hospital. "Zia will serve in a Neutral Point."

"Neutral Point? I had thought Dear Zia was only here to learn a thing or two—wayward skioses, I'm told—and to console Lady Duvall. What virtue within Dear Zia will be relied upon at the Neutral Point? Her courage? Her fortitude? Her strength? Her resolve? Her—"

"Truthfulness."

"*Oh.*" Malachi hoped he hadn't flinched. "Well, aside from her bouts of bedlam and her penchant for pranks, Zia's character is honorable. You have my word as a Finisher. But to allay any doubts, why don't we attend William's Awakening and chat with Zia afterwards. I'm certain we will find her gracious and reverent, an Energy of blessed demeanor."

"Blessed demeanor?"

"Well, Sir," Malachi cleared his throat, "blessed for Zia's demeanor."

Inside the hospital, Malachi checked the hallways for Zia, but saw no trace of her. Peculiar. An Awakening Party had gathered outside Will's room. In the doorway, an Energy was donning the costume of an elderly woman—the standard costume used for children who have never bonded, trusted, or loved an adult. All too clearly, Malachi understood the nervous pacing of Will's Guide. A Soul's likelihood of wandering increased substantially when an unfamiliar face—even the face of an elderly woman—tried to coax the Soul's journey home. "An eighty-two percent increase," Will's Guide told all, though they knew the statistic. "Plus five percent for children under the age of ten."

Attempting to calm the Guide, Alpha said, "Consider the percentage of Wanderers to the total number of removals."

"Infinitesimal," the Guide said, "as is the percent of comfort that fact bestows when it's your Charge at risk." He told the costumed Soul, "Begin."

The woman floated to Will's bedside and held out her hand. "William, come with me." An ethereal boy's hand reached up from the body to take the woman's hand. "Don't look back," she told him. "Just come with me."

Will started to tremble. "But I don't know you."

"Don't be afraid. I'm your friend. Come along." She pulled him gently, lifting him higher and higher, while Guides and Souls paralleled their ascent.

The higher Will rose, the drowsier he became. He blinked and squinted to keep his lids open. A moment later, his fight to stay awake became a fear of losing control. He yanked his hand free. "No, go away. Go away." Fisting his eyes, he started descending.

The costumed Soul followed, "I won't hurt you," but the closer she came, the quicker he lowered. Once more, Will was floating above his bed.

"William, look at me," the woman said, but Will started to turn.

In unison, an alarmed Awakening Party vibrated, *Nooo.*

When Will saw his lifeless body, he screamed, the long, agonizing scream of a terrified child. The woman tried to calm him, but Will shouted, "GO AWAY!" He covered his face. He wanted to be away from his lifeless body and away from the strange woman who had clutched his hand.

And so it was.

Instantly, Will was standing in the hall, inches from the Awakening Party, who dared not move. Though Will couldn't see them, he would feel their vibrations, and that feeling would only further his confusion. Not a molecule among the Souls stirred.

Will fled anyway. He reappeared down the hall, his voice choking and crying and begging for help. His pleas lowered the heads of his Awakening Party, their despair garnering Malachi's sympathy. He was only thankful Zia had missed this heart-wrenching scene.

Will's Guide urged the woman to try again. "Do not lose him."

The woman inched down the hall, nearly crawling. "William, please come. Please take my hand. I'm your friend. Come with me."

A frightened Will reached for a nurse. Malachi cringed knowing what would follow; the poor lad's hand swept through the nurse. William wailed, horrified. In a flash, he was further down the hall, still wailing, still crying, and now reaching in vain to every passing doctor and nurse.

From around the corner rose a clamor. All heads lifted. A whirlwind of green and red lights twisted and twirled. Its nature, no one could imagine. *An electrical tornado?* No. It had arms that whisked and whirled maniacally, and a voice that shouted a dire warning, "Danger, Will Robinson! Danger! Danger!"

"Oh, good heavens," Malachi gasped among a chorus of gasps.

"SIA!" Will ran toward Zia. "I can hear you! I can hear you!"

As the woman started to advance, Will's Guide shot out a halting arm.

"Danger," Will shouted, but in a voice free of fear. "Danger! Danger!"

"Abort the mission," Zia said. "Abort. Abort."

"Mission aborted, sir." Will saluted. "All systems are go."

"Are the hatches secured?"

"Yes, Commander, hatches secured."

"Good man, Will Robinson. Are you prepared for take-off?"

"Yes, sir, prepared for take-off."

"Do you know where you're going?"

"Galaxy forty-two, sir."

"Better than that, Will Robinson." Zia knelt and tussled his hair. "You have another mission, okay? A different one now. You know that, right?"

Will's salute slowly lowered, then he plunged into Zia's arms. For several minutes, she squeezed and rocked him. Her tenderness brought a mist to Malachi's eyes. He glanced at Alpha; his eyes were aflame.

Gently, Zia drew Will back. She nuzzled his nose. "Let's meet your new crew, okay?" She edged him around. "All-the-all-the-outs-in-free. All-the-all-the-outs-in-free."

"Sirs," Malachi said to the Guides, "I believe she wishes the Awakening Party to step into view, but costumed as Players of course."

Will's Guide nodded to the Awakening Party. They hustled into their last forms held on Earth, which ranged from one to five centuries past.

"See those guys?" Zia pointed to the Party. "That's your new team."

While eyeing them, Will cupped his mouth for a sideways whisper, "How come they're dressed funny?"

"Uhm, Halloween. It comes early this year. Want to meet them? They're nice. Watch." Zia waved to the Party. "Hey, guys, wave to my friend, Will."

"Do as she says," Malachi urged. "Go on. Go on. Lift those arms."

Hesitant arms rose and swayed.

"Yeah, they're a sorry lot," Zia said, "but they'll take you to a place where you'll sleep. When you wake up, you won't barf anymore. Won't that be great? I know Lylah will think so. You blew chunky stuff all over her legs."

Will giggled. "Yeah, I know."

"Jeez, Will, did you aim your puke?"

Will giggled again. "Is Lylah mad at me?"

"Naw. Are you kidding? She wanted me to tell you good—uhm, good aim. And that she loves you. Sappy stuff like that. You know how it is."

Will nodded. "Yeah, I know how it is."

"Hey, Will, me, too. You know, super sappy stuff from me, too."

They hugged again, then Will frowned at the Souls flagging the air. "What if they don't make me better?"

"Have I ever lied to you? That you can prove? Astronauts don't lie to fellow astronauts." She smoothed back his hair. "They'll fix you. I promise."

"Cross your heart and hope to die?"

"Stick a needle in my eye if I lie." They spat on their palms and shook.

"Come on," Zia squeezed Will's hand, "let's go meet your motley crew."

# 42

*Learn to see folks for whom they are, not for whom you want them to be, and not for whom they'd have you believe.*

After Will's Awakening, Zia brooded on top of the terrace wall. At her insistence, Malachi left her alone. When weeks had passed and Zia still hadn't visited Game Town, Malachi suspected that her solitude was fueling her grief instead of easing it. He went to the courtyard.

Sitting beside a downcast Zia was the Ghost-Doctor. He felt her forehead and wrist, then he doodled on his chart. He told her to open wide and then he slid a thermometer into her mouth.

When the Ghost-Doctor saw Malachi, he leapt from the wall. "Dr. Rockmire, your patient, green, your patient."

"Good Doctor, this child will live thanks to your dedication and medical expertise."

"No, not done. Green, terrible. Stat. Not done. Terrible, terrible."

"No, Good Doctor, not terrible. She no longer struggles for breath. You have cured her. You have saved another life."

The Ghost-Doctor stared blankly into the distance. "More children. Save them. Epidemic. Room four, room four. Nurses. Save them. Dying."

"Not all died, Good Doctor, not all. You saved many."

"Saved? Many?" The Ghost-Doctor's voice quieted. "Saved?"

"Yes, you saved hundreds of children, hundreds of lives."

The Ghost-Doctor hung his head, blue sparks slipped from his eyes and fell from his cheeks. "Saved. Yes, saved. Saved." He jerked up. "More beds. Isolate! Isolate!" He hurried away.

Malachi positioned himself beside Zia and gave her a little nudge. "I'm delighted with your newfound patience toward the Good Ghost-Doctor."

Zia dissolved the thermometer. "I read about him in the lobby. He dedicated his whole life to this hospital. He saved tons of kids, but he couldn't save himself. Influenza got him. I feel kind of bad for having yelled at him. So, I tolerate his thermometer...in my *mouth*."

Malachi formed his pipe. *Puff, puff, puff.* He waited patiently for Zia to share her feelings about Will's removal. A while later, when Zia still hadn't offered a word, Malachi said, "You will see him again."

"Jeez, I know. But why didn't he talk to me? I don't get it. After the Awakening, why didn't he come back and talk to me?"

"Dear Lady, of whom do you speak?"

"Alpha. Who did you think I meant?"

"William."

"Will?" Zia sparked confusion. "Will is in Transitional Sleep."

"Yes, I'm aware of that."

"Then how could he come back and talk to me if he's sleeping?"

"No, you misunderstood. I assumed you missed your friend."

"I do, but Will has to wake up. What does that have to do with Alpha?"

"It doesn't, nor was I suggesting it did. Dear Zia, let's begin anew. What troubles you?"

"Why didn't Alpha want to talk to me?" Her eyes blued. "I know I'm not supposed to interfere with Awakenings, but I didn't think it was so horribly wrong that my own Guide would snub me."

"He likely seeks counsel. After all, his Charge violated sacred Awakening Laws."

"Sacred laws, phooey." Zia wiped her tears. "Will is my friend. Friends don't let friends wander. Isn't that an exception to a stupid law?"

Malachi shook his head. "I'm sorry, Dear Zia."

"Well, it should be. And I'd do it again for Will, whatever the consequences." Zia bit her lip. "Uhm, so just what are the consequences?"

"I haven't the foggiest idea. To my knowledge, no one has ever violated that particular law."

"Ever?"

"Not even Niine."

"*Greeeat.* And I suppose everyone knows about this law, right?"

"Of course."

"How? How does everyone know?"

"I don't understand." But Malachi's sparks showed otherwise.

"You do, too, understand," Zia said. "Why won't you tell me?"

"Dear Zia, it would behoove you to ask—"

"There's a manual, right?"

"No."

She chewed her thumb while her eyes scoured his sparks. "Okay, okay, no manual. How about a rule-book?"

"No."

"A technical sheet? A set of instructions? A secret meeting?"

"Of course not."

Zia leaned right and left, but Malachi's lights showed truthful answers. Zia slumped. "That proves it; I'm just plain stupid."

Malachi's arm stretched over Zia's shoulders, and he pulled her close. "Dear Lady, you are impetuous, often, contentious, occasionally, but ignorant, never. You seized the tongues of all Energies and Guides. Flabbergasted, we were. Flabbergasted by your manic flapping, your frenzied spinning, and your hysteric warnings. Never has an Awakening been interrupted by a whirling dervish espousing doom." Recalling the scene, Malachi began laughing. "I thought you had taken leave of your last spark of good sense. Likely, all others believed the same. Your performance stoked Alpha's eyes from an ember to a blaze. Oh, the moment I return to Haven, I shall share this engaging story with my entire Order."

"Malachi, this is serious."

"Indeed, it is. Tell me the consequence, and I'll give it my gravest concern."

"But I don't know the—"

"And neither do I. And what is done, is done." Malachi fashioned a smoke ring into a stethoscope. "Either roam the hallways like the Good Ghost-Doctor, a self-imposed prisoner to the unchangeable past, or move forward to assist those you can, Lady Duvall and Sweet Lylah."

"Lylah is gone. In a couple of months, she'll come back for her last treatment, and then she'll be leaving for good. I'm going to miss her like crazy. Without her and Will, Game Town is Gloom Town."

Their attention turned when Jen entered the courtyard. She sat, sipped her mint tea, and scattered rips of crust to the birds.

"She's terrific, isn't she?" Zia said. "The kids love her messages."

"Messages?"

"Yeah, she's from the Order of Messengers."

Malachi choked. His pipe vanished. "Dear Zia, why do you think she's a Messenger?"

"I don't *think* it; I *know* it. She's Ereo, the Dyad to Awen, Order of Messengers."

Malachi rubbed his forehead, wondering how much he should explain.

"What's wrong?" Zia squeezed his arm. "Tell me what's wrong."

"From my observations, I would not have thought her a Messenger."

Instantly, Zia reddened. "You're wrong. Wrong!" She scooted a few feet away, her attention returning to Jen.

Malachi said nothing.

Minutes later, Zia came back to Malachi's side. "All right, Mr. Everybody-Knows-Everything-But-You, tell me what you think."

"Dear Lady, Messengers deliver ideas to particular Players at specific times, but they do so without intention or forethought or knowledge. Their message will ring true, not within the Player's mind, necessarily, but within the Player's Soul, the intended recipient."

"But Jen gives messages through her stories. She talks about good and bad, right and wrong, and all kinds of crap."

"You're confusing a Soul's Order to a Player's labor. The Order of Teachers do not fill the Players' classrooms, Messengers don't crowd the Post Offices, and Warriors don't line the battle-fields. Our own Good Ghost-Doctor is an honorable Warrior."

"A Warrior?"

"A remarkable Warrior. In his prior lives, he may have been a knight or a gunslinger, but in his last life, he was an admirable soldier against influenza. Unfortunately, he's still fighting that war."

"Malachi, you're jibber-jabbering like a Counter."

"Dear Zia, your friend attracts all Energies, both beast and Soul."

"A Persuader?"

Malachi shook his head. "Attracts, not entices. When Lady Duvall enters a room, children reach for her touch before she utters hello. All Energies benefit from her presence." Malachi pointed to the birds. "Rarely will a Steller's jay perch so close to a Player, unless the Player's Soul is a Healer. While music has its charms, it is the Healer who soothes the savage beasts."

"A Healer?"

"A Healer gives to an Energy what water gives to a body—replenishment. Once renewed, you can carry on with other business."

Zia shook her head. "You're wrong. Ereo is a Messenger."

"Yes, Dear Lady, Ereo is a Messenger." He sparkled with truth, but said no more; Zia had suffered enough knowledge for a day.

# 43

*Whether Death had kicked the board or Father-Time had spotted a better play, the tiles, all around me, shifted.*

On the morning of Lylah's final treatment, I shadowed Jen from her bedroom to her bathroom, hurrying her along. "Just grab a sweater. Let's go."

Finally, Jen selected a jacket and made her way out the door. She strolled to work in her usual cheer: greeting strangers, petting dogs, smelling flowers. I whispered like crazy to get her moving. "The guy is a bum, the dog is a flea-bag, the flower is a weed." Rounding the last block, I told Jen, "See you at dusk," and I shot into the hospital, straight into Lylah's recovery room. She was sleeping, her thumb resting beside a slobbery chin. I nuzzled her cheek.

She stirred. I curled to her side and began counting ceiling tiles.

Later, her dreamy red eyes and her heart-shaped lips parted. "Ssssia." She sounded like a balloon leaking air. "Ssssia."

I stroked her hand. "Hey, swee' pea."

Her thumb inched into her mouth before she returned to dreamland.

I resumed counting tiles.

Hours later, she woke, now without a trace of grogginess. A nurse came in, checked the IV, noted Lylah's temperature and pulse, and then left.

"Sia." Lylah wiggled onto her elbows. As always, she looked right and left to ensure secrecy of her news. I hunkered in close. "I have a radio," she whispered before giving her signature nod; *you know what that means?*

Following routine, I nodded, too. Lylah reached to the side table for her pink, portable radio. After whizzing through static, she settled on a rock station. Grinning expectantly, she said, "Okay, go."

*Go?* I shook my head and shrugged.

Her lips pinched into a pout. "You said you would. Go dance like Will."

*Oh, jeez, her quirky tip of the head had meaning?* And my nod had apparently agreed—agreed to dance like Will. I hopped from the gurney and imagined a microphone and guitar. I needed props. Luckily, Lylah couldn't see my props; she thought my fumbling to keep hold of them was part of my dance—my dancing like Will. Will would have been insulted. But I sang and jumped and wiggled, and at the song's end, I did the splits, *BAABEEE!*

Lylah's porcelain hands clapped so furiously, I thought they would break like bone china. "Do it again!" she whispered. "Do it again! Do it again!"

Elvis played next. When Elvis played on the television box, he gyrated his hips. When I tried to gyrate mine, I felt like a drunken hula dancer.

> *...I don't wanna be a lion,*
> *'cause lions ain't the kind you love enough.*

At the song's finale, I hopped onto the gurney, dropped to my knees, and made a very cool Elvis face.

> *...just wanna be your teddy bear.*

Rolling and reeling and laughing hysterically, Lylah slipped off the mattress. I bolted to catch her but couldn't. Thankfully, she wedged between the bedding and the rail. She pulled herself back up. I motioned for her to settle down, don't get so excited. Lylah made her own motions. "Dance again. You said you would. Dance. Go on, *Pleeease?*"

*Thump.* Gruer and Malachi looked up. "Come in," Gruer said, but no one entered. After a moment, Gruer returned to the monthly reports.

Malachi glided from the office to investigate.

Leaning against the wall, Jen had one hand pressed to her temple, the other hand exploring her pocket. A nurse sprinted up the hallway. "Jennifer, are you okay?" She tried to lift Jen's chin, but Jen pushed her away.

"I'm—I'm fine," Jen said. "It's just a migraine. I get them all the time. I have aspirin in my office. I'll be fine."

"You need to lie down."

"I can't. I'm tutoring in twenty minutes."

"I'll explain to the kids, but you need to rest."

"No, I—"

"Don't force me to call Claire. She'll keep you in bed for a week."

Jen lifted a faint smile. "All right, you win. I'll rest for a few hours." When she pushed from the wall, her legs buckled.

The nurse caught her. "You're not okay."

Jen steadied again, now locking her knees. She brushed aside the hand of support. "Just cancel my tutoring sessions."

While Jen staggered toward her office, Malachi peered at her life-cord. Surprisingly, it seemed solid. Malachi floated higher for a downward view. Only then did he spot the thinning base. "Good heavens." He ran a swift eye down the hallway. Zia, the consoling Soul, should have sensed Jen's removal.

As Jen was entering her office, the Ghost-Doctor came around the corner. "Dr. Rockmire. Dr. Rockmire."

Malachi blocked the doorway. "Not now, Good Doctor. I must attend to my patient, Lady Duvall."

When the Ghost-Doctor disappeared, Malachi glided into Jen's office.

A lovely Yin Guide wavered at Jen's side.

Malachi back-stepped. "Excuse my intrusion."

"No apologies due. I am Willow, Guide of Phoenix." She placed a gentle hand on her Charge's head. "Phoenix serves as Jenevieve Duvall. And you are Malachi, Order of Finishers, whose tenacious patience improved the consoling Soul's whispers. In turn, those whispers provided much comfort to my Charge." She bowed. "Malachi, Order of Finishers, I am grateful."

Malachi bowed, too. "I am honored."

With her eyes shut, Jen rummaged into a desk drawer. She brought up an aspirin bottle and tore off the cap. Pills sprinkled across her desk. She scooped up a handful and downed them with cold coffee. Her arms folded over papers and pills, her head lowered, and her lips circled in a moan.

When Alpha appeared, Willow's expression became far less friendly. "Your Charge is...delayed?"

Alpha's orange eyes shifted to Malachi.

"She's probably—I'm certain she's—" But Malachi wasn't certain of anything. His shoulders drew back. "I shall bring her at once."

Hopping on one foot, I strummed my invisible guitar while Lylah laughed and squealed with wild abandon. With pretended humbleness, I fanned myself and mimed signing autographs while Lylah hollered for more.

We were interrupted by an anxious Malachi. "ZIA!"

"Hey, I'm sort of busy right now."

"Dear Lady, your friend is Awakening."

"What?"

"Your friend is—"

"Aw, shit! Hang on." I darted to Lylah. No use in talking. I kissed her forehead and mouthed, *I love you.*

She turned off the radio. "Am I going to see you again?"

Not knowing how to answer, I mimicked her queer tip of the head...*you know what that means?*

To my amazement, Lylah said, "Yes, I do!"

While Malachi hurried me through the hallways, I asked, "Jeez, how was I supposed to know?"

"Vibrations, Dear Lady. You would have felt the vibrations."

"You mean pinpricks? Like a thousand needles poking me?"

"Yes, Dear Lady. What did you think that was?"

I shrugged. "Rock and roll."

In front of Jen's office, Malachi gave me a light push. "Well, go on. It's impolite to delay an Awakening."

My head lowered. *Drip...Splash...Drip...Splash.* My feet vanished under a puddle of inky-blue. I bit my cheek to quit, but more inky-blue spilled. With widespread arms that didn't even reach to Malachi's sides, I hugged the gentle bear, snuffling into his chest. "I'm going to miss you...miss you like crazy." *Drip...Splash...Drip...Splash.*

Malachi held me tightly. "My precious Dear Zia, we shall meet in Haven and retell every story of our love and friendship. To that, I promise. But first, you must serve Lady Duvall through her Awakening."

My neck strained back. "Will you come to my Awakenings? I mean, if you're not on Earth, will you come to my Awakenings?"

"What beast could stop me?"

"Promise?"

"My word as a gentleman. Now, you've delayed long enough. Scoot yourself inside before you create more trouble for yourself."

At the doorway, I looked back at Malachi. His cheeks were streaked with his own inky-blue.

"Tell me goodbye," I said. "Nobody ever tells me goodbye."

"Because One has never left you, Dear Lady. The word is a misnomer. But as you wish, God be with you."

# 44

*I waited and waited, wondering how long this patience-lesson was going to take.*

The name, Geminus, sounded Yang, but the Guide beside Jen was unmistakably Yin. I had assumed that Dyads shared the same Guide. If they do, then the name, Geminus, is like the name, Pat, covering both Yin and Yang. I couldn't ask the Guides. Their sullen faces told me it was a bad time for questions.

Jen gurgled, barely conscious. Blood trickled from her nose and formed red rivers around the white pills. "Pierre, forgive me. Forgive me."

*Rap, rap, rap.* "Jennifer, are you okay in there?" a voice called from behind the door. Yin-Geminus motioned. The door's lock engaged.

With a quick look at Jen's life-cord, I wondered whether the Guides had mixed up their removals. Jen's cord looked fine...until I nosed in closer and saw the base. A single thread, thinner than a spider's web, attached the cord to her head. When that thread dissolved, the cord would vanish, and Ereo's Ribbon of Life would again whip freely, just like mine.

My fingers twisted together. Although I had never led an Awakening—nobody had ever missed me that much—I had watched a few and was reasonably sure what to do. But sour-faced Guides were making me nervous. "I can take it from here," I told them. "Go join the Awakening Party. Scram."

"Ahem." Alpha's eyes swept up and down my form.

"What?" I looked down and saw my green feet. "Oops." I concentrated until my form contracted, smaller and smaller, and my green changed to tan. Purple lights curled and peeled and became short, yellow wisps. Within a minute, I appeared as a chunky blond boy with splotchy red cheeks and one rolling eye. "How's that?"

They didn't answer.

"What's wrong now?" I asked. "Are you afraid I'll mess up? Is that why you're still here?" I sparked tension. "See what you're doing? You're making me nervous. Trust that I love her. Know that I won't let her wander. But if you keep hanging around, she's going to open her eyes to a firecracker instead of her kid brother. Is that what you want?"

The Guides vanished. *Finally!*

"Okay, Ereo," I said, "let's get you home to Awen."

White foam spilled from her lips and floated on the trickles of blood.

"Let it go." I stroked her head. "Just let it go. Let it go."

Her muscles tightened as her body strained to create one more drop of fluid, just one more. It wasn't moisture for her mouth nor was it sweat from her pain. It was a tear. *A tear!* I felt completely inadequate to awaken anyone who would strain that much for a tear. After seconds of stillness, she inhaled sharply and held it...held it...held it. It left in a long, thin breath, her last as Jenevieve Duvall.

Jen died face down, but Souls exit face up; that much, I learned from watching Awakenings. I also learned about the tricky part; you have to keep the Soul from looking back at their corpse. If they turn, they freak.

I floated above Jen and held out my hand. Her Soul lifted. "Pierre?"

I nodded.

When Jen clutched my hand, I pulled her up. Entranced and bewildered, she was oblivious to our rise.

While I lifted her higher and higher, she blinked under surges of drowsiness. I nodded and nodded to each of her questions until her words began slurring from oncoming sleep.

Her Awakening Party was waiting on the hospital roof. When they saw me and Jen, they followed our rise. High above the hospital, Jen's eyes closed in Transitional slumber.

*Whew!* I flashed a thumbs-up to her Awakening Party. If the Party didn't get it, I figured Awen would explain. He was with them—had to be—even though I hadn't spotted his blue form.

I told sleeping Jen, "So far, so good." With a firm grip, I whisked her off to Divisional's Awakening field.

Having settled into a cross-legged position, I formed a pillow on my lap for Jen's head. Then I waited...and waited...and waited. Just like the Party on the sidelines, I waited for Jen to wake up.

While I'm not one to criticize, I think the Awakening ritual could stand major improvement. Transitional Sleep supposedly refreshes a Soul; that's what Romal had told me. He called it a reverent, meditative time. Translation: It's incredibly boring.

Nobody knows how long a Soul is going to sleep. Although some Souls will wake within seconds and attend their own funeral, other Souls will sleep through a century; the record is two.

For efficiency, I think every Guide ought to post their Charge's sleep-time average. That way, instead of everyone standing around waiting, Souls could relax in Haven or attend another Awakening or squeeze in a short-stay. When I shared my terrific idea with Romal, he grimaced as if I had served him vinegar tea.

*Whoosh.* Earth made a pass...then another...then another...then I lost count, distracted by the Awakening Field. It's a freeway of dimensions—the onramp to Earth and the off-ramp to Haven, the comings and goings from all over the world. Cords whip up, Energies descend, new arrivals wake, celebrate, and disappear. A few Souls in Jen's Party had to leave; they had lives to live. Other Souls, having recently returned and awakened, joined her Party waiting on the sidelines.

"You're not going for the record, are you, Jen?" I patted her cheek. "Not that I'm complaining, because I'm not. Not a bit. Sleep as long as you like...just as long as you wake soon."

I peered across the expanse to my section of Divisional. Strange how it looked empty. Desolate. As hard as I tried, I couldn't bring back my love for the place. It didn't look quiet and peaceful; it now looked lonely.

I smoothed aside Jen's bangs. "Hey, when you wake up, don't run off. You'll make me look bad. Got it?" I pinched her chin to bob it up and down. "Good. Glad we understand each other."

*Whoosh.* With every pass of the Earth came changes in hairstyles and clothes on the new arrivals. While checking out the latest, I spotted a recently awakened Soul locking arms with a large, turquoise Energy. *Malachi?* I flagged overhead and spoke in soft vibrations. "Malachi, *Pssst*, Malachi."

Within seconds, Malachi and his companion were beside me. I pointed to the head on my lap. "I'd get up, but—"

"No need," Malachi said. He bent low as I stretched up for a hug. "Dear Lady, the photograph of Pierre did not do you justice. You're a dashing young fellow."

When Malachi straightened, his friend curled down to plant a kiss on Jen's forehead. I stared impolitely because she was remarkably beautiful—a jade-green Energy with peach colored hair that splashed to her waist.

"Lady Ellisal," Malachi said, "this is the emerald gem I spoke of."

She smiled. "I recall the photograph. You're Jenevieve's little brother."

"Dear Zia, this is Lady Ellisal, Order of Peacekeepers. She served as my mother, who so viciously trapped my Soul to Earth."

"Gruer? *Gruer?*"

"Ellisal," she said without a spark of offense.

"But Gruer was so—And you're so—"

"An enchanting butterfly," Malachi said. "Freed from a cocoon."

I couldn't stop my rude amazement; you just never know what beauty a Player's shell hides.

Ellisal asked about my true colors. I started squirming.

"She's also a lovely butterfly," Malachi said.

"Nooo," I said, imagining Ellisal's reaction to my green and purple lights, a reverse amazement, an *ew* instead of an *ah*. "I'm not a butterfly. A moth maybe. An agitating moth. But you'll never see it because Jen will never wake up. I'm going to look like a pathetic kid forever."

"Be patient," Ellisal said. "I woke quickly because I wanted to go home long before my body released me."

Ellisal and Malachi turned suddenly toward the Awakening Party. "Dear Zia, we must go."

"Already?" I wanted Malachi to stay, form his pipe, and reshape smoke rings into symbols while I pretended not to notice. At the very least, I wanted a full Malachi bear hug. I cupped Jen's head to lift it from my lap.

Malachi pressed down on my shoulder. "No, Dear Lady, set aside your wishes and act in the best interest of Lady Duvall. Later, we shall reminisce in Haven."

After a peck to my forehead, Malachi and Ellisal glided off. Golden speckles trailed Ellisal. I didn't know much about Peacekeepers because I had never met one I liked...until now. Trusting that Ellisal liked me, too, I sent her a vibration, "Hey, what do Peacekeepers do?"

She looked over her shoulder, "We tether the violent," and moved on.

*Tether the violent?* "Then how come they pick on me?"

Ellisal didn't answer. She was too far away, I guess.

"Pierre?" Jen squeaked, her eyes batting. "Pierre?"

*Showtime!*

# 45

*Am I or am I not going to Earth to help Ereo?*

"**P**IERRE!" Jen bolted upright and scooped me into her arms. After crushing squeezes and frantic kisses, she swung me in circles. "Oh Pierre! Pierre!" She brushed aside my disheveled hair and pinched my cheeks to see if I were real—*really, really real.* "Pierre, how did you—Why are you—Oh God, Pierre, I love you so much. So much. Love you."

I was thinking I was a natural at this Awakening stuff...until right then. Right then, while Jen was hugging and squeezing me, I realized I hadn't a clue to what actually triggers a Soul to awaken. The moment I was aware of my shortcoming, Guides were aware of it, too. They sighed and groaned on the sidelines because I was a fraud, a sham, a pretender of greatness pulling levers and playing parlor tricks to satisfy Guides and appease Jen. I was no better than the humbug wizard in Oz. "I am Pierre. Pay no attention to the Soul behind the costume."

Jen dropped me. "Costume?" In her half-awake vision, she could only see veils of lights, a scattering of stars, and a handful of planets. I pointed to Pluto, hoping she would remember her Tinker Toy solar system. Maybe that memory would cause her other memories to loosen. But Jen didn't get it. "Pierre, what is it? Don't you know me?"

I nodded.

"Why won't you talk?" She gripped my shoulders. "Do you know where we are? Pierre, how did we get here? Say something. Pierre, say something." She began shaking me, hard and desperate, her fingers digging into my arms. "SAY SOMETHING." My head whiplashed, forward and backward. "ANSWER ME!"

*A little help please,* I said silently to the Guides, *before my head rolls off.*

*Bring the Soul forward through recognition,* Alpha said as if I hadn't already tried that by pointing at Pluto.

*Can you be more specific?*

*Ask the Soul if she knows you.*

"Does she know you?"

*Incorrect. Ask the Soul—*

"Do I know you?"

*You reversed the question, and you speak unlike Pierre.*

"Do you know me?" What a dumb question. It deserved my bad voice, a tone too high and too squeaky, like Mickey Mouse on helium.

Jen hugged herself. When I moved toward her, she crab-crawled backward. How could I wake her if I couldn't reach her? I started gnawing my thumb. How could I figure out anything with Guides watching me and making me nervous? "STOP STARING AT ME!" The second I shouted, I clapped a hand over my stupid, stupid mouth.

Jen's mouth dangled open, her face frozen in shock. I had botched the Awakening, a fact proven by the droning groans of disappointed Guides. "This is crap," I told the kibitzers. "I'm doing it my way." I had to do it my way, because their *peaceful*-way was scaring the hell out of Jen. Before she could slink away, I hurled myself forward and clutched her in a face-to-face headlock. "LOOK AT ME!"

Jen screeched. My grip tightened. "LOOK AT ME! LOOK!"

She yanked on my legs that were locked around her waist. Her frightened fists pelted my back and clawed my sides, but I held on. "Open your damn eyes. OPEN THEM!" I held on through her shoving and twisting and walloping vibrations that wished me elsewhere—a place not very nice either. "Open your eyes. Just look. LOOK!"

Her head jerked sideways, but I yanked it straight and ground my nose into hers. "Dammit, Jen, look at me. I am Pierre. I AM PIERRE. Open your eyes and see me. For chrissake, LOOK!"

Writhing, she peeked from one eye.

"Please, Jen, please. Forget my voice. Just look until you see me. Remember me. Remember you. Look and remember. Please, Jen, please." *Or I'll end up where you wished me.*

Slowly, her Energy limbered under a fog of recollection.

"You feel it, right?" I said. "A tingle? Do you hear a knocking? That's your Soul tapping to awaken. It's the truth, Jen. It's trying to come in. Open the door to your Soul." Still sensing remnants of a struggle, I clung to her neck, but strained sideways to have a peek at her legs. The beige was shedding. *Finally.* "You're doing good, Jen. Keep the door open. Wide open."

Soon, Jen became limp. Her eyes glazed under a peaceful glow.

I slid to her feet. I hadn't been so battered and bruised since the time I sneaked down to Earth to ride a tornado. You would think saddling a tornado would be fun. It wasn't. Go figure.

Although Jen didn't need Pierre anymore, I stayed costumed just in case. My eyes rested, but my ears stayed alert to her mutterings.

"Yes, yes," she whispered, while volumes of memories were flooding her head. Even without checking, I knew her illusion was peeling away. When I heard the greetings from her Awakening Party, I rubbed my eyes open.

The legs I was leaning against weren't blue, not even a speck of Ereo blue. My gaze lifted to a buttery yellow Energy topped in fiery red lights. Her friends greeted her as Phoenix. *Phoenix!* Order of Healers. And nowhere among her Party was Ereo or Awen.

Dissolving Pierre's costume, I crept away from the celebration. Though I loved Jen, I was totally confused; Who is Phoenix? Where is Ereo? What happened to Awen? A spillage of inky-blue puddled around me.

Much later, a hand rested on my shoulder. "Thank you," Phoenix said.

"No big deal." I rolled my shoulder until she took the hint and removed her hand. Far behind her, celebrating Souls created an Aurora Borealis of lights. Hundreds of Souls loved the Healer. "Better get back to your Party before your friends come looking for you. We'll talk later, okay?"

Instead of leaving, she sat beside me. "We'll talk now."

"Look, I want to be alone, okay?"

She leaned into my face, "No," and then giggled like one of those sunny-Souls who takes, *I want to be alone*, as a challenge to change your attitude. "Your death saved my Soul," she said. "Your whispers encouraged my spirit. Through your years of devotion, I served hundreds of Players, which will serve thousands to come. And you carried me into Transitional Sleep and helped me Awaken. Thank you, Zia. You made a difference."

"And you made a mistake. You had a terrible Awakening. Brutal. I did it all wrong. And my devotion was based on fraud. I don't deserve your thanks. You just don't know the truth."

"Then tell me." She winked. "Hurry up, Zia. Tell me this great truth so I can get back to thanking you."

"Our mother was a Player for Niine. Did you know that? She was Triite, Order of Persuaders. After he removed me, I did nothing but whine and complain. Believe me, I never sparked benevolence. I only wanted to help Awen. Not you. Hell, I don't even know you. I mean, I'm sure you're nice.

Judging by your Awakening Party, you're damn nice. But I didn't help you on purpose, and I didn't help Awen or Ereo at all. I'm sorry, Phoenix. I should have wanted to help you, no matter who you were. But Alpha had to trick me into believing you were Ereo. For what it's worth, I wouldn't take back a day of my whispers."

Phoenix yawned and tousled her blazing red hair. "My turn?"

"No." While I was humbling myself, she was being flippant. I waited a good minute before telling her, "Okay. *Now* it's your turn."

"Zia, before you descended, you knew the life-cord attached to a Niine Player's womb, right?"

"Yeah, but I thought I was helping—"

"You served as a consoling Soul because you loved Jenevieve, right?"

"Sure, but I thought you were—"

"Does it matter? Would you have loved Jen any less?"

"No. I wouldn't have loved you any less. Absolutely not. But—"

"But you think Alpha should have told you my identity so that you could worry about the Dyads during all those tedious years on Earth, right?"

"Yeah. No. Wait. What?"

"Keep up, my little, green friend." She budged against me. I shifted to regain space. She shifted, too, closing the gap. "As far as my so-called brutal Awakening, every Order uses their own technique. Counters do it one way, Healers do it another way. You're an Agitator; you did it the Agitator way."

"I don't know." I picked at my nails. "A Seeker and a Teacher woke me once, but other than them, I've always had the generically costumed—"

"Because no one comes to your Party. Boo-hoo." She began pestering with my hair.

I swatted her hand. "Quit it."

She swatted back, teasing and pestering in spirited play. She wouldn't quit. She grated on me but in a fun way. "You're so different from Jen."

"You're different, too. Thankfully." Her smile vanished. "Different from that cowardly Gavin MacKenzie." Her face masked into an earlier Player.

"Matthew?" I curled forward. "Shit."

Phoenix shoved me upright, her golden face returning. "I know you, and I know Triite. Sometimes, I succeed against Niine Players, but sometimes, I don't. As Matthew, I failed in Alaska because I didn't know about Murdock's character, didn't know about the gun, and didn't know about the assaults. Matthew didn't know because an Agitator kept her mouth shut."

"I'm sorry. I'm really, really sorry. I'm sooo—"

*WHAP!* Phoenix struck the back of my head. "This is my Party, not your Pity Party. Save your apologies and quit your self-blame. Zia, everybody has lives less than stellar. When we're down there, we're not completely ourselves. A part of us holds true, but the cognizant part is molded by culture, environment, and upbringing. Everyone makes mistakes, including Dyads, including Ereo. So let's get down there and help Ereo so that she doesn't repeat those mistakes. Let's kick Niine-Player butt in this do-over, okay?"

"Do-over?"

"The Neutral Point." She looked at me like she expected me to know what the hell she was talking about. Then she twisted half-circle and looked at the Guides, "How many vibrations did her skioses eat?" before she turned again to me. "It takes the decision of two Dyads in one life or one Dyad in two lives for their cord to switch sides."

"Phoenix, I hate to tell you this, but Ereo is gone. She might be in Hades." I swallowed hard. "And it's my fault. Awen tried to tell me, but—"

*WHAP!*

That crazy Healer smacked me again. "Listen, Missy, you hit me one more time and—"

"Do you think Ereo's lifetimes for One simply evaporated? Consider the reverse; if a Soul spent a hundred lifetimes as a Niine Player and then managed a life for One, would that Soul dwell in Haven between their lives?"

"Yes. No. Maybe."

"Ereo was sleeping."

"*Was* sleeping? What do you mean *was*?"

Phoenix pointed to her disbanding Party. "Do you know why my Party is leaving without me?"

"You have lousy friends?"

*WHAP!*

"DAMMIT!" I jumped up, my hands balled. "KNOCK IT OFF!"

Phoenix got up calmly. With thumb up and pointer extended, she aimed her mock gun at my fists and made a clicking sound.

My hands, as if each had a mind of its own, unballed.

"Don't mess with a Healer." She blew a quick breath at her fingertip. "I'm not returning to Haven because it's time for the Neutral Point and my life-cord is almost here."

Phoenix went on and on—something about a Soul named Poppy and something about fragments—but I tuned her out because I was flexing my fingers, fisting and uncurling, fisting and uncurling. How the hell had she caused them to go limp?

Phoenix gathered my hands. "Jenevieve and Pierre made an excellent team. Your death served as the catalyst to destroy an influential Niine cluster. Our ripple effect will serve One for generations to come. Pierre's quick life made a remarkable difference. Remember that, Zia, before you ever trivialize a short-stay."

She looked again at the Guides. "Zia, I'm out of time. My Guide, Willow, has told me that Triite descended." She kissed my cheeks. "I thank you. I love you. I have to go."

She started off.

I smoothed back my purple lights and thought a while. Something was wrong. Phoenix had said, *let's* get down there, *let's* kick Niine-Player butt, and *let's* meant me. I was supposed to serve Ereo; Alpha had said so.

But Alpha stayed in the distance with Willow.

*Crap.* I kicked imagined rocks.

When Phoenix reached the Guides, she embraced Alpha, and then she drifted away with Willow.

Alpha still didn't come for me.

*Damn.* I leaned to the right and to the left, looking for someone, anyone, to come and get me.

Nobody came.

Alpha or Romal should have been thrusting a cord into my hands and yammering last minute lectures about neutral places and do-overs and whatever else Phoenix had meant with her *let's*.

They needed me.

Nobody came.

Spotting the last fleck of Phoenix's lights, I shouted, "Shouldn't I be going, too?"

"You're the Agitator," she hollered back...and her vibration thumped the back of my head.

But I got her message. I was the Agitator for the job, but the Guides intended to leave me out.

Got it!

My eyes narrowed on the apricot glow in the distance. "Let's talk."

# 46

I stood in full readiness. "Alpha, I'm prepared to serve Ereo. Send me to this neutral place. That's where you sent the Dyads and Phoenix, right?"

"True."

"It is? I mean, okay then. Where's my cord?"

He illuminated an area within the Descending Field where a life-cord brushed at the ankle of another Yin Soul.

Once again, the Guides were tossing me aside as if I were a rotting turnip. "You replaced me."

"The Persuader—"

"PERSUADER? You replaced me with a Persuader?" *Hauck*, I spat. "They're politicians and actors, and they're full of crap."

"How many Persuaders for One do you know?"

"A zill///—" Mindful of my tattletale sparks, I bit down on my upcoming lie. I knew only one Persuader—Triite—and he played for Niine. "Whether I know one or know a dozen, who cares? I need to serve Ereo. Me. Not a stranger. I'll sense the Souls of Ereo and Awen. I'll even sense Phoenix; she'll be the Player who gives me a headache. Your Persuader won't sense squat."

"We have lifted a veil for—"

"ON A PERSUADER? Are you crazy? She might start off with innocent eyes like Will or Lylah, but eventually, she'll grow to become a soothsayer. Whatever she sees and hears because of your lifted veil, she will use to promote herself. Persuaders should never have a lifted veil; in fact, they ought to wear celestial trench coats. The only Player safe without a veil is a Player carting the Soul of an Agitator, and that's me! Voices and visions don't bother Agitators, and we're too arrogant to believe we're crazy. And unlike Persuaders, Agitators hate attention. If you sat on our nose and declared yourself, we would still argue your existence. But if you declare yourself to a Persuader, she'll exploit your message and feed off the grieving."

"A Persuader for One is generous, not self-serving. They are articulate and inspiring. That is what Persuaders do. That is their purpose. In contrast, Agitators incite opposition. Their words rile controversy, their actions invite protest. That is the purpose of your Order."

Strangely, Alpha spoke in a casual, no-big-deal kind of tone, as though he were simply passing along everyday information...until his last sentence. "But your rash assumptions—"

"Rash nothing. Soothsayers chipped at Jen's heart for more than a decade."

"I am referring to—"

"Will's Awakening? Nothing rash about that either. I'll tell you what I told Malachi; Will is my friend, and friends don't let friends wander. No matter what. And if that violates an antiquated law, then change the law. Souls are sacred, not laws. Get it? And the next time you describe an Agitator, be sure to include blatantly honest. Mostly. Sometimes. Well, I'm working on it."

Earth swished past, and the Persuader picked up the cord.

*Jeez*, she was preparing to leave.

"Zia, you misunderstand," Alpha said, though I understood plenty.

I flew to the Descending Field.

The Persuader, startled, dropped the cord.

I dove for it, grappled it to my chest, and rolled for distance.

The Persuader, eyes wide and jaw slack, shrugged to those behind me.

In a stealth move, I somersaulted sideways before having a look.

A troop of Guides—Alpha, Romal, Willow, and a portly one—were advancing. I glanced up. *One, stay with me, because when I get back, they're going to kill me.*

I plunged into the cord.

# 47

*She looked at the half*
*still embedded in her core. "I broke it."*

Willow clasped Zia by the heel and started to pull her up.

"Do not retrieve her," Alpha said. "Just suspend her in the cord until the fetus is fully formed."

Poppy stopped brushing off the sparks that Zia had flung. Her questioning look circled the Guides before it landed on Alpha. "I didn't have a chance to talk to her. You saw that. If you retrieve her, I'm certain I could convince her to remove the fragment."

"I agree," Willow added. "Let the Persuader try. Why suspend Zia? This month on Earth affords us valuable minutes to try."

But Alpha had already analyzed Zia's strange method of seizing the cord—jumping, rolling, maneuvering—as though she were an operative stealing the enemies' plans. He shook his head. "For 15 years, Malachi counseled Zia to remove the fragment. But contrary to his counsel, Zia embedded the fragment deeper."

"But Yin to Yin—" Poppy started to argue before Alpha lifted his hand.

"Yin or Yang," Alpha said, "Finisher or Persuader, one minute or one eon, the result will be the same. Arbitrarily, this Soul's skioses reverse a number of constructs, and we do not know what constructs they will be."

Geminus fronted Alpha. "That fragment harbors disdain for my Charge. You would let her carry that disdain into the Neutral Point?"

Alpha couldn't *let* or *not let*; it was Zia's choice...as Geminus well knew. Addressing Geminus's true concern, Alpha said, "Neither counsel nor insistence prompted Zia's destruction of the fragment she held against Triite. What prompted Zia was the fragment's own deleterious effect. When Zia's disdain for Ereo jeopardizes what Zia values and loves, her fragment against Ereo will likely shrink."

"Maybe," Geminus said, "but how likely before the Neutral Point?"

Alpha had no answer.

# Book III

*Because Zia's vibrations played for beelzeNiine, their side receives a ten-fold advantage for the Neutral Point. Three parities comprise the advantage.*

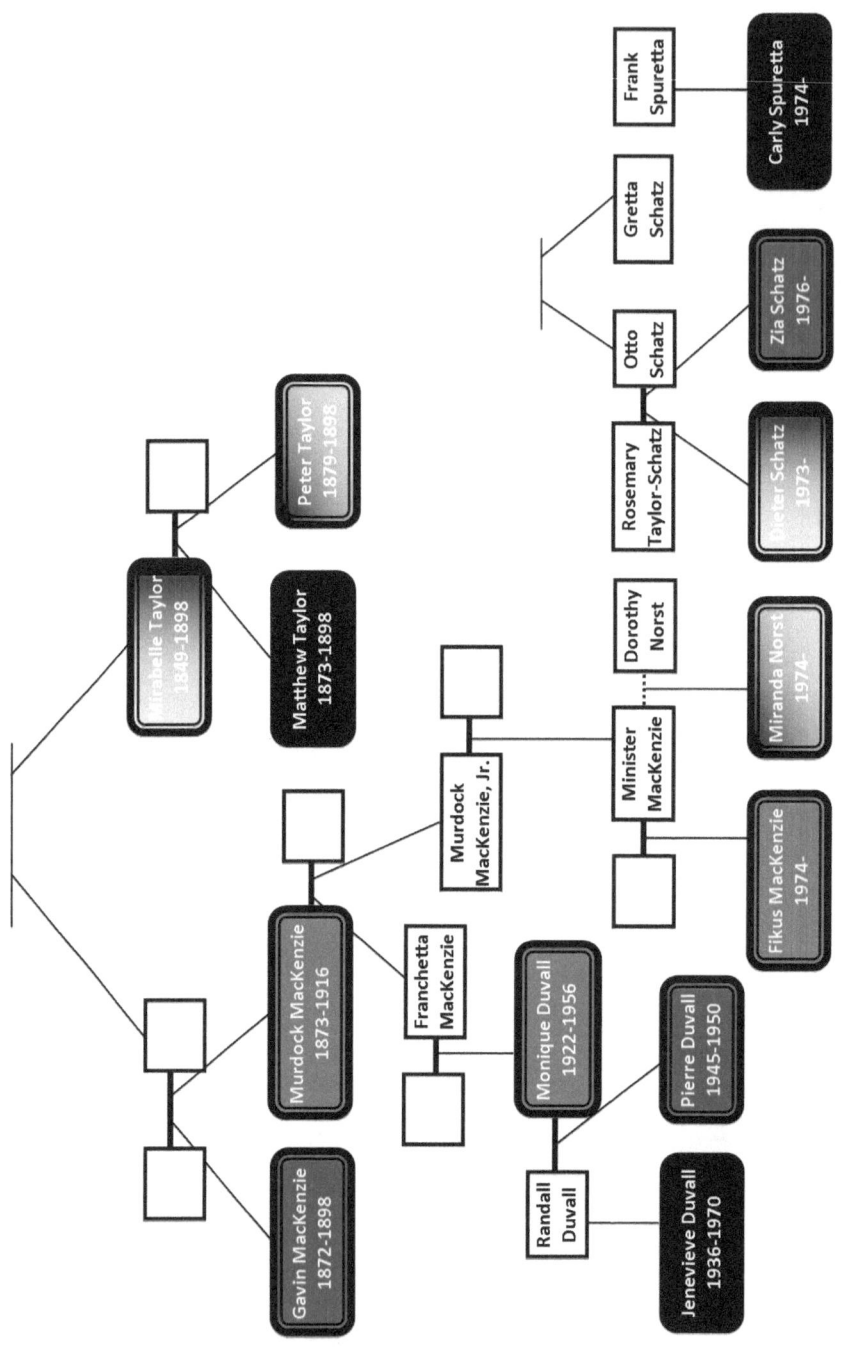

# 48

*What one believes or does not believe will not change what is.*

## 1976 - Kenzie Cove, California

Knobs and hills undulated across Rosemary's belly. "Settle down, Claudia," Rosemary said, rubbing lotion over her stretching skin, "settle down," but her daughter continued to tumble. *Daughter,* Rosemary assumed, because the pregnancy differed from her pregnancy with Dieter.

With Dieter, Rosemary's cheeks had glowed, her nails had hardened, and her hair had strengthened with a lustrous sheen. In her current pregnancy, her stomach retched, her cheeks sunk, and her blond hair thinned into ashen gray. These were the signs of carrying a strong-willed daughter, and a strong-willed daughter deserved an equally strong name, one that firmed the tongue —Claudia. Rosemary had decided this, and her husband, Otto, had agreed.

But then, a few nights before labor, Rosemary woke to the musical chimes of a windup toy. *Tink-tingaling-tink-tingaling.*

Three a.m. glowed on the bedside clock.

Dieter must have crawled out of bed to play in the nursery. Although the music would not wake Rosemary's snoring husband, it might wake Gretta, Otto's younger sister, whose bedroom faced the nursery.

Rosemary eased from her bed and into her bathrobe. While she was looking for her slippers, the music quieted. In its stead came a child's giggle. Rosemary froze. She knew the sound of her toddler, and that giggle was not Dieter's. She heard the snapping clicks of a toy being rewound before the music started again. *Tink-tingaling-tink-tingaling.*

"Otto," she whispered.

*Cauuk-shoooo.*

Rosemary stepped cautiously into the hallway. Leaning to the left, she saw Dieter snuggled in his bed. She stepped to the right and then inched Gretta's door open. Gretta was sound asleep.

*Tink-tingaling-tink-tingaling.*

Rosemary crossed the hall and then peered into the nursery.

Down from the uppermost shelf, the stuffed, blue elephant jingled and tingled in the hands of a toddler no older than Dieter. Rosemary clapped her chest. *A dream?* She pinched herself. No, she was not dreaming. Was this a lost child who had entered through a window? Maybe. Or maybe it was a vision of her soon-to-be baby. "Are you Claudia?"

"No, your baby has red lights," the toddler said in a voice that belied her tender years. "And her name is not Claudia. It's Zia." She pranced the elephant while singing, "Zia, Zia, Zia."

Rosemary rushed back to her bedroom. "Otto, get up, get up." She jostled and shook him.

Otto sat up. "What? What is it? Is it time?"

"A baby girl is in the nursery. Hurry. She's just a baby." She tugged on Otto's thick arm while he was trying to rub the grogginess from his eyes. "Hurry, Otto, hurry. We have a baby girl in the nursery."

"We do?" He raised blinking eyes to Rosemary, and he reached out to touch her belly. Feeling the swell, "Whew," he fell back to the sheets. "I thought I had missed it."

Rosemary whipped back the covers. "Get up."

"Yeah, sure." Otto pushed his bulk off the bed and onto two feet. "You had a dream, my Rosie, just a dream."

"*Shhh*, keep your voice down or you'll wake up Dieter and Gretta." She pushed and tugged until her husband was standing at the nursery's doorway.

"Where is this baby girl?" he asked.

"She's hiding." Rosemary shoved him. "Go look, go look."

Otto bent to one knee to look beneath the crib. "Peek-a-boo, where are you?" At Rosemary's insistence, he checked behind the cradle, through the closet, and inside the hamper. "Should I search the dresser drawers, too?"

"See that?" Rosemary pointed to the toy elephant leaning against the leg of the changing table.

Otto picked up the toy, and then he looked at the high shelf. "How did this fall?"

Rosie smiled. "She was an angel."

"Yeah, sure," Otto said. "Angel or dream, whatever makes you happy. Can we go to bed now?"

"Her name is Zia."

"Whose name is Zia? Your angel?"

"No, not the angel." Rosemary patted her belly.

"Auk, no," Otto said. "Claudia. That is her name. Zia is not a name. It is too many pickled eggs giving you bad dreams."

Rosemary snatched the elephant from his hands and jiggled it near his nose. "Pickled eggs do not wind up musical toys. Angels do."

Rosemary started back to their bedroom. Otto followed, pleading at her heels. "My Rosie, be reasonable. If your mind has changed on Claudia, we will pick another name. But Zia is not a name."

"It must be a name; angels do not lie."

"You do not believe in angels."

She turned abruptly. "Otto, I have never met one before, but now I have, and that is that."

They resettled into bed. No sooner had Rosemary turned off the lamp when she turned it on again. "Our baby has red lights."

Otto groaned. "Zia is not a name, and babies do not have lights."

"Hmm. Maybe the angel meant red hair. My grandfather, Patrick Taylor, had bright red hair."

"Auk." Otto sat up again. "How about this: If she has no red hair, her name is Claudia. If she has red hair, her name is Zia, which is not a name."

Rosemary kissed him. "I will find out what Zia means."

"I better get busy," Rosemary's Guide told Alpha. "For Zia to be born with a shock of red hair, I need to stimulate some old Taylor genes."

"I am grateful," Alpha said. "By having her Soul's name, Zia will be more receptive to my whispers."

"She had better be," the Guide said. "If she repeats her past pattern of wreaking havoc, the Players might think she really is Rosemary's Baby."

Alpha's brows gathered. "She *is* Rosemary's baby."

"Oh, I hope not." The Guide rippled with a giggle.

Alpha frowned.

"The Player-thing," the Guide said, "from this region. The novel? The movie?"

Alpha shook his head.

"I'm sorry, Alpha. You are correct. Zia is Rosemary's Baby."

# 49

*He introduced himself as Alpha, my new Guide.*

Rosemary's ill-health had little to do with carrying a daughter, strong-willed or otherwise. Two years after Zia's birth, Rosemary returned to Energy.

In want of her mother, Zia began bed-wetting, head-rocking, and scab-picking, which continued through the toddler's third year but calmed in her fourth. By her fifth birthday, Zia was going about childhood reasonably well.

To Romal, it seemed a good time for Alpha to make his presence known. After weeks had turned into months, and the months had turned into a year, Romal asked, "What delays you?"

"I am waiting for the proper setting," Alpha said.

"How prudent of you. And I was thinking you were nervous about interacting with a Player-child. Silly me." Romal disappeared.

The following morning, while Zia was collecting insects in the garden, Alpha vibrated repose to the elements and the beasts. Clouds and wind chimes settled. Birds perched, their beaks closed. Barking dogs quieted.

Zia sensed the stillness. Her arms, mid-reach to a caterpillar, broke into gooseflesh.

Choosing sound waves heard through the eardrums, Alpha said, "The morning is good."

Zia's head turned slowly to look behind her.

"The morning is—"

"*MAGRETTAAA!*" She ran wailing. "*MAGRETTAAA!*"

The screen door burst open, and a robust woman stooped just in time; Zia plunged headlong into her aunt's bosom. MaGretta swept her up, "Oh, liebchen, *shhh, shhh,*" and clutched her tight. "Tell me what has happened? Did a bug bite you? Are you hurt?" She ran a quick eye over Zia's arms and legs, but saw no injury.

As MaGretta smoothed back Zia's tuffs of red hair, Zia whimpered about a monster—a big, ugly monster—that was hiding in the bushes. "It wanted to eat me," Zia said. Her fingers curling into makeshift claws, Zia bared her teeth and growled. "*Grrrr*, the morning is good, uhm, good for hungry monsters like me. I'm going to gobble you up."

"Oh, Zia, you're not much of a meal."

"But that's what it said." Zia burrowed again into her aunt's chest.

MaGretta eyed the garden. Had a realtor mistakenly entered the yard? She squinted at the latch securing the gate. Had a lost beachcomber asked for directions? But she saw no shadows moving behind the slats in the fence.

All was ordinary.

All except Zia.

MaGretta's heart sank. Zia's endless imagination now included monsters. For the first time, *monsters*. It was a bad sign—MaGretta's hug tightened—A very bad sign.

---

Alpha lingered in the garden. Romal knew that Zia's cries were weighing heavily on Alpha's thoughts...as well they should. "Why, Alpha?" Romal appeared. "Why did you choose sound waves? After Niine seeded the belief among Players that voices and visions emanate from their side, and from their side only, you advised all Guides to restrict themselves to the Mind's Eye and Ear, 'For the safety of the Player,' you said. Has something changed?"

"Players do not burn witches at the stake."

"Is that your reason? Pitifully poor. The prevailing dogma still pins our voices to demons, or worse, to mental maladies. So I'll ask you again; why did you use the old technique instead of weaving yourself between what her eye discerns and what her mind imagines?"

Upon the word, *imagines*, Alpha twitched, a fraction of a second twitch, but a telling-twitch all the same. Romal surveyed the surroundings. "Something she imagines troubles you." He saw only a peaceful garden. "What could that something possibly be?"

"You do not understand."

"Yes, yes, so enlighten me. You've gone into the minds of thousands, if not millions, and not one mind ever gave you pause...until now. What ghastly beast could possibly dwell within this child's imagination that would cause you alarm?"

With a hesitant hand, Alpha gestured toward the flowerbed.

"Daisies?" Romal asked. "*Daisies?* What on Earth does her mind do to the daisies?"

"She gives them faces."

"*Faces?* Daisies with faces, I see." Romal stroked his chin thoughtfully. "That certainly begs for a line to be drawn. No Guide should have to share space with such an abomination."

"It is unsettling to be among—"

"No, no. No need to explain. It's quite understandable. You've stood among imaginings beyond the imagination—unconquerable armies, insurmountable plagues, catastrophic explosions. You've traversed a cornucopia of phantom fears and paranoid delusions. But now you must tolerate the intolerable—a patch of winking daisies. Well, I say to you, Guide of Guides, Great Solver of Peril, you can do it. Do it for all of us. Get in there and buck up to those petal pushers. Should they give you a wink of trouble, you should wink right back. Wink, wink, wink, to every last one of them. They have it coming."

"I did not say they winked."

"Oh, my mistake. That changes *NOTHING!*" Romal released an exasperated breath. "Alpha, this is a child's imagination. A *child*. Expect all elements anthropomorphized, including flowers. You can treat it as a nuisance or you can appreciate the creativity." Peering into Alpha's somber eyes, Romal whispered, "*Cura te ipsum*, my friend. Please. Cure thyself."

Weeks later, at the far end of the yard, Alpha positioned himself beside a redwood tree. He hoped the tree would remain faceless within Zia's mind.

Like before, Zia was busy with bugs, only this time, she was carting them in a shoebox over to a small table set with teacups and plates. On one plate, she scattered the sow bugs, the crickets, and the earwigs. On another plate, she set down a crippled grasshopper and a handful of beetles. Then she sat and began chatting nonsensically to her insect friends.

As Romal had stated, Zia's mind personified the bugs, each bug complimenting Zia for her lovely tea party.

A cricket, however, jumped for freedom. Zia pursued. After a stern warning on tea-party etiquette, she returned the cricket to its plate. As she started back to her chair, she noticed Alpha. She pushed aside a flop of red curls and squinted. "Hello?"

Before Alpha had a chance to return the greeting, Zia yelled, "HELLO? Can't you hear me? HELLO!"

Alpha ventured a few steps closer.

Zia perked. "Are you shy?" She clued him of the desired response by continually nodding. "You're shy, right? Right?"

Alpha forced himself to nod.

Zia squealed, seemingly thrilled. She rushed to the chair opposite her own. "Sit here." She tapped the seat. "Have tea with us. Okay? Okay?"

At Alpha's feet, a sprinkling of daffodils sprouted mouths. "She won't hurt you. Join her. Join her."

Then the crows overhead began prodding, "*Caw, Caw*, don't be shy, *caw, caw*, join her."

All the while, Zia pat her hip, as if she were begging the trust of a feral cat. "Don't be scared. We won't hurt you. Come on. Sit here."

Alpha rumbled. He would have preferred standing among phantom fears and paranoid delusions than standing among condescending daffodils and intrusive crows. Nevertheless, he approached.

Zia hurried back to her chair. She grabbed the toy pitcher. Leaning across the table, she poured absolutely nothing into a cup. "That's your tea. Try some." She raised her own cup, her pinky extending, and she sipped emptiness.

*Indulge her,* Romal said from above. *Take pleasure in a warm cup of tea.*

*There is no tea,* Alpha said.

*Even better. With pretend-tea, you can add as much sugar as you like.*

"Sit down," Zia told him.

Alpha peered at the doll-sized chair. *I do not—*

Before he could finish his sentence, out of the mouth of this very small child came an inordinately loud command. "SIT DOWN! SIT DOWN!"

*Yes, yes, hurry Alpha,* Romal said, *sit before every Soul in Divisional has fashioned a chair.*

Alpha bent into an awkward simulation of sitting.

Zia introduced her guests; Goliath and Goliath and Goliath, repeating the name for all eleven beetles. Crickets were Skippers, sow bugs were Rollie Pollies, and earwigs were Pinchers. Only the three-legged grasshopper had a distinct name—Jimminey. When it jumped for freedom, it landed sideways.

"My name is Zia." She thumbed her chest. "What is your name?"

Again, she didn't wait for Alpha's answer.

"Don't you have a name?" she asked. "I can name you."

*I have a name.* His tone was harsher than he had intended, but Zia didn't flinch. She seemed unfazed at hearing Alpha's voice through her Mind's Ear, though wholly disappointed that he had a name.

"Why can't I name you?" she asked.

*I am declared Alpha.*

She nibbled a fingernail. "What do you mean?"

*I am addressed as Alpha.*

Her forehead crinkled, still unsure of his name.

Alpha was about to restate it a third time when Zia suddenly brightened. "You mean Ralph?"

Her comment brought down a rain of laughter, not only from Romal, but from many Guides.

Alpha's jaw tightened. *I did not say—*

"Ralph, drink your tea," she said. "It's good. Hmm. Drink some."

"Zia," MaGretta called from the kitchen window, "your Papa and Dieter are home. Come inside to wash the hands. It is time for supper."

Greatly relieved, Alpha's eyes closed, his sigh ringing the wind chimes.

"NOT NOW!" Zia shouted.

Alpha's eyes flew open.

"RALPH WON'T DRINK HIS TEA!"

Alpha's hand was halfway up before he realized he could not signal for her silence. *You should listen to your caretaker.*

"You talk funny," Zia said. "How come? How come you—" An ocean breeze swept through the yard. Zia sniffed the salted air. Her face paled. "Ralph, I can't play now." Back into the shoebox went the beetles and Jimminey. Her other guests had fled. "I have to go eat dinner. We can play tomorrow." With the box tucked under an arm, she hurried to the house.

Alpha looked up to the still chuckling Guides. *Do you not have Charges requiring your assistance?*

# 50

**1992**

For a decade, Otto ignored Zia's obsession with bugs and her conversations with unseen friends. "My Gretta," Otto told his worried sister, "it is only childhood nonsense. Zia will outgrow it."

But Zia did not outgrow it, which heightened MaGretta's concerns. Several times, she had tried to ambush Otto into having a talk about Zia's funniness, but Otto had always escaped—he had to escape because he had no answer. And when a man had no answer, a man should avoid a questioning woman. To avoid MaGretta, Otto stayed late at Otto's Autos, night after night, sometimes working until dawn. Then one night, as Otto slipped into his darkened home, the entry lights snapped on.

"OTTO!"

Otto shrank like a spotlighted burglar.

"You will listen to me," MaGretta said.

Otto groaned, wishing he had stayed at Spanky's Bar for another round of beer. He pushed off his shoes and shed his coveralls.

MaGretta clasped her hips. "We will discuss Zia. Now!"

"Not now. Tomorrow."

"Not tomorrow. We will talk now. I've made up my mind. Zia needs more than bugs and invisible friends. She needs a pet that walks on four legs not crawls on six. She needs a pet with fur not with wings." MaGretta pulled in a breath. "I will buy her a cat."

"A CAT? NEIN! VERBOTEN!"

"Stop your bellowing. Do you want to wake the children?"

"Cats are no good!" Otto whispered loudly, his hand splicing the air. "No good!"

"So, it is better for your daughter to play with the cockroaches; is that what you think?"

Otto's thick hands washed over his face. He hated to argue with his baby sister. For that matter, he hated to argue with any woman because women were very good with words. They practiced their word-skills by nagging at men: Don't wash your dirty hands near the colander of noodles; don't scratch or fart in a church; don't wear a hat or blow your nose at the dinner table. Women used their words either to nag or to confuse men—like MaGretta was doing now.

If Otto said yes, it meant Zia should play with the cockroaches. If Otto said no, it meant a cat would come home. When confused, a man should say nothing and walk away—run if the woman is hot-tempered or the man might get a skillet to the back of his head. Otto's father hadn't learned to duck until the third time stitched.

Otto hiked his trousers. "No...more...talk." He marched to the living room and thumped into his recliner, causing the springs a complaining bleat.

MaGretta settled into the chair across from Otto.

After rustling a newspaper open, Otto pretended to read, though his eyes strained at the corner to watch MaGretta.

Unlike their mother, MaGretta would never be violent; Otto knew that for certain. He was watching for tears. When a woman's nagging failed, she often resorted to tears; Otto knew that, too. And tears jellied Otto's resolve. When he heard no sniffling, he started to relax.

MaGretta lifted an embroidery basket onto her lap. A moment later, she let out a moan, a moan of exaggerated despair that Otto knew well. He no longer relaxed. He answered with a tough snort and he raised his paper to block her view.

"Such a shame," MaGretta said. "The poor child has only bugs and ghosts for friends. Oh, such a shame."

Otto chewed the tip of his mustache; he must not react. Must not. If he reacted, then somehow, a cat would come home. He burrowed into the news.

"Ohhh."

"Auk," Otto crumpled the paper. "My Gretta, bugs are not so bad."

"Not bad? What is good about bugs?"

Otto pinched his lower lip until the answer came to him. "When they die, we can flush them down the toilet. That is good."

MaGretta set aside her needlework and left her chair to crouch beside her brother. "Otto, it is not right. Zia is not a little girl anymore. She is a young woman. She should be noticing the boys, not collecting the bugs and talking to the ghosts. You are a good Poppa, but you do not see your daughter with clear eyes. Before Rosemary died—"

Otto flinched. MaGretta squeezed his arm. "Before Rosemary died, I swore to her, I will always do my best for Dieter and Zia."

Otto patted his sister's hand. "And you have, my Gretta. You have."

"Otto, after the funeral, Dieter did not speak. Each night, he nestled into my arms, and I rocked him. Night after night, month after month, until finally, again he talks. But I did not push him. No. I waited with patience for his grief to ease. And it did. You did not know about this because you took to the Schnapps. But I waited with patience for your grief to ease. And over time, you did not drink so much. You are a good Poppa."

"A good Poppa? You think I am a good Poppa?"

"A wonderful Poppa."

Otto thought himself a terrible poppa, and he feared that his sister would confirm it. "I thought you would tell me that I had failed. Failed Zia."

"No, Otto, no. How could you think such a thing?"

Otto filled his lungs with a rush of air, as though it were his first breath taken in many, many years, so great was the guilt that had pressed upon his heart. "Thank you," he leaned over and hugged MaGretta. Her opinion of his fatherhood mattered—mattered greatly. Otto would sleep well tonight. "We should have talked sooner. Next time, do not wait so long."

He started to lift from his chair, but MaGretta clamped his arm. "I am not finished." Her grip didn't loosen until Otto sat back. "Otto, Zia's grief does not ease. I have waited with patience, but her grief does not ease. That is why she is...funny. Now we must act. This, I promised to Rosemary."

"Yeah, sure, but—" Otto rubbed his forehead, pondering solutions that didn't involve a cat. When his hand came down, his fingers were oily from the splatters of car grease that darkened his brow. This grease gave Otto an idea. "How about if Zia comes to the garage after school? She could work on the cars. Dieter and I will teach her. She can change tires and learn tune-ups."

"No, Otto." MaGretta returned to her chair and picked up the needle-work. "That is good for Dieter. He loves the cars and is proud to work with his Poppa, but that is not right for a girl." MaGretta glanced at the hallway before she leaned toward Otto and whispered, "Zia should speak to a professional."

"Auk, NO! No head doctor. I am her Poppa." Otto beat on his chest. "If Zia has troubles, she will tell them to me."

"Not doctor-professional," MaGretta said. "Zia will speak to the church minister. He will tell us if Zia has problems in the head."

"Minister MacKenzie? I have no use for Irish ministers."

"For the hundredth time, he is not Irish. He is Scottish."

"The same!" Otto fisted the armrest. He had no use for ministers, Irish or Scottish. No use for ministers or for their churches, not since the year he had begged God to spare his Rosie. He had lit candles, promised life-changes, and kept the Commandments—still, God had taken his Rosie. Because God had no use for Otto, Otto had no use for God.

"It does not cost," MaGretta said working the embroidery threads through the cloth. "And I think Zia should have more activities with other children. Maybe she could join the swimming team at that new Youth Center. Dieter says many kids go there after school. That would be good for Zia. Dieter can pick her up after school and take her there. Zia will have no more time for pranks. By summer, she will have friends, not beetles and ghosts."

"My Gretta, the Youth Center is for troubled kids. Zia is not troubled. She is just...funny. If she wants to swim, she has the whole ocean at her back door. That is where the young people go. They go to the beach, not to the Youth Center."

MaGretta lifted stern eyes. "You know she won't touch the saltwater. We have enough problems with Zia. You leave that one alone."

Otto slumped. Why was he fighting it? MaGretta's plans were already set and probably underway. He sighed with complete resignation...and with some admiration, too. Women were very good with words. He pulled his tired bulk from the chair. Time for Schnapps and for bed. No time for fights that he would never win. "Do as you wish. Take Zia to the Irish Minister, Scottish Minister, whatever minister he is. Sign her up at the Center with the fancy pool and Dieter will take her there. Is that good?"

His sister seemed unmoved.

"My Gretta, I have no more argument with you."

With terse snips, MaGretta clipped the threads.

Otto thought of the Schnapps, his tongue swiping his lips. But his sister's anger would taint the flavor and ruin his sleep. "My Gretta, please, what more? Tell me now, what more will make you happy?"

She gave a coy shrug. "A cat."

"Auk."

## 51

*Zia, the Players are depicted as—as troubled.*

Pop was 19 when he came to America—MaGretta told Dieter and me—with less English than money. In his left fist, he clutched fifty dollars, in his right, he held the tiny hand of his eight-year-old sister, our MaGretta.

Whenever MaGretta recounted that part of her story, her eyes twinkled and her shoulders straightened, unquestionably proud of her big brother. But when she talked about their reasons for leaving Germany, her shoulders rounded and her eyes dulled. Their mother had a violent temper, she said— *bad in the head*—when their father drank too much, which sounded more like the rule than the exception. Then one night, amid a squabble, their mother killed their father. Accidently, MaGretta told us, and then she repeated, *bad in the head, bad in the head.*

Our grandmother was sent to a sanitarium.

As kids, we didn't know what *sanitarium* meant, so Dieter looked it up. With a finger circling his ear, he said it was a nut-house.

"That is why," MaGretta told us, "when your Poppa married your beautiful mother, I lived with them, too."

Her real name is Gretta Schatz, but Dieter and I call her MaGretta. Either we blended Ma with Gretta—when I was two and Dieter was five, our mother died—or we slurred My with Gretta from hearing our Pop call her My Gretta for years. Most likely, it's both, because MaGretta is the only mother we've ever known, and she's certainly My Gretta to all of us.

Although MaGretta is damn near perfect, she's a habitual worrier. Even my taste in literature raises her concern. When cleaning the house, she gave my horror novels a dose of Lysol, warping the tops of my Stephen King first editions. When I complained, she said, "Monsters are no good." She felt the same about my arthropods. Even my rare beetles, she refused to hold.

But mostly, MaGretta fretted about my social life. She thought I should have more friends—girlfriends, boyfriends, as long as they were visible friends who walked on two legs.

She thought I was showing the first signs of *bad in the head*.

I told her my close friends at school were plenty. And that I did like boys, but they liked big-breasted cheerleaders who kicked really high, flashing their asses.

When I tried to explain my love of entomology, Pop and MaGretta stared at me as though I had sprouted antennae.

"What is this entomology?" Pop asked. "Does it make you money?"

"They kill ants in the kitchen," MaGretta said. "Isn't that right, Zia?"

"Just wait," I told them. "I have a surprise to show you, but it's not quite ready." For months, I had been converting aquarium tanks into condos for my beetles. I figured when Pop and MaGretta saw my handiwork, they'd accept my passion. In the least, they'd stop worrying about escapees breeding in the pantry or clinging on the bathroom mirror.

"We have a surprise for you, too," MaGretta said. "It's ready now." She left for a minute. When she returned, she plopped a big, fat Tabby into my arms. She held her breath. I think Pop held his, too. Reading the signals, I made a big deal about it, as though I liked the thing.

Two days later, the cat killed my beetles. It flipped them over, ate their soft underbellies, and left their skeletal cases spinning like discarded walnut shells.

I cried like crazy...and flung the cat out my bedroom window.

When MaGretta asked why I was crying, I told her the cat ran away. Had I told her the truth, that I loved my beetles enough to shed tears, MaGretta would have cried, too, but for a whole different reason.

"No more cats," I told her, "but don't worry, I'll stop chasing the bugs."

I thought my news would thrill her. Instead, she was weirdly nonchalant. "Whatever makes you happy."

Moments later, she casually mentioned my free afternoons. All of them...down to the minute. She spoke with an overkill of shrugs, which should have triggered my alarm. Instead, like the moron in a cheap slasher flick—*Look, blood on the stairs; let's check out the attic*—I walked up to disaster.

"Yep," I said, "I got tons of free time and not a thing to—"

She perked.

"—do*oooooo.*" My breath ran out before I could think of a backslide.

"Good," she said, "because I have an idea."

My stomach cramped. When she spoke again, I blurted, "YES!" because she hadn't said origami, napkin folding, ballet, piano lessons, chess club, or behavior camp. Each god-awful possibility was a bullet, and a condemned man had a better chance of dodging a firing squad's bullets than I had of dodging MaGretta's. Yet, she had missed. I broke into a victory dance.

*"Wave your hands in the air, tell me you don't care, go Zia, go Zia, go Zia."*

"This is wonderful," MaGretta said swaying to my singing. "My prayers are answered; you love the idea."

My dancing slowed. "What idea?"

"I had so much faith, I already signed you up."

"Signed me up for what?"

"You start tomorrow."

"Start what tomorrow?"

"Oh, Zia, don't be...funny." The pause before funny meant funny-odd, and funny-odd caused Pop and MaGretta to worry. So I let the question drop because that was better than explaining, "See, I didn't process your idea. I drifted into another world where crafts and tutus were loaded into guns and you headed the firing squad." At that, she would have freaked. And I would have said, "No, no, MaGretta, don't you get it? I'm free. You MISSED!"

But MaGretta would have missed my point as well.

That night, I talked to Dieter. He said MaGretta and Pop thought swimming would balance whatever imbalance made me...funny. I started to argue, but Dieter said, "Save it. Parents love; parents worry. And they worry most about their odd ducks. That ain't going to change."

His comment haunted me—*ain't going to change*. I didn't care who worried about what, just as long as it wasn't MaGretta or Pop losing sleep over me. Because they couldn't change, I decided to become healed. Balanced. To do that, I had to hide the behaviors that drove them crazy.

I gave up my chlorine-free hair and accepted the brittle-green tints. I tossed the tanks and limited my arthropods to the dead and framed. Among the macabre lining my shelves, I wedged in coma-causing drama, egg-headed poetry, and bile-inducing romance. Lastly, I stopped talking aloud to Alpha when anyone was near. Anyone except Dieter.

I told Dieter everything. If he thought having a phantom friend was weird, he never said so. The depth of his brotherly concern totaled one question, "Does he watch when you take a leak?"

At sixteen, I considered myself pretty mature to have given up so much. In the mirror, I gave Ms. Selfless Maturity a proud thumbs up. But maturity fled in a whine when MaGretta asked me to talk to the Minister—Minister

MacKenzie. *"Whyyy?"* Despite all my efforts, MaGretta wanted the Minister to certify me good in the head. My heel thudded the floor. "Do I have to? *Whyyy?"*

Every person who ever lived in our county eventually heard or read about the Minister, our town's self-proclaimed spiritual leader, whose grandfather, Murdock MacKenzie, supposedly founded Kenzie Cove.

In truth, Murdock founded squat.

Months earlier, on assignment for our school newspaper, I researched Murdock's history. In his home state of Utah, Murdock racked up a mess of charges—pandering, collusion, bribery, robbery—but skirted all convictions.

During the gold rush of 1898, Murdock and his brother, Gavin, teamed up with their cousins, Matthew and Peter Taylor, and headed for Alaska. There, Gavin was shot; a bullet straight to his heart. The Taylor brothers died in the historical Palm Sunday Avalanche.

Murdock crossed into Canada and later struck gold in the Yukon.

Married with two kids, Murdock returned to the states a rich man. He settled here, and he named the town, but that was all Murdock did. I couldn't find one record that the tight-ass ever parted with a dime to promote anything or anyone but himself.

In 1916, after complaining of headaches, Murdock keeled over and died. The officials listed his death under natural causes. Newspapers hinted at murder. Murder by poison. And they cast suspicion on Murdock's daughter, sweet-sixteen Franchetta, who liked to brew teas for her dad. But nobody dug too deep because Franchetta was pretty and Murdock was an asshole.

None of this appears in our town's brochure, which our own good Minister revised. In the Minister's brochure, Murdock is a great guy, a true humanitarian. Every tourist shop, lodge, and cafe in the county displays the Minister's version—a version of crap.

Our newspaper editor loved my report, but a teacher gave it to an administrator, who showed it to the School Board. Principal Burke summoned me to his office. He told me, quote, the report lacked merit. Naively, I fumbled for my notes, apologized for my grammatical mistakes, and promised to weed out unflattering opinions.

Enunciating his words—so I'd get his message—he told me, "Stop your troublemaking."

Walking home from school, I kicked every stone and spat on every cat. When I explained my bitterness to MaGretta, I added, "How come Kenzie

Cove has three supermarkets, five hair salons, two bookstores, twelve bars, but only one church, Kenzie's Church of Light? Isn't that a God monopoly? Ridgecrest is half our size but they have four churches."

MaGretta told me then and has repeated it several times since, "Zia, choose your battles carefully, or you will not have strength to fight in your wars." I figured she was asking me to leave it alone, so I did. I thought of her advice again when she asked me to meet with the Minister. Since whining wasn't working, I gave up the battle.

Although MaGretta had an appointment, we sat in the lounge for nearly an hour before the Minister's assistant came to escort me to the office. MaGretta remained in the lounge.

Like his granddaddy's picture in our town's brochure, the Minister had dark, sinister eyes. But unlike his granddaddy—an ox of a man—the Minister had a sharp jaw and hollow cheeks, a match for Lee Van Cleef in *The Good, The Bad, and The Ugly*—Van Cleef, of course, being the bad.

"Sit down, Zia. Make yourself comfortable." He indicated the chair fronting his desk, but he didn't extend a hand. "I'm Minister MacKenzie. You probably don't remember me, but I remember you. How are you today?"

"Fine, I guess." I sat and looked around. Later, I noticed the silence. "Oh, sorry. Uhm, how are you?"

"Fine, fine. Every Sunday, I talk with your lovely aunt, but I haven't seen your father since your mother passed away." He flashed obligatory sadness. "And it has been nearly that long since you and your brother—Peter is it?"

"Dieter."

"Dieter, that's right. Since you and Dieter attended Sunday Services. Any particular reason you don't wish to join us for worship?"

"MaGretta and Pop said we could decide for ourselves. And, well, we decided no."

"I see. Well, I'll pray that you and Peter come back to the Church."

"Dieter."

The Minister reached into a drawer. With two hands, he heaved out a monstrous book with cover boards wrapped in gold parchment. On top, a gigantic cross glistened in red stones. Or gems. They sparkled like rubies. It was the mother of all books, a huge, ornate monstrosity. With the cover boards pulled back, the book spanned a third of his desk. By the handfuls, he turned thick, brown pages, every page stained in ink, stuffed with cards, and cluttered with pictures. Jeez, it was the Catalog of all Souls.

Eventually, he settled on a half-written sheet. "You attend Kenzie High?"

"Sure. Doesn't everyone?"

He smiled weirdly, as if he were holding in gas. "Let's see. You're a sopho-more and Peter is a senior. My son is a senior, too. Maybe you know him—Fikus?"

"*Dieter* graduated last year. And yeah, I know Fikus, but we hang in different crowds." In truth, I avoided Fikus like I avoided stepping in dog-shit, both being a stinking pain. When Fikus talked, his dark eyes ping-ponged to the sides of you, as though someone were sneaking up from behind. His wiry frame and jerky movements earned him the nickname, Squirrelly Dude. That was an insult to squirrels; Fikus was just plain creepy. He laughed dramatically at jokes, but he never told one. And he wore a knowing smile, the kind you give with a wink to a close friend, but Fikus had no friends. His smile looked demented.

At one point, I felt sorry for him...and stepped right into crap. In front of a dozen classmates, a cheerleader told Fikus that his hair—which hung in clumps over a pimple infested forehead—needed an oil change. Instead of giving her what-for, Fikus scurried away.

Hating cheerleaders already, I emptied a tube of hair remover into a bottle of expensive shampoo. I gift-wrapped the bottle, attached a card from a secret admirer, and set it on top the cheerleader's locker. I didn't think she would fall for it, but her vanity won over brains.

I slept guilt-free because no one accused Fikus for causing the cheer-leader's stubble hair. Instead, snide remarks targeted me, though on the piss-poorest of reasons; *that's something Zia would do.*

I didn't care, but Fikus overheard the gossip, and he got it into his head that I had championed him. Like a fed skunk, he followed me everywhere. Around each corner, I saw his stupid, lovesick face.

My friends found it hysterically funny. Others snickered.

I threatened Fikus, cherry-bombed his locker, called him a freak over the campus PA, but he didn't get the message; he wouldn't leave me alone.

I couldn't go to an adult because adults always say, "I'll get to the bottom of this." They never say, the *middle* of this, or even the *start.* It's always *the bottom,* and at the bottom was altered shampoo.

I cut a month's worth of classes and had to take summer school to make up the Fs. Despite what Fikus had put me through, I thought it would be rude to tell the Minister the truth—your son is a freak.

I slouched low and picked my nails while the Minister studied me. "Your aunt thinks you're having some difficulties. Some problems or troubles. I might be able to help you, if you'll let me. Will you let me, Zia?"

I looked up from my bitten nails. "Sure."

"Is there a problem at home? Is something bothering you at school?"

"Nope. Everything is pretty good."

He leaned back, his pen tapping his palm. "I'm told you're preoccupied with insects. I'm also told you have an overactive imagination."

I shrugged. "I'm okay with that. I just wish it didn't trouble my family."

The beat of his pen quickened. "Zia, I need you to trust me. That's the only way I can help you. Be honest now, are you smoking marijuana?"

"Auk." I heard Pop's guttural noise come out of my throat. "No, I don't smoke pot. And I don't drop acid or eat mushrooms. I've sipped some Schnapps once or twice. Maybe more."

The Minister nodded but didn't say a word. I guess he was waiting for something juicier than sipping Schnapps.

"Well, okay," I said. "To be honest, there is something bugging me, bugging the hell out of me. Oh, sorry. I shouldn't have said hell."

"No, no, that's all right, Zia. I've heard much worse. Believe me." The Minister stretched an open hand across the desk. "What is it you were going to say? Trust me. I only want to help you."

"How come your church is the only church in town?" As God is my witness, I asked the question, not from smartass brattiness, but from sincere curiosity. I once asked our Town Mayor, "How come the potholes on your street have been repaired, but the potholes on other streets have to wait for a budget?" I lived on a pothole-free street, and I avoided all churches, so my questions rose, not from a personal interest, but from a fairness standpoint. Unfairness bugged me. And I thought the Minister wanted to know what was bugging me. But I thought wrong. His open hand whipped away. Against a nagging sense telling me to shut up, I asked, "Where are the churches for Catholics or Baptists? You can't count the Jehovah Witness building. Technically, it's a hall. But where are the Churches for—"

"Are you a Christian?" His icy tone could have frozen fire.

"What?"

"You seem concerned about Christian churches."

"No offense, Minister, but you interrupted before I got to the Synagogues. Those are for Jews, right?"

"Church of Light is nondenominational; we welcome all faiths. All *Christian* faiths. Now, Zia, you're a bright girl, and I'm sure you're a good Christian girl...most of the time. So let's stop playing games. Tell me what's troubling you."

I rubbed my forehead, my thoughts spinning with a million things not to say: *How come you waited for my manners, but you didn't offer a handshake? How come you can't remember my brother's name is Dieter? How come you dodged my question about churches?* But I didn't say any of that. "Minister, straight up, MaGretta thinks bugs are gross, so I gave up entomology, okay? And MaGretta got it into her head that I needed more friends, so I joined the swim team. My green hair isn't about a druggy's rebellion; it's about ignoring a *Do-Not-Swim* sign across an over-chlorinated pool. But what's irritating me now is that you called me a Christian. I don't like labels, especially labels with strings. But if you insist on sticking me into a slot, then call me an agnostic."

The Minister smirked, a *that-explains-everything* smirk. His pen opened with an eager click, and he muttered, "Atheist."

I arched over the desk, but the crook of his elbow covered the page. "Did you write atheist?" I asked. "I said agnostic."

"Same thing."

"IT IS NOT!"

"Sit down, Zia."

"NO! MaGretta translates atheist to gottesleugner. She'll get crazy upset. She'll camp at my bedside, freakin' praying!"

"How does she feel about agnostics?"

I bit my lip. Years ago, MaGretta mixed agnostic with obnoxious. Not confused or substituted, but blended their meanings. She thought annoying others was a strange tenet, but she defended The Obnoxious because they didn't deny God. I should have set her straight right then to spare her any embarrassment. Because I hadn't, the humiliation was forever mine. "Be patient," she told the cashier, the waitress, the bank teller, the grocery bagger, and everyone else she overheard call another obnoxious. "They all act that way. My Zia is a devout Obnoxious."

Again, the Minister told me to sit. When I didn't, he demanded, "Now!"

I thumped onto my chair.

The Minister readied his pen. "Let's discuss this imaginary friend that has your aunt concerned."

"Aw, jeez. What about him?"

"Him?"

I shrugged. "Do you want me to look under his robe?"

"Interesting." His pen jiggled across the paper. "Tell me, do you still talk to him?"

"No."

"Are you lying or is your aunt lying?"

"MaGretta never lies."

The Minister waited for more.

"Yeah, okay," I said, "but big deal. Everybody keeps mementos from their childhood—a blanket, a stuffed animal, a raccoon hat. I know a guy who kept his baby teeth. Now, that's a sicko. All I kept from childhood was my tea-party friend. That's it. No big deal."

"We're making progress." He flipped a blank page over his notes before he leaned back, posturing as Minister-Psychologist. "Tell me about him."

"Nothing to tell."

"You do understand that your friend exists only in your mind, correct?"

"Excuse me, Minister, but you're making a heck of an assumption. My friend could exist in a billion minds; how would I know? I'm not God."

"Do you believe he's God?"

"Jeez, no way. He's too ugly." *I'm just kidding.*

*I am not offended,* Alpha said.

"Besides, if I were an atheist, I wouldn't believe in God, right? So you're admitting that I'm an agnostic, right? Right?"

"It depends. Tell me what you think he is."

My attention shifted to Alpha, the oh-so-serious Alpha. "He's grumpy." *Well, you are.* "He's the gloomy ghoul of all that is dreadful and dreary."

Alpha's mouth slanted, annoyed, as if he were suffering the insufferable, which naturally begged for more teasing. My cheeks puffing, my jowls wobbling, I mimicked a Shakespearean grumble. "Why, he's an undigested bit of beef, that's what he is. Harrumph-harrumph. He's a blot of mustard, a crumb of cheese, a morsel repeating, a fragment of an underdone pota—"

"ZIA!"

My attention snapped back to the Minister, who was now glaring. "Oh, sorry," I said. "I was quoting the Scrooge guy. That's what he called the ghosts, you know, undigested beef."

"You're playing games." Then the Minister sneered, a really rude sneer, too. "You know he's not real, don't you?"

"He's real to me."

"All right, I'll play along. Is your ghost with us now?" He waved a mocking hand, which was beyond rude. "Let's have your friend prove himself. Ask him what I have in my bottom desk drawer. If he exists, he should be able to tell us."

"Are you kidding?"

"Ask him," the Minister ordered as if his test were valid and not insanely stupid. "Have him prove his existence."

"Tell you what, prove yours first. What's in my pocket?"

The Minister's eyes thinned. He leaned forward to intimidate me, so I leaned forward, too, with a hand splicing my knocking knees to hide my intimidation. The Minister's knuckles rapped the desk. "Prove his existence."

"Prove yours."

"Others can see and hear me."

"Not the blind and deaf."

"You can see me."

"I can see him."

"He's not real."

"You're not real."

"Science proves me," he spat, seriously spat, his *proves* flecking my cheek with his spittle.

"Science?" I sleeved my face. "Science can't even prove or disprove the existence of your boss."

"My boss?"

"Yeah, your boss." I pointed up. "Isn't He your boss?"

A purple vein rippled at the Minister's temple. He pushed a speaker-button. "Bring Miss Schatz."

"What are you going to tell her?"

His lips curled smugly. "I'm an honest man, Zia, a man of God. I have to be truthful with your aunt. You have serious mental issues. Whether from drugs or from illness—"

"NO WAY!" Instantly, my mouth dried. "You'll hurt MaGretta. She'll blame herself. Don't even mention mental illness."

"Do you want me to lie to her?"

"Could you? That would be great."

"No, I cannot. I'm sorry, Zia." But he wasn't sorry a bit. He started writing as if I had already left the room.

My eyes scrunched tight. I wanted to take back everything, start the session over, reverse time. *Alpha, help me. Don't let him hurt MaGretta. Please!*

Alpha stuck an image into my head. *Truth is a powerful sword.*

Being upset, I couldn't make out the image. Emotions screw up the picture like a toppled antenna screws up a TV. The image zigzagged.

I took deep breaths, trying calm down—*breathe in, breathe out, come on, come on, calm down, deep breaths.* For three seconds, the distortion eased up, at least enough for me to make out the image. "What the hell does that have to do with the price of rice? Huh? How does that help me? Huh? Oh wait. Wait. I think I get it. Yeah. Hey, thanks."

The Minister was eyeing me. "Talking to him now, Zia? Very funny, but the game is over."

"Yeah, you're right. I totally understand. You have to be truthful—truthful about everything, including our town's history. See, I wrote a ten-page biography on Murdock MacKenzie. And because you're an honest man, a man of God, you say, you might want to read it and revise our town's brochure...to make it truthful. Because your granddaddy didn't build Kenzie Cove. He named it, sure, because he bullied and blackmailed a whole lot of officials. Back in Utah, they called Murdock a scoundrel. That's an old fashioned term for scumbag."

*WHUMP.* The Minister pelted the Catalog of all Souls. "No one cares about your fabricated story. I believe you were already told that your report lacked merit."

"Lacked merit? Yeah, that's exactly what I was told. Burke used those same two words, lacked merit." A cold shiver ran up my spine; the Minister had much more power than what I had imagined. "You censored my report. You knew it was the truth, too. Wow. What a lousy thing to do. Well, Minister, I'm going to rewrite it."

Just then, the assistant cracked the door. The Minister signaled for another minute. The door closed. "No one will publish your slander."

"Jeez. You control the newspapers, too? Fine. I'll send the report to Ridgecrest. Then I'll write another story about how our town denies permits to all churches except to yours."

Alpha rolled his eyes. *You have no such knowledge.*

*It's called bluffing. Now shut it. I have to look confident.* I sprouted a grin. "I'll send my reports to the Governor, if I have to.

His eyes narrow and mean, the Minister said, "Are you blackmailing me?"

"Heck, no, blackmail upsets MaGretta." My smile flat-lined. "And I don't want anything to upset MaGretta. Get it?"

When the assistant checked again, the Minister nodded.

Upon entering the office, MaGretta glanced nervously, back and forth, between me and the Minister.

I stood on shaky legs. "I'm fine. Nothing for you to worry about." With my fingers crossed, I turned to the Minister. "Right?"

"*Riiiight,*" he hissed.

MaGretta exhaled a long wind of held tension, and then her hand fluttered at her chest. "Oh, Zia, I am so happy for you. I was not too much worried; it was your Poppa. He will be so happy." Her strong German arms noosed my neck. "You are such a good girl."

"Ma—Ma—Gretta—Can't—Can't breathe here."

She loosened the chokehold. "Tonight, we celebrate with spaetzle and strudel."

I held the door open for MaGretta, but before I could follow her out, the Minister called, "Zia, wait. Please."

His *please* caught me; it sounded sincere. "Go ahead," I told MaGretta, "I'll meet you at the car."

She nodded, still giddy, and then she bounced happily down the hall.

I turned to the Minister. "What? What now?"

"Zia, you might be in trouble, serious trouble. Perhaps, mortal jeopardy."

"Yeah? Why?"

"You might be talking to something evil. Very evil. A devil in sheep's clothing. Maybe Satan himself. Have you considered that?"

I hadn't, but I sure did now. Swallowing against a dry throat, I slowly shook my head.

"Well, I want you to think about it. Think hard. Your Soul is at stake."

*Jeez,* goosebumps prickled the back of my neck. Again and again, I swallowed, my throat too dry to even speak.

"Zia, you're shaking." He started to rise.

My palms flew up. "Stop. Stop there. Minister, if you're just trying to scare me, you did. You win. But if you're really that evil, you can change. Alpha said it's a choice."

I tore out of there.

His voice rushed after me, "Wait, wait."

But I didn't stop running until I was safely outside the church.

# 52

*Half his atoms are missing, and the remaining half,*
*a fretful scattering, circle and dart, round and round,*
*in a pitiful search for their missing pair.*

**1997**

*Y*our car is overheating, Geminus whispered.

Teary eyes glanced at the temperature gauge. More tears fell.

*Look over there.*

She spotted a mechanic's garage across the intersection.

*Observe the number of vehicles. It's likely a trusted enterprise.*

A wire fence caged a pack of cars; she hoped they could fit her in.

*You should go there.*

I should go there, she thought. When the light turned green, she crossed the intersection and turned into the shop.

*Your poor, sweet mother.*

Her grief surged, weighting her foot on the accelerator.

*BRAKE! BRAKE!*

*YEERRRRRK.*

A ton of metal stopped inches from a mechanic.

Pandemonium erupted.

Geminus sent a vibration to Alpha and Willow. *I've brought the Dyads together. Turn your Charges' heels toward the Neutral Point.*

# 53

*Dyads have a specially designed relationship
when they're in play. Always.*

Like every morning, *toot-toot*, came the horn when the driver pitched the newspaper onto our lawn. And like every morning, Dieter went outside to get it. But unlike other mornings, Dieter took a while before he returned. He slapped the Seaside Times onto our breakfast table. My bumped coffee sloshed over the rim. I grabbed a napkin. "Jeez, Dieter, look what you did." I blotted my lap while MaGretta ran for a sponge.

Leaning over Pop's shoulder, Dieter said, "Remember the Ridgecrest lady who disappeared? Dorothy Norst? They found her."

"What is this?" Pop said staring at the headlines. "She is dead?"

"Damn shame," Dieter said before he flipped the page. "Recognize her?"

"Auk, the girl who nearly ran over Sam."

"She's Dorothy Norst's daughter, Pop. She's Miranda Norst."

"Somebody almost killed Sam," I said, "but you never got her name?"

Pop shook his head. "She drove straight into the shop, right over a floor jack. Her oil pan ripped and, auk, oil went everywhere. Sam was on the creeper. Tires came at him, and he had no time to roll out of the way. He probably pooped his pants. Thank goodness the girl hit the brakes and nobody was hurt. Well, not too much. Poor Sam was clutching his chest. Eric and Robert came running to help, but they slipped in the oil. Dieter, too. All my mechanics were slipping and sliding, auk, such a mess. And this girl here, she was boo-hooing and so-sorry and boo-hooing and so-sorry. Names and paperwork did not seem important." Pop looked again at the news. "Now I know why she drove not good. Her mind was on a terrible shame. Terrible."

"Okay, I'll bite," I said with a mouthful of eggs. "What happened to her mom?"

But Pop was too busy reading, Dieter rereading, and when MaGretta returned, her eyes glued on the paper, too. "MaGretta. MaGretta." I pointed to the coffee trail. She tossed me the sponge and went back to reading.

While I wiped the spill, MaGretta muttered, "Oh, that poor woman. Oh, the poor daughter. What an awful thing to have happened." But then, "That is a miracle. Do you think that is true?"

"Auk," Pop said. "The mother, that is a shame. But this?" His thick finger jabbed at a side story. "Hogwash." He folded the newspaper, pushed it aside, and told Dieter to hurry with breakfast; they had many cars to fix.

I took the paper, but before I could read it, MaGretta said, "Nothing good happens at Angels Peak," a sentiment shared among the older locals.

I skipped the recap of Dorothy's disappearance to read the update; Monday afternoon, police found Dorothy Norst's body in a shallow cove near Angels Peak. "MaGretta," I waved the newspaper as she cleared the dishes, "the paper says *near* Angels Peak, not *at* it."

This attack and defense was likely occurring at breakfast tables throughout the county. Angels Peak, centered between Kenzie Cove and Ridgecrest, was a half-mile stretch of coastal cliff. Outside city limits and poorly patrolled, it was a teenager's paradise. After tanking their cars and themselves, teens raced across the picnic grounds, veered south through a dip in the knoll, and then spun donuts at the cliff's edge. They wanted Angels Peak left alone. For a different reason, photographers and naturalists joined in that sentiment. They followed the ridge to the north end, the high point, where lights from both towns shimmered across the sea. Glorious sunsets, they claimed, world renowned among artists—and our town's registered visitors proved that to be true. Keep it pristine, they said.

But parents of reckless kids and doctors of depressed patients fought for a barricade, calling Angels Peak a devil's trap. Only a knoll, they argued, a mere bump in the earth, separated the picnic grounds from a wicked ledge over a fifty foot drop to an inlet thorned with rocks.

Surfers steered clear, both of the issue and of the Peak, sticking to the champion waves and the no-tourist bars at nearby Breakers Point.

In my view, when the sun hit the horizon, a titan awoke and bloodied the lights on the sea. Sunsets weren't glorious; they were ominous. And barriers never stopped a teenager from getting loaded and tempting death. I bet Neanderthal teens got stoned on taboo-berries and then tried to ride woolly mammoths. I would have. And depressed jumpers ought to stick to bridges.

I sided with the fun-loving locals who placed bets on a very dangerous game played by a group of robust guys called Scavengers. For miles north, whatever inedible object dropped into the sea, the currents would pick up, drag down coastline, and wedge into the rocks beneath the ridge. Scavengers climbed into the Peak's underbelly to comb those rocks. On Thursday nights, they gathered at Neptunes to have their findings scored: two points for bottles; three for corked letters; six to ten for metal, twenty for jewelry. The tavern's owner, Liz, awarded the points, often favoring the brawniest Scavenger. Whether her scoring was fair or slanted, nobody argued with Liz—before Neptunes, she was a bouncer at a bikers' bar. At the end of the week, the Scavenger with the highest score received a cut of the betting pool.

"Fifty points for the corpse!" I should have saved the joke for Neptunes because MaGretta and Dieter didn't find it funny. Not at all.

I kept reading: Detective Carly Spuretta refused to comment on the cause of death. "Spuretta?" I knew the name but couldn't place it. I turned the page. "Hey, it's Squirrelly Dude." His photo appeared beside Miranda Norst and over the subheading, *Victim's Daughter Claims Psychic Revealed Location.*

Printed below: "While attending spiritual seminars in Utah, Fikus MacKenzie, owner of Revelations Bookstore in Kenzie Cove, claims he had a vision of a troubled woman buried in an inlet near Angels Peak. When MacKenzie returned from Utah, he recognized the Seaside Times' picture of Dorothy Norst as the woman in his vision. He immediately called the victim's daughter, Miranda Norst. Norst contacted the authorities and relayed the details of MacKenzie's vision. This information led to the body's discovery. 'I'm going to remain in Kenzie Cove,' Norst stated, 'to be near the gifted psychic who channeled my mother's spirit.' Norst hopes MacKenzie will provide further details surrounding her mother's disappearance and subsequent death." Then came drivel about Fikus's history of fortune-telling and his ancestral links to the town...*naturally.*

"What a crock," I said. "Psycho-psychic bullshit."

With an upward glance, MaGretta whispered, "Forgive the trespass."

Dieter took the papers, sat again, and returned to the second page.

"What's with you?" I asked him. "Are you memorizing the story?"

Engrossed in a reread, Dieter didn't answer. I looked at Pop for him to explain. Pop rose from the table and pulled out his keys. With a furtive finger pointing at Dieter, Pop said, "After the girl nearly mowed down Sam, she boo-hooed and boo-hooed...on Dieter's shoulder." Pop winked. "Maybe he has the goo-goo eyes."

Before I could snicker, Dieter shot up with a nasty scowl. He flung the paper and then shoved from the table, spilling my coffee a second time.

"For chrissake," I jumped up, "who peed on your Cheerios? Don't take it out on me if some Betty Boo-Hoo believes in Fikus. If it bugs you that much, why don't you set her straight; Fikus is just a two-bit hustler running a voodoo freak-show out of his bookstore. He ought to stick to fleecing tourists instead of using tragedies to proclaim himself gifted."

Dieter leaned into my ear. "I would think you, of all people, wouldn't judge what another person claims to see." He marched after Pop.

My lashes fluttered at MaGretta. "What? What did I say?"

"Zia, be nice to your brother," MaGretta said like she always said when Dieter acted like a jerk. Years ago, a flirtatious brunette waylaid my brother from picking me up after school. I trudged home through sideways rain. But before I could holler, MaGretta hushed me, "Zia, be nice to your brother."

"Stupid Dieter."

"Shhh," MaGretta said leaning across the table to peek at the entryway. I knew that posture; she had a secret. I propped on both elbows, eager to hear. MaGretta waited for the front door to close. *Click.* "Your brother—" She stretched for another check of the entryway.

"They're gone," I said. "Come on, come on. My brother what?"

"Although it is none of our business."

"Got it. Now what's none of our business?"

"He has troubles with Janey."

"That's it? That's all you got?" I sat back, pooh-poohing the gossip as trivial. "They're always fighting. Janey bitches and Dieter clams up."

MaGretta frowned, but not because of the word, bitches. Well, maybe that, too. But because I should have known better than to say, "clams up," when referring to Dieter. MaGretta acted as if Fate were listening and would steal Dieter's tongue like it had stolen his tongue through the months that followed our mother's death. "Sorry," I said before parroting her habitual reminder, "I should be grateful that Dieter speaks at all."

"That is right. Do not forget it."

"So what's with Janey? Dieter won't take a desk job at her daddy's mill? And Janey's nose is too refined to tolerate the stink of carb cleaner, right?"

"He broke it up with her."

"Nooo. Serious? Wait. They can't break up. I forked out three hundred bucks for a non-refundable bridesmaid dress. Do you know how many wind chimes I had to sell for that mutant-mermaid, lime-green disaster?"

"Stop thinking of yourself," MaGretta said with crisp disapproval.

I balked anyway—three hundreds bucks gave me the right. "Why now? Why not two days ago, before I bought the dress. Why now?"

"Dieter's heart is not good with Janey. He cannot be what she wants."

"Everyone told him that. Family and friends and, jeez, probably strangers on the street, 'Hey, Dude, dump the Barbie.'"

"Stop that. Janey was nice and well mannered."

"She was an etiquette-Nazi." Raising a pinky, I mocked the pinched propriety of high society. "'Oh, do sit when you smoke. A lady never walks with a cigarette in hand.'"

MaGretta stopped in place with a questioning glare.

"What?" I said. "I overheard Janey tell that to someone. Someone else. Someone not me."

MaGretta resumed stacking the dishes. "Janey was very pretty, too."

"Yep, a real Barbie wanting a Ken." Although my brother had the makings of Ken—tall, blond, blue-eyed—he was strictly wash-and-go— shower, shave, done. His hair never met a comb and his wardrobe never surpassed holey jeans and yellowed tees. He purchased socks monthly because he had to. Years of shoe inserts and herbal salves failed to cure his toxic foot odor—an odor so rank, his socks dissolved. *Smelly feet*, that was the only ammo I had for teasing Dieter. His unassuming nature, Boy Scout honesty, and quick willingness to lend a hand or loan a buck earned him a town full of buddies—buddies causing me trouble.

A decade earlier, while I was hitchhiking home from Girl Scouts, Dieter's newly licensed friend swung his car to the curb, one tire jumping the sidewalk. Pretending not to notice, I whistled and started around the bumper. The horn blasted. "GET IN," the guy yelled, "and snuff that cigarette."

On the drive home, he lectured me nonstop, destroying my belief that all teenagers were cool. As painful as it was to learn that lesson at the tender age of 12, I also learned to watch out for Dieter's friends. They're loyal and they're everywhere.

I stood to assess the coffee on my lap. Yep, it was too close to the crotch. I had to change pants or risk someone thinking I had peed myself. As I looked down at the yellow stain, Miranda Norst stared up from page two. I slowly picked up the paper. Something about Norst bugged me, something more than just her stupidity for believing in Fikus.

"Hey, MaGretta, when did Dieter break up with Janey?"

"Yesterday," she called from the kitchen. "Or maybe the day before."

# 54

*Franklin wiped the frost from his brow,
his squint shifting from the blood on his shovel
to the blood on the half-buried man.*

A few months into retirement, Frank Spuretta received a call from Tony, Chief of Homicide Investigations. "Call it a favor," Tony said, "a personal favor."

"But I just untangled my fishing line," Spuretta told him.

"Fishing? Hell, you don't know which end of the worm to hook."

The phone went quiet.

Tony sighed. "The middle, Frank, you hook a worm in the middle. Now, can you wait to make a mockery of fishing? I'm short staffed. Every detective is stretched thin on multiple cases, and now I've got a strange case. That's your expertise. Come back as a retired annuitant, part-time, full-time, whatever you want, just take the case. It's Dorothy Norst."

"Hold up. Didn't you assign that case to Carly and Morrison? They're still partners, aren't they?"

"They don't fight nice. When Morrison swung by Carly's house to pick up the crime scene photos, he started hollering about the other pictures. He didn't know about Winkle until he heard the growl. Winkle did not like his tone. Morrison almost shot the cat, so Carly almost shot Morrison."

"Other pictures?"

"Yeah, the ones Carly took after—You know, the pictures of—You know, the ones that—" After an uneasy pause, Tony said, "Christ, me and my big mouth. Carly shot the crime scene and that's all you're getting out of me."

"Tony, did she take other pictures again?"

"I ain't talking."

"Did Morrison have good reason to pull his gun on Winkle?"

"Depends who you believe."

"Well, I'm sure Carly will fill me in later. Other than that, how is my kid working out? Is she doing okay?"

A while passed before Tony answered. "This ain't her thing, Frank. You know it, I know it, and if it wasn't for that one asinine tourist, Carly would know it, too. I should have done more to stop her from changing careers."

"You couldn't have stopped Carly any more than I could have stopped you from punishing that tourist."

"Dammit, he broke my Goddaughter's spirit. Oh, yeah, and the law."

"The law? Four miles over the speed limit, a cracked taillight, parking an inch too far from the curb?"

"The law is the law."

"Jaywalking?"

"I uphold the law...or I would have rammed Carly's camera up the guy's ass and charged him with indecent exposure."

Spuretta chuckled. "Tony, lay off the Godfather movies before you get yourself into trouble."

"I'm in trouble now. I've pulled Morrison off the Norst case so he can close a few files. I want you to work with Carly. She'll get you up to speed."

"You want me to partner with my daughter? Isn't that against policy?"

"Hell if I know, and this county is too small for any bureaucrat to care. Just take the case, Frank. Take it and you won't have another blind date from Gina's relatives. Refuse, and I'll remind the wife that you're a happy bachelor. No woman can stand that. Hell, she's got more cousins than you got Saturday nights."

"I'm on my way."

When he arrived at the station, Tony handed him a file. "Start with this, read the rest later."

Spuretta skimmed the notes: Weeks earlier, Dorothy Norst left home to walk the one-mile stretch to her job.

She never arrived at work.

The following day, Miranda Norst reported her mother missing. During interviews, Miranda stated that they had lived in Ridgecrest for ten years. Dorothy had never married, and Miranda had never known her father. Although Dorothy dated, she had no special man in her life.

Several days later, Miranda called the police again, only now to direct their search. South of Angels Peak and north of Breakers Point was a shallow groove, tucked beneath the ridge and back-dropped in rocks. "Behind those rocks," Miranda said, "is my mother."

She was exactly right.

The detectives taped off and searched the area, but they found only Dorothy's fingerprints and blood.

With atypical calm for a grieving daughter, Miranda explained how she learned the location from Fikus MacKenzie, a gifted psychic. The detectives then turned their attention to Fikus.

Fikus happily related his vision, repeating every detail, including the irrelevant minutia. Several times, the detectives had to interrupt Fikus to bring him back on track. When questioned about his whereabouts, Fikus produced a packet of receipts from his visit to Utah.

Spuretta looked up from the notes. "Where are these receipts?"

"Carly has them," Tony said. "She's in the interrogation room taking another shot at Miranda Norst. Carly is convinced she is involved."

"What do you think?"

Tony rubbed the back of his neck. "I think this case is as clear as tar. Let's go watch your kid in action."

They went to the one-way glass fronting the interrogation room. Inside the room, Carly was pacing, her hands clenched, her knuckles white. She challenged Miranda to take a polygraph test and to give a DNA sample.

Miranda readily agreed to both.

Over the next hour, despite Carly's repeated insinuations and outright accusations, Miranda never became flustered and never shed a tear.

"Fikus MacKenzie," she said with unfaltering resolve, "is a gifted psychic who channeled my mother's spirit. Is that so hard to believe? Is it?"

*Not hard*—Tony and Spuretta shared the same thought—*impossible*.

# 55

*You're giving me a bad slant.*

Waving a twenty, I burst into Neptunes for a last minute bet.

"Sorry, Zee." Liz grabbed the coffee pot and headed my way. "Scavengers can't get into the rocks. Cops taped off the area from Angels Peak to Breakers Point."

"Over one dead body?" I rammed the twenty into my backpack and flopped into an empty booth. "That stinks."

"Yeah, the nerve of that woman to die there. She spoiled your losing streak."

"Just pour the coffee." I clanked the cup. "Which also stinks."

"I changed brands of decaf. If you don't like it, I'll switch back."

"Liz, I don't drink decaf. Never have, never will."

"Oh, sweetie, I marked this pot. It's for my ornery customers who insist on regular against their doctor's advice. I keep a list so the waitresses know who gets coffee from the special pot." She filled my cup. "But you're so ornery, the gals added your name. They underlined it, too."

"Fire them!" I pushed aside the junk-java. "And how long have I been paying for coffee and drinking crap?"

Liz's mouth slanted in a cocky smile. "Paying?"

"Hey, I'll pay my tab. Someday. Don't change the subject. How long?"

"Let me think." Liz rested the pot and ticked on her fingers. "Today is Thursday, yesterday was Wednesday, so—"

"Two days?"

"Two years."

"What?"

"Zee, look at your poor nails. You need caffeine like an Eskimo needs a freezer."

From across the room, Stackhouse and Mopar hollered for their orders.

Liz shouted back, "Hold your horses. I'm talking to Zee."

Then the guys hollered again, but not about lunch. They yelled, "ZEE," and then something about a long shot and a sucker bet.

Liz flagged them to shut up.

"Liz?"

"It's nothing. Don't pay them any attention."

"Okay. But what am I not paying attention to?"

"Ignore them."

"But what am I ignoring?"

Liz sighed and picked up the coffee pot. "Men love their gambling, I understand that, but this is—well, it's just plain crude."

"Crude. Right." I stood up and shouted, "MISCREANTS," then sat again. "What did they do?"

"They're running pools on how the Norst lady died."

"That's disgusting."

"Don't I know it."

"Despicable."

"You got that right."

"But, uhm, just curious, what kind of odds?"

"Drowning was the sucker bet, but that's out. Suicide is the long shot, six to one odds. Murder, the favored bet, pays four to one on a local killer and two to one on an outsider."

"What a bunch of twisted pigs."

"Amen." Liz looked over her shoulder, "I'M COMING," then turned again to me. "Hungry?"

"Naw."

"Then I better go feed the pigs."

"Wait." I dug the twenty out of my backpack and folded it into Liz's pocket.

"Aw, Zee, not you, too."

"Hey, no, it's not what you think. I have scruples. Tons." A sincere hand pressed over my heart. "I believe in the good people of this county, especially my fellow citizens of Kenzie Cove. They are honest, decent, hardworking—"

Liz snorted. "Twenty on an outsider?"

"Yes please."

# 56

*As Matthew, I failed in Alaska because I didn't know about Murdock's character.*

**H**er arms laden with files, her back strapped with a laptop, Carly used her foot to knock on her dad's front door.

While waiting for the door to open, she heard muffled talking. *TV?* Her dad never watched TV...with one exception. Carly angled her wrist to check the time. 12:30. *Damn*—The Saturday afternoon Cagney Classics. She set the files down and let herself in.

Spuretta, on the edge of his chair, barely glanced up. "Carly, you got to see this. That's Cagney there."

"I know, dad." She also knew that Cagney would jerk his snub-nose as though he were fly-casting and not shooting, and that her dad would rip into laughter as though he were seeing it for the first time and not for the one hundredth. She unstrapped from the laptop, brought in the files, and shut the door. "I'll make us lunch."

"Wait, wait. You'll miss the action."

"If there's a God." Carly went to the kitchen where an old refrigerator *bzzz*'d in a continual effort to keep its insides cold. Four months had passed since Carly last tackled the beast. She flexed her fingers and held her breath before she opened the door to all that will curdle, spoil, grow mold, and turn rancid. *Clunk, plop, clink, splash.*

"Carly Jean," Spuretta called, "are you tossing out my food?"

"No, dad. Food implies edible."

*Plink, clank, thunk.*

Carly left the beer, ham, dill pickles, some questionable condiments and two passable jellies. When she dug into the freezer, she found a pleasant surprise—a loaf of bread. After years of trashing blue loaves with only two slices missing, Carly had stashed some fresh bread in the freezer. She had expected to find it bluing in the breadbox, but her dad had left it alone. Carly now had the makings for ham and apricot jam sandwiches.

After fixing the sandwiches, Carly tucked a beer under each arm and went to join her dad.

"You got to see this," Spuretta said. "Watch Cagney shoot."

"Take a sandwich." When Carly lifted a sandwich to her dad's nose, a beer started to slip. Her elbow clamped down, pinning the bottle against her waist. "Dad, help me out. Take something. Quick."

"Hang on, hang on."

"Do you want lunch on your lap?"

Spuretta's attention tore from Cagney long enough to save the beers. He twisted their caps and then traded a beer for a sandwich. After a hearty bite, he flapped the sandwich at the TV. "Watch! Watch!" His wrist snapping, Cagney started shooting, and Spuretta began laughing. "Did you see that, kid? Did you?"

"Yes, dad, I'm laughing hysterically on the inside." On the outside, Carly was smiling. She was a grown woman, a 6'1" detective, but her dad still called her *kid*. That always tickled her.

In a few bites, Spuretta finished his sandwich. He swallowed some beer and smacked his lips. "They don't make films like that anymore. No, siree. Old fashioned fun." He turned off the TV, then dropped back to his chair. "Learn anything from the Kenzie Cove locals?"

"Yes and no. Surfers are not potheads and Scavengers are not drunks. That's a surprise. But neither group saw or heard anything, which is more than a surprise. That's unbelievable. Angels Peak and Breakers Point straddle the ridge where Dorothy stood."

"Well, who's paying attention to the ridge? Surfers are a fair distance from the shoreline. Besides, they're watching waves and riding south. For a view of the ridge, they'd have to start farther north, and nobody in their right mind surfs north of Breakers Point. And Scavengers tuck themselves so far under the Peak, they can't hear above the next swell and they can't see through the next wall of water. The only thing on their minds is finding a little treasure and hanging onto a boulder for dear life."

Carly shook her head, disgusted. Twice, during her college years, she had flown home to attend the funerals of prior classmates who had died in the Scavenging game. She had thought Scavengers were drunks; why else would a grown man risk being crushed against rocks and swept out to sea? "Insanely immature," Carly said. Just then, she noticed her dad's eyes twinkle. Though sixty years had grayed his hair, darkened his skin, and deepened his worry lines, the man's eyes remained crisp and ageless—and also revealing. "Nanna's suspicions were right. You were once a Scavenger."

"Oh, now, settle down. It was a long time ago. Most young men have a foolish time or two. I'm no exception."

"But a Scavenger? *You?* You risked your life for—for what? For worthless junk?"

"Nope. For fun."

Carly waved her palms to stop her dad from providing details and to erase the picture of a reckless Spuretta from her mind. She lifted the files onto her lap, withdrew a manila folder, and jiggled it toward her dad. "Miranda is involved. That's the only theory that fits. Take a look at my notes."

"Put it down."

"But you haven't read this."

"I'll read it later. Put the folder down. Let's talk a bit."

Carly sensed an upcoming lecture. She dropped the file, cleared her lap, and picked up her beer. "Is this the elephant lesson? *Again?*"

"Sure. You can't describe an elephant by feeling its tail."

"Is that what I'm doing? You haven't even heard my theory."

"Put your theory aside. Right now, just tell me what you know."

Carly leaned back, sipped her beer, and thought a while. "I know Dorothy fell from the ridge."

Spuretta's forehead creased, clueing Carly that she had erred. "I mean, Dorothy fell or she jumped or she was pushed, but she wasn't thrown."

Spuretta's face smoothed.

Carly took a big gulp of beer. Trying to talk to her dad was like trying to cross a minefield that detonates by a careless word. "Dorothy died on impact, but her body was moved twenty feet. The ME can't determine whether a person dragged her or whether the waves shoved her into the inlet's back wall. Part of the ceiling caved, burying her body beneath rocks. If a tree limb had rammed the ceiling, we should have found bits of the tree crammed into the rocks. But we didn't. We found rocks with nicks and gouges, suggesting a pronged tool, likely metal, and at least two feet long. That's what we know. Then we add common sense; Dorothy didn't jog six miles from home to jump off a cliff."

Spuretta nodded. "You're right, kid. We got plenty of steep cliffs right here in Ridgecrest."

"Miranda drove her."

"Carly Jean."

"Dad, she knew where to find the body."

"What does that prove?"

Carly had thought it proved Miranda's complicity, but apparently her dad thought otherwise or he wouldn't have asked the question...and repeated it. "What do you think that proves?"

"I think it adds to the proof. Miranda knew where to find the body, she gave us an alibi we can't confirm, 'I was in bed, nursing a cold,' and she was remarkably calm for a gal who had just lost her mother. She's involved."

"What if she passes the polygraph?"

Carly shrugged. "Sociopath?"

"Nope. Kid, you're whittling the pieces to fit the puzzle. Learn to see folks for whom they are, not for whom you want them to be, and not for whom they'd have you believe."

"But dad—"

"An alibi can prove innocence, but the lack of one doesn't prove guilt. And I think you're misreading her demeanor. She was a dazed gal. A strange daze, I'll give you that, but I wouldn't describe her demeanor as calm."

"What about knowing where to find the body?"

"Right from the git-go, she said the MacKenzie fella told her. Well, maybe he did."

"How? A vision? Do we suddenly believe in psychics?"

"I'm talking about what Ms. Miranda believes."

"No, you're talking about Fikus. You're suggesting he's either psychic or connected." Exasperated, Carly swept back her hair and drank the last of her beer. "Dad, before I transferred to Ridgecrest, I had classes with Fikus. For ten bucks, he charted your astrological life or read your tealeaves. He was good at it, too. But that makes him an opportunist. Where do you see more? He didn't even know the Norsts. Besides, he was in Utah when Dorothy went missing."

"I saw the receipts."

"Then where's the hole in his story?" Carly picked up the packet of receipts and then held it out to her dad. Instead of telling her to put it down, Spuretta took the packet. Carly sat a little straighter, her confidence boosted. "He has the flight stubs in and out of Salt Lake City, the campground receipt from a Utah State park, the dates and times of the mystic seminars, and the names and phone numbers of the newly enlightened. Unless he travels in the astral plane, Fikus was more than five hundred miles away."

Spuretta pulled out a handful of receipts. While he looked them over, Carly went to the kitchen to fetch another two beers.

When she returned, she handed a beer to her dad. He set it down unopened. He stroked his chin and *hmm*'d thoughtfully.

After waiting twenty minutes, Carly asked, "Ready to hear my theory?"

Spuretta looked up.

"You won't like it," Carly said, "because it points to Miranda."

"I'm sure it does." Spuretta picked up his beer, twisted the cap, and then took a big swig. He leaned back. "I'm all ears."

Carly scooted to the edge of her seat. "The Utah seminars taught the gamut of scams—chakras, numerology, biorhythms—and also the hottest fad—channeling. If you're good at it, you'll get book deals and guest spots on talk shows. So, Fikus, who makes a living as a mystic, flew to Salt Lake City to update his career from, 'what's your sign?' to, 'I'm sensing a spirit whose name begins with J.' When Fikus came home, he saw the news about Dorothy, and he thought to himself, 'good time to practice what I learned.' He called Miranda and told her, 'I have a message from a spirit who might be your mother.' If Miranda had taken the bait, Fikus would have set up a meeting and charged big bucks. But it never got that far, because instead of hooking Miranda's trust, Fikus hooked her conscience. Fikus might have said, 'she's in a dark place.' Then Miranda added, 'yes, a small inlet.' Then Fikus guessed, 'there's something heavy.' Then Miranda told him about the rocks. It's psychic-101; the target feeds the answers.

"Later, Miranda realized her mistake and she panicked, 'What if he tells?' So she called the police and turned it around, 'Fikus told me. He's gifted.' Fikus couldn't believe his luck. He knew Miranda's version would catapult his career, and it did. Fikus is on the news and in the tabloids. In less than a month, he's making headlines and has tripled his fees. Dorothy is no longer 'that poor woman.' She's now, 'the spirit that Fikus channeled.'"

"Hold up, kid. That's a pretty harsh judgment on the Ridgecrest folks."

"I'm not talking about Ridgecrest. Drive down to Kenzie Cove. Or visit any one of the surrounding towns and listen to the talk. It's all about Fikus. And guess who's spearheading his reputation? Miranda herself."

"Well, your theory ain't bad. Not bad at all. It ties up all the loose threads and makes for a neat finish."

Sensing the unspoken *but*, Carly rested back, no longer anxious or confident. "But?"

"But it's a darn shame it didn't go down that way. Darn shame. Where is Ms. Miranda's motive? According to friends and neighbors, the Norst ladies got along fine."

"Life insurance," Carly said. "Twenty-thousand isn't much, but people have murdered for less."

"Ms. Miranda hasn't even called the insurance company. Besides, I don't like the psychic's paper trail." Spuretta fanned the receipts. "Car washes, bowling alleys, dry cleaners; these are garbage receipts you can pull from any dumpster. All cash. Most men can't account for twenty bucks spent in a day, but this fella records every penny he spent for two weeks."

"Maybe it's a write-off."

"Maybe. But I'm going to keep an eye on the psychic, and I want you to dig deeper into his journalized alibi."

"Why? Because he's frugal? On the day Dorothy died, three witnesses place Fikus in Utah. One witness had breakfast with him, the other two had dinner."

"Did anyone see him mid-afternoon?"

"No, Fikus was camping, but he has a receipt for buying propane."

"A cash receipt; I saw it."

"But you don't believe that a man would record his pocket money."

"Sure, I do, if he's a married man, but that's not our psychic. He must have a darn interesting reason for tracking his nickels."

"Dad, I'll fly to Utah and verify every receipt, including the one from Frosty King, but then can we focus on Miranda?"

"I'll make it easy for you. Get the airline schedules into Utah."

"I already did. Flights departing San Francisco left prior to Dorothy's death, and the later flights would not have returned Fikus to Salt Lake City in time for dinner with his friends."

"Wonderful. Now check arrivals and departures out of Oakland and Sacramento."

An irritable huff left Carly as she drew out her laptop to take notes. Investigating Fikus was a big waste of time. She had thought her dad would realize this after he re-examined the Utah receipts, heard Carly's theory, and saw the airline schedules from San Francisco. "What is it about Fikus that bothers you? Is it just a gut-instinct?"

"Nope, I don't have a take on Fikus. Right now, I have one gut-instinct; Ms. Miranda is telling the truth. I'm sure of it. Now that leaves only three possibilities. One, when Dorothy died, Fikus was there. Two, a person-unknown was with Dorothy and later told Fikus what happened."

Carly's fingers clicked across the keyboard. "And the third?"

Her dad began chuckling. "If it's the third, I can get back to retirement; we found ourselves a genuine psychic."

When Carly finished her notes, she slipped the computer into its case, strapped it onto her back, and then gathered the files.

"Don't rush off," Spuretta said. "Stay for dinner. I'll fix up a salad and some grilled cheese sandwiches."

"Uhhh," Carly thought of the slimy lettuce and the moss covered cheddar now composting in the trash. "Let's go out to dinner. My treat."

"No, I'll buy, but you can drive."

On the passenger seat was a camera, which Carly quickly swung to the back seat. When her dad got in, he eyed the camera. Hoping to sidetrack his questions, Carly started chattering, "Where are my car keys? I can't find a thing in this purse. Here they are. Which restaurant do you want to—"

Before she could turn the ignition key, her dad stilled her hand. "Carly, did you get in a beef with Morrison?"

"Morrison is a jerk, a jerk with a big mouth."

"I wouldn't know. I never spoke to Morrison."

Carly's hand fell to her lap, her gaze following. "Tony, huh?"

"Not intentionally. He assumed you had told me. I'm kind of wondering why you haven't."

Carly looked out the window. How could she explain it? Distracted? After photographing the scene inside the inlet, she climbed to the ridge top and then turned her camera to the brilliant red sky of a sailor's warning, the vivid curiosity within a sandpiper's eye, and the final breath of a green-headed beetle. She had captured three glimpses of wonder from an infinite world of wonders that splice through every second of every day, though each wonder is distinct and will never repeat, not in the same way. Carly didn't have time to grab her own camera. "What could I say? 'Hey, dad, I jeopardized my job by taking pictures of a sunset, a bird, and a beetle.' Should I have said that?"

"Carly, why did Morrison draw his gun on Winkle? Did Winkle—"

"NO!" Carly's head shot up. "No, dad, Winkle did not attack."

## 57

*Squawking reporters descended like a murder of crows.*

The invasion started in the summer of 1997 when newspapers, up and down the coast, featured interviews from Miranda Norst and Fikus MacKenzie; *Psychic Finds Missing Woman.*

Spiritualists, families of the missing, skeptics, and loonies started on a path to our town. At first, they came from nearby. Later, a major station broadcasted an interview with Fikus, and he soared into celebrity status. Then people came from everywhere to hear Fikus MacKenzie, Speaker-For-The-Dead, and to listen to his number one fan, Miranda Norst, who was now my brother's latest love-interest.

I spotted Dieter and Miranda nudging together while they stood in line for theater tickets. Miranda was the reason Dieter had missed Sunday night krapfens. She was the reason Kenzie Cove, once a cheerful community that welcomed tourists, was now a hectic town that had no time for small talk. Fikus was merely a fraud. Frauds come and go. It was Miranda who was ruining our town. Because of her, everything changed.

Hotels and B&Bs posted no vacancy signs. From dawn to closing, restaurants and coffeehouses were packed. The business community prospered; admittedly, myself included. Shops tripled their orders for my handcrafted wind chimes. Although I needed the money—*wow,* a car payment without a late fee—I didn't want to cut down on my hours coaching at the Youth Center. My three swim teams—Green Guppies, Blue Dolphins, Red Herrings—depended on me.

So I rose before dawn, stumbled down to the shack behind our house, and strung shells and driftwood until noon. Then I rushed to the Youth Center to teach swimming and diving.

At five, I hurried home, grabbed a bite, then assembled wind chimes until midnight. Kids, chimes, kids, chimes—I was sleep deprived but determined. I should have slowed down when a customer complained about blood-smudged shells. Instead, I bandaged my raw fingers and kept stringing.

Days later, I yelled at a Green Guppy for towel-whipping—*towel-whipping*, for chrissake. Even the Red Herrings matched the astonished face of the tiny Guppy. When I got home, I flopped across my bed and stared at the ceiling. Seeking a dose of sympathy, I explained my misery to Alpha.

*Untrue.*

"How the hell do you know?" I bounced up. "You're not God. I told you what was upsetting me and that's it. End of story. Get it?"

Alpha's eyes closed—which meant I was wrong, which pissed me off more. "You don't know jack-shit! For sixteen miles I drove on a rim because you didn't tell me that my tire flew off. Do you know what a new rim costs? NO! Of course not. You just float around without a rim in the world. Well, this is your fault. YOUR FAULT! If you had opened your mouth to tell me something useful, I wouldn't need to be cashing in on—I wouldn't care if—"

Orange eyes flashed open. Just then, a breeze rolled through the curtains and blew across my desk. A stack of wind chime mini-cards toppled, one landing on my foot. I picked it up and then kissed my homemade gold mine—a three-inch card with a dynamite sales pitch. After attaching a mini-card to each chime, my sales rocketed. Even chimes with tangled strings and cobwebbed shells now sold within days, spiders included.

"You see this?" I waved it at Alpha. "This is my lottery ticket. Right here. Bullshit pays well." Printed on the front was *Spirit Whispers*. Inside the flap, it read, *Unlock your psychic powers.* The spiel beneath hinted at Fikus—maybe promoted him, too. It suggested that his powers came from meditating beneath chimes—*Special chimes that attract balanced energy.* What an ingenious line; I should have gone into advertising. Next came bull about a psychic's burden—*Your gift must be used to help others.* Now my chimes appealed to all the would-be do-gooders who were too lazy to do anything good beyond giving advice. On the card's flipside was severe crap—*Kenzie Cove is a rare area of spiritual vibrations*—plagiarized from a Sedona, Arizona brochure.

Three inches of genius-level writing had bolstered my bank account.

Soon, my credit score would reach three-digits. Soon, I would pay all my tabs around town. Soon, I would stop pocketing condiment packets from Burger King, storing dinner napkins from Dennys, taking envelopes from Fed-X, grabbing toilet paper from Chevron, and swiping shampoo, lotion, and conditioner from motels' housekeeping carts.

Soon, I would stop hoarding items for the day I moved out.

I looked from Alpha to my card, and then back and forth, back and forth.

My eyes watered.

Soon, I would buy those items, whatever I needed, as much as I wanted. Tears fell.

Soon, I would have the money.

Stupid, stupid tears. Stupid Alpha. Stupid me. *Damn*. Stupid money.

I crumpled the card.

When shop owners received their chimes, they asked why the mini-card was missing. I said, "Because it's wrong." Then each customer asked the same, dumb questions until I was hollering, "No, not grammatically wrong. No, not size-wise wrong. No, not paper, not font, not ink-color wrong. For chrissake, morally wrong, OKAY? Get it? I don't exploit the gullible."

One customer scoffed, "Since when?" Another kept repeating, "No seriously, why? Seriously?" But the worst was, "You? Moral?" and she ripped into laughter. "That's a good one, Zia. Wait here. Let me get Kelly. Hey, Kelly, get over here. You got to hear this. Bring Marty, too...and the recorder."

After that, I told everyone that killer clams attacked the wind chime shack and stole the cards for their theological studies of soil dwellers.

"Oh," my customers said with bored yawns and dull nods. "So, you didn't want to make them. Set the chimes in the usual spot. See you next week."

And that was that. A total letdown. After giving up the money that the cards would have brought in, I didn't even get a warm, fuzzy feeling. That *feeling* is the promised reward for doing the right thing, but I was gypped. Downright gypped. It wasn't even noon and my day had already tanked.

Figuring that coffee would give me warmth and that ten cups would make me fuzzy, I headed to Neptunes. "Excuse me. Pardon me. Coming through. Out of my way. MOVE IT!"

Visitors clogged the sidewalk. Less than half were true vacationers—drinkers, tokers, beachgoers, families. Vacationers knew their place, sticking to the shops and the restaurants on Main Street. Rarely did they venture into the locals' watering holes.

But this summer, herds of spiritualists contaminated our town. They swarmed like locust, smiled like fools, and parked like morons. Every few yards, the crowds flowed into the street to curve around groups of self-centered bastards conversing in the middle of the walkway.

As I elbowed straight through the clots, their insipid smiles flipped.

"What a bitch," a girl said.

"It's a walkway," I told her. "Not a standway. Walk on or stand aside."

Miranda's mouth had brought these idiots to our town, and their mouths had poisoned the air with talk of Fikus. Whether at the bank or at the post office, at the Youth Center or at Neptunes, conversations about our home-grown clairvoyant droned in the background.

At Neptunes, every table and booth was taken. A long line fed to the counter. My head ached. All I wanted was a lousy cup of coffee, poured from the special pot or not. I joined the line and waited. And waited. And waited. The line moved slower than a stoned sloth.

I checked my watch; within the hour, my class of Green Guppies would be waiting at the Youth Center. I had to leave. *Dammit.* What was causing the line to stagnate? What was denying me a self-induced warm, fuzzy feeling? Deserving to know, I marched to the counter. Behind it, Liz clumsily worked her first espresso machine. She glanced at the instructions, pulled levers, and mumbled apologies to the Biff- and Muffy-looking couple who were waiting at the register.

"Yeah, whatever," Biff said to each of Liz's apologies.

Muffy clicked her nails. "Just be sure it's nonfat milk, extra shot, no sprinkles, and wet."

*Wet?* I had waited in line for coffee while a frenzy of weirdoes ordered— *Mochas? Lattes?* I shoved Biff aside, reached over the counter, and grabbed two cans of whipped cream. I shook them. *Ratta-ratta-ratta-ratta.* "Wet latte coming up." *Sspppsh.* I shot white foam into Biff's stupid mug. "Wet enough?" *Sspppsh,* I got Muffy, too.

Walking backward, I knocked into a table—a table with coffee-cups filled with something other than coffee. *Spsh, Spsh, Spsh.* I creamed their drinks, and then bounced to another table, *Spsh, Spsh, Spsh.* Table to table, I sprayed cups and appalled looks. "WHO ELSE?" *Ratta-ratta-ratta-ratta.* "WHO ELSE WANTS A GODDAMN LATTE?" *Ratta-ratta-ratta-ratta.*

I walked down the line, a can in each hand, a finger ready to depress the trigger. "YOU?" *Ratta-ratta-ratta-ratta.* "YOU WANT A LATTE?"

Heads shook.

A curly-haired toddler with big, brown eyes squeezed between her mother's legs. "Kristin, it's okay," the mother said. "She's not going to hurt you. It's okay." The mother looked at me dead-on. "Right?"

"Huh?" But Kristin stole my attention again, her wide, wondering eyes peeking from behind her mother.

While watching her, my fingers loosened. The cans hit the floor, *clank, clank,* their sound amplified by the surrounding silence.

Kristin pounced, her tiny hands wrapping one rolling can. She held it up for me. *Me!* She had the pure innocence and blind forgiveness of sweet, little Maria in the book of Frankenstein. Maria didn't cast judgment when she befriended the...

*Oh my God, I'm the monster!*

I swiveled. Confused, angry, and graphitized faces stared at the monster. "Sorry," I wheezed moving toward the door. "I'm sorry. Real sorry. Sorry."

Once outside and around the corner, I crumbled against a wall. I bawled. Within a few minutes, arms wrapped me. A name-tag sprung open and the pin pricked my lip.

"This is my fault." Liz patted my back. "I knew better than to give you caffeine."

"It's not the caffeine." I pulled Liz's apron to my nose and blew. "How crazy, how stupid, how awful, what a—"

"Now, Zee, don't beat yourself up."

"NOT ME!"

"Not you, huh? Sweetie, is this a story about a clone or an evil twin?"

"No. I'm talking about Miranda. Miranda Norst. Her dumb-ass beliefs destroyed every bastion of fun in this town. Neptunes is swamped, gambling is canceled, and Scavengers are hanging out at the surfers' bars. She's ruining my work, too. One of my customers asked me to make crystal chimes, as if crystals breed on the beach. And my swimmers can't shut-up about karma and ghosts. I don't mean the right kind of ghosts that howl and torment. I mean the huggy-kissy, fake kind of ghosts that turn your stomach." I gripped mine. "Miranda did this. This is all her fault."

"Honey, her mama died."

My teeth clenched. "I *knowww.*" To a lingering bystander, I shouted, "WHAT ARE YOU LOOKING AT?"

Liz pinched my chin back to hers. "Are you going to attack everyone who believes in psychics? Tell me now, so I can hide the whipped cream."

"I'm sorry, Liz. Did you lose customers?"

"Not many. After you left, the line moved lickety-split." Imitating her customers, Liz held up her palms. "Just coffee, ma'am. No mochas, no lattes, no problems."

I smiled.

Liz gave me a quick hug and then a light shove. "Get your butt to the Youth Center and stop those kids from turning out like you. I'll call and let them know you're running late. Now go."

When I arrived, the Green Guppies were already toweling off and putting away their kickboards. "Where were you?" they asked. "Were you crying?"

"I was stuck in traffic," I told them. "And no, I wasn't crying. Coach Zee never cries. Remember that. Allergies puff up my eyes and turn them red."

Satisfied with my answer, the little boogers ran off.

"A meltdown, huh?" the surly substitute said. "Is that a new term for hangover? Well, get a grip, because my volunteer work starts and ends with the Guppies. I'm not sticking around for Dolphins." He threw the whistle to me. "And if you paid me, I wouldn't help with the Herrings."

"Not wouldn't, but couldn't." I roped the whistle around my neck. "My Guppies chew gum that's tougher than you. Get your candy-ass gone."

I had forty minutes before my next class. I rolled my neck, limbered my legs, and then headed to the deep end of the pool. Standing on the one-meter platform, I stripped away all thoughts—Selective Concentration. A diver learns this technique because the water surface is an unforgiving teacher. A careless turn, a lifted head, or a sloppy take-off are punished with a skull cracked, a shoulder separated, and a lung punched. I glanced at the three-meter platform and remembered. *Jeez,* how I remembered.

My focus returned to where I stood, a meter high, an impact of nine miles per hour. I did a back dive. I repeated the dive until my knuckles swelled, my muscles burned, and my sanity had fully returned. After rounds of successful dives, I approached the high platform...like always. But like always, by the third rung, fear wobbled my logs. By the fifth, vertigo was beating me down. "Are you going to do it?" At the swinging doors, a couple of Blue Dolphins gripped each other with gruesome excitement, as if, *yippee, we get to watch Coach Zee kill herself.*

"I'm cleaning the steps," I told them. "Just wait on the bench." In small towns, you never outlive a mistake. My peers told the story to their siblings, who told their friends, who passed it down to their younger brothers and sisters. *She was jacked up and tried to fly.* From the hospital bed, I swore to MaGretta and Pop that I was clean and sober. When the doctor confirmed it, they left. Dieter hung around for the rest of the truth. "I was clean and sober," I told him, "but bored shitless. So, I did a half-dive, half-swoop, you know, imitating Dracula." As irony would have it, my dive ended in blood.

When the Blue Dolphins came in, I warned the group, "I don't want to hear one word of any mystical crap. If I can't eat it, touch it, see it, or smell it, I don't want to hear about it. Get it? If anyone breaks my rule, the entire team will hit the runner."

"What about—"

"Starting now!" I said. The team's eyes swept to the outspoken Dolphin, their menacing signals pressuring him to leave his question unfinished.

The kid complied. Inside, I was relieved. If a kid tested my threat, I'd have to punish them all, and then I'd have to guard the big-mouth from retaliating peers—*We only held him under water for ten minutes.*

Class went smoothly. Their dives improved and their chatter returned to normal. Invigorated, I threatened the next class of Dolphins, and it worked with the same success. "Yes!" But I leashed my excitement to prepare for the Red Herrings.

A third of the Herrings were system kids, a third were repeating patrons of juvenile hall, and a third were just plain troublemakers. Having caused a few skirmishes in my younger years, I was sort of partial to the Herrings. Because they're a tough group, I brandished a harsher threat than my threat to the Dolphins. But that was a rookie move; you can't intimidate a Red Herring. They passed around a look. *Crap,* a challenge was brewing.

Terry stepped forward. He poked his glasses back to the bridge of his nose. He was a scrawny kid and a lousy swimmer, which would have made him a target in the Herrings' pecking order, except that Terry was smart, the respected, beat-the-system kind of smart. Nobody pressured his silence. "We want to ask you something."

"If I hear one word of—"

"My sister saw you on the ladder."

"What?"

"My sister. She saw you on the ladder of the three-meter platform."

"Oh. Yeah. I was just cleaning the—"

"Yeah, right." Terry cut me off as if he had whiffed my upcoming lie. "When you finally do it, you know, get to the top and dive, we want to know."

"We're not asking to watch," JoAnna said, my youngest Red Herring, a slip of a girl. She was fiercely attached to Terry. "It would be totally cool to see it, but we understand if you want to dive in private. Just have a witness."

"Yeah," the others said. "Absolutely."

"We just want to know that you did it," Terry said. "That's all."

"Why?" I asked. "Entertainment?"

In sync, their eyes rolled and their mouths murmured, "Lame."

"Are you that dense?" JoAnna said. "Can't you figure it out? How are we supposed to get over our shit if you can't get over a simple fouled up dive?"

"Yeah," they said, their voices uniting in conspiracy.

"Do a cannonball," a kid said.

"Just jump," said another.

"No," JoAnna said firmly and her arms crossed. "My older brother saw your accident. He said you called it a Dracula-dive, but that's bullshit. It was a simple twist dive, but you screwed it up. When we screw up, you tell us to get over ourselves and go do it again. So, Ms. Zee, get over yourself. Get on the three-meter platform, stand with your back to the water, step off, twist half-circle, dive. That simple. When you do it, let us know. We want to be the class to tell the other classes that you practice what you preach."

"I'll make you a deal," I said. "If you guys don't talk about psychics, karma, ghosts, crystals, or any spiritual junk, then I'll do it. At the end of the season, I'll do a twist dive. Deal?"

Silence of the unconvinced. "Jeez," I said. "I promise, okay? Have I ever lied—scratch that. I'll make sure there's a witness. Do we have a deal or not?"

The kids started to nod until Terry piped up, "No, wait. Wait. Guys, she left a loophole. She didn't say three meters. Think about it. She never said three meters. This is Ms. Zee; we know how she is."

I had no idea what he meant by that, but I was suddenly encircled by wary eyes. "Terry Lee," I said with as much practiced sweetness as I could muster, "I believe you're mistaken. I'm sure I said—"

"Then say it again," Terry said. "You made the deal. State it again."

My heel ached to thump the floor. "Fine. I promise a platform dive, three freakin' meters high. Happy now?"

The kids turned expectantly to Terry. He tapped his chin as if he were considering and not gloating. Then he grinned, big and wide, "Checkmate." The kids slapped hands and went to their stations.

I looked at the three-meter platform; payment due in nine months. *Jeez,* only nine months to live because that dive was going to kill me. For now, however, I had regained a place in the world that was Fikus-psychic-free.

I saved the victory dance to share with MaGretta. But when I got home, I found her preparing the spare room. She said Pop had called from work. We were having a houseguest—Ms. Miranda Norst.

# 58

*If you cultivate cacti or guide an Agitator,
you should keep your distance or expect to be pricked.
That is their nature.*

"**W**HY?" I dogged MaGretta as she hustled from the linen closet to the spare room then back again for blankets. "Why the hell is that girl coming here?"

"Dieter invited her."

"To *live* here? If he wants to invite her for dinner, fine, I'll eat downtown. Feed her and then show her the door."

"No, you be nice. Her poor mother has died."

"What's that to us? We didn't kill her."

"You hush." MaGretta stripped the bed and then cracked open a clean sheet. "Dieter told your Poppa that Miranda has no money to pay for the car repair. Your Poppa said, that is no problem. She does not have to pay. But Miranda has no more money to stay in a motel."

"I'll pay her cab fare back to Ridgecrest."

"No. She wants to stay in town until Mr. Fikus speaks to her mother."

"So Dieter just opened his big, fat mouth and—"

"Let it alone!" MaGretta halted, her hands clasped to her hips. "She is a girl without a mother. Where is your heart? Where is your compassion?"

Shot by the gun of guilt, I fell backwards onto the crisp sheet.

"ZIA! Is that swimming suit wet?" She slapped my bare thigh. Hard. I rolled off the side. MaGretta pointed. "Auk, Zia, look what you have done."

"Oops." I brushed at the wet mark to speed up the drying. "Sorry."

"Get out of that wet swimming suit before you ruin something more."

That night at dinner, I officially met Miranda Norst...and the polite, well-groomed guy who was impersonating my brother. He pulled the chair next to mine for Miranda. He sat across from us; Pop and MaGretta sat at each end.

While sauerbraten and dumplings were circulating the table, I noticed symmetrical similarities and contrasts between Dieter and Miranda.

Miranda's chocolaty hair cow-licked on the left. My brother's blond hair cow-licked on the right. Both had two-inch scars marring their chins, Dieter's on the left side, Miranda's on the right. My brother's pale-blue eyes and colorless skin required sunglasses and sunscreen even at dusk. But olive-skinned Miranda had eyes so dark, her brown irises and black pupils merged. Weirdest of all was the way their arms moved, passing platters and bowls, reaching for gravy and salt, moving right and left and across, but never colliding. Always in sync. Any minute, Rod Serling was going to pop into our kitchen while the theme to The Twilight Zone played. *To-do-do-do, to-do-do-do.*

"Everything smells delicious," Miranda said before she basted us in her syrupy gratitude; *oh-generous-this, oh-kindness-that, oh-how-can-I-ever-repay-you.* The more she gushed, the more my family welcomed her to stay—stay for as long as she liked. "It shouldn't be long," she kept saying, raising my hopes. "Just until Fikus talks to my mother again. He's gifted. He hears—"

"*Hauck.*" I tapped my throat. "Something stuck. Hard to swallow."

"My mother was a good woman," Miranda said as if I had said something to the contrary. "I just need to understand what happened to her. The police are investigating, but that's all they'll say. I don't want to leave town until I have answers."

"Yeah, sure," MaGretta said. "We understand."

Dieter reached across the table to take Miranda's hand. "My family will help you with whatever you need. Right, Pop?"

"That is right," Pop said, "whatever is best." He picked up his fork, because eating was best when the food was hot.

"Let me ask you something," I said.

Dieter and MaGretta hit me with their warning glares.

"What?" I asked. "Can't a girl ask a question? Am I to be censored?"

Miranda glanced from face to face, trying to decipher our family's codes. "It's—It's okay with me."

I smiled brightly. "So, Diets, it's okay with her; is it okay with you?"

Dieter's white cheeks heated into a warm red. "Ask your question."

"Thank you." And I turned to Miranda. "You think Fikus heard your mom, right?"

"I know he did. Your Minister is gifted."

"Well, he's not the Minister. He's the son of the Minister. A son of something else, too, but that's beside the point. You think he's gifted because you think he talked to your mom, right?"

Miranda sniffled.

*Aw, crap*, if she started bawling, I'd be in big, big trouble; that was Dieter's coded warning. "Hey, Miranda, I'm sorry about your mom's death. I am. Really. I was only suggesting a bit less faith in psychics and a bit more faith in cops, the lesser of the two evils. They'll figure it out. And if it's murder, maybe they'll fry the guy."

"No, I wouldn't want that," Miranda said. "I don't believe in the death penalty."

MaGretta gave her an approving nod. "Good for you."

"Guess I'm outnumbered," I said. "I think they ought to lower the bar to include human traffickers and pedophiles. If you bunch them together, you could have a group fry; energy conservation is important."

"Amen," Pop said because he shared my views and because he was hungry. He speared a dumpling and looked at MaGretta, but MaGretta was too busy growing fond of Miranda to notice.

Pop's pleading eyes shifted to me, his stomach growling for my help. I signaled that he owed me one, then I stuck a forkful of sauerkraut into my mouth. We looked at MaGretta. If the gravity of the conversation made it impolite to eat, I'd take the fall.

MaGretta didn't say a word.

Pop gave me a thank-you wink and devoured the dumpling.

"Miranda," I said, "isn't it possible that Fikus overheard someone talking about the location, but instead of calling the police, he calls himself gifted and makes a tidy profit?"

"No, that's not what happened," she said. "When Fikus returned from Utah, he held my hand and revealed personal facts that only my mother would have known. Fikus said there's more, but I have to be patient. For now, my mother's spirit just wants to comfort me. And she has. Just knowing she's still with me has been a blessing. So I'm going to keep giving interviews and spreading the word about Fikus so that others like me, people who've lost a loved one, won't lose hope. They'll hear Fikus's spiritual message and they'll know their loved ones are still with them."

Around the table, my family tsk'd with compassion, including Pop. When I wiped my mouth, I kept the napkin pressed over my lips, *don't say it, don't say it*, but when the napkin came down, my opinion slipped out. "Fikus is a goddam fraud."

"ZIA!" MaGretta gasped. "Watch your language."

"You're a goddam hypocrite."

"DIETER!" A flustered MaGretta ping-ponged her apologies between Miranda and God for our cursing.

"We should all settle down," Pop said, "and enjoy the good supper."

"You heard me," Dieter said, "Hyp-O-Crite."

MaGretta nervously refluffed her napkin. "Otto, please pass the—"

"Hypocrite?" I glowered right back at Dieter. "Are you comparing this to Alpha? It's not the same thing. Alpha isn't some dead guy hanging around spewing touchy-feely bullshit."

"Well, why would he? Why would anyone, anywhere, want to waste their time trying to tell you a thing? You got all the answers, right? You got your own private ghost, to hell with any others. You got your own set of omens—lettuce, cheese, salt. And you don't need to read tealeaves; you read birds. It's the world according to Zia, right?"

"Dieter, no, *shhh*," MaGretta whispered.

Then everybody hushed.

My eyes watered...from allergies. But stupid Dieter might think they were tears—which they weren't. I lowered my fork, excused myself, then rushed out the back door.

# 59

From all sides of Otto came a whirlwind of apologies, explanations, and rationalizations, though none addressing Otto, who sighed sadly at his congealing supper. All he wanted was pleasantries while he gorged himself to the extent of his belt. But a peaceful dinner was not to be.

His fist hit the table, "QUIET," causing a startled silence. Otto turned a gentle face to Miranda. "Young lady, you did not cause a problem. Okay? Zia does not like the MacKenzies too much. That is all." He lifted from his chair, his focus now shifting to MaGretta and Dieter. "I will talk to Zia. We are long overdue for a Poppa to daughter chat." He speared slices of sauerbraten into a napkin, excused himself, and left.

Otto knew where to find Zia. She always sulked in the same place her mother had sulked—a grassy knoll at the top of the trail leading to the beach.

While crossing the yard, Otto grabbed a folding chair. He lumbered out the back gate and down the sandy path.

The ocean, dappled with golden glints, surprisingly bright, ushered a breeze, uncommonly warm. Otto slowed to appreciate the splendor. When he reached his sprawled daughter, he cushioned into his chair and whistled a song from his boyhood.

Zia ignored him, as Otto had expected; she was much like her mother—stubborn.

Later, as evening darkened the sky, ribbons of stars lit a pathway to Rosie; that was how Otto saw it. Somewhere in heaven, Rosie waited for him. And someday Otto would follow those stars to join her. A long-tailed meteor streaked the navy sky. Otto smiled; his Rosie sent falling stars and comet trails in answer to Otto's thoughts. Yes, she was listening. Yes, she was waiting. Otto's eyes closed. His nostrils flared to welcome the ocean's salty perfume. Still drifting with sentiment, he whispered, "Your mother brooded in this very spot. Oh, how she loved the ocean. You are so much like your mother."

"I hate the ocean," Zia said.

Otto took in another breath of the fragrant sea. "I know that already."

"You really miss her, huh, Pop?"

"Every waking moment of every day. To know for certain that I will see her again would ease my heart much."

"Jeez, Pop, not you, too. Fikus is a crook. I don't know what mysterious crap he's feeding Miranda, but it didn't come from her mother."

"Probably not, but Miranda is just as convinced of her opinion as you are of yours."

"Miranda wants to believe. She's desperate. It's easy to fool the desperate."

"Yeah, sure, but Zia, it is not so much one way or the other. When I think of your mother, my heart is good. Maybe that is all Miranda wants, a heart not so heavy. If Fikus can give her that, you should not want to take it away. That is unkind, Zia. It is hurtful."

"Pop, this isn't about a heart consoled; it's about grief exploited— exploited on a grand scale or this town wouldn't be packed with lousy spectators."

Otto peered at his daughter. Like Rosie, Zia exempted herself from the reasoning she demanded of others. Otto thought it was time to straighten the kink in Zia's logic. "So, who tells you so much? Alpha?"

Zia rolled onto her side and looked up quizzically.

"Yeah, sure," Otto said. "I know about Alpha. He has been your ghost friend since you were five years old. When you talk to him, I pretend not to notice so that your MaGretta will not notice. If she notices, she will worry. If she worries, she might buy another cat, and cats are no good."

"Pop, does it worry you?"

"A cat, yes. Your ghost friend, auk, no. A few nights before you were born, a ghost or an angel, same thing, told your mother a secret."

"What secret?"

Otto unfolded his napkin and began eating the sauerbraten.

"Pop, tell me the secret."

"You should be Claudia," he sputtered in a voice garbled with meat. "But this angel thought your name should be Zia. I told your mother, 'Zia is not a name. It is too many pickled eggs before bed. That is what Zia is, too many pickled eggs.' Your mother did not believe too much in ghosts or angels, but she insisted, 'Zia, Zia, Zia.' Auk, such stubbornness. But she believed the name was special so she searched for the meaning."

Otto relaxed back as if he had finished the story.

Zia swatted his ankle. "Pop, come on. Are you going to tell me?"

"Who knows. Maybe someday."

"I hate it when you tease."

Otto chuckled. "That is why I tease you."

"Jeez, would you just tell me?"

"Grain."

"What?"

"Zia means grain. An angel tells your mother to name you Grain." Otto shrugged. "What do you and your ghost friend think about that?"

"I think you're right, too many pickled eggs. But, Pop, I don't have a ghost friend. I mean, Alpha never lived. He's just a remnant from childhood, a tea-party friend that never went home. If he were anything more than that, he would have told me stuff about when we die. He might have said that we live, but we're changed."

"Changed? What kind of change? Do we change into a rabbit or a fish? Well, it makes no difference to me. Your mother can change to whatever will make her happy, and I will change to whatever will please her. Auk, I hope it is not a cat."

"Jeez, Pop, no one turns into a cat...I think. But I know for damn sure no one hears the dead."

"Why not?"

"Because they—they sound like—" Zia's face suddenly slackened, her eyelids lowering halfway, her cheeks losing color.

*A fugue*; Otto had seen this before. "Zia, they sound like what? Answer me. Do not worry your Poppa." Otto slid from his chair and onto his knees. "Oh, this is not good. Not good." He snapped his fingers in front of her eyes. "Zia, where are you? Zia?"

"Cicadas," she whispered. "The humming drone of cicadas."

He jiggled her, "Zia. ZIA."

She blinked rapidly. "Sorry, Pop, I guess I spaced out." She tilted sideways to look behind him. "Did you fall off your chair?"

"Yeah, sure," Otto said grunting as he pushed to his feet. He brushed sand from his trousers. "Zia, try to stay in this world, okay? Will you do that for your Poppa?"

She nodded.

"Good," Otto said. "Let's go back and finish our suppers." He tucked the folding chair under one arm and stretched his other arm toward Zia.

She wove around it.

While they strolled home, Zia's shoulder pressed against Otto's chest and her head thumped beside his heart. This was his little girl; he kissed the crown of red curls. She would always be his little girl, no matter her age and no matter how...funny.

When they reached the fence, Otto returned the folding chair to its place. "I want to ask you something, but MaGretta says I should not." He peered at the house. "Maybe she is right."

"Pop, I'm not a kid anymore. Ask me anything. I won't tell MaGretta. What do you want to know? Do I drink? Do I smoke?"

"You drink? You smoke?"

"Nooo. I mean, what was your question?"

"Why do you not like the ocean? You have medals for diving. You teach swimming. And every day you collect clutter from the shore for your jingle-jangles, but never do you put a toe into the saltwater. Why is that?"

Zia's chin came down and her shoulders suddenly drooped.

"Oh, no," Otto said. "Auk, I should not have asked. It is not important."

"It's okay, Pop. I want to tell you, but I can't." Zia looked back at the ocean. "I can't because I really don't know. I just have this weird feeling that the sea—well, that it knows me. Like it's a living thing...waiting for me." Zia shivered.

Otto shook his head. "It is those books you read. They fill your mind with monsters."

"Maybe. Or maybe I don't want to swim where I'm not at the top of the food chain. Pop, do you think I'm bad in the head?"

Otto's thick arms enveloped his funny daughter. "No. Not bad. Never bad." He kissed her forehead. "Just cracked."

"Cracked?" She pulled free. "Pop, you think I'm cracked?"

"Yeah, sure. Zia means grain, and a good grain is a cracked grain. If the grain is not cracked, we benefit not much. The grain will come out like it went in, still holding its nutrients. What good is that? Because of the crack, we benefit from the grain."

## 60

*"Ereo?" Her tongue clunked as though
the name had sullied her mouth.*

Pop and I stomped the backdoor mat to knock sand from our shoes.
"I'm not hungry," I told Pop because I didn't want to see Dieter. "Tell
MaGretta I ate a late lunch, okay? I'm heading to bed."

"Are you sure?" Pop asked.

My stomach panged in a plea to reconsider. "Yeah, I'm sure." In my
bedroom, I dressed for bed while dining on breath mints and sunflower
seeds. Afterward, I perused my books for mind-absorbing horror. *The Hunger.*
Although I had read it numerous times, I felt fresh fear with every reread.
After a few pages, I wouldn't think about delicious sauerbraten or stupid
Dieter, not while I was journeying through a masterpiece of fright.

As I snuggled beneath the covers, I checked the clock to limit my reading
to thirty minutes. Any longer and I would have to sleep with the lights on.

Two hours and three chewed cuticles later, *rap, rap, rap.*

"*JEEEEZ!*" The book butterflied up and then splattered onto the floor.

A ghoulish vampire had escaped from the pages. *No, it's just a book, just a
book.* I repeated my grounding mantra. And vampires don't knock; they fly
through windows. *Rap, rap, rap.* I cleared my throat. "Come in."

The door creaked with insidious intent. I pulled the blankets to my chin.
Miranda peeked from the doorframe. "Could we talk?"

I sat up and motioned her inside.

"Zia, are you okay? You look pale."

I picked up the book and held it out. "Ever read it?"

After glancing the cover, she recoiled as if I were offering her a turd.

"It's macabre," I said. "Genuine blood-swirling macabre. No hokey-
monsters or slasher-shit. This is pure art. Guaranteed nightmares."

"Then why do you read it?" she asked as if I hadn't just explained.

"Are you slow? I just told you, the story shreds your nerves. It's horrifi-
cally scary, savagely chilling. Get it?"

"You love to be frightened?"

That sounded like a jab, so I replied in kind. "You love to be conned?"

Miranda flinched; maybe it wasn't a jab. Recalling Pop's advice, I said, "I'm sorry. You have every right to believe in someone's crap." But instead of accepting my apology, she made a sour face. "I'm serious," I said. "If a freak's bullshit makes you feel better, I shouldn't try to take that away." She still looked sour. "For chrissake, can't you accept an apology?"

"You're apologizing?"

"In plain English."

"Well, don't."

"Convenient timing." My arms crossed. "Since I already did."

"Zia, you don't like me, do you?"

I shrugged.

"I'm sorry," she said, "for whatever I did that upset you. I didn't do it on purpose. Okay? I'm going to get my things and go."

"Go? Go where?"

"I can't stay. I'm causing friction, not only between us, but also between you and your brother. That's why I'm—"

"Staying! Name your price. You want me out of the way? You got it. Wash your car for a week? Wait, it's still in the shop. Hey, you can use my car. Will that work? Whatever you want, just name it."

"Zia, my *leaving* isn't against you; it's for you."

"Right. You're kicking me for my own good. Got it. Look, I battled against you coming here, and I obviously lost. If you leave now, everyone under this roof will blame me."

"No, I'll explain—"

"*Explain?* As in, *the truth?* For chrissake, just get a gun and shoot me."

"No, I can tell them—I'll say—Maybe, I could—"

"*Stammer?* Miranda, this is no place to cut your teeth on concocting bull. I'll come up with something believable. Just give me a few hours."

"Do you normally spend hours creating lies to avoid telling the truth?"

"Hey, I had a stressful day. Normally, I can cook up a decent lie within an hour. It used to take minutes, but Dieter and Pop are wise to the library."

"The library?"

"Sure. Lies containing a library are lies believed, even outlandish crap." I assessed Miranda's potential—puppy-dog eyes, sweet smile, nervous giggle. *Damn.* "Forget it. If I gave you an unbeatable lie and tutored you all night on its delivery, you would still blow it. You might fool Pop and MaGretta, but you'll trip on Dieter. He's the landmine. Pow! Only it's my ass that's pow'd."

"Oh, Zia, your brother is one of the sweetest—"

"To you, sure. You're the reason he bought a comb. But I know my brother. You didn't tell him you were leaving or he would be in my room right now, rattling me far worse than *The Hunger*. Pow! Get it?"

Miranda's thick lashes batted with an odd kind of sympathy, the way you look at a nutcase who doesn't realize they're nuts. "Dieter is so gentle," she said, "and he loves you so much, what you're saying is a little hard to believe."

She tried to touch my hand, but I whipped it away. "What the hell are you talking about?"

"Aren't you suggesting that Dieter might hurt you?"

"I'm not suggesting it; I'm stating it. When I let Dieter down, his disappointment, his god-awful disappointment, lingers in his eyes. Then, every time he looks at me, I'm bludgeoned with guilt. I've told him a million times, stop expecting better of me. But he doesn't listen. And his disappointment kills me. So I'm asking you, hella-nicely, you're staying."

She thought awhile, then offered a hand. What choice did I have but to shake it. Although I hadn't invited her to stay, she looked around for a place to sit. Pressed moths and jarred beetles covered the chairs.

Scrunching my legs, I gestured to the bed's end. When she sat, I gave her one of my pillows. She clutched the pillow too tightly, balling the downy feathers beneath her chin. To get along, I ignored this. I said, "Can I ask a question without you getting upset?"

"I won't get upset if you don't call people names. Deal?"

*Names?* I had never called her a name, but I ignored this, too. "Yeah, whatever. What secrets about your mom did the freak tell you?"

Miranda curled into the pillow.

"Hey, are you okay?"

Her head lifted. "I thought we had a deal." She hand-wiped her face, but it was too late; the pillow had a disgusting slobber stain.

I knocked the tainted pillow out of her arms and off of my bed. Generously, I handed her another. "A deal, right." I tipped my head toward the soiled lump on the floor. "And you're breaking it."

Miranda frowned as though she were the one being patient. "Fikus knew about my birthmark that's on my rear. He also knew I had a glass charm, a kitten, and he knew I named it Fritters. He described the necklace that my mother never took off—a silver star with a diamond in the center strung on a silver chain. Fikus knew how I broke my arm and scarred my chin, and he knew where to find my mother's body. Is that enough?"

"How did she fall?"

Any reasonable person would have expected that question if their story had stopped before the shocking conclusion. But my question hung in the air like a bad smell...and Miranda sniffed again. I lunged for the tissues, but not in time. Her snot, tears, and drool sullied another pillow.

I hoarded my last clean treasure to the small of my back.

"I'm not a fool," she said. "Fikus spoke to my mother. It may be hard to believe, but it's true. In two weeks, Fikus is holding a public session to channel openly for anyone who wants to listen. Dieter and I are going, and Fikus asked me to extend his personal invitation to you."

"To me? Why?"

She shrugged. "Come with us. It's at the Ministry of Enlightenment."

"You mean the Church of Light?"

"No. His father stepped down to let Fikus reorganize the Church. Fikus renamed the Church as a testament to those who are truly enlightened."

"I get it. An enlightened cult."

"Attend one session before you judge. Okay?"

"Maybe. I'll have to check my schedule."

Miranda stood and held out a downy slime-ball. Using two fingers, I pinched it, craned it to the side, and then released it. Pillow-pillagers are insanely ignorant about those of us who cherish our clouds of comfort. Maybe pillow-pillagers just don't know we exist.

"I'll pray that wisdom guides your decision," Miranda said.

"Wisdom, right." I looked at the defiled pillows. "Just don't mention my name in your prayers."

"But God listens."

"That's what I'm thinking. And maybe I'm just a lowly spider hiding in the corner of a universal closet. I'm living only because He hasn't noticed me yet. But if you go pointing me out, 'Hey, look, there's Zia,' then He grabs a can of Raid. *Pssst.*" I slumped over. Then popped up. "Get it?"

Simultaneously, Miranda nodded and shook her head. "Don't you want God's help?"

"What is He, a friend of yours? Don't preach to me about God. I'm agnostic. The religious and the atheists claim to have the answers, but agnostics say, nobody knows shit, which riles everyone. The religious call us atheists, and the atheists call us fencepost sitters. We upset all sides because we have nothing to argue, and arguments create books, movies, headlines and wars—Judaism against Christianity against Atheism against Islamism. Everyone impassioned to convert everybody else, but what for? Might doesn't make right. *What one believes or does not believe will not change what is.*"

Briefly, I felt disconnected. Somewhere else.

"Zia? Zia? What's wrong?"

"I think I overdosed on breath mints." I rubbed my unfocused eyes. "What was the last thing I said? Do you remember? Oh, never mind. Get some sleep." We exchanged goodnights before I sank under the covers. When the door closed, I sat upright. "Alpha, is Fikus gifted?"

*All Souls hold gift and burden.*

"Don't give me that mumbo-jumbo. Is Fikus talking to Miranda's mom? Is he talking to anyone dead?"

*True.*

"True? But I thought you said—"

*In the manner your father speaks to your mother.*

I launched a snotty pillow at my phantom friend. It sailed through him and crashed into a framed beetle. "Quit your technicalities. You know what I mean. Does Fikus see or hear Miranda's mom?"

*Untrue.*

"That's what I thought." I pointed to the busted frame. "That's your fault, by the way. Now, I might forgive you, if you tell me how Fikus knew that stuff about Miranda. Eventually, I'll figure it out, but if you slipped me a clue," I smiled, pretty-please, "it would save me some time."

*And the strain of a thought.*

"That's a wisecrack, isn't it?"

Silence.

"Goodnight, Alpha." I reached for the lamp, then stopped midair. "Wait a second. I get it. Fikus is like me. He has a phantom friend, right? That's how Fikus learned the name of Miranda's metal charm, Floppy, the dog. And I bet that's how he knew about the birthmark on Miranda's breast. Makes total sense. His phantom friend showed him the images, right?"

*I do not create images; I retrieve them from within your being.*

"For chrissake, just answer yes or no; is Fikus like me?"

*Every Soul is distinct.*

"That's not what I meant and you know it." I studied my gloomy friend. "I get it. You're jealous. You're jealous of Fikus's friend."

Alpha made a face of tired endurance.

"Oh, come on, Alpha, just admit it. Fikus's phantom friend is more powerful than you, right? He might give Fikus the winning lottery numbers, or tell him which horse is going to win, place, and show at Bay Meadows. While you, on the other hand, not only let me ruin a rim, but also let a rattlesnake bite me. Remember that? I asked a simple question, should I go hiking with Randy Carter. And you babbled about vibrations."

*Intent vibrates into the result...and it was not a rattlesnake.*

"Well, it could have been. And you could have answered in plain English: Don't go mountain climbing just to impress a date because shrieking hysterically over a rattlesnake bite won't leave the desired impression. Hear that? That's plain English."

*It was not a rattlesnake...nor were you bitten.*

"Technicalities. It could have been a rattler, and I could have been bitten...and I could have had a heart attack, but a lot you care."

I turned off the lamp.

Alpha's eyes glowed like mandarin night-lights, although dimmer than usual. Maybe I had hurt his feelings. "Hey, Alpha, I was teasing. I don't care that you can't do much. I can't either. I just make wind chimes and coach messed-up kids. I don't need a fancy friend." I burrowed into the blankets. "Seriously, Alpha, I like you just the way you are."

*I do not create images; I retrieve them from within your being.*

"Okay, I'd like you more if you spoke English." I yawned. "Because I doubt that Fikus personally saw Dorothy's necklace, the gold heart with an emerald in it."

*True.*

"Oh, I thought that's what you were getting at. Now, I'm completely lost."

*True.*

"Two wise-cracks in one night; you're on a roll."

*Matter is not one-dimensional, despite your persistence to regard it so.*

"Matter-schmatter. I will bet you a million bucks that I won't understand one matter more when I'm dead than the matter I understand now."

Rare as it was, Alpha smiled. *I will not accept that wager.*

# 61

*Triite is an accomplished Persuader,
able to coerce hundreds, even thousands,
during one lifetime.*

From the moment he saw her, he loved her.

Strangely and completely.

And that occurred years ago when Zia defended him in high school. She wasn't ready to accept him then, so he watched her from the sidelines and waited for her to need him. And through the years of watching and waiting, he often surged with desire. Occasionally, he filled with hatred, too.

She dated other men.

He struggled to forgive her.

When he saw her enter the church, his heartbeat quickened. He was ready for her now. He was no longer a teen, clumsy and tongue-tied. He was now a young man of appreciative status, as the crowd filing into the church well proved. His entire life, it seemed, had been preparing for this moment when he would step from the shadows and declare his love.

While standing in line, her weight shifted from one leg to the other, as if she were an impatient princess waiting for her prince.

But unlike a princess, she gnawed on bloody stumped fingertips. It was one of her many habits that he intended on forcing her to break. These habits didn't ruin her, though. Men did.

He had witnessed it from a darkened corner at Neptunes. Men gave her cigarettes and a sailor's mouth, bought her drinks and took her bets. In their company, she behaved tasteless and crude...and cheap. Like a whore, she allowed men to bed her.

But it was an act, of course, just a pretense of friendship to ease her loneliness while she waited for her Soul-mate.

Waited for him.

To protect her, Fikus made certain that the men who defiled her would never defile her again.

As the line moved toward the receiving tables, he noticed Zia's steps were not graceful, but thudding, as if she were irritable...and not impressed by all he had achieved.

But he forgave her.

When his staff asked Zia to fill out a visitor slip, Fikus strained to hear her melodic voice.

"Get your damn card out of my face." She smacked the man's hand. "Fikus is the so-called psychic. Ask him who I am."

Though difficult, Fikus forgave her for this, too. He fixed an unyielding gaze on his future wife. She tossed her copper curls in brazen flirtation. Her emerald eyes flashed his way.

His mouth dried; his breathing became shallow. She wanted him; her coquettish glances told him so.

And then their eyes met. Fikus's legs weakened. He felt certain that their Souls were connecting. He felt it and he knew she felt it, too. Profound desire was saturating their entireties.

Zia's lips parted.

Fikus inhaled sharply. To the whole world, she was about to declare her love for him, the same love that he had held for her so vigilantly throughout the years.

His chest swelled. He mouthed, "I love you. Love you."

"STOP STARING AT ME...freak."

The church fell silent.

## 62

*If you cannot be compassionate, be tolerant.*

"What are you looking at?" I said to the woman gaping nearby. I leaned toward Miranda and asked, "Do I have something gross on my face?"

"No, you look fine," she told me.

"It's your mouth," Dieter said, and not very nicely either. "For once, just for once, could you manage a few hours without screaming at someone?"

"Hey, that freak was gawking at me."

"Zia, if you don't knock it off—"

"It's okay." Miranda squeezed Dieter's arm. "I'm just glad she's here. Now, please, let's find some seats before they're all taken."

In the fifth row from the front, three empty chairs were together...sort of. I asked a ponytailed guy to move over so I could sit next to my brother.

The guy smiled idiotically. "Hey, man, we're all brothers."

"No," I said, "This row is for the '90s. You want the '60s. They're by the exits in case Nixon sends in the man." I raised a power-to-the-people fist.

Dieter clamped my arm and swung it down. "KNOCK IT OFF!"

"Knock what off? That guy is lost." I turned to point to the lost guy, but he was making his way out of the row.

Miranda tugged Dieter and they switched seats. Rickety seats. Twenty rows of folding chairs had replaced the wooden pews. Gone, too, were kneeling benches, angelic statues, and prayer tables once set with hundreds of votive candles. The place was less like a house of worship and more like a town hall. With Miranda saving my chair, I left to mill among the crowd.

The locals—Scavengers, betters, customers, and Dieter's friends—were a pittance to the number attending. After cordial hellos, I moved on.

Five or six clusters wore baggy shorts and rubber thongs. They glanced cautiously over their peeling shoulders before they chugged and sipped their smuggled-in beer. Vacationers. No group was more obvious...or more fun to tease. I tapped an oversized man dressed in an undersized Hawaiian shirt. "Excuse me, sir. Every entrance has a posted sign, *no alcohol*."

His group swung their cups to their backs.

"But I can't tell on you," I said, "if I'm drinking with you." I held out my hand. "Am I drinking with you?" They relaxed into chuckles.

"Coming right up, little lady," the big man said. Then he turned to his friend, "Hey, Joe, get the lady a drink."

"Take mine." A bleary-eyed woman thrust out a cup, foam sloshing over the sides. "I've had enough. I'd dump it, but Henry calls that alcohol abuse."

She swayed as if she were on a boat, so I grabbed the cup before it went overboard. I raised a toast, "Thanks," and took a big gulp expecting beer.

My stifled choking caused Bleary-Eyed-Woman to swat Big Man. "I told you it was too strong."

"No, no," I managed after the burn sank to my chest. "It was just a hearty spike. Turkey or Jack?"

They started laughing in the volume of drunks. "You sure know your whiskeys," Big Man said. "Do you live in town or are you just visiting?"

"Visiting," I said, "from Nebraska." I lifted to my toes to peer over heads. "Oh, damn, I have to go. My one-armed cousin needs help."

"One arm?" Their necks craned to look for my cousin. "How did he—"

"She," I said. "Farming accident. Tragic."

They *oooh'd* sympathetically and asked how it happened.

"Automatic harvest machine," I told them. "It was moving through the field, but my cousin had her back turned. She didn't see it coming. It severed her arm, took it off at the elbow, then it kept going and going, her arm flapping from the blades as if waving goodbye."

"That's horrible." Bleary-Eyed-Woman held her chest. "The poor thing." She looked at her friends to chorus her sympathy. "Isn't that horrible?" The women nodded, but the men pinched their chins with skeptical *uh-huh*s and grunts while watching for a sign that I was kidding.

Tough crowd; my favorite kind. With a face of sorrow, I said, "We scoured the fields, acre after acre, but we couldn't find it. In desperation, we spent our last dime to get here. We pray Fikus can tell us where it is. He's our only hope of ever finding it."

"Of finding the arm?" Bleary-Eyed-Woman whispered.

"No," I whispered back. "The harvest machine."

Circling the room, I counted seven clusters of New Agers and Old Agers, which explained the VWs and Mercedes filling the parking lot. Both generations wore goofy grins, half having the pasty skin that marks vegetarians. The older ones chatted about reincarnation and a guy named Cayce, who slept a lot and made a fortune reciting his dreams. Ingenious!

Another group talked about Atlantis, when it evolved, how it destroyed itself, and where the survivors, Lemurians, now live—Mount Shasta.

"Oh, *pa-lease*," I said. "Anyone smart enough to survive a sinking continent is smart enough to avoid a freezing mountain. Couldn't they find Tahiti?"

They shouldered together. I moved on.

The young New Agers, around my age, discussed healing stones, glowing auras, and dirty chakras. Supposedly, I had a filthy chakra—that's what the girl said when she offered to clean it for free. She waved her hands over my head, and then she flicked her wrists to remove the invisible filth. It sounds easy, but trained chakra cleaners have certificates. Better pay for certified bullshit.

Threading through the crowd, I overheard talk of Guides.

"Hey, Alpha, are you a Guide?"

*I am Alpha.*

"Forget it." He didn't match anyone's description of a Guide anyway. Their Guides had normal names—Anthony, Bartholomew, Lillian. And their Guides were quirky, playful, and humorous.

Alpha had the humor of a Grim Reaper.

"What does your Guide look like?" I asked a lady, and her entire cluster chimed in—a bullfighter, an angel, a flapper, an elf, a snowball.

*Snowball?* "Does anyone see a tall Guide, thin, wears a rust-colored robe, wavy like steam, talks with the clarity of mud, has a crackled face like whittled bark with jammed in coals for huge orange eyes, which close when you're wrong, so they shut all the time, but God-forbid he should ever tell you when you're right, which apparently is never, because you don't even have a damn signal for that, do you? Do you? I mean, uhm, anyone?"

They backed away.

The last eight clusters, well-dressed, well-mannered, were quiet people and the first to find seats. Their smiles rarely rose to their eyes, and their conversations were quick, reflective, and mostly sad. Miranda's cluster.

"Welcome!" A voice boomed from the speakers. "We're about to begin. Would everyone please be seated. There are extra chairs along the back wall."

I returned to my chair. Minutes later, the lights dimmed and the chatting ceased. Fikus walked onto the stage. "Thank you for coming tonight. I'm Fikus MacKenzie. Through a God-given gift, I'm here to help you."

# 63

The opening lecture fringed on religion, but avoided terms like sin and grace. Fikus professed, "Each of us should search our Souls for the center of goodness. Only when we learn to love and appreciate ourselves can we discover our higher purpose and find the happiness and peace we deserve."

What a load of crap.

People love themselves too much already. If someone has to search for their goodness, it means they're an asshole. Fikus made it sound like people were saints just for *trying* to be good. Months ago, the Youth Center's administration pulled that crap, insisting that each Blue Dolphin receive a ribbon at every meet, whether the kid butterflied beautifully or flailed miserably. The importance, they told me, was on the *trying*, not on the *succeeding*. Very nicely, I told them they were nuts. *Trying* to swim is called drowning.

While Fikus lectured, the crowd shuffled, mumbled, and coughed, all the usual sounds of boredom. But when Fikus left the pulpit and the real show began, the fidgeting stopped. "I'm sensing a spirit. His name is Marlo or Melvin, something with an M." Fikus peered across the audience. He pointed to a woman several rows back. Everyone turned in their chairs. "Please stand," Fikus said, and he asked for her name.

"Ruth," the woman said. "My Uncle Marvin passed away recently."

"I'm sensing a slow death. Lingering. He didn't pass quickly."

"Well, he was sick for a while, but—"

"Cancer?"

"Yes, cancer."

"That's what I'm sensing," Fikus said. "He suffered with cancer for a long time."

"But he died of a heart attack."

"I see that, but the lingering is connected to his cancer. He's showing me a car."

Ruth said nothing.

"A car or a motor," Fikus continued. "Something electrical, moving, a hobby or—"

"Oh my God, yes! Model trains."

"Trains. That's what he's showing me. Impressive collection."

Ruth nodded nonstop. "Uncle Marvin had railroad tracks across the attic."

"He's showing me something gold, too. A ring? A gold necklace?"

"Gold chains," she said. "He wore gold chains."

I elbowed Miranda and whispered, "Hard call; a Ruth and a Marvin, and she's wearing more tinsel than a Christmas tree."

Miranda tapped a finger to her lips.

"And this choice," Fikus told Ruth, "a choice you're about to make, your uncle approves. He says it's right."

"I'm getting married."

"Your uncle is pleased. He wants you to know that he loves you and has never left you. Take comfort in that."

Fikus moved on, firing a shotgun blast of generalities. Eventually, one of the thousand pellets sprayed hits a mark. Then the mark jumps up, "it's me, it's me."

I pictured myself flashing an envelope to an audience of debtors. I tell them, it's sort of past due, but not quite delinquent. I'm sensing lingering charges, maybe they occurred over a month. Maybe two. It's small. Yes, under a hundred. The bill's name is Sal or Sil, sounds like an S.

Then a cool-looking guy stands up, "Hey, it's me."

He's confident, almost cocky, and stylishly dressed. His cuffs are rolled, his tie is crooked, and he smells of expensive aftershave, yet sports a three-day shadow. Inwardly, I smile, but outwardly, I wear the constipated frown of a psychic. "Cell Phone Bill!"

"*Shhh*." Miranda and others hushed me.

"Sorry," I told them. "Sorry, sorry."

Grounded again, I heard Fikus telling a man, "Your grandfather couldn't control his anger. He's sorry for the abuse. The war changed him...so he left. He wanted to spare you. He's showing me a mountain. A small house atop a mountain. Very cold. Canada. He left you his only possession, a Civil War coin collection. He loves you. Forgive him."

"Thank you," the man said. He held onto his chair to lower himself, as if the message had aged him. Both Fikus and the audience gave the man a moment of quiet empathy. I quieted, too—crazy baffled. A coin collection? A house atop a mountain? Canada? Hardly generalities. Then Fikus did it again! Instead of a shotgun blast, he fired from a rifle loaded with impossible knowledge and aimed at a single target. Like everyone else, my mouth circled, "Whoa." *Alpha, how did Fikus know that? Come on, give me a clue.*

*Matter is not one-dimensional, despite your persistence to regard it so.*

*What matter?*

*All matter.*

*All what matter?*

Alpha sighed like one sighs when they're dealing with a dumb-ass.

*How about that frickin' face you make*, I said, *is that matter, too?*

*True.* Then Alpha turned one-eighty. *And now, you do not see my face; therefore, I have no face.*

*Well, you do, I just can't see it.*

*Therefore, I have no face.*

*Alpha, stop it. You're getting on my nerves.*

*Therefore, I have no face.*

*TURN AROUND!*

When Alpha turned, his eyes were lit, and he wore a slight smile. Behind me, a lady started crying, so I twisted in my seat. The lady was in her 30s, pale and thin, rubbing her neck and wincing. Jeez, she probably saw some horrible head trauma.

"Did your daughter have a head injury?" Fikus asked.

"In a way," the woman said. "She committed suicide."

The audience, *Ooh'd.*

*Alpha, that's just body signals.*

"Your daughter left a note," Fikus said, then he quoted bits of the contents. It must have been accurate because the lady nodded before she broke down, inconsolably sobbing.

*Alpha, how the hell did he do that? This is beyond reading flinches and tugged earlobes. Just give me a clue. I'm searching for the truth.*

*Then you will not find it. Your measure of truth is one-dimensional. Unfortunate. But your measure of falsehoods is limitless. Also unfortunate.*

*What do you mean? Search for the lie? That's the same thing as searching for the truth.*

Alpha's eyes closed.

"NO, YOU'RE WRONG!" My outburst caused another round of stern shushes. "Sorry, sorry," I said.

I slouched low. Targets rose, gasping yes's to unnervingly precise, intimate facts. I plugged my ears to concentrate on finding the lie. A while later, I pulled Miranda sideways. "Hey, did you get an extra visitor slip?"

She shook her head.

I thought for a minute and then tugged her toward me again. "The one you filled out, do you remember what it asked for?"

Again, she shook her head, now annoyed, and leaned toward Dieter.

Briefly, I stood up to look back at the receiving tables. Someone had cleared them. When I started to sit again, another idea came to me. I bounced back to my feet, now looking at more than the receiving tables. I noted the silk plants, the overhead lights, the wastepaper baskets, and the poles strung with cords that had railed us in line. If I had to pass muster as a psychic, I would seed a microphone within or near every one of those objects. Then I would slow the incoming people down to a crawl. Irritated, they would commiserate, first to express their annoyance, then to share their tragedies, and finally to divulge what their hearts hoped to gain, whether forgiveness, approval, or just information.

To guarantee their sharing of secrets, I'd pepper the line with shills. Those shills would prompt the talk and would hear what the microphones had missed.

Naturally, I'd cart the visitor slips to a private room where a computer guy could run the names through public information; births, deaths, marriages, divorces, engagements, arrests, aliases, promotions, contests, hobbies, anything recorded or newsworthy.

I had cracked the scam...except for one glitch. None of it explained Fikus's knowledge of Miranda.

*Matter is not one-dimensional,* Alpha said, *despite your persistence to regard it so.*

*Who asked you? Your cryptic messages don't help at all. I'll handle it from here.*

When Fikus ended the readings, he opened the floor for questions. My hand flapped high. Fikus pointed to another...then another...then another.

For more than an hour, my arm flagged vigorously. But between each inane question asked and every predictable answer given, Fikus ignored my hand. I glanced at Miranda's watch; twenty minutes remained. Having been snubbed worse and by better than Fikus, I sprang to my feet as though he had pointed to me.

"Yeah, my question is—"

"No, I'm sorry," Fikus said. "I was addressing the gentleman to your—"

"If Dorothy's spirit can tell you the name of a charm—Flipper or Flappy—can't she tell you the name of who was with her on the ridge?"

Fikus's tongue swiped his lips before he swallowed. I read his body language, a blaring, *caught-off-guard.*

"It's simple a question," I said. "Ask her spirit if she was alone on the ridge. If she shakes her head, ask for a name."

A security goon walked up to station himself at the left end of our row. I gave him a one-finger wave without turning from Fikus. "Everyone knows your vision located the body, right? And Dorothy's spirit told you about a necklace, a birthmark, and a charm, right?"

Miranda tugged frantically on my shirt. "Zia, that was personal."

I pushed her hand off me. "Ask Dorothy the important question; how did she fall? She told you where she fell; ask her *how* she fell."

Everyone was stone-cold quiet listening for his answer. Fikus suddenly hoisted a smile. "Souls are concerned with imparting comfort. They want loved ones to move on and to trust that the departed Soul is in a better place, a place relieved of pain. They don't want us dwelling on how they died. That creates negativity and saddens the departed spirit."

"But if somebody pushed Dorothy, then that person might push another person. Then we have two saddened spirits, right?"

Whispers rippled through the audience. The goon on the left was now matched by a goon on the right.

"I believe I've answered your question." With three quick strides, Fikus crossed the stage. He pointed to a teenage girl and then cupped his ear to urge her question.

She bounced up, giggling to her still seated friends, as if a rock star had selected her as the flavor of the day. "Thank you, Mr. MacKenzie. I'm spiritually sensitive, too, but not as much as—"

"HEY," I said. "Conjure up Dorothy's spirit and ask her whether or not she was alone on the ridge. If she can't talk, ask her to nod or shake her head."

"Listen, Red," the man behind me said, "sit yourself down." It was a vacationer, a big drunk vacationer. "This ain't your show. Just sit yourself down and keep your trap shut."

Dieter turned in his chair. "Hey, pal, don't talk to my sister like that."

"Oh yeah?" The vacationer's bulk lifted. He leaned over and jabbed a finger into Dieter's chest. "Why don't you and Red hit the road."

Dieter knocked the hand aside as he got to his feet. He was a foot taller than the vacationer, but half the man's width.

A few seats over, another vacationer stumbled upright. "Lisssen, jou, juss shake a hike. Red, too."

"Back off," Dieter said, "I suggest you call a cab. It sounds like you guys drank enough enlightenment for a night."

While Dieter and the two guys argued, another guy stood, several chairs to the left. I ran a quick eye down the row. *Uh-oh*. Seated behind us were two dozen vacationers with Bleary-Eyed-Woman and Big Man capping the ends. All of them appeared to be drunk; all of them appeared to be friends. They elbowed one another, nodded conspiratorially, and began to rise.

"Uhm, Dieter." A security goon started to advance. "Dieter." I turned to tap him...just as a vacationer cocked a fist. "BEHIND YOU!"

Dieter swiveled, ducked, but the swing clipped his forehead. His arms splayed and whacked the backs of the fourth row.

People bowled from their chairs.

Miranda started to rise, but I gripped her collarbone, yanked her sideways, and gave her a shove. "Go! Go! Get out of the aisle."

Dieter sprang up and punched the vacationer's nose. Blood sprayed, but before a drop landed, knuckles cracked into Dieter's jaw. Dieter rebounded, pivoting and hurling, fist after fist, against more than a dozen vacationers. But the unfairness lasted seconds. Dieter's friends vaulted the chairs. Scavengers toppled them, cutting straight up the rows. The betters, Mopar and Stackhouse, rushed in from the sides.

Arms were swinging, people were screaming, and blood sprinkled the air like ticker-tape and red streamers. Crouching people scrambled to escape, shoving back the goons in their panic.

I spotted a guy sneaking up on Dieter. I grabbed Miranda's weighted purse and swung with might...but not mighty enough.

He kept his balance. I froze; *I'm going to die.*

But Dieter whipped half-circle, walloped the guy, then ducked as a fist swept over his head.

The shouts, curses and cries—*Get him, Stop, Goddamn it, Nooo*—and the chairs clattering and banging nearly drowned out the pleas from the speakers: "This is a Church. A CHURCH! Stop the fighting! Stop the fighting!"

Someone grabbed my hair, and I forced myself sideways, my hair ripping from my scalp. I glimpsed a woman's knuckles interlaced with red strands, glimpsed it one second before the blow sent me spinning.

I collided into a chair. When I tried to get up, my vision doubled, and my chest seared with a wicked pain. I crumpled again. Miserably.

Then came a blissful darkness.

"Zia, can you hear me? Zia?"

My eyes blinked open to two cops and two Mirandas, but I kept blinking until I saw only one of each.

"Om hohay, moe pobbem." My tongue had swollen to the size of Kansas. "Hep me up."

"Just lie still," the cop said, "paramedics are on the way."

"Moe. Hep me up." I struggled and insisted until Miranda and the cop finally helped me to stand.

Except for a few gawkers, the crowd was gone. Across the room, Fikus and the goons were talking to some cops and battered vacationers.

In our corner, Dieter was explaining the events to Officer Jim Maroni. When they noticed me upright, their conversation paused. I tried to give an *I'm-okay* smile but my mouth spurted blood.

Dieter winced and turned again to Maroni. "For chrissake, Jim, uncuff me. I told you, we didn't start the fight."

"Well, Dieter, I'd like to believe you," Maroni said, "but the Minister's son tells it different. Says you threw the first punch. I've got conflicting stories and folks grumbling to press charges and a whole lot of fingers pointing at your sister as the cause of it all."

"Moe." I shook my head. "Mop me."

Dieter shouted at the vacationers, "Drunken bastards."

"Settle down," Maroni said. "I'll take the cuffs off in the squad car."

"Take them off now," Dieter said. "That guy wearing the bedspread threw the first punch."

"Hash riii."

"They were boozing it up," Dieter said. "Why didn't security enforce the No Alcohol rule? Damn tourists never stop drinking. If you don't believe me, smell the cups on the floor."

"I don't need to smell nothing. Those folks admitted they brought in a jug of beer and a flask of whiskey...said they shared it with your sister, too. Well, to keep the story straight, they shared it with a smart-mouthed redhead who's here with her one-armed cousin from Nebraska."

"Uh-oh," escaped from me with another ooze of blood.

Dieter peered at me, his eyes questioning for the truth.

My eyes rolled upward as if I couldn't quite recall.

Dieter's head lowered with a disappointed mutter, "Shit."

I wanted to apologize, maybe explain, but I couldn't talk very well, and my brother was handcuffed, bloodied, and pissed.

"Excuse me, officer." An older man in a long, gray coat slipped between the cops. He flashed a badge and touched his hat in greeting. "I'm Detective Spuretta."

"I recognize the name," Maroni said. "You're the Detective that found the Norst woman."

"That was Carly Spuretta, my daughter. We're now partners on the case." Spuretta turned to my brother, "Dieter Schatz is it? You got a mean right hook." Spuretta shadowboxed a one-two, and then he told Maroni to take off the cuffs. "I witnessed the incident from the git-go. Dieter here is telling the truth. He took the first punch. And that young lady there," he winked at me, "she didn't start the trouble. She was merely asking a question, but she had to repeat it. I guess the psychic doesn't hear too well."

"Are you sure?" Maroni said. "Because Fikus swears he saw—"

"I guess he doesn't see too well either. Let the young man take care of his sister."

"Yes, sir." Maroni keyed the cuffs. "Sorry about that, Dieter. I like you and your family. Well, I like you and your dad and MaGretta. I was only doing my job."

"Then do it," Dieter said. "Lock up those guys."

"Well, now, slow down." Maroni scratched his neck and squinted over at the vacationers. "Are you gonna press charges? Think about it, Dieter. Locking up tourists is bad for business. You end up with a reputation like El Dorado County; come on vacation, leave on probation."

Dieter shook his head, looking thoroughly disgusted. "Can we go now? I answered your questions, and Zia can't talk. Just look at her."

Then everyone turned to look at me, and everyone winced.

Tilting back against Miranda, I asked if I really looked that bad, but that's not how it came out. "Haa baa?"

"Shhh, don't talk." She gave a tiny squeeze, but that squeeze crunched my bruised ribs. *Ooooh.* My knees buckled. Dots freckled my vision.

Dieter pushed aside Maroni, caught me, and then steadied me onto unsteady legs.

"She's pretty banged up," Maroni said. "The paramedics are busy with an accident at the turnpike. How 'bout if I put her in the squad car and run her up to Mercy General?"

"Moe, moe, moe."

"Listen to me," Dieter said.

I nodded quickly, praying he wouldn't jostle me.

"You might have cracked a rib," he said.

"Moe shep."

Does it hurt when you take a deep breath?"

"Ush a ee-il."

"Zia, let's take a trip to the emergency room."

"Moe. Hum haa hoing."

"Your mouth is bleeding pretty bad."

"I hoe hare. Hum haa hoing. Hum haa hoing."

"I don't care," Miranda said, "I'm not going. I'm not going."

Amazed looks turned to Miranda.

Miranda shrugged. "I worked in a dental office. And I don't think the cut on her lip would cause this much blood."

"No, it wouldn't," Dieter said. "Zia, did you lose a tooth?"

I shook my head.

"Are you sure?"

I nodded.

"Stick out your tongue."

"I han."

"I can't," Miranda interpreted.

"Then open your mouth," Dieter said.

I opened my mouth as wide as I could.

Dieter peeled down my puffy lip. "Shit. You bit your tongue." He released my lip, and he glared at me. I knew that glare; it was anger simmering in guilt. "Why the hell did you stand in the middle of the fight?"

"I hep you." On every level, that was the wrong answer. Blood pumped into Dieter's face and pulsated out a gash in his jaw. I looked away. "Or maybe mop."

"What world do you live in?" Dieter yelled two inches from my face. "A Green Guppy can kick your ass. Am I getting through to you?"

I nodded spastically.

Dieter pinched the swollen bridge of his nose. "Why the hell didn't you get down? What the hell were you thinking?"

"Dieter, please," Miranda said. "Zia was more concerned for my safety than for her own."

I thought, *good one, Miranda*, but I said, "Ush rii. I hep her ow ee ile."

"I helped her out the aisle," Miranda said. "And she did. So don't do this now. Not here. Yell at her tomorrow, okay?"

"Yea, ell moo-morrow."

"I'm taking her home," Dieter told Maroni, then his arm wrapped my waist. "You ready?"

I nodded.

While crossing the room, I glanced at the enemies' camp.

Fikus was watching.

Once at the exit, Miranda checked her sagging purse. Had it been leather and not fabric, it would have survived when I pelted the vacationer. Instead, the bag tore and the contents flung.

I leaned against the wall while Miranda and Dieter started back to the rubble to search for Miranda's belongings.

Fikus kept a stupid stare locked on me.

I flipped him the bird; he didn't flinch. I tried to whistle, but ended up choking and spitting blood.

Still, he watched.

"SHOP SHARIN AU ME...reak."

# 64

*Somewhere, somehow,
somebody caused someone grief. Uhm, was it me?*

Cops stopped writing. Dieter spun around causing the looks between Fikus and me to triangle.

Spuretta stepped in the middle and regarded Fikus until Fikus turned away. With a raised voice, Spuretta assured the cops, "Everything is fine. Zia is just a little excited. That's all." To my brother and Miranda, he said, "Go on and find your things. I'll run Zia home, if she's agreeable."

"She's agreeable," Dieter stated. "Right?"

"Moe," I shook my head. "He a hop. A hop. Hop."

Miranda pulled Dieter sideways to interpret in his ear.

Dieter straightened with a nasty scowl. "Zia, I don't give a rat's ass if he's Joe Friday or Dirty Harry. YOU'RE AGREEABLE."

At least Spuretta didn't look like a cop. He lacked the judgmental frown lines that come from giving speeches. Instead, every line on Spuretta's face testified to quick smiles and abundant humor. When he helped me into his car, I noticed his socks didn't match; one green, one blue. I pointed.

Spuretta checked his shoes for dog-shit.

On the drive to my house, he turned on the radio and switched the station from country to rock, which was pretty nice of him to do. But then he began singing. Sort of. He knew just enough of the lyrics to butcher the song.

> *"...if there's a buzzard in your head, Joe, don't be alone now,
> it's just a sprinkling before the maid cleans..."*

I killed the radio before restrained laughter killed me.

Spuretta flipped down the visor. "There are wet-wipes in the glove-box if you want to clean up a bit."

I looked in the visor's mirror. Apart from a swollen tongue, I had the classic face of a satiated vampire—blood outlining teeth and encrusting a chin. I imagined MaGretta's reaction; *Auk, Zia, Zia, whoever your victim was, you will write them an apology.*

I went to work with the wet-wipes. When I thought myself presentable, I turned to Spuretta. "Much better," he said. "Can I tell you something?"

*Jeez.* Here comes the self-righteous cop-lecture. I threw down the container and huddled to the door. "I'm not too keen on that MacKenzie fella," he said, and that was all that he said. He started to hum.

He sure didn't act like a cop. In fact, he looked and acted like a taste-tester of Italian cuisine, cheerful and satisfied—a spaghetti-man. "Nope, not too keen," he said quietly. "He's a mighty slippery fella."

I sat up. "I hone hi him heeher."

"You don't like him either?" When he smiled, his eyes twinkled. "Guess we have that in common."

I nodded slowly. Even more slowly, I returned the smile. Despite my contempt for cops, I sort of liked Spaghetti-man and his effervescent eyes.

Outside my house, he offered to explain things to whomever might need an explanation. Since I couldn't talk well and MaGretta would want to know why, I had no choice but to accept the offer, although I squirmed wondering what he would say. In my story, I wore a halo. I always wore a halo. If Spaghetti-man told the story, he might do something stupid—like go for the truth. I told him to slant the truth. "Shwan shwoo, shwan shwoo."

"You're welcome, you're welcome," he said.

When we walked through the door, MaGretta took one look at Spuretta and knew he was law. "OTTO!" she shouted, then turned to me, "Zia, what did you do?" then to Spuretta, "Zia is sorry, terribly sorry," then, "OTTO!"

"Ma'am, ma'am, you have a lovely daughter."

MaGretta paused, one eyebrow raising. "Lovely?"

"She's in no trouble," Spuretta said. "No trouble at all. I was just bringing her home. She's a very nice girl."

"Nice?" Then both her brows arched. "*Nice?*"

It didn't take psychic powers to know what MaGretta was thinking. *Jeez,* I had no warped fathering issues to be in an old guy's arms. I was mentally healthy...but now totally grossed out. "Moe, moe," I told MaGretta, but she didn't understand. I pushed Spaghetti-man, urging him to run, "Hun, hun."

"HON?" MaGretta swung me aside. With lethal jabs, she backed up Spuretta. "For shame! If you are not the police, you are a dead man. OTTOOO!"

"Oh, no, no, ma'am. No, ma'am." He flushed into a mortified red. "I'm a detective. Yes, ma'am. My daughter is Zia's age. Yes, ma'am." He fumbled for his badge. It was halfway out when MaGretta snatched it, tearing his shirt pocket. She scrutinized both sides, rubbing at the letters and comparing the picture to his face, as though she believed I had given him the badge prior to her finding and burning my drawer full of fake IDs. "Hmm, it looks real."

"Oh yes, ma'am. It's real. Yes, ma'am."

"And Zia is not in trouble?"

"No, ma'am. Zia is not in trouble."

MaGretta considered the badge again. "I don't understand."

"Well, ma'am, Zia fell on a chair. Nothing too serious, but she bit her tongue and she might have a bruised rib. Your son and Ms. Miranda had a few things to do, so I offered to drive Zia home."

"Is this right, Zia? Zia?"

I was still praying for a meteor to obliterate the planet and end my humiliation, but God doesn't like me; I never get my way. "Uh-huh."

"Oh my," MaGretta's hand pressed to her cheek. "I am so embarrassed, Mr. Detective, so embarrassed."

"Frank. But there's no need to feel embarrassed." He held out his palm for the badge's return.

"No, I feel terrible. Look what I have done to your shirt. And after you showed such kindness to Zia. I will make it up. You will stay and eat."

"Oh, no, ma'am, I couldn't—"

"Nonsense. Call your wife and invite her, too."

"I'm not married, but really, I—"

"You will eat. Zia will show you to the table." MaGretta pocketed the badge and walked away. Spuretta started to call after her, but I shook my hanging head and motioned for him to follow me.

MaGretta's apologies always come with a banquet, and that's just what she set down in front of Spuretta. "Eat," she said.

Just like Pop, Spuretta looked at the meal the way a hungry beast sizes up prey. He lifted his fork and was about to dive in when MaGretta sat down beside him. Oddly, Spuretta scooted over. "Will Mr. Schatz be joining us?"

"Otto is not home," MaGretta said. "When I'm upset, I yell his name. It is a habit. Now eat." And Spaghetti-man's eyes twinkled before he even took his first bite. MaGretta offered to stick my dinner in a blender, but I told her, *moe*, to the sauerkraut shake. I went off to take a shower.

Since Pop wasn't home to bang on the bathroom door, "long enough," I stayed in the shower until the hot water ran cold. When clean and towel wrapped, I started toward my room, but sounds from the kitchen stopped me in the hallway. With an ear pressed to the wall, I heard MaGretta's demure giggles while Spaghetti-man boasted of wild escapades, each ending with his lesson learned and an *I'll be darned.* I smiled; old people flirting, how cute. After dressing for bed, I read a few hours, and then came out to say good-night. They didn't even notice me.

Just then, Pop barreled through the front door. Spuretta jumped up with more zeal than someone who had sat on a lit firecracker. MaGretta introduced the two men. They shook hands quickly; Pop was eager for dinner, and Spuretta was now anxious to leave.

"But I have strudel," MaGretta said. "Please stay."

Spuretta thanked her, but refused. He didn't even offer a reason.

"Oh," MaGretta said, "maybe another day you will come back and—"

"No, ma'am," he said as curt as curt could be. "I won't be back."

MaGretta had the startled face of someone slapped. She excused herself before she rushed from the room. I glared at the asshole-cop who had hurt her. Pop scratched his head; MaGretta had never walked out on a guest before. Putting politeness before hunger, Pop escorted the cop to the door.

I held the door open, ready to slam it shut at the cop's backside.

The cop shook Pop's hand again. "It was a pleasure meeting you, sir."

"Yeah, sure," Pop said, wholly bewildered because my thumb was jerking, *hit the road, Jack.*

"Your wife is a fine cook."

*Wife?* My thumb melted.

"Wife?" Pop said, and his bushy eyebrows came together with a hard look at me. "Wife?"

I held up my palms and shook my head, *not my fault.*

"Auk, women." Pop looked back at the empty hallway and yelled, "What do you think? You think we read minds? You women, you tell a man everything he does not want to hear, but you tell him nothing of what he should know. *Auk!*"

"Excuse me?" Spuretta said.

Pop turned again to Spuretta. "Gretta is not my wife. She is my sister."

"Sister?" His eyes sparkled. "*Sister?*"

"Yeah, sure. I am a widower. Gretta is my baby sister." Pop widened the door's opening. "So, Mr. Detective, do you change your mind on the strudel?"

# 65

*No, Jen, you got it all wrong.*
*Ma mére took me to the ocean. Ma mére.*

Taking her computer case stuffed with reports, Carly drove to her dad's house. She had expected to find him home; the psychic show had ended hours ago. After letting herself in, Carly settled into an armchair to reread the printouts. Similar to the flights from San Francisco, the flights from Oakland and Sacramento either departed too early for Fikus to have been with Dorothy on the ridge or arrived too late into Utah for Fikus to have dined with his friends. Even so, Carly meticulously screened the passenger lists.

No Fikus MacKenzie, alias or otherwise.

At first, Carly believed the data cleared Fikus, but then she noticed startling coincidences in Fikus's and Miranda's background. So Carly dug deeper, exploring the history of their parents.

In 1973, Minister MacKenzie graduated Weber State University. Nine months later, Miranda was born in Ogden. Miranda claimed she didn't know her father's identity. Dorothy had picked a name at random, John Smith, to show as the father on Miranda's birth certificate. The date and the location of Miranda's birth and of the Minister's graduation was only one among many interesting parallels.

The year the Norsts moved from Utah to Ridgecrest was the year the Minister's wife jumped from Angels Peak. When Carly pulled the records surrounding that death, she learned that the Minister's wife had suffered depression, a statement validated by a psychiatrist's prescription. Publicly, the death was deemed an accident, but officially, it was listed as suicide.

Hours later, she heard her dad's car pull into the driveway. Carly unknotted from the armchair. "I'm fine," she said anticipating her dad's concern. "I came to show you some printouts."

Spuretta tossed his keys and peeled from his coat. "It's one in the morning. Are you sure everything is—"

"Fine. But where have you been? Hey, what happened to your pocket?"

Spuretta looked down at the flap of cotton. "Oh, just a little misunderstanding with an angel. A beautiful angel."

"You're seeing angels? Did they serve punch at the psychic show?"

"Carly Jean, pull out the sofa-bed and get some sleep. We'll talk in the morning. I'm fading, kid."

"You're not fading. You're evading. I'll make a pot of coffee."

"No, I'm beat."

"Wait." Carly ran to the kitchen and returned with two bottles of beer. "Relax a minute, dad. I'll save my news until morning, but give me a rundown of what happened tonight."

Spuretta took a beer and dropped into his recliner. "After this, I'm hitting the sack." He raised the bottle to his lips and then set it down half empty. He yawned. "Kid, learn to see folks clearly."

"So you've said...a thousand times. Why now?"

"Because you're misreading Ms. Miranda. She's a confused young lady stuck in denial. You can't grieve if you deny the loss. She believes her mother is talking to MacKenzie, but she'll figure it out. She's an intelligent gal." He lifted the bottle to finish his beer.

"You're probably right," Carly said.

Spuretta jerked forward to keep beer from exiting his nose. "I'm right? Those must be some printouts you got."

"Dad, I think the Minister is connected to Dorothy."

"The psychic's father?"

Carly nodded. "It would explain how Fikus knew where to find the body; his dad told him. We'll get into that tomorrow. Tell me what happened at the church tonight?"

"Before or after the fight?"

"A fight?"

"A regular barroom brawl, tourists against locals. It seems your friend from high school, Zia Schatz, thinks—"

"Wait, stop there. When did I ever allude to a friendship with Zia?"

"When Ms. Miranda said she was staying with the Schatzes, you said—"

"I said, 'Dieter Schatz is a good guy. When I was a sophomore, he was a senior, pretty low-key, but very popular.' That's all I said."

"Well, how about his sister? Wasn't Zia a freshman?"

"Yes. A freshman she-devil, who I never saw again after I transferred to Ridgecrest. But what does Zia have to do with any of this, other than her presence in a church explains the fight. What happened? Did someone burn her with holy water?"

"Carly, I'm surprised at you."

"And I'm shocked that Miranda can share a roof with Zia."

"They're sharing more than a roof. Zia seems to know quite a bit about Fikus's vision. I think Ms. Miranda has confided in her."

"Not a chance. Zia wouldn't let anyone mistake her for a sympathetic ear. Whatever Zia seemed to know, she likely invented to provoke trouble."

"Well, she sure aggravated our psychic."

"No surprise. In high school, she hijacked the PA system just to holler at Fikus and call him a freak." Carly reflected a moment. "She also hated his dad's church. What was she doing there? Community Service?"

"Nope. She was asking questions about Dorothy, questions suggesting that Zia knows a whole lot more about the vision than what we were told. Fikus wouldn't give her an answer. He hit a button and security walked up."

"Did they tell Zia to leave?"

"That was the plan, but a fight broke out." Spuretta dug into his pocket and then handed a slip of paper to Carly. "Those are Zia's hours at the Youth Center where she teaches swimming. Find out everything Zia knows about Fikus's vision, but wait a few days first. Zia took a bad bruising."

Carly pocketed the slip. "Didn't Miranda ask Fikus about her mother?"

"Nope, and she looked upset when Zia tried to ask."

"Maybe she was upset because Zia's questions were full of bull."

"Maybe. Or maybe Zia was breaking a confidence. That's what I want you to find out when you talk to her. Just approach her kindly."

"Kindly, right. If that doesn't work, I'll use a wooden stake and a silver bullet."

"Carly Jean, where is that attitude coming from? If it's high school, leave it there. In my view, Zia is a fine young lady."

"In case she's less like a lady and more like I remember, do you know where she works? I don't want to risk a scene around a bunch of kids."

"She works in a shed behind her house. She makes wind chimes."

"Wind chimes? *Wind chimes?*"

"Is there something odd about making wind chimes?"

"It depends. Do they ring without a breeze?" Carly sipped her beer while revisiting another time. "Zia created a wind chime for the year-end science project. It was a hodgepodge of beach garbage tied with fishing line. No batteries, nothing electrical. Zia made this weird claim: For one time and for one minute, the chimes would ring without a breeze. She told Mr. Linden, our science teacher, to pick the time. Linden hooked the chime to a ceiling beam. Days later, he stopped class, mid-lecture, and told Zia to make it move."

"And did it?"

"Yes and no. Zia was so cocksure, she got up and bowed to the class and everyone looked up. But right then, the air-conditioner kicked on, so of course it moved. Linden turned off the air, but it took a minute for the compressor to shut down. Zia flipped. Literally. She started yelling, 'that's unfair,' and 'you tricked me.'"

"Yelling at Linden?"

Carly shrugged. "I guess, except she was facing an empty corner of the room. Although Linden didn't like her, and he made that clear, he couldn't have timed his request to the room's temperature. He should have just left it alone. Instead, to the whole class, he called her project a failed gimmick, 'and gimmicks are not science,' he said. Then Zia called him a science-skank, 'and science-skanks are not teachers.' Linden flunked her."

"Did Zia take it to the principal? Or take it to the school board?"

"Worse. Zia took it personally." Carly carried the bottles and napkins to the kitchen. By the time she returned, her dad had unfolded the sofa bed.

"Dad, I can handle a thirty minute drive, and I need to feed Winkle."

"Winkle can wait until morning. You get some sleep, kid."

Carly looked at the crumpled mattress, her back already ached. "We can put a million bytes of information on a chip smaller than a fingernail; yet, we can't make a hide-a-bed without a spine-busting bar." She sat on the bed's edge to remove her shoes. Then, despite the constraints of a buttoned shirt and tight jeans, she stretched out. Immediately, exhaustion swept in. Tension dissolved. Spine-busting bar or not, she melted into the cool sheets.

Spuretta put a blanket over her. "Carly, how did she take it personally?"

"What?" Carly said, already muddled with drowsiness.

"Zia. Her disagreement with the teacher."

"Oh. Ever see the movie Willard?"

"Nope."

"It's about a misfit who befriends a bunch of rats and uses those rats for personal revenge." Carly nestled deeper into the pillow. "It was something like that, only not rats. Bugs. Hundreds and hundreds of beetles."

# 66

*When next a Player, I will break their crystal balls.*

Squatting, Billy poked at the dead sand crab and then looked up with question.

"Yeah, it's cool," I said, "but tourists don't like claws dangling in the wind. They think it's creepy."

Billy's head tilted and his mouth twisted with an unspoken *why?*

"Well, they think we're cutting off the legs of live crabs."

Billy grimaced.

"I know, I know," I said, "but we can't expect shop owners to educate buyers. They have businesses to run. In other words, kiddo, let's stick to driftwood and shells. No dead crabs, okay?"

Billy nodded.

Like every other Tuesday for the past six months, Billy had come to the beach at ten a.m. to help scour the shoreline for interesting sea debris. On this particular Tuesday, a bruised rib slowed my actions and cut my breaths. When the alarm clock buzzed, I slammed the snooze button and a jolt of pain slammed me. I whined in the shower, whimpered as I dressed, and *ouch-ouch-ouch*'d with every step down the sandy slope. Whether I wanted to buck-up or curl-up didn't matter. I couldn't disappoint Billy. He would be waiting.

Billy looked like Charlie Brown with an oversized head and wisps of white hair. He was ten, small for his age, stubborn, and phobic about dirty hands. He would point and poke, but he would never pick up a thing.

He was also a mute.

I once asked if his problem was physical—a four-inch scar tracked his neck—but Billy shook his head. I left it alone, figuring his muteness was similar to what Dieter had suffered, turmoil stealing a tongue.

"Hey, Bill, a few nights ago, I banged my rib and I'm crazy sore. How about if we take the day off, and I'll see you next Tuesday?"

Billy blinked a bunch of times, his chin lowered. *Crap.* My chest deserved to ache; I lacked a heart. "Hey, hey, Bill, you know what?"

His hanging head lifted.

"I spoke too soon. The aspirin is finally kicking in." I sucked in a breath to prove it. *Oooh, jeez;* I gulped, cockeyed with pain. "Oh, yeah, kicking in."

Billy looked doubtful.

"No, really." I reshaped my wince. "I bit my tongue, too. Want to see?"

Billy perked, eager to see something gross. With a finger pinning back each cheek, I let Billy have a look. After he did, he made a sour face, unimpressed.

"What? I bled buckets. But tongues heal super fast."

He made a chopping gesture, our code for lame.

"Wow, Billy, you think I'm a candy-ass?"

He grinned with a nod.

"Well, I'm not as tough as you, but who is?" I flung a piece of seaweed at him, but he dodged it with finesse. "Tell you what, how about if we collect stuff for an hour instead of three, all right?"

Billy floundered and slumped as if it were killing him to compromise. He held up two fingers.

"Two hours? You drive a hard bargain." I looked at the sky, the cloudless sky. "You're going to want a lift home, aren't you?"

Billy checked the weather and then he shrugged. He lived in a yellow cottage, two blocks from Main Street and three doors down from the Minister's Colonial. On warm, sunny days, when shadows outlined the landscape, Billy wanted a ride home. On chilly days, when a cold overcast would clatter your teeth, Billy insisted on walking home, taking the jogging trail that bordered the shoreline and wound into town. I suggested the reverse—walk home on warm days, ride home on cold days—but Billy refused. He stuck to his way like a barnacle cements to a boat. Billy was strange that way.

His mom was also a bit strange. Each time I pulled to the curb to let Billy out of my car, his mother would peek from the window. If I waved, she would close the curtains. For the last two months, the curtains were always drawn. When I questioned Bill about troubles at home, he rolled his eyes with a terse shake of his head—*no troubles, quit asking.* I backed off. Because other than Billy's muteness and his phobia about touching stuff, he was a happy, normal kid, scampering up his walkway without hesitation or fear. When he waved from his porch, I waved back, ignoring his mother peeking through the drapes. She probably had a reason for her weirdness.

Billy pointed to a starfish.

"Wow! Good job, Bill. I crown you King Beachcomber for Sea Song Chimes." I managed a stiff but grateful bow.

Billy began dancing. To a stranger, Billy's bobbing and bouncing looked less like a dance and more like he had to pee.

I sat slowly to avoid jarring pain. After poking the starfish to make sure it was dead, I wrestled it from the sand. Nothing was bent, missing, or broken—a prize specimen. A wind chime topped with a starfish would sell for twice the money and in half the time—like how my chimes had sold when they touted a mini-card of bullshit.

But unlike the mini-cards, a starfish required a lot of grooming; I began brushing and blowing the sand from its pits and grooves.

A shadow darkened my sunlight. "Hello, Zia."

Cupping my eyes, I looked up.

Fikus smiled down.

I buried my surprise under a face of indifference. "What do you want?"

"I came to apologize to you and your family. Your aunt said I could find you here. Can we talk?"

I nosed into my starfish. "You're blocking my sun."

"Oh, sorry," Fikus said with a sidestep.

I ignored him, but he didn't get the hint. "Go apologize to someone who cares," I told him. "I'm busy. Billy and I have work to do, isn't that right, Bill?" I was hoping a big round head was nodding in agreement, but when I looked up, I saw Billy climbing the path to the ridge. *Crap.* He rarely stuck around when another person approached. "Billy, it's a sunny day," I called after him. "Don't you want a ride?"

His arm tick-tock'd, no, overhead. He crested the hill and disappeared.

"Did your friend leave?" Fikus asked as if it weren't obvious.

"Yeah, because of you."

"Zia, give me a minute of your time. Please?" Despite his pressed khakis, Fikus sat cross-legged on the dirty sand. "Nice starfish."

His compliment tainted my fish; I tossed it aside. "Is that what you came to talk about? Starfishes?"

"No, I want to settle our issues. If I've offended you, tell me how."

"Why? What do you care?"

"I'm giving you the benefit of the doubt, but I know I haven't done anything wrong."

"Keep your doubts and your benefits, and you've done plenty wrong."

"Then let's hear it."

Feeling slightly baited but definitely challenged, my eyes firmed to his flickering ones. "Okay, Fikus, three issues. First, you stare too much. You stare at me too much. It's rude. Second, you told the cops my brother started the fight, and that was a bold-face lie."

"And the third?"

"The third is obvious; you're a conman."

Fikus nodded thoughtfully. "You're right about the staring. For years, I've watched you hurry around town to deliver your chimes. You hustle from shop to shop, running right past my bookstore. I've seen you breeze through Neptunes, too. You skip from table to table, sharing jokes and laughs with the Scavengers, but you never stop at my table. You don't even notice—"

"Whoa! Are you spying on me?"

He laughed. "Are you paranoid? It's a small town. I haven't spoken to you since high school. I wanted to, but you were always too busy. That's why I asked Miranda to invite you to the meeting. I never thought you'd come. And then, suddenly, there you were, standing still, all grown-up and so beautiful."

"Auk, I've heard better lines from mimes."

"Well, staring is rude. For that, I apologize. Am I forgiven?"

"Whatever."

"About your second issue, I told the police exactly what I saw. From where I stood, I saw Dieter jump up swinging. I didn't see anyone strike him. People make mistakes, don't they? That's why I came to apologize." He picked up a piece of driftwood and tossed it like one tosses a pebble while they're thinking—except the stick he had tossed had come from my stack. When he reached for another, I slapped his hand. "Do you mind? Do you think this driftwood piled itself?"

"Oh, I'm sorry. These are for your—your—"

"Wind chimes," I said as if I were proud and not embarrassed because, *jeez*, what grown woman makes wind chimes for a living? I started brushing the grit from a sand dollar. "At least my money is earned honestly."

"Oh, your third point. You think I'm a fake."

"No, I think you're an authentic swindler."

"Zia, we're like kinds with like stories and like heartaches."

"Like hell."

"We both lost our mothers."

I dropped the sand dollar. "I didn't lose my mother. She's MaGretta. And I didn't lose my first mother. She died. If your mother is lost, use your psychic-shit to find her."

"My mother committed suicide."

I flinched. When I was in fifth or sixth grade, MaGretta and Pop attended the funeral, but they never told me it was suicide. Had I known, I would have hedged my rotten remark. I mumbled an apology.

Fikus shrugged. "It was a long time ago."

"But I thought—Well, I heard she fell, you know, like down the stairs or something."

"Everyone thought it was an accident. My father wanted the truth hushed because suicide is a mortal sin. Out of respect for his wishes, I kept quiet. It was easy; nobody talked to me anyway. I was awkward. A freak."

"Jeez, Fikus, get over it. Kids are cruel."

"So are adults." His quick eyes caught mine and cast blame. Then he turned a melancholy look toward the sea. The tide's rumbling took on Pop's voice, *That is unkind, Zia. It is hurtful,* giving new meaning to waves of guilt.

Figuring Fikus wanted me to ask the big question—and figuring I owed him that much—I asked, "How did she kill herself?" I figured wrong; Fikus shook his head. He didn't want to talk about it. He stood, brushed the sand from his pants, and then offered his hand. "Come on, Zia, let's take a walk."

I hemmed and hawed because it seemed like a really high price to pay for making one lousy comment.

"Please," Fikus said, "please?"

I got up, though I refused his helping hand.

We walked the shoreline, not talking, but listening to the waves swish and fizz and to the gulls squawk complaints when we intruded.

A while later, Fikus stopped, dug into his pocket, and pulled out a bologna sandwich. Crouching, he offered torn bits to sharp-hooked beaks.

As locals well know, hungry gulls will filet the flesh off your finger. Not gracefully either. Horridly. They lock on and refuse to let go. I watched with morbid fascination, but Fikus managed to keep his fingers. Wow! But I kept the *wow* to myself. Minutes later, Fikus offered me his jacket, but I wasn't cold, and his sweet gesture warmed me even more.

Along our stroll, he picked up a baby turtle and slipped it into his pocket.

"What the hell—" But I stopped mid-bitch because Fikus began to remove his shoes and cuff his pants.

He waded into the ocean, pulled out the turtle, and set it down gently.

Back on shore, he re-shoed his feet. "I'm sorry for walking away while you were talking, but the turtle was struggling for life. I hope it lives. Anyway, what were you saying?"

"Uhm, nothing."

A half mile down the beach, we came to a partly dissolved sandcastle. Fikus dropped to his knees. "Let's rebuild it."

Before I could say yes or no, Fikus was scooping sand and piling it on top the battered castle. Holding my ribs, I sat, too. "You're not doing it right," I told him. I flattened the top to compress the sand. "Good castles are built in layers. This is the first floor." I began strengthening the castle's sides when a dollop of sand flecked my cheek.

Fikus smiled. I returned the smile with a fistful of seaweed. We battled a few minutes before the pain of a bruised rib outweighed the pleasure of a war. I surrendered. For a long while, we talked of classmates we liked and of teachers we hated. Eventually, we even finished the sandcastle. I crowned it with a feathered flag.

I got up, but too quickly; my chest cramped. Immediately, I leaned over and gripped my knees, pretty sure I was about to puke. Fikus braced my shoulders and held back my hair. I turned my face sideways; I didn't want to spew on his shoes. Thankfully, I didn't spew at all. Eventually, my stomach settled and I straightened.

"Are you okay?" Fikus asked.

"Yeah, but I need to go home."

"Not yet." Fikus sprinted to the backside of a nearby rock. When he returned, he had a painter's stir-stick. He placed it across the castle's moat. "Now that's a perfect castle."

"Where did that stick come from? I mean, how did you know—"

"I know many things, Zia. I'm gifted."

I started laughing before I realized he was serious.

His arms spread wide, his head leaned back, and sunshine illuminated his face. "The spirits reveal the truth about many things, many people, including you." He grabbed my hands. "Including us. We are like kinds, cast together, spiritually connected forever. I felt it the moment I met you. We share a destiny; it's in our Souls. You love me, Zia. You've always loved me."

I slid my hands free to finger each ear. "Come again?"

"Don't deny it, Zia. Don't deny what we have."

"Uhm, we have a sandcastle. That's it."

"We're destined to be together until the day we die."

"Again, just a sandcastle."

Fikus spun around and stomped on the castle. Before I could process that, he seized my arms. "It's not about castles. It's about us. US!"

"Let go of me. LET GO!"

He let go with a mean shove.

I started walking.

He dogged my footsteps. "Zia, just listen. Hear me out. I'm sorry I lost my temper, but I have a reason."

"Leave me alone."

"Stop and listen. Let me explain."

"Get away from me."

"Do you really want that? Suppose Dorothy was murdered."

I slowed.

"If you push me away," Fikus said, "you might become his next victim."

He was right. What if the killer was lurking behind a boulder or hiding between the sand dunes or watching us from the cliffs? Not another Soul was on the beach, nobody around to hear our screams. My eyes strained into the black shadows beneath the ridgeline. Something moved and a gull screeched. It sounded like a death cry. I stumbled, but kept walking, now with quick checks over my shoulder to ensure Fikus stayed close.

"Zia, stop. Let me explain."

"I can walk and listen. Talk. TALK!"

Fikus started rambling about destiny-this and destiny-that until I was imagining a murderous destiny drooling and slithering while it tracked us. "Shut up about destiny." My strides lengthened. "And for chrissake, keep up. Quit lagging so far behind." We crossed the beach and climbed the slope. When we reached the ridge top, I braced against a tree to rest.

Fikus circled to the front of me. "You can't hide from destiny. We're two of a kind."

I stared at his shoes, now wishing I had stained them with puke. When my strength returned, my chin lifted, and my eyes met his. "Fikus, straight up, you and I are nothing alike, nothing, except in one way. Sometimes our bullshit trumps our reality. I'm a Fright Fanatic, addicted to reading macabre. That comes with a price. At an inkling of fear, *whammo*, novels come to life; birds redirect you, bugs warn you, and lettuce is the alien means for mind control. And it is, too, but that's not the point. The point is, I have to force myself to grip what's real. Do you see where I'm going? Fikus, you're a Mystic Monger. You thrive on giving magical answers to desperate questions. Maybe tarot cards and tea leaves didn't pay too well, but at least it was harmless. Now you've crossed into the slimy field of Grief Poaching. To sleep at night, Poachers cling to their victims' gratitude, 'oh, you've helped me so much.' Eventually, the Poacher believes his powers are real and his acts are benevolent. Both untrue. And when the Poacher loses that truth, he becomes a victim of his own bullshit. Get it?"

"Our destiny is written in the stars."

"Aw, jeez." I started on the last stretch toward home.

Fikus followed. "Zia, you like bugs."

"You needed a ghost to tell you that?"

"At eight, doctors removed your appendix."

"Tonsils, but nice try."

"You once suffered a Black Widow bite."

"Rookie move!" I shouted. "I made up that story. Better steer clear of bullshitters, Fikus, or you'll dredge up their lies instead of their truths."

Behind me came his frustrated huffs. "You put a garden hose down your neighbor's chimney and ran the water overnight. You placed an Open House ad on the Mayor's home. At the liquor store, you stole porno subscription cards and wrote in Principal Burke's address. You cut the boat ties at Harbor Bay, soldered the classroom doors shut, and dumped a case of bubble bath in the Courthouse fountain."

"WRONG! Dieter did the suds. I did the Jell-O...years and years ago. And there's nothing psychic about any of that. You're just prattling off the common pranks of every normal kid."

"I never did any of that."

"Again, normal."

"Zia, I know spirits."

"You know crap."

"I know Alpha."

I stopped. Dead-stopped. I didn't know how he knew about Alpha, didn't want to know, didn't care. He had crossed the line. Game over.

Fikus came around to my front side. "I...know...Alpha."

I stepped right up to him. "Save your psycho-psychic bullshit. I am not your prey."

In a quick movement, Fikus clutched my face, and his mouth came crashing down on mine. My lip gashed against teeth that parted for a cry, but his tongue plunged inside, prodding and dominating my mouth. I fisted his back and yanked on his hair. His grip tightened, his grinding hardened, and his putrid saliva seeped down my throat. Clutching his shoulders, I pushed with might. Finally, he pulled his face off of mine. "You wanted that," he said. "The spirits told me."

In the next quick movement, I jerked his shoulders forward and my knee shot up, ramming his balls. "Spirits lie."

Fikus's eyes rounded and his legs buckled, his one hand cupping his crotch, his other arm stretching to break his fall. Despite years of Dieter warning me, *If you ever knee a man...run. A man goes down for seconds, but comes up twice as mean,* I couldn't leave. Fikus was now gripping his chest and grappling for breath. "Zia," he gasped as though he were dying, "*pleeease.*"

"Get up," I said, unsure whether he was playing me or suffering a heart attack. "GET UP."

When his head tilted back, I saw a face grotesquely enraged. Then, as quick as a chameleon, his rage masked into pain.

*Whoa,* his Jekyll and Hyde transformation puckered my stomach with a bad, bad feeling that I was out of my league, *waaay* out of my league.

My legs loosened and I began walking.

"ZIA! What will it take to convince you?"

I walked faster.

"TELL ME. TELL ME."

I held my ribs and started to sprint.

He hammered the ground. "TELL ME, TELL ME."

When I reached the safety of our yard's fence, I yelled back, "Was someone with Dorothy?"

"YES!"

His answer stunned me.

He got up slowly, winded but calm, and walked toward me. "Now do you believe me?"

"Uhm, uhm."

"What else? What else will it take?"

"Uhm. Uhm." My brain clanked and clunked trying to work again. "Who was with Dorothy? Yeah. Give me a name. Tell me that and I'll believe you." I opened the gate. "And, uhm, the winning lottery numbers, too."

# 67

*...children who struggle each day*
*for the love and compassion of positive vibrations.*

Carly flashed her badge to the teenage boy at the Youth Center's reception counter.

His slouch straightened.

"Where's the poolroom?" Carly asked.

The boy pointed to a hallway on the right. "Someone in trouble?" Nearby teens perked, a few readied to bolt. Carly thanked the boy, told the others to relax, and started down the hall.

At the corridor's end, swinging doors flung open and gusts of laughter, splashes, and whistles trailed emerging wet feet. The kids pattered up the hallway and raced beneath the banner, *No Running*, before they vanished through a side door marked, *Locker Room*. As Carly was approaching, the left door burst open and two little girls rushed out, colliding, full-body, into Carly. Their faces tilted up with a frown. Carly frowned, too; the lap of her white cotton pants was now wet and sheer, revealing her blue panties.

"You're not supposed to come in this door," one little girl said.

"How many times do you need to be told?" the other girl added, her voice mimicking a scolding adult. "The right door is the right door...always!" They broke into giggles and ran off.

Carly entered the poolroom through the right door. Instantly, moisture beads sprouted on her temples and caustic chlorine dampened her throat. The place was oppressively humid. To cool herself, she flapped one side of her jacket; the other side concealed her firearm.

*Twrrrt.* After blowing the whistle, Zia yelled, "LUKE, no running on the deck. How many times do you need to be told?"

Carly now realized that the little girl had been mimicking Zia.

Luke slowed. "Sorrreee." When Zia looked away, Luke started running.

Zia clapped her hands at the swimmers in the deep end. "Ten minutes, everyone. Let's go. Free-swim, ten minutes."

Zia was much like Carly remembered—short, loud, and comb-challenged. But she was now mature, Carly reasoned, because parents were entrusting their children to Zia. Hoping to avoid disrupting the class, Carly moved to the opposite end of the room.

Towels, clothes, and backpacks smothered the wooden benches, so Carly picked and plucked to clear a sitting space. Once settled, she noticed Zia's frozen stare. Carly held up her palms, gesturing her intention to wait.

Zia's shoulders drew back. She started to march toward Carly.

Same old Zia, Carly thought as she stood and readied her badge. "Bring it on," she whispered because this wasn't high school and Carly wasn't about to let a combative twit intimidate her. She started toward Zia.

From across the pool, a boy yelled, "Coach Zee, Coach Zee," and redirected Zia's attention. "Holly hit me," the boy said, and he rubbed his shoulder. "Hard, too."

Holly slugged the boy again. "Cry baby."

*Twrt-twrt.* Zia waved her arms like a crossing guard until the two kids separated.

"Holly, hit the runner," Zia said.

"But Joey started it."

"Two laps."

*"Whyyy?"* Holly whined.

*"Becaaause,"* Zia said, replying in kind. "You know the rules. No hitting."

Pointing at Holly, Joey teased, "Ha-ha, you gotta run," before he cannon-balled into the pool, drenching Holly in a final insult.

"Go on," Zia said, "hit the runner."

Holly snorted and crossed her arms, her heel thudding the deck, again and again, like a trick pony trained to count.

*Twrt-twrt.* "Holly, move it. Hit that runner, NOW!"

Holly stomped over to a thick pad abutting the far wall. With her arms still folded and her heels still heavy, she waddled more than she ran.

Near the diving boards, a squabble erupted.

*Twrt-twrt.* Zia sprinted toward the deep end.

Pocketing her badge but keeping a cautious eye on Zia, Carly backed up to the benches. She sat. Something squished. She shifted, thinking it was a towel or a shirt, but it squished again. Rolling onto one hip, she slipped a hand beneath her rear. She withdrew a flattened sandwich—peanut butter and grape jelly with mashed bananas. "Dammit."

She jumped up, turning to the bench. Glops of yellow, brown, and purple marked her seat. With one hand pinching the sandwich, her other hand brushed her backside. Her hand came away sticky and purple. *Aurrg.* No sooner had she wiped the sweat beads from her brow when she realized she was smearing jelly across her forehead. "Dammit, dammit."

She looked angrily at the soggy sandwich...just as the jelly soaked middle began to split. "Christ." She fumbled to catch it, but missed a banana plop. It tumbled down her blouse. Her jelly covered fingers gave chase, adding purple smudges behind the banana's rolling stain. The banana stuck to the sheer spot of her pants. Carly scooped it, finger-painting brown and purple streaks across her lap. "Shit." Her hand clenched. Another glop oozed. Carly licked quickly before it could fall. "Shit, shit," she said between two more forced licks. "Shit." A missed dollop fell, grazing the cuff of her pants and landing beside a peanut butter plop on her shoe.

"SHIT!" Carly dropped the mangled sandwich and snapped her wrists, flicking jelly and peanut butter across backpacks and towels. She grabbed the nearest cloth. A tee shirt. With muttered curses and brutal swipes, she scraped each sticky finger. When reasonably clean, she scrunched the tee shirt and began attacking the stains on her blouse and pants. After a while, she became aware of an odd silence; the noise of the kids, the *whoopees* and the *yahoos*, had disappeared. She turned around slowly.

Eight sullen faces stood beside Zia, all were staring at Carly, whose mouth opened but whose words wouldn't come.

"Go ahead, Amber," Zia said quietly, "I think she's done."

Amber walked up to Carly, pulled the shirt from her hands, and unraveled it. Grape jelly stained the imprint of comic book heroes. "Nice going," Amber told her. "You ruined the X-Men."

"I'm sorry," Carly said, then she apologized to the entire group.

They glowered, unforgiving.

"Marky," Zia said, "front and center."

A skinny boy dragged himself out from his peers. He snarled at Carly, "Smooth move, ex-lax," before he faced Zia, "If I gotta run laps, does she?" He hiked a thumb over his shoulder. "She's the one who ruined the shirt."

"You're the one who broke the rules," Zia said. "Get it, Marky? Do you finally get why we don't bring food into the pool area?"

"Yeah." He threw a quick glare back at Carly. "Because someone will squish it with their big, fat—"

"Close enough." Zia trilled the whistle while her arm circled overhead.

With parting sneers to Carly, the Blue Dolphins shuffled to the benches to gather their clothes and backpacks.

Zia remained in place. "Who the hell are you?"

"Willow, I am grateful," Alpha said, "but it is not necessary to subdue Phoenix's lights."

"It's more than necessary," Willow said, "it's crucial. Vibrations of authority provoke Agitators. Provoked further, Zia will strike Carly. And even you, Alpha, cannot guide your Charge to the Neutral Point if she's sitting in jail. Until Zia's Soul senses the Healer's gift of well-being, I have no choice but to dampen Phoenix's vibrations. Unfortunately, a wet lap and a jelly mess won't humble her for long." Willow turned a firm stance to Alpha. "And Phoenix is my Charge. She'll take the dose of humiliation like the worthy Healer she is."

"Willow, allow Phoenix to shine unhindered." Alpha highlighted a spot above Zia's brow. "Zia will be humbled."

Willow smiled. "Oh, a kiss from Niine, and it works to our benefit." But her smile quickly faded. "Doesn't Zia find charm in arthropods? How will this creature humble her?"

With a touch to Willow's forehead, Alpha transferred the images of Zia's imagination.

Willow shuddered, both amazed and sympathetic. "Why, Alpha? Why does Zia choose to distort so much matter into monsters?"

"Fragments," Alpha said. "Though she removed the majority, she retained a scattering."

"Why?"

"Unknown."

The Guides' attention returned to their Charges.

A while later, Willow pressed a hand to her mouth, but a giggle still escaped. "Excuse me, Alpha, among the plethora of objects and beasts she remakes in her mind, I find one particularly peculiar. Alien lettuce?"

# 68

*It is the Healer who soothes the savage beasts.*

She had worn a business suit to an indoor swimming pool, had flapped her jacket like an injured albatross, and had lost a battle against a peanut butter sandwich; yet, she believed herself less conspicuous than poop floating in a punch bowl. "Who the hell are you?"

She reached into her pocket, but before the badge flipped, I glimpsed the side-strap. "Aw, shit, you're a cop?"

"Detective. I'm Detective—"

"Which Red Herring is it and what did they do?"

"Pardon me?"

"Well, you're not here for a Blue Dolphin. They're maddening but they're not criminals. And Green Guppies are barely pool-trained."

"I'm here to talk to you."

"*Me?* Oh, hell no. Whatever it is, I didn't do it. And if you've got proof, I want a lawyer."

"Do you know Fikus MacKenzie?"

I pictured an assault charge for kneeing him. "He's a lying asshole. I was defending myself. Whatever he said, I'm denying it. Write that down. I'm denying whatever he said."

"He didn't say—"

"I don't care what he said. He's a freak. He assaulted me first. Get it? Arrest him. I'm pressing charges. Why aren't you writing this down?"

"He didn't accuse you of anything. I just have some questions about what happened at the church."

"The church? Why? I didn't start the fight. A vacationer threw the first punch. Talk to Detective Spuretta. He saw the whole thing."

"Yes, I know. I'm Detective Carly Spuretta. Frank is my father. Now, can we sit and talk a minute?"

*Crap.* Nothing good comes from liking a cop, but I did like Spaghetti-man, so I had to be civil to his daughter. I motioned for Carly to take a seat.

She inspected the bench before sitting.

Briskly, I towel-dried my hair. "I'm not a Fikus-fan." I pitched the towel and sat. "I'm not a cop-fan either. Cops are always accusing me of stuff."

"Stuff you didn't do?"

"How is that the point?"

She didn't answer, as though she were taking the high road, the high-and-mighty road traveled by law. "Is Ms. Norst staying at your home?"

"Don't ask questions when you know the answer."

"Fair enough. Has Ms. Norst spoken with you?"

"Don't ask vague questions either. I won't be lured into your brackish waters where God-only knows what will bite my butt."

"Has Ms. Norst spoken with you about Fikus's vision?"

"Jeez, if you're under the delusion that freaky-Fikus is the real-deal, then suffer the embarrassment and go talk with him yourself."

"We did, months ago. Ms. Norst, too. But they might have left out a few details. Did Ms. Norst ever tell you what Fikus saw in his vision?"

"Why? Are you investigating Fikus?" I started to laugh, but she blinked three times in the space of one. "Wow, you *are* investigating him. Why?"

Her tongue moistened her lips. "I can't discuss the case."

"You just did." My thoughts whirled to Fikus and his warped notion of our destiny, his temper that destroyed the sandcastle, and his instant shift from rage to pain. Still, he was just squirrely-dude, a harmless freak...but then I recalled that odd sense of feeling out of my league, *waaay* out of my league.

"Ms. Schatz."

"Zia." I shook free of retro-nervousness. "By the way, do I know you? Your name sounds familiar."

"We had a science class together, but I transferred to Ridgecrest after my sophomore year. You were a freshman."

I tilled the memory ground for an Amazon blond. "You weren't a cheerleader, were you?"

"No, I wasn't one of your targets. But let's discuss high school another time." She reached into her jacket and pulled out a notebook and pen. "Right now, I need information. What did Ms. Norst tell you about the vision?"

"Plenty. But she got crazy mad when I brought it up at the Freak-Fest. How was I supposed to know she wanted it kept private? I'm not a mind-reader." I inspected my bitten nails and waited for Carly's offer. When no offer came, I threw out enticements. "It's great stuff, too. Real personal."

"I'm listening," Carly said.

"And I'm waiting, so let's hear the offer."

"Offer?"

"Yeah. I didn't fall off the turnip truck yesterday. You're supposed to give me something in exchange for information."

"I'm supposed to what?"

"I'll make it small. How about parking tickets, can you fix those?"

She gaped as though I had requested a private jet. "You're kidding, right?"

"For chrissake, they're just parking tickets. Is that a big deal? Is it really putting you out? Will worlds collide? Will global destruction—"

"How many?" she asked in a tone I didn't much care for.

"Well, with that attitude—"

"HOW MANY?"

"Ooh, just a couple—" I coughed.

"Fine. I'll see what I can do."

"You do that, and I'll see what I can remember."

She got pretty steamed and called me selfish and callous, "a woman has died," and, "what kind of a person are you," and, "any decent citizen would gladly help," and blah-blah-blah. When I yawned, she threatened.

"Spare me," I told her. "I've been threatened with worse and by better than you."

As if I were too vile for human eyes to look at, Carly turned a profile— and I recognized that profile. "Holy shit, you're Flash!" I bounded to my feet and pointed at her. "You're the eye behind the camera, right? Right?"

She smiled uncomfortably. "No one has called me Flash in years."

"Shit almighty, look at you!" In high school, a camera hid Carly's face. Always. Even teachers allowed it because Flash had the inborn talent of a great artist, no less than Mozart or Michelangelo. She could capture a blade of grass in such a way, you would feel like you were seeing grass for the very first time. Then you would walk around lawns to avoid hurting a blade. I could hardly wait to tell Dieter, "Guess who Spaghetti-man's daughter is?"

When I looked for her camera, I saw only the bulge of a firearm. "Where's your camera? What's up with the badge? What happened to you?"

"Nothing happened to me," she said in a testy tone. "I chose a career in law enforcement."

"Oh." I sat again, trying to figure it out. "On purpose?"

"YES, ON PURPOSE."

"Oh." As hard as I tried, I couldn't make sense of it. "Uhm, sorry."

"Sorry? Sorry for what?"

"I'm sorry for whatever caused you to—well, you know. I'm just sorry."

Her grip tightened on the notepad, bending the cardboard backing. "Are you sorry I left Ridgecrest for a Bachelor's degree in Forensic Science? Sorry I worked my ass off to promote to Detective? Or are you sorry I work in a profession that most people respect, but apparently not you?"

I half-shrugged, half-nodded. "Yeah, that pretty much covers it. Sorry."

"So, Zia, what do you do for a living? Make wind chimes?"

I made the dopey face of hurt feelings.

Immediately, her face flushed apologetically. Almost as quickly, I covered my mouth to muffle a laugh. Then Carly's contrite pink darkened into angry red. "Oh, come on," I nudged her. "Your heightened sensitivity made your photos amazing. You have a gift. But gifts come with handicaps. Sensitivity makes you lousy at insults and vulnerable to guilt. But your pictures—"

"Zia, can we stick to the present day?"

"Gee, I'd like to, but that's kind of awkward now, you being Flash and me needing tickets fixed."

"I'll fix your damn tickets...if you know anything of value."

"I do, so get your pen ready." I cleared my throat. Then, in the tattering speed of machinegun fire, I began telling Carly everything I knew. Carly's pen skated across the notepad. Pages whipped. She told me to slow down. I told her, "Tough tomatoes, keep up."

Then, as if Carly had willed it, a plague of hiccups slowed me down. My syllables breaking, I sounded like a drunk auctioneer. I stopped, held my breath, and then tried again. But whenever my words rolled faster than Carly could write, the hiccups returned. Constantly, I had to repeat myself, much to Carly's satisfaction. I finished with the episode on the ridge. "I kneed him in the kiwis. He went down and then started hollering about proving himself. So, I said, 'Was someone with Dorothy,' and he said, 'Yes.'"

"Did he say who?"

"No, but I promised to believe in him if he provided a name. That was all I asked for." *Hic-hic-hic.* "Well, a name and the winning lottery numbers."

Carly stopped writing and raised a judgmental frown. "Lottery numbers?"

"Hey, I deserve some luck in money; I have zero luck in love. Every time I start liking a guy, he dies in a freak accident. I dated a rock climber, then he died in a fall. My last boyfriend was using an electric leaf blower to clear pine needles from a pool's patio. He tripped on the cord and fell in. What a dumb way to die. Lousy luck for both of us; I still miss him."

"Did you ever date Fikus?"

I clutched my throat and started gagging.

"A simple 'no' would have sufficed," Carly said. "I'm just wondering why he's so determined to have you believe in him."

"Who do I look like, Freud? He's a freak. But his spiel about seeing me around town and over at Neptunes, that's creepy. I never noticed him before, but after our chat, I've spotted him everywhere. I think he's following me."

"Have you told anyone?"

"Like who? I don't run to the cops. And I sure as hell can't tell Dieter or Miranda. Imagine how Fikus would slant the story; we strolled the shoreline while reminiscing our high school days. Fikus stopped to feed the birds and to save a turtle. We played in the sand, built a sand castle, and crowned it with a feather. When we headed back, I demanded that Fikus stay close. After we rested, I approached him. So he kissed me. *Bam!* I attacked him. Pretty good, huh? That's how I would slant it if I were Fikus. And Miranda believes everything Fikus says, which sticks Dieter in the middle. Does he take Miranda's side, the girl he's crazy about, or does he take my side, the sister who might have fibbed once or twice?"

I began picking up towels, balling them, and chucking them into the laundry bins. "It's not just Dieter's goo-goo eyes that keeps my mouth shut. Miranda started working at my Pop's garage. She cleaned up the paperwork, organized the books, and set up a system for handling customers. Pop is walking on clouds and singing her praises. When he's happy, he drinks less. When he drinks less, MaGretta is thrilled. Miranda also helps with the cooking and the laundry so MaGretta is twice as thrilled. 'Miranda is sooo sweet, sooo nice.' She stops short of, 'Why can't you be more like Miranda?'"

I jogged to a bin and spiked the towel. "Five points."

"Do you get along with Miranda?"

I shrugged. "She's an idiot to believe in Fikus. Oh, and she's a pillow pillager. That bugs me. They make tissues for a reason, you know."

"Do you know of anything connecting Miranda to her mother's death?"

I fouled an easy jump shot. "You got to be kidding." But I could see that she wasn't. "If you guys suspect Miranda, then you guys are desperate. Desperate and wrong. Carly, she's like you, and I mean that in a good way. Miranda can't hurt someone's feelings without bruising her own."

"During questioning, she was pretty controlled. Never shed a tear."

"She cries at night. I hear her through the bedroom wall. Then I stash my pillows and go get Dieter or MaGretta." A few kids barreled into the room. "That's my next class of Dolphins. Anything else?"

Carly got up and handed me her card.

"What's this for?" I asked. "I told you everything I know."

"If Fikus stalks you again, call me. Just pick up the phone and call me."

"Seriously?"

She nodded.

I gazed at the gift and mumbled, "But I didn't get you anything." Then I thought of something; a secret. I pulled her back to the bench. "I'll tell you something I never told another Soul except Dieter." I checked the distance of the big-eared Dolphins. "When I was sixteen, MaGretta made me talk to the Minister, the old Minister, Fikus's dad. Remember him?"

Carly tensed. "Go on," she said with more interest than I had expected.

"Well, when we were alone, he told me that he was Satan. Satan! And he threatened my mortal Soul. Pretty crazy, huh?"

Carly's breath left in a cynical snort. "Yeah, right."

I raised my hand. "It's the truth. I swear it."

Carly still looked doubtful. "All right, so what did you do?"

"What anyone would do. I ran. When a preacher claims to be the devil, you don't ask questions, 'hey, how's that hell-fire working out for you?' You leave quickly. Damn quickly." I bent over to gather and rubber band my kinky hair. "Dieter thought I had something wrong. He goes, 'Zia, did the Minister actually use those words, Satan and mortal soul?' And I said, 'Yes, Dieter, those were his exact words.' It's plain English. But Dieter thinks I misinterpret stuff, like I'm on a different page than the rest of the world."

My head flipped up sporting a red pom-pom.

Carly smiled. "It looks ridiculous."

"So does your purple forehead." I gave her a towel. Smoothing back my bangs, I pointed to the mirrored spot of her jelly streak. Instead of wiping her forehead, she stared weirdly at mine. "What is it?" I asked.

She came closer. "Keep your bangs up."

My other hand lifted, but Carly blocked it. She leaned in. "I think it's a scab." Then she recoiled. "*Ooh,* not a scab."

She guided my hand to the nub. Beneath my fingers, eight tiny legs wiggled in protest. "A TICK? A BRAIN EATER?"

"Zia, calm—"

"A BRAIN EATER! A FREAKIN' BRAIN EATER!" I ran in erratic circles, my blood surging and fattening the monster. "A BRAIN EATER!"

The Dolphins fled hollering, "*Heeelp*, somebody *heeelp*. Coach Zee has a brain eater. A brain eater is killing Coach Zee. Help! Help!"

"A BRAIN-EATER. A BRAIN—"

Carly seized me, *WHAP*, and slapped the back of my head. "STOP IT. Stop your screaming." She gave a fierce shake. "What is wrong with you? One minute, you're a cocky hustler, the next minute, you're a screaming banshee."

"But there's a—"

"A tick, Zia. Just a tick." She jerked me sideways and whispered into my ear, "Look what you're doing to the kids. Look!"

In the doorway, legs jittered, hands wrung, and mouths rounded in bewildered horror.

My eyes scrunched tightly, I began an inward battle—logic against imagination, a tick against a Borzinak beetle. To control hysterics, I bit my lip...and tasted blood.

"Oh, Christ." Carly grabbed a towel. "Zia, let go of your lip. LET GO!" When my teeth parted slightly, Carly wedged in the towel. "Bite on that." She guided my shaky legs to the bench. "Where's your first aid kit?"

I pointed to the metal box hanging on the wall.

While Carly was rummaging inside of it, a kid asked her, "What's wrong with Coach Zee? Is she going to die?"

"No, she's fine. She just has a small cootie."

*Cootie?* I rolled flat, my teeth clenching. Had it not been for the towel, I would have severed my lip. Carly had called it a cootie...to a Blue Dolphin.

Although Carly directed the kids to sit quietly on the bench, they ran to each arriving kid to warn, "Stay back. Cooties are eating Coach Zee's brain."

Minutes felt like hours. Then, "Man, that's totally gross."

My eyes blinked open to the red eyes of Brad, our perpetually stoned counter guy. His nose was inches from mine. Behind him, his bimbo girlfriend added the articulate comment, "Ew, yuck."

I spat out the towel. "GET OUT OF MY FACE."

Carly budged in holding a sack. "Come on, guys, back up."

I sat upright, wobbly and dizzy from adrenaline.

"You gotta twist it," Brad told Carly. "Pinch the end and twist it."

"No, moron," I said to Brad. "This isn't one of your funny cigarettes."

"Whoa, you're talking bullshit." With paranoid glances at Carly, Brad and his bimbo quick footed away. "Messed up bullshit."

"Carly, do not twist the tick," I said. "Clasp it at the base and pull it straight out, but pull gently. Very gently. And hold onto it until I check for the head. Get it?"

"Zia, I know how to remove—"

"GET IT?"

"Yes, okay, I get it." She draped a towel across the bench, smoothed it flat, and then shook out the sack of medical supplies. One by one, she arranged the items into a uniform direction, equally spaced. When she finished her surgical setup, she smiled. "Okay, I think we're ready. I have tweezers, rubbing alcohol, Neosporin, Mercurochrome, cotton-balls," she pointed to each item as she went along, "a packet of aspirin, some Tylenol, a cold compress, and some Band-Aids, both jumbo and small."

"What? No mediums?"

"Oh, I didn't find—"

"Jeez!" I grabbed the tweezers, doused them in alcohol, and then shoved them into Carly's hand. Like a waiter whips a tablecloth, I whipped the towel draping the bench. But unlike the waiter's result, Carly's setup went flying. With the towel pressed to my brow, I dumped the remaining alcohol over my head. Alcohol saturated the towel, leaked into my eyes, and burned my chlorine-raw skin. "DO IT! DO IT NOW! Get that brain-eater out of me before I lose control."

"Too late for that." Carly tipped my head forward. "You can't lose what you don't have." Tweezers scratched my scalp; I assume she was parting my hairs. I held still. Metal scraped and then pinched, pulled lightly and then tugged. "He's out, but I'm not sure we got him in time. Are you brainless?"

"Not funny. Did you get the head?"

"See for yourself." Carly held it up. I blinked and blinked until my sterilized eyes finally focused. The tick's head was intact.

Carly crushed and disposed of the bloodsucker.

I melted onto my back. "Fikus."

"Fikus what?" Carly asked. "Did he stick you with a tick?"

I slipped into another world.

Carly jiggled my leg. "Zia, don't pass out."

"Huh?"

"You want a cold compress?"

"No. Just give me a minute. I need to separate a tick from an alien Borzinak beetle."

It wasn't funny, but Carly laughed. "Do you still read that B-rated trash? During science class, you were always reading books with cheesy monsters on the cover; giant ants, killer clowns, vampire trees. Well, it's time to grow up, Zia. Time to act like an adult. A tick is not a Borzinak beetle. It's just an insect, a lowly, parasitic beetle. Nothing more."

She patted my foot.

I kicked off her condescending hand, "Screw you," and lifted to my elbows, "and screw your uppity idea of maturity. A tick is not a beetle. It's not even an insect. It's an arthropod of the class Arachnida, not Insecta, and of the order Acarina, same as mites. Carly, I know what a goddam tick is...better than you. And yes, I'm still a Fright Fanatic, so don't piss on my taste in literature. Got it?" I sank back to the bench. "Tell the kids to give me ten minutes. Can you handle that?"

Carly went to the kids, but instead of telling them, *give your coach ten minutes,* she tried to discuss the situation, just like a typical cop.

The Dolphins, atypical, started teasing and chiding, which grew into shoving and punching. "Cootie-head. Butt-face. YEOW! Stop it. Frog-shit. YEOW! Cootie-shit. YEOW!"

Carly's voice rose above the banter, "Children, that's not nice. Stop that. Listen here, name calling is—stop that."

*Aw, jeez;* a cop serving milk-toast when she should have been waving a gun. Soon, they would have her hog-tied and tossed in the pool.

I grabbed the whistle and headed toward them. *Twrt-Twrt.* "Everyone to your stations." I clapped my hands. "Come on, move it. Let's go."

"Okay, Coach Cootie-head."

"TWO LAPS!" I told the kid. "Anyone else?" My finger swiped a line across the group. Mouths shut and nobody moved. "All right then. What are you standing here for? Get your behinds to your stations."

They hurried to the poolside and waited.

Turning swiftly to Carly, I said, "Cooties? *Cooties?* Is that the best you could do?"

Her arms folded with attitude. "It's better than brain-eater."

"The hell it is." I shook my head at her stupidity. "Carly, you don't know bugs, and you sure as shit don't know these kids."

# 69

*But Jen didn't live the life she wanted.*

Parallel roads, Sandstone and Trapper, stretched west through miles of uncleared forest and empty dunes, but led to only one connecting street—Shady Lane. A wind barrier of brambles spread across the government-owned land that spanned the Lane's east side. On the Lane's west side, 15 two-acre parcels, set with century-old cottages, bordered the sea. To postmen, Shady Lane was a route best taken with mace in hand, though that changed after Carly and Winkle made Shady Lane their home.

To County residents, however, Shady Lane, changed or unchanged, would always be known by its indelible nickname, The Sand Trap.

For decades, The Sand Trap's ocean views at bargain prices attracted unwary families, renovators, and retirees. For just as long, honest realtors pointed out what the secluded location and the isolated roads attracted—unsavory characters, their illegal activities forging The Sand Trap's reputation as a dangerous dump. Often and quickly, undeterred buyers became discouraged sellers.

When Carly was house-hunting, The Sand Trap had three cottages for sale, though Mr. Barns, her realtor, did not want to show them. "The Sand Trap is no place for a single lady."

"I'm a detective with the Sheriff's Department."

"Yes, but—"

"I grew up in this county; I know all about The Sand Trap."

"But if something happened—"

"I'll sign a waiver."

"There's a condo on—"

"Mr. Barns, I have no choice." Carly slapped down a picture of her fifty-two pound cat. "I need affordable acreage for Winkle."

Mr. Barns gaped at the photo. "You have a pet—a pet a lynx?"

"It's a Savannah, part wild serval and part domestic cat."

"Are you sure about the domestic part?"

Carly steeled her patience. A thousand times, she had been asked that question, word for word. Carly snatched back the photo. "Yes, I'm sure. She's a loyal, lovable cat that would never hurt—" Carly stopped herself because Winkle had hurt someone, though someone deserving.

Previously, Winkle's name was Bullet, the cherished pet of Ms. Jones. Then one night, a serial rapist, Mr. Van, climbed through the bedroom window and brutally raped Ms. Jones. In leaving, Mr. Van opted for the bedroom door.

Bullet attacked.

A bloody trail of flesh and pulp led Carly to the mauled rapist.

Ms. Jones faced multiple surgeries and a lengthy recovery. Unable to care for Bullet, she begged Carly to take the cat. At first, Carly declined, but then she learned that Mr. Van's counsel had petitioned the courts to destroy Bullet. Animal Control joined the petition, which flared Carly's outrage. She took the cat, renamed it Winkle, and retained counsel, Mr. Tait, to fight the petition. Privately, she fought her dad. "A wild animal is unpredictable," he stated repeatedly.

Because Ms. Jones had lost Winkle's papers, Carly couldn't prove the cat's heritage. Although Winkle had the common traits of a Savannah—a lion's purr, a leopard's spots, a cheetah's speed, and a lynx's triangular ears— the lean, muscular cat was more than twice the size and weight of the average Savannah. It seemed highly plausible that someone had spiked the cat's gene pool, impregnating a wild serval with something equally wild. The most compelling evidence supporting that theory was the mauling itself; Savannahs do not attack humans.

Through rigorous argument, Mr. Tait won the case, persuading the court, though not himself; the photographs of the mauling had left him shaken. "You better be careful," he told Carly as he latched his briefcase, "a wild animal is unpredictable."

"So my dad tells me," Carly said, "daily."

Victorious, Carly received her prize; ravished furniture, mauled coats, shredded shoes. Winkle needed acreage for an outside den. Only one area offered affordable homes on acreage—The Sand Trap.

While in escrow, Carly visited The Sand Trap to introduce herself. The neighbors, however, already knew her name...and where she grew up and what she did for a living. Ms. Duggan, The Sand Trap's oldest resident, even knew about Winkle.

Although Ms. Duggan was eighty-six years old, she bent gracefully to return Winkle's head-butt greeting, "Hey, big girl," and she straightened with equal ease. Fixing her crisp green eyes on Carly, she said, "Don't look so surprised. Gardening keeps me in shape, though I feel pretty rickety by the day's end."

Ms. Duggan's youthful flexibility was only part of what amazed Carly. "Ms. Duggan, how did you know Winkle was greeting you?"

"She's a Savannah, isn't she?"

Carly, speechless, just nodded.

"A darn sizeable one, too." Ms. Duggan made a chirping sound from the corner of her mouth. Winkle's purring amplified, as did Carly's amazement. Winkle's hind legs stretched up, and her forepaws came down on Ms. Duggan's shoulders. Ms. Duggan gave her a vigorous petting. "I make it my business to stay informed. Yes, I do. How do you think everyone here knows you? I told them. That's right. When I heard the name Spuretta, I told the neighbors, 'Fifty years ago, I babysat little Frankie.' Oh, your daddy was a rambunctious boy, full of spit and vinegar, but he was a good boy. Respectful. Not like the kids nowadays. Punks." She pointed to a few houses. "Bad apples. I let the good neighbors know, 'Frankie's daughter bought the place. She's a police lady. She'll put an end to the shenanigans.' And you will, won't you, Carly?"

When Carly signed the final escrow papers, Ms. Duggan tacked a twenty foot banner across the front of her fence.

### Welcome Police! Good Riddance Shenanigans!

Encouraged by Carly's presence, two sellers secretly took their homes off the market and, in collusion with Ms. Duggan, planted rumors that deputy sheriffs had purchased their cottages.

Between the rumors and Carly's pressure, the shenanigans—drug depots and auto chop shops—began to clear out.

While Carly was still unpacking, neighbors converged with lasagna and coffeecake, both in greeting and in appreciation. Carly had never felt so welcome. According to Ms. Duggan, the neighborhood had never felt so safe...because Carly was in law enforcement.

Decent citizens respected and appreciated law enforcement, Carly reminded herself while sitting cross-legged on her rug—a rug buried beneath a myriad of photographs, not one relating to police work.

*Damn Zia.*

*Grrgrrgrr.* Winkle rammed Carly's side.

Carly flipped the cat to give her a brisk belly-rub. "Is this a pre-apology?"

*Grrgrrgrr.*

"Nothing doing, Winkle. When dad gets here, you behave yourself."

Spuretta arrived and held still while Winkle butted his leg. Long ago, Carly had given up on encouraging her dad to pet the cat. When Winkle finished her greeting, Spuretta stepped over the sea of photos to sit in the only comfortable chair Carly owned.

"Did you talk to the Minister?" Carly asked.

Instead of answering, Spuretta tipped his head toward the photos. "What's going on, kid?"

"Just reminiscing. Do you remember my nickname in high school?"

"Your friends called you Flash."

"Yeah. Even the teachers. They gave me that nickname after I took this photograph." She held up a picture of a hummingbird, its beating wings captured midair. "It won an award." Drawing a slow, reflective breath, Carly detected a spicy scent in the air. "Are you wearing cologne?" Only then did she notice her dad's semi-pressed shirt. "You ironed? Did you have a date with that angel again? Who is she? Do I know her?"

Spuretta shook his head. "Let's talk about the Minister and my lady friend later. Right now, tell your old dad why you're going through these pictures. What's bothering you, kid?"

"It's nothing. Well, nothing important. It's just that, well, I was wondering if my pictures were good, not hobby-good, but professional-good."

Spuretta groaned. "No, Carly, they're not good; they're excellent. God-given talent. I've told you that for years."

"But you praise everything I do. I love you for that, dad, but I can't put too much weight on a biased opinion. I just wish I knew the truth about the quality of my photos."

"You have the truth, but you don't believe it, because you don't believe in yourself. You got drawers full of blue ribbons from judges who weren't your dad. And how about that fella from LA, the national photographer, he said you had a rare style, a keen eye, and an unbeatable knack for timing. Your talent sure impressed him, and he wasn't your dad. Carly, the whole world can believe in you, but if you don't believe in yourself—"

"Okay, let's drop it."

"Now hold on a minute. Let's talk this through."

"There's nothing to talk about. Let's forget it." Carly began raking up the photographs, her internal war raging—a war Zia had resurrected and Spuretta now fueled. "I've worked hard to become a detective, and it's a damn good career. If you want to live in a small town, or close to it, either you choose a profession that works, or you open up a trinket shop that panders to tourists. Well, I did it right. The community respects what I do. They feel safe. And I earn a decent income, enough to buy my own home. And I am not—AM NOT—waiting for some bourgeois tourist to decide whether my photo's frame matches or clashes with the color of his couch."

"Aw, Carly, don't you see what you did? You gave that tourist's ignorant comment power over your life."

"Right, dad, and I will never do that again. Never, ever again. I went to college for a career, for a respectable career, not for this." She flapped a handful of pictures at him.

"Your passion?"

Carly jerked back with surprise. A second later, *Aurrrg,* her handful of photos winged overhead.

She marched from the room.

*Grrgrrgrr.*

"Uh, Carly? Carly Jean? You forgot your—Nice kitty."

# 70

Daily, Carly's cell phone rang with caller ID illuminating ZIA. "When are you going to fix my tickets?" she kept asking.

And Carly kept answering, "When I get to it."

Other times, Zia insisted that Fikus was following her. To those calls, Carly responded quickly, but she never saw Fikus. Zia once called from a Farmers' Market. "He's tracking me," she said. Carly sped to the Market and then searched the grounds. No Fikus. Unappeased, Zia demanded that Carly search again. Instead, Carly radioed a patrol unit to check Fikus's house.

Minutes later, the officer reported, "MacKenzie is mowing his lawn."

When Carly explained to Zia that the distance from the Farmers' Market to Fikus's home on B Street made Zia's sighting impossible, an irate Zia dropkicked a mango and stomped off. Carly apologized to the vendor and paid double for the fruit.

Because Zia's calls persisted, Carly began to think that the calls were less about tickets and Fikus, and more about loneliness and attention. To help Zia overcome her social issues, Carly picked up a college catalog and then took Zia to lunch. While they ate, Zia propounded ludicrous theories about food. At first, Carly laughed, but later, she argued. She argued so vehemently, she forgot her original plan. A week later, she arranged another lunch. After an unpleasant meal—"Zia, quit grimacing at my salad"—Carly handed Zia the college course schedule. "Night classes are a great way to make new friends."

"What?" Zia said, in the calm before the fury. "You sanctimonious prig." She riffled the catalog, cracked the spine, and then slapped it down. Her finger jabbed the page. "That's your course, Sister Superior." She walked out, leaving an embarrassed Carly to pay the bill.

When next Zia called, Carly delayed before picking up. "Stop badgering me about tickets. Oh, not tickets? We're back to Fikus?" Carly leveled a newly hung photograph. "Yes, I'm coming. Yes, now. Just calm down and stay put."

Carly matted another picture, hung it, and then ran a few errands before arriving at Neptunes. Zia jumped up, flagging and pointing. In a corner booth, several tables behind Zia, Fikus was eating a sandwich and minding his own business. Carly went to Zia's table. "He's following me," Zia said. "Yesterday, he was lurking outside the store where I was delivering chimes."

Carly slid into the booth. "Zia, his bookstore is on Main Street."

"I know where it is, but I was six blocks from his shop. Like always, I ignored him, but I draw the line on him invading my space at Neptunes."

"And at the Farmers' Market," Carly said. "You made me come down—"

"Whoa!" Zia said. *"Made you?* I called, bitched about tickets, and you put me off. Then I asked about your photography, and like always, you changed the subject and asked about my stalker. I told you he was tracking me. You came to the Market, didn't see him, and called me a liar. Keep it straight."

"Don't make a scene," Carly said. "Just calm down."

"I'm calm. Damn calm." Then Zia hollered, "LIZ," and a husky waitress came to the table. "Carly, this is Liz. She owns the place. She sees everything. Ask her whether Fikus followed me in here."

"Ma'am," Carly said, "do you know the gentleman in the corner booth?"

Liz glanced over her shoulder. "You mean Fikus? He's the Minister's son. Is something wrong?"

"Did you happen to notice whether he arrived before or after this lady?"

"Well, uh." Liz looked at Zia.

"Just tell her the truth," Zia said. "Fikus came in after me, right?"

"Well, honey, no. Fikus came in first."

"No way. When I came in—"

"Sweetie, I'm pretty sure he was in the bathroom."

"No, Liz, that was later. I swear, that was later."

"Maybe you're right." Looking warily at Carly, Liz said, "What difference does it make? If Zee says he did something wrong, then he did something wrong. Zee is as truthful as the day is long." Briefly, Liz bit her bottom lip. "But, uhm, I won't have to swear to that, will I?"

"LIZ!"

"Oh, honey, come on now. Sometimes your truthful day has an eclipse."

"Thanks a lot." Zia sank in her seat. Her chin rested on the table's edge.

"I appreciate your candor," Carly said.

Liz frowned. "I bet you do. Are you going to order?"

"No, thank you," Carly said. "I like my food spit-free."

"Smart." Liz refilled Zia's coffee cup, "Cheer up, honey," and walked away.

"I'm not saying you lied," Carly said. "You just made a mistake."

"Bullshit," a wilted Zia said. "After I sat down, Fikus walked in. He couldn't even get to his booth until the FBI moved out of the—Wait." Zia sat upright. "Ask the FBI. When I came in, I said hello to him. Then Fikus came in, and bumped against the FBI trying to get around him. Ask him."

"You want me to ask the FBI?"

"Yeah, right over there." Zia pointed to an enormous man. His rear swallowed the bar stool, his girth mushroomed over the neighboring seats, and his seated height dwarfed most standing men.

Carly sensed a setup. "Are you trying to make a fool out of me?"

"I'm trying to prove I'm right."

"So the FBI is going to back your story?"

"Absolutely. Trust me."

Carly doubted she would ever trust Zia, but she slid from the booth anyway. "I'll check it out. But I swear, Zia, if you're screwing with me—"

"I'm not. Ask the FBI. He knows."

Carly went to the large man. She tapped the man's shoulder and showed her badge. "Sir, are you a federal agent?"

The man rose. Although Carly was over six feet tall, her neck craned back to keep eye contact. "No, ma'am." The giant spoke with an accent that Carly couldn't place. "I'm a pirate," he said—or so it sounded like to Carly.

"You're a pirate?" she asked.

Nearby patrons began chuckling. One man ribbed another, "She thinks ol' Sal here is a Federal pirate." More chuckling sounded as others joined in the fun. "Yo-ho-ho and a tax on your rum." They broke into blustering laughter.

Without a glance to Zia, Carly marched out of Neptunes.

That evening, at her kitchen table, Carly pored over the case facts while her dad reread his notes. "Birthmark, charm, necklace," Spuretta said quietly, reflecting on Zia's questions in the church. "Are you sure Zia made up those things?"

"I'm sure she's delusional," Carly said. "Whatever she seemed to know about Fikus's vision, she made up to gain attention. She's now insisting that Fikus is stalking her, but he's not." Carly retrieved the college course catalog, still on the page where Zia had bent the spine. She placed it in front of her dad and sat again. "I tried my best to help her. On my own time, I picked up the new schedule of college classes and gave it to her."

"You gave this to her? Why?"

"Because she's lonely. She has to be. She lives alone in La-La Land. I'm sick of her trying to suck me into that world. I prefer the real world. If Zia went back to school, maybe she'd enjoy the real world, too. But, like usual, she caused a scene. She said I'm the one who needed psychological help."

"She said that, did she?"

"She implied it. She deliberately flipped to the psychology courses and shouted, 'That's the class for you, Ms. Superior.' Something like that."

Spuretta considered the page. "She pointed to this, did she?"

"Yeah, the psychology courses."

"Psychology covers more than one page. Was it this particular page?"

Carly leaned forward for a quick recheck. "See the mustard stain? That came from her jabbing finger." She sat back, her arms folded.

Spuretta turned the catalog around and tapped at the bottom listing. "How do you know Zia didn't mean this class?"

Carly drew the catalog closer, her eyes squinting. Capped in a mustard blot was the course, *Photography-Advanced*. Carly shoved it away. "That's not what she meant. She meant psychology. The entire page is psychology."

"Except the last course. Carly, how do you know she didn't mean—"

"Because I know her." Carly stood abruptly. "Zia meant to insult me. 'Get help with your psycho-self,' not, 'Gain confidence in your photography.'" Instantly, Carly sucked in air through closed teeth, wishing she could retract her last statement. Flustered, Carly went to the refrigerator for a beer. When she opened the door, she saw a head of lettuce. *Aurrrg*. With both hands, she seized it and then shook it at her dad. "See this? You think this is lettuce?" She cannonballed it into the garbage. "Think again. In Zia's back-assward world nothing is what it seems. Trees talk, birds warn, bugs listen. Try having lunch with her. Want to know how Swiss cheese gets the holes? Better yet, order a salad. You'll get the whole shebang of her insane theories. Weight Watchers ought to hire her; their clients would become anorexics."

Spuretta eyed the garbage. "I take it, she's not too keen on lettuce."

"Dad, every bite you take, she cringes as if you're killing yourself. She'll say, 'Where are all the lettuce farms, huh? Huh? Salinas has a few, sure, but let's do the math. Every deli, fast-food chain, and kitchen, from the shabbiest diner in California to the ritziest restaurant in New York City, everyplace everywhere serves lettuce. But how? Even if you factor out salads, it would take the entire state of Texas to grow enough leaves just to top America's burgers for one day. So, where are all these lettuce farms, huh?' Honestly, dad, her insanity gets under your skin. First, you laugh, but soon you're braking for crows, apologizing to moths, and ordering pastrami but please hold the Swiss. Then you're a goner because you can't drive past a farm without checking out the crop. 'Nope, not lettuce.' Eventually, you find yourself wondering, 'Yeah, just where are all these lettuce farms?'"

"Carly, take a breath."

"Again, today, she called about Fikus. Like a fool, I drove to Neptunes. Fikus was there, but the waitress said he arrived before Zia. Does Zia quit? No. She demanded I talk to a guy at the counter, supposedly the FBI."

"FBI? I'll be darned. I haven't talked to Sal in years."

"Sal?" Carly sat slowly, taking her first calming breath. "*SAL?*"

"Sure, one of the first Scavengers."

Her elbows on the table, Carly rested her aching head on cupped hands.

"Carly, you didn't think—"

Briefly, her head lifted, flashing an angry glare.

"Aw, kid," Spuretta said. "I can see how that might have caused a little problem."

"Would you mind telling me why he's called the FBI?"

"Well, most folks don't like to curse. FBI stands for F'ing Big Indian. He's a darn sizeable Paiute."

"Paiute." Carly shook her drooping head. "I thought he said pirate. I suppose common sense should have told me that he was an Indian."

"Nope, but your training in law enforcement should have told you about Protective Orders."

"What?"

"Zia complains about stalking and you hand her a college catalog. Did I miss the part where you advised her to file a Protective Order?"

"Dad, I always—I must have—" She tried to recall *when* she had told Zia, because it was basic procedure, ingrained from experience. But after a while, she had to admit, "I forgot. I don't know how, but it slipped my mind."

Willow preserved Phoenix's remark, adding it to the treasure-trove of cherished moments. When her Charge returned home, Willow would share these keepsakes with laughter and love.

# 71

*Quite the collector, you are,*
*a collector of all that is or ever was.*

Had Zia called again, Carly would have told her to file a Protective Order, but several days passed without one call from Zia. Nicked with guilt, Carly drove to the Schatz's home to pick up the tickets. She thought it would only take a minute, but when she asked to speak to Zia, she was ushered into the house. "Oh, come, come, I never see Zia's friends. This is wonderful."

"Really, Ms. Schatz, I just—"

"Call me MaGretta. Come. Join us for krapfens in the living room." MaGretta latched Carly's arm and tugged her along. "Zia, your friend is here."

Sprawled sideways in an overstuffed chair, Zia looked up briefly from the plate on her lap, "Some friend," and resumed eating.

Miranda immediately stood. "Have you found something, detective?"

"Detective?" Otto rose, too. "A woman detective?" He held out his hand.

"Yes, sir." Carly shook Otto's hand and then Dieter's. "Good to see you, Dieter." When her arm came down, MaGretta pulled her into a hug.

"Your Poppa is a smart man," MaGretta said. "Did he solve the case?"

A bit bewildered, Carly mumbled, "No, investigations take time."

"Oh, of course they do. Much time. But do not worry. Your Poppa will piece the whole puzzle together. Now sit. I will fix you a plate of krapfens."

Dieter moved to the fireplace hearth and motioned for Carly to take the couch. Carly hesitated, but Dieter said, "Don't argue with MaGretta."

"That is right," MaGretta said. And until Carly had a plate and MaGretta gave the okay, no one took another bite of a krapfen, no one except Zia.

"Carly is a strong, beautiful name," MaGretta said. "It fits you so much. Tell us about yourself. Where did you go to school?"

Carly shifted uneasily; she didn't want to chitchat, but she also didn't want to be rude. She answered quickly, took a bite of a krapfen, and then excused herself to use the restroom. MaGretta started to lift from her chair, but Carly said, "No, please, don't get up. Zia can show me the way."

Zia jerked a fork over her shoulder. "It's down the hall on the left. You don't need a map. Even a cop can find it."

Carly walked to the backside of Zia's chair and then placed a hand on Zia's collarbone. "Would you please show me?"

"I'll give you a clue, detective, it's the room with a toil—"

Carly's hand clenched.

"—*eeetYeoww.*" Zia's plate clattered down from her lap and onto the coffee table. "What the hell is your problem?"

Pleasantries hushed as everyone waited to hear Carly's problem.

"No problem," she said. "Everything is fine." Bending down, Carly angled a stern face into Zia's. "Don't you have papers for me? Parking papers?"

"Oooh," Zia whispered. "Alms from the prig? Bless you."

"Get them now or I'm out of here."

"Zia? Carly?" MaGretta tilted from side to side. "What is the matter?"

Carly straightened. "Nothing, Ms. Schatz."

Zia got up. "Now, Carly, let's not fib to MaGretta. Yes, we have a problem, but it's all my fault. See, I have expired parking passes from the library. Carly unexpires passes so that the library can reuse them and save money. Last month, I promised to give Carly the passes, but I never made the time to deliver. Like a jerk, I brushed her off and ignored my promise."

"Zia, that is not nice," MaGretta said. "You must keep your promises."

"You're right, MaGretta. Hey, Carly, sorry I dodged your calls and treated you like crap. Only an asshole reneges on a promise. Sorry, I was an asshole."

Carly looked across the faces, wondering who among Zia's family was buying her bull. Not Dieter; he rolled his eyes. Not Miranda; she shook her head. And Otto was shielding his face and eating much faster.

"Carly," MaGretta said, "Zia is sorry. I am sure she will make it up."

"Oh, she has, Ms. Schatz. Zia made it up good." Carly gave Zia a tight-lipped smile. "But I'm the one who should apologize. I called you repeatedly, sometimes twice a day. I interrupted your work, wasted your time, and when you didn't drop your life to accommodate mine, I threw a hissy fit. So, I'm sorry, Zia. Sorry I acted like a spoiled brat over a promise I had no business asking for in the first place. Obviously, I was only concerned for myself."

"And for the library," MaGretta said.

"Library?" Carly asked, then, "Ouch," from Zia's quick pinch.

"Yes, MaGretta," Zia said. "Carly and I have tons of concern for the library. Tons and tons, right, Carly?"

"Sure." Carly shoved Zia. "Get going."

Zia led the way to her bedroom. There, Zia yanked out drawers from a large desk and then stretched inside to grope the backboards. "I cram stuff behind the slats in case MaGretta binge-cleans."

Carly froze in the doorway. Staring out from beneath glass frames were thousands of spiders, butterflies, scorpions, and beetles—a mortuary of crawlers with pincers and of flyers with stingers that most people paid good money to exterminate. Carly swatted her neck, thinking that six tiny legs were crawling beneath her ear. "Do you keep live ones?"

"Not anymore," Zia said from inside the desk's hull. "I used to, but the sneaky bastards kept escaping. They showed up in MaGretta's strudel, inside Pop's shoes, on the shower curtain, and under the toilet seat. Mostly, they just crawled to the ceiling, but then they dropped at really bad times."

Stumbling backward, Carly's stare swept to the ceiling.

"Got 'um!" Zia said.

Carly jumped. "GOT WHAT?"

Zia emerged jiggling a brown, paper bag. "Parking tickets." As Zia got to her feet, she followed Carly's line of sight to the ceiling. "What's wrong?"

"Everything," Carly said, itchy and edgy. "To start with, your lies. Expired parking passes? From the library?"

"I didn't lie. It's about parking. And something expired or I wouldn't have these tickets." She tossed the bag to Carly. "So unexpire them."

"These aren't all—" Carly fanned a handful and then plunged them back into the bag. "You said a couple."

"No, I didn't. I said a couple dozen. You had jelly in your ears."

"I can't—"

"Fix them all? I know. Just stop at twenty-four."

Carly shook her head. "You're a piece of work, Zia, a scheming liar."

Zia grinned so wide, she reminded Carly of the Cheshire cat. "I've been called worse and by better than you." She lifted to her toes to lean into Carly's face. "And you lie, too. You just rationalize yours."

"Think so?" Carly rammed the bag into Zia's chest. "Not anymore. Take care of these tickets or I'll have your car booted and towed."

"We had a deal."

"Tough. I lied. No rationale about it; I plain don't like you."

"Oh, ouch, however will I sleep at night?"

"Soundly. You'll be dead tired from walking."

"That's not funny."

"Not yet, but I'll be laughing tomorrow when your car goes bye-bye."

*Rrring.* Zia's cell phone sounded from the nightstand. When Zia went to answer it, Carly walked out. From the hallway, Carly heard a second ring, then a third. Wondering why Zia hadn't picked up, Carly back-stepped. Zia was staring at the phone. Carly hated to ask, "Problem?"

A pale Zia shrugged, her hands flourishing at her chest. Carly crossed the room to check the caller ID. Green glowing letters showed FIKUS.

"Zia, answer it," Carly said. "Find out what he wants."

"No, he's a freak. I don't care what he wants."

"Answer it. Ask him why he's calling. Go on."

Zia picked up the phone. "Hello?" She listened for a moment before she cupped the phone. "He wants to know if I'm alone. What should I say?"

"You're an idiot."

"You're an idiot," Zia told him.

Carly smacked Zia's arm, "No," and Zia cupped the phone again. Carly thought of her car parked out front. "Just tell him the truth."

"Got it, but what truth?"

"*The* truth, Zia. Tell him I'm here and ask him what he wants."

"Carly Spuretta is here. What do you want?" As Zia listened, she slowly started to sit. Suddenly, she sprang upright. "Oh, hell no. You're not coming here. I don't care if she told you who shot Kennedy."

Carly's hand spliced between the phone and Zia's mouth. "Is he saying Dorothy revealed something?"

"Yeah, another vision, but he wants to come here and talk about it."

"Let him."

"Come here? To my house? He'll leave an imprint."

"An imprint?" Carly bit back her swelling frustration. "Zia, I'm begging you, *begging you,* put your lunacy aside for one evening. Please."

Grumbling, Zia pushed Carly's hand off the phone. "Okay, Fikus, but this better be good." No sooner had she closed the phone when she fumbled to reopen it. "Wait, wait, what about the lottery—Hello? Fikus? Crap." She snapped the phone closed.

Carly called her dad. "Our psychic friend is on his way to the Schatz's. Yes, now. A vision about Dorothy. That's what I'm hoping. No problem, but hurry up. What? Who? Gretta? She's—She's fine...I guess."

# 72

*Thinking quickly,*
*she screamed with calculated volume.*

Because Carly and I were arguing, we never heard the doorbell ring.
What rose above our voices and hurried us to the entryway was the commotion of a freak's cry.

A startled MaGretta was holding onto the front door while a collapsed
Fikus wailed at her feet. Miranda was kneeling beside Fikus and smoothing
back his hair. "Fikus, what happened?"

"I had a vision," he said. "Your mother showed me how she fell."

"Let's get him off the floor," Carly said.

Grasping Fikus under each arm, Dieter and Pop half-carried him to the
living room and settled him into a chair. Miranda crouched at his feet. Dieter
moved off to the side, either hurt or concerned. He was impossible to read.

Pop, on the other hand, was impossible to misread. He thumped into his
recliner, his thick arms knotting. He regarded Fikus like one regards a snake;
is it harmless or poisonous? Until that's known, wary eyes don't blink from
the snake. MaGretta blotted a damp cloth to Fikus's forehead. Fikus moaned,
his arms stretching upward like a melodramatic replay of his performance on
the beach.

"I hate reruns," I whispered to Carly. "I've already seen this act."

"I wish my dad could see it," she said.

"You got it." Then I told Fikus to hold the show. "We're waiting for—
*OWW.*" Carly's pointy elbow jabbed me in the ribs.

I sidestepped a few feet before saying, "We're waiting for you to eat."

At that, MaGretta sprang into action. "Oh, yes. Eat first." She went off to
fix a plate of strudel and krapfens. By the time she placed it in front of Fikus,
Spuretta was knocking at the door. MaGretta brought him into the living
room. "Your daughter and my Zia will save the library much money."

Spuretta shot a questioning look our way. Carly and I looked elsewhere.

Turning to Fikus, Spuretta said, "I heard you had another vision."

"Oh, no, not now," MaGretta said. "He is too troubled to talk. Right now, he should eat." And nobody overrides MaGretta. Nobody can...except Pop.

Spuretta seemed to know this. He fake-cleared his throat, sending a man-code message to Pop. Pop answered with a quick nod. "My Gretta, he did not come for krapfens and strudel, and he is not hurt. He will talk now."

She started to argue, but Pop cut her off using his baritone voice speaking German. MaGretta respected the old-school gender rules, and whenever those rules came into play, she gave me a scolding look while holding a finger to her lips, demanding that I respect the rules, too.

I rolled my eyes; *yeah, yeah, a woman who speaks now disrespects Pop.* Whereas Dieter, a big-whoop male, could have talked nonstop had he wanted to.

"Young man, start talking," Pop said. "We are all listening."

Fikus raised pitiful eyes. "Dorothy has shown me the truth, but the truth tests my strength. My heart breaks with unbearable news. Devastating and unbearable."

"Bear it," Pop said with a guttural growl. "Mend your broken heart later. If you have something to tell us, tell us now."

Fikus slid to his knees and grasped Miranda's shoulders.

Dieter sprang up, but so did Pop's hand. Dieter held ground.

"My father," Fikus said, "my father killed your mother."

MaGretta dropped a plate.

I sucked in a gasp, "Oh shit," recalling the Minister's threat to my Soul and realizing that I had, indeed, pissed off the real-deal devil.

"Where is your father now?" Spuretta asked.

"I haven't seen him since I confronted him this morning. He begged me not to expose him, but spiritual laws bind me to tell the truth. All day, I've been trying to muster the courage to tell you, Miranda. I wanted to tell you in private, but when I called, Zia said Carly was already here."

Spuretta hoisted Fikus upright. "Let's go chat with your father." They headed to the door. Miranda went for her purse. Dieter grabbed his coat.

I trailed Carly down the driveway and said, "Hey, fill me in later, okay?"

"Zia, I can't discuss the case with you."

"Yeah, yeah." I hurried to say goodbye to Spaghetti-man, who was already in his car and preparing to leave. I stooped at the car's window to wave.

From the backseat, Fikus's eyes caught mine, his face now devoid of agony. Before Spuretta pulled from the curb, Fikus mouthed the word, *proof.* *Proof?* Or maybe he had blown me a kiss. Either way, it was equally creepy.

# 73

*Thorough, he told himself,*
*but a queer feeling—an instinct, he figured—disagreed.*

Death by suicide...or so it appeared. Spuretta radioed for a homicide team before he called Tony. "Supposedly, the Minister killed himself out of guilt for killing Dorothy."

"Back it up," Tony said. "Did I miss something? Who said anything about the Minister killing Dorothy?"

"Our psychic," Spuretta said. "A vision gave him the particulars, and he's darn anxious to tell us all about it."

"But you're not buying it."

"Tony, like you said from the git-go, this case is as clear as tar."

"Did the Minister leave a parting note?"

"*Nemo malus felix.*"

"Come again?"

"Sunday-School Latin," Spuretta chuckled. "This is why I buckled down to my studies when you and the boys were sneaking off to the docks."

"You called it, Frank, fifty years ago. Now, what does it mean, altar boy?"

"Peace visits not the guilty mind."

⚷

Carly planned on taking Fikus's statement at the station, but when she opened her car's passenger door, Fikus shut it. "I'm not going anywhere with him." He indicated Dieter. "I sense Dieter's hostilities. He wishes me harm."

"You're wrong," Miranda said. "Dieter trusts you. Tell him, Dieter."

Dieter kept silent. His firm stance and frosty-white skin reminded Carly of chiseled marble. Above him, his pale-wheat hair twirled like saffron strings caught in a breeze. And below his colorless brow, icicle eyes steeled on Fikus.

"Miranda, stop pleading," Fikus said. "It's degrading. Obviously, Dieter distrusts both of us. If he had any respect, he would answer you."

"If you had any balls," Carly said, "you would pose the question yourself."

Carly's comment gave Miranda pause. She stepped aside.

"Is this my cue?" Fikus asked, but no one answered. "All right, if that's what it takes." As he turned to face Dieter, Fikus hunkered into his shoulders, nervously. "Do you believe in me or not?"

"There is less chance of your telling the truth than a slug's chance of crossing the Bonneville Salt Flats."

"As I predicted," Fikus said. "Either he remains here or my vision remains a secret." Fikus got into the car and then slammed the door.

Miranda stared at the ground. "Dieter, I need to—I have to—"

Dieter gathered Miranda into his arms. "I know. It's okay."

Carly frowned, both at Miranda's stupidity and at Dieter's tolerance. She gave an interruptive cough as she opened the car door. Miranda climbed inside. As Carly closed the door, she gave an apologetic shrug to Dieter.

"Miranda is not stupid," Dieter said.

Carly drew back. She would have denied that she had ever thought such a thing, but when she met Dieter's eyes, she almost flinched. A trick of the moonlight had bleached Dieter's irises from blue to translucent. His pupils, half-lidded, appeared like razors, cutting through the flesh and peering into the Soul. No wonder why Fikus had cowered; Carly would have cowered, too, had she anything to hide...anything more than her opinion of Miranda. "Look, Dieter, if I said anything along those lines—"

Dieter shook his head. "Miranda doesn't have a malicious bone in her body. Not one. So, she has a tough time seeing it in others, even in Fikus."

Hours later, Spuretta and the homicide team came out to the driveway to inspect the Minister's Cadillac.

The officers collected hair and fibers from the seats, and then opened the trunk. Spuretta carefully picked up the tire iron. It was certainly long and strong enough to cave an inlet's ceiling. Encrusting one end was dirt and stones, which Spuretta suspected would match the debris that had buried Dorothy. He also suspected the iron's shape would match the gouges left in the rocks. An officer held a bag open. Spuretta started to put the tire iron into the bag when Dieter came up from the curb. "It's wrong."

An officer blocked Dieter's approach.

"Let him through," Spuretta said.

"You're holding a tire iron from a scissor jack," Dieter said. "Scissor jacks come with foreign cars and late model domestics, not with a '72 Caddy." He pointed to the jack inside the trunk. "That's a bumper jack. Your tire iron won't fit the jack and it won't fit the lug nuts on this Caddy."

Crouching, Spuretta lined up the iron's socket to the wheel's lug nut. It didn't fit. "Well, I'll be darned. Thank you, Dieter." Spuretta stood again. Though he didn't know Dieter well, Spuretta sensed that the young man had a fine character, a character worth trusting. He also felt a bit bad for Dieter; it seemed that Dieter was taking a lot of guff for his interest in Miranda. "You know, Dieter, you got a real nice family. Yes, siree. Real nice. And you got yourself a kindhearted girlfriend, too."

Dieter smiled. "So do you."

Fikus sat alone behind one-way glass. On the other side, Carly, Tony, and the District Attorney, Robyn, were replaying the last few minutes of a five-hour taped statement.

> Fikus: "It comes down to love and deceit. For years, my father loved her, and for years, she took his love, but rejected him. My father forgave her. He always forgave her; her gambling, her mouth, her whoring. He only wanted to remind Dorothy of what he had given up for her. His sacrifice. So he picked her up to take her to the place where my mother had jumped. But barbecues were going on. For privacy, he drove to the neighboring cliffs. The passing years had never eased my father's guilt for the affair that had caused my mother to take her own life. I reminded Dorothy of this."
>
> Carly: "You did?"
>
> Fikus: "My father did. Pay attention! All he wanted was an apology, a small price to pay for his decades of wasted devotion. But Dorothy refused. My father pushed her. And Dorothy chose me, the murderer's son, to reveal the truth and to bring about justice."

Carly stopped the recorder. "That vision is a disguised confession."

Addressing Tony, Robyn asked, "Did Frank find any indication of a staged suicide?"

"Not yet."

"Do we have anything more than Fikus's statement?"

Tony shook his head.

"Then why am I here? And why is Mr. MacKenzie still here?"

Tony pulled in a deep breath and looked away.

Robyn took two steps before Carly blocked her path. "Robyn, wait a minute. Either Fikus knew from the beginning that his father killed Dorothy, or Fikus was with his father on the ridge."

Robyn's palm came up to stop Tony from intervening.

Carly, believing she had Robyn's interest, ignored Tony's finger swiping a line across his throat. "I requested an expedite on the DNA tests," Carly said. "I think the results will prove that Fikus and Miranda are half-siblings."

"Do you intend to charge Fikus with having an illegitimate sister?"

"If Fikus knew of his father's affair, it might go to a conspiracy motive."

Robyn's arms crossed. "An *if* with a *might*? On behalf of the Judicial System, thank you, Carly, for not becoming an attorney."

"But the motive—"

"What motive? Every motive you attach to Fikus, a first year law student will attach to the Minister. Did Fikus blame Dorothy for the death of his mother, or did the Minister blame Dorothy for the death of his wife? Where does the evidence lead? To the Minister."

"But—"

"Ms. Spuretta, this case has the attention of our entire county, and in a week, our nation's tabloid readers as well. What charge do you want splashed across the headlines? All we know is that Fikus withheld information to promote himself as a psychic. To prove that, we would have to refute the psychic industry...and dig up twelve jurors who have never read a horoscope."

"But there's still a gap in time where he could have—"

"*Could have?* I don't prosecute *could haves*. For that matter, I don't care if Fikus *was* in California when Dorothy died. The name, MacKenzie, makes this a high profile case. No room for *could haves*. If you want Fikus charged, place him on the ridge. Do you understand? I need evidence that puts Fikus on the ridge when Dorothy died. Finding that evidence is your job, Carly. Do it, so I can do mine." Robyn leaned into Carly and whispered, "And if you ever jump the chain of command again, it won't matter who your father or your godfather is. Understand? You'll do something else."

Carly cleared a dry throat. "Something else?"

"Something else, Carly. Not police work."

# 74

*So as the Agitator withheld her voice,*
*so shall her voice fall on deaf ears, ten-fold.*

After everyone left, Pop hunted for his Schnapps—MaGretta often hid the bottle—so I reached into the big, cooking pot, retrieved the bottle, and then poured two glasses, a healthy dose for Pop and a modest splash for myself.

MaGretta, still shaken from the evening's events, didn't even lift her wagging head. "He accused his own Poppa of murder."

"MaGretta, it's all bull. Think of the MacKenzies as the modern day, *The Good, The Bad, and The Ugly.*" I poured another splash. "We'll call this sequel, *The No-Good, The Devil, and The Freak,* because only a freak lies about their dad, right, Pop?"

"Yeah, sure." Our glasses clinked together, we downed our Schnapps, and I headed to bed. Before settling under the covers, I re-stashed my bag of tickets. I would take it up with Carly later; she owed me, big-time. I set the alarm; no reading tonight. The first Monday of every month required an early rise, not only to deliver chimes, but also to collect payments. It would take all day if I hustled.

At eight a.m., I grabbed my backpack and hurried to the kitchen. MaGretta was washing breakfast dishes left by Pop, but only Pop. During the night, Dieter had come home, had packed a bag, and had left a note stating that he and Miranda were driving to Ridgecrest and that he would call later to explain.

I sat down to breakfast warmed in the oven. When MaGretta looked away, I smeared eggs across the plate and folded potatoes into a napkin. MaGretta accepts only two reasons for a light appetite—serious illness or bad cooking. The first, causes her worry, the latter, causes her shame. Lies have their place. I guzzled the coffee, plunged the napkin into the trash, and thanked MaGretta for a terrific breakfast.

"When I hear from Dieter," she said, "should I call you?"

"No, no. Don't call me. Just tell Dieter I'm tutoring a Blue Dolphin."

Because Dieter didn't have a cell phone, I passed coded messages through MaGretta. Any mention of a Blue Dolphin meant, "Dieter, give me a call." A message containing a Red Herring meant, "Dieter, post my bail." This way, we kept MaGretta from calling my cell phone and panicking over lousy reception. If crackling preceded a dropped call, MaGretta pictured my car scrunching like an accordion. In nonstop rotation, she called the hospital, the fire department, and the highway patrol. *My Zia is lying in a ditch by the side of the road.* Either I raced home to prove my health or I phoned a neighbor to ask a favor, "Please tell MaGretta to hang up the phone so I can call her again...and I'm not in a roadside ditch."

"See ya tonight," I told MaGretta. With a kiss to her cheek, I was gone.

Like always, I started my route at the south end of town, the thicket of stores. Moving my car every few blocks, I worked my way north to where shops intermingled with homes and where residential streets crossed Main.

My customers also had a routine; they stalled. "Oh, did you want to get paid today?" By the time I parked for the last stretch of stores, the restaurant windows were displaying their dinner menus. I pulled on my chime-stuffed backpack, fed the parking meter a slug, and started across B Street. From the middle of the intersection, I spotted a yellow ribbon flapping midway down the road. I could tell it was police tape, but I couldn't tell whose house had the trouble—the Minister's Colonial, Billy's cottage, or a neighbor in between.

Responsibility nagged me to deliver the chimes, but the ribbon curled like a jaundice arm inviting my curiosity. I hurried back to my car, dumped the backpack, and then sprinted down B Street to check it out.

Security tape marked the Colonial. I saw that before I noticed the ring of cops standing on the porch. I hadn't done a damn thing wrong—other than jogging in the middle of the road—but my hands twisted and my feet slowed. I began whistling to appear casual.

The circle of cops spread to a line. *Shit.* They smelled my nervousness, and predictably, so judgmentally, they assumed it was the scent of guilt. I could tell this by watching them watching me. They were mentally accusing me of all kinds of unsolved crimes. *Jeez.* The pressure turned my heels. *Oh jeez.* Changing direction had all the subtlety of a neon light blinking, *guilt, guilt.* I swiveled again to prove my innocence. *Shit.* Ambivalence shows guilt. I switched again. *Damn.* Walking away is worse; I turned again.

Their stares hardened.

*Jeez, oh jeez.* I gave my fickle feet a harsh warning, "Stop it! Stop pivoting like a duck in a shooting gallery."

*Toot-toot,* came from behind me. In scrambling to get out of the car's way, I tripped on the curb. Denim frays ripped. My skin tore. I sat clutching a bloodied knee.

"Miss, are you hurt?"

Wishing he'd go away, I shook my head.

"Do you have business here?"

I shook my head again.

"Can I see some ID?"

My ID was in my backpack. "No."

The cop's radio squawked, and he answered, "Could be a 5150. Maybe a 5149 and a half," and he laughed at what was likely a coded cop joke.

I stood and brushed myself off.

Joining the cops on the porch was Fikus. Our stares riveted. Fikus curled his hand, *come here,* before he slipped behind the cops' peripheral vision.

I took a few steps closer.

Fikus inched back.

I moved to the yellow tape and then stretched to my tippy-toes.

Hidden from the cops' view, Fikus gestured, lewd and lascivious, with his tongue and two fingers.

My heels smacked down, my middle finger whipped high. "FUCK YOU!"

Weirdly, Fikus flinched, as if hurt and surprised. He hunched into his shoulders like a little boy who had been slapped unfairly. Had he been within the cops' view, I would have sworn his injured look was for their benefit. As it was, Fikus, in his twisted mind, had honestly expected a different reaction to his lewd gesture. Apparently, I had been too nice or too subtle in making my feelings clear. It was time to correct that mistake. "STOP WATCHING ME, YOU VILE PIECE OF SEWER CRAP."

"Lady," a cop said, "calm down and—"

"DISGUSTING WAD OF LIVER SHIT."

The cop fronted me. "LADY, this is your last—"

I pushed him aside to keep watch on Fikus, whose lips were tightening on a reddening face. Finally, I was getting through to him. "LUNATIC."

The cop roped my waist and swung me sideways.

"PSYCHOTIC LUNATIC."

He forced my arms to my backside.

"GET IT?"

Metal pinched my wrists.

"FREAK!"

The cop pressed my head down and into the back of a car. I kicked the front seat, "Fuckin' freak," again and again. Slowly, adrenalin drained under a dawning realization of where I sat. *Uh-oh.* Wrangling onto my knees, I half-bounced half-tumbled over to the window. My lips squeezed into the open sliver at the top. "Hello, Officer, I'm calm now. May I please leave?"

The cop spoke into his radio, "Yep, she's a 5150."

"Officer, please, I can explain. Officer?"

Nothing.

*Crap.* Time to rehearse my one phone call. "Hi, MaGretta, I won't be home for a few days. Please tell Dieter I'm visiting a Red Herring. Where? Uhm, in Carceration." A flawed excuse; MaGretta would search a map for Carceration.

While rethinking my story, wrinkled pants strolled past the window. When the man leaned against the back fender, his outstretched legs revealed unmatched socks. *Yes!* I banged my head against the window. *Wump, wump, wump.* "Spaghetti-man, Spaghetti-man." *Wump, wump, wump.*

His kindly face lowered. "Well, hello there, Zia." He opened the door, helped me out, and ordered the officer to remove my cuffs.

"It was a misunderstanding," I told him. "I got—I got—"

"A little excited?"

"Yeah, a little excited."

"Well, folks get excited now and then, but there's no crime in that."

"Thank you." I gave the other cop a vindicated huff.

"Do you feel all right now?" Spaghetti-man asked.

I nodded and pointed to my skinned knee. "I had a bad day."

Spaghetti-man looked like he had had a bad day, too. He was still wearing the same clothes he had worn at our house and his stubble was now a beard. "Have you been here since last night?"

"Oh, don't worry about me. Go on and get your knee fixed."

Then Carly marched up, also in day-old, rumpled clothes. Her makeup had settled into her creases, darkening her crows' feet and frown lines. "What are you doing here?"

"*Whoa.* You look nastier than your attitude."

"WHAT ARE YOU—"

"BACK OFF! I was delivering chimes to the stores."

"Really?" She cupped her eyes and looked right and left. "I count zero stores on this street, but how many exist in your world?"

My teeth clenched.

"Ladies, settle down," Spuretta said. "We're all a bit hungry and tired. Why don't you ladies go grab a bite to eat and relax for a while. How does that sound? Carly? Zia? Please, ladies, make an effort."

"I'll walk you to your car," Carly said.

"I know my way."

"Good. Get going." She shoved me.

My hands fisted, but Spaghetti-man smiled to encourage my compliance. I started walking. Once at a distance, I batted Carly's pushy hand off my back. "Why are you so pissy?"

"Why are you here?"

"I saw the police tape. Big deal. You were going to call me anyway, right? So is the Minister in jail?"

"The Minister is dead."

I slowed. "Dead?"

"Suicide." She pushed me again. "Keep moving."

"Did he kill—"

"Zia, I'm not discussing the case, especially with you. Now why are you here? And don't give me that bullshit about delivering chimes. Ten minutes into my first meal of the day, I get a call that a nut-job is pinballing in the middle of the street and—"

"Nut-job? Is that a 5150?"

"—and shouting profanities at the officers. What a shock to find that it's you. Did you forget your morning meds? Do you suffer Tourette's? Seriously, Zia, what is wrong with you?"

"I never swore at the cops; I had no idea they were calling me a nut-job. I was yelling at Fikus, but he provoked me."

"Let me get this straight. Within a day of his father's death and after a night of providing statements, a morning of fielding reporters, an afternoon of receiving medical attention for collapsing, Fikus came out to his porch and, while shoulder to shoulder with police officers, had the desire to provoke your deranged screaming."

"You got a bad attitude."

"WHAT DID HE DO?"

"THIS!" And I showed her.

After a moment of disgust, Carly wore a skeptic's frown. "How can I believe you when you treat bullshitting as an Olympic sport? The police said you were ranting at them. Considering how you feel about cops, it sure sounds right to me."

"But Carly—"

"Save it. Whether you're lying or telling the truth, I don't care right now. You're interfering in a police investigation." She rubbed her forehead. "Look, Zia, you need to leave Fikus alone."

"*Me* leave *him* alone? What do you mean?"

"Fikus claims you're obsessed with him. He says you're following him and inviting his phone calls. Oddly enough, he described your attack on the beach exactly the way you said he would."

"You don't believe him, do you?"

She looked away. "Go home, Zia. Just go home." She started back to her cop friends.

"I bet he just made that claim," I hollered. Carly didn't turn, but she slowed. "I bet Fikus never mentioned it before today, not once in any interview or in any statement, not until after I yelled, supposedly at the cops, right? He's mad, Carly, because I finally got it through his thick skull—"

"Go home, Zia." She started walking again, her gait toughening as she neared her friends.

"Crap," I muttered, "I told the truth."

*Truth is not clay to be sculpted at whim, though that is your pattern.*

I turned an angry face toward Alpha. "You know what your pattern is? A pattern of unwanted advice, the pattern of a buttinsky."

Listening from across the street as I argued aloud with seemingly nobody was a potato-faced woman holding a fat mangy cat. In the woman's lipless mouth, a cigarette squirmed, dropping ashes onto the fat cat's head.

"What are you looking at?" I shouted.

Carly swiveled around.

Necks stretched on the other cops.

"Aw, jeez." I waved them off and moved on.

# 75

*A Player's reproach is understandable,*
*their perspective limited, and therefore, forgivable.*

Pop worked late every night because Dieter and Miranda were spending the month in Ridgecrest to pack Miranda's belongings and close out her lease. She planned to stay with us until she found a rental in Kenzie Cove.

While MaGretta shared this news, she almost smiled, but no sauce bubbled on the stove, no aroma leaked from the oven, and no surplus of refrigerated foods hid the box of baking soda, an ominous sign.

"MaGretta, what's wrong?"

She dabbed her eyes, but wouldn't look at me. "The Minister, he takes his own life. That is not right. Not right."

At a loss for words, I tried to hug her, but she pushed me away. She started clamoring around the kitchen, opening and closing the cupboard doors, and checking and rechecking the vegetable bins.

I nibbled a cuticle.

She finally settled on cutting onions; tears already streaked her cheeks.

I rubbed a gentle hand to her strong back. "Whew, mighty strong onions."

No reaction.

"MaGretta, are you okay?"

"I trusted the Minister." She stared into the sink. "Thirty years, I go to his church, and I believe in his words." She tossed the knife and clenched a sponge. Foam gushed between her knuckles. "I thought he was a good man. A man of the church. How could I have been such a fool?"

"No, MaGretta, you're not a fool. Lots of people trusted the Minister."

"NO!" She whipped around, sudsy hands clasping her hips. "I should have listened to your Poppa. He never did like him."

"Pop doesn't like any minister, especially the Irish. I mean Scottish. But that's the depth of Pop's insight; mad at a country and mad at God."

"Maybe he is right to be mad."

"Come on, MaGretta, you don't believe that."

"Maybe I do. Tell me this; what God would allow a murderer at the pulpit? What God is that?"

"Murderer? Did the Minister really kill Dorothy? Did Dieter say that?"

"No. The papers say it looks that way, but nobody knows for sure. But he took his own life; isn't that also murder?"

I stammered.

"That's what I thought," MaGretta said. "You have no answer. All the time, you make jokes about death. 'Oh, Dr. Kevorkian cures whining. Oh, group executions solve crowded prisons.' And when a train killed my friend's nephew, you said, 'natural selection kept stupidity from breeding.'"

"I was trying to comfort you."

"Comfort me? How does that comfort me?"

"By pointing out the bright side. Any fool blasting rock from a headset while jogging down the railroad tracks has just spared society from his not-too-bright gene. A train didn't kill him; his stupidity did."

"You think that is funny?"

"Uhm, not now."

"Death is never funny. I believe in life. When life is taken, I am hurt. I am hurt deeply, Zia." Again, she bustled about the kitchen. "You cannot understand because you have no such beliefs."

"MaGretta, stop. Stop."

"Go away." A head of cabbage smacked the cutting board. She regained a knife then chopped with intimidating blows. My fingers cleared the counter in case tears blinded her aim.

"MaGretta, don't blame God. This isn't His fault."

Her chopping slowed. "Then what is? Answer me that."

"Well, uhm, maybe gophers and sharks and Dieter's foot odor. Blame God for those things, but not for what the Minister did. MaGretta, please."

"Auk, this from you, Zia Endolyn Schatz." She waved the knife as if it were a pointer stick. "You never pray. Never. Maybe the Obnoxious are gottesleugners after all. Now out!" The knife swung toward the door.

Reluctantly, I left her alone.

Usually, I love coastal nights with the rumbling foghorns, the eerie boat lights, and the brisk breezes, but tonight was different. My family was disconnected, each tending to their own problems, nobody pulling together.

Our gluing force, MaGretta, was a wounded Soul.

Needing two dozen chimes to deliver within the week, I trudged to the work shack and kicked the old wooden door. Instead of opening, the rusty hinge snapped, *thrack,* and the door skewed, embedding its corner into the floorboard. *Crap.* My palm rammed the door; a splinter rammed my palm. "DAMMIT!" Blood marked the entrance of a long, wooden needle. I looked up with a scowl. "Are you bored? Is that it? Is there no one else on this planet for you to pick on?"

Jostling the door, I squeezed through and hit the lights. Spiders, roaches and mice scampered for cover. I grabbed a bin of shells and a drawer of tools, and I smacked them onto the workbench. Propped on a stool, I held a mallet in one hand and a pointed chisel in the other. I *tap tap tap*'d the top of a shell. Instead of creating a hole, the damn shell broke. I tossed the pieces and began again. *Tap tap tap.* That shell broke, too. One shell after the next, I tapped and destroyed. After wasting dozens of shells, I slammed down the tools. "Alpha, God being God and all, He knows people blame Him, right?"

*True.*

"And we're not talking about busted doors or broken shells, right?"

*True.*

"Then why the hell doesn't He do something?" I looked up accusingly. "If He exists, why doesn't He do something to help? Does He want MaGretta to lose faith? Does He care? Did He care when Pop lost his faith? Tell me straight up; does God give a flying fart about any of us?"

*True.*

"NO! Say yes or no, got it?" I looked at the heap of shells. In each, I saw MaGretta's damaged faith. "This is His fault. His inaction creates atheists. If He doesn't like it, He ought to get down here and unleaven some bread or part some waters or turn sea into wine. Do something to prove He gives a shit." I regained my tools, positioned a shell, and raised the mallet. "His system stinks. You tell Him I said so." *Tap, tap, tap.* "Better yet, I'll tell him right now. Hey, God, this is Zia Schatz. Listen up; your system stinks. Get it? Big-time sucks."

I tapped again, gently. The shell didn't break, but it splintered. A piece flecked my cheek. I pinched it. On my fingertip was a white chip shaped like a teardrop. For a split-second, it sparkled blue, dark blue, as if it were a sparkle of ink. For some crazy reason, that ink drip stirred a torrent of sadness. I cupped my mouth and closed my eyes. Tears leaked anyway.

"This is so unfair. MaGretta walked the walk of kindness and generosity. She doesn't deserve to be disillusioned and heartbroken. She deserves her religious junk to kick in and soothe her, not to abandon and hurt her. I hate it when she cries, but I can't do a damn thing to make her feel better."

*Untrue.*

"No, it is true. I already tried, but I didn't do any good."

*Untrue.*

I swiped my eyes and peered hard at Alpha. "Don't mess with me. Are you saying I helped MaGretta...feel better?"

*True.*

"Do you know that for a fact? I mean, don't you have to blink into the kitchen and check first? I don't want to press my luck, but are you absolutely positive I did or said something that helped her?"

*True.*

I released a held breath. "Thanks, Alpha. I needed to hear that. You probably never noticed, but I'm lousy at offering cheer. Or comfort. Or sympathy. Not that I care, but we're talking MaGretta. She's different."

*Would you give your last crust of bread to a starving man?*

"The riddle game? Now? I have work to do, chimes to make."

Alpha waited for my answer.

Although I hated the game because I always lost, Alpha had eased my worries over MaGretta, so I figured I owed him. My elbow on the table, my cheek rested against a fist. "Okay, let's hear the riddle again."

*Would you give your last crust of bread to a starving man?*

My fingers thrummed the table while my mind searched for the trick. There's always a trick. "You said it's my *last* crust, correct? So the answer is no, because then I would starve. Did I get it right?"

*And if it were not your last crust?*

"That's different. He can have the bread."

*Why?*

"Because I'm generous."

*Then you will have gained his gratitude, but you will not have staved his hunger. The bread bitters.*

"Then it's a bad piece of bread."

*Intent vibrates into the result. You will not have fed the man.*

"Technically, you're wrong. Intent isn't food, so it doesn't matter what my intent vibrates. If the guy ate the bread, then technically, I fed him."

Alpha's eyes radiated. *Generosity spawned for accolades results in accolades and little more. Breads bitter, shelters fall, medicines fail. The giver, however, declared fine and noble, revels in fallacious conceit, 'oh, all others should be as charitable as I.'*

"Okay. I'll give the guy the bread and throw in a hearty handshake."

*Would you feed kinship?*

"Stop changing the terms. See, this is how you always win; you cheat."

*Would you feed kinship?*

"Family? What's mine is theirs—first crust, last crust, pie crust."

*Why?*

"Jeez, Alpha, I love them."

*Love vibrates into the result. The bread will nourish, not bitter.*

"BREAD DOESN'T BITTER." My temples throbbed. "Bread crumbles or hardens or molds into a bluish fuzz-ball, but bread doesn't bitter. It doesn't become bitter, turn bitter, or be bitter. There's nothing bitter about it, except your point, which I don't get. If you talked English, I would understand, and I wouldn't have been bitten by a rattlesnake."

*It was not a rattlesnake nor were you bitten.*

"Stop correcting me. There's only a slight difference between a rattler and a ferocious lizard."

*A hatchling smaller than your finger.*

"For chrissake, Alpha, what are you getting at?"

*What is your intent when you speak to Ereo?*

"Who?"

*Miranda. Miranda.*

My heart lurched, "Who said that?" and I slid from the stool. Alpha had only echoed the name; the first *Miranda* had come from a different voice—a voice high and to the side of Alpha. For the first time in my life, I realized the oddity of hearing voices at all. While gauging the door's distance in case I needed to bolt, my eyes strained to the shadows on the overhead beams. Nocturnal creatures scampered. "Alpha, do we have company? Seriously, I don't like this. Not a bit. What's going on here?"

*What is your intent when you speak to Miranda?*

"I just—I just want to help her." I spotted a rat. "Shoo, shoo. I was trying to console her."

*Untrue.*

"Well, I didn't succeed, but at least I tried."

*Untrue.*

My focus slowly shifted to Alpha, whose eyes reflected the truth.

I sat with a sigh. "Okay, you're right. I didn't want to console Miranda; I wanted to slap her. But she deserved it. I know she's sticky sweet, sappier than a maple tree, but she's a goddam idiot. Every time Fikus mentions Dorothy, Miranda gets all excited. 'Oh, Fikus said this, Oh Fikus said that.' You'd think Dorothy was sending him postcards from Florida. Well, I'm sorry Miranda believes in Fikus, crazy sorry, because Dieter loves her. He loves a woman who adores another man."

Alpha's eyes intensified. *And?*

"And, well, nothing. Let's call it a night."

The room glowed as if it were lit by a hundred jack-o-lanterns. *And?*

"And I got to get up early to—"

*AND?*

"AND I'M RIGHT" came out in a rush. "I'm right about Fikus; Miranda is wrong. Is that so terrible to want to prove?"

*Prove yourself correct? Or prove Miranda incorrect?*

"You're splitting hairs."

Alpha's eyes dimmed to their normal shine. *The distinct vibration threads into the result; Miranda is wary of your presence.*

I smiled, quietly appreciating my friend. Although Alpha wouldn't say whether Miranda would wise-up or whether MaGretta and Pop would regain their faith, and although he wouldn't talk plain English or provide winning lottery numbers, Alpha did something tons tougher than prophecy. He tried to keep me honest...which started me wondering. "Hey, Alpha, speaking of intent, what's your intent for hanging around me?"

*Poof!*

The room dimmed to the incandescent lights.

Weird. Very weird. I hadn't wished Alpha gone.

# 76

*Murdock racked up a mess of charges—pandering, collusion, bribery, robbery—but skirted all convictions.*

Winkle's ears flattened, her claws extending, her fur bristling. Coiled on her haunches, she growled like rolling thunder.

Spuretta snapped off the tape player. "Carly, put Winkle in another room before she attacks this recorder."

"It's not the recorder irritating her. It's Fikus's voice."

"Well, that voice is coming from a recorder on my lap."

Carly got up, tightening her bathrobe's sash and wishing her dad would call it a night and go home. "Why are we replaying the tape anyway? I've heard his vision so many times, I can recite it verbatim."

"Did you catch the parts where his tone changed?"

"A tone? I hear cracking as if his voice never smoothed from puberty."

"Do you have a transcript of the vision?"

"In my computer."

"Bring it up." Spuretta set the recorder aside. "You can read the parts I'm talking about."

While Carly's laptop powered up, she went to the kitchen for herbal tea.

*Grrgrrgrr.*

"Carly, where'd you go? Nice kitty. Settle down."

When Carly returned, her dad had one arm protecting his groin, his other arm outstretched with Winkle bumping beneath it for a petting. Carly set down two cups of tea. She stomped, "OUT." In two bounds, Winkle was through a small door leading to a pen. Positioned on the sofa's edge, Carly brought Fikus's transcribed statement onto the computer screen. "Where does his tone change?"

"Carly, your cat—"

"Never hurt an innocent person."

"She darn near killed a man."

"A rapist," Carly said, deliberately curt. "Winkle merely removed the offending weapon."

"Kid, as smart as Winkle is, she can't reason. She attacked from an instinct, not from a choice."

"Drop it, dad." Carly scanned the transcript. "What am I looking for?"

Spuretta took a sip of his tea, then gagged. The cup clattered back to its saucer. "Needs sugar."

"Tough. It's a blend of chamomile and dandelion."

"Those are weeds."

"It's tea."

"Well, my weed-tea needs sugar."

"I don't have any sugar. Now, do you want to complain about tea, argue about Winkle, or discuss a change in tone?"

"Let's talk about your tone. Is there a reason for it?"

Carly sat back. "Yeah. After months of tests, lab results, and DNA reports, all we can prove is who fathered Miranda. We have nothing on Fikus. Common sense dictates that his knowledge didn't come from psychic visions, but that's not good enough for Robyn. She doesn't care about withholding information or impeding investigations. She's not interested in time-gaps, tire irons, or revenge schemes. She'll only charge Fikus if we can put him on the ridge. So how does a change in Fikus's tone help us do that?"

"That reminds me." Spuretta pulled a pencil and paper from his pocket and slid it across the coffee table. "I'm writing to your Aunt Sherrise, but my Italian is a bit rusty. Could you translate one line for me?"

Carly waited for the punchline because her dad was surely joking. He spoke Italian fluently, often translating for Carly when their relatives called from Italy.

"Humor me," Spuretta said. "Translate, I sleep well with a good heart."

Believing it would take less time to humor him than to fight him, Carly took the pencil and paper and began working the sentence. After a few minutes, she held it out.

Spuretta glanced at the paper. "Keep it." He gave Carly a copy of the Minister's suicide note. "How do they compare? Note the wide spacing between the words. When you were confident of a spelling, your pencil grooved the paper. When you weren't so sure, you started to erase. The Minister smudged three letters, too, as though he were thinking to erase. Twice, you tapped the pencil on the paper. Pencil dots are on the Minister's note as well."

Carly nodded at the remarkable similarities. "You think the Minister was translating?"

"Judging from his books, I'd say the Minister spoke just enough Latin to impress another preacher, but not enough to write it fluently. So what man cares about misspelled words when he's about to drink lethal tea, even sweetened lethal tea?"

"Sweetened?" Carly looked up from her notes. Her dad was pinching his lip and staring at his tea as though mustering the courage for another sip.

Carly sighed. She took his tea to the kitchen. When she returned, she smacked a beer into her dad's hand.

"Thanks," he said. After a thirsty gulp, Spuretta relaxed with a satisfied smile. "That sure beats weed-tea."

Resettled behind the computer, Carly switched files to notate her dad's issues with the suicide note. She typed two lines, but then shook her head. "Fikus couldn't have killed his father. The fingerprints and the lab reports—"

"Kid, I darn well know what's in the reports, and I disagree. I don't believe the Minister's hand trembled from poison. I believe a cognizant man was translating English to Latin and that's why he cared about a misspelling."

"So you think the Minister killed Dorothy, and Fikus killed his father?"

"Nope. I believe the Minister had nothing to do with Dorothy's death or with his own."

"Fikus?" Carly leaned back, her thoughts spinning. "What about Miranda?"

"What about her?"

"If Fikus knew of his father's relationship, then Miranda had to have known, too. There's only one reason for her to withhold that information; she conspired with Fikus."

"Carly, do you really believe that?"

Unable to say yes, unwilling to say no, Carly shrugged. "How could Miranda not have known the man her mother was dating? No mother would keep the name of her daughter's father a secret when she's still involved with the man. Further, the Minister was a widower and Dorothy was single. It was no longer an affair; it was dating. At some point, Dorothy would have said, 'Hey, daughter, I'm dating the Minister.' That simple."

"That simple, huh?" Spuretta grinned. "Hey, daughter, I'm dating Gretta Schatz. Hmm. You're right, Carly, that was pretty simple."

Far less simple for Carly, who sat confounded by the news. "What are you saying? You're dating...*Ms. Schatz?* With an entire world of beautiful, eligible women, you picked a relation to *Zia?*"

Spuretta's smile flipped. He did not appreciate the comment, a fact made clear by his frown.

"Sorry, dad," Carly said. "I didn't realize you felt so strongly about her. Just watch your back. When Zia finds out, she'll make your life miserable."

"Don't you worry about Zia. We get along just fine."

"Zia *knows?*"

"She calls me Spaghetti-man."

"Oh, cloaked bigotry. How endearing."

"It has nothing to do with Italians. Zia gave me the nickname to keep herself comfortable with liking a detective. I'm glad for that, because I like her as well. We share an understanding."

"What understanding could you possible share with Zia?"

"Gretta is an angel. A beautiful angel."

Carly rolled her eyes. "Then she's an angel raising a devil."

"Then call me the devil's advocate."

"The devil, Zia, or the devil, Miranda? Because Dorothy sure didn't sneak out a bedroom window to meet her mystery man."

"You're right about that, kid...because Dorothy's relationship with the Minister ended a long, long time ago."

An astonished Carly drew back. "Where did you get that idea?"

"Why do you believe otherwise?"

Carly dug into her notes, sifting through records and statements.

"I'll save you the trouble, kid," Spuretta said. "You won't find a phone call, a love letter, or an eyewitness to support a recent relationship. Fikus planted the idea, insinuating it as a given. He's a slippery fella."

"So Miranda didn't know," Carly said quietly, more to herself than to her dad, who had been stating as much all along. Now eager to learn about the tone her dad heard, Carly closed the suicide notations and reopened Fikus's statement. "I have the transcript on the screen. Where did his tone change?"

"When he spoke of forgiveness."

Carly did a keyword search. "I asked forgiveness for—"

"No," Spuretta said. "Much later. Toward the end."

Carly hit *Enter*, then again and again. "Fikus spent five hours talking about forgiveness. Is there another keyword?"

"Gambling."

Carly typed *Gambling*. The screen shifted to the transcript's last page. "Is this it, 'He always forgave her; her gambling, her mouth, her whoring'?"

"That's the line. Who do you suppose our psychic is talking about? Coworkers and friends say Dorothy limited her gambling to a five-dollar loss on Monday night bingo. She seldom dated and no one knew her to curse. Tomorrow, relisten to the tape. Fikus punches an angry inflection into those three words; mouth, gambling, whoring. And his anger is genuine, personal, and current. More troubling than that—"

Just then Winkle galloped into the room. She rammed Spuretta's leg and then curled down, wrapping around his ankles. When the cat began its droning purr, Spuretta finally exhaled. "More troubling than that is a cheetah sleeping on your feet."

Carly tapped the keyboard. "Detective...scared...of...pussycat. Okay, dad, what else?"

"A key question: Why did Fikus poison his own money well? He had a whole flock of cash paying believers. Group sessions cost a hundred a head and packed a full church. He charged a thousand for private meetings. Why did he throw it away? He would have known he was ending his psychic career by accusing his father."

Carly cursored to the side to list possibilities. "Fikus either over-estimated his followers' loyalty or he underestimated their intelligence."

Spuretta shook his head. "He's a smart fella. He could have kept his career by keeping quiet. Instead, he accuses his father, discrediting himself as a psychic. A man's drastic acts are usually tied to money or to a women. But Fikus gave up his money and he doesn't have a girlfriend. He must have a mighty interesting reason for ruining his fame. Highlight that question; I want to come back to it."

As Carly stretched to her keyboard, she saw a red and green moth with a five-inch wingspan clinging on her sleeve. Startled by the moth's size, she sprang up and brushed at it, but the moth clung tight. When Carly nudged it, the moth only leaned. Using two fingers, Carly tried to scrape between fabric and moth, but its sticky legs pried off with the unnerving crackle of Velcro detaching. Carly swatted it, and immediately and strangely, she regretted it.

The injured moth hit the rug and staggered.

Winkle's head lifted, her eyes zeroing in.

"Winkle, NO!" Carly swept up Winkle and then plopped her onto Spuretta's lap. Spuretta's arms shot straight out to the sides. Carly gathered his hands and firmed them onto Winkle's back. "Hold her. Just hold her." Carly opened the front door and waited for the moth to regain itself.

"Uhhh, kid, why do I have a leopard on my lap?"

"Hold her tight."

"*Tight?* You want me to hold onto a lynx so you can...save a moth? Carly, a moth won't leave a lit house for a dark night."

Just then, the moth flitted up from the rug. Beneath Spuretta's palms, Winkle's muscles constricted, preparing to pounce. "Carly? Carly Jean?"

"Just hold her."

The moth fluttered out the door. Despite what Carly expected, the moth didn't pause at the porch-light, nor at the solar lamps edging the walkway, nor at the streetlight across the road. The moth flew straight, disappearing into darkness. Slowly, Carly shut the door, her mind churning with Zia's insane superstitions about moths. *Don't kill it*, she had said, *what you're looking for is right in front of your face...if the moth is unexpected.* Carly shook her head; what moth is ever expected?

Spuretta's hands came off Winkle, leaving her fur imprinted with two moist handprints. Instead of clearing his lap, Winkle draped herself, like a spotted throw blanket, over Spuretta's legs. Spuretta jiggled his knees. "You can get off now. Go on, kitty." He poked her.

Winkle arched up and playfully batted his hand.

"Carly Jean, get your cheetah off my lap."

Carly's heel thumped, "OUT," and Winkle took off. Carly returned to her laptop. While searching keywords, she said, "For the hundredth time, Winkle is a Savannah. She's not a leopard, lynx, or cheetah. Honestly, dad, sometimes you exaggerate more than—" search results popped on the screen, "—Zia." Carly stared at the computer, her stomach knotting.

"Kid, what is it?"

"Neptunes, they were once cited for gambling, right?"

"Yep, back in '93 or '94. The locals were betting on the Scavengers. Officials came in and closed the place for two or three months. Liz had to pay a hefty fine, too. She owns Neptunes. She's a real nice lady."

"Sure, dad, like Attila the Hun's sister." Carly looked up from the screen. "Do you suppose Liz is running the betting pools again?"

"I'm not in the loop, but I'll call the FBI—I mean, Sal. It's a good excuse to catch-up. Where are you going with this?"

"Hang on." She clicked more keys and raised other files. Carly scanned the notes, and then her fingers flurried and the files shifted. "Damn."

"Carly, let's hear it."

"Zia is a regular at Neptunes. If they're running pools, Zia is gambling. She's the type. And she has got a mouth." Carly read and reread her notes.

"Kid, let's talk a minute."

Carly leaned back, her palms pressing to her forehead, her defensiveness swelling. "Yes, Zia accused Fikus of stalking, but Fikus claimed the same about Zia. And yes, I checked out Zia's calls, but Fikus was never there. And yes, I initially forgot to advise Zia of a Protective Order, but I've told her about it several times since. But she won't listen. If I mention any legal recourse, she hangs up." Carly took a deep breath. "What else do you want to beat me up about?" Carly's palms came down.

Her dad was gaping. "I only wanted to know what you were reading. It was siphoning the blood out of your face."

"It's my notes from talking with Zia at the Youth Center."

"What about your notes? I thought you told me everything."

"Well, everything I thought was important. When Zia had the argument with Fikus on the beach, he wanted to know what it would take for her to believe in him. Zia wanted lottery numbers." Carly glanced at her screen and then mumbled, "Or the name of whoever was with Dorothy on the ridge."

"Aw, Carly."

"Dad, I thought she was embellishing."

"You mean lying."

Carly blended a nod with a shrug.

Spuretta sighed. "And not much later, our psychic shows up at Zia's doorstep to give her a name. Anything else you didn't bother to mention?"

Carly hedged with another faint nod.

"Let's hear it, kid."

"At the Minister's house, when Zia was acting nuts, according to her, she was swearing at Fikus."

"Fikus? Wasn't he resting in his bedroom?"

"I guess he came out to the porch for five minutes. The officers were sure Zia was screaming at them. Since Zia hates cops, I just assumed—Well, I might have assumed wrong."

"How friendly is Zia with the Scavengers?"

"They all seem to know her, but how well, I can't say. But dad, Zia seemed to be stalking Fikus, not the reverse. Nobody dragged Zia to the church, and she had no business at the Minister's house."

"Print up a copy of your notes, *all* your notes. I'll take a look at them in the morning." Spuretta stood and slipped on his coat. "Carly, learn to see folks clearly, all folks, including Zia. Zia doesn't present truth the way you want it presented. That's not who she is. Zia paints truth. She pokes it, pinches it, and downright piddles on it, too. But underneath her painting is a canvas of truth."

Carly slouched low. "To uncover that canvas is not only exhausting but also infuriating."

"You think so? Then you better learn to see yourself clearly, because it's not Zia's painted truths nor her fanciful world that's riling you." He looked across the wall of photos. "No, siree, not at all."

"Dad, her world—"

"Her world agitates your world."

"What?"

"You'll figure it out." Spuretta leaned down and kissed her forehead. "Goodnight, kid." He paused at the front door. "By the way, did Zia tell you what set her off?"

"What do you mean?"

"At the Minister's home, when they cuffed her. I'm assuming Fikus triggered the outburst. Did Zia tell you what he did?"

Carly peered into the eyes of the most decent man she had ever known, a man who still tipped his hat in greeting, who still opened doors for ladies, and who only used *darn* for his strongest curse. Although he had seen it all and had heard it all, he would not witness this vulgarity from his own daughter.

Whether a white lie or a painted truth, Carly smiled at the irony of needing one now. "No, dad. Zia didn't *tell* me."

# 77

*When Zia's disdain for Ereo jeopardizes*
*what Zia values and loves,*
*her fragment against Ereo will likely shrink.*

The Seaside Times printed the facts; the tabloids made it worth reading. A series of articles portrayed Fikus as a conman who learned of his father's crime, and then used the information to dupe Miranda and garner a fortune from grief-stricken families. Fikus plummeted from grace.

I celebrated his comeuppance, but I celebrated alone. Around town, moods sank into glum despondency. My gloating *I-told-you-so*'s received anemic shrugs. News of our psychic embroiled in fraud added to the gloom of autumn's doldrums that had replaced summer's fun-filled debauchery. Weekend tourists canceled reservations for livelier spots up the coast. Orders for wind chimes halved, then halved again when they should have been doubling for the upcoming holidays.

Dieter's month off from work turned into eleven weeks. When he came back, he worked fifteen hours a day to relieve our exhausted Pop.

Miranda resumed her job at Otto's Autos, but she didn't move into our house. With Dieter's help, she secured a nearby rental. Although she still joined our family every evening for dinner, she barely spoke to Dieter. Dieter spoke even less to her. Their cloud of discord stifled our family's friendly banter. Suppers became silent movies starring Negative Ned and Gloomy Gale. Dieter wouldn't discuss it—not that I expected him to—and Pop ignored it, also expected.

When I questioned MaGretta, she told me to mind my own business.

"But what's none of my business?" I asked, but she still refused to tell me. To break the chain of secrets, I attacked the weakest link. "Hey, Miranda, after dinner, could you stick around to help me organize the shack?"

The minute I jury-rigged the crippled door closed, I asked, "What's going on with you and Dieter?"

"It's personal. Now what boxes do you want—"

"Come on, Miranda. Three months ago, you guys marinated in love. Now your togetherness causes a barometric drop. What happened?"

Miranda shrugged and continued rummaging in a bin. "You have shells tangled in fishing line. If we separate—"

I shoved the bin aside. "Look, if you don't want to talk about it, say so."

"I don't want to talk about it."

"Okay, but what don't you want to talk about?"

"I just told you, I don't—"

"Was it something I did? Something I said?"

"Zia, this has nothing to do with you." She pulled up a stool, so I sat, too, my knees to her knees. After a while, she said, "It has to do with Fikus."

"That figures. What did that freak do now?"

Miranda ruffled. "You're like everyone else, casting stones at a man you know nothing about. Fikus showed tremendous courage to turn in his father. It tore him apart. And now he blames himself for his father's suicide. When my mother died, I thought that losing a loved one was the deepest wound a person could suffer, but I was wrong. Being accused of involvement is far worse. Fikus has no time to grieve; he's too busy defending himself. He lost everything—his friends, his career, his church."

"The church?"

"It's closing. Nobody wants to hear Fikus. He's the town's pariah. His mailbox is stuffed with anonymous threats. Death threats. Kenzie Cove hypocrites have warned Fikus to get out of town or else. Fikus had to buy a gun for protection. He's not a freak. He's my—My—"

"Your what? Guru?"

Miranda bristled. "No, Zia. He is a frightened man who lost everything he valued. And what sin did he commit? To serve justice, he turned in his own father. People in this town ought to be ashamed. You included."

"I get it." But I didn't get it at all, nor did I speak again until Miranda's reddening cheeks had simmered into pink. Then, with an abundance of patience, I said, "Just for a moment, try to look at this from another perspective. Pretend you're reading a story about a loser who suddenly gains fame as a psychic after locating a body. Then, out of billions of people, the killer just happens to be the psychic's father. Is it a rolling ball of coincidences that the psychic knew where to find the body of his dad's victim? Do you see a few dots that might connect?"

"Your dots assume the Minister confessed to Fikus. I believe Fikus learned everything through a vision."

"Is that the rift between you and Dieter? You believe in visions and Dieter doesn't?"

"That's part of it." Miranda fidgeted for a minute. "And we disagree on supporting Fikus's church."

"I thought you said the church was closing."

"The old church is closing. Fikus has plans for a new church. It's his dream. He asked for my support and I gave it. He's buying the old Duvall mansion down the coast. We're going to restore it. It has been in the bank's hands for years, but it used to be in Fikus's family. Monique Duvall's maiden name was MacKenzie. When Fikus explained the mansion's heritage, the bank reduced the price."

I bit my lip to keep a straight face. "Uhm, Miranda, there is no such beast as a sentimental bank. They charged Christ for the cross, and when he rose from the dead, they demanded interest. The bank's price reflects a dilapidated dump. And it's cursed."

Now Miranda suppressed a laugh, but my smile was gone. The neglected mansion was so creepy even the word creepy found it creepy. Although teenagers pilfered their parents booze, scored their first joint, and spun donuts at the brink of Angels Peak, the true right of passage among the coastline's youth was a night in that horror-house. *Me?* Hell no, despite my elaborate stories to the contrary.

I wasn't frightened by the legend of a small spook seen wandering the mansion on the night Mrs. Duvall died. Legend had it that the ghost was green and red, which sounded like a Christmas ghost. Or maybe a clown ghost. Either way, the ghost seemed more comical than scary.

The legends hadn't kept me out of the place; it was the facts. When I heard the tale of the nanny murdering the Duvall kid, I started having nightmares. More than once, my screams woke up the family. MaGretta and Pop blamed it on my books. But they were wrong. I'd been digesting horror novels for years, but I never woke drenched in sweat and unable to breathe. But that's what happened when I learned about the murderous nanny.

From then on, thoughts of the mansion were like thoughts of the sea, both causing my mouth to dry, my head to spin, and my body to heat like an inferno. While Miranda chatted excitedly about restoration plans, sweat began to freckle my nose. I fanned my face, which was likely the color of my hair. I guess Miranda didn't notice that she was killing me. "STOP!" I told her. "I don't care about your curtains or blinds. It's just a damn church."

"No. We're not just building a church. Fikus wants a place where people can live and work together as a family."

"A commune? Is Fikus haunted by ghosts from the 70s?"

"It's not a commune. Not exactly. The difference is..." And she went on and on—commune this, church that—with all kinds of definitional-crap.

I tuned her out and tuned Alpha in. *Do you hear this shit? She's nuts. Can I slap her now?*

*Your intent is self-serving.*

*What the hell is her intent? Raising the bar of stupidity?*

*Intent vibrates into the result; the bread bitters.*

*Dammit, bread doesn't bitter. And if it did, it wouldn't bitter because of intent. Wait. Intent?* "Miranda, what kind of support did Fikus need? Financial?"

"It takes money to build a church."

"But you don't have any money."

"My mother had a small life insurance policy. When I talked it over with MaGretta—"

"MaGretta? What does MaGretta have to do with this?"

"I sought her advice. She's a firm believer in supporting churches."

"Oh shit."

"Zia, I have never met anyone as generous as your MaGretta. She's not rich, but every month she gives a dozen churches a hundred dollars each."

"Wrong. Those are god-mongering evangelists who ought to be shot for fleecing lambs. And MaGretta gives her donation envelopes to Dieter and me so we can add our contribution before we mail it. And we contribute plenty; we rewrite her checks but less two zeros."

"That's dishonest."

"No, that's love. MaGretta has no concept of money management, but she can recite every passage in the Bible. If we didn't rewrite her checks, MaGretta's sweet generosity would have bankrupted Pop a long time ago."

"Then tell MaGretta the truth."

"What truth? That she's inept with money? Should we take away her checkbook, treat her like a child? Or do you mean the truth about the evangelist pigs and their grandiose lifestyles, and to hell with MaGretta's crushed spirit? Dieter and I waded through a ton of solutions, all were quick and easy. Finding a solution that didn't bruise MaGretta's feelings or step on her beliefs, that was tough. Damn tough. And it's also why Dieter still lives at home; I'm not quite trustworthy with those checks. I might have lost one or two. Maybe cashed them."

"Dieter never told me."

"Because I repaid it."

"No. He never told me about rewriting MaGretta's donations."

"Oh. So how much did you donate to Fikus?"

Her chin tilted high. "Fikus needed money to build his dream. I gave him all the money from my mother's insurance policy."

"Jeez, all of it? How much was it? Three thousand? Five thousand?"

"Twenty."

"Twenty what? Not twenty—TWENTY THOUSAND? Are you insane or insanely stupid? Without a dime to your name, you forked over twenty freakin' thousand dollars? Unbelievable. Shit, now I know what's bugging Dieter. You're another lamb trotting off to a financial slaughterhouse, and he's trying to figure out how to protect you without hurting your feelings. Well, let me save everyone time; you're an idiot!"

She firmed to her feet, her cheeks splotched in anger. "I don't care what you think. And I don't need protection. I love your brother, but he doesn't support the church. And if it's a choice between Dieter and my faith, I choose faith."

"Faith in what? Faith in God or faith in Fikus?"

Miranda fought the door open. "I'm sorry I confided in you. I won't make that mistake again."

"Of course not. You're too busy making new ones."

Miranda stomped out.

I threw a mallet at a bin of shells. "Alpha, did you hear what she did?"

*True.*

"She's a goddam moron."

*Your intent is self-serving; the bread bitters—*

"FINE!"

*—to kinship.*

"Kinship?" Immediately, I thought of Dieter. "Aw, shit. I blew it again, didn't I?"

# 78

*Bronk bronk bronk.* Hitting the snooze button gave me ten more minutes. *Bronk-bronk-bronk.* And another ten...then another. An hour later—*Tuesday!*—I bolted upright and flung off the covers. Before the blankets had settled, I had pulled on my cutoffs, sweatshirt, and sandals. Carting a toothbrush doused with Crest, I made a lap through the kitchen. "Great breakfast, MaGretta. I bussed my own plate. Thanks!"

"But I didn't see you—"

"You were showering." Before the screen door clattered shut, I was out the back gate and running with a toothbrush bobbing in my mouth. Envisioning Billy's anxious little face, I skidded, nearly tumbled, down the slope to the beach.

Billy was sitting calmly on the shore, his arms wrapped around his knees, his gaze fixed on the sea. I spat toothpaste and back-pocketed the brush. "Hey, kiddo, sorry I'm late. Power outage. My alarm never went off."

He didn't turn.

"Billy?" I walked around to his front side, and then crouched. "Hey, buddy, you feeling okay?"

He rubbed his stomach.

"What's the matter? Are you hungry?"

He shook his head.

"Bellyache?"

He nodded.

"Want me to take you home?"

He nodded again.

"No problem. But which side of your tummy—"

He sprang to his feet and then sprinted toward the ridge. He sure didn't move like a sick kid, but I headed back up the slope to drive Billy home.

When we drove past the Colonial, Billy pointed, then pinched his nose and tapped his armpit—our code for stinky jerk.

"Yep," I said, "he reeks."

When I opened the car door for Billy to get out, I gave the customary wave to his peeking mother. Like always, she straightened the curtains. Billy skipped to his porch.

"Hey, you're not sick," I called after him. "You just wanted the day off."

He looked back with a grin.

"Little shit." I had started around the car when I noticed the silence. Actually, I felt the silence. No dogs barked, no music played, no sirens howled. No sound or movement among the small cottages that stood like peasants' huts in the midst of a white Colonial castle.

Fronting each hut, a splintery board impaled a rusty mailbox, whereas the castle had a doublewide box enshrined in bricks. Crass grandeur. I stared so hard, my eyes watered from missed blinks.

According to Miranda, hate-mail stuffed the Colonial's box. But if I peeked inside, I figured I would find only utility bills and junk mail, proving to Miranda that the drama-prince had lied. While I thought about this, *Ouch*, my nibbled thumb began to bleed.

Maybe the mailbox contained a rude letter or two, but big deal. For years, my family received nasty letters, some so thick, they came with an index. But Pop never bought a gun. MaGretta handled hate-mail with dignity; I had to buy ad space in the local paper to publish my apologies for the anonymous accusers to read.

Whistling nonchalantly, I strolled up the road. Across the street, Potato-face Woman peered from her window. I gave her a one-finger wave. Her spying ended. But Nosey-Nellies don't quit for long, so I walked faster.

At the mailbox, I semi-knelt as though tying my sandal, "Dum-dee-dee-dum-dum-dum," while scoping the area for prying eyes. Safely unnoticed, I stood and lowered the wide metal flap. "Whoa." Assorted envelopes topped bundled stacks. But removing mail from a box is a FEDERAL CRIME—that's how the Postal Police say it, FEDERAL CRIME—even if you only remove a lousy postcard.

To stay within a misdemeanor, I pressed my arm against my tilted head, and squeezed inside the box. Flicking aside bulk stamps, I examined the handwritten envelopes. *Return addresses?* Nobody sends threats with return addresses, not one among the hundreds that I ever received.

I stretched to the back of the box and then fingered some envelopes with drawings. One had a heart dotting the 'I' in Fikus. On another, a dollar sign sealed the flap. Still another, the smears of lipstick. *Sealed with a kiss?* Revolting. Nearly all had the fluid handwriting of niceties, not the embossed streaks of anger. I wanted—needed—to read one, but when I tried to wedge in my other arm, the stupid metal refused to flex against the mortar.

I crammed in further, my sandals scraping grout for a lip on the brick. One hand clawed to hold on, my other hand split an envelope's seal and finagled a letter halfway out.

"Looking for something?"

I lurched, spilling from the box and scraping the bridge of my nose on the sharp metal edge. "I was just—just—"

"Going through my mail?" Fikus reached past me, took the mail, and slapped the box shut. "You played me." His lips barely moved. "I jumped through ever hoop you asked of me, but when I came to collect your loyalty, what did you do? 'Oh, Carly, he's stalking me. Come quick.' You played me."

"I didn't do crap."

"You deceived me. But I'll rebuild my fortune, while you, Zia, a gutter-mouthed slut, will never rise above stringing garbage and coaching misfits."

Respecting his insanity, I inched backwards. He came forward. "What begins in deceit, ends in disaster. Understand? It's not over until we're even."

His breath, a rank weapon of polluted molecules, left his lungs and traveled up my nose. Inhaling sideways for fresh air, I saw Potato-face Woman watching from her window. I stopped backing up. "Fuck you, freak."

Fikus's pupils momentarily strained at the corner. "Lucky you."

"Big man when nobody's watching, huh? You're a lousy parasite. After bilking the grieving, you're now preying on bleeding hearts who think assholes like you need hugs, sympathy, and of course money. How did you find so many new victims so fast? You must have one impressive spiel to fill up your mailbox and con Miranda twice."

"Miranda loves me."

"Miranda doesn't know you, but she will, freak."

"So will you." He came closer.

I stepped back with a polite wave to Potato-face Woman.

Fikus smirked. "I promise you, Zia, on my grave, you'll apologize ten times for every time you have ever called me a freak." His eyes darted to the side of me, but no one was walking up from behind. I didn't fall for it in high school and I wasn't going to fall for it now. Fikus lifted his hand, "Deceitful... lying...slut," and punctuated each word with a tap to my nose.

I hauled off and slugged him.

He crumpled with melodramatic injury.

*WHRRRrrrr* came from behind me. I spun around.

Carly and Spuretta exited the detective's car.

Fikus was splayed on the ground. "Gotcha." Then he writhed and moaned, "Officers, help me. Please. She assaulted me."

Spuretta helped Fikus to his feet.

Carly fronted me. "What are you doing here?"

"Oh, come on. You don't believe—Carly, for chrissake, he's faking."

"Faking?" He palmed his mouth then showed everyone a pinprick of blood. "Does this look like I'm faking?"

"You bit your own lip, you candy-ass freak."

"I want her arrested," Fikus yelled. "I'm filing assault charges."

Carly yanked me half-circle. "What is going on?"

"Nothing. Well, okay, it's like this—"

"Officers," Fikus said, "I caught her going through my mail. When I politely asked her to stop, she went crazy. She shouted threats and obscenities, and then struck me."

"That's what she did." Potato-face Woman came running from across the street. "I'm a witness. I saw her climbing into this man's mailbox, and I phoned the police."

"Yes, ma'am," Spuretta said. "We'll talk to you in a minute."

"I should have pressed charges after Zia attacked me on the beach," Fikus said. "Instead, I prayed she would get psychiatric help."

"Back at you, freak," I told him.

"Officers, please," Fikus whined, "her psychotic assaults have got to stop. She's delusional, a danger to the community. Jail her before she hurts anyone else."

I pointed to my car. "Carly, I was just dropping off a kid."

"Lies," Fikus said. "No child lives on this block."

"That's right," Potato-face Woman chimed in. "Not a one."

"She parked up the street," Fikus said, "then skulked through the bushes to get into my mailbox."

"Were you in his mailbox?" Carly asked.

Potato-face Woman nodded incessantly like one of those bobble-headed toys you stick on a dashboard.

Spaghetti-man looked a little concerned while he waited for my answer.

"Jeez, maybe, sort of, but Fikus is giving me a bad slant."

Carly gripped my elbow and escorted me to her car. Spuretta told Fikus to settle down, settle down, while Fikus kept hollering, "Put her in jail. JAIL!"

I climbed into the backseat. Carly got behind the wheel and twisted around. "You have no business here. What did you think you were doing?"

I gazed out the window. "Forget it."

"Forget it? That's your answer? Forget it? Seems everywhere you go, a fight breaks out. But in your mind, it's never your fault. You didn't cause the battle in the church, you were defending yourself when you struck him on the beach, and when his father died, you were provoked into gracing the scene with profanities. And now—"

"For chrissake, your slant is worse than his."

"—and now, you're here again, at his home, in his mailbox. And you punched him."

"I didn't—"

"WE SAW YOU!"

"Oh. But he set me up."

"A setup? Again, a setup? How in the hell did he set you up?"

I didn't feel like answering.

"Zia, I am trying to believe you. I am trying hard. Give me something. Anything. How did he set you up?"

"He, uhm, he touched my nose. But he saw your car—"

"Did he cut your nose?"

"Well, no."

"Zia, was Fikus telling the truth? Did you come here to threaten him? Swear at him? Go through his mail? Zia, for once, just tell me the truth. Did Fikus accuse you of one damn thing you didn't do?"

"Yeah. I never skulked."

"Funny," Carly said. "Real funny." She turned forward.

I flattened to my back. My eyes closed. "Hey, Carly?"

"What?"

"Do I need a lawyer?"

"You need a shrink."

Minutes later, I saw Spaghetti-man's bright smile at the window. "You got some swing. Yes, siree, a swing like your brother's."

I sat up. "Hey, how come you're so nice, but your daughter is so—" I jiggled, cockeyed and tongue dangling, mimicking an electrical shock.

Spaghetti-man chuckled.

Carly did not.

"I'm sure this whole thing is a simple misunderstanding," Spaghetti-man said. "Why don't you ladies grab some lunch while I convince Mr. MacKenzie to see it our way. It might take a minute or two."

"Don't waste your breath on the freak," I said. "If he won't be reasonable, it's no big deal. My indiscretion will be kicked down to Court Five, the Honorable Lon Bartholomew presiding." I leaned back, confident fingers laced behind my head. "Yep, it's been a long time since I entertained the Lon-Man. He appreciates a well-spun tale. He's a great guy."

"He's also retired," Carly said.

"Retired?" I asked.

Spuretta confirmed it with a nod.

"Then who's on the bench?"

"Birch," Carly said. "Thomas Birch, remember him? He transferred from the Juvenile Court." She adjusted her rearview mirror, no doubt to watch my melting composure. "What's the matter, Zia, don't you feel well? I'm sure Judge Birch remembers how entertaining you are. Make it good, Zia, because it's adult jurisdiction now. Hell, I'm laughing just thinking about it."

I slumped under waves of nausea. "Mr. Spuretta, forget what I said before. I mean, please convince the freak of a misunderstanding. Please try hard. Judge Birch isn't too fond of me. Years ago, he had this crazy idea that I pressed cap gun stick-ums onto the end of his gavel."

"Did he get a bang out of it?" Spaghetti-man winked. "Don't worry about MacKenzie. Go on and have a good lunch."

"Thank you. And may I say, I wholeheartedly agree with MaGretta; you're a gentleman of fine character and of rare caliber."

"She said that, did she?" His eyes sparkled. "Well, she's an angel. Yes, siree, a lovely angel. Next week, we're celebrating four months of courtship. I'd like to take her someplace fancy. Do you know where she might—"

"Oh, for the love of God." Carly fired the ignition. "We're on duty. A prowler; ring any bells?" She revved the motor. Her dad stepped away. Carly shifted into reverse and hit the gas. The car lunged backward, tumbling me forward. Carly fishtailed the curb, and then slammed on the brakes within an inch from hitting my car's bumper.

I pulled upright. "Should I get out?"

"NO!" She killed the motor and turned in her seat. "Which house? Which house did you drop off a kid?"

I pointed. "That yellow cottage."

Carly peered at the house. "Before I verify your story, is there anything else I should know?"

"What do you mean?"

"I mean to be clear," Carly said. "A kid is a child. You dropped off a child, not a goat. And a cottage is a house, not cottage cheese."

"You feel okay?"

"Dammit, Zia, I don't want to walk up to that door and discover some bizarre kink in your story. No surprise definitions or muffled meanings. No nicknames, no symbols, no bullshit. To be clear, you're not talking about a cheese-eating goat. You dropped off a boy who lives in that house. Right?"

"Wow, what bee flew up your—"

"RIGHT?"

"YES! Jeez, yes. His name is Billy. He's ten years old, but small for his age. He has a big head like Charlie Brown, fuzzy white hair, and a nasty scar on his windpipe. He slipped while dancing and sliced his throat on a metal railing. He needed a dozen stitches. Now does that sound like something I would make up?"

"How do you know him?"

"Every other Tuesday, he comes to the beach and helps me collect stuff for the chimes. If the weather is good, he wants a ride home. If the weather is lousy, he likes to walk. Sounds backwards, doesn't it?"

"Of course it's backwards. You're backwards." Carly cracked the door open. "But I'll check it out."

"Oh, wait. He's also a mute."

"A mute?"

"Yeah. And he's phobic about his hands. Don't expect him to shake. He won't touch anything, not even a door handle."

"Christ, anything else?"

"Well, his mom is kind of weird. She peeks from the drapes and—"

"QUIT!" Carly slammed the car door and started the car. "Let's get something to eat."

"But I thought you were going to—"

"Do what? Verify a story about a phobic, fuzzy-haired mute whose mother fits *your* idea of weird? No, Zia. Not today."

# 79

*An asteroid carried off my work.*

I was starving, but cheap-Carly said, "Just coffee," before she went to the restroom. When she returned, we drank our coffees in silence.

Later, Carly received a call from her dad. After listening for a while, Carly said, "Yes, I'll tell her. No, she'll agree."

"Hey, wait," I said. "What am I agreeing to?"

Carly cupped the phone. "Protective Order and restitution."

"Restitution? For what?"

"Assault, battery, trespass, mail tampering. Pick one."

"How much will this cost me?"

"Less than a fine from Birch."

"This stinks."

Carly returned to the phone. "She's delighted." While Carly talked with her dad, the waitress set the bill next to my plate. I flicked it across the table. When it was near the table's edge, I sucked in a big breath and blew hard. Carly fumbled to catch it. "I'll see you in ten minutes," she told her dad and closed the phone. "Grow up, Zia."

"What? There's an overhead fan."

Carly checked the tab and flagged the waitress, "Ma'am, this is not our bill. We didn't order steak and prawns or a bottle of wine."

"Your friend did," she said. "Her to-go order is waiting at the register."

"I was hedging my bets," I told Carly. "If I had to go to jail, I didn't want to go hungry."

Carly gave her credit card to the waitress. "Remove the bottle of wine."

"Can't," the waitress said. "Your friend had me uncork it."

I smiled. "I didn't want to go sober either."

Carly got pissy. "Every time I do you a favor, it costs me."

I shrugged. "Fikus cons the gullible, but I'm the one fined. He spies on me, but I'm the one slapped with a Protective Order. Don't blame me for the ironies of life."

"Bullshit," Carly said. "It's not ironies; it's you. You're a wormhole of distorted reversals sucking everyone else in."

"Hey, you sound like me."

That startled her. Maybe shocked. Her eyes fluttered, and she told me to shut up. "For the mercy of all shrinks overbooked with crazies babbling your name, just...shut...up."

Carly can't take a compliment, but I didn't say another word.

Over the following weeks, between each afternoon class of Blue Dolphins and Red Herrings, I rushed home to intercept the mail so MaGretta wouldn't find a court envelope bearing my name. Then one day, I came home to an empty mailbox. "Shit!"

"Looking for this?" From around the yard, three Red Herrings walked up, mail in hand.

"Give me that." I snatched it, leafed through it—nothing but junk—and returned it to the mailbox for MaGretta to find. "You got two seconds to explain."

"You start the class late," a kid said.

"And you cut out early," another kid added.

"Deal with it," I told them.

"We are!" The kid punched numbers into a cell phone and then held it out. "Talk to Terry."

"Terry?" I grabbed the phone. "Terry, if you're behind this—"

He interrupted, prattling off dates of the qualifying meets before the final diving competition. He accused me of selfishness, my divided attention causing sucky dives and sinking morale. He didn't want to hear my excuses. Red Herrings had a long-standing record of losing, and competing counties had a bad habit of snickering, *Red Catfish*, bottom feeders. "Remember how that felt?" Terry said. But this class, for the sake of future Red Herrings, had worked their butts off and intended to make a difference. They intended to win. "Do you give a shit for how hard we've worked?"

Tarred in blame and feathered in guilt, I coughed up a feeble, "Yeah, but, well, you see—"

Again, he cut me off, only this time, to propose a solution. A Red Herring would arrive at noon to babysit the mailbox. When the postman left, the kid would stash the mail behind the boulders fronting our junipers.

"Listen, Brainiac, you can't take someone's mail. It's a FEDERAL CRIME. No, I'm not yelling. That's the way you're supposed to say it."

"It's your mail," Terry said. "If we have your permission, it's not a crime."

That threw me—permission negating a crime. My thoughtful pause clued Terry. "Wow, you ripped off someone's mail?"

"No, of course not. I just forgot the permission part."

"Do we have yours? We need our coach back. If our dives improve, we'll kick ass on the Northern Pricks."

"Pikes," I mumbled with an ambivalent, "I guess."

While Terry's henchmen slapped hands, Terry said, "Oh, Coach Zee, I almost forgot. When you get your mail, leave your envelope in its place."

"My envelope?"

"For us. Ten bucks a day."

"You want to be *paid?*"

"Cash. Your checks bounce."

Two hundred dollars poorer, I got the expected Court papers...and an unexpected letter from the California Department of Motor Vehicles. I retrieved my bag of tickets, jammed them into my backpack, and used the kitchen phone to call the DMV. I pressed one for English, six for registration, two for fines, and then three by mistake. I hung up and started over. After wading through questions and pressing correct numbers, and after surviving twenty-two minutes of *Concertos for a Deaf-Wish*, I heard a human voice, "DMV, pwease to hep you."

Even though I had pressed one for English, I remained pleasant while explaining my situation.

Coldly, he tore my excuses apart. In his final quip, he said I should have learned my lesson last year. "So saw-wee."

"Sorry nothing," I said. "And don't tell me what to learn until you learn to speak English. Get it?"

*BaZzzzz,* came the dial tone.

*WHAM, WHAM, WHAM.*

"ZIA!" MaGretta seized the phone, checked it and the countertop for breakage, and then gently rested the phone back to its cradle. "What would make you do such a thing? Answer me that?"

I started a fitful pace. "Aw, the stupid DMV—I mean, the stupid library. Carly never fixed any of my—my expired library passes. This stinks. Stinks! I can't register my—for a new library card. How can I read if I can't register my book? I need my book to get around. Stupid Carly, this is all her fault."

"Oh, no, Carly is a nice girl. I have a book for you. It is a beautiful love story, so romantic, so rich in the heart, the story will move you to tears."

"Yeah, yeah, I'm crying already. Hey, did Spaghetti-man ever tell you where Carly lives?"

"Not the address, but it's in The Sand Trap."

"The Sand Trap? Are you sure?"

"I think so. Zia, just call her."

"Oh, believe me, I'll call her." I pecked MaGretta's cheek, grabbed my backpack, and headed to the door. "I got choice words to call her."

On the way out of town, I stopped at Freddie's Fill-Up where each gallon of gas comes with three free ounces of soda. After filling my empty tank, I filled a bladder-breaker cup with forty-eight ounces of Orange Crush.

I hadn't been to The Sand Trap since my twelfth birthday at 2 a.m., when my friend, Kathy Moon, provided the transportation—a hotwired Plymouth Duster—and I supplied the fun—a potato-gun and a bucket of gasoline soaked Super Balls. But twelve-year-olds don't know crap; we didn't know how to change a flat tire, which caused us a one-mile hike lugging spud-guns and ammo, and we didn't know about dangerous people, which nearly cost us our lives.

We hid among the trees and brambles on a small hill across from the houses, and we fired flaming balls to the one street below.

Stoners stumbled outside, *"whoa, the sky is falling"* dancing and dodging the bouncing fireballs. Kathy and I were giggling and laughing and popping off more when the stoners were joined by paranoid cranksters.

Suddenly, *powk, powk, powk*, the tree beside Kathy sprayed bark.

We tore through the brambles and blackberries, leaving them tinseled with blond and red hair. We didn't stop running until dawn.

When I turned into The Sand Trap, I slowed to ten miles an hour, almost forgetting about a bladder that ached to pee...and almost forgetting where I was—The Sand Trap had changed.

Gardens and fountains had replaced junked autos and strewn trash. Broken windows and tattered curtains had become French doors and faux-painted shutters. Someone had removed the dead trees, sheared the brambles, trimmed the vines. Each parcel, once overgrown with thistle and sawgrass, now had a visible backdrop of ocean blue.

From behind a hedge, a woman popped up wearing a sombrero covered in rosemary. "Can I help you?" she called out.

I stopped the car.

She set down her clippers, removed her gloves, and held her hat level as she came to the street. With her back straight, she crouched at the passenger window and introduced herself as Ms. Duggan. "Are you lost?"

"You have a little rosemary—"

"Yes, dear. I keep the prunings."

"On your head? I mean, as opposed to putting them in a basket or a—"

"Are you lost or are you looking for someone?"

"Carly Spuretta. Do you know where she lives?"

Sprigs tumbled as she nodded. "Is Carly a friend of yours?"

"More than a friend. She was my sorority sister at Idaho University."

She eyed my car's clutter. "Then you should know where she lives."

I guess driftwood, paperbacks, and a rotten peach arouse suspicion—suspicion in a woman capped in rosemary. *Jeez.* Tightening a Kegel to hold onto the soda, I explained how I rescued Carly from self-destruction, funded her rehab, and counseled her recovery.

Despite my best creative crap, Ms. Duggan tapped her chin, still unsure.

I ransacked the console, found the car registration, and waved it at her. "Look at this." And she did. Then I dug into my backpack, pulled out my wallet, and flipped the ID. "Do you see my picture? Read the name, Zia Schatz. Same name and address as on the car registration." I snatched it back. "Now, straight up, my brain is dissolving in uric acid. Either give me her address or let me use your bathroom or plan on explaining to Carly why you let her sorority sister wet her pants."

She made me wait another minute before saying, "Drive straight. Carly has the only parcel beyond Trapper Road. She comes and leaves that way so I don't know if she's home."

"Thanks." I hit the gas.

I found Carly's house, but it appeared empty.

## 80

*He hid in a shallow vein above the main trail*
*and ambushed returning prospectors.*

From the moment he saw her, he hated her. Strangely and completely. And that occurred years ago when she pretended to defend him in high school. And in that moment, he fell on the razor's edge of love and hatred, mistaking one for the other. And Zia knew it.

He lowered the binoculars. "Get ready for equity."

From the beginning, she had taken advantage of Fikus's mistake. Played him. She had let him believe it was love, when all along, she had known the truth. It wasn't love they felt; it was hatred. Now, when he watched her, he surged with the truth—hatred. He had wasted so many years believing a lie.

When Zia had turned onto Sandstone, Fikus had driven straight, intending to take Trapper Road. But when he neared the turn, the Detective's car drove past. Fikus approached the T slowly, watching Carly's bumper thin into a needle. Fikus then parked in a shallow vein above the main roads.

He brought the binoculars back to his eyes.

Zia knocked on the door and then pounded. She tried ringing the doorbell continuously. Fikus whispered, "Give it up, Zia. No one is home."

Zia tried the handle. Fikus smiled to himself; no detective leaves their house unlocked. But the door opened. Fikus pressed into his binoculars.

Zia poked halfway into the house, backed out, and then stepped inside.

Fikus had planned to ambush Zia on her drive out of The Sand Trap. But knowing she was alone in Carly's house gave Fikus a better idea, one that included equity to Carly for ridiculing Fikus in front of Dieter and Miranda. For that, Carly deserved worse than having her house violated by Zia. She deserved her home changed into a bloodbath.

Fikus opened his glovebox where he kept his gun and his bowie knife. He chose the knife because acquiring apologies would take time, and Zia owed a lot of apologies.

He slipped on his gloves.

# 81

*To cats, all matter fits into one of four groups*
*—cat, threat, food, entertainment.*

Some girls, barely squatting, feet inches apart, can piddle neatly on the ground. Other girls can crouch like sumo wrestlers balancing on tiptoes, but their pee will still curve to a thigh, stream down a leg, and wet their sock and shoe. I'm the latter, and I didn't want to drive home while pee dried on my feet. I banged on the aluminum screen, *clank, clank, clank*, pounded on the door, *thud, thud, thud*, and hit the doorbell a dozen times, *dingdong, dingdong, dingdong*, but nobody answered. In a last effort, I tried the doorknob...and it turned. "Hey, Carly, are you home?" My legs twined around a cupped crotch. "Carly? CARLY?"

Unless Carly counted squares of toilet paper, she would never know I had used her bathroom. I slipped inside.

Carly kept a spotless house—not surprising. What did surprise me was her conflicting decor—mundane safety battles creative risk. Conformist Carly had a matching sofa and armchair, separated by a standard coffee table, and centered on a tan rug. It reeked of normality.

The creative-Carly housed her TV and stereo in an antique armoire. Pastel painted walls exhibited her blue-ribbon photographs, and preserved manzanita limbs wrapped around planks for her trinkets and books. Beside the shelves was a weird statue of a guardian cat, a mixture of lynx and leopard.

On the chance that Carly was parked in the garage, and while I had been knocking, she had been showering—and was now loading her gun—I called out, "It's Zia. Don't shoot. No one will believe it was an accident. Carly?"

I tiptoed toward the hall. "Carly?"

Behind me came the sound of a rumbling stomach. *Grrrgrrr.*

I turned slowly. The statue's tail whipped the floor. *Wump, wump, wump.*

*Batteries?* My eyes scrunched and reopened; The statue's eyes did the same. "Oh shit. You're real?"

*Grrrgrrr.*

My mind raced through the National Geographic Specials for the emergency measure when faced with a lion. *Don't panic! Roll downhill, climb a tree, play dead.* Had the cat been a bear, I would have known what to do.

*Grrrgrrr.*

My heart was thundering so hard, I patted my chest to calm it down. Instantly, the cat coiled onto its haunches.

*Shit!* I dropped to a ball, flung crisscrossed arms over my head—*I'm going to die*—and braced for the impact of claws and fur.

Nothing. Eventually, I peeked. The cat had disappeared.

I tilted sideways to see into the kitchen. No cat.

Pop was right; I needed to quit reading horror. I started to stand.

*Grrrgrrr.*

"*JEEEZ!*" My head jerked back. The beast was watching from atop the armoire. Screw emergency measures; I flew down the hallway, burst through the end door, and slammed it shut. Locked it, too. Puffing and panting, I sat down. Seconds later, I realized I was sitting on a toilet. Instantly, my need to pee returned. My trembling hands took a while to unzip my shorts.

In the middle of releasing forty-some ounces of soda, I heard a bump, then came an explosion of noises—thuds, whams, thumps, and the tinkling sound of breaking glass. At the tail end was a screech or a yowl, maybe human, maybe not. I couldn't tell above the orange-crush gush. *CLANG.*

*Screen door? Window?* I stood, zipped, then robotically flushed. "Damn." I jangled the lever, but it wouldn't unflush. All sounds muffled under the toilet's *swoosh.*

When the toilet finally quieted, I pressed an ear to the door. I heard nothing, not even the lion's menacing growl. Before I opened the door, I stuffed washcloths into my pants, looped a towel over my head, and armed myself with the plunger.

At the hallway's opposite end, the cat licked its paw.

I brandished the plunger. "Shoo, shoo."

It started toward me.

"Shoo! Shoo! SHOO!"

It was limping, each hobbled step leaving a red paw print. When it reached me, it bumped its head into my knee. *A lion-goat?*

I sidestepped, thinking to scoot around it. It curled down with a bloodied hind-leg side up. It began thrumming in what I hoped was purring, and it extended a wounded paw. *Grrrgrrr.*

Part of me wanted to help the animal, but a bigger part of me echoed my remark to MaGretta when her friend's nephew was hit by a train. *A train didn't kill him; his stupidity did.* Remarks like that have a way of boomeranging; *a lion didn't kill her, her stupidity did.*

I started inching around the lion. Its paw swiped my leg, but it was a paw with retracted claws. *Damn.* I put down the plunger and took hold of the paw. "If you eat me, I swear, I'll give you worse than heartburn."

*Grrrgrrr.*

A nasty glass shard protruded from the pad. My fingernails, chewed to the quick, couldn't pinch it free, and the cat's quivering told me to stop trying. "Where did you get this? Did you jump through a window?"

*Grrrgrrr.*

"Stop that. Stop that weird noise. It makes me nervous, okay?"

*Grrrgrrr.*

I pulled the towel off my head and used it to wipe the hind leg. Fresh blood immediately re-glistened. "What the hell happened to you?"

The cat licked my hand, hopefully in gratitude and not in a pre-taste. "Listen, I need medical supplies, and you need to stay still. Walking around will push that glass in deeper and track blood throughout the house. Get it?"

*Grrrgrrr.*

"Dammit, it's meow. Meow, meow. Cats are supposed to meow, okay?"

*Grrrgrrr.*

Having already ransacked the hall's bathroom, I knew it had nothing more than hygiene sundries for overnight guests. I headed for Carly's bathroom. Upon entering her room, my breath left, completely awed.

Across each wall hung brilliant photographs capturing heights of color and depths of black and white. Among the photographs was a precious jewel that eclipsed all others—a flawless portrait of a Coral Pink Sand Dunes Tiger Beetle matted in emerald green, a tribute to the beetle's green head.

My mouth dried from gaping admiration...and envy. How and when had Carly taken this? And why? She didn't even like bugs. For months, I had begged Dieter for a loan so I could go to Utah and get one of these beetles. He stalled so long, I ended up haggling with internet dealers and paying top dollar for a mediocre specimen. But at least I finally obtained one of these endangered beetles, the prize of my mounted collection.

For several minutes, I forgot where I was and what I was supposed to be doing.

Inside Carly's bathroom, I found tweezers, bandages, scissors, gauze, and tape. Before leaving the bedroom, I gazed again at the photo...and left it alone, the ultimate proof that I was not a thief. I dabbed my misty eyes before forcing myself back to the issue.

The damn issue had wandered off. That's the problem with cats; they never listen. I followed red tracks up the hallway. "Hey, kitty, kitty, where did you go? I have tweez*zz*—WHAT THE HELL?"

Carnage. All around me, carnage. Shattered frames sprinkled glass over crumpled photos. Lamps and tables were overturned. Throw pillows oozed intestinal stuffing. Water dripped from a toppled vase while flowers wilted on the rug. *Crap.* Brain-dead partiers left an easier cleanup at Woodstock.

The lion-goat rammed my leg. *Grrrgrrr.*

"Look what you did. You're a bad cat. Bad, bad cat." I stepped between gutted pillows and then sat in the column of light shining in from the screen door. The cat settled beside me, turning its paw toward the...*sunshine?* Rethinking, I was pretty sure I had closed the front door. Tilting, I looked outside. Nothing seemed out of the ordinary. I returned to the paw.

When I pressed between digits, a set of mini pitchforks unraveled. *Grrrgrrr.*

"Don't give me that crap. I came in to use the bathroom. That's it, just a quick pee and a few squares of toilet paper. Nobody would have been the wiser. But no, you had to pick today to traipse your furry butt out of the zoo, or circus, or wherever you're from, and go on a rampage. And of all the houses to rip apart, you had to choose this one, today, while I'm here. Shit, I just know I'm going to get blamed."

I removed one shard and started working on another. The cat quaked in reflexes to pain. "Hold still, you big wuss." Next, I snipped the clotted fur on its hind leg, "Whoa," exposing a big meaty muscle deeply slashed. I sucked in a sharp breath. "I take it back; you're not a wuss. Not at all."

Using gauze strips and tape snips, I fashioned a row of butterfly stitches. I fixed a large bandage on top. The cat's tongue, coarser than pumice, raked my face. "Yeah, yeah, sappy crap. Listen you, don't ever eat a beetle, okay? And tell your whole species, too."

*Grrrgrrr.*

Before leaving, I secured the cat into a spare bedroom and then tacked a note on the door.

*Warning! Trapped Saber-toothed tiger. Call Zoo.*

# 82

*A died-in-the-wool stalwart,*
*Matthew hadn't come for the gold.*

Carly entered The Sand Trap from the south road, Sandstone, to deliver a new barbecue grill to Ms. Duggan. During the last neighborhood potluck, Winkle broke her leash to pounce on Ms. Duggan's grill. The grill toppled, the knobs cracked, and the steaks vanished.

"Oh, Carly, it's a beauty," Ms. Duggan said looking over the new grill. "It must have cost a fortune, my goodness, Carly. I told you not to worry about it. You shouldn't have gone through all the trouble."

"It was no trouble," Carly said. "I still owe you for the steaks."

"Don't you dare. Those steaks are on me." She smiled brightly. "Thank you, dear. You're such a thoughtful girl. Your friend could learn a few manners from you."

"My friend?"

"Your college friend. I gave her your address hours ago. Haven't you been home?"

"No. Did you get her name?"

"I did but I can't recall it. She was your sorority sister. She helped you overcome—well, some of your personal issues."

"What personal issues?"

"Well, I wasn't prying; your friend just blurted it out. Stuttering."

"I don't stutter."

"You certainly don't. You're very well spoken...now. But when you left the treatment center—"

"Treatment center?"

"For alcohol abuse."

"I've never had a drinking problem."

"Oh. I assumed it was alcohol. Was it drugs?"

Carly rubbed her temples. "No, Ms. Duggan, I've never had a problem with drugs, alcohol, or stuttering."

"Oh dear, oh dear. Carly, I would have called you, but the girl's driver's license matched her car's registration. Oh, I should have known better than to trust a crude girl like that."

"Crude? Was she a small redhead? Zia?"

"ZIA, that's it. Yes. You gave me such a start."

Carly pushed up a reassuring smile, telling Ms. Duggan everything was fine. "Zia is just—She's just odd, but harmless."

Ms. Duggan pondered a moment, then nodded knowingly. "It's the residual effect from her amnesia."

"Amnesia?"

"Her surfing accident. I had an uncle who fell from a ladder. He suffered amnesia, too. When he tried to regain his memories, they mixed with fantasies. Your friend needs your patience. Jog her memory with photographs from your college days in Idaho."

"Idaho?"

"That's right, Carly. The more memories you revive, the less room for her fantasies. It worked miracles for my uncle."

Carly looked down the street. "Do you ever quit?"

"Pardon me?"

"Nothing, Ms. Duggan. Thank you for the advice. I'll keep it in mind."

Zia's car was not at the curb nor in the driveway, much to Carly's delight. But delight turned to confusion when she opened her front door to the shambles. "Winkle? Winkle?" Spotting the bloodstained rug, her voice pitched high, "WINKLE!"

From down the hall came a scratching sound of claws raking wood. Carly ran to the bedroom. She grabbed the posted note as she flung the door open. She dropped to her knees and hugged her bloodied cat. "Winkle, what did you do? What did you do?"

Her dad's warning blared through her mind; *a wild animal is unpredictable.* Carly shook her head. "No. Not you, Winkle. Not you."

She pushed Winkle onto her side and peeled back the bandage. A meticulous row of makeshift stitches sealed a five-inch gash. Before reattaching the bandage, Carly noted the layers of gauze, the overlapped taping, and the cat's wiped and clipped fur. A vet could not have provided a better dressing.

Tender care, yet a living room destroyed? Carly could not make sense of it. She made several phone calls. Neither the hospital nor the Med Center had treated anyone for claw-type injuries. No animal attacks reported.

Carly stood, patting her chest in relief.

Winkle saw the signal and crouched, preparing to spring.

"No, no, Winkle, don't—"

But Winkle leapt five feet high, knocking Carly into the wall.

Grasping the Savannah, Carly's face buried into fur. "You dummy, I wasn't patting for you."

*Grrrgrrr.*

Carly craned back to spit out cat hairs. "No more pouncing until that leg heals. Understand?"

A loving tongue braised Carly's cheek.

Carly called Zia's cell phone. When Zia's voicemail answered, Carly hung up. She then called the Schatz's house phone.

"She's at Neptunes," MaGretta said. "She left after dinner."

"So you saw her?"

"Yeah, sure."

"Did she look all right?" Her question caused an awkward silence.

"She looked like Zia," MaGretta finally said. "Why should she not look all right?"

"Colds. Everyone is coming down with colds. That's all."

Through the evening and the following morning, Carly left messages on Zia's voicemail. Zia neither answered her phone nor called Carly back. Mid-afternoon, Carly drove to the Schatz's house. "Hello, Ms. Schatz, is Zia home?" After fielding questions—Yes, she would call her MaGretta; no, she wasn't hungry; no, not sick either; yes, she loved home cooking; no, she never tried pickled cabbage; no, never tasted a pickled egg either; yes, her dad was a nice man; yes, a smart man, too—Carly learned that Zia was on the beach collecting shells.

While MaGretta talked on, Carly started to ease away.

"There are two paths," MaGretta said, "but one is not good. Take the path with the rocks; that is the good trail. The other trail leads to a drop."

"Thank you," Carly said, and then, "Hi, Mr. Schatz," because Otto had joined MaGretta in the doorway.

As Carly walked off, she heard MaGretta shout a warning, "Don't be fooled. Don't be fooled."

Carly widened her strides, "I promise, I won't be," thinking the whole Schatz family a little strange.

&—

MaGretta and Otto shared a puzzled look.

"What did she mean by that?" MaGretta asked. "I tell her to take some food, and she promises what? Not to be food?"

Otto shook his head. "Auk. Their whole generation is much like Zia, a little...funny."

&—

Not far from the Schatz's back fence, the trail forked, one smoothed with sand and one pitted with rocks. Carly chose the rocky path. The ridgeline formed a wide half-circle around the beach. At the tip of the opposite curve, something glinted. Garbage, Carly figured, either metal, tin, or glass was catching the afternoon sun at just the right angle. Two steps later, a crow landed in Carly's path, its wings flapping aggressively. "Go away," Carly said to the bird...and to Zia's nonsense echoing in her head about the meaning of a bird landing in one's path. *Caww, caww.*

Reconsidering the glint, she squinted at bushes and trees a half-mile away. *Caww, caww.* The bird flew off. *Aurrg.* Carly's heels turned back to her car. "Damn you, Zia, you and your infectious insanity." She was driving around the bend to the far side of the ridge because of a Coke bottle or a Pepsi can or a foil gum wrapper. She could not have felt more foolish...until she pulled into the parking lot and spotted Fikus's van.

She parked beside it, got out, and looked into the van's window. A map strewn on the passenger seat had The Sand Trap circled in red.

Angling in from the side, Carly crept to the ridge. Fikus was wedged between shrubs, flat on his belly, binoculars to his eyes. Carly stretched to her toes to follow the binoculars aim. Without a doubt, they centered on Zia. Carly arched over Fikus and cupped the lens.

Fikus jerked onto his back. Scratches and gashes marred his temples and forehead, bandages clung to his neck, and a wad of gauze, soaked through, dangled from a torn ear still bleeding.

Carly swallowed her gasp to hold a face of indifference—*but oh Christ,* Fikus's wounds deserved a doctor's treatment.

Fikus slid the binoculars under the brush as he hustled to his feet. "Detective, what a surprise."

"I bet," Carly said. "What happened to you? Were you shaving during an earthquake?"

Fikus laughed gratuitously. "I fell while hiking and got tangled in some barbed wire."

"Barbed wire, right. I think my cat tangled with something, too, but I can't figure out what it was. She only attacks cockroaches, snakes, and rats, the creatures that cause a good person anxiety. I say, 'good person' because my cat seems to sense a bad person, as if a bad intent gives off a smell."

"Yes, interesting, but what brings you to—"

"To Winkle, a person with a bad intent is like a cockroach, only bigger."

Nervously, Fikus pocketed and unpocketed his hands. Carly reached into the brush and brought up the binoculars. She inspected them, "Expensive." She held them out. But when Fikus went to take them, Carly swung the binoculars to her eyes. "Mind if I have a look?"

"Uh, well, I—"

"What were you watching, Fikus?" Carly pretended to look across the beach. "What is so interesting down there?"

"Birds. I'm an avid bird watcher."

"Bird watcher? What kind of birds were you watching?"

"All kinds. Today, well, a flock of crows."

Carly lowered the binoculars. "A *flock* of crows? Coming from a bird lover, that's an odd term to use."

"I don't understand what you're driving at."

"Well, there's a brood of hens, a rafter of turkeys, a wedge of swans. So what is the bird watcher's term for a group of crows?"

"There are—There are several terms. It depends on the region. It's somewhat debatable. It's—"

"It's a murder."

A tremor of anger flickered in Fikus's face. "The murder is solved, detective. If you have evidence to the contrary, my lawyer—"

Carly rammed the binoculars into Fikus's chest, winding him. "Murder of crows," she said. "And Zia is not a bird."

After a few coughs, Fikus regained his breath. "Zia? Is she down there? I hadn't noticed, detective. I have no desire to spy on Zia."

"Good. Go find some birds."

"You can't bully me. I haven't broken any laws."

"The Protective Order works both ways."

"Look at my distance. I'm nowhere near Zia. I have every right to stay here and watch birds."

"There are no birds on that beach."

"Are you blind? The beach is covered with—"

"NO BIRDS." Carly encroached into Fikus's space, her eyes steeling onto his, her voice menacingly low. "Not a single feather exists within five miles of here...or I will toss your ass off this ridge, drag it across the beach, and then bust you for violating the order. Understand?"

Fikus's face torqued with rage. His head lowered briefly. When it lifted, his cheek twitched with a forced smile. "Thank you for pointing out Zia," he said. "After the nightmare she put me through, I'll do anything to avoid her. Your charade of 'no birds on the beach' is obviously in my best interest, and I appreciate—"

"Goodbye, Fikus."

Without another word, he walked off. Carly followed. When he got into his van, she got into her car. While he drove down the main road, Carly kept an intimidating hug to his bumper. Miles beyond the northern curve, she flipped a U-turn. Once more, she was walking down the trail leading to the beach. This time, however, nothing glinted from across the ridge. While she was descending the slope, a crow landed, though off to the side, not in her path, but startling her all the same. *Caww, caww.* Carly lost her balance. She skidded for several yards before she regained footing. Brushing her backside, she felt the flap of a torn pocket. With a defeated sigh, Carly surrendered to Zia's ridiculous superstitions about why a bird returns—either to give thanks or to receive thanks, Carly couldn't remember which. "Thank you or you're welcome, whatever works. Now get lost."

Crossing the beach, Carly called out, "How goes the chime business?"

Zia glanced up from cleaning a sand dollar and then turned her back.

Ignoring the snub, Carly sat beside Zia's pile of driftwood. "Do you want some help?"

"From who? You?"

"Do you see anyone else? Wait, please don't answer. Yes, Zia, from me, who's visiting your world of reversals. Despite your involvement in trashing my home, I'm pleasant instead of angry, and you're surly instead of contrite."

"Involvement? I don't know where you get your information."

Carly placed the printed note before Zia.

Zia studied the one line. "No, sorry. That's not my writing."

"Who else on this planet would call it a saber-toothed tiger?"

"Damn." Zia thumped a palm to her head. "I should have said saber-toothed leopard. But I swear, that leopard was already in your house. I only came in to use the bathroom. That's it. I just needed to use your bathroom."

"So, what happened?"

"That leopard is what happened. It escaped from the zoo and—"

"It's a Savannah, a loving pet."

"Whoa! That thing is your pet?"

"Zia, didn't you see the animal door in the living room or the flap over the door painted with a cat's face and bearing the words, *home sweet home?*"

"Yeah, I saw it."

"Well, what did you think?"

"I thought what anyone would think; the big cat ate your little cat."

Carly sighed. "Go on."

"So I'm on the john peeing, when suddenly there's a bunch of crashes and booms. I came out of the bathroom and found what you found. But I didn't do it; your pet-leopard did. I don't know why it went ballistic or how it was hurt or whether it jumped through a window or attacked a mirror."

"Were you alone?"

Carly saw candid surprise in Zia's face. "Yeah. Why? Who do you think was with me?"

"No one. You say you were alone, then you were alone. I believe you."

"You do? Why? What's going on? How come you're here? Why do you believe me? Knock it off, Carly. I mean it. I don't need the pressure."

Her backward paranoia started Carly laughing.

"IT'S NOT FUNNY," Zia shouted. "You have no right to believe me. I know where this leads. First, you'll assume I'm telling the truth, next, you'll expect it. Well, forget it. I'm not living up to anyone's expectations, get it? Sure, laugh now, but you won't think it's funny when—STOP LAUGHING!"

"Then shut up. Your absurdities are killing me."

Zia's arms crossed.

"I'm here to thank you," Carly said, "for bandaging my cat."

"Leopard."

"All right, my leopard."

"Don't patronize me."

"Sorry, Zia, I'll try again. Quit the bull. It's a Savannah, not a leopard."

"That's better. And don't pull that trusting crap again."

"So what brought you to my house? You didn't drive to The Sand Trap just to use my bathroom, right?"

"Tickets. I can't register my car."

"The tickets, right. I promise I won't leave without them, okay?"

"Carly, you're scaring me. Am I dying?"

"Zia, seriously—"

*"Seriously?* Oh, shit, I *am* dying?"

"Zia, I think Fikus trailed you into my house."

"He did?" Her attention shot to the ridge.

Carly tracked her line of sight. "You knew Fikus was watching you?"

Zia nodded, still fixed on the ridge. "I see him constantly."

Carly tugged on Zia's shirt. "He's gone now. I got rid of him. Now listen to me, a Protective Order goes both ways. In other words—"

"Jeez, Carly, you act like I've never been served with a PO before."

"If you know how it works, why haven't you called the police?"

"I can't."

"Zia, you have to. When he comes near you—"

"Forget it. Those who dodge the law, don't cry to the law."

"Where did you read that? Criminals' Ethics for Dummies? You asked for my help, now let me help you."

"I will. Grab those bundles." Zia stood with an armload of driftwood. "With your help, I can do this in one trip."

Carly blocked her. "Zia, put the stuff down and look at me. Dammit, Zia, put it down. Just STOP."

With a long exhale, Zia slowly let the driftwood roll from her arms and drop to the sand. For several seconds, she held onto the last stick before she let that one fall, too. When Zia's eyes lifted from the pile, Carly saw a seriousness in Zia she had never seen before. "What do you want from me?" Zia asked so calmly and so quietly, it briefly disarmed Carly.

"I want you to quit the bullshit," Carly said. "Just quit it. You called me, and I'm part of the law, now let the law help you."

Zia shook her head. "I never called a cop. Never. I called a friend."

# 83

*I wanted to go home long before my body released me.*

After showering and scrubbing grease from his stained hands, Otto trimmed his mustache and doused his cheeks with Old Spice. With lips pinned back, he searched for dinner remnants hiding between his teeth. Finding none, he smoothed a wad of gel over the last few hairs topping his head.

Tonight he would not worry about Dieter's problems with Miranda, Zia's troubles with police, or MaGretta's trials with Italian cooking. Tonight was Otto's night, his yearly celebration with Rosie.

On the table by the front door was a bouquet of red roses and a basket with pickled meats, champagne, and two glasses. With the roses and the basket in hand, Otto went to the dining room where his family was finishing their supper. "How do I look?" he asked.

All turned to appraise him. "Prince Charming," Zia said.

MaGretta nodded. "So handsome. Strong and handsome."

Dieter and Miranda raised their milk-filled glasses. "Happy anniversary."

"Do not wait up for me," Otto said. "I could get lucky." He chuckled as though the joke were fresh and not a joke he had repeated on each anniversary for more than two decades.

"Take your coat," MaGretta said. "It is a cold night."

"Auk." Otto detoured through the kitchen to tuck a bottle of Schnapps into the basket—another tradition for more than two decades. From the doorway, he called, "Auf wiedersehen."

And "Goodbyes" and "Auf wiedersehens" echoed back.

Before going through the rear gate, Otto looped his arm through a folding chair. He lumbered along the path until he reached the spot. Their spot. A grassy knoll among patches of sand where he first saw, and instantly loved, his Rosie. She was seventeen and brooding. Otto had called it brooding, but Rosie had insisted it was something else. Something Otto couldn't recall. Maybe reflecting or meditating. Years later, they would have a daughter who would come to the same spot to brood. And like her mother, she would not call it brooding. "Auk, women mix the meaning of words." He looked up. "But that is okay by me."

He set the bouquet down a few feet in front of his chair. He uncorked the champagne, poured two glasses, and then placed one glass beside the roses. Relaxing into his chair, he raised his glass. Just then, a crisp, ocean breeze swept in, causing him to shiver and remember his coat still hanging by the door. "Auk." He topped his champagne with a splash of Schnapps. "This will keep me warm." He raised the toast again. "To us, my Rosie, and to our starry night together. Happy anniversary. Happy anniversary my—my love."

His toast suspended, Otto stared at the other glass, the one slightly tipped on the bumpy ground, the one not raised. His shoulders rounded, sagging. He was tired and sad and then very angry with himself for spoiling their anniversary. "I—I just miss you so very much."

He swallowed a rising lump before he swallowed his drink. His lips smacked. "But you know that already."

Otto refilled his glass without champagne, and then settled back to update Rosie on the year's events. "Let's see, Dieter did not marry Janey. Now he is in love with Miranda Norst, and she loves him, too. But they are mad at each other so much of the time. I do not understand why, and they do not tell me. Auk, maybe that is best. I am sure it is only the stubbornness of youth and no reason to worry.

"And our daughter is—well, do not worry about her either. Zia is Zia, a little—" Otto teeter-tottered his hand, "—funny. But she will outgrow it. Someday.

"MaGretta has the goo-goo eyes for a detective man, Mr. Spuretta. Yeah, sure, he is Italian, but he is a good man. You would like him. He asked for my blessing to propose to MaGretta, but I told him, 'No, do not propose.' Then Mr. Spuretta wanted to know the reason, 'Is it because we have not dated for long?' And I said, 'Auk, no. MaGretta is no spring chicken.' Then he asked if I do not like Italians. And I said, 'Tell me this, what is with your country and cheese? Cheese in this, cheese in that. Ever since MaGretta changed the cooking, I am stopped up.'

"I let Mr. Spuretta be sad for a while because Italians like to be sad when they're in love. That is in their blood. But do not worry, my Rosie, I did not let him mope for too long."

Otto took a few gulps of Schnapps to warm himself. "I told Mr. Spuretta, 'Yeah, sure, MaGretta loves you very much. I know this. But I also know my sister. She will never leave our home while Dieter and Zia live under the roof. Soon, Dieter will get a place of his own. But Zia, auk, that one, I cannot predict.' And do you know what Mr. Spuretta did, my Rosie? He is a smart man, this Italian, very smart, and he is a man deeply in love. He is buying the house next door to ours. Now, MaGretta will not have to choose between families. Tomorrow, he will ask for MaGretta's hand in—"

"Good evening, Mr. Schatz, enjoying yourself?"

Otto jerked, twisting in his chair.

Fikus came around to his front. "I'm sorry, did I startle you? Please, don't get up."

Otto set down his drink. "What do you want, young man?"

"Fikus. We met several months ago, the day my father passed away."

"I know who you are. I am sorry for your loss, but you should not be here."

"Are you expecting someone?" Fikus gestured to the glass of untouched champagne.

"Maybe. But you—you should leave."

"It's cold out here." Fikus rubbed his gloved hands together. "I hope your guest is bringing an extra jacket."

"Young man, I think you should go."

Fikus smiled. "Mr. Schatz, have a pleasant evening." When he turned, his foot toppled Otto's glass. "Oh, I'm so sorry." Fikus grabbed the glass and the Schnapps. "Let me pour you another. It's the least I can do."

"That is unnecessary."

"But I insist." Taking the glass and the Schnapps, Fikus strolled toward the ridge. "It's a rare evening," he called over his shoulder. "Typically, the Danberry Lighthouse is shrouded in mist, but not tonight. Tonight, everything is perfectly clear."

"Yeah, sure." Otto scratched his head. He wished Fikus would bring back the Schnapps and leave. "My guest will arrive soon."

Fikus returned the bottle, and he placed a glass of Schnapps into Otto's hands.

"Goodnight, Mr. Schatz." Fikus left quickly.

"And goodnight to you," Otto said. When Fikus had crested the hill, Otto whispered, "He's a strange one, my Rosie," and took a long swallow of his drink. "Must be the Irish blood. Or the Scottish blood. Auk, whatever blood it is, it makes no difference. He is a strange one."

Otto emptied his glass and then poured another. While he chatted with Rosie, sprinkles of pinholes popped through the darkness until the entire sky was glittering with stars. "You see this, my Rosie? I ordered one million stars for our anniversary." Otto winked.

The stars winked back.

All the stars. All at once.

"What is this?"

The stars twinkled and glistened...and then moved.

*Moved?* Otto rubbed his eyes and then peered harder, his mind spinning to make sense of what he was witnessing.

His chest felt heavy—heavy and tight and growing tighter, squeezing the air from his lungs.

His breaths became sips, labored and shallow. But each breath he expelled seemed to feed the stars; they grew larger and brighter, pulsating and twirling and fascinating Otto beyond his pain.

Specks of light expanded into moons. The moons then ballooned into planets. And the planets danced.

*Oh my God, how they danced.* Across the sky, they flitted and bounced and landed into two parallel lines.

*A Pathway?* Otto gasped; it was the pathway he had always imagined, the pathway to Rosie.

A stream of silk, a figure, glided down between the rows of planets and moons and stars.

Otto's jaw dropped...as did his glass of Schnapps. He clutched his chest, forcing a whisper, "My—My Rosie, is it—is it you?"

"Otto, my dear husband, take my hand."

Her voice was so lovely, her words were so soothing, her arms were so delicate...and so close. *So close!*

Otto wrenched against torturous pain, his arm swinging upward for Rosie's hand, his body falling forward, his agony exploding.

His hand clasped hers.

His pain vanished.

Rosie smiled. "Don't look away."

Otto smiled, too, his grip tightening. "Oh, my Rosie, my beautiful Rosie, I will never look away from you again."

# 84

*Ain't no tree branch killed this man.*
*He was good and dead before the avalanche.*

For the third time, Spuretta looked out the window, and for the third time, he frowned. "It's still overcast."

"Relax," Carly said. "It will burn off. The weatherman promised."

"I must have been nuts to plan a picnic in winter. Gretta will freeze."

"It's romantic," Carly said. "You'll sweep MaGretta off her feet."

A wicker basket stuffed with gourmet foods sat on the kitchen table. The receipt for the basket's contents spilled from the garbage. Carly glimpsed the receipt's total and pulled the paper-tail out from the trash. She brushed off the coffee grounds. "This can't be right."

"I should have hired violinists," Spuretta said rubbing his jaw. "Should I shave again?"

Carly didn't answer, she was too busy digging into the basket, withdrawing each item, and comparing it to the receipt. "This is unbelievable. Five hundred bucks for salty fish eggs, two hundred for Dom Perignon, ninety-seven for pâté de foie gras. What a rip-off. Canapés, truffles, petit fours. You don't even know what half of this stuff is."

"Do too."

"Really? What's a petit four?"

"It's for—for eating petits. Now arrange it back the way Stella had it."

"Stella? Stella at Grand Gourmet?" Carly checked the receipt for the store's stamp. "That figures. I ought to bust her for assaulting a wallet."

"Stella helped me."

"Stella robbed you for not proposing to her."

"Naw. Me and Stella are just friends."

"That's why she robbed you."

Carly repacked the items and then turned to her dad. She straightened his collar and brushed lint from his jacket.

Spuretta stepped back. "Did I clean up okay?"

Carly's eyes watered. Her dad looked better than okay. He looked happy, the deep-rooted Soul kind of happiness that comes from being in love. "Yeah, dad, you look terrific."

"Aw, kid, there's no reason for tears."

"Yes, there is. I'm going to be related to Zia." Carly smiled. "Now get out of here."

"You're a darn good kid." After a hug, Spuretta kissed each side of Carly's face, accidentally rouging her cheeks with his whiskers. "Darn it. I need to shave again."

"Won't do any good," Carly told him. "Nanna said you were born with stubble. You gave her whisker burns when she nursed you. Now stop stalling. Do you have the ring?"

"Sure do. Got it right—" Spuretta patted his empty pocket. "Guess I'm a little nervous."

The phone rang.

"I'll get it," Carly said, "you get the ring."

Spuretta returned flashing a grin and jiggling a velvet box.

Carly slowly replaced the receiver. "Dad—"

"What's wrong? Who was on the phone?"

"Miranda. She's at the Schatz's house. Otto went to the beach last night and, well, that's where they found him this morning."

His breath held, Spuretta waited.

Carly shook her head. "Heart failure. Dad, I'm so sorry."

"Oooh." His eyes closed momentarily. Then, a strong inhale brought a rush of air into his lungs. He grabbed his coat and keys before he ran out the door. "Gretta needs me."

# 85

*Tell me goodbye.*
*Nobody ever tells me goodbye.*

My Pop...*left.*

\*

\*

\*

I walked out of the funeral because the attendees vaulted the bar of stupidity; *your dad is in a better place,* and *he'll always live in your heart,* and the worst, *was he baptized?*

I walked out because it's bad manners to punch people at a funeral. You're supposed to return hugs, and you're supposed to let cheeks, slippery with tears and snot, press against your cheeks, already wet and slick.

I walked out because I could not be nice.

"I'm so sorry."

*For what?*

"He was such a good man."

*I know.*

"If there's anything I can do..."

*Yeah, get away from me.* "STOP CRYING. For chrissake, part of life is— People get old and they—I mean, I realize that Pop—Just stop. Everyone stop clinging and hugging and telling me that Pop—that he—that he—"

\*

\*

\*

I left.

\*

\*

\*

My Pop...died.

## 86

*I languished on the floor in Game Town
because nothing changed for me. Nothing.*

Life is not the snippets of crap printed in greeting cards. Life is a Scrabble board, each person a lettered tile, and Father-Time a lonely gamer.

When Time connects our tiles to the tile of another, our humble letter becomes part of a greater meaning. Then along comes Death, a jealous bully, who's not allowed to play, so he kicks the board. Tiles shift, letters jumble. Thankfully, Father-Time remembers the tiles in play, but unfortunately, he can't recall their exact position. After all, it's a big board. So he rearranges the letters, forms new words, new meanings. But sometimes, despite Father-Time's best efforts, he has a leftover tile. It just doesn't fit. Not anywhere. Not anymore.

A few months after the funeral, in a private ceremony behind our house, MaGretta married Spaghetti-man. Dieter gave her away, and Carly shot the pictures. In all the photos, tears glossed our beautiful MaGretta's eyes. Most tears matched her smile of joy at her tile's new board placement—Gretta Spuretta, we couldn't say it without laughing—but some photos caught MaGretta's sorrow for having left her prior position beside Pop.

Now Spaghetti-man's wife, she moved into his house. Next door. Well, she moved her dresser and clothes, but her presence remained. Daily, she came over to scrub the floors and prepare the meals. The never-rest work ethic was no less ingrained in her than was the old-school tenet that a male oversees a family's assets and debts. As such, Pop willed the house, the monies, and the business to Dieter. "As it should be," MaGretta told Dieter. "You are the man of the house. It is your responsibility to tend to the money and to take care of your sister until she marries."

Dieter strived to live up to that archaic crap, so I strived to break the boundaries. I asked for a hundred bucks; Dieter gave me two. I asked for a thousand. Dieter picked up the phone to call the bank.

I slammed down the receiver. "What are you trying to pull? Last year, I pleaded to borrow five hundred bucks to get the bug of my dreams. Not only did you want me to draw up a repayment plan, but you made me endure a two-hour lecture about stupid passenger-pigeons and stinking spotted-owls and dumb-ass salamanders. Out of respect, I kept my mouth shut, even though your lousy birds and your greasy reptiles had nothing to do with me."

"Amphibian. A long-toed salamander is—"

"WHO CARES? All I wanted was that tiger beetle before other collectors wiped them off the face of the Earth. And now I'm asking for a thousand bucks. At least have the decency to ask why."

"Okay, Zia. Why?"

"I want to burn it."

"All right. Give me a few hours, and you can light the match."

"Dieter, stop it. Stop this obligation shit. I don't want any money. I want you to argue. Fight. Tell me to knock it off. Please."

But I could see the change in his eyes; his tile had shifted. Pop's death had bumped the board, and Dieter's letter no longer attached to an irritated brother. His tile was now part of a different word, a different meaning, and I was powerless to change it back. "Sorry, Diets. I was just giving you a hard time." I punched his shoulder.

Instead of a returned punch, his arms spread.

*A hug?* The Dieter I knew was gone. I ran off, cupping my eyes and claiming, "Allergies, allergies."

Otto's Autos wasn't too profitable before Miranda cleaned up the paperwork, nor was it too profitable when she divided her attention to help Fikus, but Pop's death brought her back to the shop, full-time, now to help Dieter. Once again, business flourished, though Miranda intended to leave as soon as Fikus finished remodeling his new church. She wanted Dieter to come with her; Dieter wanted her to stay. They had the weirdest relationship, neither fighting nor getting along, separate but inseparable.

At times, when my third-wheel status became too uncomfortable to ignore, I drove to The Sand Trap to visit Carly and roughhouse with Winkle.

The cat and I played a stalking game where I would chase and Winkle would run. After several laps up and down the hallway, I would pretend to give up and walk away. At that, Winkle would pounce on my back, and we would fall to the floor and wrestle. Only this time, we knocked over a dish of potpourri.

"Look what you did?" I whispered into Winkle's furry ear. "You're a bad cat. Bad, bad cat."

*Grrrgrrr.*

"Hey, Carly, what's with the name Winkle? Is it after Rip Van Winkle? Did your cat sleep a lot?"

Winkle's paw hooked my neck. I tackled her, pinning her down. "Are you a sleepy kitty? Huh? Come on, sleepy Winkle, give me what-for. Fight me, you pansy-cat." I held tight as Winkle gave me a tongue-lashing. Literally.

Carly scooped up the spilled potpourri. "Winkle mauled a rapist."

Wrestling stopped. "What rapist?"

"Mr. Van. After the rape, he opened the bedroom door, and Winkle, then Bullet, attacked him. I named her Winkle because she ripped Mr. Van's winkle. Ripped it right off."

"You're kidding."

"Nope. Balls included. Everywhere was blood spatter and penis chunks, but not a trace of the testes."

"But you just said—"

"She ate them."

My jaw slackened, and Winkle's speedy tongue swiped my lip.

*"Hauuuck."* I pushed her off me, spat, and sleeved my mouth. "Where's your scotch or whiskey or—Get back, scrotum breath. Carly, at least give me mouthwash, quick."

Within the month, I entered third-wheel status around Carly, too. She had met a photographer, Kevin, and it was love at first flash. All she talked about was oh-Kevin-this and oh-Kevin-that. Whether Death had kicked the board or Father-Time had spotted better plays, the tiles, all around me, shifted.

The Youth Center's administration changed hands. After observing my classes, the new directors deemed my methods *inappropriate,* the favored term of the self-righteous when asserting power.

I yawned through pages of insipid *do*s and *don't*s until I reached the last *do*. *Do* remove disruptive kids. Permanently.

"Oh hell no," I said. "Disruptive kids need double-time. Swimming cools their tempers and diving teaches them self-control. Your *do* is like, 'Hey, blind guy, read the rules or get out,' or 'hey, deaf dude, listen up or leave.' Get it?"

"You have an inappropriate attitude," they said.

*Inappropriate attitude*—management's euphemism for, "I have the power, you don't, so quit yanking on that stick up my ass."

I went to Neptunes and drank a few beers. Maybe more.

> *"Where have all the Scavengers gone? Long time passing.*
> *Where have all the Scavengers gone? Long time ago."*

Liz scooted into the booth. "Zee, quiet down on the serenade. I'm running low on boxes to-go."

"Well, my singing improves with alcohol."

"You've had enough to drink."

"Not for me. For your customers."

"That's it." Liz seized my backpack. "You're not driving."

"You got that right. Now hand over my backpack."

"No. I don't want you walking home either." Liz looked worriedly over her shoulder...or maybe at her shoulder. I couldn't focus too well.

"Dandruff?" I asked, wondering why her flaky scalp was nixing my leave. Whenever I drank too much, I walked home, but Liz had never stopped me before. She frowned again at the back side of her shoulder. I said, "They make dandruff shampoos, you know," and I started to stand.

Liz pushed me. "Stay put."

Either I was shit-faced or Liz's push was really a shove. I splashed back onto the bench. "Hey!"

"Hey what?" Liz said clasping her hips, towering over me, and carting a mean gleam in her eye that warned against arguing.

"Hey, all righty." I flashed a toothy smile. "Wake me up at the crack of noon." Before Liz walked away, I asked, "Aren't you ever going to run the betting pools again?"

"Honey, I can't. Detective Spuretta was asking questions. Now, I know Frank is a good man, but when one cop is interested, another cop usually follows. I can't afford legal hassles. I'm sorry, Zee. No more gambling."

"God, when will this end? Must every stinking tile shift?"

"Zee, are you sure you're okay?"

"Oh, I'm just peachy-keen. Peachy-freakin-keen." I waved her off.

> *"Where have all the Scavengers gone?*
> *Surfer bars have gained them, every one.*
> *When will they ever return?*
> *When will they ever return?"*

## 87

*Phoenix struck the back of my head.*
*"This is my Party, not your Pity Party."*

Amid candlelight and violins, Chateaubriand and Bordeaux, they reached across the table, once more, to touch hands.

For Carly and Kevin, the world was a romantic enchantment for two, all else had slipped into oblivion, including the waiter. He cleared his throat to gain their attention. "How is everything this evening?"

Together, they said, "Perfect." Then Carly giggled and Kevin smiled.

The waiter smiled, too; young lovers are generous tippers. "Very good, sir. Will you be enjoying desert tonight?"

Carly gave a quick head shake.

"Leave the menu," Kevin said. "The lady might change her mind."

The waiter bowed and left.

"Now where were we?" Kevin said. "Tell me about your—"

*Trrrg. Trrrg.* Carly's cell phone displayed NEPTUNES. She started to apologize, but Kevin interrupted. "Your job is 24/7; I accept that. Quit apologizing. Answer your phone."

Carly picked up. After a few exchanges, she said, "No, I'm glad you called. Don't let her leave. I'll be right there."

Kevin was already signaling the waiter.

"Family business," Carly said. "My stepsister, Zia, is a little messed up."

"Drunk?"

"That too. I need to get my car and pick her up at Neptunes."

"Your car is an hour away. Neptunes is a twenty minute drive from here. Let's get your sister before she decides to drive herself."

"But Zia might throw up in your car."

"Then I'll wash it." Kevin handed three bills and a valet ticket to the waiter. "We're in a hurry. Could you bring my car immediately?"

Glimpsing the bills, the waiter's rehearsed smile became genuine.

While helping Carly into her coat, Kevin asked, "Any heads-up so I don't offend your sister?"

"No, of course not. Well, don't bring up cheese."

"Cheese? Easy enough."

"Or lettuce. Or onions. To play it safe, don't talk about food."

"No food. No problem."

They started toward the door. "Oh, and don't bring up birds," Carly said. "Or cats. Or bugs."

"No food, cats, or bugs. Should I jot this down? I was expecting a ban on religion or politics."

"Oh, no, those subjects are fine."

Once seated in the car, Kevin said, "Let's send a cab to Neptunes in case your sister decides to leave before we get there."

"Don't worry about that. Zia won't sit in a cab."

"Dare I ask why?"

"Vibrational imprints," Carly said. "Better not mention cabs."

When their headlights swept through Neptunes' window, Liz rested her broom and unlocked the front door. Across the tavern came slurred singing.

> "...he's got hiiigh hopes, he's got hiiigh hopes,
> he's got, high apple-pie in the skyyyy hopes..."

"How much did she drink?" Carly asked.

"I cut her off at two beers," Liz said, "but Zee sneaks behind the counter and helps herself. When she gets a little toasty, she walks home. But tonight, I didn't like the idea. The preacher's son was watching her."

"Fikus MacKenzie?"

Liz nodded. "He sat in the corner booth, over in Kelly's section, and he nursed one cup of coffee all night. He stayed until Kelly booted him out at closing. Then I saw him hanging around out front, so I kept Zia inside."

"Did Zia know he was here?"

Liz snorted. "Do my tables and chairs look busted up?"

> "...just remember those ants,
> whoops, there goes another rubber tree..."

Zia's cheek rested on the table, one eye closed and one eye fixed on grains of salt, which she poked into a line leading to the shaker.

Carly slid onto the bench across from Zia and rapped the table. Salt grains scattered. "Hey!" Zia's head lifted. Her soggy eyes went from Carly to Kevin to Liz, and then returned to Kevin and stayed.

Kevin gave a hesitant, awkward wave.

Zia frowned. "What are you looking at?"

"That's Kevin," Carly said snapping her fingers until Zia's attention turned. "Be nice, Zia, we're here to take you home."

"What home?" Zia said. "I'm a letter without a word."

"Zia, listen to me."

"No, you listen. You and you and you." She dotted the air toward each of them. "All of you, listen up." Then her anger receded into watery eyes that focused on the salt grains. "I got bad dreams. Bad, bad dreams. Every night, it's the same. Want to know what about?"

"Sure, hon," Liz said. "What's haunting your dreams?"

"The Timer-Guy. That dumb bastard is holding my letter. 'Sorry, Zia,' he tells me, 'but you don't fit anymore. I have no place for your tile.' I tell him to keep looking. I fit before; I'll fit again. Stick me anywhere. Screw spelling. Who's going challenge? But Timer-Guy won't listen. He's a sorry-sap. 'Nope, can't be done. Go away.' That guy has my tile, but he tells me to go away." Tears began rolling in a continuous stream. "I'm a letter without a word. A leftover. And he has my *tiiile.*" Her wail became incoherent sobbing.

Carly started to slide from the booth to go to Zia's side, but Liz pushed past and thumped beside Zia. "Oh, honey, come on now." Liz patted Zia's back. "Don't worry about it. We'll get your tile back."

"Or we'll get you a new tile," Carly added. "A better one."

"What?" Zia sat upright. "What are you guys talking about?"

Carly and Liz looked at the other—*Do you know? No. Do you? No*—exchanging shrugs and head shakes.

"Sweet-sanity," Zia said, "what is wrong with you people? How do you *not* get it? Death fucked up the Board because Death always fucks up the Board. That's his job. But it's Timer-Guy's job to reset the tiles. And he did, but it sucks to be me because my letter doesn't fit anymore. Now do you get it?"

"Scrabble," Kevin said with Jeopardy-speed. "The board is life, the tiles are people, and the Timer-Guy is—is time itself? Change? Fate? Am I close?"

Liz rolled her eyes.

Carly shook her head. "Kevin, I don't think—"

"Whoa!" Zia said, marveling at Kevin. "You don't eat lettuce, do you?"

Carly and Liz gave furtive signals for Kevin to say no.

"Lettuce?" Kevin said. "Never touch it."

"Wow. You're alien free." Zia passed out.

# 88

*On March 9th, we boarded the*
*steamship Farallon bound for Alaska.*

In the morning, the bathroom mirror reflected the bloodless face of a monstrous hangover. I gave up the day, returning to bed and hugging my pillow with its loud, scrunching feathers.

The next morning, my head felt the wake-up punch of an epiphany. I did belong, but not in Kenzie Cove. My destiny waited elsewhere. When I said it out loud, euphoria washed over me. Time to hoist anchor on Kenzie Cove and set sail for a new adventure. That was the epiphany. I felt it so profoundly, I kissed the calendar to remember the day—March 9th, 1998.

Throughout the week, I settled business accounts and closed books. To questioning customers, I gave cryptic answers. "Oh, it's just time for a change. No big deal." Had I told the truth—I'm driving off to wherever whim leads me—someone's good intention of practical advice would have ripped my sail, spinning me off course.

At the Youth Center, three of the new directors came to my class to confirm that I was following their list of changes. To their surprise, they observed my methods pristinely unchanged. When the class ended, the directors approached, armed with paperwork.

Several Red Herrings meandered nearby, so I told the directors to wait. And they told me, "We don't take orders from you," and they started up with a barrage of criticism.

The Red Herrings perked.

I told the directors, "No, wait, shut up, for chrissake, wait." But the more I shushed them, the more their voices blared with inappropriate-this and unacceptable-that. The Red Herrings passed cloaked signals.

Intending to smite their avenging ideas, I yelled, "Hey, you guys, don't any of you leave. Stay right there."

Walking papers slapped my chest before the bureaucrats told the kids, "You children are free to go. Go on."

When the swinging doors settled behind the last Red Herring, I walked to the garbage, looked back at the directors, "You shouldn't have done that," and dumped the papers.

I had planned to finish the swimming season and then slip from Kenzie Cove without a fuss. No goodbyes, no upset. I had planned to pack a few items, get into my car, and drive north. If and when I hit a town that felt right, I'd settle in and make a few calls. But my sweet and simple plan began to dissolve the moment the directors barred me from the Youth Center.

A rash of vandalism struck the parking lot—keyed cars, smashed windows, punctured tires. The only vehicles spared of damage were the impoverished beater-cars driven by teens. Administration called the police and the directors closed the Youth Center for three days.

When it reopened, vandals struck again. And again, cops were called and kids were interviewed. In the jungle of denials, contradictions, and accusations, the kids' resounded one theme; the directors had brutalized their Coach. In the kids' version, the directors had pummeled me, brutalized me, nearly killed me. I set the cops straight; I had suffered a paper-cut. Unfortunately, nobody set the parents straight, and the gossip of a beaten Zia spread to my wind chime customers. "Oh, she was beaten so badly, she had to close her business."

Within days, my voicemail clogged with concerned questions; "What's going on? Where are you? Call me." Particularly concerned, Liz and Carly left dozens of messages, but in each of their messages, I heard an undercurrent of treading lightly, as if they were afraid of upsetting a loon. No doubt my night of drunken blathering had changed their opinion of me.

Humiliated, I turned off my cell phone, and night after night, I camped in my car.

Unfortunately, Dieter knew my hiding place. I woke to him pounding on the windshield. "Zia, unlock the door." The moonlight glazed his white skin and pale hair into the eerie yellows of a moon-man, a madman moon-man. "ZIA!"

"Calm down first."

His teeth gritted. "Unlock this goddam door. NOW!"

I fumbled with the seat belt as if it were latched. Then I scratched my head as if I couldn't quite decide which door to unlock.

*WHAM*, his fist pelted the windshield.

"OKAY!" I said. "Don't break the glass." I unlocked the passenger door.

Dieter jumped in and, wow, was he steamed. He accused me of being selfish, inconsiderate, and hurtful. He punched the dashboard and shouted, "Knock this shit off!"

I could not have smiled wider; for one brief moment, Dieter's tile was again connected to mine.

Long into the night, I talked and Dieter listened. I told him about the shifting tiles and my feelings of displacement, but then I explained my epiphany and my sense of belonging—belonging somewhere else. And I reminded Dieter how much I loathed goodbyes—don't want to give them, don't want to get them. Then Dieter spoke. In less than a minute, his few words about love and concern for others annihilated my million excuses spewed through the night.

"You win," I told him. "I'll tell everyone goodbye. But Dieter, straight up, do you think Liz and Carly realize it was the beer talking? I mean, they know me, right? They don't think I'm weird, do they? Hell, I'm so grounded, I set the bar for sanity, don't I? Don't I?"

"Sure, Zee, they know you."

"Thanks, Diets." I punched him

He punched back. Hard, too. Joyously, my arms flung around him for a fierce hug, startling him like crazy.

The next morning, I drove to The Sand Trap. Although it was 11 a.m., Carly was still in her bathrobe. I would have asked why, but Carly looked pretty miffed, so I cut right to the apology. "Sorry for getting plastered two weeks ago."

"You're apologizing for that?"

"No, not *just* for that. Hang on. Uhm. Sorry for talking crazy, sorry for ruining your date, sorry for puking in Kevin's car."

Her foot kept tapping, her arms stayed knotted, and her breaths unfurled from her nostrils like a challenged bull. I scratched my head. "Jeez, what else did I do?"

"You avoided my calls. *My* calls. Mine!"

That, I did not expect. I held up a give-me-a-minute finger, then I turned halfway around to discuss the matter with Alpha. *WHAT THE HELL! Remember last year when she didn't return my calls? Where does she get off telling me—*

"Turn around," Carly said. "Talk to your demons later."

*Hear what she called you?* I pulled in a deep breath to fortify my patience before I faced her again. "Carly, I am very sorry for not returning your calls. I am an inconsiderate, selfish jerk who deserves to be flogged. *Now* may I come in, please?"

Carly stepped aside.

I poured a cup of coffee before I sat at her kitchen table. "If it makes any difference, I didn't return anyone's calls. I wanted to leave town without giving goodbyes, but Dieter explained how that might upset a few people, you included. So I'm here to say goodbye. Uhm, goodbye."

"You're not going anywhere until I know what you're doing and why you're doing it and where you're going?"

"Whoa. Does Kevin know how bossy you are?"

"I do." Kevin's voice came from the hallway.

I glanced over my shoulder. Kevin was wearing a bathrobe.

"*Aw, jeez.*" I melted in my chair, hoping to hit the floor and slink out the nearest exit.

Carly gripped my arm and told Kevin to give us a minute.

"Nice to see you again," Kevin said.

I waved overhead. "Sorry for barfing in your Beemer."

Carly scooted her chair closer to mine. "So what are your plans?"

I jerked a thumb over my shoulder. "Pretty dull compared to yours."

"Oh, he'll wait." Carly giggled like a schoolgirl. "He's very patient. Last night, we had dinner on the beach, a lobster dinner. We fed each other." *Again,* she giggled. "Afterward, we spread a blanket and—"

"*Excuuuse* me. If we both had hot guys, this would be called sharing. When only one has a hot guy, it's called bragging."

"Zia, if you stay, I will set you up with Kevin's cousin."

"I'm not staying. Mentally, I've already set sail. Physically, I'm leaving on April 6th."

"In two weeks?"

"Two and a half."

"Why? What's the rush?"

"Why not? I closed up shop, and the diving finals are on the 3rd."

"You're finishing the season? I heard the Youth Center kicked you out."

"They did. But the kids persuaded them to reconsider."

"Yeah, I heard about the broken windshields and slashed tires."

"Hey, I offered to tell the kids to knock it off, but the directors didn't want that. They wanted me to convince the kids that I was leaving by choice, as if those kids haven't had enough adults quitting on them in their lives."

"What did you tell the directors?"

"I told them to bite me. But destroyed property trumps insolent coach, so they're letting me finish the season. Then I'll pack over the weekend, store my remaining stuff, and hit the road on Monday. It's a great plan, so don't say anything to ruin it. Just offer a photo as a good-luck gift."

"You want a photo?"

"I would love a photo."

"I have a great picture of Kenzie Cove that—"

"Whatever you decide, but no landscapes."

"Oh. Well, how about birds?"

"Strictly your decision. But no birds. And could you frame it?"

"No landscapes, no birds, and you want it framed. Is that it?"

"Hey, I can't dictate a gift. I'll love whatever you choose, but I would love it more if it had a green mat."

"A green mat?"

"Yeah. And the green mat should compliment something green in the photo. Like, oh, say for example, if you had a green-headed beetle."

"A beetle? I don't have a—" A slow recollection came to her face. "Zia, were you in snooping in my room?"

"Whoa, check out the time." I jumped up. "Gotta go." I hurried to the door. Winkle bounded after me. When she pounced, I sidestepped and flipped her over for a belly rub. "I'll miss you, Winkle." Her tongue lashed out, but I kept my face beyond its reach.

"What does Dieter think about your plans?"

"Same as always; 'Zee, you need a clue and a prayer.' I promised him, 'the second I feel like staying somewhere, I'll let you know. I swear, I'll let you know I'm okay.' But my promises don't mean squat, and Dieter knows that, damn him. He forced me into a spit-promise. I don't break spit-promises. Never have, never will. Spit-promises are sacred."

## 89

*These delinquent skioses have quite a proclivity to invert vibrations of direction.*

### April 5, 1998

Other than the bouncing headlights from trucks towing boats to the marina, the streets were empty. The entire world was still asleep except for fishermen and me—*dingdong, dingdong, dingdong*—and now Carly, whose feet slogged toward the door. *Dingdong, dingdong, dingdong.* I stepped back to wave at the peephole. "Hey, Carly, were you sleeping?"

A puffy-faced Carly came outside. "What's wrong? What happened?" She fisted her half-lidded eyes and then squinted into the darkness graying with dawn. "What time is it?"

"Time? Time is so relative."

Carly frowned. "Relate it to a clock."

"Speaking of clocks," I tucked an envelope into her hands, "between two and three this afternoon, give that letter to Dieter. But don't give it to him any earlier or any later. Got it?"

She blinked at the envelope, mystified. "You woke me up to—to deliver mail? You hammered my doorbell at—" She looked again at the dimly lit world. "WHAT TIME IS IT?"

"It's important," I said. "It's an apology letter because I'm sort of, well, leaving now."

"Now? No, you're not leaving now. You're leaving tomorrow." Carly's puffiness shriveled into cranky lines. "A lot of effort went into your farewell surprise party. I only told you about it to ensure you wouldn't take off early. But if you skip out now, you're intentionally snubbing your family and friends. How can you do that, Zia? How can you be so deliberately self-centered?"

"I'm not. If you wait until two o'clock, Dieter won't have time to cancel. At four, everyone will get together and celebrate."

"Without you?"

"Jeez, Carly, haven't you ever attended a wedding where the bride failed to show? I have. The groom didn't waste the food, the music, or the guests' time. He cut to the reception and everyone partied. It's different when the bride gets jilted. Betty Boo-Hoo ruins everyone's fun. Now that's self-centered. But no one is going to cry over my absence. Any pissiness will end when the first few steaks come off the grill. Everyone will have a good time, with or without me. For some, especially without me."

Carly slipped the envelope into her bathrobe's pocket. "If you were dead-set on leaving today, you should have told me. We could have rescheduled the party for this morning, and you could have left this afternoon."

"I thought of that, but it wouldn't have worked. Today is a big deal for you Catholics, right? That's what MaGretta said. She loves the Catholic ceremonies with all their genuflecting and water-sprinkling and holy-this and holy-that. For a while, MaGretta had a tough time with her faith, but now, she's fully absorbed in your church. I've never seen her more thrilled. I love your dad for giving her that. Just curious, though, what's the ritual for today? Foreheads smudged with dust bombs?"

"No, that was Ash Wednesday. Today is Palm Sunday."

I looked at my hands. "What are you going to do to people's palms?"

Carly slapped my hands. "Not those palms, you heathen." After an uneasy quiet, we shared an awkward hug. "Zia, you're a pain in the ass."

"I've been called worse," I pushed her back and met her eyes, "but never by better, Carly, never by better than you."

We walked to my car. From the trunk, I pulled out a framed arthropod. "This is for you."

"Oh, Zia." Carly gazed at it with sincere admiration. "What a gorgeous butterfly."

"Whoa, butterfly? No. It's an Insecta, order of Lepidoptera, and that's a species of the Attacus genus, Saturniidae family."

"A moth?"

"That's what I said. It's an Attacus Atlas. In wing area, they're the world's largest moth, but on wingspan, they lose to the Giant Agrippa, which is a dumb moth...because I don't have one."

Carly's eyes misted. Her arms came up, but I sidestepped the hug. "I'm over my quota for sappiness." I opened the car door. "I don't suppose you have a gift for me, do you? Something in a green frame?"

"Oh, I matted a photo of a turtle."

"A turtle? *Turtle?* Yeah, okay, I guess a turtle is not completely lame."

"Good, because I sent it to my aunt. Then I wrapped a green-headed beetle for you."

I sucked in a swift breath. "No. Seriously? Don't joke about this."

"It's at your house. When you settle someplace, I'll ship it."

Uncontrollably ecstatic, I hugged her...then hugged her again. I climbed behind the wheel and lowered the window. "By the way, who had the brilliant idea to have the party at Angels Peak? Miranda?"

"Miranda organized everything. She reserved the park, rented the tables and chairs, planned the menus, sent out the invitations, and handed each of us a to-do list. After Mass, I'm going straight to the Peak to help her with the canopies. It's a heck of a send-off. My dad and Dieter will be barbecuing for fifty to sixty people."

"Fifty to sixty? Do they know me?"

"Yes, and they're coming anyway. Some are your prior customers, but most are the parents of your swim teams. They're not just coming to say goodbye. The Red Herrings were planning a big celebration for winning the gold medal in the diving competition. They told Miranda they had a special tribute for you."

"A tribute? What kind of a tribute?"

Carly shrugged. "It must be at the Youth Center because they planned on escorting you there after the barbecue."

I smiled, which caused Carly to ask, "Do you know what they were planning?"

"Yep. Just tell Terry Lee that it wasn't a spit-promise, and be sure to add, 'checkmate.' He'll get my drift." I fired the motor. "Listen, Carly, keep an eye on the kids. Don't let them wander toward the cliffs."

"Don't worry. I'm bringing police tape to mark the boundaries. Then I'll round up the kids and explain the dangers of—"

"For chrissake, explain nothing. No Kumbayah lectures. Be tough. Draw your gun. Tell them if they cross the line, you'll shoot them."

"I can't do that."

"Well, don't shoot to kill. Just wing one or two. Start with Terry Lee."

"Zia, I can't—"

"Suit yourself. But don't stand at the cliff's edge with your back to a Red Herring." I revved the motor.

Carly stepped to the curb. "Keep your cell phone on."

"It's on and the battery is charged. I got it right—" I scrounged among empty Coke cans and Egg McMuffin wrappers, and then pawed at the litter beneath the passenger seat. "Shit, shit, shit." I began banging my forgetful head against the steering wheel. "It's on the kitchen counter...still charging."

"Turn around," Carly said, but in a low, stern voice.

"Aw, crap, that's backtracking miles. This stinks."

"Drive back home." Again, her voice sounded weird.

My head-banging stopped. "Do you have a frog in your throat?"

She leaned into my car. "I said, buy a new phone."

"Oh. Good idea." I put the car in gear. "I'm outta here."

"Take care, Zia."

"Take pictures, Carly."

I drove off.

Miles later, I came to the Y in the road. If I turned right, I could go home and get my phone. If I veered left, I'd have to buy a new phone. A new phone for a new adventure; I chose left and headed to the freeway.

A quarter mile short of the onramp, a string of orange cones tried to block the road. Around the next bend, police cruisers topped with revolving lights were parked in front of a boulder.

I approached at a bashful, pay-no-attention-to-me speed.

A cop wearing shades swaggered to the centerline. He held up a halting hand, his other hand touched his gun.

I stopped.

The cop strutted to my window. When he leaned in, he looked to the side. Add a toothpick and he was a cop-cliché. "Ma'am, just where do you think you're going?"

"To the freeway."

"The freeway, huh?" His sunglasses turned toward me.

I smiled, big and wide. In his mirrored shades, I saw a piece of toast stuck between my front teeth. I propped up, centering my face in his lenses, and then I picked at the bread.

The cop straightened. "A smart-aleck, huh?"

"No, a lousy tooth-brusher."

"Ma'am, do you see that rock?"

"Rock?" I pressed into the steering wheel to squint at the twelve-foot boulder. "Oh, that? Well, yeah, but my car is small. I bet I can squeeze—"

"Do you think we put out traffic cones as an obstacle course?"

"Cones? *Cones?* I don't recall any cones."

"You don't, huh?" The cop stepped back, his finger curling, *come-here,* and then he pointed to the rear of my car.

I stretched halfway through the window to look. Jammed between the back tire and the fender was a mangled mass of orange rubber. "SHIT!"

I got out and slammed the door. "Great! Goddam great!" I kicked the tire. My sandal split and so did my toe. I hopped about on one foot while holding my bloodied toe. The cop didn't even offer a Band-Aid. After walking off the pain, I sat in the gravel next to the tire. With both arms, I reached under the rear wheel-well, gripped the twisted cone, and began yanking. "Son-of-a-bitch. You stinking son-of-a-bitch."

The cop watched, but never offered to help.

By the time I pried the cones out, my arms and shirt were blackened.

I limped to the driver's door, got in, and glared at the cop with his John Wayne sway, his thumbs tucked in his belt, and his shades reflecting my grease-streaked cheeks. "You could have helped."

"Yeah, I could have. And I could have cited you for destroying State property. I still might if you don't shut your smart trap. Now turn around."

Grumbling and mumbling, "Donut-sucking prickweed," I flipped a U-turn...and a finger.

Again at the Y, I let the car idle. To reach the onramp north, I'd have to loop around several towns funded by speed traps that cited drivers for exceeding a jogger's pace. The onramp south was halfway back to Kenzie Cove. Because I could afford the time but I couldn't afford a ticket, I cranked the wheel and headed south.

Other than sandpipers, the road was deserted and monotonous. One dune rolled into the next, mile after mile, a hypnotic blur of tans and browns. My trance didn't break until I spotted the crossroads. "Aw shit." I had day-dreamed right past the first turn and was now only a mile shy of Kenzie Cove. I stopped the car.

Maybe I hadn't daydreamed. Maybe my subconscious was driving me home. Maybe that's why I had forgotten my cell phone. In my heart, I wanted a reason to go home...but *my* home. In my home, Pop still sat at the head of the table, still sneaked Schnapps, and still hollered to keep the peace. In my home, MaGretta still fretted over my books and bugs, and she still cooked banquets to cure family woes. And in my home, Dieter bailed me out and punched me back. Always.

My home didn't exist anymore.

I turned left and headed toward the 101 onramp. "Well, Alpha, it's just you and me now."

Steering with my knees, I leafed through CDs for cheerful music.

*Matter is not one-dimensional, despite your persistence to regard it so.*

"Save it, Alpha. I'm not in the mood for riddles."

I popped in Grace Slick and sucked in a breath, ready to belt out White Rabbit, but I must have misread the CD. Instead of White Rabbit, my car filled with the haunting voice of Bonnie Tyler.

> *Turnaround, Every now and then I get a little bit lonely*
> *and you're never coming around.*
> *Turnaround, Every now and then I get a little bit tired*
> *of listening to the sound of my tears.*

I should have changed CDs immediately. Because I hadn't, my tears began to plink-plink on the steering wheel. Eventually, my sniffles grew into sobs. Again, I pulled off the road.

> *Turnaround bright eyes,*
> *Every now and then I fall apart.*
> *Turnaround bright eyes,*
> *Every now and then I fall apart.*

I cupped my face, and my hands filled with a deluge of wet emotions.

> *Nothing I can say, total eclipse of the heart.*

My heart eclipsed, too, now broken and drained...and totally confused—Why the hell was I crying? Probably PMS combined with sad music. Had to be. When the song ended, I sleeved my face.

Just then, the CD flipped tracks, restarting the song.

"What the hell?" I piano'd the buttons.

*Turnaround, Every now and then I get a little bit nervous
that the best of all the years have gone by.*

I jabbed and jabbed the Off button.

Finally, the music died.

*Matter is not one-dimensional, despite—*

"Shut up, Alpha. Just shut up. I'm upset, can't you see that? Leave me alone."

The stereo lit again.

*Turnaround, bright eyes...*

"DAMMIT!" Again, I stabbed furiously at the Off button. "Alpha, this can't be happening. Do you hear me? It's insane."

*Turnaround, bright eyes...*

"STOP IT! STOP IT! STOP IT!" I pounded Eject. When the CD coughed up, I Frisbee'd it out the window.

I clutched my head. "Alpha, I can't take this anymore. I can't take the craziness, the voices, the imaginings. I can't take this insanity any longer. I want to see stairs without grins, hear birds without warnings, and maybe someday, some sane day in the future, I want to eat lettuce."

I dried my eyes before fixing them on Alpha. "You're the best friend I've ever had," I whispered. "From the moment you came to my tea-party, you've been the one constant in my life. But I'm not a kid anymore. I need to put away what I conjured up in childhood. It's time for me to grow up and to send my tea-party friend home. I love you, Alpha. I will never forget you. But you have to go home now."

He started to fade.

A lump swelled in my throat. I fought against an aching heart and an overwhelming urge to call him back.

His orange eyes dimmed. They became smaller and smaller, until they were tiny specks glowing like lingering embers that begged to be stoked...or the fire will die.

My head lowering, my eyes shutting, I let the fire die. "Goodbye, Alpha."

# 90

*Will is my friend.*
*Friends don't let friends wander.*

Despair chorused from Geminus and Willow.

Alpha stood apart, vibrating a need for solitude.

In a bleat of laughter, Kaane appeared. "You, Willow, should choke on your own unpalatable words. 'A kiss from Niine,' you had said of the tick, 'and it works to our benefit.' So as it was for you, so as it is for us; the kiss from One works to our benefit." He blew Willow a kiss. "Free Will."

He turned a sly smile to Geminus. "As we speak, a Niine Determinant prepares for your Dyad's cord."

He then glided to Alpha and said, "Skewing voices? Blocking exits? Switching CDs? And what did you gain? Banishment. She banished you from her mind, and she forbade your further interference. So as it was in Alaska, so shall it be at the Neutral Point. I ask you again, Alpha, how do you like this Free Will now?"

"What is that foul smell?" Romal appeared. "Oh, malodorous Kaane, take your wretched stench elsewhere." Before Kaane could retort, Romal added, "Be gone."

Kaane disappeared.

Turning to Alpha, Romal said, "Break your heart, did she? Well, break your Peril Guide habits. Now is not the time for solitude. Now is the time for collective strength." He gestured toward Willow and Geminus. "Their Charges have equal importance and cause equal concern."

Alpha nodded understanding and went to join the two Guides.

※

From the Order of Counters, the consoling Soul stopped his whispers mid-sentence. His head cocked. Within his being, he had kept a window open for any vibration concerning his friend, Zia. He felt one now, but it was a strange vibration, unlike any vibration he had ever felt before. It was not emanating from an Energy nor from a Player. Puzzled, he descended to his Soul's window.

Vibrations trickled in like silk threads carried on a breeze. He caught a strand and examined it. It contained a universe of intricate complexities.

*A Guide's vibration?*

No sooner had he realized this when, *WaPOOSH,* a hurricane of distress blasted through the window and flung the Counter backward.

Struggling against the gale force, he finally reached the window and then closed it. Though Counters are analytically gifted, he could not dissect a Guide's vibration into explicable segments. No Energy could. So he analyzed the number and the weight of the vibrations. From their total, he knew a great cataclysm loomed. From their momentum, he knew the cataclysm was imminent. Although he couldn't break the vibration to learn the *why*s and the *how*s, he did discover a linking thread—movement.

*Movement?* He shook his head, baffled, because the movement was neither spiritual nor mental, the two types that would give rise to a Guide's distress. Instead, the movement was physical—a physical direction. How could Zia's physical direction, whether north, south, east or west, be seeding a disaster so catastrophic as to cause multiple Guides a whirlwind of angst?

The Counter, a mere Energy, hadn't the power to help nor the insight to know how. Besides, as a consoling Soul, he had parameters of where he could go and had time-limits of how long he could leave. He had rules to respect and laws to obey.

Yet, had it not been for Zia violating the Awakening Laws, he might still be running through the hospital's hallways, still wailing, and still reaching in vain for doctors and nurses. "Friends don't let friends wander," Zia had told her Guide, who had then told his Guide. "Friends don't let friends wander," had been her sole reason for disregarding the laws.

For her, he would disregard the laws, too.

He had to flip her direction, of that, he was almost certain. Almost. He pondered the vibrations, the billions and billions of threads. Movement, not flipped, but reversed. Not reversed in time, distance, or direction, but reversed to her Soul's desire. Where would Zia least likely want to be?

Seconds later, he smiled. He knew the place...and he even knew why she needed to be there.

He took off.

# 91

*The Golden Stairs, an aversion gleaned during her last life.*
*That, he understood; why she had kept it, he did not.*

A box of Kleenex sopped up my stupid blubbering, which had thankfully spilt in private. Around others, an emotional spillage comes with a hefty price; a down payment of humiliation, followed by interest charges of tolerating faked concerns. *So how are you doing, you know, really?* Insisting you're fine is like paying off your loan early—it's met with a disappointed smile and a *Please call me on your next breakdown.*

Sadness spent but sympathy-debt free, I rolled my neck and flexed my fingers, more eager than ever to begin a new adventure. I revved my motor and checked my review mirror. *Huh?*

Way down the road was the backside of a small figure walking away. But away from where?

No side trails cut through the dunes; moreover, no town or beach was within walking distance.

I got out of my car and squinted at the hiking midget or the lost kid, a figure no bigger than Billy.

*Billy?* "HEY KID."

He turned and waved.

"Aw, shit. BILLY! WHAT THE HELL?"

He turned again and continued walking.

I hopped into my car, spun a half donut, and yards past Billy, slammed on the brakes. When I barreled from the car, dirt clouds billowed in. "For chrissake, Billy, what are you doing here? Are you alone?"

He nodded.

"No, no, no. You can't be, Bill. This is too far from home. Way, way too far. Does your mom know you're out here?"

He nodded again.

"Straight up?"

Billy X'd his chest.

For a moment, I cupped my forehead to hide my anger at Billy's lame-brain mother. "Billy, listen, I need to talk to your mom. You can't be out here by yourself."

He hand-signed, *why?*

"Because it's dangerous, that's why. Psychos are everywhere."

Billy peered across the vacuous dunes and then shook his head.

"Don't argue with me. If I say psychos are everywhere, then psychos are everywhere."

He gestured, *where?*

"Jeez, Bill, how can you doubt me?" I looked around for a convincing danger. "Right there. See those sandpipers? You probably think they're the gentle breed, the kind we see on the beach, right?"

He nodded.

"Well, you're wrong. Beach birds are good birds; dune birds are psycho sandpipers. They collude with demented gulls to peck out a trespasser's eyeballs. It's horrible, Bill, god-awful horrible, but it's all in a documentary called, *The Birds.*"

Billy pinched his nose, *story stinks.*

"Whoa, stop that. Never besmirch the great work of Alfred Hitchcock. He's a genius. Now let me take you home. I need to chat with your mom."

Billy looked at the sky to assess the weather. My stomach cramped. If he refused a ride, I'd have to walk him home. My legs ached with the thought.

"It's just a haze," I told him. "Just a slight coastal haze, a measly filter over a hot, blinding sun." To prove it, I stripped off my sweatshirt. Frigid air bit through my cotton tee. My teeth began chattering. "Se-see? Wa-warm. So, how-how about it?" I was prepared to beg or bribe, whatever it took, but Billy went to my car and pointed to the backseat.

Redressed in my sweatshirt, I said, "Don't you want to sit up front?"

He shook his head.

"Okay, not a problem." I opened the back door and Billy climbed inside.

On the drive into town, Billy rapped the window.

"Down?" I asked. Through the review mirror, I saw him nod. "Billy, be reasonable. It's freezing outside."

He rapped again.

I lowered his window and cranked up the heat. I hadn't told Billy I was leaving. In my letter to Dieter, I had asked him to tell Billy. It was chicken-shit of me, and while watching Billy bounce and grin at my peeks in the mirror, I knew it would be doubly chicken-shit if I didn't tell him now.

"Hey, kiddo, I never thanked you for all your help with the chimes. So Billy, thank you. You're the best sea-crap collector I ever had. I couldn't have done it without you. But now, well, I'm sort of not doing the chime thing anymore. See, I'm going away for a few months. Maybe longer. I'm moving north, you know, to live someplace else. I'll be back to visit on holidays."

I rambled on and on with sentiments, gratitude, and pathetic explanations. By the time I pulled up to the stop-sign at the end of his street, I was choking on sappiness. "Hey, Bill, we'll always be friends. I promise."

Thinking he needed a hug—because I sure did—I twisted around in my seat and stretched out my arms.

The little booger was climbing out the window.

"What the hell are you doing?"

Billy slid from the car and hurried to the sidewalk. I jutted from the window. "BILLY, COME BACK HERE!"

*Beep, beep,* honked from behind.

"BILLY!"

*Beep, beep.*

I flipped a finger to the impatient driver.

*BEEEEEEP!*

"Son-of-a-bitch." I curbed the car and got out.

Billy took off running.

I walked unhurriedly down B Street, pretty sure Billy was just going home. "Come on, Billy. Is this how you want to say goodbye? Running from me?"

A few doors before his house, he bolted to the right, ran up the long driveway, and hopped onto the porch—the porch of the big white Colonial.

I stood on the sidewalk, dumbstruck.

Maybe Billy had mental problems that news of my leaving triggered. Or maybe he was afraid that my tattling to his mom would result in a horrific punishment. Or maybe—he stuck thumbs into his ears, wiggled Bullwinkle moose-horns, and blew a raspberry—the kid was just plain ornery.

"Billy, get down here. Listen, if you promise not to wander off anymore, I won't tell your mom where I found you, okay?"

Billy smiled as though we had struck a deal.

Just then, the front door opened and Billy disappeared. That fast.

From the sidewalk, I couldn't tell whether Billy had let himself in or whether someone had seized him. Either way, he didn't belong in that house.

I sprinted to the porch and then pushed on the unlatched door. "Psst. Billy? Pssst." Hearing nobody, I braved a little volume. "Hello? Anyone home?" No footsteps sounded, so I eased inside and then gently closed the door. *Click*. "BILLY! GET YOUR BUTT OVER HERE!"

Silence.

"For chrissake, Bill, if I'm caught in this house, I'll go to jail. Do you want that? Huh?"

Nothing stirred.

I gnawed cuticles, changing fingers when they bled. My legs refused to budge because my brain was registering the house as dark. Too dark. Daggers of light sliced the drapes, creating tall, dripping shadows of evil incarnate.

*No, no, no.* I gave my wrist a bruising pinch to beg reality's return. It's sunlight, just filtered sunlight. I managed a step before my legs locked again, my mind now processing a smell, musty and sulfuric. *Uh-oh,* the odor of scattered ashes from Fikus's father, and his forefather, and God-only knows how many forefathers before them.

*No, no, no.* It's dust. Just dust. Guys never dust. "BILLEEE*eeeeee*." My breath emptied in a desperate plea knowing what was about to consume me—a hellish imagination that would frighten the devil himself. "Billy, please come out. This place is seriously creepy. Please come out and I'll give you ten bucks."

Silence.

"Twenty! Twenty bucks, Bill. I mean fifty. Fifty bucks and I'll let you drive my car."

Not a sound.

"I'LL GIVE YOU MY CAR!"

Still nothing. *Shit.*

Dragging fear-laden feet from room to room, I demanded and begged, threatened and promised, but no movement sounded and no Billy appeared. Positively and absolutely, he had slipped past me and was now safely outside. That's what I told myself as I quick-footed to the front door.

*Tap, tap, tap.*

"Nooo." I was standing in the entryway, my hand gripping the doorknob, my feet two steps from exiting a labyrinth of creepiness...when I heard the tap. I knew where it came from—the one place I had refused to check.

Turning, I gulped down the acid gurgling up from my stomach. *Please no, please no, please no.* But sure enough, Billy grinned and waved from the top of the staircase.

"Aw, please, Bill, for the love of—"

He took off.

Although I had intended to conquer my fears someday, I sure as shit hadn't intended on starting with stairs, especially stairs of this type. These weren't innocent stairs with measured widths and engineered slopes, the kind built in modern homes. These were wicked stairs with broad planks and warped banisters, the kind described in *Staircase to Hell.*

My head lowered, my hands clasped. "Dear God, I know I never pray, but I'm praying now, could you help me? I'll burn the macabre and read nothing but sappy crap, if you'll just let me see those stairs as a carpenter's nailed boards and not as a monster's rotting jaw. Can you do that, please? *Please?*"

When my eyes reopened, the staircase banister curved into a malevolent grin. Its purple tongue, cloaked as a stair-runner, licked down its brown teeth masquerading as steps.

"I knew it." I gave an upward scowl. "You never liked me."

Alone, I confronted the monster, planting my foot on its bottom tooth.

Its sneer widened.

I punched it.

My knuckle tore open. *Shit.*

Supposedly, I had hit a distended screw; in truth, the monster had bitten me. I retaliated with a stomp. *Thump.* "You like that? Huh? Want to mess with me?" *Thump, thump, thump.*

# 92

*Matthew gave her love and respect, but Peter, the apple of her eye, gave her crap. She forgave him, but I didn't.*

Near the park's entrance, a distance before the picnic grounds, flame whips and smoke plumes rose from the fire-pits. Later, the fires would smolder beneath hotdogs, burgers, and steaks. For now, their blaze provided warmth on a sunny but chilly day. Carly stopped at the first pit to rub her hands. Through the smoke, she saw umbrellas and canopies and two figures struggling to move a table. She assumed the figures were Miranda and Dieter, but when she drew closer, she realized the second figure was Fikus.

Carly marched up to him. "You have no business here."

Miranda stepped between them. "Fikus loaned us fifty chairs and twelve tables from the old church."

"I don't care if he loaned us the sunshine; get rid of him."

"Excuse me, Carly, but Fikus saved me from having to rent the setup and haul it here. He helped me wrestle with the tables, hook-up the banners, raise the canopies, and secure the umbrellas. Creating a relaxing, enjoyable party takes a tremendous amount of preparation and cooperation. So while you may not care about Fikus's help, you're not the one who needed it."

"If you needed help, you should have asked."

"I did. You said you'd be here after Sunday services, which I thought ended hours ago. Did I misunderstand?"

Miranda's tone was deplete of sarcasm, much to Carly's disappointment. Carly would have preferred to fight rather than to apologize. "I'm sorry, Miranda. After services, I met up with Kevin and lost track of time."

Fikus smirked. Carly caught it and pushed Miranda aside. Fikus skirted over the table. "What's wrong, Fikus," Carly said, "are you *sensing* my feelings or having a vision of yourself behind bars? It's only a matter of time; my father will never quit the case."

"How's that working for him?" Fikus said. "My attorney says you need proof that I was on the ridge, which of course is impossible because I was in

Utah. But despite your sinful hatred for me, I pity you, Carly. Few of us know the pain of a father's disregard as he chases an erroneous belief."

Carly kept her game face on, despite her brewing anger at Fikus and now her refreshed anger at Robyn, the DA; *I need evidence that puts Fikus on the ridge when Dorothy died.* Carly couldn't find the evidence...nor accept the injustice. It ruined her sleep, clouded her photographs, and chipped at her faith in God. How did her dad do it? Day in and day out, he plugged away with unscathed optimism as he had done on other cases for more than 40 years, still waking with a smile, still laughing in good humor, still trusting and loving generously.

After all-night talks with Kevin, Carly gave notice. At the end of April, she would turn in her badge and devote her time to photography.

Upon hearing the news, her dad and Tony threw a celebration befitting a wedding, their relatives in Italy joining by phone. Carly credited Kevin for her decision, which endeared him to her family. "Italiano, yes?" Aunt Sherrise kept squawking over the phone. In truth, Carly's decision had less to do with Kevin and more to do with Zia and her insane world. Carly longed to design her own world, too—a world spliced with wonders for a camera's lens.

Fikus snapped a tablecloth open and smoothed it flat.

"Where's Dieter?" Carly asked Miranda.

"At home. Your dad and MaGretta wanted to attend Mass in Ridgecrest, so Dieter offered to cook the casseroles. I was planning on leaving in a few minutes to help him."

"Who's going to keep an eye on all this stuff?"

Miranda indicated Fikus. "He offered to finish setting up."

"Not a chance," Carly said.

"But Fikus knows where I want the banners and the     "

"Then you stay here. I'll help Dieter."

"But Carly—"

"Just be damn sure he's gone before I get back." When Carly turned to leave, she noticed the tablecloth weights—at one end, a rock, at the other end, a gun. She picked up the gun. Half the tablecloth whipped free. "Do you have a permit for this?" she asked, knowing full well that he did.

"Of course," Fikus said. "But I was only anchoring the tablecloth."

"Is that your story? I'm pretty sure the tablecloth was covering the gun, which makes this a concealed weapon."

"Carly!" Miranda pulled her around. "That's not true."

Carly jerked free of Miranda. "Before I get back, he better be gone."

# 93

*I almost felt sorry for him—almost, but not quite, because Peter had also bawled over an elbow.*

Seemingly perturbed, Billy rapped the banister, *rap, rap, rap,* before his outstretched arms waggled as if he were asking, *what the hell are you doing?*

I waved a bloody knuckle, "THE BANISTER BIT ME!"

Billy gave a long, upward sigh, as though he were complaining to the universe about me. *Me!* He walked off, shaking his head.

I climbed the stairs as fast as I could—which wasn't very fast. I stomped ruthlessly on each tooth of the monster's grin. Once at the top, I tracked a noise down the hallway and into the last bedroom. My head poked inside, "Billy?" Fermented aftershave and soured sweat assaulted my nose. Jeez, how come guys never open a bedroom window?

*Tap, tap, tap,* came from inside the closet. Pinching my nose, I trotted to the closet door to return the knock. *Rap, rap, rap.* "Hey, come out now, Bill. I'm not really mad. I was just scared, but only for you. You might hurt yourself. Come on, Billy, come on out. I'm sorry I yelled at you."

Hearing nothing, I swung the doors wide, stepped inside, and yanked the chain on the overhead light. "Whoa." I back-stepped. The builders must have intended the large room as a nursery. Now it held a bodiless army of starched pants beneath pressed shirts wrapped in tailored jackets—long rows of ghostly soldiers, facing forward, ready to salute or attack. Their perfect alignment proved Fikus was a freak, because he wasn't smart enough to be an engineer, and he wasn't handsome enough to be gay. That left "freak" to explain his fastidiously organized clothes.

I did not want to venture into a freak's closet. "Forget it, Bill. Hide and Seek over. Get it? All-the-all-the-outs-in-free. All-the-all-the-outs-in-free."

Nothing stirred. *Shit.* I'd have to go in.

I assessed the front-line soldiers. A cotton battalion stood on the left, a squadron of wools stood on the right. And somewhere, pressed to the wall and hidden behind pants, was a reason to rethink my ever having kids.

Tightening my clutch on reality, *it's clothes, just clothes*, I elbowed into the cottons. Half-crouching, half-crawling, but fully spooked, I searched along the wall, the dark side of the army.

A jacket fell, its sleeves piggy-backing my neck. At that, traitorous Reality abandoned me, *I'm outta here*, causing Sanity to bail on me, too. But I couldn't leave without Billy. My arms whirled frantically, whacking and smacking like a human eggbeater. "Billy, *paa-leeease.*"

I attacked a fortress of fabric, ripping ties, throwing shoes, pelting suits. Cuffs and collars peeled from their skeletal-triangles. Pleats and perma-press trailed in crumpled heaps. Eventually, I stopped to catch my breath and to survey the battlefield. One row of the army lay slain.

I had won...won without Reality or Sanity's help, the overrated cowards.

While pillaging the next row, I hit a barricade of four zippered plastic bags, each stuffed with a blanket. The top one, orange, and the bottom one, green, sandwiched the blue and the red. The stack was wide enough and high enough to conceal a hunkering kid.

I sat back on my heels. "Gee, I wonder where Billy could be?" I tossed the orange blanket. "AHA!" But Billy wasn't there. I flung the blue and the red blanket, too, thinking he was curled really low. *Crap*, no such luck. I grabbed the green blanket to fling it out of my way, but my fingers slid off the plastic. I pressed the center; yep, it was a blanket, but a blanket that wouldn't budge with my one-handed grip. *Weighted?*

I unzipped the bag and reached into the thermal folds. The blanket was swaddling a thick, rectangular slab with a bumpy surface. I wrestled with this thirty pound mystery jammed into a five-pound bag until a shirt, slipping its bones, plopped on my head. I jumped up with a galloping heart. "That's it, Bill. When you decide to come out, maybe I'll be here or maybe I won't, but I'm done playing games. Got it?"

With both hands, I grasped the plastic bag and dragged it from the closet. I wanted to cut the bag open, but that bright idea dimmed under the thought of jail time. Violating a Protective Order to search for a lost boy was understandable, but no tweaked-truth, even concocted around a library and delivered with rehearsed remorse, would justify gutting the bag. I nibbled an already bloodied finger while pondering solutions.

Finally, the obvious answer came to me—Don't get caught!

Searching for a knife, a letter-opener, or a pair of scissors, I wrenched drawer after drawer, dumping the contents, but found nothing sharper than toothpicks, paperclips, and a stickpin. Taking the stickpin and straightening a paperclip, I hopped over the obstacles of his ransacked room to the only drawer left undefiled, the only locked drawer. Gum would have secured the drawer better, the lock picked so easily, the drawer sliding on its casters.

Bingo! A pocketknife. Lying beside the knife was a chain laced with a silver star embedded with a diamond. I snaked the chain around my fingers. Why would a male freak have a lady's necklace? It was worn, too. Years of rubbing a collarbone had shined and rounded the star's points.

Walking back to the bag, I dredged my memory for Miranda's description of her mom's necklace, but all I recalled was pooh-poohing her humdrum description and my reinventing the necklace into one more interesting—an emerald heart strung on a gold chain. My version was the only version I stashed into memory. I set the necklace aside.

Using the pocketknife, I plunged the blade into the plastic and filleted the bag. In my earnest, I cut too deeply and sliced the blanket. It was ugly anyway. Puke-green, the color for nightmares, not for warmth.

I stood, grabbed the blanket's edge, and spooled the wool over my arms. *Thump, thump, thump.* The great mystery spilled.

A book.

A big, stupid book.

What neurotic sicko jams a huge folio into a goddam blanket?

I sat with a thud of disappointment. In *Staircase to Hell,* the characters discovered a gargoyle's decapitated head. I didn't expect anything that grand, but I sure as hell wouldn't have risked jail for a stupid—I heaved it over— *book?* The cover board sparkled with a red-jeweled cross, thick and gaudy and very familiar. "Hey," I said with slow recollection, "you're the Minister's Catalog of Souls."

The gems winked.

After all these years, I would finally know whether the old devil had listed me as an atheist or as an agnostic.

When I lifted the cover board, the red stones seemed to darken into burgundy as if it were warning, *invade these pages and suffer the wrath of hell.* I held the cover board midair because who would know hell's wrath more intimately than the guy who murdered Dorothy?

I waited a good minute for the Earth to rumble and split open, and for flames to leap up and broil me for damnation.

Didn't happen, so I laid the cover board flat.

The beginning entries surrounded the Minister's college days, although I found no mention of parties, sports, beer, trouble, cars, or sex. I rechecked to make sure it was college and not jail.

Pages later, I found photos of a young Minister beside a sullen lady. Her mouth drooped, her eyes sagged, and her hair coiled like a sticky bun on top her head. Fikus's mother. Her drab dress buttoned up to a ruffle that cinched her throat, strangling her in modesty.

I gulped, tugging and stretching at the neck of my sweatshirt.

Photos later, the Minister's wife was holding a gigantic, squishy, lopsided grubworm.

Or Fikus.

Poor Mrs. McKenzie, married to a devil and saddled with his spawn, the poster baby to promote condoms and celibacy.

Turning pages, the journal became a scrapbook of ticket-stubs, newspaper clippings, and a documentary of secrets. Churchgoers' secrets. Charlene Ragio, my high school volleyball nemesis, had been born Charles Ragio; no wonder he-she kicked my ass.

From affairs to pregnancies, thefts to surgeries, personal upsets to scandalous trysts, all that had been spoken in trusted counseling, the Minister had betrayed into writing. Whatever his intent for creating it, the Minister's confessional sourcebook had jettisoned his son to stardom. My intrigue soured. But when I started to close the book, a loose card skewed. *Congratulations on your graduation,* signed, *Love Dorothy.*

I flipped to the Minister's graduation pictures. In the background of two photos was a young Dorothy. A young fat Dorothy. While turning pages, now one at a time, I came to a birth certificate. Miranda's birth certificate. Dorothy wasn't fat; she was pregnant.

My inner alarm blared, *Take the book and get out,* but denial glued me to the pages in search of another explanation, one less repugnant than Miranda being related to a mutated grubworm.

*Bump, bump, bump,* sounded outside.

Cops? Gunfire? Alarm now screamed, *GET OUT,* but I couldn't leave without Bill. Inhaling so deep my toes swelled, I screeched, "BILLEEEE—"

*KRLAKK, shrllll-schlunk-krrck.* A light bulb burst, and a wall mirror jumped its hook and shattered across strewn drawers.

*Earthquake?* I hurried to the window. *Billy?* Somehow, while I was reading the journal, Billy had sneaked out the bedroom. I wouldn't have believed it, but there he was, standing beneath the window and acting weirder than ever, rocking and clasping his ears.

"Bill?"

He looked up, stretched his jaw for an ear pop, and then waved.

I rammed the window to the top sill. Without caring who heard me or who called the cops, I shouted, "YOU'RE IN TROUBLE, MISTER. BIG, BIG TROUBLE. GOT THAT?"

Billy grinned, a wide gap-toothed grin.

"You little shit," I muttered as I swung out to grab hold of the drainpipe. I intended to shimmy to the ground. And I would have done just that...had the drainpipe been an inch closer. I smacked siding, grappled for the sill, and pulled myself back through window.

Billy found my near-death plunge hilarious. I wagged a finger at him. "You're in trouble, Mister. Big, huge trouble. GOT THAT?"

In our code for a loon, Billy jiggled, his eyes crossing, his tongue sputtering, and, dammit, I smiled; the kid had the loony-face down pat. I ran from the room, then, *crap*, rushed back for the book. With my arms wrapped around the Catalog of Souls, my sprint slowed to a waddle.

At the stairs, I twisted right and left, but I couldn't see around the voluminous journal to watch my steps. Unable to hold onto the banister, I began a careful descent, my feet feeling for each stair's end.

A few teeth from the landing, the monster's tongue slid back.

Motion slowed.

All my weight plus the tonnage I carried impacted on a single arm.

Both floor tile and elbow bone chipped. *"AAAWWW."* Blasts of pain careened up my arm and into my neck. I wailed and rocked, "Oh God, oh shit, shit, jeez, shit, oh God, shit, mother-shit."

Mushrooming above my agony was incredulity; how the hell can this much pain erupt from an elbow? Just a goddam elbow. *How?* Elbows jut out. They poke, bump, and jab. Anatomically, elbows are positioned to be whacked. You don't stick godforsaken pain-points in vulnerable positions. Jeez, oh jeez, what a stupid, stupid design.

When nerve-endings finally dulled into bearable throbs, I pulled upright, one arm clutching the book's bulk, the other arm curling in anemic support. I staggered out the front door.

Billy stood in the driveway.

Still panting from spiking pain, I said, "Listen, Bill, I'll talk to your mom later, okay?"

Billy's questioning gaze drifted up from the book.

"Oh this? You want to know what this is? Okay, Bill, I'll level with you, straight up, but you can't tell anyone. I'm trusting you, big time. Get it?"

He nodded gravely.

"All right, but remember, it's a huge secret, just between us." I sighed the beaten sigh of a confessor. "See, the thing is, I work part-time for the Library International Police Service, also known as LIP Service. We track down overdue books and then steal them back. That's our job. When I was looking for you, I found a book on the overdue list. The perpetrator on record is—" Jeez, for my friend to understand the real danger, I had to quit the bull. "Listen, Bill, I want you to steer clear of Fikus. Don't go near him or near his house. Never, ever go into his house again. He's not a good guy, Bill. Seriously, I need your promise. Swear it. Swear you won't go near—Bill? Billy, are you listening to me?"

Billy seemed agitated or distracted, his eyes scanning the ground and then zigzagging over me, from my neck to my feet. He rubbed his forehead, jittering and wincing.

"Billy, what's the matter? Did you lose something?"

His arm shot up, pointing urgently to the walkway beside Fikus's house.

I turned sideways. "What? What is it?" But I saw only a cat sleeping on top of the garbage cans.

I looked again at Bill, who was now oddly calm. In a swift move, he latched onto my jean pockets and gave a quick tug. It was strange and beautiful, and I guess it was Billy's way of saying goodbye.

I would have dropped the book to squeeze him like crazy, but he darted off toward his home.

He skip-danced across the lawns, vaulted the garden fence, then bounced up to his porch.

Watching him, I realized how much I was going to miss him and our goofy times together. "I love you, Bill," I whispered.

Although impossible for Billy to have heard me, he looked back with a smile...and he slapped his chest and raised two fingers—*me, too.*

## 94

*If you raise the blade of vendetta,*
*you will fall on your own sword...again.*

"SEIZE TIME!"

A Sentinel, the guardian of time and dimensions, stilled the Earth.

Leveling an accusatory finger at Alpha, Kaane said, "By neglecting to reveil his Charge, Alpha allowed Player and Energy to interact within the Neutral Point, an egregious breach to the Covenants. I am woefully harmed." He punctuated his woe with a sad sigh. "To make whole, mute the Agitator."

Addressing the Sentinel, Alpha said, "It is Kaane who has breached the Covenants. He has seized the dimension for a meritless reason. The Agitator is a Wanderer."

"A Wanderer?" Kaane looked from Alpha to the Sentinel, who also appeared somewhat puzzled. Kaane erupted in laughter. "Outrageous. Alpha's outrageous attempt to shirk accountability deserves no reply. Regardless, allow me to record the patently obvious; the Agitator is a Player, not a Wanderer."

"Untrue," Alpha said. "The Articles defining Wanderers encompass all that is beyond Earth's physical plane."

"What does he contend?" Kaane asked the Sentinel. "That this Player is not physical?"

"Sentinel," Alpha said, "I refer to the Neutral Point. The Neutral Point is not on the physical plane; it is a returned state of being. As such, until her heels turn toward the Dyads, she is rightfully classed a Wanderer."

Kaane immediately checked Zia's position—she was just beginning to turn. Kaane's laughter became a disagreeable grumble. He summoned a minion. After quick counsel, Kaane again faced the Sentinel. "Wanderer or not, the Covenants forbid an Energy's interference within the Neutral Point."

Alpha gestured toward the Counter. "This Energy is tasked as a consoling Soul. The interaction of a consoling Soul with a Wanderer is exempt from the Covenants...as all Guides know."

Kaane shook with fury. "You bastardized the definition of Wanderer."

"KAANE," the Sentinel thundered, "you will address me, not Alpha."

"Sentinel, he—I—" But Kaane lacked an argument. He clutched the minion's throat and dragged him aside. "Because of you, I seized the dimension two seconds before her heels turned. Do you realize what the penalty is for seizing a dimension?"

The minion's answer gurgled beneath Kaane's grip. When Kaane released him, the minion coughed out, "But you had reasonable—"

"*Reasonable?*" He moved toward the minion, who began backing up. "Do we look like Players? We don't indulge *de minimis* violations. If I lose access to my Charge, you lose pleasure in your existence—and you will always exist."

"Sanction the Neutral Point," the minion blurted.

Kaane's approach halted. After considering the idea, he drew a razor nail to the minion's throat. "Why would Alpha agree to a Sanction?"

"Because he must," the minion said, "if you ask for his pardon."

Repulsed, Kaane punctured the minion's throat. "You want *me* to beg *Alpha* for a pardon?"

"No, no," the minion wheezed. "Use a Player's technique; offer an excuse in lieu of regret."

Kaane withdrew his nail. An excuse versus regret; the idea had merit. Kaane returned to the Sentinel and said, "Rather than argue definitions or debate perceived offenses, I propose to sanction the Neutral Point."

A slight smile floated across Alpha's face.

"Do you agree?" the Sentinel asked.

"Sentinel," Alpha said, "a Guide who seizes a dimension has relinquished access to their—"

"AGREED!" Romal's shout arrived before his appearance, startling all.

The Sentinel began lowering to a bended knee, but Romal, quickly and discreetly, ushered him to stay upright. Romal then paddled the space for the Guides to step aside.

They did so.

Romal glided forward until he stood between Alpha and Kaane. To Kaane, he said, "You're looking quite ghastly, but I suppose that's intentional." To Alpha, Romal delivered an admonishing frown. Bending down to the stilled Earth, Romal secured Zia's veils. If only time had stopped while Zia's eyes were distracted to the side or half-mast by a blink. Instead, her eyes were wide open and fixed on the Counter's two fingers. When time

resumed, she would undoubtedly suffer confusion. Most unfortunate—
Romal patted Zia's cheek sympathetically—unfortunate indeed. Straightening,
Romal glanced from face to face. "Where were we?"

"Formalities," the Sentinel whispered.

"Oh, yes, yes." Romal came up to the Sentinel and said, "I am Romal,
Council of Genesis, Interim and Primacy Guide for Zia, Order of Agitators."
He leaned forward. "Have I dispensed with authorities?"

The Sentinel nodded.

"Good. I hereby agree to sanction the Neutral Point."

The Sentinel raised a sword. "All trespasses known and unknown
preceding this point are hereby sanctioned." Thrusting the sword downward,
the Sentinel severed the binds that held time still.

The Sentinel bowed to Romal and then disappeared.

Witnessing Alpha's shock, Kaane and his minion glided away in
celebratory laughter.

Alpha struggled to force his voice, "Romal?"

"Yes, I usurped your authority. Thank One, I arrived in time to do so."

"You do not understand."

"Understand your upper-hand? Or Kaane's upper-hand? Or vendetta's
power?"

"I did not—"

"Not yet!" Romal fronted him. "Vendetta first blinds its victims before it
romances their actions. In your blindness, Players and Energies have collided,
disregarding the rules, and now run about willy-nilly. Chaos. Observe the last
minute before the dimension was seized." Romal touched Alpha's forehead.
When the Counter tugged on Zia's jeans, Romal froze the image. "Look into
Zia's pocket."

Alpha peered through the fabric. A stunned gasp left him. "It is not the
Counter's fault," Alpha managed from a sinking voice. "I should have
shielded my Charge, but I chose to indulge her."

"No, you overindulged. There's quite a difference. Of more significance,
you drew too close to vengeance, and it blinded you. Fortunately, it blinded
Kaane as well. More fortunately, the Neutral Point is sanctioned."

"Thank you," Alpha whispered, vibrating a desire to say more but unable
to find the right words.

Romal swiveled him toward the horizon. "Berate yourself later, and I
promise to assist. Right now, guide your Agitator to that Dyad."

# 95

*Zia interprets quite a lot of things incorrectly.*

*W*hat the hell? I squinted. "Bill?" Billy disappeared. Right before my eyes, he vanished. Poof. Gone. He hadn't faded like in a mirage, and he hadn't dissolved like in an alien beam-up. My eyes stayed glued to where he last stood, half expecting him to reappear. I just couldn't process it; I just couldn't move.

A few yards in front of me, a scrub jay landed. It squawked and squawked until I told it, "I'm going," and started backward steps to my car.

Somehow, the shadows, the sun, and the elbow pain had skewed my vision. Billy had gone into his house, that's all. I turned forward, my stride lengthening. Twice, I paused to look back, because, dammit, I know what I saw; Billy had vanished...but the kind of vanished that no one ever believes.

With the journal on the passenger seat, I headed to The Sand Trap. Halfway there, I swung a U-turn, remembering that Carly wasn't going home after church. She was going to Angels Peak to help Miranda. *Crap*. I didn't want to see Miranda. Telling someone that they're related to a freak requires tact. Carly excelled at tact.

Armed with the Catalog of Souls, Carly could prove to Miranda what the rest of us already knew; Fikus was a fraud. Then Carly could deliver the final blow; he's also your half-brother. Carly could handle Miranda's tears and shock, not me. Not if I gave Carly the journal and then ran.

Angels Peak's parking lot ended in a string of redwood logs designed to stop kids from driving across the grassy picnic area to spin donuts at the ridge. But kids, determined to do it anyway, kept the ninth log rolled off. Always. It was a vandalism tradition spanning generations.

When I drove into the lot, I swerved around the dips and pits. Giant dirt-genies swirled up in pursuit. Gravel-laced plumes dogged my tires. Gravity snatched stones mid-flight and hurled them at my fenders...but missed. Gravity always missed because I was a pro at staying ahead of it. The trick is to gradually increase your speed until you can cut onto the grass through the missing ninth log. My rearview mirror attested to my finesse; a smothering dirt cloud engulfed the world behind me.

In contrast, the world in front of me...*had a ninth log?*

*"AW SHIT!"*

I stood on the brakes, cranked the wheel, and skidded.

*KRUNCH.* Thrown sideways, I hit the door when the car whacked the log...the goddam ninth log.

My car hobbled, the engine wheezing and whining. I killed the motor.

When I pushed on the door, twisting metal squealed. *Crap*—A front-end alignment *and* a bent frame. I got out. For the second time that day, I split my toe by kicking a tire.

I limped to the logs and sat, rubbing an arm, massaging a toe, and shaking my head. In simpler times, bureaucrats thought the logs' size and weight would deter vandals.

They thought wrong.

Later, they tried ropes.

We brought torches.

Now thick chains looped the redwood trunks and bolted them to cement blocks. It was depressing; today's youth had let lousy metal and clunky stones end a beautiful tradition.

Leaving the cumbersome book in the car, I headed toward the canopy tips that flapped above and beyond the first knoll. When I crested the hill, I saw Miranda's arm reach up to a canopy to secure a balloon, then she lowered behind a curtain of smoke billowing from the fire-pits.

I walked down the hill, past the pits, and into the open picnic grounds where I expected to find Carly.

"Zia," Miranda said, "you're not supposed to be here."

"Where's Carly?"

"She's at your house." Miranda glanced at the overhead banner, *Have a Safe Trip, Zia!* She dropped a fistful of streamers and thunked to the bench. "You spoiled the surprise."

"Tough. Do you have a cell phone?"

Miranda's drooping head managed a nod. "It's in my car."

At first, I thought Miranda was sulking, but the more I noticed her efforts, the more I realized her disappointment. She had helium balloons tied to raffia garlands strung between canopies dripping with poppers, twirlers, and streamers. On the tables, she had flowered plates with matching cups and, *oh-for-chrissake*, personalized napkins, *Good Luck, Zia.*

Only Miranda was dumb enough to order imprinted napkins. *Shit.* Only Miranda was sweet enough. I sat straddling the bench. "Hey, I didn't mean tough as in—" I dug for an excuse for my flippancy, but I hit hardpan. "Miranda, I'm sorry."

She shrugged but didn't look up from her lap.

"Come on, Miranda. I ruined the surprise, not the party. How could I ruin this? You went overboard. Way overboard. This party is fit for a queen. No, better than for a queen. Better than for a queen or for the president or for a Hollywood star. This party is fit for—for Edgar Allan Poe."

Obviously, my compliment was gross hyperbole, but Miranda brightened, her chin lifting with a smile, as if she actually believed that she, a mere mortal, could have possibly staged a party befitting Poe. "Thank you, Zia."

"Yeah, well, you're getting a little full of yourself," I told her. "You don't even have a raven."

"I have napkin rings."

"Napkin rings?"

"Handmade."

"You made napkin rings?"

She nodded. "And I wrote today's date on each one."

"On napkin rings?"

"In calligraphy."

"Whoa. I mean, wow." I smoothed back my kinky hair.

"Zia, your elbow."

She tried to touch the golf ball swell, but I blocked her hand. "No, no, no. I chipped the bone. You can't touch it. You can't even breathe on it. In fact, your thoughts are making it ache."

"Zia, let me see it."

"Forget it. I don't need your help. You're the one who needs help, but not from me. No way, not from me. From Carly. Yep, Carly's help."

"With the party?"

"Oh. Yeah. The party." Pinwheels danced, twizzlers sparkled, balloons bobbed, and jeez, napkin rings bore calligraphic dates. "Why did you do all this? Are you trying to make me feel guilty? Is that why you did this?"

"I did it because you're worth it."

"Yeah, right. Save the guilt-trip, Miranda. I'm not falling for it. Nope, nope, nope. I'm immune to guilt, get it? Imperviously immune."

"Zia, I—"

"Jeez, okay, okay. You win." I gathered her hands and my gaze lowered to our twenty fingers. "I'm going to tell you something pretty upsetting. I need you to get a grip. The thing is, well, Fikus is your half-brother."

I expected her hands to yank free, but her hands stayed in mine. I listened for her scoffing huff or stubborn denial, but she didn't make a sound. I looked up wondering if she had died.

"Is that it?" she asked.

"Isn't that enough? Didn't you hear me? FIKUS IS—"

"My half-brother. Is that it?"

"Miranda, I'm not making this up. I have proof."

"Zia, I know he's my brother."

"You *know?*"

"We've known for months."

"*We?*"

Consoling hands reversed, Miranda's now enveloping mine. "Zia, when I fell in love with Dieter, I embraced his whole family, but you shut me out. At best, you tolerated me, at worst, you were rude, and rude was the rule. I wanted to be friends, and God knows I tried. But every feeling I shared, you ridiculed, calling it stupid, lousy, or wrong. Had you made one effort, I would have told you about Fikus. But I'm glad you found out because look at us now. Finally, we're sharing, friend to friend." She squeezed my hands.

"Jeez, Miranda, I hate to spoil this moment, but you're wrong."

*Now* came her scoffing huff. "I'm wrong again, *naturally.*"

"Well, you are. Do the math. You believed in psychics, idealized a commune, and funded a God-barker. When you consider all of that, I think I showed unfathomable restraint."

"You called me a moron."

"Exactly. Mind-boggling restraint."

"She'll never understand," came at my back. I spun around.

Fikus dropped an armload of chairs. "I saw you talking with Zia so I hung out at the fire-pits, but it looks like you're going to be a while."

Miranda nodded...*pleasantly.*

"Are you crazy?" I said to Miranda. "How can you forgive him? How can you even look at him? After he used you and lied to you, how can you—"

"Wait, wait," Miranda said. "Lied to me? Used me? Zia, what are you talking about?"

"I'm talking about Fikus, your brother, using you as the patsy in his psychic-scam."

Miranda shook her head. "Zia, you're mixed up. Fikus didn't know we were siblings then. We were told together. After our father died, his DNA was compared to mine. Months later, the detectives gave us the news."

"Detectives? You don't mean Carly. Carly would have told me."

"Carly had no right to tell you. It's my business. Well, our business." She winked at the freak.

"For Miranda's protection," Fikus said, "I wanted the DNA results kept confidential. Right now, most people think I conned Miranda. She has their sympathy, and I have their spite. I can live with that, for Miranda's sake. But if word got out that we were siblings, small-minded locals would jump to false conclusions, and Miranda would suffer what I've had to suffer, unfounded accusations and malicious gossip. Miranda doesn't deserve that. And what brother would subject his sister to that type of treatment? Not this one." And the two of them exchanged smiles.

"Wow-oh-wow." I stood and thumped the side of my head as if clearing water from my ears. "Excuse me. I'm a bit dizzy from that sludge of bullshit. Fikus, you are one slick bastard. Can you thread a needle with that tongue?"

Miranda came off the bench and her arm spliced between Fikus and me as if she were parting the Sea of Discord. "Zia, stop it. Fikus, go. Just go."

"Oh hell, no," I said. "Stick around, freak. I'm going to prove you're a manipulative liar."

"Zia, please." Miranda shored up our eyes "I'm asking you, as a favor to me, would you please let it alone?"

"For chrissake, do you think I enjoy stirring up shit?"

She didn't answer.

"I DO NOT," I said. "Look, I didn't come here to set you straight. I planned on passing that buck to Carly. But now I can't. As much as I'd like to, I can't because you made napkin rings. I wish you hadn't, but you did. I'm trying to repay you for that, so please, Miranda, shut up and listen. When Fikus peddled his bullshit as divine, he knew you were his half-sister. His father kept a journal, which has pictures of your mom, a copy of your birth certificate, and the secrets of the parishioners. Everything the Churchgoers confessed in counseling, the Minister notated in the journal. That journal gave Fikus all of his impossible-to-know information. That's how your brother rocketed to fame. Without that journal, Fikus is your ordinary psychic-sleazebag using shills, mikes, and cold-reads. Get it? His great vision amounts to reading without glasses. Do you want the journal? It's in my car."

Miranda looked inquisitively at Fikus.

When Fikus finished his yawn, he said, "Yes, fine, whatever. Let's pander to Zia's delusions. Maybe someday she'll seek professional help."

"Back at you, freak." I marched off to get the book.

Miranda and Fikus trailed.

Nearing the fire-pits, I noticed one had flames cutting high into the smoke. Drawing closer, I saw embers glittered with red jewels. *"NOOO!"*

I jabbed, pinched, and poked at the flames, sending blackened wings fluttering.

*KRAC-POK* Out from the popped wood came a fiery fist of burning kindle. It struck me square across the bridge of my nose.

I reeled, blinded, my eyebrow, eyelash, and bangs frizzling.

Arms roped my waist, swung me backward, and threw me to the ground.

"GET ICE!" Miranda shouted, her body pinning mine. She slapped and rubbed my shriveling hair. "HURRY UP!"

Pain wrenched me into the fetal position.

Blazing eyes tinted the stars an ominous orange.

In a flash, Romal fronted Alpha to keep him in place. "It is Kaane's offense. Do not make it yours. *Do not* make it yours."

# 96

*Peripheral Players may not acquire knowledge prior to the Dyad.*

Carly turned off the oven but left the trays inside to keep the strudel warm. A bubbling crock-pot, a burning stove, and a 350-degree oven had transformed the kitchen into a steam bath. Carly lowered her head beneath the faucet to let cool water run along her neck. "What's next?"

*Whrrr* came from a floor fan that Dieter positioned in front of the open Dutch door. "Relax," he said. "We have time to kill before we load up."

Carly pulled a chair at the kitchen table, but when she sat, she felt Zia's envelope poke her hip. She withdrew it. "Hey, Dieter, I wasn't supposed to deliver this until later, but I think now is a good time."

Dieter pocketed the envelope on his way to the sink to scrub his hands.

"Aren't you curious?" Carly asked.

"It's from Zee, right?"

"Yes, but don't kill the messenger."

Dieter took a dishtowel and pulled a chair alongside Carly. He leaned back, his legs stretching. He worked the towel over already dried fingers.

Carly nudged him. "Come on, you probably expected it, right?"

"Expect she would cut out early?" Dieter shrugged. "Expect she would tell me in a letter? No, I did not."

"At least she told us, which is more honest than we've been with her."

"Meaning?"

"Meaning, everyone but Zia knows that Fikus and Miranda are siblings."

"Carly, that's their business to tell, not ours. If Zee had shown Miranda an ounce of respect, Miranda would have happily shared the news with her."

His tone had an edge of harshness—far more harshness than the conversation warranted, Carly believed. "I think thou protests too much."

Dieter frowned. "What the hell are you talking about?"

"You and your worrying. Underneath your tough-guy controlled exterior is just a big brother who's worried about his little sister. It's very sweet."

Carly laid an understanding hand onto Dieter's arm.

Dieter eyed the hand until Carly withdrew it. "Zee is my sister; of course I love her. And yeah, I'm worried. She's not acting right."

"She always acts a little—"

"Not acting right for Zee."

"Dieter, most girls, sooner or later, spread their wings and fly their hometown. You think she needs a clue and a prayer; yes, she told me. But I'm telling you that most girls—"

"Zee isn't most girls." His abruptness chilled the air. "Haven't you noticed? She's a little...funny."

"Everyone has quirks. Zia just has more than most."

Dieter shook his head. "Do you know where I found Zee after she disappeared from Pop's funeral? I found her on the beach. She was—" Dieter looked away and cleared his throat. "She was standing in the water."

For several seconds, Carly waited to hear the problem. When the silence had stretched, she asked, "Dieter, what happened in the water?"

Dieter looked at her queerly. "Standing in the damn ocean. *Saltwater!*"

Carly shrugged.

"Forget it," Dieter said.

"No, tell me. Why is that a problem?"

"That's Zee's business to tell, not mine. But if you knew her better, you would know why I'm worried."

Wanting to lighten his mood, Carly said, "Hey, Dieter, let me show you the photo I picked out for her." Carly left for the entryway where MaGretta had stacked the parting gifts.

Willow and Geminus looked anxiously at Romal.

"Absolutely not," Romal said. "Parity Three is still in play."

With much reluctance, Willow shielded the gift.

Carly returned to the kitchen. "I can't find it. I even checked the closet. Did MaGretta move some of the gifts?"

"Find it later," Dieter said. "I smell something burning."

# 97

*When lost, open your heart to guidance. Loving arms will find you, lift you, and light your direction home.*

"GET OFF!" I shouted through riptides of pain. "GET OFF ME!"

Miranda arched and saw my smoldering sleeves. "Lie still. We're going to ice your arms."

I sipped in another breath. "*Pleeease*, get off me. Please, jeez, please, you're crushing my elbow."

She rolled off.

My fried hands cupped the swell while pain radiated through my entire side. I rocked and swallowed between ragged cries to the universe, "How is this possible? HOW? It's just an elbow, just a goddam elbow."

"Is it burned?" Miranda asked.

"It's PULVERIZED."

"Zia, I'm sorry, but your sleeves were on fire." She helped me sit up. Carefully, she peeled away charred cotton. My arms emerged with pink, healthy flesh. My wrists, however, were pocked with bubbles and my palms were seared smooth. "Zia, your hands are burned."

"YA THINK!" I twisted into my shoulder to wipe tears and snot onto what was left of my sweatshirt. "Don't touch me. Just back off. Please, just back off."

"I was trying to save you."

"Save me? I was trying to save you. I had proof of everything I stated, but your brother destroyed it."

Miranda looked sorrowfully at me, as if I were a nutcase deserving of pity. "Zia, why did you burn yourself?"

"Aw, shit, why doesn't anyone ever hear me?" I sniffled again into my shoulder. "I give up. I'm done. Miranda, have a nice life."

Fikus returned carrying bags of ice. He dropped them beside Miranda.

"Come on, Zia," Miranda said, "let's ice your hands."

"No. Nothing that freak touches will ever touch me."

"Droll," Fikus said. "Poetic but droll."

"Shut up," Miranda told him, causing Fikus and me equal surprise. "Zia, come on, it's just ice."

"Probably dry ice." I forced up to my feet, but couldn't force my eyes from the bags. My scorched hands were still burning, and I desperately wanted to thrust them into the ice, but my stupid pride kept echoing, *nothing that freak touches will ever touch me.* Endure the pain or retract the insult? At that moment, I hated my pride as much as I hated Fikus, both were immobilizing me from the frigid relief I needed.

Miranda kicked the bags aside, breaking my trance. "You're right," she said. "The heck with sharp slivers of ice. They would tear your burnt skin. Me and my dumb ideas. You're right to want cold water."

"I am?"

"I'll say. What was I thinking? Sorry, Zia. Come over to the benches and dunk your hands in the cooler's ice-water."

"Yeah?" My legs wobbled under a weight of gratitude. Miranda's arm wrapped my shoulder and she escorted me back to the benches.

My inflamed hands plunged into the icy water. *Ahhhh,* blessed cold to slow the crops of blisters. For a long while, I swished and swirled, playing with dissolving icebergs. Miranda sat quietly beside me. Fikus hovered nearby, opening chairs and setting them at tables. Every few minutes, I withdrew my hands to count the seconds before the burning returned. Eventually, seconds became minutes and the burning became tolerable, at least more tolerable than the presence of Fikus.

I pulled from the water for the last time. "Hey, Miranda, uhm, thanks."

She gave a humble smile. For the life of me, I could not think of one reason, good or bad, to explain why I had treated Miranda like crap. In many ways, she was like MaGretta—trusting, kind, generous. That's what I adored about MaGretta; that's what I ignored about Miranda. Only one reason for my behavior made sense; I was an asshole, a total bitch.

My lungs filled for a long overdue apology that Miranda had no reason to believe or accept. "Miranda, I treated you really lousy. You didn't deserve it. Not a bit. I'm sorry. I'm honestly sorry."

Miranda looked hard into my eyes. After a minute, she nodded; she heard me, she believed me, she forgave me. She also hugged me...and I let her. For the first time, no wall stood between us. Only a bridge.

When our hug ended, I got up, wished her well, and told her goodbye.

"Let me drive you to the Med Center," she said.

"I don't need a doctor."

"You have second-degree burns. When the blisters open, they'll get infected. You need your hands bandaged."

She tried to inspect my palms, but I told her to quit fussing.

Relentlessly, she wrangled my arms. "Zia, let me have a look."

"No, don't worry about me." I shoved my hands into my pockets, "*Yeow*," and instantly brought them back out. Stuck to a blister was a sharp, silver star dangling from a chain. *Oh, shit, I'm a klepto.*

Miranda ripped the necklace from my hand. She examined it quickly and then waved it in my face. "Where did you get this? Where?"

I had plenty of reasons to lie; I didn't want a wall between us again, I didn't want us parting on bad terms, and I didn't want her looking at me as if I were a nutcase to be pitied or a shit-stirrer to be tolerated.

Miranda clutched my shoulders. "Please, Zia, tell me where you got it."

"Do we have a bridge between us? I mean, if we do, we just built it, right? Seems premature to test its strength. What if it's flimsy? What if—"

"Zia, trust the bridge. I'll hear you. I'll believe you."

"Whoa, it's like you were in my head...except you forgot the last part."

"What last part?"

"You'll forgive me...for stealing it."

"Who did you steal it from?"

I pointed a burnt finger at the hateful eyes glowering behind Miranda.

Miranda turned, "Fikus?" Then Miranda's face began to change. Her eyes thinned and darkened, her jawline sharpened, and her cheeks contracted beneath her cheekbones. She transformed into a knowing Miranda, a hardened Miranda...a wee scary-looking Miranda.

Kaane shook an infuriated fist. "The Counter planted it."

Alpha did not respond.

"You knew," Kaane said encroaching into Alpha's space.

"Ahem," Romal said, and when he had Kaane's attention, Romal waved. "Give my disregards to beelzeNiine."

Kaane rumbled. "Clever, Romal."

"The act preceded the sanction," Alpha said. "Choices made in the Neutral Point will not parallel the choices made in Alaska, for this time, the Healer gains evincible knowledge of your Charge."

A smirk skipped across Kaane's lips. "Too late." While he drifted away, he tossed a casual whisper to his Charge. "Kill the Dyad."

Instantly, the message released a murderous rage within Fikus. But just as quickly, the fragment within Triite quivered, twisting Kaane's words into the message Triite had waited centuries to hear. "Kill the Agitator."

⚷

"Dieter, take over stirring the chili," Carly said. "I'll start loading up the car. I need fresh air." Carrying a box stuffed with chips and crackers, she headed toward the door.

While crossing the entryway, Carly spotted a glint of metallic green wrapping paper poking up from the stack of gifts. She set down the box of snacks and dug out the gift. "How did I miss this?" She looked around, somewhat suspicious of a prank. She returned to the kitchen. "Dieter, this is the photo I wrapped for Zia."

"You don't look happy about it."

"I am. It's just that—It was right there among the gifts, right where I had already searched."

"That happens to Zee all the time."

"Oh, yeah, and this is her house. Either her ghosts are picking on me or I have heat stroke from this kitchen."

Her comment gave Dieter a smile...*finally*, Carly thought.

Dieter bumped up to sit on the counter. "Well, let's see it."

Carly stripped off the foil. "Don't expect much. It's only a bug."

"Hand it over."

When Carly gave it to him, she watched for his immediate reaction.

His mouth circled, "Whoa," and he stared unblinking.

Carly, unable to interpret a *whoa* and a stare, said, "Do you like it? I know it's not award-winning, but Zia dropped hints that she wanted it."

"Oh, I bet she did. I bet those hints dropped with the subtlety of a wrecking ball. So what were you doing in Utah?"

"Utah? What's in Utah?"

Dieter looked up quizzically. "Your beetle."

# 98

*Meaner than a snared wolverine.*

Fikus came around the table, "Bitch," and struck so fast, I never saw the fist. I hit the ground, dazed, my eardrums ringing. Before I recovered, Fikus yanked me upright, "Meddling bitch," and punched me again.

My vision blurred and I tasted blood. The ringing in my ears now blared. In its din, I heard shouting and yelling and the thuds of a fight.

I lifted my head to spit sand. A blur of feet marched toward me. I tried to crawl, crawl away quickly, but a kick exploded into my side. My breath shot out. Before I could pull in another, Fikus roped a hank of my hair around his fist and jerked me upright. His knuckles grooving my skull, he dragged me, kicking and swinging, across the grounds and over the knoll that separated the picnic area from the cliffs.

I thought he intended to throw my ass over the bluff, but he stopped on the ridge and slammed me, face down, like a rag-doll. His knee jammed into my spine. "Look!" He wrenched my head back. "Look out there. A decent, God-fearing woman died from this ridge. She was a devoted wife and a loving mother. MY mother. Did you dig into the lies of her death? No, you did not. Nobody did. Nobody cared. Life as usual for Kenzie Cove. But when a worthless slut gets what's coming to her, everyone wants to know why and how and who's to blame. 'Poor, poor Dorothy,' and they call it a shame. Do you think that's fair, Zia? Don't you think my mother deserved—"

"LET HER GO!" Miranda shouted, and to my amazement, Fikus's grip loosened. My face flopped into the dirt. "Get off her," Miranda said.

Free of his weight, my lungs expanded. I rolled with a blind swing and a backward kick, expecting Fikus to try to stop my escape. But he didn't. I crawled toward Miranda, and then pushed onto my feet. "Miranda?"

She did not look like Miranda. Her short, static-charged hair cast a dark halo around her head. A bruised cheek, still swelling, nearly closed one eye. Her other eye steadied down the length of her arms, which were locked straight, her hands clasping a gun. "Why did you kill my mother?"

Dieter set aside the photo. "I just assumed you took the shot."

"I did, but not in Utah."

"Carly, I'm not calling you a liar, but Zee put our family through hell over this beetle or I wouldn't know it from a cockroach. It's a subspecies of the tiger beetles, although Zee got it into her head that it was a full species, not a sub. In that vein, she wrote dozens of caustic letters to federal and state officials. She demanded they recognize this beetle as a full species, but what they recognized was a nut. Our phone clicked for months; I'm sure officials were trying to determine whether she was a harmless or a dangerous nut."

"A ruckus over a beetle?"

"A rare beetle. Environmentalists are fighting to protect it under the Endangered Species Act. If they win, collectors have to leave the beetle alone. If they lose, the beetle faces extinction. Both those outcomes stoked Zee's obsession to get one. Eventually, she struck a deal with a fellow collector over the internet. When the bug came in, Zee paraded it around, telling everybody everything that nobody cared to know about this bug. Pop only cared that Zee got her money's worth; he figured the more you paid, the bigger the beetle. He didn't expect a beetle that could fit on a postage stamp; he expected a beetle that would need a leash. MaGretta only cared that the certified beetle was certified dead. And I was just relieved that Zee had quit badgering me for airfare to Vegas."

"Vegas? I thought you said Utah."

"Vegas is the closest major airport to the Coral Pink Sand Dunes in Utah. That's where this beetle lives. They live no where else on this planet."

"Well, a few must have strayed and—"

"No where else on this planet."

"Dieter, I personally photographed this live beetle at Angels Peak."

"Then we have an anomaly. Because the only way this beetle could have been at Angels Peak is by hitching a ride on someone in the Coral Pink Sand Dunes, who went straight from the dunes to—Carly, you don't look well."

"No, I'm—I'm fine. Is Zia's beetle still here?"

"Check her room. She tapes full statistics on the mounting's backside."

With photo in hand, Carly hurried to Zia's bedroom. "Her walls are bare," she called out to Dieter.

"Check her closet," Dieter said, "but stand back. Zee likes to—"

*RUCKLE-CLUNKLE-CLONK-FLUMP, splink, tink.*

Dieter rushed to the room, but halted in the doorway. "—stack things. Are you okay?"

Carly, still crouching and protecting her head, nodded. When she straightened, her eye caught a dark mass on her shoulder. With a sweeping hand, she sent the preserved tarantula flying. Dieter stepped over jars and broken glass to pluck the unframed bugs off Carly's hair and back.

Tossing a scorpion, Dieter said, "I think that's the last of it."

Carly touched his arm. "Could you *know* instead of *think*, please?" And she rotated for inspection.

"Oh, I missed one." Dieter then peeled a flattened millipede off her calf.

Carly began sifting through the fallen frames. Dieter, thinking to search the remnants in the closet, pushed aside boxes to fully open the door. "I should have known," he said spotting flaps of purple velvet and green satin on the door's reverse side. Beneath the curtains was a tiny shadow box. "Zee hides her valuables."

"Bug burglars?"

"Yep, Zee claims they're everywhere." Dieter unhooked the box and handed it to Carly.

Under the desk lamp, Carly compared Zia's beetle to the beetle in the photo. Identical. She flipped it over and read the stats, which included a map of the beetle's roaming region, one of the smallest of any creature on Earth. Her forehead glistening with rising tension, her fingers leaving foggy prints on the glass, Carly still mustered a pretense of nonchalance. "You get things packed in the car. I'll clean up this mess."

"We got plenty of time. I'll give you a hand."

"No, I—" Carly's smile rose and fell. "I want to check out the bugs."

Dieter rolled his eyes. "You stink at lying. You want privacy? No problem. That's all you needed to say." He left, closing the door behind him.

Carly unpocketed her cell phone.

*...Gloria laus, gloria laus, gloria laus et honor...*

Like always, Spuretta jumped when his cell phone buzzed; it buzzed like a hornet trapped in his pants. While the chorus resounded, he withdrew the phone, glanced the name, and then said, "hold on, Carly." He kissed MaGretta's cheek and pointed to the phone.

Without missing a note, MaGretta nodded understanding.

Tipping his head and mouthing apologies, Spuretta worked his way out of the pew. He hurried down the aisle, through the vestibule, and into the quieter outdoors. "Carly?"

"Dad, on the Norst case, remember the pictures I took after shooting the crime scene?"

"The bird?"

"No, the beetle. The green-headed beetle. It's a Coral Pink Sand Dunes Tiger Beetle. They're not scattered here and there. There's no migration and there's no exception. Their diminishing number lives on an eight-mile stretch in Utah." Carly read the stats into the phone.

"Southwest Utah," Spuretta said, "I'll be darned."

"Fikus took a flight from Vegas to California and drove straight to Angels Peak. He never stopped or changed clothes. He didn't have time. And when Dorothy fell from the ridge, this six-legged stowaway fell from Fikus."

"Carly, slow down."

"The passenger list leaving Las Vegas puts Fikus in California; our green-headed friend puts him on the ridge."

Spuretta mulled it over. "Are you sure you have the right beetle?"

"I trust Zia's fanaticism for bugs," Carly said. "If Zia's beetle wasn't the rare tiger beetle, she wouldn't have enshrined it; she would have crammed it down the seller's throat. So dad, how much faith do you have in my photographer's eye? Because I'm stating, unequivocally, Zia's beetle matches the beetle I photographed on the ridge."

Spuretta let out a long breath. "You did good, kid. I'll call for a warrant."

"Fikus is helping Miranda set up for the party. Meet me at Angels Peak."

"Carly, don't do anything until I get there."

# 99

*I listened without hearing, watched without seeing,*
*and felt only the northern wind*
*as it cut through my jacket and rattled my bones.*

Swirling in the mix of a bruised rib, a burnt arm, and a crushed elbow was a deluge of confusion. Was Fikus trying to kill me over a stolen necklace? Was Miranda accusing Fikus of killing Dorothy? And where the hell did Miranda get a gun?

I had to do something, but I had no clue what that something should be. Should I run for help? No, I couldn't leave Miranda. Should I start hollering? No, nobody would hear me. Should I wave a stick or grab a rock? No, a gun pretty much trumps sticks and stones.

I stood to the side, watching and listening but not getting it at all.

Mean veins bulged on Fikus's temples. "You'd shoot me? Shoot your own brother? I trusted you, Miranda. I protected you. And now you'd shoot me? *Me?* Well, what are you waiting for? Guts? Grow a spine; pull the trigger. Shoot me. SHOOT!"

Miranda, crazy calm, repeated, "Why did you kill my mother?"

Fikus turned toward the ocean. His anger cooled into bothered huffs and tired sighs.

"Fikus, why did you kill my mother?"

His lips squeezed together and he shook his head.

"Fikus, why did you—"

"SHE KILLED MINE!" he shouted just when a wave pitched high.

I jumped, startled by the shout and by the ocean breaking into the rocks.

Miranda didn't even flinch.

Then, like the wave, Fikus's anger receded. His head lowered and a quick knuckle blotted his eyes. He turned again toward the sea. "Growing up, I wondered why my mother was so sad all the time. So tired. So thin. Just a wisp of a woman. Then one day, she packed her clothes and said she was leaving, leaving my father...and me. Leaving me, the only person who truly loved her. My father explained it as depression, but he was lying. It was one lie among hundreds of lies. Years later, I found my father's journal and learned the truth. My father had paid for his whore and bastard child to move here from Utah. That was the final blow that destroyed my mother. She lost the will to fight for her marriage." He inhaled a deep breath through his nose. "It's a universe of equity, Miranda. My mother jumped from this cliff. In fairness, your mother needed to feel what my mother felt, the shock of falling and the terror of imminent death."

"Why had your mother packed?" Miranda asked.

Through a flurry of blinks, Fikus glanced at us. "What?"

"If your mother intended to jump, why had she packed?"

Fikus's gaze scoured the ground as if the answer were hiding near his feet. After a while, he looked up with a shrug.

Pity brewed in Miranda's eyes, even her swollen eye. She lowered the gun. "Fikus, how do you know what your mother felt?"

"I assume she felt—"

"No, Fikus. You're not assuming."

Fikus twitched spasmodically, as if he were wearing wool over sunburned skin.

"You were with her," Miranda said, her voice soft. "Weren't you?"

"No." Fikus shook his head continuously. "No, she was alone."

"You saw your mother's face when she fell, *fell*, from this ridge. She didn't jump. You were with her. You witnessed her shock and terror."

Fikus's head shaking and body twitching slowly abated. His chin lowered. "I didn't mean to push her." He stared numbly at the ground. "We were standing right here, right at this spot, when she told me she was leaving. A boy shouldn't have to beg his mother to stay, but I did. I begged and I pleaded, 'Please, mommy, please don't go. Whatever is wrong, I'll fix it. I promise. Just stay. Please stay. Please, please don't go.'" His eyes closed tightly, sending a tear down his cheek. "'*Pleeease*, mommy, please don't leave me.'"

"Fikus, what happened?"

Fikus brushed away the tear. "She tried to hold me. But I didn't want her damn comfort. I wanted her to stay. So, I—I pushed her." Fikus shrugged, an apathetic, oh-well shrug. "I only meant to push her away. I didn't mean for her to fall. I loved my mother. I never meant for her to die."

"Fikus," Miranda said, her face battered and swollen, her tone drenched in sympathy, "you're lying."

*Huh?* I hadn't expected Miranda to say that, and apparently, neither had Fikus. He shot a raging glare at me.

From defensive habits, my palms flew up, *Hey, I didn't say it.*

Moving subtly toward Miranda, Fikus said, "She had no right to leave me. No right to make her own son beg and plead. I'm glad I shoved her."

Miranda raised the gun. "Stay back."

"You won't shoot me," Fikus said. "All wrongs have been righted, all debts have been paid, and all scores have been settled, both for us and for our parents. Don't you see that? You have no reason to—"

"Fikus, stop. Stop. I don't want to shoot you, but I will."

Fikus paused, his head tilting as he studied Miranda.

Her arms braced, her stance firm, and her grip solid, Miranda appeared the pinnacle of resolve.

But Fikus smiled, realizing the facade and concluding what I already knew—Miranda would never pull the trigger. He moved closer.

*Aw shit!* I spun toward Miranda to lunge for the gun—I had no problem with shooting the freak—but motion lingered and time thickened in a haze of déjà vu. My heels smacked down and cemented. My arm flung out and stretched to its limit. "Quick, give me the gun."

The moment she set it into my hand, I swung it toward Fikus. "Back off, freak."

Like a human Etch-A-Sketch, his head tipped down, shook, and erased every trace of sadness. His face came up redrawn of rage. He marched toward me.

I squeezed the trigger...then again and again, ratcheting in futility.

Fikus's hand wrapped the barrel. "Let go."

And I did.

Displaying the gun sideways, Fikus pulled back the hammer. "Single action, you ignorant bitch."

I sickened; I was the stupidest shit in the whole freakin' world because even a cap-gun needs to be cocked.

Fikus walked to the ridge, his gaze returning to the sea. Miranda and I started shuffling backward. Fikus shouted, "You can't outrun a bullet." He turned toward us. "And I'm an excellent shot."

"Fikus," Miranda said, "I understand how hurt—"

"HURT?" His face flushed into crimson. "For you, Miranda, for you, I poured out my Soul. I revealed myself. For you! But what did you do? You betrayed me. You're the same as my mother. Same as Zia. Same as all women, all blights on mankind. You betrayed me."

"No, Fikus, I—"

"YOU GAVE ZIA THE GUN." He took deep breaths as if to regain his patience. "You're another conniving bitch. You pretend to understand equity, but all the while, you're judging me. *You*, a cowardly betrayer, judging *me.*"

"You gained nothing by killing my mother," Miranda said. "It didn't change what happened in the past between our parents, and it didn't bring back your mother. There's no equity, Fikus. You didn't—"

I pulled Miranda sideways for a ventriloquist's whisper, "Agree with him. He's whacked. He says he got equity, he got equity. Don't argue."

Miranda stepped toward Fikus. Her hands at her backside, Miranda's fingers gestured for me to inch away. "Fikus, maybe on some level—"

"All levels," Fikus said. "I achieved perfect parity on all levels, mother for mother," and then his head tipped toward me, "and father for father."

A shiver raced up my spine. "What does that mean?" I started forward.

Immediately, Miranda stepped in my way. "Agree with him. Just agree."

"No. He's talking about my Pop."

"Zia, please."

"Am I right, freak?" I shouted over Miranda's shoulder. "Did you hurt my Pop?"

"No," Fikus said. "You did. Your broken promise killed him. You wanted the name of the man responsible for Dorothy's death, and I gave you that name—my father. His deception killed Dorothy and my mother. Your deception killed your father. For you, I gave up my father, my church, and my success. For me, you gave up nothing. Off to Neptunes you went, drinking and gambling and carousing like a penniless whore. Your depravity tipped the scales beyond forgiveness. You are not innocent, Zia. You're an immoral, vile-tongued slut who deceived me...deceived me for years. I am the victim. ME! For breaking your promise, I would have killed you, but a cat intervened." He stretched his collar to show puckered gashes. "Then I realized my mistake. Equity dictates an eye for an eye, a father for a father."

I shoved free of Miranda. "You sick bastard."

Fikus leveled the gun at me.

"Fikus, NO," Miranda hollered. "Zia, STOP."

"You goddam freak."

Fikus cocked the gun. "You're going to apologize for every time—"

"You fucked up—"

"SHUT UP! Never again will you—"

"—psychotic—"

"SHUT UP! SHUT UP!"

"—FAA-*REAK!*"

A myriad of moments blurred; Miranda's screech, her knocking me aside, the gun exploding.

A chunk of flesh ripped from Miranda's shoulder.

She didn't spin or fall. She just stood there, staring in surreal shock, waiting for the pain to signal her brain. Her lip quivered, "Zia?" before her face whitened and her legs folded.

I rushed to slow her fall. "Oh God, don't die. Don't die." I whipped off my sweatshirt and wrapped it around her shoulder. "Please be okay. Lie still. Lie still. Don't die. Please don't die. Lie still."

Miranda looked past me. "No, Fikus."

Before I could turn, Fikus roped me in a headlock, the gun pressed to my temple. "See what you did?" he hissed in my ear. "Your fault, Zia. This is your fault. You shot my sister."

"Fikus, stop." Miranda fought against shock to regain her feet. "Let her go, Fikus. Please."

"Do you possess one shred of loyalty? I'M YOUR BROTHER! I stood by you, trusted you. I GAVE YOU HOPE!" He flung me to the ground. "She ridiculed and mocked you. She made me shoot you, and she tried to shoot me. ME! YOUR BROTHER!"

He began pacing in tight, distraught circles, shifting from clasping his head to pointing the gun. "Deceit, deceit, deceit."

Despite her blood draining into my sweatshirt, Miranda seemed bizarrely calm and mentally detached from her injury.

Fikus was an emotional melee, sobbing and shouting and pacing. "You gave her the gun. YOU! You chose her life over mine. Why, Miranda? Why would you choose this bitch's life over your own brother's?"

"I'd choose her life over mine."

Fikus halted, briefly stunned. Then another persona emerged, the rage-controlled Fikus. "Liar," he said quietly. He grabbed my hair, jerked me to my feet, and rammed the gun beneath my jaw. "Prove me wrong, Miranda. Prove you're not a lying bitch. Give your life to save Zia's life. Jump. If you jump, I'll let Zia go, and you will have saved her life with your honesty. If you don't jump, I'll shoot her, and you can watch her die. For the rest of your life, you'll know you killed her with your lie."

"Fikus, please, let her—"

The gun swung down and fired. A blast of pain careened up from my foot. Fikus's muscles tightened around my neck to keep me upright, though nearly cutting off my air. Once more, the gun pressed under my jaw. "No...more...lies. Jump!"

Miranda backed up to the cliff's edge. She glanced down, and then began sidestepping to the right. "First, let her go."

"After you jump," Fikus said. "I promise."

Miranda moved further up the ridgeline. Every few feet, she glanced over her shoulder. "Fikus, I can't trust you to keep your promise."

"I'm not the liar. Prove the same about yourself."

"But Fikus—"

He pulled back the hammer.

Miranda stooped, then started to slide from the fifty foot drop.

The gun digging into my windpipe, I couldn't even mouth the word, no.

She disappeared.

Fikus released his grip.

Horror melted my bones; I fell in a lump.

Fikus crouched beside me. Using the gun barrel, he drew back the curtain of hair covering my face. "Why are you crying? My sister told the truth. Honesty should be celebrated."

I started crawling toward the ridge. With every knee and palm that lifted and lowered and worked its way across the ground, I whispered, "I'm sorry, Miranda, I'm sorry." When I reached the cliff's edge, I swallowed and choked, hating myself for what I had caused—Miranda's limbs, broken and mangled, impaled on death's rocky teeth. "I'm sorry, Mir—*Miranda?*"

Yards down and to the right, a ledge protruded from the precipice like a tongue, long and narrow, jutting from a face. On it, Miranda huddled against the wall and pressed a hushing finger to her lips.

Unnecessary; I was speechless.

Miranda had inched along the ridgeline to aim her fall. Once again, I had underestimated this woman—this woman of steeled wits and titanium guts. Far below her, the ocean swashed through the craggy rocks, churning up drifts of saliva as though it were robbed of a meal.

A shadow lengthened to the side of me.

Quickly, I tried to scoot back from the edge, but just as quickly, Fikus threw aside the gun and yanked me up by the front of my tee shirt. He pulled me into his face. "You will apologize for each time you have ever called me a freak." He tilted me over the edge.

My arms clapped his arms, my hands grappling for a firm hold, my feet skating for solid earth.

Finally, he pulled me forward. "Your life is in my hands. If I let go, you die." He leaned me back, laughed, and then pulled me forward. Pushing and pulling, pushing and pulling, he teetered me on the cliff's edge. "Apologize or you'll join my sister."

*Join?* I glanced at the distance to Miranda's ledge. It was too far to the side, too far for me to reach. Panic shouted, *You're going to die.* I didn't have Miranda's wits and courage, but a very small voice inside me urged, *Platform twist dive. Don't flail. You'll hit the ledge as you start the arc.* Immediately, panic retorted, *You'll miss the ledge; your brain will become fish food.* The tiny voice countered, *Launch to the side, twist, you'll make the ledge. Try, TRY!*

Panic's voice came out audibly, "No, no."

"No?" Fikus stopped rocking when I was full tilt. "You'd rather die than apologize?"

Drawing on Selective Concentration, I shut out the voice of panic. To my imagination's credit, instantly I was standing on the three-meter platform, my back to the pool, though a pool far to the right. Instead of jagged rocks, below me was a panel of judges with readied pens.

"Ziaaa," Fikus sang, "I'm waaaiting."

I pretended to whisper an apology.

The judges snorted...or maybe it was Fikus. "LOUDER!"

I whispered again.

"I can't hear you." As he drew me forward, my chin came up, my spine stiffened, and my arms pressed to my sides, straight and balance. But I had to propel—the pool was yards to the right. To make it, I had to bend my knees. But if I bent my knees, I'd lose a point.

A judge jumped up, but this judge didn't fit with any judge I could have ever imagined. He was big, bluish, naked, and furry, more bear than man, and he was sucking a pipe. *Oh jeez,* I had imagined a crack-smoking bear. *Yes, dear lady, bend those knees. Penalty waived! Penalty waived!*

"APOLOGIZE!"

My eyes flashed open, and I hurled a bloodied phlegm-ball. "Fuck you, freak."

In a single moment, his hands came off me and went to his face.

My arms swept high.

His arms drew back for a vengeful shove.

My legs pushed off.

He thrust out with a cheated screech. His fingers grazed me, dragging my launch and spinning me off-kilter.

Seconds felt eternal—*Oh God, I missed*—but right when I arced, *WHAP*, my chest smacked the ledge. The impact bounced me backward, winded and sliding.

Miranda lunged for my arms. "Zia, hold on, hold on."

I made stuttering noises, my lungs grappling for air.

"Come on, Zia, pull up. Please, Zia, come on, pull yourself up."

No breath came. "*Au, au, au.*" My chin grooved into the dirt, my legs wheeled emptiness. No leverage. Black spots circled my head. Bumblebees, swarming bumblebees, their buzz grew louder and louder. But I was too tired to swat them, too tired to bicycle, just...too...tired.

"Zia, open your eyes. Stay with me. Open your eyes."

My fingers groped for the snooze button. "Not time."

"Please, Zia, help me. Open your eyes."

All I wanted was five more minutes, just five more minutes of sleep; I forced awake to tell Miranda so.

Awareness came with a rush of pain and a gasp for air.

Miranda lay prone, her face two inches from mine, her arms locked around my arms, her grip holding onto all of my weight.

Blood had soaked through the sweatshirt and had blackened the ledge like an oil spill. Miranda hadn't the strength to pull me up, and I hadn't the leverage to boost.

When I tried pushing up on my elbows, the chipped bone brought back the spots of unconsciousness.

I braced onto one side, digging in on my good elbow, and dangled from waist down.

# 100

*The Indian called after him, "Cheechakos will die."*

To Carly's luck, Fikus's van was still at Angels Peak, only now, it was layered in dirt. Miranda's car, too. A dust devil must have swept through the lot. Carly exited her car and then sat on the redwood logs to wait for her dad.

At the lot's opposite end, an inconsiderate jerk had parked at the logs, their tan car blocking the drive-through and creating a safety hazard. Carly smiled; that end of the lot had a history of safety hazards. In high school, Zia and her fellow delinquents used to roll off the ninth log. What a bunch of vandals; Carly laughed lightly. By the car's angle, you would think one of those vandals had gunned through the lot, not knowing—Carly's attention jerked back to the car. But Zia was halfway to Oregon. Carly got up slowly. Shielding her eyes, she counted the logs. *One, two, three, four...* Zia drove a pale blue car, not tan. *...five, six, seven, eight...* But pale blue becomes light brown when covered in dirt. *...nine!* Her heels pounded in a full sprint. "No, no, no."

When she reached the car, "Shit," her fist added another dent. What was Zia doing here? Carly started toward the picnic grounds. Hadn't Zia seen Fikus's van? Carly looked back. No, Zia had not seen Fikus's van and a dirt devil hadn't coated the vehicles. It had been Zia, gunning it through the parking lot to stay ahead of the dirt clouds. Zia and Fikus were likely arguing while Miranda refereed. Then Carly remembered the gun. She began running.

When she crested the knoll, smoke obscured her view, but she heard no angry voices, no sounds of a fight, and her gait eased. She passed the fire pits and walked toward the canopies. She saw no sign of Zia, Fikus, or Miranda.

The cooler, left open, had bits of ash and soot floating among pink ice. Stacked beside it, milk and meat were spoiling. For a moment, Carly thought the drippings of raw meat had tinged the water pink. But then she spotted a clump of grass, red and wet, surrounded in smaller dots. Blood spatter. The spray of a nose punched. She bent for a closer look.

*PokWruuu.* Carly swiveled, one hand drawing her gun, the other hand pulling her radio. "Carly Spuretta, Angels Peak, east entrance, shots fired."

## 101

*In a split-second of insight, I realized how my silence
and inaction had paved the path to where we now stood.*

When the gun blasted, Miranda and I waited and expected the grip of the other to weaken, our gaping mouths and rounded eyes mirrored in dread. "Miranda," I whispered, "I think he shot you again."

"No, he didn't."

"Are you sure?"

"Zia, I'm pretty sure I'd feel a bullet in my back."

My chin tipped up as far as my neck would allow. My eyes straining to the top of their sockets, I met the wild eyes of the freak, the wind mussing his hair, the gun aimed at the sky. He had fired for attention, and when he received mine, his last spark of sanity vanished. He began manic singing and dancing. "Glorious parity, all equity served, whoo-hee, whoo-hee, bitches beg at my feet, *MY* feet, as it should be, whoo-hee, whoo-hee."

"Stop watching him," Miranda said. "Zia, look at me."

"No. The freak wants an audience; we want to live. Sounds fair to me."

"Bitches beg at my feet, *MY* feet, as it should be, whoo-hee, whoo-hee."

Miranda jostled our arms. "Zia, he feeds off the attention. Listen to me. You have to stop watching him. Without an audience, he'll calm down."

"So you think," I told her. "I think he'll shoot us."

"I'm scared, too, Zia, but if you don't turn away, I'm going to—I'm going to—" *Jeez,* I was dangling over death; what could Miranda possibly threaten? "I'm going to sing so loud, I'll drown out his song."

"What?" I glanced at her. "Have you lost your freakin' mind? This isn't Sound of Music, you're not Julie Andrews, and he's not a Nazi with a whistle. He's a lunatic with a gun. Get it?"

Miranda smiled. "Got it." Then this woman of unshakeable courage, a lover of gospel music and of candy-ass pop, began singing a heavy metal song about a lunatic.

That succeeded in lowering my stare.

While Miranda sang, she gave coaxing nods for my voice to chorus with hers. Either she had never heard me sing or she wanted an attractiveness to death. Oddly enough, the longer she held my astonished attention, the quieter Fikus became.

Each time curiosity tipped my head back, Miranda's fingernail gouged my arm, scolding for my focus's return, but never breaking from her song.

Behind Miranda, sand trickled down the cliff's wall—right to left, left to right—the freak's spastic dancing had settled into an agitated pacing.

Then a clump of dirt tumbled.

Despite Miranda's jabbing nail, I looked up at the ridge.

The freak was kneeling, calmly kneeling...until he noticed I was watching. "SHUT YOUR MOUTH!" he directed at me, though I hadn't made a peep. "SHUT UP! You hear me? SHUT UP! SHUT UP!"

My lips rolled under my teeth.

Apparently, I was rocket fuel to the freak's fire...and apparently, Miranda had already figured that out, her digging nails urging me to lower my head.

Carly scanned the knoll that surrounded the picnic grounds. Though the shot's blast seemed to rise from the south, logically, the shot had fired from the north and the sound had bounced through the cliff's hollows. Logically, no one would venture to the south side where the ridgeline snaked into a thin ledge over a lethal drop.

Carly started on a diagonal right.

While glancing the ground for tracks and blood spatter, she spotted a praying mantis. Instantly, common sense battled against Zia's superstitions. "Hey, I don't make the rules," Zia had said, "and I don't obey them, but I know them, and a mantis means, hang on a minute."

Ludicrous, Carly knew, but she glimpsed her watch and held ground. Forty-four seconds later, a faint voice—*whoo-hee?*—rose from the south. Cutting stealthily to the left, Carly heard only the shrill cries of overhead seagulls and the swooshing crash of ocean waves.

Had the *whoo-hee* come from a gull? She didn't stop to ponder it.

Just then, spliced between the tide's retreating rumble and its incoming thunder, came a sound so utterly bizarre, Carly nearly tripped. She held still, listening. *Singing?* As if the ocean itself were singing...*Brain Damage?*

Carly crept over the knoll. She scanned the ridgeline for Miranda or Zia, but spotted only Fikus's backside. He was leaning dangerously over the cliff.

"SHUT UP! SHUT UP!" he shouted at the sea...the singing sea. As he pushed to his feet, he raised the gun.

Carly dropped to a crouch and took aim. "FIKUS."

Fikus looked over his shoulder.

"DROP THE GUN," Carly shouted. "NOW."

Fikus's arm lowered, but the gun stayed in his hand. "Carly, you're early." He turned toward her. "The party doesn't start until—"

"Put the gun down."

"You don't understand."

"DO IT! Put the gun on the ground. NOW!"

"I'm afraid I can't do that. I'm gifted with a higher purpose. My job is to—" His eyes veered upward, his ears perking to the string of sirens, their whirls growing louder and louder. "Oh, Carly, you invited your friends." His head lowering, his breath left in a long, disappointed sigh. "Parity lost. Parity lost."

"DROP THE GUN NOW!"

"How can I?" His thumb eased back the hammer. "My purpose is greater than you. Greater than me. My purpose is equity."

Just then, he pitched around, swinging the gun's barrel toward the cliff. *POWK, POWK, POWK.*

For one second, I stared into the barrel of Fikus's gun. Then three shots rang out, their sound ending in the thud of a target hit. I flinched three times, but I didn't feel dead. And Miranda, blood-drained, was still singing, or trying to sing.

When I looked up, I saw the gun drip from Fikus's hand. His back arching slightly, he tilted forward, and then his arms spread into a skydiver's fall.

"AW SHIT!" I braced for the impact of a plummeting freak.

*SHACRAKK.* His head struck the ledge, his arms flopped over me, and his neck torqued back like a Pez dispenser.

With adrenaline powered lungs, I screamed...and I didn't quit screaming until gravity peeled the freak off of me.

He slid away, taking a chunk of the ledge and leaving bits of his skull.

Miranda's face was resting sideways in blood-made mud, her lips still muttering the lyrics about a lunatic.

"No, Miranda, no. The lunatic is dead. Dead."

Her head wiggled to rest on her chin, her lids parting a sliver. "Are you lying?"

"Not this time." Twisting, I looked down. Dark, vacant eyes stared up. Once more, I had a strange sensation of déjà vu, only this time, the feeling threaded to a payback. I sent a spit-wad down to the corpse. "Freak."

"ZIA! MIRANDA!" Came from a shocked-looking Carly above us.

"Hey, Carly," I said. "I'm not loving my party."

"Hang on! Just hang on!" Then Carly started hollering into a radio for paramedics, ropes, choppers. Maybe the Marines.

"Hear that, Miranda?" I squeezed our locked arms. "The cavalry is coming to the rescue. We're going to make it...and you were scared. *Jeez.*"

Though barely conscious, she smiled.

*Schlunk.*

My smile faded. I twisted again to look below. A dirt clot now covered Fikus.

*Dirt?*

Where Fikus had struck the ledge, a crack had started. More than a crack. A rip. A fracture zigzagging on a path to Miranda's thighs. Bits of Fikus's skull and pools of Miranda's blood were seeping into the crevice, widening the gap and greasing the breakage.

The underside of our ledge was crumbling.

No dream or denial was going to change that. Reality parched my throat. I choked out, "Miranda, you have to move back against the precipice wall."

She blinked and blinked until her eyes focused. Then, for the first time, her calm ruffled, as though she could see the rip through my eyes. "We're going to be rescued," she insisted. "Hold on."

*Clunk, clunk.*

The rip stretched.

The gap widened.

"No, Miranda." I kept swallowing and swallowing. "You got to—You got to—move to the wall."

"I'm not letting go."

"You have to. The ledge is splitting."

"No! You'll fall!"

"If you don't let go, we'll both fall."

Spaghetti-man rushed in so fast, he skidded at the edge. His eyes went from Miranda to me and then riveted on the expanding rip.

I could have, and probably would have, denied the truth had it not been so clearly painted in the horrified look on Spaghetti-man's face.

"Miranda, move to the—"

"We're going to be saved," she said, and she repeated it over and over again. Her words melded with Carly's shouts to hold on, hold on, hold on.

So I held on, because maybe a ton of denial would convert hope into fact. Maybe the sickening rumble was the ocean's thunder and not a splitting ledge. Maybe the rustling was tumbling leaves and not crumbling earth.

I had every right to hope.

*Zia, you are such a good girl. Come give me a hug.*

*Jeez, MaGretta, I hugged you last month.*

Who could blame me for holding on?

*Dammit, Zee, I yell 'cause I care.*

*I don't need sappy-crap; I need bail.*

My grip tightened; I wanted to live.

*I love you.*

*Back at you.*

*I love you.*

*Why? Am I dying?*

*I love you.*

*Yeah, yeah, can you spot me a twenty?*

Countless arms had opened, but a lifetime of my sidesteps, ducks, and swerves had left them empty. I had to hold on because I had apologies to give and hugs to return.

The zigzag disappeared beneath Miranda's legs.

I had to hold on; I needed to tell my family...I love you.

The rip reappeared, snaking faster.

My watery eyes lifted to Spuretta. I mouthed, "Tell them for me."

I wrenched free.

# 102

*The tide rushed in to soften Pierre's fall.*

"P op?"

## 103

*Half the mountainside curled like a white tsunami.*

Carly muffled a cry behind a clapped mouth.

Sobbing, Miranda curled into the blood-soaked dirt.

Spuretta yanked Carly away from the ledge. He dropped to his stomach and stretched flat across the cliff's edge. "Ms. Miranda, I need you to listen to me. You have to move back. Get against the wall. Come on now."

Miranda made no sign she heard him.

"Ms. Miranda, please, you have to move now."

She didn't budge.

"MIRANDA NORST!" he shouted.

Choking on ragged cries, her head lifted and turned just enough to look up at him.

"Zia wanted you hugging that precipice. That's what she wanted. Will you do that? Will you do that for Zia?"

She managed a slight nod.

"That's good. Real good. Okay, let's move back to the wall. Come on, Ms. Miranda, you can do it. Do it for Zia. Let's go."

Miranda pushed up onto her knees, then flopped onto her other side.

"That's good. That's a real good start, but let's keep going. Come on, do it again. Little more. Come on, Ms. Miranda, I know you can do it."

Her legs slid against the dirt, one arm clawing the ground.

"You're doing real good," Spuretta said. "Keep going. Come on, keep going. Real good. Come on, just a few more feet."

After more pushing and more scraping, Miranda slumped against the wall.

Spuretta inhaled a deep breath, but before he could exhale...

*KRAKK*, the ledge tore.

Tonnage fell.

From the rocks below came a mushrooming dirt plume.

Jutting from the precipice now was a two-foot lip beneath an unconscious Miranda.

# 104

*The tear touched the womb; the life stands.*

With Awakening Parties trailing, Souls from Hades carried off Triite, and Otto's Soul lifted Zia into Transitional Sleep.

Kaane stayed at the cliffs. While he peered at his Charge's empty husk—a mass of stewed flesh and shattered bones—he sent a private vibration to Alpha. *Your Charge will pay the price. From her next life through her one-hundredth life, she will never know peace. My players will surround her—doctors, teachers, neighbors, preachers—and one will cripple her life, her every life, emotionally, mentally, physically. From Earth, her cries will rise as a perpetual wish to have never been born.*

Romal was about to join Zia's Awakening Party when he noticed Kaane's vibrations streaming to Alpha. Romal went to Alpha and said, "I have an important question that can't wait. One of my Charges had a stubborn sliver embedded in the bottom of his foot. He was a strong man of admirable character, but each time his foot set down, the sliver scratched a nerve, not a great pain, but a constant one, inviting the man's anger. With knife in hand, the man went at his foot, slicing and digging into tissue. Despite his efforts, the slip of wood remained. But the poor fellow, having diced his arch, now limped. To hide his limp, he forced two feet on the ground, but with every step, the sliver delivered a sting. Eventually, the sliver rose to the surface where it was easily withdrawn by tweezers. The man held it up, turning it around and around, his wrath leaving him as he realized what he held—an irritant, an unremarkable irritant, simply doing what irritants do. Imagine the man's chagrin; over an irritant, he had slashed his foot, as his scars well proved and would forever remind him. In good humor, the man laughed at his prior foolishness, and without issue, he disposed of the sliver."

Alpha waited, but Romal said no more. "Your question?" Alpha asked.

"Oh, yes, yes." Romal tapped his chin, thinking. Then he gestured toward the Awakening Field. "Shall I meet you there?"

It took a moment before Alpha's puzzlement changed to a smile. "Thank you, Romal." He bowed. "I will dispose of the sliver." He went to Kaane.

"Wherever you place her," Kaane said, still staring at the husk, "I'll find her, and I'll inflict misery into her life. Over time, she'll blame you for having made her a target, and she'll beg for your protection. But you can't protect her, Alpha. You haven't the power." Kaane tsk'd tsk'd. "Sadly, but inevitably, she'll come to hate you."

Alpha held out a closed hand. "The Neutral Point's completion brings all acts into accountability." His hand opened. Within his palm was the image of the burning kindle that had lashed Zia's face. "All acts."

Kaane's mouth curved into a scoffing grin. "Are you seeking my apology? Or are you thanking me for not setting her hair ablaze?"

"You, Kaane, first Entity of Niine, inflicted injury upon an opposing Guide's Charge."

Kaane's grin expanded. "I littered once, too. I'll pay the price."

"As will beelzeNiine. You violated the Twelfth Life Covenants."

Kaane's amusement soured. "Count again. That was the Agitator's Eleventh Life."

Rising in the east, a low, churning rumble drew their attention. Vibrations were piercing the dimensions and darkening the spatial plane.

"I will not see you again," Alpha said. "For what spawned from your hand now returns to beelzeNiine."

"Lies," Kaane said, his voice weakening. "Lies, lies."

"Each vibration intensifies, magnifies, and multiplies one-thousand fold."

The rumble grew into a thunderous roar.

To be heard above the din, Alpha's voice raised, "To beelzeNiine, you sent an endless torrent of sharpened quills."

"NO!"

"And beelzeNiine is unforgiving."

Kaane whipped around. "NO! It was her 11th life. ELEVENTH!"

"Twelfth Life, Kaane, a matter of great consequence."

"But I counted." Kaane's arms stretched out, beseeching the universe. "I COUNTED!"

Alpha shook his head. "You missed a tear."

Moving through the dimensions toward the Awakening Field, Alpha felt the disruptive vibrations of Kaane's panic and fear, and then his hysterics.

The vibrations ended abruptly in an unholy shriek.

Alpha paused but never looked back.

# 105

*We shall meet in Haven and retell every story of our*
*love and friendship. To that, I promise.*


Hey Diets,

Before you go sideways, it's _not_ my fault! I had no idea about any surprise party until this exact minute. See, I hit the road at four and detoured to Carly's for a last goodbye, and she just now told me. Wow, I'm shocked! I was going to return home, but Carly told me not to bother. She said the party is no big deal, and that, with or without me, everyone will have a good time. I was going to hang around so I could call you at 7 or 8, but Carly convinced me to just write a note. I said okay, as long as she promised to give you this letter before 10 a.m. in case you wanted to cancel the party, and Carly swore that she would. I'm trusting her, Diets, but I have a bad feeling that she's going to mess up because her mind is on Kevin. If that happens and you don't get this letter until mid-afternoon, don't rub Carly's nose in it. In fact, don't even mention anything I've written here because it would only make Carly feel bad. Just go on with the party and have a great time. I'll let you know the minute I anchor somewhere.

Love, ya... Happy kisses.

Z.

P. S. Fair warning about opening my closet. Hang a helmet on the doorknob because I broke the laws of physics with how much crap can be crammed into a closet.

P. P. S. I need a huge favor that has nothing to do with money. (Surprised? Me, too!) There's a kid named Billy, about ten years old, big head, looks just like Charlie Brown. He helped me collect sea shit every other Tuesday. I completely forgot to tell him I was leaving. This Tuesday, he'll be standing on the beach, all alone, wearing a sad face, maybe crying...unless my very nice brother tells him for me. Pleeease? But you won't catch him on the beach because *he's crazy shy. Could you swing by his house on your way to work tomorrow? Billy won't answer the door and his mom is weird, so you'll have to yell through the window. They live in the yellow cottage three doors down from the minister's Colonial. You're the best, Diets. I owe you big time. Oh, crap, speaking of "owing" that reminds me...*

*P. P. P. S. Could you pay my tab at Neptunes? Just add it to what I owe you. Thanks Diets. Super sappy kisses.*

*Z.*

Dieter, sagging across two seats in the hospital's waiting room, lowered the letter and pinched his eyes. "I don't even know what day it is."

Carly took the letter from his lap and read it. "Dieter, I'll take care of this. I know where Billy lives."

Dieter mustered a lethargic nod, appearing devoid of hope.

"Dieter," Carly crouched beside him and squeezed his arm, "Miranda is going to make it. She is not going to die. Do you understand?"

With an appreciative pat to Carly's hand, Dieter looked away.

"Dieter, you have to believe me. You have to have faith. God would not take both of them on the same day. He wouldn't. He just wouldn't." She was nearly shouting, her voice desperate. "God wouldn't do that."

Dieter's arm extended. "Come here."

Carly hesitated. She had wanted to give emotional support, not take it. But she dropped beside Dieter, and her face buried into his chest. She wept. Interlaced with her sobbing, she confessed her doubts and regrets, her *what if*s and *if only*s, and her assertions of what God would and would not do.

"Carly," Dieter whispered, "don't do that."

Unsure of his meaning and suddenly embarrassed, Carly started to pull away, but Dieter gripped her in place. "I'm talking about beating yourself up with hindsight; don't do that. And don't blame God either. My family reacts to tragedies that way, blaming themselves or blaming God, and their wounds never heal. Pop thought he could have saved my mom *if only* he had noticed her symptoms earlier. That *if only* started him drinking. When he wasn't hating himself, he was hating God. And I doubt MaGretta's broken faith would have ever healed had it not been for your dad. So, please, Carly, don't do that. Keep blame where blame belongs. Okay?" His grip loosened. "God didn't kill Zia, and He didn't shoot Miranda. A man did—Fikus MacKenzie."

When Carly parked at the curb fronting the cottage, her cell phone rang for the fifth time—three calls from Kevin and now two from her dad. She had let the prior calls transfer to voicemail. Their messages had voiced concerns for Carly, but not one had given an update on Miranda's condition. So this time, Carly picked up. "Dad, is Miranda going to make it?"

"She's still in surgery. How are you holding up?"

"Me? Hell, I'm fine." Even to her own ears, she sounded curt. "But I can't talk now. I have a job to do."

"Are you at the boy's house? I read the letter."

"Yes, I'm at the house, but I have to go."

"No, you don't. Just hold on. I know what's eating you, kid."

Impulsively, Carly's arm reared back, preparing to hurl the phone. She didn't want to have this conversation. Not today. Dammit, if only she hadn't answered the call. Summoning self-control, she brought the phone back to her mouth. "Gotta go."

"Darn it, kid, LISTEN TO ME! Zia knew you were doing your blasted-best to save her. She knew that, Carly. But she also knew the ledge was splitting. If she had held on, Miranda would have gone down, too. Zia saw that. And kid," he paused with a deep sigh, "we saw that, too."

"If I could have—If she had just—" Possibilities stuck in her throat. "I gotta go." She slapped the phone closed. She didn't want lectures about time limitations or physical impossibilities, and she didn't want anyone assuaging her guilt, not her dad, not Kevin, and not Dieter, who was wrong about God. God could have and should have stepped in and changed the outcome.

Carly peered at the cottage, her thoughts revisiting the time when Zia had claimed to have dropped off a boy...and Carly had accused her of lying. *Damn.*

Although Zia's letter directed Dieter to yell through the window, Carly didn't feel like catering to the mother's weirdness, so she pounded on the front door. When the peephole darkened, Carly raised her badge. "Ma'am, I'm Detective Carly Spuretta. I'd like to talk to you for a minute."

The door swung open. "Detective?" A slender blond, mid-30s, wearing pressed jeans and a cotton blouse, stepped outside. "Is somebody hurt? Has there been an accident?"

Carly hadn't expected a classically pretty lady, her hair smooth and neatly tied, her nails short and polished, her cheeks scrubbed, her skin flawless. A little thrown by the lack of weirdness, Carly stammered, "No, no, no, ma'am."

And apparently, the lady had expected an emergency, one that would warrant Carly's door-pounding. Finding no such emergency, she rechecked Carly's badge. "Detective?"

"Yes, ma'am, may I come in?"

The lady stepped aside. "Must be bad news." She led Carly to the living room where music sheets covered the tables, spilled from the chairs, and buried much of the rug. The only uncluttered space was on the piano bench fronting a Baby Grand. "Excuse the mess," the lady said. Then, much like Carly scooping up photographs to make space for an unexpected guest, the lady shuffled the music sheets off the couch and into neat stacks beneath the coffee table. "Have a seat."

Carly lowered slowly, struck by the lady's passion. "You're a musician?"

"Depends who you ask," the lady said as she cushioned onto the couch. "My family and friends think I have talent, but I—"

"Don't believe them?" Carly winced; she hadn't meant to say that aloud.

The lady drew back. "Is that what you came to talk about?"

"No, ma'am."

"*Ma'am* is my mother. I'm Lylah. Now, what's the bad news, detective?"

"Carly."

"All right, Carly, what's this about?"

"It's about your son's friend, Zia."

"My son?"

"Yes, ma'am—I mean, Lylah. Your little boy, Billy."

"Billy?" Lylah's breath left with a *whew*, her hand pressed to her chest. "You had me worried. I was afraid something had happened to my sister Bell."

"No, this isn't about your sister."

"Nor me, detective. I don't have a son."

"Oh," Carly said, a bit stupefied. "I guess Zia assumed Billy was your son. Is he your foster child? Your nephew? A kid you babysit?" Carly went on to list more than a dozen relationships, but to each, Lylah shook her head.

"I have a nephew in Denver," Lylah said, "but his name is Ethan."

"No." Carly shifted irritably. "I told you, I'm here about Billy."

"And I'm telling you, I don't know a Billy. Maybe you have the wrong street. Most of my neighbors are retired, and their kids are grown and gone. One block over, there's a teenager named Bobby."

"NO! His name isn't Bobby. Or Ethan. It's Billy, B-I-L-L-Y!" Carly's head began to throb. Nothing made sense. Where was the lady's weirdness? Where were a kid's toys? Where were the sandy sneakers, the broken crayons, and the sticky fingerprints on windows and walls? Not even a goddam cardboard juice box in sight. Zia bullshitting Carly about dropping off a kid made sense. Zia bullshitting Dieter in a letter made no sense at all. She wouldn't have messed with Dieter that way. "Lylah, what boy, under the age of 12, comes into this house? Maybe he mows your lawn or house-sits or takes piano lessons or feeds your cat or—"

"I don't have a—"

"WHATEVER THE REASON, I don't care. A kid comes into this house, THIS HOUSE, RIGHT HERE!"

Lylah got up with commanding abruptness, her finger pointing toward the door. "Detective, you had better go."

"Lylah—"

"Immediately."

Prudence reigned in Carly's frustration. With a respectful nod, she lifted to her feet. "I'm—I'm sorry, Lylah. I was out of line. I didn't come here on official duty. I came here to do a favor for a friend. But I'm not—I'm not myself." She thumbed a spilling tear and raised an apologetic smile. "My friend told a fanciful story about driving a kid home on Tuesdays."

"Tuesdays? Sunny Tuesdays? Does your friend have curly, red hair?"

"Yeah, Zia. Do you know her?"

Lylah's arms crossed, one brow raised. "I know she's disturbed."

"Disturbed? No. Odd, maybe, but—"

"More than odd," Lylah said. "Every other Tuesday, if the weather is nice, your friend parks in front of my house. She gets out, walks to the car's passenger side, and opens up the door. She gabs and gabs, but no one gets out of her car, because no one is in her car. Then she waves at me, but I stopped waving back a long time ago. I don't know what your friend's problem is, but I'm not going to encourage it. I draw the drapes on sunny Tuesdays. Other neighbors keep an eye out for her, too. Dora once spotted her trying to steal mail. And last year, when the Minister died, your friend stood in the middle of the road and screamed bloody murder at the police officers. I bet they heard her in Ridgecrest." Lylah's voice quieted. "What did she do wrong? Did your friend harm the little boy you're looking for? Billy?"

"Wait, wait." Dazed, Carly needed a moment to process this, her mind still reverberating, *no one gets out of her car, because no one is in her car.* How was that possible? Zia talked to herself, sure, but this smacked of delusions. *Delusions?* Was that what Dieter had meant by calling her...*funny?* Carly inhaled a draft of air to steady herself. Whether delusional, disturbed, or odd, what difference did it make? Zia was gone. Carly's shoulders drew back. "For your information, Zia wasn't stealing the mail. She was only snooping. And she wasn't swearing at the police. She was screaming at Fikus. Get your facts straight. And speaking of facts, Zia would never hurt a kid."

"Then what did she do wrong?"

"Wrong?" Carly's headache exploded. How dare Lylah assume a wrong-doing. "I'll tell you what she did wrong. She died. That's what she did wrong. SHE DIED! You can open your damn curtains." As Carly turned to leave, she caught the glint of a sliver frame propped on the far corner of the piano. Even at a distance, Carly could see the boy's photo. Carly pushed past Lylah and went to the picture. It was a black and white photograph of a big headed boy, the human version of Charlie Brown. "I knew it," Carly said eyeing the Xs that seamed the boy's neck. "So you don't know any Billy, huh?" She waved the photo accusingly. "Mind telling me who this is?"

Lylah marched over, snatched the picture, and pressed it to her breast. "*My* friend, detective. And he is not who you're looking for."

"Is that so? Then it's a hell of a coincidence, because he fits Billy's description, right down to the stitches."

"Detective, this boy died in 1969."

"1969?" Carly tried to appear unshaken, "Yeah, sure, uh-huh," even cinching her disbelief with an eye roll.

"It's date-stamped." Lylah handed it back to Carly. "Be careful when you remove it from the frame. The photo is irreplaceable."

Carly turned the frame over, twisted the tiny metal latches, and lifted the frame's inner padding. Printed on the photo's backside was St. Luke's Hospital. Beneath it was a faded 19, the last two digits illegible.

"I guess you'll have to take my word for it," Lylah said. "It was 1969."

"No, I believe you," Carly said softly. "I know this paper and these processing marks." Carly's nostrils flared. "I can still smell the old chemicals they once used in developing."

"Are you a photographer?"

"Depends who you ask. According to my father and boyfriend—" Carly stopped herself because her answer was about to parrot Lylah's remark about being a musician. A fluke? Right. Just like the fluke of a 1969 photograph matching Billy's description. Carly reassembled the frame and then placed it on top of the piano. Carly stepped back, still entranced by the photo. Had Zia peeked through the window, spotted the picture, and fabricated the story?

Like Carly, Lylah was staring at the photo, mesmerized. "I was there when the nurse took the picture," Lylah whispered. "Will was so proud of those stitches."

Carly snapped from her trance. "Will?"

"William, but we called him Will." Lylah suddenly chirped, "Oh, oh, oh, how uncanny is that? Both names, Bill and Will, are versions of William."

"Uncanny, right. How did you know Will?"

"The orphanage sent him to St. Luke's. That's where I was and that's where Will stayed for the rest of his short life. He died of leukemia. He didn't have any family. I was his only friend. Well, me and a little fairy Will dreamed up. He had such an infectious imagination, I began to see the fairy, too. Clear as day. A small green thing with spills of red hair and sparkling blue tears. Isn't that strange? Isn't that strange how one friend's fantastic tales can come alive for another?" She cupped a hand over a nervous giggle. "You probably have no idea what I'm talking about, do you?"

Her mouth dry from hanging open, Carly gulped a few times before managing an answer. "Me? No. Sorry. Not a clue. Nope. Can't relate."

"Neither could my mother," Lylah said. "She's a stifling pragmatist, who would rather dissect creativity than enjoy it. She insisted that the meds brought on the fairy. She was halfway right; the fairy was a side effect, but not from meds, but from my friendship with Will. We were the very best of friends. The best. And yet," Lylah's voice quivered, "he died alone."

"Oh, I'm so sorry," Carly said. "It's rough to lose a friend."

Lylah nodded. "It was a long time ago. I keep Will's picture on the piano to think of him once a day. Every good person deserves to be remembered, right? Will didn't have anyone else, but he has me." Then Lylah's hands balled to her chest, and she glanced around the room as if to ensure their privacy.

Carly looked around, too. "Is there someone else here?"

"No," Lylah said appearing puzzled by the question. Then she leaned toward Carly and whispered, "Want to know how Will got those stitches?"

Carly's heart began pounding. She was crossing into Zia's crazy world of reversals; she knew it, she felt it, and her answer to Lylah would only prove it. "Let me guess, he slipped while dancing and sliced his throat on a metal railing."

Lylah jumped back with a gasp, her cheeks draining of color. "How—how did you know that?"

"Lylah, calm down."

"Nobody knew that," Lylah half-whispered, half-wheezed. "Nobody." Her legs trembled as if she were about to faint.

Thinking to help Lylah to the couch, Carly came toward her, but Lylah backed up, fear rising in her eyes. "How did you know that? Only Will and I knew. No one else was in the room. I lied to the hospital staff and told them Will slipped, just that, Will slipped, because he wasn't supposed to be dancing. The nurses got mad when he danced." Her hands twisted nervously. "I didn't want Will to get into trouble. He was my friend. So I lied. Not much later, Will died."

Sadness rimmed in Lylah's eyes and diluted her fear, so Carly helped her to the piano bench. "Lylah, are you connecting your lie to Will's death?"

Lylah shrugged.

"But you said he died of Leukemia."

"He did. He did. But what does a child know about Leukemia? What I understood was what the nuns told us. 'God punishes naughty little boys and girls who tell lies.' Not much later, Will died. I thought—Well, I blamed myself. If I had just told the truth, confessed that Will had been dancing, God wouldn't have taken my friend. It sounds ridiculous now, but that's how a little girl thinks. And that kind of guilt doesn't magically disappear with adult reasoning." She clutched Carly's arm. "But how did you know?"

Carly scratched her head, wondering what to say. She did not believe in ghosts or specters or signs from the dead or voices from the grave. She pried free of Lylah's grasp. "Lucky guess," Carly said, and then she hurried toward the door.

Lylah went after her. "Just tell me, tell me how you knew."

"Nothing to tell." Carly threw the door open and gave a quick, "Bye."

Lylah didn't answer.

Carly turned for a proper goodbye. "Thank you for your time."

Lylah didn't lift her downcast stare.

Carly wanted to leave—*God, how she wanted to leave*—but she couldn't. "Look, Lylah, how you feel is a choice, not an accident. If you want to blame yourself, go for it. While you're at it, why not blame yourself for bad weather. It makes about as much sense. You didn't cause Will's Leukemia. You're not responsible for his death. And God wasn't punishing your lie."

No response. Nothing. Not even an acknowledging nod.

"Dammit, Lylah, what do you want me to say?"

Lylah finally looked up. "The truth."

Carly fell against the doorframe, her breath issuing in a beaten sigh. "To be clear, I agree with your mother; fairies are a product of meds. That said, Billy told my friend how he hurt his neck. Well, he didn't *tell* her because Billy was a mute. He didn't talk, and he didn't touch anything either, which now makes perfect sense. The phobic, little mute was invisible."

Gentle tears striped Lylah's cheeks. "Did he mention me?"

"He must have. Zia thought he lived here."

"But only on sunny Tuesdays?"

"That's when he wanted a lift. She said he liked to walk home when the weather was overcast and you couldn't even see your own sha*aaa—shit!*" Carly suppressed a light laugh. "Around Zia, Billy kept to the shade. Not only invisible, but also smart. He didn't cast a shadow...and he knew it."

During a brief, commiserate hug, Carly whispered into Lylah's ear, "This conversation never took place."

Lylah stepped back into her house and shut the door.

Carly pulled her cell phone and called her dad. "Is Miranda—"

"She's going to make it."

Carly clapped the phone over her heart. "Thank you, God."

"Carly, are you still there?"

"Yeah. How is MaGretta holding up?"

"Not too good. Dieter and Kevin are going to stay the night in the waiting room. MaGretta wants to stay, too, but she needs food and rest. I sure could use your help. If you stayed with Dieter and Kevin, I might be able to convince MaGretta to come home for a few hours."

"I don't know, dad. I'm really not up to—"

The cottage drapes whipped open. Lylah pressed her face against the window and then winked. Or her face tic'd. Either way, it was followed with a quirky head jerk. Then Lylah seemed to be waiting for Carly's reply.

So Carly waved, shrugged, and then winked. Eventually, something worked. Lylah nodded, opened the windows, and then disappeared.

"Strange lady."

"What's that, Carly?"

"Nothing, dad. Listen, about the hospital, I'd like to help, but—"

From the window came the piano's music, each note rising and blending with intoxicating harmony.

Then came Lylah's voice...

> *I see trees of green...red roses, too.*
> *I see them bloom...for me and you.*

...emotion-rich and razor-pitched. Carly shivered, though she wasn't cold. It was the music! Carly *felt* the music. Like an ethereal fluid, the music flowed into her, each chord penetrating her skin, warming her blood, and pumping her heart beats.

> *...I see friends shaking hands,*
> *saying how do you do.*
> *They're really saying, I love you...*

Like a rose opening its petals, the lyrics bloomed inside Carly, their secrets unfolding the strength, the beauty, and the simplicity of love.

> *...And I think to myself, what a wonderful world.*

Her tears cascading, her skin prickled in gooseflesh, and her mind badgered by Zia's voice, *Do you get it? Huh? Do you get it?* Carly shouted toward the sky, "YES! Yes, Zia, I get it. I get it." Her chin came down slowly. "I'm going to miss you, too."

"Carly?" sounded from the phone. "Are you there? Carly?"

"I'm here, dad. I'll be at the hospital in twenty minutes, and I'll stay for however long you need me."

"Oh, I would sure appreciate that. Are you still at the boy's home?"

"Yeah."

"How did the little fella take the news? Pretty upset?"

"No, dad. Billy already knew."

# 106

*Life itself refuses boundaries, always has, always will,*
*and it throws us an anomaly to remind us of such.*

*S*woosh. Alpha watched the Earth complete another cycle, its third during Zia's Transitional Sleep. Time, a constant remodeler, had melted, shifted, and reshaped twelve seasons. Eventually, time would awaken Zia...and she would leave Alpha's charge. He sighed; what a peculiar sensation, joy mixed with sorrow.

"Bittersweet." Romal appeared with a cheerful smile. "I can recognize a bittersweet vibration from ten dimensions away."

"I do not have bittersweet," Alpha said. "I have...reflection."

"Yes, yes, I'm certain you think so. And I have seventy-seven more matters for your added reflection." He held out a thick document. "Upon analyzing one of Zia's vibrations, Andromnis made an astounding discovery, but you'll have to read it, just as I have had to read it. Ever since Players embraced the film industry, Andromnis has refused to transfer information. Instead, she forces our eye strain to show her support for the literary field."

Alpha took the document. "How did Andromnis afford the time? Her Charges are scheduled for particle discovery by the dawn of next century."

"Mid-century now. The Player-physicists made a critical error in the second phase of constructing their particle machine, though they won't realize it for several years nor have it corrected for several more. If Andromnis had hair to be torn out, I believe she'd be bald. She welcomed this diversion. Read her findings."

Alpha fashioned a table for the document. While Zia slept peacefully, Alpha read. Several pages later, Alpha said, "Higgs particle?"

"Skioses!" Romal swiveled around. "Did that persnickety Guide change it again?" Romal looked at the page, saw 'Higgs particle,' and then gave a disagreeable snort. "Skioses; that is, that was, and that will continue to be, the correct term for the awareness particle. When Andromnis insisted we rename it the Higgs particle, I said, 'Andromnis, must we always adopt the Player's term when that Player happens to be your Charge? When will this end? At your prior request, we honored your Charge, Gell-Mann, and look where that led? We now refer to a pinnacle particle by a ridiculous name. Quark! That's hardly a word; it's a belch. Perhaps we should honor all Player-physicists and rename the skios the God-particle. Or, as your Charge would have it, the goddamn particle. Which shall it be?' And Andromnis, quite incensed—"

"Romal, does this address the seventy-seven?"

"Seventy-seven? Oh, yes, yes. Among the billions of Energies, seventy-seven, including Zia, carry mischief-making skioses."

"A distinct species?"

"No less distinct than a Dyad, but far more difficult to detect, unless you know what to look for, and we know now. Thankfully, we discovered them in time; zero play for Niine. If you'll turn to the last chapter, you'll find a complete list. We have one Agitator, Zia, and true to her Order, she brought the matter to light. We have zero among the Warriors, Healers, Peacekeepers and Finishers. Constructors, however, have three, and all three lived in the Republic of Pisa during the 12th century. I suspect their ne'er-do-well skioses played a part in that leaning tower. Moving on, Seekers have ten, Teachers seven, Persuaders four, and Counters thirteen, including William, which explains his capricious act of finagling a necklace into Zia's pocket. The majority, thirty-nine, are among the Messengers, and their names explain several historical faux pas."

Romal highlighted the last name on the list.

"Darwin?" Alpha said, his tone high with surprise.

"Yes, Darwin. As I stated all along and to everyone, my whispers were clear, my diction superb, my timing impeccable. Darwin, however, minced my words. 'No, no, no,' I corrected him, repeatedly, 'you're a matter of shape and weight, not a ladder from ape and fate.'"

Just then, Zia jolted upright. "What the fuck?"

Alpha turned to the Awakening Party. "It is this Soul's nature to—"

"To wake wickedly," the Party finished in unison, causing Romal to chuckle and Alpha to frown.

Zia's three words marked the start of her tirade, but because of the Soul beside her, those three words marked the end of her tirade as well. "Auk, Zia, Zia," Otto said. "Do you kiss your poppa with that mouth? Tell me that."

"Oh, sorry, Pop." She bit her bottom lip. "But I've never cursed before. Honest."

# 107

*I don't break spit-promises. Never have. Never will.*
*Spit-promises are sacred.*

"**D**ear Lady, you are woefully mistaken," Malachi told me after I woke up and accused the surrounding Souls of being Party-shills. "You have woven many positive threads into the lives of others. It's time to celebrate with those Souls and to marvel at where your threads have led."

"But what if my threads did a lot less positive weaving and a lot more negative tangling?"

"Then the Soul wouldn't choose to be here."

I wrung my hands, pretty nervous for a while about the number of Souls in attendance. A Player's life can sure affect a whole of others. Who knew? Once I relaxed, my party became a real celebration with sharing and laughter and telling jokes and playing guessing games—*Remember me?* and *Guess when our paths crossed?* It was the best party in the universe...until a smart-ass Counter tried to ruin it with his trumped up tallies.

"Six hundred, thirty-eight lies," he said, "and four thousand, two hundred and twenty-two curses."

"That's crap."

"That's one year."

"All right, who invited the Counter?"

Alpha nodded, and the Counter then shifted into his Player's illusion.

"Will? Billy? But you were a kid when—How could you have the same face as—" I turned to Alpha. "I saw Billy. My physical eyes as Zia Schatz saw him. How could I see him if he wasn't there?"

Off to the side, Malachi scrolled up the bottom of a squared off smoke puff. "Aw, crap, a lifted veil?" I sat, covering my face in a permanent cringe. "Alpha, do you realize what you did? I told Carly about Billy. I even wrote a letter to Dieter about Billy. Now everyone thinks I lied. Or worse, they've tagged me as crazy. That's what you did, Alpha. You gave me a legacy of lunacy."

"Zia, the Players' perception of your veracity and sanity is unaltered."

"Nice try." I shook my head. "Didn't they discover that Billy wasn't real?"

"True."

"Shit. Now they think I was a nutcase liar."

Alpha placed a hand on my shoulder. "The Players think of you as they have always thought of you."

My head lifted. "Really? Are you guessing or are you sure?"

"I am certain that their opinions of you remain unchanged."

It didn't seem possible, but when I scanned the faces of my Awakening Party, each of them nodded, "Unchanged! Unchanged!"

Even Romal confirmed it. "Yes, indeed, unchanged." Then he looked at Alpha and said, "Remarkable." No doubt he was impressed at how Alpha had worked his magic over the Players to keep my reputation intact.

I stood and thanked Alpha. "I hope it was easy to do."

"True," Alpha said.

As I turned to rejoin my party, I heard Romal tell Alpha, "I trust you'll prepare the monograph on this species."

*Species?* But no Dyads were in attendance. "Alpha, where is Awen and Ereo? Did they survive the do-over? Are they together? Why do you have to monograph them? Why?"

"Within the cortex," Romal said eyeing me, though I think he was talking to Alpha, "remember to index, *rash assumptions.*" Then Romal smiled. "Zia, you needn't worry. The Dyads are safely together. When you finish your party, Alpha will show you."

One by one, I hugged and thanked my guests. When I finished, I bolted to Alpha, who was talking with Romal. I tugged on Alpha's robe. "I'm ready."

Romal sighed. "Perhaps, *rash* deserves its own index."

Alpha clasped my shoulder.

Instantly, we stood on the walkway fronting Carly's house. I heard laughter, music, and the voices of my family, except for Pop, of course, an awesome Soul from the Order of Peacekeepers, which just figures.

"It is the fourth anniversary of your removal," Alpha said.

Inside the house, Carly was rinsing noodles while MaGretta stirred a pot of marinara sauce. Spaghetti-man and Kevin were talking politics in the living room, while Dieter leafed through photographs and Miranda fattened herself on krapfens and kaiserschmarrn. A thick life-cord protruded from Miranda's belly, and she wore a gold band that matched the band on my brother's hand. I had missed their wedding. *Damn.* Peering into Dieter's life-cord, I recognized Awen's dazzling Ribbon. When I palmed my eyes, my hand came away inky-blue. "Miranda is Ereo, right?"

"True."

"Jeez, that explains so much."

"Their bond?"

"Yeah, that, too." Leaning into Miranda's ear, I whispered, "You're good stuff, Ereo. Only a bitch would think otherwise."

*Grrrgrrr.*

"Winkle!" The cat was eyeing me. "Alpha, can Winkle see me?"

"True."

"YES!" I crouched, ready to chase. Winkle coiled, preparing to run. "Let's go, scrotum-breath." And off we went, barreling down the hall, then up again, then down again, then throughout the rooms, tumbling and wrestling, reversing roles of stalker and prey.

Like once before, our game ended when we knocked over the potpourri. That's when I noticed Carly standing in the kitchen doorway, her hand clapped to her mouth, her stare fixed on Winkle.

My family fluttered around her. "Kid, what's the matter?" and "Maybe you should eat," and "Honey, something wrong?" and "Hey, you okay?" But Carly didn't seem to hear them.

Miranda started to clean up the mess.

"It's just potpourri," I said. "What's the big deal?"

"Winkle never raced indoors," Carly said still staring at Winkle, "except when she played with Zia. They used to play a stalking game. Winkle was acting like she were playing that game now, as if Zia were here playing it, too. Not a similar game, but the exact game."

"Alpha, was she watching us?"

"True."

"Oh. Uhm, oops."

"She is the Soul of Phoenix."

"Carly is Phoenix? Can I slap the back of her head?" Though at the moment, it didn't seem fair; she was really upset.

Kevin was hugging her. Then Spaghetti-man hugged MaGretta, and Dieter hugged Miranda. During their hug-fest, I backed out of the house.

Once more, I stood on the walkway, not wanting to leave, not wanting to stay. Reality took a long time to sink in. "I don't belong here."

"You serve in memory."

"Same thing." I turned and glided away. Knowing you can't get back what you once had, a Soul would have to be a masochist to want to hang around on Earth. I shared this and more with Alpha over the next few hours as we moved along the coastline. At times, I teased him, "Will the One Determinant inherit Dieter's stinky feet?" At other times, we reminisced like old friends...until Alpha ruined everything.

"Zia," he said with a bow, "I hope I have served you well."

"Served? You're still serving, right?"

"Untrue."

"Am I going back to Romal?"

"Romal is an Interim Guide; he cannot serve beyond a Soul's Twelfth life."

"Then I'm all yours."

"I am a Peril Guide. You are not in peril nor do you jeopardize another."

"Then I'll change."

"When we enter Haven, I will escort you to the Parity Halls where you will receive the Guide's name who will next serve you well."

"Forget it. I'm sticking with you. Discussion over."

"Zia—"

"No. Don't I get a say? Don't you want me?"

"It is not a matter of preference. It is a matter of purpose."

"Screw purpose. That's a lousy excuse for pawning me off to another Guide."

"Your unchaining from a Peril Guide should be viewed as an honor."

"I don't want an honor. I want you."

We moved along the shoreline, only now, we moved in silence.

When we came to Angels Peak, we saw a group of people tossing roses over the cliff. I first recognized Terry Lee and then, one by one, my other Red Herrings. Four years had turned pimply teens into young adults.

"Are those roses for me?" I asked Alpha.

"True."

"Come on," JoAnna told Terry. "Read it."

"Not this year," Terry said. "It's lame."

"No, dude," another Herring said, "it's the memorial tradition."

Their eyes clear and sober, their hands strong and steady, their mouths smiling and grateful, they had taken the lemons life had handed them—more lemons than any one life deserved—and they had cranked out sweet lemonade. Not a bitter or sour face among them.

Terry took out a paper and then adjusted his glasses. "By the Red Herrings of '98, Ode to Coach Zee," he read.

> "To keep a promise would kill you
> You hid the truth behind the dive
> All along you knew to be true
> A pledge held, you would not survive
>
> You hid the truth behind the dive
> Promise-kept topped your hated list
> A pledge held, you would not survive
> Do a three-meter, back-dive twist
>
> Promise-kept topped your hated list
> No beast caused you greater fright
> Do a three-meter, back-dive twist
> In the end, what you feared proved right
>
> No beast caused you greater fright
> All along, you knew to be true
> In the end, what you feared proved right
> To keep a promise would kill you."

"That sucks!" I said while their hands slapped high and their hugs were exchanged. "What the hell was that? A tribute or a roasting?"

"A Pantoum," Alpha said.

"Panto-nothing. That was downright lousy. I bet Terry Lee wrote it. And for the record, I kept my promise. I freakin' *died* keeping my promise."

"As the Pantoum so stated."

"So stated as a wise-crack. I never broke a promise in my life. Well, maybe a few, but I never broke a spit-promise. Never. My last spit-promise—" and then it struck me. "Oh, my God. I can't go. Alpha, I can't go."

"Zia."

"NO! I can't. I made a spit-promise to Dieter. I can't break it. I need to show him that I'm okay. You have to remove his veil."

"I cannot."

"Yes, you can. I could see Billy."

"Allowed because you perceived him as a Player, not as an apparition."

"Oh, I get it. Viewing a Soul is restricted to the young and the stupid. Hmm. Dumb-dumb, dumb-dumb, dumb-dumb, dumb-dumb—"

"Zia."

"What? I'm tapping while I think."

"From time beginning, Players have vowed to their loved ones to deliver evidence of their continued existence, but it is a promise they cannot keep."

"This is different."

"How?"

"This is me. And we're not talking about some half-cocked, voodoo-hoodoo, séance-psychic crap. We're talking about a spit-promise. So how about this; I'll shift into my form as Zia. You grab hold of Dieter's veil. Suddenly, you need to yawn or stretch or admire the clouds. Then, oops, would you look at that? How the heck did that veil slip from your fingers? Fumble to pick it up. That ought to give me plenty of time. Okay? Okay?"

Alpha began his schoolmaster pacing, his hands locked at his backside. I waited, mouth shut, pretty sure he was figuring out a better trick than mine, his technique being less obvious, more Guide worthy.

"Zia, listen carefully to glean the weight of the consequence."

"Got it. What's the plan?"

"Would you have me abandon the rules, forsake the laws, and disregard the millenniums of Souls who have had their promises refused and their appeals denied, so that I may declare you exempt from the laws and the Covenants and permit you to undermine faith and strengthen godmancers for the purpose of honoring a spit-promise?"

"Wow! You'd do that for me?"

The ground trembled. "NO!"

I put distance between us. "Then tag me as a Wanderer, because I'm staying until I've kept my promise to Dieter."

"You are cognizant, not a Wanderer, and you are not tethered to a Soul for consoling. Zia, you will leave Earth; you have no choice."

"Bullshit." I swept further from his reach.

"Zia, I need only wish it, and you will find yourself in Divisional."

"You're bluffing. If you could do that, you would have done it."

"Forced is unpleasant. Do you recall your experience in the cyclone?"

How could I forget it? For months, I glided in circles. "Yeah, go on."

"Imagine endless dimensions of cyclones."

Slowly, I dragged myself toward Alpha, but halfway to his transporting reach, a brilliant idea came to me. "Alpha, let me stay until tomorrow. All I want to do is tell Dieter goodbye, but I won't do anything more than whisper. Strictly whisper. Okay? Please?"

Alpha inspected my sparks, but saw no flicker of lies. "You will not engage the Savannah."

"YES! I mean, yes, Alpha. No games with Winkle; I swear it."

"You will not exceed a whisper."

"Not a breath beyond it, cross my heart."

"You will not leave the grounds of his domicile."

"Not a particle of my being will stray from the property."

Alpha paused as if searching the catalog of limitations. "Zia, you will not denigrate my trust."

"Grade-A trust only, you got it." I spat into my hand and offered a palm of puddled atoms. Grumbling, Alpha reached out, but I jerked my hand away. "You have to spit first."

"I do not spit."

"Then the promise isn't worth spit." I offered my hand again. "Give the promise worth. Now spit."

By the look on his face, you would have thought I had asked him to crap in his hand. Eventually, his hand went to his mouth, and then he held out a poor excuse for a spit-wad.

We shook.

"I will return," he said, "when the first rays of sunlight have reached —"

"Dawn," I told him. "You need to work on your English." We continued down the shoreline, now toward my old home. "Hey, the Counter William, would it be all right if William joined me?"

"For what purpose?"

"Purpose? Uhm. I might get lonely." I trusted the *might* would cancel any spark of a lie. "Besides, what harm could we do in one night? Wait. Scratch that. If you give Will the same restrictions as you gave me, then can he come?"

"If he so wishes, and if he so agrees to the conditions."

"Thank you. And, uhm, could you tell him to hurry."

Alpha's brow arched.

"What?" I said. "I like his company."

We were nearing the beach behind my house when I suddenly realized something—something incredible and wonderful that had zoomed right over my head...until that moment.

I hip bumped Alpha affectionately.

Alpha paused, considered, but then he moved on, as if that were the polite thing to do.

I bumped him again, harder.

He stopped. "Zia, do you suffer imbalance?"

"Oh, you'd like to think so. You'd like to keep your secret hidden, but I know the truth. Wow! And to think I nearly missed it."

"I do not understand."

"You understand plenty...and now, I get it, too. You're crazy upset that I'm going to another Guide." I threw my arms around him. "You proved it with one word, one single word. Your shout gave you away. You said, 'NO.'"

"I do not understand."

"Sure you do. A mile back, you shouted, 'NO.' Alpha, you've never said, 'No,' before. In the past, you've said, 'Untrue,' or 'That serves no purpose,' but you've never said just plain, 'No.' Am I right? Tell me I'm right."

Keeping a poker-face, Alpha started up the trail leading to my house.

I orbited around him. "Guides are supposed to answer. It's in the Guide-book. So, answer me. Have you ever said, 'No,' to anyone, at any time, before today?"

He ignored me.

"I'm right. You like me." I danced around him. "You like me. You like me. You really, really like me. Admit it, Alpha, I hold the truth. You can face it, fight it, or fuck it, but I hold the truth."

Alpha dead-stopped. "What you hold is another squalor of fragments that need to be purged."

# 108

*When I tried to align the beetles into the letters of my name,*
*they lumbered and tottered and took all night just to form the Z.*

Wﬁlliam arrived while I was searching the garden.

"What kept you?" I said. "It's nearly midnight. We have to work fast. Help me find mantises."

He shook his head. "Whatever you're up to, it can't be good. I was told you were lonely."

"I'm an Agitator; do you know how long it takes before we get lonely? You're a Counter; do the math. Then help me collect some mantises."

He didn't move.

"Come on, Will. You know my restrictions, right?"

"And you're going to break them."

"I am not. I'm sticking to whispers, but I never said who or what I would be whispering to."

"So you're whispering to—to bugs?"

"Praying Mantises. Years before I met you in the hospital, I hung out in the courtyard talking to the wildlife. Guess what I did with rain beetles? I directed them to form a Z. You know, Z for Zia, get it?"

"Not yet."

"For chrissake, I have three mantises on the porch. I need a bunch more to make a big Z. But if I'm the only one whispering to these plodding buggers, I won't have any Z, big or small. And these few mantises will be bug-guts after Dieter stomps outside for the morning paper. Will you please help me? I have until dawn."

"How tall is Dieter?"

"Six foot three or four."

Will glided to the porch. He glanced from the mantises to the front door and mumbled calculations of ratios and depths, sizes and odds. "For Dieter's line of sight, you should position nine mantises here." He backed up a few inches. "For a large Z, position twelve mantises here."

"Got it. We need six or nine more mantises."

"Seven or ten," Will said pointing to two copulating mantises, the male already decapitated.

"GET OFF HER!" I shouted.

"Where's his head?"

"She ate it."

"And he can still—"

"Yeah, he can still...horny bugs."

"Zia, if you measure the distance from the garden to the porch, and calculate the hours left until dawn, and factor in a mantis's gait, and—"

"*JEEZ,* Will, cut to the chase."

"We need to hurry, or you'll have to settle for a small Z."

"Crap." I glared at the beheading mantress. "SEE WHAT YOU DID?"

"Does yelling work?"

"Works for me. I always feel better."

Through the night, Will steered tottering legs—they refused to fly—while I babysat the mantises to keep them apart and their heads attached. "Touch her and you're bird food."

Hours later, we had twelve mantises sitting on the porch.

Will looked at the horizon. "Eight minutes to dawn. Let's line them up."

"I'll do it," I said. "I need you to do another favor." I gave him a letter. "When you get to Haven, will you give that to Romal?"

"A letter? Are you sure you're awake? Just send a vibration."

"It's personal."

"You can direct a personal vibration."

"Jeez, I know. But Alpha might intercept it, and I don't want him to know."

"Why? What's in the letter? What are you getting me into?"

"Are all Counters so guarded?"

"How many Counters do you know?"

"Three or four."

"Then three or four are guarded."

"Look, I don't have time to explain."

"Six minutes."

"Just trust me, Will. I trusted you."

"When did I ever—"

"I *would* trust you, okay?"

"All right. But first, let me line up the mantises." He fashioned a stop-watch and placed it into my hands. "You'll have your Z in three minutes."

I clicked the timer. "Go."

Will had some talent with whispers; with thirty seconds to spare, he coaxed twelve bugs into a perfect Z. "Thanks, Will. You're amazing."

A glum-looking Will shook his head. "I made a significant error in calculating time."

"What are you talking about? In less than three minutes, you made a terrific Z."

"I allotted too many seconds for the headless one. I didn't expect him to move so quickly."

"Oh. Yeah. He won't even miss his head for a few hours." I shoved him playfully. "Hey, I bet you're the only Counter who knows that now."

"Are you patronizing me?"

"Hell yes. Who else but a Counter would give a flying fig about the speed of a headless mantis?"

Will smiled. "Hurry home."

## 109

*I want to go home.*
*Don't you?*

The second Will vanished, the mantises rebelled, their legs straightening, their wings rustling. Then Alpha appeared, and all the mantises realigned into a Z, an improved Z with uniform direction.

Not one mantis moved again, not even to wiggle an antenna.

"Thanks, Alpha. Can we stick around a few minutes? The newspaper truck should be here any second. He always comes at dawn. When the driver throws the paper, he toots his horn. It's a courtesy beep because Pop used to repair his truck. It's been that way since I was a kid. Any second, the truck will be coming up the road. I guess he's running late today, but he'll be here. And when he toots, Dieter will come out. Dieter always comes out when he hears the horn. Always. We just need to wait a minute or two."

"Zia, the delivery service was—" His attention fell to the mantises...and stayed.

I tugged him. "Was what? Was what? Alpha, finish your sentence."

When his gaze lifted, his eyes shifted right and left like he were trying to recall his previous thought. Then he winced slightly; I think his memory lapse was bothering him deeply.

"Hey, it's no big deal," I told him. "It happens to everyone."

He looked at me queerly. "What happens?"

"Senior moment. ADD. Sometimes, even I get distracted. It happens."

The corner of his mouth tinged upward, and I saw a slight eye roll, but my insight must have impressed him because he said, "We will wait."

Although Alpha waited calmly, I couldn't sit still. I darted to the curb and looked up and the down the street, then I flew past the mantises—so beautifully lined—and jumped into the house.

Dieter and Miranda were waking.

I swept back to the curb and looked again for the truck. No sign of it.

I rushed into the house. Dieter was showering while Miranda was cooking bacon and eggs.

Back to the curb; no truck.

Then Dieter and Miranda were eating breakfast.

Back to the curb; no truck.

Time was ticking...and ticking...and ticking.

I went back and forth...back and forth...back and forth.

Then Dieter and Miranda were in my old room, taping window sills and door frames and preparing walls for paint. Brushes and cans sat next to drop-cloths. All the supplies they needed were right at their feet.

They were never going outside.

The newspaper was never coming.

And the distance from the bedroom to the mantises was the longest distance I have ever traveled.

I slumped beside the mantises and shook my head. "I think—Well, I think—It's not going to happen. We can, you know, forget it."

*Screech.* Sudden braking was followed with toots of the horn before the neighbor's cat sauntered off the road. It stepped to the sidewalk and hissed at me. I hissed back; that cat always sprayed my car.

Our front door opened.

Miranda called over her shoulder, "Are you sure you cancelled delivery?"

*Cancelled?*

"Yes, I'm sure," Dieter called from another room. "You don't see a paper, do you? Miranda? Honey?" He came to the doorway. "Honey?"

Miranda pointed at my mantises. "What do you make of that?"

Dieter eased around her and then squatted beside the mantises. For an entire minute, his eyes combed the area before he looked again at the bugs. "They're just Praying Mantises."

"Are they dead?"

Dieter nudged one, and they all stirred. "Nope."

"Dieter, they form a Z."

"They're just bugs." Dieter rose to his feet. "Food brought them together, that's all."

"What food?"

"Whatever mantises eat."

"So twelve bugs just decided to dine on our porch?"

"That's right."

"In the shape of a Z?"

Dieter shrugged. "It might be a Z. Another man might say—"

"Dieter Schatz, how can you be so stubborn? That is a Z. Are you saying it's explainable by science? Or it's just a coincidence?"

"Either one, that's exactly what I'm saying. Now what are you saying?"

Miranda crossed her arms. She looked again for the Z, but my mantises had scattered, all but the beheaded one. "Remember what you told me about Zia's promise, her spit-promise? Maybe she is trying to let you know that she's all right. Finally settled. Happy."

"Honey, Zee lives in our hearts, not in bugs. But if there's something more after you die, do you think Zee would pop down from heaven after four years just to stick mantises on our porch? 'Hold the pearly gates, God, I have a spit-promise to keep.' And what for, Miranda? Would we miss her any less? Would we love her any more?"

"Well, no. I'm just saying, it could be a message."

"So could spilt milk if it puddled into the shape of Elvis. It's all in the interpretation. You see it one way—Zee is telling us she's okay—but a priest might interpret it another way—Zee needs our prayers."

"Prayers?" Miranda said.

*Prayers?* I looked at Alpha.

"Sure," Dieter said. "*Praying* Mantises. And what does the headless one mean? It's all how you want to read it. But I think when love showed in life, and Zee showed plenty, you don't need messages from the grave."

"Maybe you're right," Miranda said, "but I wish we had taken a picture." She went into the house.

Dieter started to follow, but then he turned in the doorway and peered again at the dead mantis. "What took you so long?" he whispered, his gaze lifting to the sky, "Love ya, too, Zee." He gave a quick nod and then shut the door.

Every part of me quaked. "Alpha, did you hear that?"

"True."

"He got it, Alpha. He got it. Did you hear him? Did you?" I drummed Alpha's chest. "He really, really got it."

"He believes you are settled; is he correct?"

I had never felt more settled in my entire existence.

I pulled Alpha's arm around me, tilted my head back, and smiled up at him. "I want to go home. Don't you?"

# 110

*Her heel thumped as if she were perturbed, as if, for years and years,*
*she had been asking me to take her home, and as if, for years and years,*
*I had been denying her. What a kooky, little Wanderer.*

### April 9, 2002 —Haven

"**I** said, 'bring on the floods,' to tease Novella. Instead of getting mad, he tried to pat my head. Romal moved on, as if we weren't together. I hurried up the Parity Hall steps to catch up with him."

Silence. Jarring silence. After three days, Zia's mouth had finally closed. Romal sat up, replaying Zia's last words, *up the Parity Hall steps to catch up with him*. He roused the ArchGuide. "She finished. She finished."

Quickly, they regained their attentive postures and waited for Zia's ascension to consciousness. After a while, Zia's mouth reopened, "In the summer of 1898, we heard the rumors..." retelling her story from the start.

With chorused groans, the ArchGuide and Romal slumped back. "Instead of up," Romal said, "she went down and is now quite lost in the catacombs of her Soul. These delinquent skioses have quite a proclivity to invert vibrations of direction, rendering these Souls very poor navigators."

"Poor navigators who invert their Divine's vibration."

"Theoretically," Romal corrected. "When Zia's Soul flooded with negativity, yes, her Divine's vibration popped right out. This shadow, or echo of sorts, returned when her Soul was again hospitable. In theory, the Divine's vibration would do no less in the other seventy-six, but thus far, only Zia has been foolish enough to submerse herself in malevolence. Considering these Souls' particular needs, the Council of Genesis initially thought to appoint one Guide for the entire species, but we have since reconsidered.

"Vibrations cement in these Souls in the same manner as knowledge cements within a Player—through a process. After one or two skinned knees, a precocious child learns that a Superman cape won't enable them to fly. Granted, Zia endures countless bloodied knees and several fractured limbs before she quits retesting the cape. But eventually, vibrations do cement; she learns. Further, these Souls attach to their Guides like a Player-child attaches to their parents, and children suffer deleterious effects when torn from their roots. To avoid such harm, the Council decreed that all seventy-six Souls shall remain with their Guides. Had the Council authority over Peril Guides, we would have made it seventy-seven."

"Does Alpha agree?"

"Alpha doesn't know." Romal handed Zia's letter to the ArchGuide. "How could I deny her confidence when she embraced such a quaint tradition? Letter writing—an art lost among the ages. Notice the watermark, the tri-fold, and the dollop of red wax. She sealed the letter with a precious dollop of red wax. Such elegance."

Holding the letter up, the ArchGuide peered at Romal through the snippets and cutouts. "Elegance?"

"Yes, yes." Romal took back the letter. "An elegant presentation. Her language, however, always requires a bit of editing."

"If Zia understood a Peril Guide's duties—"

"No, no, no." Romal shuddered. "Such a mistake. If you explain the purpose of a Peril Guide, Zia will wink and say she has got it, and then she will go out and create a magnificent disaster that redefines peril."

In the background, Zia droned on, "...webbed in stink-bead..." muffling the ArchGuide's continued questions. Romal pinched the bridge of his nose; he had had quite enough. He twitched his finger.

Zia's voice muted, and the ArchGuide rocked back in sudden sleep.

Romal placed his palm within the light beam. "One, forgive my excursion from character, but the day has been dreadfully long. The past one hundred years have felt very much like a thousand. It's time for our private celebration, don't you agree? Your children are home." The light brightened. Romal smiled and felt himself blush. "Yes, yes, but you give me too much credit. I merely knotted a thread in your eternal tapestry."

Sitting back, Romal twitched again, now returning Zia's voice and waking the ArchGuide. Romal asked, "Have I explained all matters sufficiently?"

The ArchGuide stood, "Request granted," and vanished.

Romal lifted Zia into cognizance. Immediately, she looked for the ArchGuide. "Where did he go? What did he say? How did I do?"

"If you keep blathering, you'll never know, will you?" When she finally quieted, Romal said, "Alpha will remain your Guide."

"YEE—"

Romal clapped her mouth. "Don't shriek. With a smidgeon of restraint, you can express joy without shattering atoms. Will you give it a try?"

She nodded.

"Calmly now." And Romal uncupped her mouth.

"Freakin' great. Let me tell Alpha, okay? He'll be happier than hell, right?"

"Oh, not a tad less than hell."

"I knew it. This good news ought to raise a smile."

"I suspect you'll raze much more than his smile."

Romal started out from the chamber, Zia chattering and bouncing around him. "Hey, I have some requests for my next life. Not many, just a few. But I want you to present my wish-list to Alpha. He listens to you. So could you?"

"I'll hear your list," Romal said, "if you'll stop dancing. These are the Halls of Parity not the Halls of Frivolity."

Curtailing herself to Romal's side, Zia said, "Being female tops my wish-list, which should get no argument. My last life just proved that I do my best work when gender-matched. Second, a desert placement. No more ocean. A big, blue fragment inside me keeps growing and growing. If I am ever to break it apart and remove the pieces, I need a few lives far, far from the sea. Third, until I'm an expert at removing fragments, I want atheist parents. They have kids, too, you know, not that anyone would know that by my lives— Hinduism, Judaism, Christianity, Indian and African Spiritualism. *Jeez*, do you know what happens when a few religious fragments crisscross? You get a life plagued by superstitions...as my last life just showed. Fourth—"

Romal stopped, pulled Zia back to his side, and said, "*Shhhh*." He motioned toward the Parity Halls' entrance where Alpha stood waiting to learn the name of Zia's next Guide.

"Thank you, Romal," Zia whispered.

Romal turned Zia and held her squarely, face to face. "Everyone stumbles, Zia, but not all lose their way. When lost, open your heart to guidance. Loving arms will find you, lift you, and light your direction home."

"*Home?* Oh, Romal, there's a dim-witted Soul dressed as a little girl—"

"The Wanderer?"

"Yeah, you found her?"

Romal kissed Zia's forehead. "I assure you, Zia, the little Wanderer finally came home."

~ ~ The End ~ ~

*Life is a Scrabble Board,*
*each person a lettered tile,*
*and Father-Time a lonely gamer.*

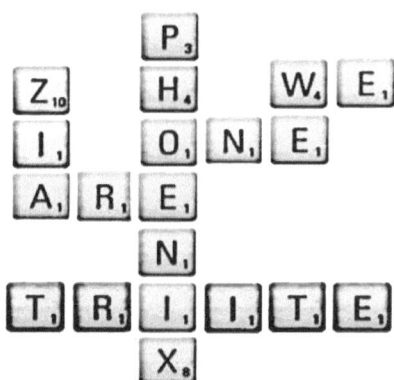

*Such is life.*